"The tattoos. You don't recognize them?"

He squinted at her inked forearms. "Vagrant tattoos. She's a rebel mage?"

"Not just any, you fool," Sindra whispered. "You haven't heard the tales? The *warnings*? That's no outlaw."

She pointed a baleful finger at the woman.

"That's Sal the Cacophony."

And a cold deeper than winter wrenched his spine.

He'd heard. Everybody who ever hoped to help people in the Scar had heard of Sal the Cacophony. The woman who walked across the Scar and left misery and ruin in her wake. The woman who had killed more people, made more widows, and ended more townships than the fiercest beast or the cruelest outlaw. The woman who painted the Scar with the remains of her enemies—Vagrant, Imperial, Revolutionary . . .

Sal the Cacophony, it was said, had tried to kill one of everything that walked, crawled, or flew across this dark earth.

And maybe that was true. Maybe all of it was. Maybe she had done even worse things than what the stories said.

Praise for

SAM SYKES AND
SEVEN BLADES IN BLACK

"Sykes is a master at taking familiar elements of fantasy and stirring them to a wicked, wholly original churn. In Sal the Cacophony, Sykes has crafted a protagonist for the ages. Ludicrous, wicked, delightful."   —Pierce Brown, *New York Times* bestselling author

"*Seven Blades in Black* offers villains that are as memorable and unique as the heroes. Action, magic, romance, and humor mingle well in this mammoth tale. It's an immersive read in a well-realized world."
      —Robin Hobb, *New York Times* bestselling author

"Exciting and inventive. I never realized how much I needed wizard-hunting gunslingers in my life."
      —Peter V. Brett, *New York Times* bestselling author

"*Seven Blades in Black* is terrific. The tale of Sal the Cacophony is delightfully sarcastic and deeply sorrowful."
      —Nicholas Eames, author of *Kings of the Wyld*

"Gunslingers and mad mages and monsters, oh my. Sykes's latest is a brutal and vulgar epic, yet still fun enough that it—and I say this as the highest of compliments—makes me wish like hell it ends up with an adaptation into a role-playing game."
      —Chuck Wendig, *New York Times* bestselling author

"Sykes's writing is full of heart, hilarity, and the frank understanding that as humans we are all disasters. Come for the adventures, stay for the weirdos."   —R. F. Kuang, author of *The Poppy War*

"By the end of the first page, you'll know Sam is in love with his characters. By the end of the second, you'll know you are too."
      —Myke Cole, author of *The Armored Saint*

BY SAM SYKES

THE GRAVE OF EMPIRES

Seven Blades in Black

Ten Arrows of Iron

The Gallows Black: A Grave of Empires Novella

BRING DOWN HEAVEN

The City Stained Red

The Mortal Tally

God's Last Breath

THE AEONS' GATE TRILOGY

Tome of the Undergates

Black Halo

The Skybound Sea

An Affinity for Steel (omnibus edition)

TEN ARROWS
OF
IRON

THE GRAVE OF EMPIRES:
BOOK TWO

SAM SYKES

www.orbitbooks.net

Copyright © 2020 by Sam Sykes
Excerpt from *Legacy of Ash* copyright © 2019 by Matthew Ward
Excerpt from *Ashes of the Sun* copyright © 2020 by Django Wexler

Cover design by Lauren Panepinto
Cover illustration by Jeremy Wilson
Cover copyright © 2020 by Hachette Book Group, Inc.
Map by Tim Paul
Author photograph by Libbi Rich

Orbit
Hachette Book Group
1290 Avenue of the Americas
New York, NY 10104
orbitbooks.net

First Edition: August 2020

Orbit is an imprint of Hachette Book Group.
The Orbit name and logo are trademarks of Little, Brown Book Group Limited.

The publisher is not responsible for websites (or their content) that are not owned by the publisher.

The Hachette Speakers Bureau provides a wide range of authors for speaking events. To find out more, go to www.hachettespeakersbureau.com or call (866) 376-6591.

Library of Congress Cataloging-in-Publication Data
Names: Sykes, Sam, 1984– author.
Title: Ten arrows of iron / Sam Sykes.
Description: First edition. | New York : Orbit, 2020. | Series: The grave of empires ; book 2
Identifiers: LCCN 2019059644 | ISBN 9780316363471 (trade paperback) | ISBN 9780316363495
Subjects: GSAFD: Fantasy fiction.
Classification: LCC PS3619.Y545 T46 2020 | DDC 813/.6—dc23
LC record available at https://lccn.loc.gov/2019059644

ISBNs: 978-0-316-36347-1 (paperback), 978-0-316-36346-4 (ebook)

Printed in the United States of America

LSC-C

10 9 8 7 6 5 4 3 2

For every reader who still carries scars.

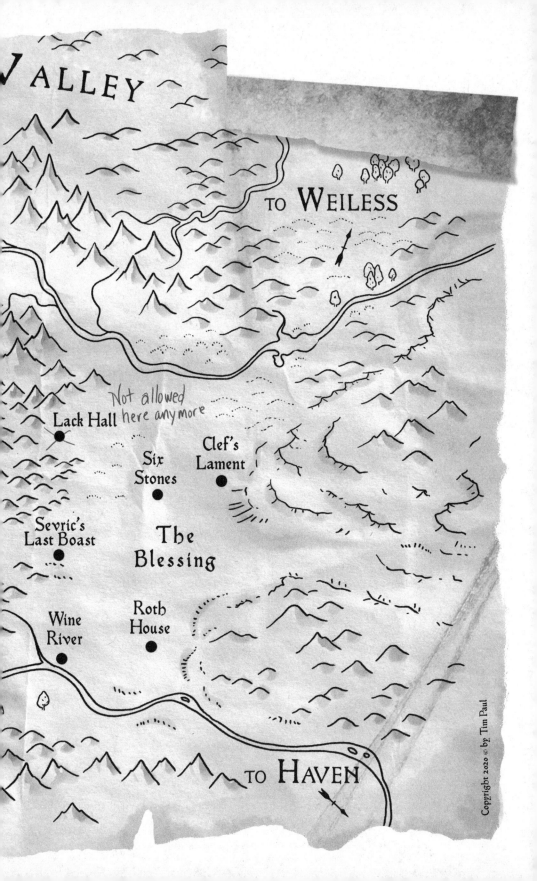

FOR THOSE
RETURNING TO
THE SCAR...

*P*erhaps you've heard the tales of Sal the Cacophony. Wielder of the magic gun that brings ruin, destroyer of Lastlight, avenger of Stark's Mutter, slayer of Vraki the Gate, and she who leaves only cinders in her wake.

Then again, perhaps you haven't. Or perhaps you just don't remember. I won't hold it against you.

Bear with me, though. I was kind of drunk for a lot of it.

It all started when I was "captured" by one Governor-Militant Tretta Stern, a saltslick of a woman in the service of the Glorious Revolution of the Fist and Flame: the people who come in with big guns, kill everyone, and leave. On behalf of said people with big guns, she inquired what happened that led me to preside over such a ruin across the Scar and, I suspect more pressingly, what had happened to one of the soldiers she was intended to rescue.

I was on the hunt for certain wicked people—we don't have time to go into all the reasons they deserved to die, but trust me, they did. Each of them a Vagrant who broke their oath to the Imperium—same as the Revolution, except big magic instead of big guns and, oh, they both want to destroy each other—in a bid to bring it to ruin, and led by the fiend Vraki the Gate.

Pursuing them led me to the door of my former lover, Liette, who had very good reasons to be a former lover and even better reasons not to help me, but what can I say? I'm just that charming, probably.

Together, we followed those people to a township named Stark's

Mutter, only to discover—after narrowly escaping gruesome death at the hands of lunatic zealots from Haven—that they'd summoned a horrific beast known as a Scrath that had promptly fled from their control. In an attempt to summon a new one and provide it a suitable host, they abducted children from Stark's Mutter, and I was determined to kill them.

The, uh, names. Not the children. I saved those ones.

That led us to cross paths with Cavric Proud: soldier of the Revolution, future abduction victim and the object of Tretta Stern's interrogation. After "borrowing" his vehicle and him—kidnapping is bad, sure, but I was in a hurry and I couldn't fucking drive that thing—we followed their trail to the Weary Mother, *a barge serving as the mobile fortress of the Ashmouths, the largest crime syndicate in the Scar.*

It was revealed to us—after a thrilling battle—that Vraki had taken the children to a source of great power: the Husks, a battlefield so suffused with magic from battles between the Revolution and Imperium that he could draw from its latent energy to summon another Scrath. We found the town of Vigil, a former Revolutionary garrison that had been utterly destroyed by an Imperial Prodigy named Red Cloud—a mage who requires no Barter.

I knew it well. Because I was Red Cloud.

Once, anyway.

I revealed to Tretta my former identity as a celebrated hero of the Imperium and she was kind enough to refrain from putting a bullet through my head long enough for me to explain what had happened.

Vraki and I... we were once members of the Crown Conspiracy, seeking to overthrow the Empress and her non-magical son to replace them with a true heir. That all changed when it turned out the plot involved me being betrayed by him, by my friends, by my former lover—the other one—Jindu the Blade. They stole my magic. They took my power. They left me for dead.

And I was eager to return the favor.

Liette and I... we had a fight. She left at Vigil. I found more enemies there that led me and Cavric to the town of Lastlight, a great city built by an amazing inventor known as Two Lonely Old Men. It was a beautiful, magnificent town, a triumph of alchemy, engineering, and spellwrighting so majestic that even the Imperium and Revolution wouldn't fight inside its walls.

In hindsight, I probably shouldn't have destroyed it.

But I did. To flush out Vraki's associates. And it worked. I followed them to Fort Dogsjaw, a ruined Imperial fortress famed for being the site where the Imperial Mages, upon learning that the Empress's son had no powers, rebelled and became Vagrants.

What happened was incredible. I fought Vraki and his followers, rescued the children of Stark's Mutter, foiled Vraki's attempt to summon an inhuman monstrosity, and narrowly escaped with my life.

It was thrilling. Incredible, really. Life-changing, epic, astonishing.

You should have seen it.

Anyway, I escaped to a ruined Lastlight, barely alive. With the help of Cavric and Liette's timely return, I was able to escape back to the town of Lowstaff.

And I was followed.

Vraki and Jindu, eager to take vengeance, returned and destroyed the town . . . and so did I. I ruined that city, I killed people, I shook that region to its foundations. I left Vraki dying in his own dust, and Jindu, the man who betrayed me, the man who held my heart in his hands and put a dagger through it . . .

. . . I let him get away.

I don't know why. To this day, I don't know why. And neither did Liette. She left me. Again. I didn't follow her. What I'd done to Lastlight, to Lowstaff . . . I couldn't do that to her.

I hope she's doing all right.

Tretta Stern, my captor, was ready to execute me, having gotten my full story. But an intervention from Cavric—who, as you can imagine, came to forgive me for kidnapping him—allowed me to escape.

And then he left, too.

And all I was left with was my namesake. The Cacophony. The gun that shoots magic, burns bright, and, sometimes, talks to me. And while Vraki and his underlings had been slain, those were only seven names on my list.

And thirty-three of them had betrayed me.

And so, in search of the others, I went out.

And that's when things got worse . . .

ONE

LITTLEBARROW

The day the sky rained fire began like any other.

Meret awoke before the dawn, as he always did, to grind the herbs he had dried last week into tinctures and salves that would cure by next week. He gathered the medicines he needed to, as he always did—balm for Rodic's burn that he had gotten at the smithy, salve for old man Erton's bad knee, and as always, a bottle of Avonin whiskey for whatever might arise in the day—put them into his bag, and set out. He made his rounds, as he always did, and visited the same patients he always had since he had arrived in Littlebarrow three months ago.

The name was a little unfair, he thought. After all, it was a long time ago that a woman had built a shack to live in beside the cairn she had constructed for her only child. Since then, enough people had found it a good place to stop on sojourns into the Valley that it had grown to a township worthier of a name that matched its thriving circumstances. But as it wasn't his township, he thought it not his place to protest the name, no matter how much he had grown attached to the place.

While it was nowhere near as big as Terassus or even the larger towns in the Valley, and it still had its share of problems, Littlebarrow was one of the better places his training had taken him. The people were nice, the winter was relatively gentle, and the surrounding forest was thick enough for game but not so much that larger beasts would come sniffing around.

Littlebarrow was a fine place. And Meret liked to think he had helped.

"*Fuck me*, boy, you missed your true calling as a torturer."

Not everyone agreed.

He glanced up from Sindra's knee, now wrapped in fresh antiseptic-soaked bandages, to Sindra's face, contorted in pain, with keen distaste that he hoped his glasses magnified enough to demonstrate how tired he was of that joke.

"And you apparently misheard yours," he said to his newest patient. "I would have thought a soldier would be made of sterner stuff."

"If my name were Sindra Stern, I'd agree," the woman growled. "As the Great General saw fit to call me Sindra Honest, I'll do you the courtesy of pointing out that this shit"—she gestured to the bandages—"fucking *hurts*."

"It hurts much less than the infection the salve keeps out, I assure you," Meret replied, cinching the bandage tight. He dared to flash a wry grin at the woman. "And you were warned about the importance of keeping the joint clean, so in the interests of honesty, I believe I could say I told you so?"

Sindra's glare loitered on him for an uncomfortable second before she lowered her gaze to her knee. And as her eyes followed the length of her leg, her glare turned to a frown.

The bandages marked the end of her flesh and the beginning of the metal-and-wood prosthetic that had been attached months ago. She rolled its ankle, as if *still* unconvinced that it was real, and a small series of sigils let off a faint glow in response.

"Fucking magic," she said with a sneer. "Still not sure that I wouldn't be better off with just one leg."

"I'm sure you wouldn't be able to help as many people without it," Meret added. "And the spellwrighting that made it possible isn't *technically* magic."

"I was a Revolutionary, boy," Sindra said with a sneer as she pulled her trouser leg over the prosthesis. "I know fucking magic when I fucking see it."

"I thought that the soldiers of the Grand Revolution of the Fist and Flame were so pure of ideal that vulgar language never crossed their lips."

Sindra's face, dark-skinned and bearing the stress wrinkles of a woman much older than she actually was, was marred by a sour frown. It matched the rest of her body at least. Broad shoulders and thick arms that her old military shirt had long given up trying to hide were corded with the thick muscle that comes from hard labor, hard battles, and harder foes. Her hair was prematurely gray, her boot was prematurely thin, and her heart was prematurely disillusioned. The only part of her that wasn't falling apart was the sword hanging from her hip.

That, she kept as sharp as her tongue.

"It's the *Glorious* Revolution, you little shit," she muttered, "and it's a good thing I'm not in it anymore, isn't it?"

"True," Meret hummed. "Otherwise, I wouldn't be able to treat you."

"Yeah, lucky fucking me," Sindra grumbled. "I wouldn't mind a couple of alchemics our cadre medics used to have, though. A hit of those and I could fight all night."

"I am but a humble apothecary, madam," he replied. "And while herbs and bandages take longer, they heal just as good."

Sindra sighed as she winced and hauled herself to her feet, her prosthesis creaking as she did. "You're just lucky that it's a choice between keeping you around and keeping soldiers around. If it were a choice between a smart-mouthed apothecary who couldn't heal for shit and, say, a Hornbrow who hadn't eaten in days, I'd slather myself in sauce and pry its jaws open myself."

He agreed, but kept it to himself.

Littlebarrow had been fortunate enough to escape most of the battles between the Revolution and its inveterate foes, the Imperium, which had raged through the rest of the Valley. The wilderness surrounding it had seen battle, he had been told, and there was the incident with farmer Renson's barn that was turned into kindling by stray cannon fire. But by and large, the two nations kept their fighting focused on the cities and resources. A township like Littlebarrow was worthy only of a few scuffles between Revolutionary cadres and Imperial mages.

One such scuffle had deposited Sindra here two years ago. After a savage battle that saw her grievously wounded after bringing down an Imperial Graspmage, she had been left for dead by both her comrades and her foes. The people of the township had taken her in, nursed her back to health, and begged her to put her sword and strength to the defense of their township, which she, in possession of a generous heart that nonetheless burned relentlessly for justice, reluctantly agreed to.

At least, that's the way Sindra told it.

Meret suspected the true story was perhaps less dramatic, but he let her have her stories. It was true enough that she had the injuries that came from defending the town against the occasional monster that came wandering out of the woods or outlaws that came searching for an easy hit. But if the war ever came back to this part of the Valley, a middle-aged woman with a sword wouldn't do much to stop it.

Hell, neither would a hundred.

He'd been to the rest of the Valley. He'd seen the tanks smashed into the earth by magic, their crews buried alive inside them. He'd seen the towns and cities reduced to blackened skeletons by cannon fire. He'd seen the big graveyards and the little graveyards and the places where they just hadn't bothered to bury the bodies and had left the bird-gnawed bones to rot where they lay.

It hadn't put him off. After all, the wounds inflicted by that terrible war were the whole reason he had come to the Valley once the Imperium claimed victory and started settling it again. But part of him wondered if the reason he hadn't lingered so long in Little-barrow was because, deep down, he knew that he'd never come close to mending even a fraction of those wounds.

"I can't pay you, you know."

He snapped out of his reverie to see Sindra leaning over the small table—an accompaniment to the small chair, small cabinet, and small bed that were the only furnishings of her small house. Though she stared at her hands, he could see the shame on her face all the same.

"It's not like Terassus here," she said softly. "We don't have rich people. I know you've done more for this town than we deserve, but..."

She couldn't bring herself to finish the sentence. He couldn't bring himself to press her.

Wounds, he'd learned, came in two kinds. If you were lucky,

you got to treat the broken bones, the split-open heads, the horrible burns—wounds that herbs and bandages and sutures could fix. If you weren't, you had to treat the wounds like the kind Sindra had, like the kind all soldiers had.

The war had left them all over the Valley: soldiers who woke each night seeing the faces of their best friends melting off their skulls, soldiers who were visited by the ghosts of people they'd strangled to death, soldiers who had seen all the fire and blood and bodies that had heaped up across the Valley and simply lay down and didn't see a reason to get back up.

Sindra was a strong woman. If half her stories were true, one of the strongest the Revolution had seen. She had been a sword of the Revolution. But she had been left behind. Too broken to be used by her comrades.

How did you fix a sword that couldn't kill?

Meret didn't know. He only knew what his master had taught him: how to keep wounds from getting infected and how to set broken bones, and one important cure that almost never failed.

"Do you have cups?"

Sindra looked up, confused. "Huh?"

"Cups. Glasses. Bowls will do, if you've got nothing else in this dump." He slid a hand into his satchel and pulled the whiskey out, giving it a come-hither slosh. "You want to pay me back? I just finished my rounds and I hate drinking alone."

Sindra grinned. "Close the fucking door, then. Snow's coming."

He smiled, walked to the door, looked up to the clouds. She was right. Winter was coming early to the Valley, as it always did. Snow fell gently, a layer of cold, black flakes falling softly upon the town's—

"Wait." Meret squinted. "Black?"

Somewhere far away, beyond the thick cloying gray of the sky, he heard a sound. Like a voccaphone, he thought, that strange crackling machine warble that couldn't ever *quite* sound like a human. A tune, growing louder, one he could have sworn he'd heard before. What were those lyrics? What *was* that song?

"Is that," Sindra muttered to herself, glancing out the window, "the Revolutionary anthem?"

And then the sky exploded.

First, sound.

A roar split the sky apart, a wail of breaking wood and shrieking metal fighting to be heard. The gray clouds shuddered and swirled, chased away to reveal a bright red flash, as though someone had jammed a knife into the sky and cut a wound lengthwise.

Then, fire.

In cinders, in embers, in fist-sized chunks and shards as big as Meret, it fell from the sky. A splintered timber crashed in Rodic's field and lay smoldering like a pyre. A blade of metal as long as a rothac speared through the roof of a house and belched fire through the wound it had just cleaved. All around the town, the fires fell, erupting in gouts of flame, an orchard of laughing red blossoms in the span of a soot-choked breath.

And then, the ship.

Its prow punched through the clouds, the gray parting for the great iron figurehead of a stern-looking man, his hand thrust out in defiant warning. A hull followed, riddled with wounds of black and red as fires burst out of its timbers. Propellers across its deck and prow screamed in metal agony as they came apart under the stress of the flame. For one glorious moment, the sky was alight with the beautiful view of the ship, as magnificent as any he had seen in the richest harbors across the Scar, burning as bright as a tiny sun.

And then it crashed.

Meret had the presence of mind to scream as it plummeted into the earth. If there was a god, they must have heard him, for the ship veered away from the town and smashed itself into the fields nearby, carving a blackened scar into the earth as it tore through the trees there. A cloud of smoke roiled up, sweeping through the town and casting them into blackness.

"*Shit.*"

He hadn't even noticed Sindra standing beside him that whole time. She was still staring at the wound in the clouds, mouth agape despite the ash gathering on her lips.

"That was…a ship," she whispered reverently. "A fucking *air*ship. The Great General's very own fleet. I remember the propaganda, the paintings they made." She swallowed hard. "That thing's a

Revolutionary prize. They won't let it sit here. We have to get every-one and get away from the town before they come."

That was very good advice, Meret thought.

And had he caught the whole of it, he'd probably have agreed.

As it was, he only managed to catch about half of it before run-ning off toward the wreckage of the site like a fucking idiot.

It was stupid, he knew. But he had been stupid to come to the Valley to help people, stupider still to become an apothecary in the first place, so he saw no reason to stop now. He slowed only to shout warnings to get clear to the curious and horrified onlookers who had gathered out-side to see the sky fall. He didn't stop until he found the first body.

He tripped over it, planting face-first into the burned dirt. He looked back and grimaced at the sight of a blue coat laden with fancy-looking medals. Treating Revolutionaries always came with risks—they tended to "thank" you for your service by conscripting you into their armies.

Fortunately, this guy was dead.

Unfortunately, it had been magic that killed him.

An icicle jutted out of his chest, as long as a man's arm, still whis-pering frigid mist even as fires burned around him. Only a mage could do something like that. And there weren't many mages who weren't part of the Imperium. Which meant war had brought this ship here.

And this ship had brought war here.

He pulled himself to his feet and beheld the other bodies scat-tered like ash across the field, half hidden in the cloud of dust and grit. Most were burned to death, smoldering alongside the ship's rubble. A few had been crushed or broken like toys, tossed when the ship had been struck. A few others were dead of more unusual cir-cumstances. But they were all dead.

More than he'd ever seen in one spot.

"You *fucker*."

A hand grabbed him by the shoulder. He whirled, fearing the Revolution had already come to claim their war machine or that the dead had risen due to some magical birdshittery. Seeing Sindra's angry face made him think that either of those might have been preferable.

"Do you not understand what's happening here?" she snapped. "Everyone in the Valley must have seen this ship come down. Either the Revolution will come to pick up the pieces or the Imperium will come to finish the job and *both* of those things end with Littlebarrow and everyone in it *dead*."

"But I had to help—" Meret began weakly.

"Help *what*?"

Good question. There was nothing left for him here. Even if he *did* find survivors, what could herbs and salves do for people who had been crushed by a giant airship or electrocuted by doomlightning or whatever the fuck those mages did?

But he could still help the people of Littlebarrow. And they'd need help. Whatever else happened after this day, it would not end well.

He sighed, turned, and nodded at Sindra. She nodded back, cuffed him lightly across the head, and together they started walking.

Until the rubble started moving, anyway.

The groan of timber caught his ear. He turned and saw a pile of debris shifting. He walked toward it and, as if in response, something reached out.

A hand. Wrapped in a dirty leather glove stained with blood. Tattoos of blue-and-white cloudscapes and wings stretched from the wrist down to the elbow. It reached out of the rubble, fingers twitching.

Alive.

In need of help.

Or so Meret thought when he started to run toward it. But when he came within ten feet of the pile, it shifted suddenly. A great beam of wood rose, pushed upward by a shape shadowed in the cloud of ash. Two tattooed arms lifted the great beam and, with a grunt of effort, shoved them aside.

The smoke cleared. The fires ebbed. And Meret saw a woman standing there.

Alive.

She was tall, lean, corded with muscle that shuddered with labored breathing, her dirty leathers not making much of an effort to conceal it. Or the numerous old scars and fresh injuries she wore. An empty scabbard hung at her hip. Her hair, Imperial white and cut rudely short, was dusted with ash. Pale blue eyes stared across the field, empty.

He started to move toward her. Sindra seized him.

"No." No anger in her voice, just quiet, desperate fear. "No, Meret. You can't help that one."

"Why not?"

"The tattoos. You don't recognize them?"

He squinted at her inked forearms. "Vagrant tattoos. She's a rebel mage?"

"Not just any, you fool," Sindra whispered. "You haven't heard the tales? The *warnings*? That's no outlaw."

She pointed a baleful finger at the woman.

"That's Sal the Cacophony."

And a cold deeper than winter wrenched his spine.

He'd heard. Everybody who ever hoped to help people in the Scar had heard of Sal the Cacophony. The woman who walked across the Scar and left misery and ruin in her wake. The woman who had killed more people, made more widows, and ended more townships than the fiercest beast or the cruelest outlaw. The woman who painted the Scar with the remains of her enemies—Vagrant, Imperial, Revolutionary…

Sal the Cacophony, it was said, had tried to kill one of everything that walked, crawled, or flew across this dark earth.

And maybe that was true. Maybe all of it was. Maybe she had done even worse things than what the stories said.

But at that moment in that ash-choked field, Meret did not think about what may be. He thought about the only two things he knew to be true.

First, he should definitely turn around, start walking, and keep going until he forgot Littlebarrow's name.

Second, he was not going to do that.

"Meret."

Sindra, a woman who had once screamed the whole town awake when she thought someone had touched her sword, sounded strange, whispering his name as he started walking toward the white-haired woman. She didn't go after him, making little more than a fumbling reach for his shoulder as he headed deeper into the ash.

Sindra, who had once slain a Bittercoil Serpent by leaping into its mouth and cutting her way out, was scared to draw the notice of this woman.

Truth be told, maybe he was, too. Or maybe he thought that the closer he was to the damage, the more he could keep it from reaching Littlebarrow. Or maybe some dark part of him, the morbidly curious part that had driven him to come to this war-torn land, wanted to look into the eyes of a killer instead of a corpse.

He didn't deal with what may be. He dealt with what he knew to be true.

Someone was injured. And he could help.

"Madam?"

His voice was so timid he barely heard himself over the mutter of nearby fires and the groan of fragmenting metal as the gunship's remains continued to crumble. Sal the Cacophony, breathing raggedly and staring out into the distance, did not seem to notice. He came closer, spoke a little louder.

"Are you hurt?"

She didn't look at him. She didn't even seem to notice the fact that her immediate vicinity was almost entirely on fire. Trauma, perhaps; he'd seen it before.

"We saw the ship come down..." He glanced toward the ruin of the machine, wearily sighing plumes of flame. "I mean, everyone did." He looked back to Sal. "What happened—"

Or, more specifically, he looked into a gun.

A polished piece of brass, its barrel forged to perfectly resemble a grinning dragon's leer, stared at him through metal eyes. Steam peeled off the cylinder, almost as if the thing were alive and breathing. A polished hilt of black wood clung to her hand—or she to it— as she leveled the gun at his face, finger on the trigger, and pulled the hammer back with a *click* that carried through the sounds of hell.

Including the sound of his own heart dropping into his belly.

Meret stared into the weapon's smile, into that black hole between its jaws. For every story about the woman, there was another one about her weapon. The Cacophony could set fires that never went out. The Cacophony warped metal and broke stone. The Cacophony sang a song so fierce it killed anyone who listened to it.

He hadn't heard as many stories about the gun. But even if he hadn't heard a single one, he would have believed them.

Weapons ought not to look at people.

Not like that.

"Imperial?"

A ragged voice caught his ear. He looked up the barrel to see her looking down it. Her blue eyes, no longer so distant, were fixed on him. A long scar carved its way down the right side of her face, and a cold stare punched through him just as cleanly as the gun's brass eyes had.

"W-what?" he asked.

"You Imperial?" Sal the Cacophony asked again, with the slightest variation in tone that suggested the next time she asked, it would be to a corpse.

He shook his head. "No."

"Revolutionary?"

"No. I'm just…" He, without taking his eyes off the gun, gestured in the direction of Littlebarrow. "I'm from the village over there. Unaffiliated. Neutral."

She stared at him for a long moment. Slowly, her eyes slid to the gun with an expectant look, like she expected it to weigh in on whether he was lying or not.

Could it do that? Was there a story about that somewhere? He thought he had heard something like that once.

"You know this gun?" she asked.

He nodded.

"You know what it can do?"

He nodded.

"Am I going to need to use it?"

He shook his head.

She either believed him or realized that she could probably wring his neck just as easily as shoot him. The gun lowered and, with a hissing sound, slid into a sheath at her side.

Without the threat of imminent death by firearm, he had a chance to take stock of her. Her breathing was steadier and she seemed unbothered by the wounds decorating her. Was that part of her legend? he wondered. Did Sal the Cacophony simply not feel pain?

"You a healer?"

Apparently not.

He noticed her eyes on his satchel. "Y-yeah," he said, opening it. "I've got salves and…and stuff." He swallowed hard, looked over her wounds. "What sort of pain are you feeling and when—"

"Not me."

He looked up. She stepped away, pointed down to the earth.

"Her."

There, nestled amid the wreckage, was a woman.

Pale, slender, dressed in clothes that weren't Revolutionary, weren't Imperial, weren't anything special. Her black hair hung limp around a face peppered with cuts and scratches. Her skirts were torn and her shirt was stained with blood and soot. A pair of shattered spectacles rested on her chest.

She didn't look like a Vagrant. Or anything that the stories said Sal the Cacophony was interested in. She was just a woman. A plain, ordinary woman you might find in a plain, ordinary place like Littlebarrow.

Why, Meret wondered, would a monster like Sal the Cacophony be around her?

"Help her."

A good question. One he'd answer someday, if he had the time. But that would be another day, another place, another person. Right now, he was here, the only one who could help.

He knelt down beside the pale girl. He performed all the tests he had been taught: moved her as gently as he dared, listened to her breathing, studied her many cuts. He did not look back up to Sal the Cacophony, did not dare give her hope. Whatever monster she was, right now she was like any of the other fretting people who doted over their injured. She did not need hope. She needed information.

He could give it to her.

"Her breathing's difficult," he muttered. "Probably not surprising, given the fall. But it's dry. No internal bleeding that I can tell." He looked down at her leg and winced. "Thighbone is broken. Her left arm, too. And I'd be shocked if that was all." He dusted the considerable amount of ash that had gathered on his clothes as he rose. "And that's without however many cuts and wounds she's got."

"Can you help her?"

When he turned to face Sal the Cacophony, her stare was no longer so distant, nor quite so cold. It was soft. Wet. It didn't belong on a monster. It didn't belong in a place like this.

"Tell me what happened here," he said, "and maybe."

Those eyes hardened. Cold and thin as scalpels in a corpse's body. She spoke in the voice of someone who was used to speaking once and did not repeat herself without steel to accompany it.

"You don't need to know that," she said, as slow and calm as a sword pulled out of a ten-days-dead body. "Help her. Help yourself."

Despite the flames, he froze. His legs turned to jelly. His breath left him and was replaced by something weak and rotten in his lungs. He hadn't felt that wind, that cold, since the day he had come to the Valley and seen the bodies.

He hadn't turned away then, either.

"N-no," he said.

"What?"

"No." He forced his voice hard, his spine straight, his eyes on hers. "Whatever happened here, it concerns this town. And if it concerns this town, it concerns me." He swallowed lead. "I'll help her. But you have to tell me."

She stared at him. Did the stories say she never blinked or had he just made that up?

She raised a hand. He forced himself not to look away.

Her hand shot out toward his waist. He felt ice in his belly, terrified that he'd look down and see a blade jutting out of him. His breath left him as she slowly drew her hand back.

In it, she held the bottle of whiskey he packed.

"Avonin." Her eyes widened a little. "Damn, kid. What do you use this for?"

"Disinfecting wounds," he replied.

She looked at him like he had just insulted her mother, then gestured at the unconscious woman with her chin.

"How much of this do you need to treat her?"

"I...I don't know. Half, I think?"

"You sure?"

"No."

"Get sure."

He looked over the woman on the ground, nodded. "Half."

Sal the Cacophony nodded back. Then she pried the cork out with her teeth, spat it out, and upended the bottle into her mouth and did not stop to breathe until she had drained exactly half the bottle.

She handed it back to him, licked her lips, and spat on the ground.

"I'll tell you," she said, "but you have to promise me something."

He stared at her as she looked over the wreckage. "All right."

"I won't ask you to promise to forgive me," she said. "But when I'm done…"

She closed her eyes, sheathed her weapon, and let a black breeze blow over her.

"Promise me you'll try."

TWO

THE VALLEY

Anyway, what was I talking about?

Oh, right.

The massacre.

It took me a second to notice through the blood weeping down into my eye, but his guard had dropped. Weary arms could no longer hold his blade quite so high, the tip of it dragging in the earth as he charged toward me, a scream tearing out of his throat, dust rising in a cloud behind him.

"DIE, CACOPHONY!"

He roared, swinging his sword up as he came within spitting distance. I stepped around the blade, into his path, bringing my own blade up. Steel flashed. A splash of red stained the air. His sword rushed past me, biting into my cheek and drawing blood.

As for *my* sword . . .

His body stiffened on my blade. His eyes were frozen in unblinking horror, yet he couldn't look down to see the four inches of steel thrust into his belly. His lips trembled, struggling to find his last words, to make them meaningful. I have no idea if they were or not. When he spoke them, they came out on a bubbling river of blood that spilled out of his mouth and onto the dirt.

Where he fell, three seconds later, after I pulled my weapon free.

And there he lay, unmoving. Another dark stain on another patch of dark earth.

Just like the other four.

Once the air stopped ringing with steel and screams, I let my blade lower. My breath came out hot and my saliva came out red. My spittle fell and lay on the cheek of a woman's body, but I didn't think she'd mind—after all, it wasn't the worst thing I had done to her. To any of them.

I'd given them every opportunity. I came wandering into their valley, my blade naked in my hand and my arms open and waiting. I came screaming my own name and cursing theirs. I came with no surprises, no stealth, no subtlety—just a sword and harsh language. And they were dead.

And I was still alive.

Assholes.

Credit where it's due, they'd given it their best shot. My body was littered with cuts—grazes, a few gashes, one good gouge that I thought might have ended it—but the blood drying in the cold mountain air on my chest was mostly not my own. My breath was coming harsh in my lungs. My scars ached, my bones ached, my body ached. But it wasn't ready to quit.

Which meant I still had a mage to kill.

I heard the click of a trigger, the thrum of a crossbow string, and the shriek of a bolt. I glanced up. A bolt as long as my arm flew past my head, jamming itself into a dead tree ten feet away.

I stared down a long stretch of dark earth. The young man holding an empty arbalest far too big for him stared back at me, dumbfounded. I sniffed, wiped blood from my cheek.

"Shit, kid," I said. "I was standing still. I didn't even see you. And you still missed." I gestured to my body, spattered with the drying life of his comrades. "Do you need me to get closer?"

I started walking toward him, my sword hanging heavy in my hand. Then I started jogging. Only once I saw him grab a bolt did I start running.

He ceased to be a person and became a series of fumbles—fumbling lips struggling to find a word, fumbling hands struggling to load the arbalest. If I had waited long enough, he *might* have killed me.

But I wasn't going to have it said that Sal the Cacophony was killed by some shithead who couldn't even shoot straight.

The sound of dry earth cracking under my boots filled my ears. My sword sang in the air as I raised it high. All my aches and cuts were lost in the feel of my legs pumping, my heart beating, and the weapon in my hands screaming for more.

He fired again. The shot went even wider than before. He gave up, dropping the arbalest and reaching with shaking hands for his belt. I thought he was going to pull out that sword that was too big for him at his hip. Instead he pulled out a dented brass bugle and pressed it to his lips.

He let out two and a half blasts that echoed across the valley. The last half fell flat, just as the bugle fell from his hands as I brought the sword down across his chest. His life spattered the sky. He crumpled to his knees, along with his bugle and his crossbow, just another useless thing that hadn't been able to kill me.

I watched him collapse, facedown, in the dirt. I felt a passing urge to flip him over, to give him the dignity of dying with his face up. But I couldn't.

I didn't want to know how young he was.

He'd died too quickly for me to get a good look at him, but I could tell from how he had fought that he wasn't cut out for bandit life. Probably some peasant shithead, terrified of settling down and dying in whatever backwater township he'd been recruited from. I didn't have to kill him, I knew. I could have disarmed him, broken his wrist, beat him savagely enough that he would have to crawl back to whatever life he'd had before.

Then again, he could have killed me. And we wouldn't have been in this mess.

So, if you think about it, it's really his fault.

A cold wind blew across the valley, sending my scarf whipping about my face. I pulled it up tighter over my head, stared down at his body, and wondered if he knew he was going to die like this when Cassa the Sorrow had pulled him into her gang.

My eyes were drawn to the great manor looming over the kingdom of cracked earth and dead trees that was the valley. Well, once-great manor. Long ago, some aristocratic Imperial fop had made it his vacation home among gentle brooks and rolling forests. War with the Revolution had found its way here, dried up the brooks, set fire to the forests, and the dilapidated estate had been left for whatever human scavengers could claim it.

Which, today, was a Vagrant whose name I had written down on a list long ago.

I'd tell you what she did to end up on that list, just like I'd tell you what that list was for. But given that I had just killed five people, I'm guessing you can probably figure it out.

I left the corpses in the dust as I walked toward the manor. My eyes drifted toward the boarded-up windows, searching for crossbows poking through the slats. But all that greeted me were shadows. Shadows and a big-ass pair of doors.

I stared at them for a moment, smacked my lips. I reached into my belt, pulled a flask free. I took a long swig and let the whiskey burn its way down my throat.

"No snipers," I grunted. "They must have heard the bugle, though. So you figure that Cassa either doesn't have enough weapons to go around or not enough thugs to use them. She hasn't had time to recruit and arm herself. She came here in a hurry."

I stared up at the crumbling, decaying manor.

"She's scared," I muttered.

In the cold, I could feel his warmth even more sharply than I normally could. Something burned at my hip, seething in his leather sheath. In a rattling brass laugh, the creature that always accompanied me spoke on a voice of smoke and flame.

"*She should be.*"

"Right." I sniffed. "Still, she's heard us coming. I'll bet she's waiting for us behind those doors, with whoever she's got left, right?"

I reached into the sheath, pulled him free.

The Cacophony stared back at me through brass eyes.

"What do you say we knock?"

You'd call him a gun to look at him—a black hilt, a brass chamber and hammer and trigger, a barrel carved in the shape of a grinning dragon. But that's only because you didn't know him. He wasn't like the crude hand cannons and gunpikes you see in the hands of fallen soldiers who thought too much and outlaws who thought too little.

The Cacophony was more than a weapon—particular in his tastes, elegant in his sensibilities, and absolute in his destruction.

"*Let's,*" he hissed.

Also he talked.

So, that's pretty weird.

I nodded, flipped his chamber open. I reached into my satchel and found a silver shell of a bullet. I ran my finger over the script on its surface.

Discordance.

Sloppy. Noisy. Perfect.

I slid the shell in. I slammed the chamber shut. I felt the Cacophony burning in my hand as I raised him and aimed him at the door.

And I pulled the trigger.

I know you've heard the tales about him—about the lone Vagrant's grinning gun that shoots magic. Maybe you've heard the bullets that fly from him are enchanted, sorcerous, spellwritten. Maybe you've heard stories about what happens when that lone Vagrant pulls his trigger—laughing fires light up the sky, freezing ice blossoms in patches, walls of sound erupt and drown the screams of those people they sweep away like human trash every time the Cacophony fires.

They're good stories.

But nothing like seeing it in action.

The shell flew from his barrel and struck the doors. Discordance erupted an instant later. The air rippled, wailing wind and cracking earth going silent in the wake of the percussive force that erupted to thunderous life. The force sent my scarf whipping about my face as a symphony was born into shrieking life. The Discordance shell tore earth apart, split timbers into splinters, sent shards of wood and rock flying as it punched a hole through the doors.

The stories you've heard are mostly true.

Mostly.

Loud as it was, I could still hear the screams.

The wall of sound dissipated after a moment, leaving behind a faint ringing in my ears and shattered timbers falling from the jagged hole torn through the doors. I waited a moment—for outlaws to come out with brandished blades or for a flurry of crossbow bolts to answer me—before I was convinced no one in there could kill me.

I sniffed, flipped the Cacophony's chamber open, and fished three more shells out of my satchel: Hoarfrost, Hellfire, and . . . Steel Python?

I shook my head.

Not Steel Python. Just because we were trying to kill each other was no reason to get desperate.

I exchanged it for a Sunflare shell and slipped it into the chamber, slamming it shut and sliding the Cacophony back into his sheath. Sword in hand, I walked through the jagged hole, through a veil of rising dust, and into the manor-turned-fortress.

Scattered ancient opulence greeted me: overstuffed chairs that had been broken down into kindling, tables once used for decadent feasts repurposed as barricades, various portraits of various Imperial ancestors torn and turned into bedding. On either side of an extravagantly large living room, staircases rose to a balcony overlooking me. Once, before age and necessity had taken their toll, this manor must have been quite stately.

And, you know, before it was littered with bodies.

Cassa's boys and girls lay scattered across the floor. Discordance had flung them, their weapons, and their makeshift barricade all over the room. Some lay groaning with twitching limbs, reaching for fallen swords and gunpikes. Others lay screaming, shards of wood lodged in legs or ribs from landing on a shattered banister or jagged plank. Some simply lay, motionless, soundless.

I paid them only as much attention as it took to find the least injured.

I wasn't here for them.

I found him, a grizzled-looking older fellow, inching across the floor, using the only limb that still worked. His trembling hand reached out for the heavy arbalest lying nearby, fingers shaking. He let out a scream as my sword came down, punching through his hand.

I'd have felt bad about that.

You know, if he hadn't been reaching for a weapon to shoot me with.

I waited for the screaming to abate to a whimper before I squatted down beside him. He looked up at me, his face mapped by a respectable amount of scars and wrinkles—no wide-eyed youth taken in with the romance of banditry. I was dealing with a veteran. Hopefully that meant this would be easy.

"Where's Cassa the Sorrow?" I asked.

"Fuck...you...," he spat.

But you know what they say about hope in the Scar.

It's about as much use as a hand with a sword through it.

"He's feeling pugnacious, isn't he?" the Cacophony giggled from his sheath. *"Draw me. Let us show him our diplomatic skill."*

I refrained from taking that advice. While I had no doubt that the Cacophony was indeed skilled in diplomacy, I also knew that his definition of diplomacy usually involved shooting people until the ones left alive gave him what he wanted. And while that was occasionally tempting, I knew a better way.

I sighed, laying my hand on the hilt of the sword, and leaned closer to him. He flinched away, anticipating a fist in his face or worse.

"What's your name?"

He hadn't anticipated that.

"W-what?" he gasped.

"Your name," I said. "Either the one you were born with or the one you took when you started working for her. I know Vagrants like their henchmen to have fancy names."

His eyes hardened as he sucked back pain through his teeth.

"Rishas," he answered.

I kept his eyes in mine as I nodded slowly, weighing the name on my tongue.

"How old are you, Rishas?"

"Fuck y—"

He hadn't been anticipating my fist that time, but it found his cheek all the same.

"There's no need to be uncivilized about this," I said, as soft as my blow hadn't been. I glanced at my sword. "Any more than we already have been, anyway. I'd hate for your last impression of me to be unmerciful, so let's just make this easy, shall we? How old are you?"

He hesitated, whether through pride or pain, I didn't know. He eventually answered, all the same.

"Forty-four," he grunted.

"Forty-four," I repeated. "That's old for an outlaw. You didn't get that old by being stupid, did you?"

He said nothing. The silence drew out between us for a long moment before I broke it.

"You know my name?"

He stared at me, opened his mouth like he wanted to curse. Instead, a thin dribble of blood came out as he pursed his lips and nodded.

"She tell it to you?" I asked.

Again, he nodded.

"You know who I am, then," I said. "And you know that I didn't come all the way to this valley to kill old outlaws." I glanced over my shoulder at his companions—the ones who were still moving and the ones who had stopped. "Your friends might think that loyalty will be rewarded, that they'll get rich or favored if they keep fighting. But it's not going to make their bones any less broken." I looked back at him. "Is it?"

He shut his eyes tight.

"I'll bet Cassa isn't the first Vagrant you've fought under," I said. "You've probably served with dozens of renegade mages, am I right? You know what they're like—they see you as tools, like their magic, except less impressive and more disposable. You know that they wouldn't die for a nul like you."

I drummed my fingers upon the hilt of the blade.

"I'm ready to kill you to get to her, Rishas," I said. "Are you ready to die to keep her from me?"

Rishas drew in a breath and held it. He shuddered with whatever pain wracked his body. He looked away from me, down to the pool of blood that had formed beneath his hand.

"Joined with her six days ago," he grunted. "She told me that a Vagrant was after her. When I heard it was you, I damn near turned right around. Thought, after what I'd heard you and that fucking gun of yours had done in Lastlight, there'd be no sense in fighting a legend like you."

I was grateful my face was hidden behind my scarf. After I'd put a sword through his hand, it would have just seemed cruel to show him the shit-eating grin on my face.

"Of course, you look beat to fucking hell right now," he grunted, looking back at me. "So you can't be as legendary as she thinks you are."

And then I was decidedly less pleased that my face was hidden, because I would have really liked him to see on my face what I was about to do next.

I twisted the blade, drawing a scream out of him. Not that it served any purpose, really. Regardless of what you've been led to believe, torture doesn't actually do anything other than get someone to tell you a bunch of lies you want to hear. Maybe I did it out of spite.

Or maybe I just didn't like being reminded that, for all my best efforts and theirs, I was still alive.

"*FUCK*," he squealed.

"Did she tell you I'd do that?" I asked. "Did she tell you everything else I'd do if you don't tell me where the fuck she is? She can't be worth it, Rishas."

"Yeah...I used to think so...," he rasped. "Had a thought that I wouldn't be much more than a distraction to someone like you."

"You should have listened to it."

"As it turns out..."

He looked at me. He smiled a grin full of blood and laughed.

"Sometimes that's enough."

I'd have asked him what he meant, but I didn't have to.

Not once I heard the Lady Merchant's song.

A single note resonating off broken glass. A breathless whisper from a dying woman a thousand miles away. The language of the wind, the sound of time speeding up, the last words you hear before you head to the black table—everyone has their own way of describing what the voice that heralds magic sounds like.

To me, it sounded like crackling flames and hissing smoke.

No. No, wait.

That was the fire.

A bright flash burst at the corner of my eye. My feet were moving before my brain knew what was happening. Fire swept down in great red curtains, chewing through rotted timber, ancient dust, and the screams of Rishas as he vanished beneath the flames.

Hope that last laugh he had was worth it.

Heat kissed my skin. Soot and char stained me like ink blotches on parchment. I could feel that telltale ache in my scars that told me I should have died.

Around my neck, my scarf hummed. Upon its fabric, tiny sigils glowed with a faint purple light before winking out, their magic spent. Luckwritten cloth—rare, costly, and exceedingly good for saving my ass when my guard had dropped. It was the first gift I had ever gotten from her. And I had it to thank for keeping me alive.

Not like *he* had fucking helped.

I drew the Cacophony, met his brass grin with a glare. "That almost killed me. You didn't think to warn me?"

"Please," he rasped. *"If you had been slain by an art so primitive as common fire, you'd be unworthy to wield me."*

I might have responded, had I not been so rudely interrupted by a scream.

"NO!"

The flames parted, leaving behind blackened, smoldering chunks that had once been Rishas clustered around my sword. Through the ebbing fire, my eyes were drawn to the balcony overlooking the living room and the haggard figure standing there.

Cassa the Sorrow had looked better.

She'd been born to peasants, and while the manifestation of her Embermage powers had saved her from toiling in fields all her life, it hadn't spared her the ruddy cheeks, thick arms, and solid stature. She did not cut an imposing figure, it was true.

But then, when you can shoot fire out of your skin, I guess it doesn't matter.

"Damn it," Cassa growled. Beneath a thick brow, her eyes glowed violet with the magic coursing through her. Flames ran from her shoulders to her clenched fists, crackling with anger. "Why the *fuck* did you have to move, Sal?"

"Yeah," I replied, "the problem is clearly me and not the fire-shooting wizard bitch."

"He was a good man," she snapped. "They were all good. They didn't deserve what you did to them!"

"Well, you probably shouldn't have killed him, then." I leveled my stare at her like a blade. "You could have made this easy, Cassa. You know why I came here."

Cassa stared me down from the banister. She took in the scope of the scarred woman before her: skin kissed by fire, body trembling with ragged breath, eyes three nights sleepless and locked on her.

"I heard you were unkillable," she said. "But here, you look barely able to stand. Was that just one more lie?" She snorted. "The stories say that Sal the Cacophony comes to kill, she comes to destroy, she—"

"She comes looking for someone less chatty and better smelling than you."

I glanced over my shoulder toward the remainder of her outlaws—some had managed to crawl away, a few more were stirring back to consciousness, but there was no helping the dead ones.

"Your boys and girls got in my way, but I've got no interest in killing them," I said, looking back to her. "So we can do this quick or slow. We do this quick, we talk like mages—face-to-face, no tricks or threats. We do this slow, I find out what I want to know from you or from them."

I pulled my scarf down from my face. I gave her a good, long look at the scar running down my right eye.

"And no one walks out of here."

The Lady Merchant's song went soft. The light left Cassa's eyes even as the flames sputtered down to a low smolder across her skin. As the fire abated, I could see the woman a little better. That solid physique couldn't hold up her sagging shoulders, and her furrowed brow couldn't hide the dark circles under her eyes.

Her old Imperial uniform hung loosely on her now. It had been torn and shredded in places, enough that I could see the twisting tattoos of flames coiling around her collarbone. Fresh ink, not worn and faded like the storm clouds running the length of my arms.

Back when she'd served as an Imperial mage, Cassanara yu Althama had a reputation for rationality. Despite her destructive powers, she'd always been reluctant to fight as a first resort. Her value for the soldiers she commanded had made her a favorite among the Imperium's forces.

Everyone wondered why she'd gone Vagrant.

But that proud Imperial mage was gone. Cassa the Sorrow—the Vagrant, the outlaw, the fugitive—was a tired, ragged, broken-down woman dealing with people she didn't like, doing work she didn't care for in a world she didn't understand.

Maybe that's what made me think I could walk out of here without having to fight her.

Or maybe I was just kind of stupid. I was tired; it was hard to tell.

Regardless, she didn't make another move. "Speak."

I made a show of holding up my hand and easing it slowly into my scarf. From a hidden pocket inside, I produced a thin scrap of paper, folded up delicately and wrinkled with time and weather.

"You've heard stories about me," I said. "You know what this is?"

Cassa nodded slowly. "There are thirty-three names on that list. Vagrants. All of whom wronged you . . . or so you say."

At her words, I felt a pang of agony lance through my chest, running the length of the scar that wound from my collarbone to my belly. I hid my wince behind my scarf as I slid the list back into its folds.

"Twenty-four names," I replied. "Nine of them are crossed out. But you're not on this list. And neither are any of your people here. If you're willing to answer me one question, we can leave it at that."

Cassa regarded me down the length of her nose.

"Ask."

I stared up at her. And the scent of ashes filled my nose. And my scar itched in that way it does when things are about to go terribly wrong.

"Where," I asked, "is Darrish the Flint?"

And that's when she *really* started trying to kill me.

The Lady's song rose in my ears, swallowed by the sound of fires crackling to life, which was in turn swallowed by the furious shriek that came red-hot from Cassa's throat. Flames erupted from her hands, racing up her arms, her shoulders, her neck until she wore a lion's mane of fire.

She thrust her hands toward me. Waves of flame cascaded from her fingertips, washing down the banister toward me.

"Lively now, darling."

The Cacophony leapt into my hand. I aimed him upward. I pulled the trigger.

The Hoarfrost shell burst from his mouth, exploding in an

eruption of cold. A mouth of blue-and-white ice opened wide in a crackling, freezing hiss to swallow the flames. They tore through each other, smothering and searing one another until frost became water and water became steam. Curtains of white mist flooded the living room, blinding me.

I heard her scream cut through the steam. I felt her through the floorboards when she fell from the balcony and landed with a crash. I saw her, a distant light in the fog.

And then I felt her heat.

I tried to bring my gun up, but her fire came faster than I could shoot. Hands ablaze came lashing out, sending embers scattering from her fingertips. Those few that found my skin burned, filling my nostrils with the reek of my own cooking skin. I hissed, leapt backward, tried to get room. But she knew me and my gun and she wouldn't give either of us the space we needed.

The steam continued to roil around us, rising up to mask us. I could see her, of course, but as I was not currently radiating fire, I doubt she could see me. All I had to do was get far enough away to lose her in the steam. All I had to do was keep backing up until I could get an opening to escape.

It would have been a great plan had I not bumped into one of her boys just then.

He acted quicker than I did—possibly because he wasn't distracted by a ragingly furious Embermage—and lashed out, wrapping an arm around my neck and holding me tight with a snarl. I don't know if he thought through his plan, as she'd incinerate us both.

Fuck if I had time to explain it, though.

I didn't have time to do anything, in fact, but dig my heels in and push back as much as I could. He was bigger than me, but not by much, and he didn't have the fear of being burned alive driving him.

Cassa came lunging out of the steam, shrieking, rushing, raking fiery hands as she reached for me. I pushed back against my captor, shoving as much as I could against him, but he was finding his footing and held me fast as she closed in. I saw the fire in her hands erupt into a glorious blaze that lit up the steam like a lighthouse in the fog.

If it wasn't about to kill me, I'd have called it beautiful.

As it was, I had to think fast. And since this battle was already turning messy, the first thing I thought of was just as bad.

Promise you won't judge me.

I brought the Cacophony up, then swung him down, past my leg and between my attacker's. I'm not sure if the gun's hilt smashed into what I was aiming for, but from the cracking sound and ensuing scream, I assumed I was close enough.

His footing lost—among other things—I seized him by the hands and swung him around, wearing him like a cloak of flesh and leather, just as the Lady's song reached a crescendo in my ears. The fire stoked itself to a roaring blaze.

Flames washed over him, drowning out the sound of his screams. I pulled free of him as his grip suddenly was concerned with trying to futilely smother the flames engulfing him. I fled into the curtains of steam and didn't stop until I felt the heat ebb to something merely painful instead of agonizing.

I whirled, saw Cassa burning brightly, a red-hot beacon in the veils of white. But she wasn't looking for me. Her eyes were on the smoldering heap of a minion on the floor, his attempts to extinguish himself ending as his limbs stopped flailing and his body stopped twitching and he lay still and let himself be swallowed by fire.

"NO!"

Cassa's shriek cut through the steam as surely as any flame. She collapsed to her knees, eyes wide as she stared at the fallen man with the same horror with which she might have watched a lover fall. Maybe she just had.

In which case, she probably shouldn't have killed him.

"I'm sorry!" she shrieked to a man who couldn't hear her. "I'm sorry! I just had to...I couldn't...I..."

She reached out to touch him, then pulled away, as if afraid he might crumble to ash. Her fire ebbed, guttering out to smoke.

I admit, the sight made me pause. Just as there are legends about every Vagrant, there are legends about Cassa the Sorrow. Serving the Imperium, she was dutiful, thoughtful, and careful. Serving herself, she demanded the highest honor from her boys and gave it in return.

Throwing off the Imperium and going Vagrant does things to

you, sure, but seeing her so reckless, so emotional, wasn't something I had expected. What did that name on my list mean to her that she'd fight like this? Why did she abandon reason and logic for it?

And why, even as her fires went quiet, did I hear the Lady's song growing louder?

"If any of you are left alive," she called out into the steam, "run. If any of you can't, I'm sorry."

Something sparked through the veils of steam. A fire grew bright.

"But I can't let her leave."

And hot.

"Forgive me."

And huge.

It rose in one great, discordant roar: the angry howl tearing out of her throat, the fires roaring to burning life, the Lady's song wild and vicious. It filled my ears. And the fire filled everything else.

I raised the Cacophony to fire, but it was too late. A great wave of flame burst from her body, cutting through the steam and banishing the white mist in a great eruption of light and heat. I collapsed to the floor, scrambled to get away—blind from brightness, choked by burning air, biting back pain as cinders and ash fell upon my skin.

The fire rose around me like a living thing, tongues of flame licking out to taste any flesh it could, dead or otherwise. It chased me across the floor as I crawled on all fours, everything forgotten except escape. But through the burning and the smoke and the endless heat, I had no idea where I was going.

Not until I came across a charred corpse and a piece of steel.

"Sal."

Her voice was soft as it came from behind me, her footsteps unhurried. There was no escape—from her or her flame—and she knew it. And though I didn't turn around to see her, I could feel the remorse in her eyes as she stared at my back, as she raised her hand.

As her fire burned.

"It didn't have to be this way," she whispered.

"Yeah," I replied.

I reached out, wrapped my hand around a hilt.

"It did."

The heated metal burned through the leather of my glove, but that was fine. It wasn't the worst pain I'd ever felt. Nor even the worst burn. I held the sound of her voice in my head, the direction it had come from, as I jerked my sword free from the corpse's hand and whirled about, the red-hot blade screaming as it arced through the air.

There was a meaty smack.

There was the sound of something wet sizzling as it spattered across the floorboards.

There was the disappointed sigh of a thousand magical flames as, one by one, they dissipated into smoke and dying embers.

And in the center of the blackened ruin, Cassa the Sorrow stood, bleeding from a bright red line across her throat.

She slumped to her knees as I rose to my feet. Her magic no longer feeding them, the flames went quiet and the Lady's song was just one more smoky silence among them. She reached for her throat, maybe to sear shut the wound or something. But she knew as well as I did that this was over.

Maybe it was her hesitation that had cost her the battle. Or my resourcefulness. Or maybe it was just dumb luck.

I wasn't going to waste words speculating on that. Neither of us had that many left.

"I won't tell you that you can fix this by telling me what I want to know," I said to her. "All I want to know is whether it was worth it." I stared down at her, the Embermage who had won a hundred victories for the Imperium, now dying on her knees as she tried to keep her blood in her neck. "Was it worth it to save Darrish the Flint?"

Cassa looked up at me, the last violet light dying in her eyes.

"Yes," she rasped through a voice thick with liquid.

"If you knew why I hunted her," I said, "you'd know it was stupid to try to save her."

"I know why," she gurgled. "I know…the stories. You hunt… because you're a monster…You kill…because you're a killer. I tried…to save…"

She narrowed her eyes at me.

"Because soldiers…kill…monsters."

I wish I could have told you that hurt me. I wish I could have said that her last words struck a part of me and carved open a wound that bled regret and remorse into my heart. Maybe, in a fairer world and a gentler life, I would have.

But this was the Scar.

I was Sal the Cacophony.

And no one stood in my way.

"You're wrong."

I squatted down beside her, met her gaze.

"I hunt her," I whispered, "because when I needed her, all I could do was stare, begging, pleading, trying to understand why she wouldn't save me."

Cassa's mouth hung open. Her eyes widened. A rim of moisture appeared at their edges.

Her body jerked suddenly.

"Yeah."

She slumped to the floor. I rose to my feet. And I stared at the red life weeping from her throat as she bled out onto the ashes.

"Like that."

THREE

THE VALLEY

When you get down to it, people aren't too different from scars. You go through life collecting them. And when you get a new one, you feel it. The pain, at first, is so raw and vibrant that you feel it with every step you take beside them. But then, things are said and apologies aren't, and over the course of years, that pain fades to a slow ache.

Then one day, before you even know it, you wake up and just feel a numbness where something else used to be.

But you never forget it's there. Not once.

I awoke from dreamless sleep. Pain sang through me. My body ached. The scent of stale blood and ashes filled my nose.

A woman was on top of me.

Her hair dangled down in messy black strands brushing across my face. I stared up into a pair of keen brown eyes, thick with disgust. Her voice escaped on a rasping hiss through an ugly, angry sneer.

"You left me."

She raised her hands and pressed them against my throat. I felt my breath go short as her fingers dug into the flesh of my neck.

"You betrayed me."

Something hot and wet struck my cheek, slid down the trail of my scar. Tears fell from her face. Or maybe mine. I couldn't tell.

"I loved you."

Couldn't move.

"I hate you."

Couldn't breathe.

"She isn't real."

I felt a surge of warmth, as though someone had lit a tiny fire. It seeped into the numbness of my flesh, gave my fingers enough feeling to move. They crawled across the floor, toward the heat, and wrapped around a black wooden hilt.

"You are dreaming."

The heat coursed through my flesh, awakening me to every cut, every bruise, every burn that scored my body. The numbness began to fade. And every time I blinked, she grew a little hazier, until I closed my eyes.

"Wake up."

And opened them.

And she was gone.

I let out a groan as I sat up, my body screaming from its many injuries. I was beaten, battered, damn near cooked. But I was alive. And I was alone.

Sometime after I left Lowstaff burning to cinders and left Vraki's corpse on the floor of a dirty basement…I lost something. I've retraced my steps, my injuries, my kills, trying to find it, but I'm not even sure what it is. It's like…I got cut somewhere, deeper than I knew, and something inside of me just spilled out onto the dust. What was left behind was something vast, hollow…

Empty.

And from it came the ghosts.

Not actual ghosts, mind you. But I didn't know what else to call them. I started…seeing things. People.

Sometimes I woke up to Vraki, his chest scored with cuts, cursing my name as blood spilled from his mouth. Sometimes it was Jindu, weeping in the corner as I tried to sleep. Sometimes it was people I had killed, people I was going to kill, people who would kill me one day.

Sometimes, on dark days, I woke up to her.

And sometimes, I almost wish she really was here.

I glanced to the empty space beside me. The bedroll wasn't anything fancy. Just a thick blanket, a thin sheet, and a dirty pillow. It was barely enough for me, let alone two people.

Yet somehow . . . we had always made it work, she and I.

She'd complained, of course—of it being too cold, of me snoring too much, of the stupidity of agreeing to sleep outdoors with me in the first place instead of just staying at her nice house in her warm bed. She'd complained. A few times, she'd even cursed my name. But she'd never left.

When I awoke, Liette was always still beside me.

Always smelling pretty, even when she stank of the same sweat and road that I did. Always beautiful, even with her hair stiff and messy. Always waking up with the same slow opening of her eyes and the same slow smile that made everything hurt a little less.

Today, though, she wasn't there. Just like the last three months.

Today, I awoke to the bitter cold. Today, everything hurt. Today, I got up and found no one waiting for me.

Except him.

Evening had settled across the valley. Darkness seeped in through the broken walls and shattered windows on a cold wind. In the manor's upstairs, there was not a single light to break the gloom.

And still, I could feel him staring.

"Oh, good." His voice rang out, a brass rasp in the dark, from beneath my fingers. *"You're still alive."*

He was what kept me from slipping into that empty place inside me. He was what saw through the ghosts. He was what kept calling me back.

Somewhere, I didn't know where, he had stopped being a weapon and started being a companion.

And I hated that.

"Don't get dramatic. I was just resting for a moment," I muttered, rubbing a kink out of my neck. "Let's not forget which one of us just had to kill a fucking Vagrant."

"Had you simply shot her instead of indulging delusions of being a decent human being, you'd feel much more spry."

"I'll take that under advisement when I start feeling the need to take advice from talking firearms." I waved a hand at him. "There's a certain way we do these things. The Vagrant's code requires me to—"

My words slid into a seamless hiss. Across my palm, I could feel a sudden searing heat, deeper than Cassa's had reached, and crueler.

In the darkness, I could feel the Cacophony burning. Even from so far away, I could feel him reaching out.

And into me.

"Do not forget our bargain," he whispered on a burning voice. *"Do not forget what I have given you. And do not forget who I am."*

I bit back the pain, the anger, the scream brewing behind my teeth. I wouldn't give him the satisfaction of any of it. The Scar was full of people like him—people who fed on pain, who drank screams, who grew fat off suffering. I knew how to handle them.

Most of the time, anyway.

Those people ate to satiate a hunger that never would be filled. I suppose, on some level, the Cacophony did, too. But more than that, he ate for another reason. He ate to grow.

The pain slowly abated. The heat withered away, leaving the chill of the evening to settle back over me. But his voice lingered in my ears.

"I can feel her slipping away," he whispered. *"Take me to her body."*

I winced, though not from pain.

I'd seen a lot of shit since I arrived in the Scar—murderers atop mountains of corpses, beasts who tore villages apart, mages who could split open the sky. Those got easier to see over time.

This next part never did.

Through his black wood hilt, I felt a faint pulse, echoing in the brass. A slow, steady rhythm that trembled in time with my steps as we walked, hand in hilt, down the hall and toward a black door.

Like the beating of a burning, brass heart.

I pushed the door open. Cassa's corpse, still warm, greeted us. I had laid her out upon a table, wrapped her in some nice-looking clothes I had found in the basement, and lit a candle that still burned quietly next to her.

A shitty funeral. Far shittier than someone like her deserved. But she deserved something.

Something far better than what I was going to do.

"Yes. YES." The Cacophony's voice was an excited squeal, the pulse growing swifter as we looked over her body. *"I can feel her strength, her magic. Lady Above, it burns so brightly. Let me taste it. Let me drink from it. Let me FEED."*

I hated when he got this way. You wouldn't think a talking gun could get any creepier, but he somehow found a way.

I held him up. He left my hand, floating in midair above the body. His brass trembled and shook, glowing brightly. Cassa's corpse, once pale and empty, began to glow as well.

I looked away. But it didn't help.

Light left her. A bright purple glow emerged in wispy tendrils from her eyes, her mouth, her skin...and from the wound I had carved in her. They danced over her body, those lights, hovering aimlessly as though confused as to what they were doing out here. That lasted only a moment, though.

Then, the Cacophony fed.

The light swept into him, every last drop of it disappearing into his brass. His glow became brighter, his blaze hotter, his laughter louder as he hungrily drew every scrap of light into him. They didn't make a sound as they vanished. But if they could, I knew they'd be screaming.

I wasn't sure how long it lasted—I never was—but eventually, like all the other times, it ended. The glow in his brass dimmed. Darkness settled over the room. And he fell with a heavy thud upon the floor.

I walked over to him, looked down, sniffed.

"Well?" I asked.

In response, his brass began to quiver. It rippled, as though liquid. It expanded, shrank, twisted. I could feel the effort with which he was straining as something pressed against the metal. By the light of the candle, I could see something pushing outward. It was joined by another something. And another. Until five small protrusions emerged from the shaft of his barrel.

Fingertips.

Five fingertips. Straining to reach out.

An angry snarl filled the room. The fingertips disappeared back into the brass. The metal re-formed itself, once again becoming whole and solid. Once more, he was just a gun.

"DAMN IT!"

A talking gun.

"It's not enough. NOT ENOUGH. I was sure that this was it. I was so close. I could feel the air on my fingers...I could...I...I need more."

"There are no more," I replied, shrugging. "No more mages,

anyway. I suppose if you wanted, I could drag Cassa's boys up here and see if you could get anything out of them. That is, if there's anything left of them after—"

"*MORE.*"

His voice rang out in my skin, a single burning note that raced through my veins and set my body ablaze. I couldn't help but scream and fall to my knees, my body forgetting how to stand, how to breathe, how to do anything but feel that pain searing through me. It smothered the sound of my breath, of my heartbeat, of every thought except one.

Fuck. He's actually going to kill me this time.

I don't know long it lasted or how close to the edge I drifted, but after a moment, the darkness at the edge of my vision stopped and then slowly began to slide away. The heat ebbed away, going cold in my veins. My breath returned in ragged gasps. Somehow, I forced my legs to remember how to stand.

"*Gracious, that was rather rude of me, wasn't it? Do accept my apologies, darling.*"

I meant it when I said he's a gun.

He's a weapon. A force of destruction. One I didn't understand at all when he first spoke to me and I made my deal with him. One I still don't understand, even all these years later.

But the deal...I understand that.

The Cacophony...whatever he is...is bound to that form, that burning brass. And he wants out. Every time he feeds, he gets a little closer. I don't know what comes out when he finally does, nor do I know what happens after he does. But in exchange?

He gives me every name on my list.

Every person who betrayed me.

Every former ally who gave me this scar that burns on my chest.

That deal is what I remember when he gets this way. That deal is what I remember when I wake up. After all...

I have nothing left.

Nothing but his burning smile and a voice in the dark.

"*Shall we, then?*"

I sighed, picked him up, and replaced him in his sheath around my waist. I made my way back to my bedroll and bundled it up, slinging it over my shoulder along with the sword. Together, he and I started down the hall and into the living room of the manor that had become a graveyard.

He felt heavier than he did when we came in.

"Well, a shame our friend Cassa was so unforthcoming. I expect our next lead will bring us closer to your desired quarry, though."

The Cacophony's voice was punctuated by a hissing chuckle. And while you'd think that a talking gun was a novelty, I assure you that the appeal runs thin when he's feeling chatty.

"Though, perhaps you'll be dead before then, no? I watched you hurl yourself into that battle with nary a care, barely an attempt to defend yourself. If your foes were not so inept, your carcass would be feeding the birds. But then...perhaps that's the aim, hmm?"

I had no desire to humor him. Each step I took down the stairs and into the living room sent a fresh jolt of pain through my body. I hurt too much to walk straight, let alone to humor a talking gun.

I hurt.

But not so much that I couldn't tell when someone was standing behind me.

I'd made it halfway across the living room before feeling eyes drawn on my back like a knife. And in the cold evening, a colder silence drew out between us. A slow breath seeped out into the darkness and filled my ears.

Easy, I told myself. *Another ghost. Another vision. Not real...right?*

I glanced down at the Cacophony. He sat, cold and still in his sheath. Which meant...

Fuck.

"I don't know what you're chasing," I said without turning around. "If it's wealth, I'm not your girl. If it's fame, you don't want it. If it's revenge"—I paused—"you can try. You can draw your steel and I'll draw mine and we'll see what happens."

No response, steel or otherwise, came.

"But if you've been chasing me, then you know me," I continued, "and you know what happens once I draw metal. No matter what happens, it won't end well. For either of us. Now you can make the smartest decision of your life and keep yours sheathed. I'll do the same..."

My hand rested upon the hilt of my sword.

"But if you really want it," I said, "just say so."

I knew they were still there. I could feel their air, could hear them shuffle from one foot to another. And for a long time, it looked like air and noise were all they were going to give me.

Then I heard them take a step forward.

I heard the creak of leather.

My hand tightened around the grip of my sword and I knew I should have felt fear, anger, despair—anything but the eager rush that bade me to draw steel.

I had begun to do just that when they finally spoke.

"Well, shit."

Or, rather, *he* finally spoke.

"I had this great dramatic thing I was going to say once you came down the stairs, but I'm starting to think it would sound a little pathetic after *that.*"

No steel. No blade. But I could feel his grin just as keenly. When I turned around, the first thing I saw was his knife of a smile, white and flashing in the dark.

"But then, what else should I have expected from Sal the Cacophony?"

Long and lean and well worn, he was a walking stick of a man who had seen too many miles and too few sunsets. A disheveled mop of brown hair draped his face and neck, despite the valiant effort of a braid to keep it in line. He stood with a slouch too easy and folded arms too cocky for the military coat he wore. And though the dark circles under his eyes and three-day stubble around his jaw conspired to smother it, even in the dark I could tell he was handsome.

Though I couldn't tell if he was ruggedly handsome or he's-going-to-say-something-that's-going-to-make-me-punch-him-in-the-face handsome.

The difference is painfully thin sometimes.

"I don't know you," I said, more to myself than to him.

"I'd be fairly shit at my job if you did," he replied. "I'm the sort of fellow who specializes in not being noticed, in whatever professional capacity that might entail." Dark eyes lit up in the gloom. "Sometimes I'm a stalker, sometimes I'm a thief, sometimes I'm just a drifter walking between names and calling the shadows friend."

Well.

Face-punching it was.

But either I was getting worse at hiding my contempt or he had been punched in the face a lot, because he immediately chuckled, holding up a hand for peace.

"Today, though, I'm just a simple courier with a simple message," he said. "I know you. So, too, does my employer. But for ease of communication..."

He stepped closer. The moonlight showed his face more plainly, revealing eyes too young for the man who wore them.

"Feel free to call me Jero."

In my line of work, if you can call it that, a face you can trust looks different than you might think. Someone who cowers when you approach them, who flinches when you raise a hand, who snarls when you speak—those, you can trust. They don't know how to hide their problems behind grins and pretty voices.

And Jero's voice was *quite* pretty.

Hence why I didn't take his hand when he offered it to me.

"Of course," he said, lowering it and offering a helpless shrug. "You wouldn't be the woman the stories spoke of if you were quick to trust, would you?"

"I suppose I wouldn't," I replied. "Of course, there are no stories that say it's a good idea for strange men to show up in the dead of night in the middle of nowhere, either." I stared down my nose at him—as much as I could, anyway, since he was roughly my height. "How'd you find me?"

He blinked, then looked around at the charred remains of the living room, replete with the charred remains of Cassa's boys, then back at me.

"Seriously?" he asked. "You left six villages in various states of mildly to completely fucked in your wake. I just followed that all the way here. Before that, I followed rumors of a name, a Revolutionary deserter by the name of Cavric Proud."

My eyes narrowed. The heat of the Cacophony called my hand to his hilt.

"Cavric," I spoke sharply, "is a name you and I would do well to keep out of our mouths. He left the Revolution for something better, and if you've done *anything* to him..."

I didn't need to finish that threat. The collapse of Jero's face told me as much. And I know we just met, but I hope you won't think me a shit to admit that it gave me a cold, bitter smile to see that I could still shake someone to their core with a few words.

"I assure you, the man isn't even aware of my existence," Jero replied. "He wasn't who I was instructed to find. You were. Granted, I lost your trail briefly in Lastlight."

His grimace deepened. My blood went cold.

"But a lot of things were lost in that city, weren't they?"

Yeah. A lot of things were lost. A lot of wine bottles from vintners who'd come to that city to sell their wares and never came back out, a lot of stuffed animals and toy soldiers left broken or half charred in the fires, a lot of shoes that couldn't run fast enough, rings pried from corpses' cold fingers, blades slick with blood, streets seared black, houses torn apart by cannons, by magic, by fighting, by screaming, by—

I felt the Cacophony's heat at my side and realized the cold that had begun in my blood had cloaked my body. It did that, sometimes, when I thought about Lastlight, whenever I heard stories about it. There were plenty, after all, about that thriving trade city, its beneficent baron and its happy people.

And none were more famous than the one of how Sal the Cacophony had walked through its gates and turned it to ash in the span of a day.

I focused on that heat at my hip, that burning pain that reached out and held my hand with searing fingers. He did that, sometimes, when he felt me going cold, when he knew I was slipping into some dark place inside my head.

Sometimes, when I couldn't find company or drink, he was all that reached out to me. And sometimes, when the dark grew dark and cold enough, I felt like reaching back.

Of course, I didn't. That would be insane.

He was a gun. It was weird enough that he had a sex.

"He doesn't blame you."

I scarce recognized the man when I looked back up at him. His smile was gone, his face hung lower, and he looked so very tired.

"If it's any consolation," Jero said.

"Who?"

"Two Lonely Old Men," he replied. "Not that he was thrilled about your part in his city's destruction, but he knows that one woman alone can't destroy an entire freehold." That grin crept back across his face. "No matter how legendary she might be."

"Well, you've put me in a bit of an imposition, sir," I replied. "As you've come all this way to tell me that, I feel as though I should give at least *one* fuck. But as you can see"—I gestured to the vast darkness around me—"I've got nothing but corpses."

I pulled my scarf a little closer around my face, grunted toward him.

"Kindly offer my apologies and regards to Two Lonely Old Men, would you?" I turned and started walking. "If he cares for neither, kindly offer him the nicest spot on my ass to kiss."

That might have seemed rude and perhaps a touch hasty. After all, it isn't often I get approached by strange men in dark places who aren't trying to kill me. I'd forgive you for thinking I was being a little too quick to walk away from him. And I promise, I'd indulge you in that argument once I finished finding that one name on my list.

At that moment, though, my thoughts were on other things. Cassa had been my best lead. She had known where Darrish the Flint was. And she had taken that knowledge to the black table with her. Now I was left with no leads, no hints, nothing but a—

"She didn't tell you where Darrish was, did she?"

I paused. I turned around. Jero was idly cleaning his nails with a broad-bladed knife.

"What?" I asked.

"Hmm?" He glanced up, almost disinterested. "Oh, sorry, did you have something else to offer my employer? A different part of your ass, maybe?"

"What the fuck did you just say about Darrish?"

"I couldn't begin to fathom what I might say about a Vagrant like Darrish the Flint." He tapped his cheek with the tip of his blade. "I suppose I know as much as anyone. A promising Wardmage, defected from the Imperium to go Vagrant, currently hunted by a woman with a giant fucking gun, last seen in the company of Cassa the Sorrow, who died without telling you where she was." He blinked. "That sound about right?"

"Your blade is far too small to be this coy, my friend," I growled. "If you know something about her—"

"I can say, in all honesty, that I don't." He flipped the blade deftly in one hand, returning it to a hidden sheath in his coat. "No more than what I just told you, anyway." He winced, catching himself. "Well, that and *one* more thing."

That grin returned to his face, sharper and keener and so bright it almost lit up the living room.

"Two Lonely Old Men knows where she is," he said. "He can tell you exactly where, in fact. He can pinpoint her precise location, down to the last step she took. He'll give that information to you."

Jero's hand slid into his coat. When he drew it out again, he held a sheaf of papers delicately between his fingers, secured with an elegant silk string.

"And more."

He approached, tentative, and held them out to me. I glanced from his hand to his eyes. He shot me an imploring look and I hesitantly took the papers from his grasp. By the dimmest light, I could make out the details of what was scrawled upon them in impeccably written ink. Some elaborate maps, some lengthy logs detailing movements and locations, a few profiles. I couldn't make sense of any of it until I saw a name printed in bold letters at the top of a page.

Darrish the Flint.

I flipped to another page. And another name glared back at me. *Yugol the Omen.*

More maps, more logs, more pages. More names.

"This is…," I whispered, but my mouth hadn't the words for what I was looking at.

"A gesture of goodwill," Jero finished for me. "You'll find there the movements of three individuals that we believe are of some interest to you, including last known residences, aliases, and acquaintances. I prefer to think of this as a gesture of goodwill. My employer considers it proof of concept, though."

I looked up at Jero. "What concept?"

He smiled back at me, softly. "The concept that nobody is beyond the reach of Two Lonely Old Men. He was the most powerful baron of the most powerful freehold in the eastern Scar. Now he's simply someone with a lot of money, a lot of time, and a burning need.

"You can take those papers if you'd like and use them however you see fit," Jero said, gesturing to the papers in my hand. "Mind you, the information is only accurate up to two months ago—my employer thought it foolish to hand you *everything*—but it should prove adequate enough for what you want to do. You can take those papers, find those names on your list, and kill them in fairly short order." He sniffed. "Or..."

He let that word hang in the darkness, giving way to a silence so deep I could hear the blood rushing through me, my heart pounding at the realization of what I held in my hands. And I wondered if Jero could hear it, too.

Because the smile he shot me was the sharpest thing I had ever felt.

"Or...what?" I finally asked, my voice breathless and cold.

"Or you could have more."

He approached me slowly, his boots crunching on the scorched timbers, until he was close enough that I could see him clearly in the dark.

"You could have every name on your list. Any name you want, he can find it. No matter where they hide, no matter who protects them, no matter how far they run, Two Lonely Old Men can find them. He can give them to you."

He raised a pair of fingers to my face. I didn't stop him. I didn't know why.

"You can find the people who gave you that."

His fingers grazed the scar that ran down my right eye. And in response, I could feel it burn.

"And you can give them worse," he whispered, "so much worse."

And that's when I knew what kind of man Jero was.

He had a pretty face, a sly tongue, a sharp smile—but that's not who he was. This close, I could see the wrinkles that faintly mapped his face: the strain of a brow too often furrowed, of a mouth too often set in a frown, of eyes that had seen more than they should.

I guess it sounds clichéd to say I know a killer when I see one, but it's true. And it's not like I held that against him—there were, after all, many killers in the Scar and a few of them were good friends of mine.

It's not killing that makes a man wicked or good. It's how he carries the killings. And it's a cruel fact of a cruel world that the wickedest and vilest of men sleep soundly and smile easily. Jero's wrinkles told me he hadn't slept soundly in a very long time. Whatever kills he'd made, he still carried them.

Maybe he always would.

I guess it sounds insane to say that made me trust him more, but that, too, is true. And so I met his weary gaze and I asked.

"And what does he want in return?"

His smile fell. And his eyes followed. And the weight of all those kills came down on him like stones, and when he spoke again, it was from a deep place.

"Same thing you want," Jero said. "Revenge."

FOUR

LITTLEBARROW

S cions."

At his breathless whisper, Sal glanced up at Meret. She was seated on the sill of his window, as she had been since they'd arrived, staring out over the village. Beneath the soot caking her face, her smile was a broad white scar, another one to join those twisting across her face.

"Scions?" she chuckled. "I didn't take you for religious." She glanced over him. "Or an Imperial, for that matter."

He wasn't religious *or* Imperial. He'd only gathered as much as he had about the Scions, those fabled first mages who founded their respective arts and enjoyed immortal reverence throughout the Imperium, in idle banter with the few Imperial patients he'd come into contact with.

But the story this woman had just told him demanded *some* kind of response and he'd already used all the curse words he knew by the time she'd paused.

Vagrants were dangerous business. Everyone in the Scar knew that. Just as everyone in the Scar knew that when a Vagrant got within ten miles of your village, you should immediately leave and return to whatever ruin they left behind when they got bored and moved on.

For a long time, Meret had been content to let them remain precisely that: some kind of amalgamation of unpredictable wild beast and fictional haunt used to frighten children into obedience. He'd never once considered, in all his time here, that they carried the same scars as anyone else, the same pains, the same traumas…

"Trauma…," he whispered.

"Huh?"

"The, uh, ghosts you described." He cleared his throat, looked up from his work. "Injuries sometimes, uh, take a toll on the mind. People sometimes see manifestations or hallucinations of people, sometimes doing familiar things or acting unusually." Suddenly very aware of her stare on him, he chuckled nervously. "I once treated a woman with a bad hip who claimed to see her husband standing in the corner a lot. It turns out the accident that injured her had killed her husband, and she was, uh…she was feeling guilty."

Sal the Cacophony took her leg off the sill. Her boot struck the floor with a resounding crack of leather against wood. She tucked her thumbs into her belt, tilted her chin up, and regarded him through a stare as long and cold as midnight.

"Do I look like I have a guilty conscience?"

Meret knew a trap when he heard it.

He looked over the Vagrant. Tall and lean, she resembled a blade that had seen too many battles and not enough care. Her leathers— from her shirt to her boots—were caked in dried blood and dirt where they weren't torn or ragged. And the expanses of skin they showed were decorated in injury: scratches, gashes, smears of blood from her or someone else.

Beneath those, though, older injuries clung.

She was used to moving with them, he noticed. Anyone else probably wouldn't have noticed the way she put her weight heavier on one foot than the other, the way her right arm was more tense than the left, the squint in her right eye. The scars, old and thick, patterned her body like a map, telling him not where she'd been, but all the pains that would follow her wherever she was going.

She didn't look guilty. But she looked like she knew regret intimately.

Of course, telling a Vagrant with a huge, fuck-off gun *any* of that seemed like an especially stupid idea.

"No," he said. "But it happens a lot of ways. Even little scratches sometimes leave big wounds on someone's heart. Or soul, or mind, or whatever you want to call it."

Her gaze softened slightly. Her voice followed.

"How do you heal that?"

He looked back up at her and frowned. The austere coolness with which she'd treated him was melting like ice beneath the sun. In her blue eyes, he thought he could see something, the same thing he saw in patients sick with an ailment they didn't understand—a yearning, a need so deep people feared to mention it or give it a name.

But…

He must have been imagining it. There were no stories about Sal the Cacophony that said she could look like that.

"There's no easy answer to that. Pain goes deeper than flesh. The recovery has to go deeper than the pain."

Her face twitched. The scar across her eye wrinkled. A surge of anger at that answer smoldered beneath the grime on her face and he half expected her hand to take that gun and put something through his skull.

But her eyes drifted away from him, down to the bed he sat next to, and the anger dissipated.

What lay behind on her face hurt much worse.

"What about her?" she asked.

Meret looked back down at his patient. The girl had been cleaned up, the grime wiped from her body and the dirty clothes replaced with some garments that had been generously donated by Erton's daughter. He'd set her broken leg and arm, disinfected the wounds, bandaged and balmed what he could but…

"She hasn't woken up," Sal muttered.

"No," he said. "But she's breathing normally. She *should* be fine…"

A long silence he spent praying that she wouldn't punch him.

"But?" she finally asked.

"But she fell out of the fucking sky," he replied. "I've only been looking her over for an hour. There could be internal injuries I don't know about, a break I haven't caught, I don't know."

"Can she be moved?"

"No." He cleared his throat. "I mean, that is…" He sighed, shook his head. "No. I still don't know the extent of her injuries, but I know they're worse than what I can deal with. Moving her would be a really bad idea."

Whatever he feared she might do, Sal simply sighed and nodded. She walked over to him, sat down opposite him beside the bed. Her eyes were locked onto the girl, twitching and appraising, as if searching for a way to simply reach out and . . . fix all of it.

"Who was she?"

Sal glanced up at Meret, eyes narrowed. He winced, looked away.

"I mean who *is* she?" he asked.

"You need to know her name to fix her?"

"No. But . . ."

Sal looked back to the girl and those searching, twitching eyes suddenly became very, very tired.

"She's . . ." She swallowed something bitter. "She's important to me. And she deserves better than what she got."

Meret would have asked her to elaborate, but he was, at that moment, keenly aware of the gun again. He could feel its brass glare beneath its sheath, staring at him, searching as keenly as Sal had searched this woman. And he couldn't help but wonder if that gun, the Cacophony, would simply reach out and pry something out of him.

Don't be stupid, he told himself. *It's just a gun.* He stared at its polished black hilt. *Just a magic gun.* He swallowed hard, found his mouth dry. *Just a magic, talking gun that eats people and has been eating people for who knows how long and . . . okay, yeah, maybe stop looking at it.*

Sal glanced up as Meret pulled himself out of his seat and headed for the door.

"Something wrong?" she asked.

Yes.

"No," he replied. "I just . . . there's an herbal concoction that relaxes muscles. One of my patients makes it. I was going to go . . ." He gestured vaguely at the door. "You know?"

"Is she going to be okay?"

No.

"Huh?"

"While you're gone," Sal replied.

"If anything changes, come get me," he said. "Otherwise, I'll be right back, okay?"

She nodded, looked back to the girl.

He stepped outside, shut the door behind him. Snow had begun to fall in earnest now, nobly struggling to smother the smoldering wreckage that still belched smoke into the air not a mile away. The wind howled, cold bit into him. Yet, he still felt rather warm.

What with Sindra's scowl boring holes into his face.

"She still in there?" the woman growled.

Meret wanted to confirm, and he also wanted to ask if she had been waiting outside his door this whole time. But the sword Sindra carried in her hand persuaded him not to do either.

"What are you going to do with the sword, Sindra?" he asked.

"You don't need to worry about that, apothecary."

Her don't-fuck-with-me-I-have-a-sword voice. He only ever heard that authoritative, soldier's edge to her voice when she was breaking up bar fights or warning people from starting trouble.

Or, apparently, when people made stupid decisions.

"I worry about all my patients, madam," he replied coolly.

"She's not your patient."

"And she's not a criminal."

"Of course she's not a criminal—she's a fucking *Vagrant*!" Sindra snapped. The metal of her prosthetic slammed on the ground as she took one menacing step forward. "You could give a hundred criminals a hundred swords and a hundred gunpikes and *still* not have a creature as dangerous as a Vagrant. She's from the Imperium, she's a conqueror, a...a..."

"An enemy?" Meret asked. "Like the kind you fought in the Revolution?"

She fixed a glare at him. "Don't talk to me like that, Meret. I left my oath to the Great General behind, but I took a new one when I came to this town." She gestured to the nearby houses. "These people are farmers. Traders. I'm the only one who can fight in this entire shitheap."

"Fortunately for you," Meret said, "she doesn't want to fight. So your services will not be required."

"No?" Sindra took a long, menacing step forward. "You see it started snowing?"

He nodded.

"You still see smoke over the ridge?"

He glanced over her shoulder, nodded again.

"So does everyone in a hundred miles," Sindra said, voice low and dangerous. "Revolutionaries will come looking for their airship. Imperials will come looking for the Revolutionaries. Outlaws will come looking for anything left over."

She held up a finger.

"We've got one chance of getting out of this all right." She reached into her coat, produced a medal. The crossed sabers and cogs of the Revolution. "I've still got this. Revolutionaries come here, they'll see one of their own guarding the town. They'll help."

"You're a deserter, Sindra."

"I'll be able to explain that." She pointed a finger toward his door. "But I *won't* be able to explain a fucking *Vagrant* hiding here."

"So," he sighed, "you're going to kill her?"

He could see by the tight set of her jaw that she was considering it. Just as he could see by the frown that followed that she had realized that if even a fraction of the stories about Sal the Cacophony were true, she was going to end up being painted on the walls.

"I'm going to convince her to leave," she said curtly. "She's wounded. She won't want to risk the fight."

"She's wounded, yes," Meret agreed. "Which means I can't let you do that."

"Be practical, apothecary," she warned.

"I am always practical. I'm also always an apothecary. And in the event those two things collide, then..." He closed his eyes, shook his head. "The woman she's with...she's injured. I can't—"

"You'll have a lot more injured if you *don't*," Sindra snapped. "All these people, *all* of them...you swore to help them, too, didn't you? How are you going to help them when soldiers come? They can't fight, they can't organize, they—"

"Can they leave?"

It suddenly got much colder.

Meret whirled, following Sindra's horrified gaze to the tattooed woman standing in his doorway. Sal the Cacophony lazily leaned against the door frame, idly scratching an itch on her belly as she offered Sindra a slow, cold look.

"Can they leave?" Sal asked again. "Do they have birds?"

Sindra furrowed her brow, reached for the hilt of her sword. "They do. But they aren't going anywhere."

"No?" Sal asked.

She took a step out of the house. Sindra took a step back, seizing her sword. Meret swallowed hard as a cold dread punched through him.

"Why not?"

"Because this is their land," Sindra growled. "They've worked it hard. Too hard to give it up to a Vagrant. They'll die before they let you—"

"I get you."

Leather hissed. Brass sang out. Falling flakes of snow became steam as they landed on the barrel.

The Cacophony was drawn. Meret held his breath.

Sindra cursed, pulling her sword free and sliding into an attack stance. But she did not move—either waiting for Sal to strike first or just too fucking scared at the sight of that grinning dragon of a weapon. She did not attack.

Neither did Sal.

"Apothecary." Sal fished something out of her satchel, flipped the chamber of her gun open. "Who lives in that house over there?"

"Which?" Meret looked over.

"The one across the road. The big one."

He squinted. Bigger and nicer than the other meager cabins and cottages, Lady Kalavin's manor loomed as a peasant over dirt. She'd come here with money, it was said, after her spouse died in the Imperial army. She'd erected a nice place—not nice enough to be considered Imperial, mind, but certainly nicer than anywhere else in Littlebarrow. She had *two* floors, after all.

"Lady Kalavin," he replied. "But—"

"Does she live alone?" Sal asked, flipping the chamber shut.

"She has a servant," Meret said, "but they both went to the market in Owltown this morning."

"Pets?" She drew the hammer back.

"Just a cat. But she takes it with her wherever she goes."

"Bedchambers and kitchen," Sal said. "Are they on the second floor?"

"N-no." Meret furrowed his brow. "She says it hurts her hip to climb stairs, so she—"

"Good."

Sal raised the Cacophony.

And fired.

The shot rang out, streaking through the snowy skies with a wail to punch a jagged wound in the upper floor's windows. A breath passed.

Discordance rang out.

In a spray of finery—clothes, chairs, the severed remains of a few sculptures—the house erupted with a blast of sound. Glass and timber rained down alongside the falling snow to plummet into the street. The remains of portraits drifted on the wind, shredded. Destroyed bottles of wine bloodied the snow.

Meret's scream had been lost in the noise. He'd never seen such destruction, such effortless horror. He was unable to look away from the jagged crown of shattered wood that the house now wore.

And yet...

The more he looked, the more he saw no one had been injured. No one had been in the streets. Even the houses nearby were spared anything worse than a shard of wood lodged in their roof.

Sal the Cacophony, killer of men and beasts and everything that had walked on this dark earth, had failed to kill anyone.

"Anybody still out there, listen up!"

In the aftermath of the sound, Sal's voice carried clear and sharp as she shouted into the snow.

"This pissberg town belongs to Sal the Cacophony now!" she cried out. "I won't take your money and I won't take your shit. But I'll take your land. And if you're still here in another..."

She glanced toward Meret. "How many people live here?"

He turned, stunned, toward her. "Huh?"

"People. How many?"

"S-seventy," he said. "Wait, no. Sixty-nine. Bennerus moved to the city last week."

"Nice," she grunted, and looked back out into the snow. Then she shouted, "If you're still here in another three hours, I'll take *everything* from you." She snorted, spat into the snow. "Anyone unclear on that, feel free to come by and see me. I'll be happy to straighten it out for you after I fuck your face, your spouse, and your life." She narrowed her eyes. "*Three hours!*"

She looked out over the silence, the snow gathering over the ruins of the house she'd just destroyed, and nodded to herself.

She slid her gun back into her sheath, fastening it.

"As long as she's here," Sal whispered, "I'm here. I don't want any trouble and I won't offer it. But if anyone wants me to leave before she's ready..."

She looked up and stared Sindra in the eye.

"Honey," she said, "you'd better bring a lot more swords than that."

She turned away, as if daring Sindra to strike. But by the time she'd walked back inside and shut the door behind her, Sindra was still rooted to the same spot she'd been in, hands bloodlessly clenched around her hilt, eyes wide and unblinking, mouth fumbling for words.

Meret swallowed hard, stared out at the devastation.

In the distance, smoke continued to climb.

FIVE

THE VALLEY

We had been traveling for hours when I felt it.

A sudden chill fell upon my brow, seeping into my skin. I blinked, touching it with a pair of fingers and bringing back water. I looked up and saw the snow beginning to fall.

The forest loomed kingly around me, ancient firs and pines that wore crowns of bare branches and sat upon gnarled root thrones. As the snow began to fall in earnest, they made tired sighs as they settled upon their roots, as though the entire forest had been holding its breath for winter.

I peeled my scarf off my neck and gave it a flick of my wrist, and when I held it again, it was a full-sized cloak. I pulled it around me, drawing the hood up—I guess you might expect something flashier from an enchanted scarf, but damn if that one wasn't useful.

A thin carpet had blanketed the old road that wound its way through the forest, pristine white marred only by the tracks of traveling caravans or passing beasts. Those few willow trees still stubbornly holding on to their leaves leaned far out to let the snow accumulate on their boughs. Far away, a bird sang a single verse of a lonely song, the last holdout to admit that autumn was over.

I closed my eyes, breathed in the cold. The woodlands of the Borrus Valley stretched out for a still, soundless black-and-white eternity.

Really, if you ignored the parts where people had been violently blown apart, the whole scene was quite tasteful.

Every now and then, you could catch a glimpse through the endless trees. In the distance, a hastily erected graveyard with wooden markers for the dead who couldn't be carried back lined the forest floor like mushrooms. Beside the road, a rusting Revolutionary tower tank, its stone-and-metal hull shredded by magic, huddled beneath the snow, a peasant among kings. Here and there, you saw the signs where mages had wrought their fury—granite statues of soldiers, their faces frozen in the horror of the last moment before the spell had struck; trees and earth sundered where great jagged spikes had burst from the dirt; the occasional Echo of a person who would form in the swirling winds, scream a soundless word, then disappear.

In the Scar, the difference between a bad piece of land and a nice piece of land was whether your life was routinely threatened by beasts and outlaws or if your life was routinely threatened by warring armies fighting over it.

And Borrus Valley was one of the nicest pieces of land in the whole fucking place.

With cool summers and bearable winters, it was already tempting to begin with. But its richness in ore, timber, game, and fish was what led the Glorious Revolution of the Fist and Flame, freshly liberated from Imperium rule, to settle it originally. Likewise, those same qualities—plus the fact that their former subjects now held it—were more than enough to draw the Imperial legions and its mages to fight over it.

The battles that had followed had been savage, as any battle between a nation of machine-riding fanatics with giant guns and a nation of magic-flinging lunatics who can shit fire would be, with the Imperium eventually claiming a bloody, if tentative, victory in the Valley. Eventually, through local efforts, rebel uprisings, and good old-fashioned body counts, an uneasy peace had settled.

A peace I was content to enjoy, for the moment.

"Squawrk."

Of course, I was probably the only one.

Underneath me, my mount shifted uncomfortably, rustling her black feathers. A long, naked neck ending in a bald avian head with a vicious beak and a pair of piercing eyes twitched, shaking off snow that had settled upon her pate. Congeniality let out another irritated squawk, stomping from one powerful clawed foot to another, decidedly off-put that this wet white stuff was insisting on ruining her lovely black plumage.

For someone who routinely ate carrion until she puked, Congeniality was surprisingly delicate.

"Easy, madam." I reached out and stroked her neck soothingly, giving her flanks a gentle nudge to keep her walking. "I've seen you tear apart warlords with your feet. Whatever *will* the neighbors say to see you scared of a little snow?"

Congeniality arched her neck and let out a quarrelsome chirrup. I sighed and reached behind me into her saddlebags, rooting around for something dead and furry. I pulled out a vole—I wasn't about to reward this obstinate behavior with anything bigger—and slipped it toward her.

Her neck twisted, beak snapping out, narrowly avoiding taking my hand off as she snatched up the rodent. She threw her head back, its legs disappearing down her craw as she swallowed the thing whole.

"Really, madam," I chided. "Just because we're on the road is no reason to forget your manners."

"Trouble back there?"

Jero had paused in the road ahead, reining his own bird—a shabby-looking Imperial Bushnester with legs so twiggy they should be ashamed to be in the presence of thews so mighty as Congeniality's—to a halt and glancing back.

"She's just not used to cold weather," I said, patting her neck and spurring her forward. "Badlanders like her are used to uglier climates."

"Ah. Well, I'd hate to subject a lady of such refinement to anything more than necessary." Jero chuckled, kicking his bird back to a saunter as I caught up. "Terassus is just up ahead. All the luxuries and amenities that a handful of rich, bored old fucks can buy await us. Soon enough you'll have everything you need. A nice, warm stable, plenty of feed…"

"Hopefully a bath," I muttered.

"Absolutely," Jero replied. "And none too soon, either. The smell was beginning to get unbearable."

"I meant for me."

He shot me a wink. "So did I."

He pointedly avoided looking at me as we continued to make our way, which I was grateful for. This man had sought me out for my reputation as a ruthless killer, after all. It wouldn't do for him to see me grinning like an idiot just then.

I couldn't help it because I couldn't recall how long it had been since I had spoken to someone who I wasn't about to kill or who wasn't about to help me find someone who I wanted to kill. Granted, I suppose Jero fell under the latter category, but he at least managed to talk to me like I was just someone else, not a hired gun or a killer. To anyone else, we would have just looked like two people traveling through the woods.

I wondered, if we walked long enough, would we look that way to me, too?

I suppose that might sound odd, but in this line of work, moments of happiness come wedged between tragedies. And, as I was walking away from one massacre into another one, I was content to hold on to this one.

After all, as the burning displeasure of the Cacophony coursing through my wrist reminded me, those moments didn't come often in the Scar.

And after this, they might not come for a long time.

"What's Terassus like these days?" I asked. "Last I heard, it was what everyone was fighting over."

"It was. But then the Imperium won the war and figured out they liked money more than blood. It's a safe place now. Mostly."

I shot Jero a sidelong glance. "Meaning?"

"Meaning..." He scratched his chin, contemplative. "You ever been with a woman, say, in an intimate setting and you ask if you can try a certain maneuver and she *says* it's fine but you can tell that just by asking you know something bad is about to happen?"

I furrowed my brow. "I don't... Wait, what kind of maneuver?"

"Does it matter?"

"Obviously."

"Oh, I don't know. Let's say ... the Oiled Shears."

"Eastern or Western?"

"Western."

"Oh. *OH!*" I winced. "Things are *that* bad?"

"Don't let me mislead you," he said, waving a hand. "Aside from the odd assassination, things are mostly easy. The Imperium wasted no time in establishing order once they'd won the war."

"Meaning they killed everyone who looked vaguely like a Revolutionary and enslaved the nuls?"

"Close. They stopped *just* shy of enslaving, preferring instead to rely on economics to do that for them. The Valley's resources made them rich enough to realize that tempting people with just a few pieces of metal while they hoard the bulk of it was easier to keep them working than forcing them to."

He clicked his tongue, pulled his bird to slow down.

"You're dead on about the killing part, though. They don't want to admit that they don't have the power here to force the magically disinclined to obey them, so the hope is that, with enough money coming through Terassus, peace will eventually settle."

"Huh." My nostrils quivered at the scent of smoke. "You think that'll happen?"

"I hope not," Jero replied. "Peace would make what we're about to do irritatingly difficult."

I would have asked, but at that moment, the scent of smoke became a reek. The trees gave way to spires and rooftops. And my grin gave way to a deep frown.

The city of Terassus loomed large overhead, its towers already cloaked with snow and columns of chimney smoke clawing their way through the white haze. The quiet of the forest was replaced with the increasing din of civilization—smith hammers banging, wagons rattling as the birds that drew them squawked, and punctuating each noise, the sound of people, shouting, laughing, weeping, cursing.

I couldn't remember when I had pulled Congeniality to a halt, let alone why. But at that moment, when I looked up at Terassus's stone gates, I recall having a profoundly ill feeling, like I was about to walk naked into a funeral.

"Something wrong?"

Ahead, Jero glanced back at me. A bored-looking guard, dressed in the violet foppery of an Imperial bureaucrat, waved the few travelers besides us through. He spared an irritated glance for the woman who had suddenly decided to hold up the line, opening his mouth to say something. Without looking at him, Jero silenced him with a single hand raised.

His eyes never left mine.

The feeling didn't leave me, but I shook my head all the same. Jero's eyes lingered on me for another second before he spurred his bird forward through the gates. I followed.

I couldn't let Jero or his employer think Sal the Cacophony was uneasy about a city.

I was about to kill people for them, after all.

Terassus had the distinct honor of being the only Imperial city in the Valley to not have begun life as a fortress. Once the Imperium's foothold in the region was secure enough for them to want in, the nobility found the various forward commands rather too . . . *severed-heads-on-pikes-y* for their tastes. Mages were shipped out, spellsmiths and wrights followed, and through immense cost, the city of Terassus had been born.

I bet it was beautiful before the war.

Not that it wasn't beautiful now, mind you. But just like the fanciest clothes can't hide a grievous scar, all the finery of Terassus couldn't hide the wounds that hadn't healed. Bombed-out shells of houses remained tucked away behind their more elegant neighbors. Here and there a crater from Revolutionary cannons hadn't gotten around to being filled. And, if you knew where to look, you'd wonder why a city as fine as Terassus had so many graveyards.

But the goal of fancy clothes is to draw the eye away from the scars, after all. And no one made things fancier than the Imperium. While the cozy houses and shops of the city were all made by the hands of honest workers, the great spires and cliffs that overlooked it, impossibly sheer and elegant, had been carved by magic.

The manors that loomed over the city were severe and ostentatious— a handful in a golden gauntlet. Sparkling gates of ivory and marble secluded gardens of moving hedges and living water. Animate figures set in stained glass windows sneered down at the rabble that kept the appetites of the lords overhead fed. The glow of spell-lights burned through the snow, illuminating spectral sculptures depicting endless phantom displays of mighty heroes felling terrible beasts or operatic lovers embracing.

The Imperials overhead had designed their various decadences to overlook the town, in full view of the populace below. Perhaps to show off their wealth or to remind the commoners that they could be bought or sold at a moment's notice. From down here in the streets of Terassus, you could see every opulence, every gaudy display of wealth, everything…

Except, of course, a way for any commoner to get up there.

An avian keen caught my ear. And a moment later, a great claw nearly caught my head.

I ducked, a stiff wind sending my scarf whipping about my face, and Congeniality squawked angrily. Though through her ire, I could hear the distinct laughter of assholes lilting on the snowy sky.

I looked up and saw them, ghostly shapes of ivory and onyx feathers twisting through the snow.

Oyakai. Black-and-white birds, each amply big enough for the gaily dressed riders astride their backs—twisting and wheeling through the sky as they scraped over rooftops and sped down avenues, sending commoners diving for cover before ascending into the snow clouds to disappear into aerie towers atop the cliffs.

I watched them vanish into their estates of glowing spell-lights and mage-twisted stones. I trotted down the city streets in Jero's wake, until those estates, too, vanished behind the falling snow.

As the snow settled on my shoulders, I started to feel a cold deeper than the wind could bite.

Not for what I'd just seen. I suppose some people might have found the senseless opulence looming overhead to be uncomfortable—after all, no one likes being reminded that there are people out there who can buy and sell them like meat. But me? I'd met a significant amount of rich assholes—first serving them when I was in the Imperial guard, then robbing them when I went Vagrant—certainly enough to know that they died screaming and covered in urine, just like anyone else.

Rather, it was what I saw when I looked down that unnerved me.

People were helping each other to their feet, helping gather up bundles and baskets that had been struck from wagons when the Oyakai had buzzed the streets. They were cracking jokes about the rich assholes dropping golden shits and laughing. Smiths were hammering at steel as apprentices showed them shoddy work for inspection. Young men and women laborers were singing work songs in off-key unison as they pulled heavy wagons down the streets. Mothers talked with fathers, each of them keeping an eye on children desperately struggling to gather up enough snow to hurl at each other.

People were talking, laughing, buying, selling, joking, complaining, insulting...

...and I had no idea how they did it.

I didn't know how they bowed to each other without checking to make sure the other person wouldn't stab them when they inclined their head. I didn't see how they could walk the streets without a piece of steel and look like that was perfectly fine. I stared at them, embracing and laughing and making it all look so easy, and wondered what the fuck I was doing wrong that that all looked...so unnatural.

How long, I wondered, *was I out in the wilds?*

"DOOM IS UPON YOU, SINNERS!"

Probably fucked up of me to say that the sound of someone screaming death threats made me sit a little easier in my saddle, but I assure you, that won't be the weirdest thing you hear out of me.

My attentions were drawn to a tiny square and the stark red figure standing at its center. Her crimson robes hung loose and tattered about her withered frame, lending the impression of someone bleeding out on the streets. Her staff, as withered and gnarled as the hand that held it, swept decisively over the crowd assembled around her. A hood, etched with a single eye wreathed in flame, hung low over her head.

To look at her, you might have called her weird-looking.

Until you saw the hollowed-out holes where her eyes should have been, a pair of pale flames burning there.

Then I guess you'd call her something worse, if you could stop screaming.

Sightless Sisters had that effect on people.

"The Seeing God judges you, and all your hedonist ways!" she shrieked to a small, attentive crowd. "He sees your opulence! He sees your pride! He shall claim both before he grants you reprieve! Your world shall end in flame! A cleansing purity shall sweep o'er the land and you shall weep upon the ashes that remain!"

"You're gawking."

I glanced ahead to see Jero shooting a smile back at me.

"I can't imagine a woman who has a song written about the time she won a drinking contest, a shooting contest, and a riding contest all in the same day has never seen a preacher from Haven before."

"*The Ballad of Two-Hundred Beers* is a classic in some regions, you heathen," I replied. I glanced back at the Sister. "I've seen, fought, and almost been killed by Haveners before. I didn't expect to see them here so . . . so . . ."

"Unskewered?" Jero chuckled. "They started filtering in a few months ago and occupied houses destroyed by the war. The guards call it Little Haven. Terassus's upper crust thought it charmingly eccentric enough to allow them to stay."

Eccentric was a weird word for "prone to tearing unbelievers limb from limb in a drug-fueled fanatical rage," but what the fuck did I know? I'd only seen them kill about six or seven hundred people in a gibbering orgy of bloodshed. Hardly enough to make a judgment.

And I was hardly the only one. The crowd gathered around the preaching Sister was small, so small you could convince yourself they were just normal people with normal curiosities.

If you didn't look into their eyes, anyway. If you'd seen what I'd seen—the hollowness, the hunger, the desperate raptness that comes from people who've seen so much misery that even the most deranged shit starts making sense if it promises to end it . . .

Well, maybe you'd have been as worried as I was.

"We're not far from the border with Haven," Jero continued, decidedly not sharing my concern. "You find these things all over the Valley."

"Right, but I expected to see them in the hills and the forests and wherever else you let religious fanatics who gouge out their own eyes dwell." I winced as we rounded a corner. "Not in respectable cities."

"You don't. So long as they stay down here, with the commoners who spend more time watching their backs around the Seeing God's fanatics than they do thinking about the rich fools who put them there, the Imperials in Terassus are happy to have them."

"But you just said Haveners don't come into respectable cities."

"And I meant it." Jero glanced toward a nearby alley. "But what about any of what I just said makes Terassus sound respectable?"

I saw it, too. A scarecrow of a man, wretched and wrapped in rags, coiled in a greasy heap at the base of a decrepit shell of a building, a beggar's bowl sitting empty but for a few bent metal bits at his feet. Whatever he'd done before he ended up like this, he must have been even shittier at it than he was a scarecrow, for a fat black bird sat perched atop his head, crying out at whoever happened to pass.

You probably wouldn't think of him as anything more than another destitute relic of the war. But then, that's precisely how he wanted to be thought of. As I turned away from the glare he shot me, I was content to indulge that fantasy.

I knew how that crow got so fat.

"Ah." Jero's voice brought my attentions back. "Here we are."

Silence descended with the snowfall as we turned into a small huddle of quaint houses posing as a square. A dead tree rose at the center, a stubborn old man refusing to give in to the uneven cobblestones crowding around him. The few houses that huddled close together seemed intent on ignoring us, their windows shuttered and their porches thick with snow.

If the rest of Terassus felt like a warm family gathered at a dinner table, this square felt like the aging relative they kept upstairs waiting to die. The silence was thick, even the crunch of snow beneath Congeniality's feet barely audible. I felt like I had walked out of a city and into a graveyard.

And, fucked up as it was, it was only here that I finally felt myself relax.

The only signs of life came from a broad, two-story building at the end of the square. Smoke wafted from a stout chimney, lights burned behind frosted-over windows, and, beneath a gently creaking sign depicting a toad being beaten and looking quite pleased about it, a severe-looking woman in a faded purple robe dutifully swept gathering snow from the steps of an open door.

"I daresay I must be dying," Jero called out suddenly, breaking the tranquility, "for I see before me a heavenly creature here to usher me to my final reward."

Distaste was not the word I'd use to describe the look the woman gave when she glanced up. One *distasted* things like noisy eaters and bad wine. The look this woman offered Jero, through a frown set in wrinkles so deep they were like scars, was less about taste than it was suppressing the urge to vomit over his shoes.

"Were I you," she replied through a measured voice, "I would not tempt me." She swept the last of the snow away from her steps. "Or I would, at least, wait for me to get something heavier and sharper than a broom."

"You wound me, madam. I had hoped my month's absence would have made you miss me." Jero hopped off his bird and glanced around the square. "I also kind of hoped you'd have asked a brothel to move in next door, like we talked about."

"The only ass in this square that anyone would look at is the one I'm talking to." The woman set her broom aside and came stalking toward us, shooting a glare in my direction. "And if you wanted a warmer welcome, you should stop bringing trash to my door."

I opened my mouth to protest.

Then I remembered how I must smell.

She carried herself well, I noticed, walking with a poise you typically didn't see in cities this small. Though her hair was streaked with gray, it was still immaculately done up in a pristine Imperial style, not a hair out of place. Her robe, too, was well maintained and of fine Cathama silk. At a glance, I'd have said she belonged up on the cliffs with the other elites. Except for the way she shoved Jero away with one hand and snatched the reins of his bird with the other.

"Well?" She looked up at me, expectant. "If you want me to stable that feathered wreck you're riding, you'd better hop off."

Congeniality let out an irate squawk. I stroked the bird's neck. "I should probably do it myself. She gets a touch...sensitive around strangers."

The woman rolled her eyes. "I've met many, *many* sensitive sorts, honey, and not one of them I couldn't bring begging to their knees with my little finger. And I intend to use my full hand with this one."

I blinked. "Was that...like a threat or..."

"I'd do what she says, Sal," Jero offered. "Madame Fist doesn't typically offer twice."

I blinked. Again. "Madame Fist? Why do they—"

"Because if I had as much luck as I had talent, I'd have an excellent job as a capital courtesan instead of my current illustrious position as a translator for the wooden-witted and obstinate."

"Wait…what?"

"It means I spend too much time talking to assholes. Now, off, if you please."

You don't typically get a name like Madame Fist because you're used to being disobeyed, I reasoned, and so slid off Congeniality. The bird glanced toward me, imploring, before Madame Fist gave her a swift jerk on her reins.

"I'm your mommy now, dearest," she hissed to Congeniality before glancing toward Jero. "Your boss is in his room. He's expecting you."

"Don't think I won't be informing him about the dreadful conduct in this establishment," Jero replied.

Madame Fist stopped midstride. A chill deeper than the falling snow settled over the square. And Congeniality—who had stared down rampaging beasts and torn the guts out of outlaw kings without blinking—let out a nervous squawk.

"Understand this, *Master* Jero," she uttered, voice like frost. "The arrangement your employer and I have come to includes room, board, and my silence on your dealings here. The furthest politeness I am willing to extend you without additional payment is abstaining from lodging my foot so far up your ass I'll wear your teeth as a toe ring." She cast the narrowest-eyed glare I'd ever seen over her shoulder. "And should your employer's money ever dry up, rest assured that this kindness, too, will vanish as surely and swiftly as my pristine boots."

I've stood within blade's reach of badlands warlords. I've held my breath as beasts with more fangs than mouth hunted for my scent. I've seen damn near every horror, two-legged or otherwise, that the Scar has to offer.

Now, I'm not saying Madame Fist was the *most* intimidating of all those. But if you'd been there, you'd have understood why people, birds, and everything else did what she told them to.

The woman, with my suddenly-very-obedient bird in tow, rounded a corner to the stable and disappeared. I glanced at Jero, who stared at her wake with an impassiveness I couldn't help but be impressed by.

"You, uh, at all worried about that?" I asked. "That was an *exceedingly* specific threat against your ass."

"Oh, please." Jero shrugged as he walked up the steps and pushed the door open. "She knows I don't have enough to pay for that."

I'd been in nicer inns than the Caned Toad. The floors, though impeccably washed, were old and creaky under my boots. The scents of the kitchen were of predictable stew and bread. The selection of liquor I could see behind the bar could charitably be called a war crime. The bath was nice enough, but smelled too much of sweat and desperation.

But the stew was filling.

The whiskey was warm.

And goddamn if the steam didn't feel good on my scars.

I'd been in nicer inns than this one, true. But at that moment, if I closed my eyes, this one made me feel like I could pretend I was just normal.

Like anyone else in this city.

"We should get going. There are a *lot* of people we need to kill."

I hadn't known Jero long, but he seemed to have a talent for ruining the mood. He certainly hadn't let me enjoy the amenities for long—I had barely been allowed to stick my head into the bath before he hurried me upstairs to the inn's rooms.

"If that's all you wanted, there are others you could have gotten for less effort," I replied as he led me down the carpeted hall, closed doors flanking us. "I mean, not that I'm not *good* at killing, but…"

"Rest assured, I would not have been requested to seek you out if my employer could be satisfied with a few dead bodies. He didn't get to be the greatest Freemaker in the Scar by limiting his vision to mere corpses, after all. What he has planned is something far greater." He shot a smile at me over his shoulder. "And there aren't nearly as many stories told about someone who's merely *good* at killing as there are about you, Sal the Cacophony."

He was either attempting to praise me or this was an extremely fucked-up way of flirting. Either way, I was just a little flattered. Not that reminding me of dead bodies was the best way to go about that, but…

I guess it had just been a while since someone had smiled at me like that.

"That is, of course, if I decide to accept your offer," I reminded him. "I'm not agreeing to anything until I know exactly what he wants."

"Of course," Jero replied. "In which case, you'll be free to take what information we've offered, indulge our hospitality as long as you please, and leave with as much whiskey as you want." He paused, then added, "Without the location of Darrish the Flint."

And just like that, all those pleasant smiles and warm feelings and illusions of pretending to be normal melted, like snow on the windows. My scars ached, the Cacophony burned at my hip, and in the pocket of my scarf, I could feel the tiny scrap of paper I carried there suddenly feel as though it weighed as much as a boulder.

The list.

For a moment, I had forgotten about it, and all the names on it. I had forgotten that until each and every Vagrant written on it was dead, all I'd ever be doing was pretending things would be normal.

I couldn't pretend. I was tired of it.

"Ah, here we are."

I looked up at his voice to the dead end he had led us to. A wall, bare except for a portrait of a sailboat, loomed before us. I shot him a look that was still struggling to decide whether it was confusion or a scowl to be swiftly followed by a punch in the mouth if he had dragged me this whole fucking way to see a painting.

It didn't even have any naked people on it.

"Just a moment." Jero knelt down, pulled a piece of paper out of his pocket, and ran it along the edges of the wall. "This normally works on its own, but sometimes it needs a little—Oh, here it is."

He pressed the paper hard against the wall. A sigil glowed upon its surface. In response, a small line of similar sigils tracing the edge of the wall glowed with a faint light. There was a hushed sound as the wall began to slide away, disappearing into the building and exposing a hallway hidden behind it.

"Spellwrighting," I whispered.

"A command sigil, specifically," Jero replied, standing up. "One of our employer's own making. He is a fairly talented wright, himself." He shot me an inquisitive glance. "You know anything about them?"

I opened my mouth to reply. But I forgot how to speak—that knowledge was buried under a slew of images that came flashing into my head. Dark eyes hidden behind thick glasses. Quills worn in a tight bun of black hair. Hands that used to feel so good on my scars...

"No," I settled for saying. "But I used to know someone who did."

"Basically, the command sigil is what persuades an object to think it's something else," Jero said, beckoning me to follow him down the hall. "Such as persuading a wall that it's a door."

"I see," I grunted. "This job going to feature a lot of magical bullshit?"

"I'd tell you myself what the job requires," he chuckled, "but he's only ever divulged pieces of the plan. Any one of us knows only a fraction of his full vision."

" 'Us'?" I quirked a brow. "There's more?"

"You didn't expect a mind as keen as his to come up with a plan that could be accomplished with only two people, did you?" Jero said, grinning. "I was the first moving part in this machine of his and I've spent the last four months finding others. You're simply the last one before we can get this thing rolling on its way to—"

His metaphor was cut short as he rounded the corner and collided face-first with what appeared to be a moving wall of extremely fine cloth.

"Jero, Jero, Jero..."

As a deep voice chided him and a pair of large hands took him by his shoulders, I could see that the moving wall was, in fact, just a woman in extremely fine cloth.

"There are *astonishingly* easier ways to get your face in a woman's breasts."

A very...very tall woman.

Her admittedly fine wardrobe couldn't do much to hide the muscle packed onto the six-and-a-half-foot frame that loomed over Jero like an exceptionally dapper tower. Tight-fitting breeches and boots strained against powerful legs, and she wore a red silk vest over a long-sleeved white shirt contouring a powerful chest and broad, brawny arms.

She pulled Jero off his feet like he was a toy, bringing him face-to-much-prettier-face. You wouldn't think a woman that tall could be coquettish, but the smile she shot him was a fine match for the fluttering of her eyelashes, her elegant features framed by short-cropped jet-black hair, oiled and slicked back.

"I'm vaguely insulted you didn't offer me at least a bottle of wine beforehand, though."

You wouldn't think a woman that tall could giggle as effetely as she did, either, but damn if today wasn't just full of surprises.

"For you, I'd need far more than a bottle." Jero, it had to be said, did not share her amusement and regarded her flatly. "Put me down, for fuck's sake. We have company."

"We do?" She glanced over him at me and her eyes lit up. "We *do*!"

She dropped him rather rudely and strode over him as though she had already forgotten that she could step on him. Smiling, she extended a large hand replete with perfectly manicured nails to me.

"Madam," she said, "don't we look lovely today?"

"Uh, thanks?" I reached out and took her hand. "I'm—"

"Oh, I know full well who you are." She brought my hand up and gently kissed the first two fingers in the old Imperial style. "I've heard the stories. The nice ones, anyway."

I couldn't help but grin. "There are no nice ones about me, madam."

"Oh? Is it not true you once fought ten outlaws to a standstill to defend a young gentleman's honor?"

It was true.

Well, it was partially true.

Well, it was *vaguely* true.

He wasn't honorable, just a rich spawn of a richer sire who ran away to go start his own outlaw kingdom and who I had to drag back to his father...who, at the time, was willing to let slide the fact that I had robbed his caravan not three days earlier if I did. The part about fighting ten outlaws to a standstill was true, though.

I mean, I guess they were standing still after I blew them up, so yeah, like I said, vaguely true.

"You have me at a disadvantage," I replied, "Madame…"

"Agnestrada," she said, voice smooth as silk.

I furrowed my brow. The name sounded familiar. And there were only so many women *that* tall in the world, let alone the Scar. Still, I found my thoughts more consumed with what, exactly, Jero and his master were planning that they needed someone like her around.

"Agne." Jero rose to his feet and dusted himself off. "Am I to assume your presence here means something's gone awry? We were on our way to see Two Lonely Old Men."

"You *were*, yes. But now you're on the way to help me with something else." Agne jerked a thumb back down the way we came. "The man himself asked me to come find you and help find the others. That delightful little horned man took off this morning and the twins are doubtlessly scribbling away somewhere."

Jero clenched his teeth. "Then go find them."

She shook her head. "The one twin only listens to his sister. And *she* only listens to you. She doesn't like me for some reason." She leaned over to me—well, *over* me—and whispered conspiratorially, "I suspect she's envious of my feminine mystique."

I certainly wasn't about to argue that. And neither was Jero, who rubbed his eyes and threw up his hands.

"All right. Fucking fine. I'll help you find them." He glanced to me, gestured down the hall with his chin. "He'll be expecting you, though. Last door. Knock first."

"A pleasure to meet you, my darling." Agne took Jero's hand in hers, sparing the other to offer me a dainty wave as she hauled him off. "I simply can't *wait* to start killing people with you."

She seemed nice.

I continued down the hall, coming to a pair of double doors at the end of it. Simple, unassuming—not the sort of thing you'd expect a Freemaker, secretive as they are, to be hiding behind. But I leaned out and knocked, all the same.

No answer came back.

I waited a moment before putting my hand on the knob and pushing the door open.

And I came face-to-face with the city I had killed.

It was Lastlight. Lastlight's streets, polished and pristine. Lastlight's homes and shops and buildings, marching down the avenues. Last-light's spires rising high above everything to look down upon it through sparkling windows behind flying red-and-white banners. Lastlight's canals, beautiful and blue, wending their way through the streets and under bridges like veins of precious ore.

And the lanterns...

Tiny lights scattered across the city, hanging from every eave, decorating every tower, floating down every canal. When Lastlight had still stood, these lights had lit up the whole city, a sky full of red and white stars under which people had traded, laughed...

And died. The night I had brought a war to their doorsteps.

The detail on the city was so perfect that it took me a second to realize it was entirely miniature. The re-creation sprawled across an immense table, the sole furniture in the room, beneath the glow of an alchemic light overhead. Each building was a perfect replica of its life-sized original, down to the last window on the last house on the last lane.

It was incredible. I felt like I should have been marveling. And if I was anyone else, I probably would have.

But I was Sal the Cacophony. And I couldn't look at that tiny city without seeing a little cemetery. Each building a grave. Each spire a tomb.

Too many of them wrought by my hand.

"Three months."

A voice rasped from the vastness of the room. In the shadows on the other side of the table, something stirred and leaned forward, into the pale light.

A man. Or maybe a skeleton that hadn't figured out it was dead yet. It was hard to tell.

He was tall, thin, and honestly not that old. But weariness had carved away youth and vigor, leaving behind someone too gaunt to eat, too tired to die. His hair was more white than black now, hanging in unkempt streaks about his haggard face. His body bent in the way that only once-proud postures could. His clothes were fine, but unwashed and wrinkled. And his face hung like a dead man from a tree, sallow skin sagging around a pair of deep-set, dark-circled eyes.

Two Lonely Old Men.

Once the greatest Freemaker in the Scar. Now keeper to the world's tiniest crypt.

"Three months, twenty-four days, sixteen hours, forty-nine minutes and"—he paused, closed his eyes, his lips continuing to twitch silently before he finished—"seven seconds." He waved a thin hand over the miniature city. "That's how long it took."

I stared at the city—*his* city—silently. Had it been that long since Lastlight was destroyed? Since I had disappeared into the wilds and went chasing my death? It felt longer to me, like I had vanished from a world that had kept on going for years after I was gone.

I wondered if it felt like that to him, too.

"Lastlight...the *real* Lastlight, was built in just twenty-two years," Two Lonely Old Men continued, his voice like broken glass. "Inexact, I know, but it never truly stopped building. Every year, there were more people wanting more homes. Every year, I thought we could build the towers higher or make the lanterns glow brighter." He stared at the miniature city for a long, silent moment. "The lanterns were the hardest part to get right. There were so many of them.

"But I remember each one," he said, "because I was there for each one we put up. It was my alchemics and sigils that made them glow, after all. And it was my design that every building was made from. I was there for every tower, for every tavern, for every café and shop and garden and park..."

His voice trailed off. His eyes did, too, drifting off to some dark place in the room and staring at a ghostly city much grander than this one.

"Twenty-two years."

He swayed, unsteady, and leaned on the table's edge.

"And they destroyed it in less than a day."

They had.

Or rather, *we* had.

The Scar was full of tales of how it had happened. No one could agree on who fired the first shot—whether it was Revolutionary cannons or Imperial birds dropping spells. Just like no one could agree who the first civilian casualty was—a family caught in the crossfire or an old man who was struck down in a blast. But everyone knew that the Revolution and the Imperium tore each other to pieces and, in the process, took Lastlight with them.

Sal the Cacophony was also there. Some said that she started the whole thing. Some said she just walked out of it. Some said that she individually went from house to house and put a blade in the throat of every last man, woman, and child she could find.

Honestly, when I think back, I sometimes have a hard time remembering which it was.

But I was there. And I had brought fire and blood to that city. When I walked away, I walked away from a pile of ash and dust.

I wanted to say that it had been worth it. That evil people had died because of what I did that night. And that was true. But when I opened my mouth to say that, I could taste the lie on my tongue.

No matter how many evil people I had killed, I had killed far more good people.

I didn't know what words I could say to even those scales.

I didn't know if they existed.

"I don't blame you, Cacophony."

Maybe he sensed my hesitation. Or maybe he was just talking to himself. He wasn't looking at me, his eyes still locked on that tiny city.

"You weren't the first person to bring weapons to my city," he said. "Nor was yours, impressive as it was, the most destructive one she had ever seen. All you did was start a fight. Lastlight had seen many fights before." He shook his head, sending strands of hair trembling. "It was me who let the Imperium in. Me who let the Revolution in. Me who, somehow, assumed they would never think to stain it with their ugly war."

He twitched, grimaced, shut his eyes.

"Not right. No, that's not right at all. It's not that I assumed they would *never* fight. It just…didn't occur to me." He looked back at his tiny city, despair creased over his face. "I thought everyone would look on Lastlight like I had. I thought they would see its lights and its towers and its water and see what I saw. Every morning I awoke, I stared out over that city and thought how lucky I was to have been able to build it, to have created it." He sighed so hard he almost lost his balance. "You look at your child and you wonder all the great things she'll become, all the things she'll do, she'll see. No one ever looks at their child and wonders how many people will die because of her."

His voice drifted off. His eyes followed. He wasn't staring at the tiny city anymore. His hollowed-out eyes might still be on it, but he was looking somewhere else, somewhere far away where that city still stood and its people still laughed and travelers still came from miles just to stand under its lights for a few hours.

I stared at those tiny buildings, just like him. I tried to see it. And for the most fleeting of instants, I almost thought I could. Then I blinked. In the instant my eyes closed, all I saw were ruins, ash-choked.

And silent.

"Is it true?"

I glanced up. He wasn't looking at me. But he was speaking to me.

"Is what true?" I asked.

"The story," he said, "about how you got your scar."

I didn't need to ask which one he referred to. Absently, my hand reached up, fingers alighting on the long, jagged line that wound from my collarbone to my belly. Underneath my touch, it ached, as though it had its own heartbeat.

"Depends which one you heard," I asked. "There are a lot."

"I heard," he rasped, "you got it from Vraki the Gate. I heard he took something from you. I heard you took something from him."

The scar beat faster with each word, throbbing under my fingers.

"Then it's true," I whispered. "If you want to know what he took from me, though—"

"I don't." He shook his head. "I don't want to know that. I don't need to know it. I just..." He finally looked up at me. "What do you feel...when you think about it?"

I didn't answer.

I wanted to say it was because I didn't know how. I wanted to pretend that it was beyond me, those emotions and feelings tangled up like briars that hurt just to pull on, let alone out. I couldn't possibly do it. I couldn't even try. It would hurt too much.

Yeah.

That sounded like what a normal person would say.

The truth was that I knew the answer. I knew it the day I got this scar and I'd only been honing it, sharpening it like a knife, every day I woke up still alive. And that's why I hesitated. Because it was a knife.

You didn't draw it unless you planned on cutting someone with it.

"It feels like"—my voice came so soft that I didn't even recognize it—"one day I woke up...and every door in the world was locked. And everyone but me had a key. The doors they just walked through like it was so easy, I had to break down. So I did. I beat them down, shattered them, pounded on them until my hands bled because even if I didn't know what was on the other side, I knew I couldn't stay on this one for one more second."

His gaze grew heavy as it lingered on me. "And what," he said, "was on the other side?"

I dropped my fingers. The scar's heartbeat slowly went silent.

"Another door."

He nodded slowly.

"That's why I couldn't blame you."

He looked at me with those hollow eyes. I could see within them the great void where so much had once been—so many ideas, so many stories, so much hope for so much more. And now there was...nothing. Nothing except an empty, vacant darkness in which I could just barely see, beneath all those dead dreams, a tiny light.

And it burned red-hot.

"I believe I understand you, Sal the Cacophony. And I hope you understand me...do you?" he rasped. "It's a pain, isn't it? Like a lost limb. That feeling that something *should* be there, inside you, that isn't there and you can't sleep soundly, no matter how much you drink or who shares the bed with you. It's a hole...and you don't know how to fill it, but you aren't going to feel right until you do. And the only way you can possibly think of—"

"Is to take it back from the people who put that hole in you," I finished for him.

I hadn't even realized it until the words left my lips.

And his mouth curled into a bitter smile as he inclined his head in a long, slow nod.

Liette had told me about this man once. Among normal people, Freemakers were legends—brilliant inventors, alchemists, Spellwrights, engineers, and more. And among Freemakers, Two Lonely Old Men was unto a god. The stories written about his brilliance filled ten books—she owned nine of them. I had no idea if any of them were true.

But he was right about me and him.

We understood each other.

So I closed my eyes and let out a cold breath.

"What do you want from me, then?" I asked.

He turned toward his tiny little city and stared over it with a sad, cruel little smile. And that tiny light in his eyes burned hotter.

"All I require," he said, "is the absolute destruction of the two most powerful nations in the Scar."

SIX

THE CANED TOAD

Life is measured in deals. Specifically, bad ones.

Any scar you collect, any corpse you leave behind, any tender-eyed pretty face you wake up next to comes with a cost, whether you know it or not. Scars don't come without pain, corpses aren't left behind without someone to avenge them, and any heart you get will be one you eventually break.

There are no good or bad costs, just ones you are or are not willing to pay. But, paradoxically, all deals are bad ones because any deal worth making means giving up something you can never get back.

In the case of the deal proposed to me, the cost was steep, indeed. Aside from the very likely possibility that it would end in me just dying and accomplishing nothing, Two Lonely Old Men's proposal to destroy the Imperium and the Revolution alike was more or less asking me to give up sanity entirely. After all, I had enough trouble just fighting *one* mage or *one* tank—how the hell he planned on taking out two nations positively brimming with them was a concept beyond me.

Granted, I wasn't a genius Freemaker. Then again, I wasn't out of my fucking mind, either.

He was asking the impossible. He was proposing the deranged. He was hoping to avenge thousands of fallen souls by the destruction of two nations. And in exchange...

In exchange...

He was offering me revenge.

Every last name on my list. Every mage who had ever crossed me. Every hand that gave me these scars, every eye that looked on helplessly and did nothing while I bled out in the dark, every reason I still wake up from a dead sleep screaming, stuck on this cold, dark earth.

He could give it to me, too. That much, I didn't doubt. His city might be gone, but the genius that built it was still there. Two Lonely Old Men had enough informants, loyalists, and money to guarantee that even the most elusive name on my list couldn't escape his reach. Or mine.

Like I said, the only costs worth considering are the ones you're prepared to pay. And that's why I was heading downstairs—down the halls of the inn, down past a glaring Madame Fist as I made my way into the basement, down to the door locked therein.

For what he was proposing . . . I was ready to pay.

"*Foolish.*"

Not everyone agreed.

"*I could sense his fear, his desperation,*" the Cacophony rasped from his sheath, his voice burning. "*He is no brilliant mind. He is a grieving widower clinging to a cold corpse. You waste our time indulging his delusion.*"

"I'm just hearing him out," I replied.

"*You are hearing what you want to hear.*"

"Given that I'm being lectured by a talking gun, I can't say I am."

"*He will lead us to nothing. Your quarry will grow ever farther from your grasp. Your revenge shall diminish and become nothing more than the epitaph on your grave.*"

"And your body?" I glanced down at him. "That goes away, too, right? That's why you're really upset."

He went quiet and hot. That's how I knew I was right. Reading a living weapon's emotions wasn't an easy thing to do, but I *was* Sal the Cacophony, after all—I'd done more impressive stuff.

"He's offering us a means of killing more mages," I replied. "Which means more magic for you, which means you get what you want that much sooner."

"*Don't forget why we're getting me a new body, darling,*" he whispered. "*I'd hate for you to be afflicted by hallucinations of altruism.*"

Now I went quiet. Not only because I hated the accusation he made, but also because we were at the door that Two Lonely Old Men instructed me to head to and I didn't want to be seen talking to a gun.

After all, wouldn't want this fucking lunatic old man with a deranged plot to kill empires thinking he had gone and hired a crazy person, would we?

I raised my hand to knock. The door damn near flew off its hinges before I could. It smashed against the basement wall with a groan of metal and a shower of sparks.

And the doorway was filled with the broad shoulders of Agne.

She leaned down, taking me in with a pair of narrowed eyes, and uttered through clenched teeth, "The crow flies at midnight."

I blinked. "What?"

"In Cathama, the cafés are many."

I squinted back at her. One of us was way too drunk or way too sober for this to be happening. But before I could decide which, a pair of hands appeared at her shoulder and, with no small effort, Jero shoved Agne to the side.

"Agne, for fuck's sake, we *talked* about this," he snarled. "You don't need passwords when you already know everybody."

"I'm surrounded by philistines," she said, rolling her eyes and folding her arms as she stalked away from the door frame. "How any of you expect to conduct a successful espionage without the proper theatrics is beyond me."

"Good thing you're not being paid to think, then." Jero sighed, exasperated, before turning a weary smile toward me. "Glad you could make it. I take it Two Lonely Old Men explained things?"

I nodded. "He did."

"Then that means you're going to—"

"It means I'll listen to whatever he's planning," I said. "No promises beyond that."

He winced. "This isn't really the sort of operation you participate in casually. The ruin of two nations requires a certain—"

"A certain lady like myself," I interrupted, "and I'm not the sort of lady you tell what to do."

"See?" Agne bellowed from within. "How come *she* gets to say things all dramatic like that?"

Jero rubbed his eyes before stepping aside and beckoning me in. "Fine. Let's all do whatever the fuck we want, then. Not like arranging the collapse of the most powerful nations on earth would require any sort of actual commitment, would it?"

"Commitment isn't my strong suit." I walked in and patted the hilt of the Cacophony. "But then, you didn't ask me to come out here for that, did you?"

The room was a simple wine cellar, half dirt and half stone, lit by an alchemic lamp hanging overhead. Casks and barrels had been shoved to the side to make room for a modestly long table and accompanying chairs, around which a collection of figures sat.

Agne occupied the head of it, her towering frame occupying two spaces as she kicked up her boots and idly began to file her nails. To her left, a slender fellow wrapped in a cloak and a hood sat hunched over the table, his features shrouded behind layers of cloth. To her right, a man and a woman sat, each sporting the same braided black hair and simple breeches and tunics; neither of them looked my way as I entered—the man was consumed with carving something into the table's surface with a small knife and the woman was busy picking her nose.

So, you know, already this was looking like a bad idea.

"Permit me to introduce you to the rest of our association," Jero said, stepping up. He gestured toward the man and woman. "You know Agnestrada, but the charming duo beside her are the twins, Urda and Yria."

"Yria?" I asked.

The name sounded familiar, but I didn't put it together until she looked up and I saw the tattoo across her face. From her bottom lip down to her chin, a jagged portcullis had been inked.

"That's Vagrants' ink." The realization hit me a moment later. "Fuck, you're Yria the Cell."

She grinned triumphantly—or as triumphant as one could be with a finger up one's nose. To her credit she pulled it out a second later and flicked away whatever was on it before puffing up.

"Hear that, you narrow-jawed turdkin?" She nudged her brother, who grimaced as his scrawling was jostled. "Sal the fuckin' Cacophony's heard of me."

"Is that really worthy of pride?" her brother—Urda—asked. "What if she saw your name written in an alley above a pile of trash and fe—" He paused to make a heaving noise. "*Feces?*"

"I've heard of what you've done," I said. "You opened a portal into the baron of High Hold's house and pulled his entire living room through it."

"With his wife in it." She let out an unpleasant guffaw. "I was only going to steal his fancy-ass art. Should've seen her face, all slack-jawed and sodden, when she popped her greasy ass up in her nice-ass chair in the middle of the fucking Scar. Came for a pittance, walked away with a ransom." Her smirk damn near bent her neck with its weight. "And that's when they started calling me the Cell. Finest Doormage in the Scar, at your service."

She offered me a weak mockery of the Imperial salute and that's when I noticed her fingers.

Doormages, see, pay for their powers same as any mage: with a Barter for the Lady Merchant. Only their power to leap through portals comes with the price of giving up their mobility. The more they use, the more their nerves go dead, and the more paralyzed they become.

You wouldn't have noticed if you weren't a Vagrant, but while her index and middle fingers were healthy, the other two curled numbly into her palm. She'd done something to deaden them permanently. But if she'd come as far as she had and *only* lost the use of two fingers, she was a very fine Doormage, indeed.

Not the finest, of course.

The finest was on my list.

"Not *her* service, technically," Urda muttered without looking up. "She isn't the one paying us, after all."

"It was a figure of speech, you asslump," she hissed. "We agreed to leave the talking to me, didn't we?"

"You were wrong," Urda replied, continuing to scrawl. "I corrected you."

"And *this* is why we don't have any friends. This shit right here." She absently scratched somewhere decidedly indelicate in a profoundly indelicate way. "If it weren't for you, I'd have 'em *crawling* all over me like flies on shit."

"Charming." Jero politely looked away and gestured me toward the hooded man sitting at the other end. "And this mysterious weirdo goes by Tuteng."

That name didn't sound familiar. In fact, I'd never heard one like it—Imperial, Revolutionary, or otherwise. But the minute he glanced in my direction, I saw why.

His hood covered most of his features—I could just barely make out the monochrome green eyes, the viciously sharp angles of a not-quite-human face—but there was no hiding the pair of horn stumps sprouting from his brow, protruding from his scalp.

I knew Two Lonely Old Men had money. I knew he had power. How the hell he convinced one of the Rukkokri clans to help him, though, was impressive even for him.

You didn't see many of them in the Scar anymore, mostly by their choice. The Imperium's initial incursion saw them lose a lot of land; the Revolution's rebellion took care of the rest. Tall, slender, and horned, they had mostly kept to themselves when the Imperium's first settlers arrived, their sole interactions with humans being occasional trading and occasional raiding. They were the first and possibly only creatures on this new land that *hadn't* expressed an overt desire to kill, crush, and eat every human they could.

In exchange, the Imperium had destroyed them.

Understandably, most of their attitudes toward the Scar's new occupants ranged from justified distrust to extremely justified aggression. From what I could see beneath his cloak, Tuteng didn't exactly look friendly. But whatever his feelings toward humans were, he kept them as shrouded as the rest of him as he pointedly returned to staring at the table's surface.

"Interesting collection you've got here," I muttered. "A Rukkokri, a hulk of a woman, a Vagrant, whatever Urda is, and—"

"A dashingly handsome rogue with a talent for finding the unfindable?" Jero offered.

"I was going to say 'me,' but yeah, you're special, too, I guess." I scratched an itch across my scar. "What the hell is Two Lonely Old Men planning that he needs this?"

"I am glad you asked."

I caught the rasp of his voice a second before I felt him—and that hollow, empty hunger of his—behind me. I turned and saw Two Lonely Old Men, even thinner and more haggard in the light, standing in the doorway. He gestured toward the empty chair at the table.

"If you would not mind taking a seat," he added, "we can get to the business of explaining things."

"Right," Yria said, leaning back in her chair. "Taking down the Imperium and the Revolution." She rolled her eyes. "Can't fucking *wait* to hear this plan."

"Come now, darling," Agne chided, shooting her a grin. "You can't tell me you're not a *little* excited. How often is it that you get this many magical characters in one spot?"

"Only once before, as far as I can recall," Yria replied. "Last time, they tried to overthrow the Imperium, too." She shot me the kind of grin that would one day get punched down her throat. "How'd that work out, Cacophony?"

She was, of course, referring to the Crown Conspiracy: the plot between thirty-four loyal mages to extinguish the line of Empress Athura and her son, who had been born without magic, and put a proper mage on the throne again. It had ended in a disaster I knew quite well.

I had earned my scars there.

I had lost my magic there.

I had written the list there.

Yria no doubt knew that, if her shit-eating tone was any indication. What she didn't know, however, was that I was not at all opposed to adding more names to my list of people to kill, as the Cacophony burning at my hip was quite insistent I do.

But Two Lonely Old Men had gone to a lot of effort to track me down. It'd be terribly rude of me to spill the brains of his associate on his nice table.

"If we could refrain from the shit-talk until *after* we're done conspiring?" Jero asked with a sigh. He pulled out a seat for me, smiled. "Madam."

"Sir," I replied, despite myself, as I took it.

He helped himself to a chair next to me, like it was the most normal thing in the world. Like we weren't a bunch of killers here for an insane idea. It felt nice. Which is how I knew it wouldn't last.

"Regardless of whether you believe it's possible or not," Two Lonely Old Men began, "you all agreed to come here for a reason. You can say it's for the money or for what I can offer you, but what truly convinced you to come is you've seen what the Imperium and the Revolution and their war has done. You've seen the corpses it's left in its wake and the monsters that have risen from them. You've seen the Scar, coarse and cruel though it may be, and you've seen a life you could have here denied to you by this war. Whether or not you think it *can* be stopped, you know it *must* be."

I was surprised to see that an attentive hush had fallen over the room. Almost as surprised as I was to see myself sharing in it. I had expected to walk out before he finished his first sentence. But he didn't just sound sane—he sounded certain. When he spoke, leaning over the edge of the table as he did, he looked less hollow, less hungry.

More alive.

"I won't insult your intellects by suggesting that it can be done swiftly, nor easily," the Freemaker continued. "Powers like theirs have grown like trees, watered by blood and fertilized by the dead, to be tall and strong. Peace—any peace worthwhile—will take time to grow as well. I ask you not to help me grow it. Merely to get the seed I need."

He glanced toward the other end of the table and nodded.

"Master Urda, if you please."

Urda did not meet his gaze. Rather, he looked to his sister. Only when she offered him a nod did he reach into his belt and pull out a small vial of greenish powder. He emptied a few pinches into his palm and then sprinkled it out across the carving he had been making upon the table.

Immediately, a faint green light swept across the wood, humming to life as it followed a series of sigils that had been carved with precision into the wood—sometimes jagged, sometimes curling, sometimes so delicate that I didn't see how he possibly could have made it with a knife. But I knew these sigils. I knew this magic.

That little bastard was a Spellwright.

"Recently, Revolutionary excavations on the rim of the Valley uncovered something," Two Lonely Old Men said as he walked around the table. "A few could be persuaded—"

"Bribed," Jero interjected.

"—to see the greatness of our cause—"

"Tortured."

"—enough to tell us what they'd found."

Two Lonely Old Men reached down upon the table and touched a sigil. In response, the magic hummed, as if alive, and above it a spectral image apparated into view.

Of what, though, was up for debate.

It was a shape. With faintly glowing lines—jagged and impossibly ordered all at once—etched across its surface. But what kind of shape depended on how you looked at it. Stare at it straight ahead and it was a pyramid. Cant your head to the left, it was a square. To the right, a sphere. Maybe it was all of those. Or maybe none of those. I had no idea.

Well, that wasn't exactly true.

I had *one* idea.

"*Fuck.*" Yria turned her face away. "Hurts my face just looking at that thing."

"What . . . *is* it?" Agne asked, her face screwing up.

"A Relic," I answered.

"Unlikely," Urda muttered. "Relics don't look like that."

"It is, indeed, a Relic," Two Lonely Old Men confirmed. "Though, you're correct, Master Urda, it does not look like that. This image is far too small."

He pressed another finger to the sigil. The spectral image grew immense, to a size that filled half the room. You might have thought it strange to see every eye go wide and hear every breath go short at the sight of that.

But then, you might not know much about Relics.

Long ago, when they had first thrown off the Imperium's yoke, the Revolution faced a daunting challenge: their meager weapons were no match for the endless legions of mages that served the Empress. They needed something to even the odds. Their Great General found it.

No one but him knew where they came from or how they worked, precisely, but Relics were the engines that drove the Revolution's machines. Their tanks, their living armors, their cannons, and anything else their engineers could dream up to kill people all worked only with the aid of Relics.

The biggest one I had ever seen was only about the size of a human head.

And it had provided enough power to level two cities.

A Relic as big as the one he was showing us... well, my brain damn near broke just trying to think about how much it could destroy.

"Impossible," Agne whispered. "They can't... I mean, they don't *come* that big." She glanced toward Jero. "Darling, are you sure you didn't just buy a very fanciful lie? What did your informant look like? Was she pretty?"

"The information is authentic and verifiable, I assure you," Two Lonely Old Men said.

"How can you be sure?" I asked.

"I questioned no less than a dozen Revolutionary commanders about it," Jero said. "Different cadres, different commands, all said the same thing. Their information all came from the same chain of command."

"They could have been lying," I said.

"I know when a man's lying." Jero pointedly avoided my gaze as his voice went quiet. "And it isn't after he's just seen me cut off the faces of his two best friends in front of him."

"Fuck off, you can't cut a man's face off." Yria glanced to her brother. "Can you?"

"It's possible," Urda replied, cringing. "And... *messy*."

"Any doubts I might have had about the information were banished when my spies reported movement among the Revolutionary forces on the rim," Two Lonely Old Men continued. "A sudden mobilization of forces unheard of was sent to the rim."

"What kind of forces?" Agne asked.

Two Lonely Old Men raised a hand, pressed it to the table.

"The Iron Fleet."

If eyes went wide and breath went short before, the image that next apparated over the table almost struck everyone dead.

They were tiny, pale, and ghostly, ten little round shapes floating in the air. Each one was nothing more than a tiny airship—a little ship with tiny little propellers. If you didn't know what they were, you would have called them adorable. And yet not a man or woman in that room looked upon them without a chill in their heart.

Because not a man or woman in that room didn't know the Fleet.

"Mom saw them once, she said." Urda was the only one to find his voice, muttering in the dark. "She said the first thing she heard was the noise, like locusts buzzing in her ears until she couldn't think, until she couldn't see the shadow falling over her, until she couldn't hear the bombs dropping and..."

His face screwed up, eyes shutting tight as he clapped his hands over his ears, like he could hear them in his head. He let out a low whine as Yria shot him a glance before looking back to Two Lonely Old Men.

"One typically does not see the Fleet far from Weiless," the Freemaker said as he walked a circle around the table. "Only their presence keeps Imperial birds from swooping down and turning the Revolutionary capital to cinders. In their most dire circumstances, they have never sent more than two airships away from the city. For this new Relic..."

His features trembled. His words came out dry and rasping.

"They sent all ten."

I took a special pride in my ability to not be rendered speechless— they didn't call me Sal the Cacophony because I was often at a loss for words, after all. But this...

I'd never seen one of the Revolution's airships. Hell, I was halfway convinced they didn't actually exist outside of the ramblings of drunkards and the shrieking of lost minds. There were stories about them, same way there are stories about every monster.

Among the dramatic, they were called the Ten Arrows, the greatest weapons in the Revolution's quiver. So named because they flew where the Great General told them and where they struck...tales were born.

Tales of fields of fire, blazes that burned for six weeks straight. Legends of the blackened graveyards the ships left in their wake, twisted trees and bombed-out homes to serve as headstones for the carpets of corpses. Songs of roaring engines, of screaming skies, of iron wings...

I didn't know what all ten ships would leave behind.

I didn't know if there were words invented that would describe that.

"And at their head..."

Two Lonely Old Men made a gesture. The phantom images quivered, vanished, and were replaced by a ghostly visage.

The man who stared back at us was just an image, I knew, but to look at him, I'd have believed him a ghost. He was a wrinkled, withered husk of a human, a frown so severe that it was a crater in his face that sucked in every other part of his countenance. His eyes were sunken, his nose crooked, his cheeks gaunt. You wouldn't think he was alive, let alone in command, and yet...

"Culven Loyal."

"Loyal?" The name sprang to my lips unbidden. "He's a fucking *Loyal*?"

"Is that...bad?" Urda asked, sheepish.

"You know the name."

Jero's voice was as cold as his stare as he looked toward me. Not as cold as the sensation that settled at the base of my neck at the mention of that name, though.

"Every Revolutionary gets their name from the Great General himself," I said. "Prouds, Sterns, Relentlesses, Dutifuls..."

"Erstwhiles," Jero muttered.

"There's no name higher in the Revolution's eyes than a Loyal. They have his respect, his admiration, and his trust," I continued. "Probably why the paranoid fuck's only ever given it to six people."

"Rather," Two Lonely Old Men observed, "the Loyals are entrusted with every secret the General himself knows and, thus, every secret of the Revolution and all their machines. Hence, they are never far from his side." He stared at the phantom image of Culven Loyal's face, contemplative. "Until now."

The Iron Fleet.

The Ten Arrows.

And one of the Great General's own advisers aboard it.

That was unheard of. But then, so was this new Relic.

Which meant that whatever Two Lonely Old Men was planning was also...

"That means they value this new Relic enough to leave their city defenseless," I said, scratching at a scar. "Which means they think whatever it is can change the balance of power in the Scar in their favor."

I chewed on those words for a moment. Then, realization hit me like the hilt of a wrought-iron blade across my jaw. I stared at the spectral image with cold dread.

"And that's why you want to steal it."

"'Steal'?" A wry smile creased his haggard face. "That's far too primitive a word for what I intend to do. I will use this Relic to ensure peace for countless generations. Madame Cacophony, with your aid, I will hack off the head of this war and water the Scar with its blood."

"Okay, but…" I scratched the back of my head. "You know that still sounds *extremely* violent, right?"

"You might have to elaborate, darling," Agne said, nodding.

"Think of it," Two Lonely Old Men hissed, leaning over the table. "A Relic of this magnitude has never been seen before. In the hands of the Revolution, it would become another siege engine, another cannon, another *weapon*. But in the hands of a Freemaker…in *my* hands?

"With severium, alchemics, and oil, I created Lastlight. With a Relic, I could create an immortal city: lights that never dim, water that never runs dry, food that never withers. With a Relic of *that* power, I could bring Lastlight back from the dead and spread her across the entire *Scar*. No one need go hungry, no one need fear the brigand or the beast, no one need worry for anything so long as I could make that."

"Can a Relic actually *do* any of that?" Jero surprised me by asking. Up until now, he had seemed to be the most informed of any of us outside the Freemaker himself. "I always thought they, you know, made things explode."

"In the hands of those primates in the Revolution, yes." Two Lonely Old Men waved a hand, sneering. "Their imaginations are throttled in the crib and their minds are stunted by a diet of propaganda. There's not a book in the entire archives of Weiless that isn't a military treatise or slogan scrawled on paper. Their vision blended with this Relic could only create a bigger explosion."

"They have several explosions already, darling," Agne pointed out. "What's to stop them from simply taking it back once you have it?"

Two Lonely Old Men smiled. "With such power in the hands of a Freemaker, who would dare make a move?"

He had a point, I had to admit. Regardless of the prevailing attitudes on Freemakers in the Revolution and Imperium—which ranged from branding them as lunatic menaces to outright hunting them down—there wasn't a soldier, noble, or politician who didn't recognize their intellect and aptitude.

A Freemaker left to their own devices was dangerous. A Freemaker in possession of a Relic was a tragedy waiting to happen. The most brilliant Freemaker in the Scar in possession of a Relic of unfathomable power...

"Shit." My eyebrows went up. "That might just be enough to make even the Imperium think twice about making a move. *Any* move."

"Just so." The Freemaker's grin grew broader, that fire in his eyes burned brighter. "Think of it. Just the *threat* of the Relic in my hands would be enough to curb the aggressions of *both* powers. They already were wary of my wrath before. With this, I could coerce the Imperium, the Revolution, and every warmongering bloodthirster in their ranks into pacifism.

"The prosperity I promise would walk hand in hand with peace. No more children burying their parents. No more cities turned to graveyards. No more soldiers, no more atrocities, no more orphans, no more..." He paused, looked down at his hands. "No more ruins."

"Now granted, all that latter business sounds quite lovely," Agne said, scratching her chin. "It's all the...insane things beforehand that I'm having trouble coming to grips with. Wherever this Relic is, it must be heavily guarded. Impossibly so."

" 'Impossibly' is an understatement," Jero said.

"Given that 'impossible' is an absolute, I don't see how that can be an under—"

"The Relic is currently under guard," he continued over her, "in a stronghold brimming with soldiers, cannons, and every kind of mechanical horror the Revolution's warped little minds can dream up. And that's *before* the Ten Arrows show up. Once you add airships to the mix, retrieving it from within will be impossible."

"So, what's the plan, then?" Agne asked.

Two Lonely Old Men smiled in that way someone smiles when you know they're about to say something insane.

"We're going to steal it from the airships."

See?

"I beg your pardon?" Agne said, clearing her throat. "I believe I had something incredibly stupid in my ear."

"The Great General wants the Relic brought to Weiless for study. I mean, he wants it bad enough to send all ten airships to it. Lifting it out of its stronghold is impossible. Lifting it out of Weiless is unthinkable. But the journey from one to the other provides us a weeklong window. If we can get in and get out—"

"Get out," Agne repeated. "With a gigantic Relic. How do you propose to do that?"

I glanced across the table toward the twins. "I suppose that's why you brought a Doormage."

"Birdshit."

Yria shot out of her chair, slammed her hands onto the table.

"I fucking knew this was going to be insane, but fuck, I feel my brain leaking out my ears just listening to you." She gestured wildly at the spectral image. "The Iron Fleet? Do you fucking hear yourself? You want *us* to fucking try to swipe a Relic the size of your dad's gaping asshole after I'm done with him from a fleet of airships—those are ships that fly in the *fucking air*, in case you're stupider than you sound—brimming with cannons, soldiers, and…and…fuck, I don't even *know* what else they've got in there."

She shook her head and waved a hand through the spectral image, casting it into a blurry mess as she turned and started heading for the door.

"I knew this would be crazy, but I thought it'd at least be the profitable kind of crazy. Fuck your plan, fuck your Relic, and fuck you, old man." She shot up a rude gesture—with both hands, impressively enough—as she stormed toward the door. "Come on, Urda. We're leaving."

She went without protest, without objection, without insult. As she hesitated at the door, she realized she went without her brother.

She turned. Her twin sat at the table. His eyes had turned up for the first time since I had arrived and were locked on the image of the fleet.

"Urda?" she asked.

He turned to her. And for the first time, I saw his face. He looked too young. Too young to be in a place like this, with people like this—too guileless, too naïve, with eyes too big and mouth too trembling as he looked back at his sister and whispered in a shaking voice.

"No more orphans, Yria," he said.

His sister's face didn't so much screw up as implode. Her mouth hung open for a second before she gritted her teeth, narrowed her eyes, clenched her hands into trembling fists, and tensed up like she was ready to leap across the table and beat those too-big eyes right out of her brother's skull. I saw her lips twitch with the beginnings of a hundred different curses—some of which actually made *me* blush, or had the last time I'd heard them—before she shut her eyes tight and let out a snort.

All the anger and venom seemed to ebb out of her, leaking out in a long, tired sigh. With her head hanging low and her shoulders slumping, she dejectedly stomped back to her seat.

"Fucking doe-eyed crybaby," she muttered, "always fucking going and shedding tears like a fucking piece of..."

Her voice trailed off into an unintelligible and creative string of curses, but she made no other move to leave. Soon enough, her voice fell as still as the rest of her as she fixed a pointed glare onto the Freemaker.

"If there are no other objections?"

Two Lonely Old Men's question hung in the silent air, unchallenged. Unsettlingly so.

Not that I was relishing the idea of another slew of curses—creative though Yria's had been—but I felt it would have been perfectly reasonable to meet a plot to steal a weapon of unknown and possibly limitless power from one of the most powerful armies in the Scar with at least *slightly* more skepticism.

Yet, as my eyes drifted around the table, my curiosity followed. I looked from Yria and Urda—resentful and withdrawn, respectively— to Agne, attentive and rapt, to Tuteng, who had sat so still and silent

I had barely remembered he was there. Each of them was silent in the face of this insanity. I couldn't help but wonder what Two Lonely Old Men had offered them to make them want to stay.

I suppose I could have asked, like a normal person.

Of course, then there was the chance that they'd ask *me*, and I'd have to reveal *my* reason for staying and explain why I wanted a bunch of people dead so badly that I'd indulge this madness and it'd be a whole...thing...

I was content to let everyone's motives be their own, for the moment. Granted, to the outside viewer, that might sound a touch insane—after all, you might point out, honesty is more emotionally healthy and, from a practical standpoint, knowing where everyone's priorities lay would mean fewer surprises. To which, I would reply, you had some good points.

But consider this.

Shut up.

Only in the military or at an orgy do you want honesty, and even then it's incredibly awkward. In a situation like this, the less everyone knows about each other, the less likely anyone is to let their guard down. No doubt everyone here was thinking the same thing I was. And if they weren't, no doubt they'd be dead before long.

Either way, it wasn't going to be an issue.

"Very well, then." Two Lonely Old Men gestured back to the table. "Master Jero. The map, if you would."

Jero grunted, rising from his chair and producing a rolled-up parchment.

"Oh." A note of disappointment escaped my mouth.

"What?" he asked, glancing at me.

"Nothing. It's just...it's a regular map," I observed.

"What else would it be?"

"I don't know. You had all these spooky, glowing things..." I gestured to the illuminated sigils upon the table. "I was kind of expecting the map to follow suit."

"She has a point," Agne said. "You can't really expect us to be impressed with a map that *doesn't* glow."

"Oh, I could *make* it glow," Urda offered, fumbling with a pen and inkwell. "Just give me a little bit."

"He can," Yria grunted. "Give him ten minutes and he'll make that map glow like a fat man in a—"

"*Master Jero*," Two Lonely Old Men pointedly interjected. "If you would be so kind."

Jero struggled for a moment to figure out which of us to spare the bulk of his scowl for before giving up and unfurling the map on the table. The Valley sprawled out in parchment before us as everyone gathered around to have a look.

Funny, I thought, but I never realized just how many villages were in it.

"The Fleet's route is currently thus." Jero drew a finger from an imposing-looking stronghold in the south up toward the north and west toward Weiless. "Plenty of open air, good for surprise maneuvers."

"And bad for us," I noted. "I'm assuming, anyway."

"And you'd be correct. The more room they have, the more chances they have to escape. We need them to take a more...claustrophobic route." He stabbed his finger toward a series of mountains leading east. "The mountains here provide enough room for each airship individually, but prevent any possibility of...complications."

"Such as *not* being susceptible to ambush by a bunch of ill-intentioned louts?" I asked.

Jero flashed me a grin. "Ill-intentioned louts and their extremely handsome friend."

"What are these here?" Agne pointed at a cluster of inked houses at the foot of the mountains. "It looks like the route you chose goes right over them."

"Villages. Townships. A freehold here and there. The mountains are littered with mines and people flock there for work and metal."

"The area has a name."

My heart skipped a beat. The voice—so soft that it was barely audible—felt like it was coming right out of my skull.

Not here, I thought. *Fuck me, not here, of all places. I can't be hearing things that aren't there now.*

But my breathing slowed when I saw that everyone else wore the same bewildered look I did, as though we'd heard a ghost. And in another second, we heard it speak again.

"They call it the Blessing. Humans do, anyway." Beneath his hood, Tuteng's voice came impossibly quiet. His eyes glittered softly, gemstones reflecting a dying light. "We called it something different. It was beautiful... once."

His voice ebbed away as quietly as it had come. The glitter in his eyes vanished back into the shadows of his hood, leaving him faceless and slight. Perhaps he wasn't a ghost.

But the freaky little fucker might as well have been.

"*At any rate,*" Jero continued with a dismissive wave of his hand. "If all goes well, we'll have our prize and be gone *long* before we go over them."

"And if all doesn't go well?"

"Then we'll be so high in the clouds, they won't even notice us." He rolled up the map. "The sort of people in *that* chunk of land can barely understand the word *heist*, let alone interfere with it. They'll be of no concern."

Yria folded her arms, let out a snort. "So you need these flying fucks—"

"Fleet," Urda corrected her.

"Flying fucking fleet, whatever," she grunted, "you need them to take that route. How the fuck you planning on doing that?"

All eyes—or I assume all, Tuteng's were kind of hard to see— turned toward Jero. He held them for a moment before looking expectantly to Two Lonely Old Men. The Freemaker let out a long, tired sigh as he leaned forward.

The glow of the sigils painted his face in haggard, weary shadows. The fire in his eyes sputtered out. What was left was a walking corpse, standing upright only by virtue of the table he leaned on, bereft of all but the barest spark of light behind his eyes.

"Understand this," he said. "I know what I ask of you. I know the impossibility of success. I know the many, *many* things that could go wrong. And I..." He closed his eyes, drew in a breath. "I know that if we fail, the Relic will turn this war from a spark to a wildfire. If there exists any chance of stopping it, of improving lives..."

He opened his eyes again, swept them slowly around the table.

"You stand in the doorway of a dark room, madams and masters. You can turn back now and no one will think less of you. The incentives I offered you to bring you here are yours to keep. No grudges will be borne, no revenge will be sought, provided you stay out of the way of those who remain. But if you stay...if you walk through that door...then it shuts behind you. We shall remain in the dark until we find a light that might not exist."

That tiny glimmer of light behind his eyes flickered, a candle in a breeze, as it settled upon me. Beneath his eyes, my scars ached. My blood ran cold. And the Cacophony burned.

"If you want to walk away," he said, "now is the time."

He held his breath for a second. Then a minute. Then two. Yria glared at her brother, who smiled softly at her in return. Jero watched the room for any sign of dissent. Tuteng stood still, said nothing, did nothing. And Two Lonely Old Men...

...his eyes never left me.

"Well, then!"

The silence was shattered with a boisterous bellow and a decidedly unpleasant popping sound. Agne loomed up, a grin on her face as broad as her shoulders as she slammed her fist into her palm and cracked her knuckles.

"Now *that's* decided," she said, "let's get to toppling empires, shall we, darlings?"

SEVEN

LITTLEBARROW

"HOLY SHIT!"

That, Meret thought, was possibly not what he should have said.

Granted, he wasn't quite sure what the appropriate response to... whatever he had just heard *was*. Well, that wasn't entirely true, either—he was fairly certain the correct response was to run as far away from this woman and whatever she'd dragged him into as quickly as possible.

Of course, he thought, *she'd probably just shoot you before you took three steps. Or stab you. Or strangle you. Really, she's got an awful lot of ways to kill you.*

The second-best response, he figured, would have been to condemn such an insane plot. He'd once been in a Revolutionary township and had the...opportunity to witness the Great General's justice upon a thief found guilty of stealing a weapon for defense. It had taken the town six days to find every piece of him. To try and rob the fabled Iron Fleet, of all things, was positively...

Insane, he thought. *Better not call her insane, though. She seems the type to get mad about that. What else? Bold? No, that's just "insane" with better colors. She'll see right through you and shoot you. Actually, just don't say anything—she might get offended and shoot you. Wait, no, say something or she'll get suspicious and shoot you. Shit, is she looking at you now? SHE IS. QUICK! SAY SOMETHING!*

"HOLY *SHIT*!"

Nice.

Red colored his cheeks. At the very least, he thought he ought to have sounded a little less impressed.

Sal the Cacophony seemed to agree. She looked up from the table for the first time in hours. Across features painted with grime, blood, and weariness, she afforded him the barest grin.

"Impressed?"

"I mean, a *little*, yeah," he said. "Or...or maybe a lot. That sounds... incredible. You were going to *steal* from the Iron Fleet? *The* Iron Fleet? The Ten Arrows! That's amazing! That's incredible! That's...that's..."

"Easy, kid," she chuckled softly. "If you explode, I'm stuck with a dead girl *and* a mess to clean up."

"Sorry, it's just..." The blood rushing to his cheeks weighed his head down, drew his eyes down to the floor. "I've heard rumors of the Ten Arrows, you know? So many rumors, I thought they were just legends. Like you." He blinked, looked up through eyes snapped wide. "Uh, not that you're, like, *imaginary* or anything. I just—"

"Yeah." Sal leaned back, stretched. Across her skin, her scars flexed, twitching like living things all their own. "It's always the big, noisy, bloody things that get legends." She draped an arm over the back of her chair, sized him up. "Which ones have you heard?"

"Oh, uh..." Meret rubbed the back of his neck. "The usual ones, I guess? About all the warlords you killed and the towns you, uh, destroyed." He grinned sheepishly. "Though, if I'm being honest, my *favorite* is the one about you and the woman from Althura's Nest, with the—"

"Not of me, dumbshit." She paused, considered. "I mean, yeah, that's a great one, but I meant which legends of the Iron Fleet have you heard?"

He opened his mouth, but found his throat suddenly tight, his words suddenly choked. Without entirely realizing it, his mouth was suddenly dry and his eyes suddenly stung from not blinking. An ache settled over him, a dull and distant feeling of a wound that never quite healed.

Because when he thought of the Iron Fleet, he didn't think of legends.

"Just one." He stared at his hands, noticed them twitching. "Not so much a legend as..." He folded his fingers to keep them from trembling, set them on the table. "During the end of the war for the Valley, I was going around the townships on the borders, trying to help. I remember there was this one guy...

"He was a...merchant, I think? Or maybe a farmer? I can't..." He licked his lips, found himself without spittle. "They run together in my head a little. But he was on the very edge of the Valley, right on the border with Weiless. Some fighting broke out near the freehold he lived in. Then it got worse. Then...the Iron Fleet came."

He glanced back up at Sal, finding himself hoping she would change the subject or, even better, just look away and let him compose himself.

But she was still sitting, exactly where she had been. And she was still staring right at him. And she was still listening.

"Just one airship," he said. "Not even all that big, I heard. Just... one. He said he heard the sound and looked up and suddenly..." He made a vague gesture overhead. "Suddenly, the sky was on fire. Bombs were falling, cannons firing, in the dead of night it was brighter than daytime. He wasn't even sure what they were shooting at. He didn't know where to run or...or..."

When had he started sweating so much? When had it gotten so hard to breathe? And when, he wondered, had he started seeing that man's face in his head again?

"What happened to him?" Sal asked. She was staring at him with that need again.

"Huh?"

"The man."

Meret stared back down at his hands.

"He said that. And then nothing else. I kept coming back to check on him, hoping to see some change."

"Hoping to see him get better," she grunted, nodding.

"No, not better," he snapped without realizing. "Some *change*. I wanted to see him crying, mourning, drinking himself to death, *anything*. But he just sat on his bed...staring at the wall, this look in his eyes like...like..."

He looked up at Sal. He smacked his lips.

"Like he was still trying to figure out what he'd done to deserve that."

"Did he die?"

"Yes. I mean, no. He didn't die. But he didn't laugh, he didn't cry, he didn't do anything else. Ever." Meret held out his hands, empty and helpless. "So...maybe he did."

His fingers curled without him realizing, balling up into trembling fists. His breath came out ragged, pushed between clenched teeth. And somewhere inside him, that memory of the man's face turned to something else.

"It was the same. Everywhere I went, it was the same," he said. "Sometimes it was the Iron Fleet. Sometimes it was a spell gone wrong. Sometimes it was the Revolution, sometimes it was the Imperium, sometimes there was so little left I couldn't even tell who started it. And all I could do was stitch cuts and brew teas and...and..."

He drew a deep breath, closed his eyes. He let the memories, the anger, the helplessness flow out of him with that breath, just like his old teacher had taught him. Just like he'd done a thousand times, a thousand patients before.

And like all those other times, it didn't help.

"But you..." A smile crept across his lips, unbidden and bitter. "You did something bigger than that. You took the fight to those bastards. You brought them down. *You* showed them that people like us can hurt people like *them*. And I just wish I could be like you and—"

"Don't."

Her voice came suddenly, but not harshly. It wasn't a demand. It was too soft a word for that. When he looked up, her eyes weren't quite so hard as he remembered.

"Don't say that," Sal the Cacophony said. "The Scar has enough killers. Fuck, it's got too many. Too many killers and too many blades and too many guns and too many people who don't give a shit about any of them." She gestured with her chin. "You're a healer. That's special."

"It's futile," Meret muttered. "You can't fight diseases by just cleaning up after them. You have to go to the source. You have to chop off a limb, if it'll save the body."

"How many?"

"Huh?"

"How many limbs?"

"It's just a—"

"How much blood can you lose? How many scars can you take? How much can you cut up a person before they aren't who they are anymore?"

"I . . . I don't know."

"I do." She glanced out the window. "Or I thought I did, at one point."

"But if it helps . . . if one person can make that sacrifice . . . is it worth it?"

Sal gestured toward the window. The columns of smoke from the airship's crash continued to climb high into the sky. Somewhere far away, a severium storage exploded, painting the sky in a brilliant flash of red and purple flame. And all through the sky, the snow continued to fall.

Black as night.

"I thought I knew that, too," she said.

Somehow, Meret thought, it was easier when she was just a legend. Sal the Cacophony was a murderer, a destroyer—do what she says, the stories said, and stay out of her way. Simple. He could have dealt with that. He could have treated it like anything else, a disease to cure or a wound to bind, and been done with it. But something in her voice, in her eyes, in the way she looked out the window . . . somehow, he knew he'd remember that in those dark nights when he couldn't sleep, just like he remembered that man's face. All their faces.

There was no story that said Sal the Cacophony could look as sad as that.

"Fuck me." Glass shattered as she absently tossed the drained whiskey bottle over her shoulder. "You got anything else to drink here?"

That was more in keeping with what he'd heard about her, though.

"Uh, sure." *I hope,* he added to himself as he rose from his chair and found his way to the stairs. "I'll be right back. Don't, uh, don't go . . . looking for something without asking me."

"Why? You got anything weird lying around?"

"No. Wait, why do you assume it's because I have something weird?"

Sal shrugged. "I don't know. You just seem the type." She made a gesture toward his staircase. "I'll make you a deal: you find me whatever you have to drink, and I won't go looking for whatever stained pillow you've made your bride."

"I don't have a—"

"This is a time-sensitive deal, Meret."

While he wasn't the *quickest* mind around, Meret was swift enough to realize that all ends to this conversation were bad, save one. And that one saw him hurrying up the stairs to the second floor of his house.

He padded softly to his room and peered around the door. The girl, cleaned up as much as they could manage, lay right where they'd taken her: sleeping soundly upon his bed.

He glanced over her. Her breathing was deep and steady; there were no signs of bleeding—as good as he could hope for, at this stage of her recovery.

His gaze lingered for a long moment, though, searching her. She bore no weapons, possessed no scars of great struggle, carried no trinkets or treasure that he could see, beyond the clothes on her back—and even those seemed shabby and ill-mended, even without the soot and grime. She was, to all appearances, a perfectly normal, unremarkable girl.

So why, Meret wondered, was she the only thing that Sal the Cacophony had pulled out of that wreck?

What made one person worth that much pain?

The answer, he suspected, wasn't going to come to him just staring at her. What *would* come was a murderous Vagrant going through his things in search of a pillow-bride he might or might not have. Content, he turned and busied himself in his dresser, pulling a deep red bottle from beneath his clothes.

Cathama Crimson. One of the last in the world, or so his teacher had told him. He'd received it as a gift when he completed his studies and had been saving it for something special ever since. He *thought* that was going to be when he finally found a nice young lady and got married...

But meeting an angry young lady with a magic gun who had fallen from the sky on a flaming airship was probably also fine.

He took the bottle in hand, turned to head back to Sal.

And gazed into a pair of eyes black as pitch.

His breath caught in his throat. His body froze. Dread welled up inside him, something cold and dark and forgotten. On a thousand legs, it crawled out of that dark place where he kept the memories of the patients he couldn't save and the towns that he'd watched burn, and reached through every vein and into every sinew of his being until all he could see were those two pits. And all he could hear was a cold rasp of a voice.

"I'm alive."

He opened his mouth to scream, or to beg, or to weep—he wasn't sure. But it took everything in him just to shut his eyes and escape that gaze.

When he opened them again, the black stare was gone. In its place were two normal, if tired, dark brown eyes. And standing before him was a perfectly normal, if bloodied, girl.

She was awake? She was *walking*?

"Uh...y-yes. You are." The dread ebbed away, leaving behind muscles that felt like they'd been tensed for a hundred years. "You're alive, but...are you okay?"

The girl didn't respond. Or move. Or blink. She stood there, inches away from him, trapping him between her and the dresser. Her eyes seemed to stare right through him, as if she could see that thing that had crawled out of him.

"You..." he said haltingly, "you took a really bad fall. You were incredibly injured. You shouldn't be up."

He tensed as she reached around him. Her fingers wrapped around something behind him.

"I *mean* it." He tried to sound authoritative. "You're really hurt. You've got a busted leg, a lot of bruises and—"

"Three bruised ribs, a fractured arm, and no inconsiderable amount of blood loss. As none of it appears to be internal, I suspect I'm capable of reasonable movement." She pulled back a pair of bifocals— *his* bifocals—and snapped them out, setting them atop the bridge of her nose and, somehow, looking down upon him, despite being four inches shorter. "And I've suffered a mild fracture of the thighbone. Not 'a busted leg,' as you so buffoonishly put it."

"You're...you're..."

"Twenty-Two Dead Roses in a Chipped Porcelain Vase." She paused, narrowed his eyes, appraising him. "Since you assumedly are the reason I'm alive right now, though, you can call me Liette. I *guess.*"

"Er...yes, Liette." He cleared his throat, extended his hand awkwardly. "It's a pleasure."

"Rather a bold claim to make, considering the circumstances." She turned and limped back to the bed, wincing as she eased herself back down. "Where am I?"

"Uh, my house."

"Oh, good, I was worried I might be in a river or a perfume shop." She glared at him behind bifocals that were now, apparently, hers. "I can tell I'm in a house. In which town is this house located?"

"Oh! Right. Uh, Littlebarrow. Around the edge of the Borrus Valley."

Her brow furrowed, eyes squinting. "How?"

"How?"

"Yes, *how*, motherfucker," she snarled. "I didn't fucking come here for a little bit of rest and relaxation and—"

Her face seized up suddenly. Her body began to shake. Trembling hands reached up to clutch a face contorted in agony. A shriek pried her lips apart, came out in a short, agonized sound before she bit it back behind a clenched jaw. She gripped her head, shaking violently.

All fear lost, Meret rushed to the door, ready to find his supplies to treat her. But by the time he'd reached the threshold, she'd stopped. Breathing raggedly, she rubbed the temples of her head.

"I can't remember...anything," she said. "Fire. Metal. And..." She opened her eyes again, stared out at nothing as she whispered breathlessly. "Stars. Millions of stars."

"You shouldn't be moving around," Meret said, approaching her tentatively. "It could aggravate your..." He searched for a word to fit. "Condition? I mean, once I figure out what your condition *is*, I can say for certain. If your friend hadn't brought you here, I don't know what—"

"Friend?"

"Uh, yeah. Sal? The Cacophony?"

Liette stared at him with something between astonishment and horror, provoking in him something between a pang of dread and a profound awkwardness.

"She, uh, had us bring you out of the crash," he said. "She's still downstairs if you..."

Holy shit, the thought struck him. *Are they even* friends? *What if this girl just owes her money? Shit! She's going to shoot her, then shoot me, then—"*

"She's still here," Liette whispered to herself, staring down at her knees. The horror drained from her face, leaving something soft, something pained, and something terribly, terribly sad. "She didn't leave."

"She didn't." Meret offered her a smile. "I can go get her. If you want."

She shook her head. "No. Don't tell her I've awoken." She looked up at him through her bifocals, eyes glistening behind them. "Please."

There's no healing a body without a head.

The first thing his teacher had ever told him. At first, he'd thought it a statement of the stunningly obvious—either that or there were an awful lot of people woefully underinformed about the effects of decapitation. But over the years, he'd come to see the wisdom in it.

Healing was more than stitching and binding. It was making a cup of tea for a grieving widow. It was helping a child learn that a scar didn't make them worse. It was sitting quietly with someone and listening to them tell him all the places that hurt.

And, in this case, it was keeping a secret.

To help Sal, he needed to help Liette. To help Liette, she needed to trust him. Keeping this secret didn't make sense to him. But then, he wasn't the one with a busted leg.

Mild fracture, he reminded himself. *You know that.*

He left his smile with her, gave her an understanding nod, and turned to leave.

"She's going to hate that wine."

Meret made something close to a scoffing sound. "It's Cathama Crimson. Vintage."

"It doesn't matter. She'll say it tastes like skunk-ass."

He looked at the bottle, frowned, and kept walking. Liette might have been a woman worth hauling out of a fiery wreckage, as far as he knew, but that didn't necessarily make her an expert on wine.

Besides, he thought as he headed down the stairs, *what would she even know what skunk-ass tastes like?*

"MURDERER!"

A shout came up the staircase, strong enough to shake the floorboards. He knew Sindra's voice well enough to know her anger—it was like a blade to her, only ever drawn if she intended to kill someone with it.

Which was why Meret also knew to run.

"Sindra!"

He came bursting in, eyes wide at the sight of the old soldier pressed up against the wall. And, pinned beneath her brawny forearm, stood Sal.

With Sindra's blade, naked and gleaming, pressed against her throat.

"Fucking Vagrant," she snarled. "No matter what fucking story you spin or which moron believes you, you're always the fucking same. Every last one of you a murdering piece of shit caring for *nothing* but yourselves."

"Sindra, *stop!*" Meret screamed, rushing up to grab her arm and try to pull her away. His cries and his grip were both futile—Sindra had four inches, twenty pounds, and thirty-odd years of propaganda-fueled hardheadedness on him. "Let her go!"

"When did you call them?" the old soldier growled, taking neither her blade nor her eyes off Sal. "How far away are they? *How long do we have?*"

"*SINDRA!*" Meret shrieked. "Sindra, listen to me! What are you talking about? *Who* are you talking about?"

"*SOLDIERS!*"

She whirled on him with a face he didn't recognize. Sindra had always been a flint of a woman—hard edges honed by a harder life—but the face she showed him, the mask of wild eyes and gritted teeth and desperate terror painting every wrinkle, he'd only seen that face a few times before.

Never on her.

"I saw them, Meret," she snarled. "I *saw* them."

"Saw *what*?"

"Birds. Big Imperial riders, tearing across the sky not a league from here. Do you know what that means?"

Meret fumbled for a response. Too long.

"*DO YOU?*" She lunged at him, driving him back a step before she looked back to Sal. "Of course, she fucking does. Every shit-eating Vagrant was once a shit-eating Imperial. You know what birds mean." She narrowed her eyes. "You know they're only the beginning. Soldiers will follow. Mages will follow. A fight's coming, isn't it?"

Sal said nothing. Sindra slammed her against the wall again.

"*TELL ME!*"

Sal didn't respond. Sal didn't flinch. Sal didn't even seem to notice the blade pressed against her throat, or the red line blossoming beneath it. Her eyes were on Sindra—cold and blue and empty as a fresh snowfall.

Whether it was defiance or resignation in that stare, Meret didn't have time to decide. He'd be the shittiest healer around if someone got decapitated in front of him.

"Sindra," he spoke calmly, softly. "How many birds were there?"

"Huh?"

"How many birds?" he asked again, swallowing back a quaver in his voice.

"I think...six."

"You think?"

"I...I think, yes."

"Okay, six birds. Which direction were they going? Do you remember?"

Sindra pursed her lips, grunted. "North."

"North," Meret repeated. "Away from Littlebarrow?"

"What's your fucking point?" she snarled.

He held up a hand for calm. "I believe you. There were six birds heading away from the village. I believe you." He held a breath, released it. "But if she had something to do with it, wouldn't they have come back for her?"

"They...I don't know," Sindra grunted, shaking her head. "Maybe."

"Maybe," he said. "Sindra...how many people are left in the village?"

"Not many," she replied. "They mostly left after this lunatic shot her gun off and—"

"Who's left?"

She closed her eyes, let out a breath. "Old Man Termic. And the widow Attara. They're refusing to leave."

"So, if there are soldiers coming," Meret spoke softly, "will killing this woman help Termic and Attara get out safely?"

A long moment passed. A hundred heartbeats. A breath held forever. Sindra's blade did not leave Sal's throat. Meret clenched the wine bottle in his hand. And Sal...

Sal the Cacophony never even blinked.

"Too fucking good, Meret." Sindra's voice dropped, along with her blade. She shoved Sal to the floor and sheathed her blade. "Too fucking good..."

Meret let his breath out. "I know this is hard, but—"

"And too fucking dumb."

She was over him now, looming stark black. The anger, the terror, everything had seeped out of her face—everything but that flint-eyed stare and that low, gravelly voice.

"Whatever oath you took, whatever promises you've made, whatever you *think* you have to do," she rasped, "she's not worth it. She's not worth what she's going to do and she's not worth this town."

She raised a hand. Meret clenched his teeth, tightened his grip.

"I just hope..." She squeezed his shoulder. "I hope you figure that out."

She said not another word, she spared not another glance, as she turned smartly on the heel of her prosthetic and stalked out his door.

And only when the door slammed shut behind her did he realize how tightly he'd been clutching the bottle.

He looked to Sal, lying on the floor. She pulled herself to her ass, rubbed at a bruise on her ribs, and glanced up at him.

"Which part of the Imperium did you say you were from?"

"I didn't."

"Did they not teach you how to help ladies up in I Didn't?"

"You can get up yourself," he observed. "You could have stopped her, too."

"She had a blade to my throat."

"She did. And she took her eyes off you. You looked down at her knee. You could have—"

"Kicked the joint of her leg, yeah," Sal finished. "Those prosthetics aren't built for that kind of hit."

"She would have gone down." He swallowed hard. "You could have killed her."

Sal held his gaze for a moment longer before pulling herself to her feet. She brushed herself off. She rubbed her bruise again. She limped back to the table.

"I could have, yeah," she replied. "Did you want me to?"

"No!" he snapped. "But...why didn't you?"

"Because she had good reason to kill me."

"Then... *did* you lead soldiers here?"

A cold moment.

"No."

And a cold word.

"But she was ready to kill me if I had," she continued, easing herself back into the chair. "I couldn't take that away from her."

"That..." Meret shook his head as he uncorked the wine and poured a glass. "That doesn't make sense."

"You come into this world with a name and nothing else. Everything else—the money, the blood, the people you love—you earn." She took the cup, stared into it. "And you lose them. But everyone gets one reason, one thing they'll fight for, that they'll *kill* for. And when you go to the black table...it's the one thing you get to keep."

She swirled the wine, took a long sip.

"Take that from someone, you take everything from them, and send them out of this world with nothing." She closed her eyes. "And I've done enough of that today."

Meret sat there in silence as she drained the glass, smacked her lips.

"What is this, anyway?" she asked.

"Cathama Crimson," he replied. "Vintage."

"Huh." She reached for the bottle, poured another glass. "Tastes like skunk-ass."

EIGHT

SNOWBIRD

T here had to have been a dozen of them, at least, circling me like wolves, their blades glimmering like fangs in the moonlight."

Ereth Meticulous was a proud man.

"Behind me, the maiden cowered, her screams only made silent by the reassuring comfort of my steel imposed between her and the fiends."

Thick-bodied, with muscle that was slowly but inevitably turning to paunch, and a few respectable scars, you might have thought he had good reason to be proud. He was tall, strong-looking, courageous...

"I gazed into their eyes, one by one, and whispered to my blade: 'Tonight...we dance a crimson waltz.'"

Also loud. Extremely fucking loud.

Hence why, despite being all the way across the floor of a little tavern called Snowbird and doing my absolute damnedest to appear like I wasn't listening, I could hear every masturbatory syllable dribbling from his lips. When said lips weren't occupied with quaffing cheap wine from a cheap glass, anyway.

His body too big for his shabby clothes, his smile too dumb to make his scars look good, and his wine *clearly* too strong for the amount he was drinking, he looked, sounded, and—I'm amazed I could tell from all the way over here—smelled like any number of drunken braggarts that I'd punched out before.

To look at him, you'd never have guessed he was the key to bring-ing down nations.

Which, I suppose, made sense.

After all, he'd be a pretty shitty Revolutionary spy if he looked like one.

He continued to spin his yarn through wine-slurred boisterous-ness, his voice bellowing over the low din of the tavern's other traffic, though I had stopped listening to what he was saying. The reason for that being that I didn't think I could hear the words *crimson waltz* again and not hurl myself out the window.

And also because my job was to watch, not to listen.

The war for the Valley may well have ended in a defeat for the Great General, but as any Revolutionary soldier will tell you, a crushing, bloody war in which thousands upon thousands of your comrades had died horrific deaths was no reason to be a quitter. And while he might have been a raving lunatic, a power-hungry mad-man, and an iron-fisted tyrant, the Great General was no fool.

When cannons couldn't break the Imperium's grasp on the Val-ley, he'd turned to more subtle methods.

"*Clang! Whoosh!* We danced a bloody dance, each step ruby on that uneasy night!"

As subtle as a drunk fuck like Meticulous could be, anyway.

The Revolution's spy network was legendary, a hidden army of sym-pathizers, codebreakers, saboteurs, and, apparently, sleazy drunkards. Maybe the Great General saw something in Meticulous I couldn't through his sopping, slurring flirtations. Still, at the very least, he hadn't said something as stupid as—

"When I had finished, they lay dead at my feet. The crimson waltz was done...though I knew, with a heavy heart, it was but a rehearsal."

Holy fucking shit, kill me.

"Something on your mind?"

My companion must have sensed my unease. Or, more likely, noticed the way I was getting ready to impale myself on a chair leg after listening to that tripe. Because while the look Jero flashed me was one of practiced calm, he had a twinge of worry at the edge of his grin.

"We could be done with this by now, I hope you know," I replied, sinking back into the booth at the back of the bar from whose shadows we observed. "I could have gotten whatever papers you need well before any of us had to hear him talk."

"We," he corrected. "*We* need the papers he has." He took a sip of his wine. "And how would you go about it?"

I glanced at him. "Are you asking me to do it?"

"I'm asking how you would."

"I don't know. I'd probably find parts of him to break until he gave them to me."

"And how would you intend to do that without drawing attention—and thus, the guards—down on yourself?"

"I don't know. Follow him into an alley or something."

"He's the Revolution's spymaster for this entire region. You think he doesn't know how to shake someone following him?"

"Look." I narrowed my eyes at him. "I carry a *gun* that shoots *magic*. I could figure something out."

His expression turned severe. "If you don't want this ending with us getting noticed, found out, and summarily executed, you'll keep that thing hidden." Fear began to creep into the corners of his eyes. "You *can* keep it hidden, right?"

Beneath my cloak, the Cacophony seethed at the implication that I could control him. It was true, mind you—whatever profane powers he possessed, fingers were not one of them. But as offended as that made him, the idea of drawing him for so mundane a task as intimidating a shiftless drunk would demand an answer.

And that I could not keep hidden.

"As adorable as you are when you're nervous, I can handle the gun." I glowered over the table back toward the bar. "I'm just saying, I could do *something* to speed this along. If you had let me bring my sword, we could be out of here already."

"Swords attract attention."

"Not where I'm from."

"This isn't some frontier freehold where people kill each other in the street. In Terassus, there are certain expectations."

Jero's gaze fixed on Meticulous as the large man gesticulated wildly, apparently enacting some pantomimed duel, with his wineglass serving as a sword.

"Meticulous knows those expectations. He knows exactly what he looks like. People go out of their way to avoid looking at drunks, which is precisely what he counts on. You see an imbecile—so does every Imperial in this city—but that man is the Revolution's eyes in this city."

He looked to me, all mirth fled from his face.

"That's why we need this to go off flawlessly. Which is *not* helped by swords, magic guns, or...I don't know, throwing poisonous snakes or whatever else you Vagrants do."

I bit back a curse. As gratifying as it would have been to spew, Jero was right.

Two Lonely Old Men's information revealed that the Iron Fleet's flight had been painstakingly planned to avoid any possible detection—no mean feat when you're talking about ten ships that fly through the sky. Coordination between every spy—including the ones that Jero had made disappear a week ago—was key to figuring out where the Imperium's forces were deployed so as to more expertly avoid them.

Ereth Meticulous was in possession of that knowledge.

Which is why we wanted it.

The idea, Jero had explained, was to arrange it so that Meticulous's information found its way to his Revolutionary masters, as expected. Save that it would just so happen to inform them that Imperial forces along the anticipated route were too strong and divert them to another flight path.

One that would make them significantly easier prey.

It was a complicated plan. And complicated plans required delicate touches.

"Oh, my lord," a feminine voice purred, "you must have been *dreadfully* frightened."

You wouldn't have thought a woman as tall as Agne could deliver that delicate touch. But she was just full of surprises, it turns out.

Agne sat upon a stool beside him, as primly as a six-and-a-half-foot woman could. Her legs were crossed, skirt flowing down to dainty shoes, one gloved hand resting delicately upon her knee, the other holding a fan that she half hid a demure smile behind.

I admit, I had been skeptical of this plan for her to charm him *before* I had seen her dress. The cut of its violet silk did nothing to hide her *exceedingly* pronounced muscle, her gloves clinging almost enviously to the curve of her biceps as she flicked her fan back and forth. And, while I mean no disrespect to the gender, I've known enough men to know that they'd scarcely pay a woman a head taller than them with thighs that could crush that same head any attention, let alone affection.

But fuck me, Meticulous was eating up every flexing ounce of attention she gave him.

"Well, I admit to *some* pang of nerve," he chuckled, throwing back the last of his wine and setting it on the bar for a refill. "But I knew that even if my sword was shattered, I still had *these* weapons."

He held up his arms and flexed, visibly straining with the effort. Agne gasped and, with a hand big enough to encompass his entire arm, felt at the muscle beneath, making a show of fanning herself ever more swiftly.

"By the Scions, my lord, you are like a python made man."

"Oh, come *on*."

I groaned louder than I intended to, but it's not like Meticulous noticed. I'd have been surprised if he had enough blood left in his ears to hear *anything*, the way his trousers tightened. I glanced around, wondering if perhaps there was a quicker way to avoid this situation than jumping out a window. A knife sharp enough to impale myself upon, perhaps. Or at least to gouge my own eyes out.

"Oh, hush," Jero chided through a grin. "Let her do her thing. It's amazing."

"It's *depraved*," I replied. "What's more, it's a *gross* misuse of our team assets." I gestured toward the scene unfurling as Meticulous demonstrated a few squats to Agne, who clapped with delight. "What's the sense in having our muscle do this?"

Jero shook his head, took a deep drink. "Agne's not the muscle."

I blinked. "What? She's *huge*."

"That's her strength. But it's only one of many." He tapped the rim of his glass. "*You're* the muscle. She's the charm."

"Why am *I* the muscle?"

"Because, of the two of you, only one has a story about beating a warlord to death with an empty whiskey bottle."

I grit my teeth. I couldn't rightly argue with that—hell, the bottle hadn't even been empty when I started beating him. Still, I found it odd that there wasn't *one* story about how charming I was.

A fucking mystery, that.

Maybe Jero noticed the consternation on my face, because his grin grew insufferably wide.

"Did you *want* to be the charm?" he asked.

"Of course not," I replied, sneering.

A long moment passed as we watched Agne clap at the sight of Meticulous raising a barstool over his head. I cleared my throat.

"But if I *did*," I said, "I could certainly do a much better job of it than this."

"Birdshit," Jero scoffed over his wineglass.

"Excuse me?"

"Oh, no, not you," he said, waving a hand. "That was in regards to the *other* ludicrously asinine thing someone just said to me." He chuckled. "Come on. I've heard the stories. You? Sal the Cacophony? The woman who once escaped a hanging by challenging her accuser to a drinking contest? *Charming?*"

I sipped my wine. "Well, one would *have* to be charming to get an entire legal system to agree to such a contest, wouldn't they?"

"Go on, then," he said, setting down his wine.

"What?"

"Say something charming."

"Now?"

"Now."

"Well, I can't just, you know, do it on command like that."

"Okay, well, see, that's kind of necessary to be the charm."

"Fucking okay." I slammed the rest of my wine and then the glass before leaning toward him. I shot a coy half-grin—the half without the scar—and stared at him from beneath a lofted brow. "Ah, wait, you have something in your eye."

Jero blinked. "What?"

I leaned in closer, until my breath was on his neck and my voice was a whisper in his ear.

"Our future together."

I held that closeness for a moment before leaning back to take in his expression. He stared at me, his mouth soundlessly agape and the world falling silent around our ears, his eyes wide and unblinking with dazzling admiration and—

Wait, no.

That was just regular old horror.

"What," he said, "was that?"

"Charm," I replied, smirking. "I wouldn't expect a philistine like you to be able to appreciate it."

"I wouldn't expect to hear that from anyone whose last relationship wasn't with a pillow," he said, shaking his head. "Where did that even come from? Were you high when you came up with that? Are you high right now? Am *I*?"

"Don't be so fucking dramatic." I shot him a glare. "In the proper context, I assure you that line works."

"What context?" He met my scowl with a smile—the kind I didn't want to punch off his face. "Did you have a gun to their head?"

"The next time I use it and it succeeds, you can ask them." I couldn't help but smile back. "When they're coming out of my bedroom."

"I don't know if I've got the years left to wait that long." He laughed. "Be honest with me, madam, has that *ever* worked?"

Suddenly, my smile fell.

I looked down at the table.

I blinked and, in that half second of darkness that stretched out forever, I saw her: her black hair, damp and sticking to her forehead as she rose out of bed and fumbled for her glasses; her grin, crooked as her spectacles as she put them on her face; her lips, wet with the taste of mine, as she looked at me and said...

"Has that ever *worked before?"*

I stared at my empty wineglass.

"Yeah," I said. "Once."

I could feel his stare, just as keenly as I could feel that smile disappear from his face. He opened his mouth to say something, but thought better of it. He looked up, waved down a passing barmaid.

"Pardon me, madam," he said. "We're a little empty here. Another bottle of Imperial red, if you don't mind."

She smiled, nodded, walked away. I grunted.

"Whiskey would have been better."

"We're trying to keep a low profile," he said. "In an Imperial city, they drink Imperial red." He sniffed. "Besides, whiskey makes my mouth get blisters."

I glanced at him. "Well, shit, maybe we ought to just get you a nice little cup of milk."

"Okay, see that?" He leveled a finger at me. "That right there? That's why you can't be the charm. That is a distinctly 'muscle' thing to say."

I opened my mouth to reply, but my words left me just as my attention left him when I caught a flash of movement at the tavern door. Whatever assuredly clever retort I had for Jero would have to wait.

Because the woman I needed to kill just walked through the door.

NINE

ELSEWHERE

"You missed drills again."

I remember her voice. Specifically, the way it entered a room long before she did.

Some people called her shrill. One legion commander with abominable taste in opera referred to it as "akin to a pair of lovebirds singing, if one drank heavily to block out the other." Personally, I had always found her voice to have a certain forthright charm to it. She wasn't a woman of idle banter and pointless small talk. When she spoke, she always chose every word specifically for you.

But on that morning, when I had pulled the pillow off my head just enough to glare at her from a messy nest of sheets, I was starting to see what that one commander had meant.

Maybe he had been six bottles hungover, too.

Darrishana stood in the middle of the door to my bunk, pointedly noticing neither the multiple empty wine bottles on my floor or the offensive sunlight she was letting in. Her full Imperial uniform failed to lend much authority to her petite frame—her blond braid, perfectly done up, and the soft angles of her face didn't help, no matter how deeply she might have been frowning at me.

"This is the sixth time this month," she said, putting her fists on her hips. "People are starting to notice. The nuls are getting bolder. Morale is sinking. The entire campaign is starting to shake."

She was being dramatic, of course. Back then, the Revolution hadn't scored a major victory in years. We were all starting to think of them less as an upstart rebellion backed by cannons and machines and more as how we used to see them—nuls, without magic, culture, or destiny. And I was starting to pull the pillow back over my head.

"Salazanca," she sighed. "Would you at least *look* at me when I'm describing the imminent collapse of our empire?"

Fine.

I suppose I did owe her.

With no small amount of effort, I disentangled myself from my fort of pillows and sheets, ignoring my throbbing headache, parched mouth, and *distinct* odor long enough to put my feet on the floor and sit on the bed. I clutched my head and, through strands of unwashed white hair, I could see the red rising in her cheeks.

"And could you *please* put some clothes on?"

Not fucking likely.

I owed her. But not that much.

Besides, I noted with a grin, she wasn't looking away.

"Look," she said, as modesty forced her to look down at my feet. "I know that lulls in combat can seem tedious. But I want to remind you that laxity is what led to the nuls forming their little Revolution in the first place. This Imperium, the Imperium that *we* built with *our* sacrifice, only works if we're willing to fight for it."

She gestured out toward the training ground. Noonday sun poured down on the fort's courtyard. I could see mages sparring, hurling fire and frost at each other, honing their skills. I smiled. It had always seemed so quaint.

I had sparred exactly once. With a tall, mean Siegemage—seven feet and four hundred pounds of magical, unstoppable muscle, impervious to pain or fear.

Our match had lasted two minutes. It took them an hour to pull him out of the wall I put him through.

"Everyone out there is working hard," she continued, rudely ignoring my pounding head. "Jindunamalar, Vrakilaith—everyone is preparing for orders from the capital. Something big is coming, Salazanca. There's talk that this one could come from the Empress herself. If there's a target, we need to..."

Her voice trailed off as I held up a finger, asking for a moment. Just as swift as her voice had entered, it fell silent as she watched me.

"Forgive me, Darrishana," I muttered without looking up. "My skull feels like a rothac kicked me last night, so I'm having a little bit of trouble remembering. But…who was it that covered for you when you snuck out to the freehold to see their festival?"

The red that had begun blossoming in her cheeks started to rise. "You did," she said softly.

"Ah, yes, it's coming back to me." I rose up out of bed, naked and painted with dried sweat. She turned away, her cheeks on fire. "And who was it that led the charge to the nuls' fortress and brought down their gates last month so that you wouldn't have to?"

"You did," she whispered, "Salazanca."

"Right, right."

I approached her, my hands on my hips, looking down at her until she could bear it no longer. Her face was pure red when she looked up, taking me in: tall and lean and not a single scar on me.

Fuck, I was strong back then.

"And who was it"—my fingers found her chin, tilted her face up toward mine—"that stayed behind, after the nuls had been defeated, and sifted through the rubble of their fortress all night to find that painting you had said you liked?"

"I don't know why." Her tone was indignant, but she couldn't fight the smile on her face. "It was absolutely hideous, on close inspection."

"Point being…"

I leaned in. My lips found hers. Her tongue found mine. And that voice became something soft and sweet in my mouth as she let out a hum.

"I resisted the urge to burn down a fortress for you," I said, pressing my forehead against hers. "And you know how much I love burning things. You can cover for me at drills now and again, can't you?"

Her smile ebbed. She looked away. "I'm just worried," she said. "The word from the capital is that the Empress's pregnancy is… complicated. The nobles and Judges are whispering. I worry about the Imperium." She looked back up at me. "And I worry about you. We're fighting out here for them and they don't seem to care."

"You worry about everything." I patted her cheek. "But you don't need to worry about me. I'm a Prodigy, remember?"

"As you love reminding the entire legion," Darrishana said, rolling her eyes as I walked past her. "The mighty Red Cloud, finest of the Imperial Prodigies, favored by the Lady Merchant herself, who pays no Barter for her powers and hurls magic like—*SALAZANCA!*"

"What?" I asked as I walked out into the courtyard.

"You're still naked!" she screamed after me.

"And I'm still Red Cloud." I held up a finger as she snatched a sheet and came running up behind me with it. "They can't have a war without me."

"Salazanca!"

I remember the way she said my name.

I remember her voice.

I remember the way it fell silent that night, when I was cut and bleeding out on the floor, and I cried out for her.

And she did not answer.

———— ✦ ————

Darrish the Flint entered the bar without saying a word.

No one noticed. Why would they? She was just another body in a cloak coming in from the snow. She might have been shorter and younger-looking than most of the clientele, her flaxen hair disheveled and weariness in her eyes, but she was nothing worth noticing. No one bothered looking up.

Except me.

My eyes couldn't blink. My heart couldn't beat. My blood couldn't move in my veins as I watched the door shut behind her.

She didn't notice me, deep in the booth as I was, as she cast a look around the tavern. She pulled a hood up a little tighter around her face. She took a single step forward.

I blinked.

And I was somewhere else. Somewhere years ago, in a lightless place, bleeding out on the floor as the thirty-three names on my list stood around me.

She took another step.

I was watching my blood glide through the air, carried on a beam of light that tore itself out of my chest, disappearing into the darkness above me and taking my magic with it, even as I begged it to stay.

Another step.

I was screaming, weeping, trying to find the words to ask why they had betrayed me.

Another.

I was empty, hollow, my magic gone and my body a mess of wounds. Another.

I was no longer Red Cloud. That name was no longer mine. That life was no longer mine.

Another. Another step. Another memory. Over and over as she walked into the tavern, my screams ringing out in my head with every step she took, until I was hollowed out all over again, left with only a single memory in my head.

Of me, in that dark place the night they had betrayed me, looking through the shadows for anyone, anybody who would save me. I remembered seeing only flashes of light reflected off of cruel grins and glistening eyes. I remembered seeing only one face.

I had reached out to Darrishana, my arm numb and bloodless. I had cried out for her to help me. I had watched her meet my eyes. I had watched her mouth open.

I had watched her say nothing. And turn her back to me.

"Sal?" Jero's voice was a distant whisper, barely registering as I watched Darrish walk through the crowd. "Are you all right?"

Why was she here? Where had she come from? Why hadn't she seen me?

Is she even real?

The thought crept into my mind on clawed feet, sank into my skull. I couldn't be sure. I had been seeing things lately—ghosts walking in and out of my view, my dreams. People I knew, people I had yet to kill. This might be another one of those, just a fragment of a shattered mind.

But what if she's not?

I didn't recognize the sound of my own breath, the beating of my own heart. Sound and color drained from the world around me, bleeding out through a wound in my head, until it was a formless noise, a gray-and-white mess, with only one source of color.

Her.

A small part of me—the small, practical part that told me not to trust honeyed words and to get paid up front—was screaming inside my head. It pounded on my skull and begged me to remember what was at stake. It shrieked at me to think of all the wars that would be stopped, all the good that would be done, if I could just sit still until this ghost disappeared, like all the others.

But another part of me—the cold, silent part that held me closest during dark nights—spoke softly. It asked me to remember the woman who had shown me her heart when she needed me most. The woman who had shown me her back when I needed her most. Another name on my list. One step closer to being normal. Or as normal as I could be.

How many wars, it asked me, was that worth?

I couldn't feel my legs beneath me as I slid out from the booth and rose to my feet. I couldn't feel my heart beating or my blood flowing through my body as I started walking toward Darrish—the ghost, the woman, the name. I couldn't feel my hands wrapping around the black hilt of the gun.

All I could feel was the heat of the Cacophony as I wrapped fingers around him.

And made my choice.

I pulled, but the gun wouldn't come. An indignant surge of heat shot up through my arm as the Cacophony voiced silent displeasure. I glanced down to see a hand wrapped around my wrist, keeping the gun in his sheath.

Jero's hand.

Color and sound returned, bleeding back into the world as I looked up at him. But his eyes weren't on me. His gaze was locked across the bar.

Meticulous's gaze was locked upon us.

You wouldn't have caught it if you hadn't seen it before: the moment a man drops whatever mask he wears for the benefit of society and lets his true face show. Hell, I'd seen it a thousand times and I only barely noticed it, he was that good at what he did.

But in the briefest of instants, the besotted gormlessness of a wine-drunk braggart slipped off of Meticulous's face and revealed something sharp, calculating, and uncomfortably perceptive. His stare darted between us, taking everything in in an instant: Jero's eyes on his, Jero's hand on my wrist, my fingers on the brass glittering at my hip. And just as swiftly, I watched those eyes go wide with recognition.

"He's made us," Jero muttered. "Fuck."

In the time it took him to curse, the mask came back on. A sodden smile oozed back across his face. The rehearsed lack of focus came back into his eyes. He leaned toward Agne, holding her hand in his, and whispered something to her before sliding off his stool and trundling into the back.

"Come on."

Jero released my arm and hurried out of the booth and toward Agne. I paused, glancing through the crowd of the tavern. The noise of laughing drunks and bawdy jokes filled the air. Red wine splashed on the floor and silken skirts swished across the puddles.

Darrish the Flint was nowhere to be seen.

Had she been real? Or just another ghost come crawling out of my brain? To disappear so swiftly, I wanted to believe that. But if she had been, the Cacophony would have told me.

I glanced down at the gun.

Wouldn't you?

The gun did not reply.

No time to dwell on it. Maybe later. You know, when only a few things were going to shit, instead of everything.

"You just *let* him go?"

I caught Jero's irritated growl as he leaned into Agne. The woman shot him a confused blink.

"He said he had to take a piss," she replied. "What was I supposed to do?"

"I told you not to let him out of your sight."

"And I told *you* that my dedication to your cause ended at watching a man take a wine-piss."

Jero's face screwed up. "You never told me that."

"I make it a point of assuming that I don't have to." Agne took a sip of her wine, completely unbothered. "Don't worry. He'll be right back and then we can continue." She paused, considering. "Well, maybe not *right* back—he had an awful lot to drink."

"He won't be back, you idiot," Jero hissed. "He's on to us."

"That's impossible." Agne shook her head. "I've been the vision of loveliness."

"He recognized…" Jero caught himself, shot me a look. "Someone."

I didn't bother acknowledging the accusation lurking behind that look. My response was the brass sliding into my hand, the turn of my heel, and the tug of my scarf over my face as I started heading for the back.

If this *was* going to be my fault for sending this operation to hell, I might as well make sure I sent it there in a flaming coffin.

I pushed my way toward the back where Meticulous had disappeared into. In a cozy little hall at the back of the bar, a single door marked with an old Imperium sigil for something indelicate squatted.

Indoor plumbing, along with the voccaphone and several centuries of unpaid labor, was one of the few Revolutionary innovations that the Imperium had adopted from their former thralls. Imperial sensibilities being what they were, it was rare to find a tavern that didn't have a nice, private chamber to piss in.

Nice, private, and inescapable.

Meticulous wouldn't be the first man I'd gunned down on a toilet. And, being completely honest with myself, he wasn't likely going to be the last.

I pulled a shell out of my satchel—Hoarfrost, as clean a spell as something named the Cacophony could manage—and slid it into the gun's chamber. I took him in both hands, felt his heat in my palms.

"Shall we?" I asked.

"*Let's,*" he answered.

I kicked the door in, leveled the gun into the washroom. And as ready as I had been to pull the trigger, I hesitated. I felt the Cacophony's seethe of displeasure at not being able to kill, but how could he blame me?

We'd have both looked pretty stupid if I wasted a shell on a toilet.

"Fuck." I scanned the empty washroom, found nothing but a bowl reeking of urine, an empty wineglass, and a distinct lack of Revolutionary spymasters to kill. More puzzling, though, was a lack of any way out. "Where the hell did he—"

"Sal."

Jero stood behind me. In the dim light of the hall, the wrinkles on his face stretched like black scars.

"Come on."

He swept out of the tavern and into the streets, me following close behind. We came out into a black-and-white world, snow falling in sheets. I glanced down the road, to where the street branched into a spiderweb of alleys and side avenues. It was the best place to lose a pursuer, I wagered.

But I hadn't taken two steps in that direction before I felt Jero's hand on my shoulder.

"No," he said. "This way."

"You sure?" I asked, following him all the same as we hurried down the other direction.

"Positive," he replied. "He knows we're hunting him."

I glanced back toward the winding alleys we were quickly putting behind us. "The other way looks like a place I'd go if *I* was being hunted."

"Because you're used to hunting beasts, outlaws, Vagrants," he said. "Meticulous has lived and worked in a city full of his enemies for years. We're hunting a spy. And spies..."

We rounded a corner. A cringe painted Jero's face.

"Seek the light."

Moths of a hundred different hues fluttered on hand-sized wings over the heads of lovers embracing. Opera singers long-dead stood in ornate Imperial masks, singing ballads in tongues forgotten to all but the elders who watched them. Great cats with two heads prowled the streets, snarling at girls who giggled and fled.

A riot of ghosts exploded in the sprawling avenue. Spectral images in purple and green, red and yellow, danced through the falling snow or prowled across the street, gliding intangible through tightly packed crowds, their ethereal shapes disappearing into peoples' bodies, only to elicit applause and laughter as they emerged out their backsides.

Seated upon pedestals lining the avenue, men and women in elaborate costumes and indecipherable masks controlled the ghosts, the glowing fingertips of their gloves weaving commands to be carried out by the spectral creatures, eliciting delight and proffered money from the crowds for every caper of ghostly beast or note from ethereal singer.

"Marionettes," I muttered.

Illusory magic was considered by most Imperial scholars to be not a true art—given that it wasn't particularly useful in killing people—and at best was considered the prettier, less successful cousin of a Nightmage's powerful hallucinations. Still, "puppeteers," as they were commonly called, found ample work, delighting and eliciting donations from crowds of people who didn't know how many corpses magic tended to pile up. I'd loved seeing them when I was a little girl in Cathama.

Of course, if I had been tracking a man with the intent of bludgeoning information out of him back then, I might have had a different opinion.

"Night market," Jero said, scanning the crowd. "The rich shits up on the cliffs come down to amuse themselves with the commoners, drinking cheap wine, indulging cheap tricks, and buying cheap company."

In the shadows cast by the glow of the illusory puppets, I could see what he meant. Clouds of *thesha* smoke filled the air from giggling nobles puffing on ornate pipes. Men and women in various provocative outfits—some delighted, some not—negotiated prices with clients before disappearing behind velvet curtains. Merchants hawked illicit wines, illicit wares, illicit flesh for the pleasure of the drug-addled, drunken fops.

Earlier today, Terassus had seemed so strange, so normal. Gazing upon it now, reeking of wine and weed, it felt a little more familiar.

And so did the promise of violence lingering in the air.

"Meticulous would have gone in here," Jero said, "tried to disappear into the crowd." He searched the heads of people and frowned. "And we aren't going to find him—"

"Unless someone goes in after him." I sniffed. "Well. Good thing you brought muscle, then, isn't it?"

Jero nodded. "Agne is right behind us. She'll keep him from coming out this way. I'll circle around in case he emerges out the other side." He looked at me, the wrinkles on his face deep as emptied graves. "Sure you're up for finding him?"

I wasn't.

I hadn't been sure of much ever since I saw Darrish in the tavern. I wasn't sure what was real and what was another ghost come crawling out of that dark part in my skull where I had made the list. But I *was* sure of three things.

First, I wasn't going to finish my list without Two Lonely Old Men's help. Second, I wasn't going to get that help without finding Meticulous. And third?

"I'm sure," I said.

I was a damn fine liar, when I needed.

"Watch your back," Jero called after me as we set off in separate ways. "You don't get to be a spy without learning some tricks."

The bodies of the night market pressed in upon me immediately. Vapid nobles pushed past me on their way to see some new excitement. Drunken revelers shoved into me, cackling as wine sloshed out of their cups and onto the streets. The occasional client who couldn't wait for more private circumstances fell into my path, half naked and wrapped in the arms and lips of a pretty stranger they'd just met and paid a moment ago.

I gently pushed past them, gingerly stepped over them, kindly encouraged the handsier ones away from me with a very polite punch to the kidneys. But even as I cleared a path through the crowds, there was no escaping the marionettes.

A miasma of brightly colored specters descended upon me. Illusionary koi fish swam lazily over my head, shifting between nauseating shades of lime green, lemon yellow, and beet red. The disembodied melodies of spectral opera singers permeated the crowd, punching through the din. Shimmering nightcats pursued the quavering shapes of hounds, disappearing in and out of walls and the very stones of the street.

I had thought, among the crowd of generally attractive, welldressed nobility, a paunchy man in a dirty coat would be easy to spot. But it was hard to see beyond the glow of the specters, hard to hear beyond the roar of the market, hard to move, hard to think, hard to—

"Answer to my steel, knave!"

I saw the blade before I saw the figure holding it, the tip of a longsword aimed at my chest as a looming body came leaping out of the crowd at me. I had barely wrapped fingers around the black hilt beneath my cloak when I saw the blade punch through my shirt and sink into my chest. My breath caught. My eyes went wide.

And that's when I noticed the sword was bright pink.

As was the figure holding it.

"Parry! Thrust! Ho ho! Ha ha!"

The spectral fighter danced back and forth on ghostly feet, cutting through me with his blade, the blade shimmering and disappearing as it touched my skin. Each touch was painless, except for a faint tingling sensation. At the very least, it wasn't nearly as excruciating as the smug grin the puppeteer mage sitting nearby shot me from beneath his gaudy ballroom mask.

"It seems the stylings of Lord Fyzzyl were too swift for you, my dear." He bowed low, holding up a hand in expectation of fiscal generosity. "Perhaps you'll get him next—"

He didn't get around to finishing that thought. But he *did* find the time to let out a scream as I grabbed him by his collar and shoved him ungently against a wall. Anger and agony pulsed through my body with every heartbeat, each one of them demanding I vent them on this poor dope. He must have realized that, because there wasn't a mask made gaudy enough to hide the terror in his eyes.

With one hand pressing him against the wall, my other slid down to my waist and pulled out something shiny and metal. He watched, too breathless to scream, as I took his hand, slid a pair of copper knuckles into it, and closed his fingers around it before shoving my way back into the press of bodies.

I wasn't going to have it said that Sal the Cacophony didn't support the arts.

Idiot, I chastised myself. *Don't blame him just because you didn't see that attack coming. How the fuck did you not see a hot-pink sword coming at you? What's wrong with you tonight?*

I didn't give myself an answer, even though I already knew it.

I couldn't shake the feeling from the tavern, that feeling of color and sound draining out of the world. Even now, it seemed to come back muted—voices distant, colors faded, like they weren't really there, like I wasn't really sure what was.

Because of Darrish.

Because I had seen her. Because I *thought* I had seen her. Because I didn't know if I had and I didn't know if I hadn't and I didn't know what was real or what was an illusion or what the fuck I was seeing anymore.

My breath came slow, ragged, like I had just walked thirty miles instead of thirty feet. Something was wrong with me. More than I first realized. The faces and illusions and laughter around me all blurred into one vomiting stream of noise and light—I couldn't make out people anymore, let alone the one I was looking for.

Turn back, I told myself. *Find Jero, send him in here instead. You can't do this. Not while you're seeing ghosts. Not while you're seeing...*

"Darrish."

My voice tumbled numbly out of my lips at the sight of her hood, bobbing through the crowd. There she was, just like she had been in the tavern.

Darrish the Flint. Or...a ghost that looked like Darrish. Or another illusion? I couldn't think. I could barely see as I saw her glance over her shoulder and lock eyes with me.

I didn't know what played behind that wide-eyed stare. Was it fear? Recognition? Or was it something else she had never shown me as her lips formed two words I couldn't hear?

Hello, Sal.

No...no, wait. That wasn't it. I squinted. It was...

Look out.

I heard the hiss of steel leaving a sheath.

I felt the looming bulk of someone rising up behind me.

I turned.

And Meticulous's blade found my flesh.

I snarled instead of screamed and I bled instead of died as his knife punched into me. It had only been because I had turned at the last possible moment that his blade had found my side and not my spine. And the realization of his error was in the fear painted on his face.

"Fuck," he whispered as he jerked the blade free and turned to go before anyone noticed him.

Good plan. Get out, escape, leave me to either break off the chase to seek help or risk bleeding out. If I had more brains than scars, it probably would have worked, too.

His bad fucking luck.

I grabbed his wrist as he turned, pain fueling my grip as my fingers dug into his skin, refusing to release. He tried to pull away as discreetly as he could, trying desperately to avoid attracting the notice of the people around us.

They didn't notice my blood.

And he didn't notice my blade.

Not until I had jammed it into him.

The steel punched past his coat, past his clothes, into his flesh. But the telltale quiver you feel in the hilt when you've punched something vital was missing. He took the blow with gritted teeth and a muffled growl—old soldier like him knew how to take a hit like that without keeling over from pain—and shot out with an elbow that caught me in the jaw. He tore free from my grip and my steel alike, pushing between a pair of laughing lovers and ignoring the curses they hurled at his back.

I moved to follow, winced at the pain lancing white-hot through my side. I pressed my hand against the wound in my flank, drew in a sharp breath to bite back the agony.

That was all he needed to lose me.

I searched the crowd. Darkness tinged the riot of color assaulting my senses. Pain made the world seem shaky, the spectral marionettes even more twisted than they had been. One by one, the colors sank into a nauseous blend of black and red.

I'd had a hard time hunting him before. Now, with pain clouding my senses, it would be impossible.

Impossible for me, that is.

I slid my knife back into my cloak, ran my hand across its blade. Meticulous's life was still warm on my palm as I slid it down to the black hilt at my hip, as I wrapped blood-slick fingers around it, as I felt a delighted burn coursing through my hand.

No more lying senses. No more seeing ghosts. No more games.

Now was the time to let him work.

The acrid smell of cooking blood filled my nose. Thin trails of steam wafted out my cloak as Meticulous's blood sizzled upon the

Cacophony's hilt. Through his burning brass, he drank. And with a burning voice, he purred in my ear.

"*This way.*"

And I listened.

I kept my eyes on the ground, focusing only on each step. It was all I could manage—agony shot through me with every stride and I couldn't hear the noise of the night market through my own labored breathing. I couldn't see. I couldn't hear. But I didn't need to.

"*There.*"

He told me everything.

Maybe, listening to me, you might think that he was just a weapon. Sure, he might talk and make loud noises—but he's still a gun with a barrel and sights and a trigger, right? To hear me talk, you might think I can control him.

I don't blame you. Sometimes, when he goes quiet, I almost think that, too.

But that's what he wants. Because it's when he's quiet that I realize he's not a weapon. He's listening, hungering, *thinking*. And when he tastes blood like this—when he tastes a man and knows his fears and his dreams and the steps he's taken and the things he's seen—I realize I don't truly know what the Cacophony is.

But by then, like now, it's too late.

I let him guide me. His voice was in my ears, telling me where to step, who would move when I pushed, and who would flee when I threatened them. All the while, my eyes were on my feet, watching every step, until the noise of the crowds faded and I was left with just the ragged sound of my breathing and the feel of snow melting as it struck my blood-slick skin.

Only then did I look up.

I wasn't sure where he had led me. Some cold, empty part of the city where the windows of houses were dark and the streets were empty of people and everything was so cold and quiet that I could hear the patter of my blood weeping onto the snow gathering at my feet.

"I don't see him," I whispered.

"*He is close,*" the Cacophony answered. "*Be ready.*"

I slid a hand into my pocket, found a shell. Jero had told me not to bring too many—said there was a fine line between preparing for trouble and looking for it—but I'd be fucked if I was going anywhere without Hellfire. I quietly loaded the shell into the chamber, clicked the hammer back as I listened.

Nothing. Nothing but snow falling. Nothing but wind blowing. Nothing but the hot cloud of my breath against the black sky and my heart pumping in my chest and my blood oozing down my side and the snow shifting behind me and the—

"THERE!"

I heard his warning. I felt it. I whirled.

Meticulous was right behind me—how had he gotten so close? I didn't know. I didn't care. I didn't think. I raised the Cacophony in both hands, leveled it at him as he leapt at me.

I pulled the trigger.

Snow erupted. Wood splintered. Glass shattered. The night died in a bright, glorious instant as Hellfire's flames gaped wide to swallow it all. Snow melted under its lashing tongues, sending walls of steam rising from the road like a misty garden as the flaming wreckage of doors and windows and crates fell in cinders and smoldering chunks.

I shouldered the Cacophony, waiting for the steam to dissipate.

Admittedly, that might have been rash. Jero *had* said that we needed whatever Meticulous was carrying and that wasn't *too* likely to have survived a blast of unholy flame. But then again, Jero had also said that we needed to catch Meticulous.

So if you *really* thought about it, it was Jero's fault that he was dead.

Or rather, it would be.

If Meticulous weren't standing in the center of the destruction, very rudely still alive.

A cold wind chased the steam away, revealing a thick man hiding behind a thicker shield. A circle of bronze that hadn't been there before appeared from beneath the shredded sleeve of Meticulous's coat, its surface seared black from where Hellfire had struck it. Over the shield's rim, the man cast a pair of wide, wild eyes at me.

"What the fuck is that?" he growled.

"What the fuck is *that*?" I pointed at the shield.

He flicked his wrist. The shield suddenly began to fold in on itself, concentrically twisting with a rasp of metal until it had disappeared entirely, leaving only a thick bronze bracer on Meticulous's wrist.

"Retractable shield," he grunted. "Proofed against arrow, blade, and the magic of Imperial swine. Revolutionary ingenuity at its finest."

"Sure," I replied, fishing another shell out of my pocket. "Or cheating."

He might not have known the Cacophony, but he knew what a gun was. And no sooner had I flipped the chamber open than he was running. Not away—he knew he couldn't run faster than a bullet. He charged toward me, his blade at the ready.

I checked, saw Hoarfrost in the chamber, slammed it shut—always polite to make sure he's ready before we go out. I took aim as he closed in on me—he weaved as he charged. He might shake my aim, but he couldn't shake the Cacophony's. The gun burned in my hand as I stared down his sights.

He whispered with a brass voice, *"Now."*

I pulled the trigger.

Meticulous was faster.

His hand caught my wrist, pushing it up toward the sky. The hammer of the gun clicked. The brass voice roared in anger as the Hoarfrost shell shot out into the night, exploding into crystalline fragments and plummeting to the earth amid the snowfall.

Too fast, I thought. *Too fucking fast. How does a man that big move that fast?*

Or that's what I would have thought, anyway.

If the blade flashing toward my belly hadn't demanded my attention.

I leapt away, feeling my blood hit the wind as his blade drew a thin line across my stomach. Just a graze—a warning. Not enough to stop me. Not enough to make me run.

I slid the Cacophony to my left hand, drew my blade in my right as he rushed toward me, pressing the attack. Our steel met in an ugly metal song. I felt the shock of the blow run down my arm and into my chest.

He was strong. And fast. And clever.

If I spent much longer thinking about that, I might start to realize I was going to die here.

I met his attack with a counter, sliding off his blade to thrust at his chest. He leapt away, and I pressed forward, sliding through the melted snow and the steam coiling under my feet to strike again, aiming for his belly. He parried, stepped out of range. I let the momentum carry me into him, each time snarling, cursing, swinging. Each time finding nothing but a scrap of his coat, the metal of his parry, the whistle of the wind as I struck through empty air.

I'd fought old soldiers before—Revolutionary veterans, Imperial judges, sellswords from all over the Scar. I knew this trick. He was letting me attack, wear myself out, waiting for an opening. He knew he'd cut me worse than I'd cut him. And all his fights taught him that all he had to do was wait.

But an old soldier was still just a soldier. They all came from the same place, learning how to fight in academies and dueling exams, learning to fight for the benefit of other people. Fighting for your own life, your own metal, teaches you things that even the best army can't.

Like this next bit.

I let out a rasping breath as I swung wide, offering him an opening. He took it, leaping forward to try and carve into my flank. I twisted enough to avoid a vital organ—not enough to avoid the blade, though. His edge bit into the new wound, sending fresh agonies through my skin. My body was torn between the urge to run away and the urge to fall down and die.

I did neither.

I wrapped my arm around his, trapping his blade. He tried to pull free, realizing my grip was stronger. Just as he realized what I was about to do next.

Just two seconds after I had done it.

I raised the Cacophony above my head and brought it down hard, the heavy brass of his hilt smashing against the back of Meticulous's shoulder. His body shuddered with the blow, his lips tearing apart in a pained grunt as the shoulder joint loosened. He looked at me, wild-eyed, as I raised the gun again.

"Wait," he said, "no!"

And brought it down.

The sound of his shoulder popping out of its socket was music to my ears.

But the sound of his agonized scream was a fucking twenty-piece symphony.

He lashed out with his knee. I leapt away, releasing him. Meticulous staggered back, staring at his right arm hanging limp and useless from its socket, before looking back up to me. There was no anger in his appraising stare. No hatred painted on his face beneath the sheen of sweat. He studied me like he studied a battlefield and realized that I was more treacherous than I looked.

Which made me feel pretty good about myself, until I realized that I was losing an *awful* lot of blood.

"You're not the deserter." His eyes narrowed on the tattoos running down my wrists. "You're a fucking mercenary. Fuck me blind."

"That could have been arranged," I replied, "if you hadn't decided to run."

"Forty years I served the Great General," he spat. "Thirty-two of those in the Revolutionary Spy Cadre. A *decade* of waltzing beneath Imperial noses, evading their best Maskmages, hiding from *every* scrying magic they had." He shook his head. "And I get found out by a common Vagrant."

I'd have taken offense at being called "common," if I hadn't been about to kill him.

"I don't know why you've come to Terassus," he said, "and I don't know why you chased me here. But I do know the cut I've given you will make you bleed out unless you get help. And I know whatever you're after, you can't like it more than you like money." He gestured with his chin toward some distant place. "You're too wounded to keep fighting and I've spent too much time out in the open. I've got metal stashed nearby. I'll tell you where it is. We leave this here, you can walk away with it, so long as you keep walking right the fuck out of this city."

He wasn't lying.

The adrenaline was ebbing out of me with every breath and being replaced with fresh pain. He might have missed anything precious, but the wound he gave me would be the death of me before long.

It'd be smarter to run, I knew. Hell, it'd be downright fucking brilliant to take his offer. If I just dropped my blade, I'd be able to have my life, metal, and everything else.

I could see my life painted on the red-spattered snow. I could see him, weary and broken and still ready to fight. In battle, in the fight, in the smell of ashes and the song of magic, I could see everything.

Everything...except the ghosts. The one place I was safe from them.

I swallowed hard. I let go.

My blade clattered to the ground to lie among the melted snow.

"Smart girl," Meticulous said, nodding. "This ends well for both of us."

"No," I said, "just me."

He narrowed his eyes. "You've got wounds, girl. You've got no hope of beating me."

"True." I reached into my pocket, drew a shell out. "But I do have one shot left."

I ran my finger along its side, traced the word *Hellfire*, and flipped the chamber of the Cacophony open.

"And you've got a shield you can't raise anymore."

The chamber slid shut with a click that echoed through the night. The Cacophony's excited hiss filled my ears as I raised him and stared down his sights at the old, paunchy drunk who had nearly killed me twice tonight.

A lot of men and women have stared down this barrel before. Only a few ever walked away from it. Most died cursing, spitting hate and anger at me—some of it well deserved—as cinders and frost ate them. A few left begging, parroting hollow remorse they'd been rehearsing. But I could count on one hand the number of them who gave me the kind of look that Meticulous did, breathing hard and one arm hanging limp as a fish, as he stared death right in its brass grin.

His was a look without hate, without anger. Behind all that sweat and blood and pain that painted his portly face, there was just one question.

You sure you've thought this through?

Exactly three people had given me that look before, including him.

In another three seconds, two of them would be dead.

I pulled the hammer back, heard it click. I tightened my grip on the hilt, steam peeling through my fingers. The wind died, and in the silence that followed, I could hear only blood cooling on the snow and an old man waiting patiently for me to kill him.

"*Sal?*"

And one voice. Painfully loud.

"Was that you making that giant explosion?"

And painfully, *painfully* close.

"Ah! There you are, darling."

Agne appeared at the mouth of an alley I hadn't noticed, starkly pretty against the cold dark street in her pristine dress and flawless makeup. She placed gloved hands on hips, shot me an impish smirk.

"Aren't you the little minx, scampering off when you should be hunting down a spymaster. What have you…gotten…up…" She slowly began to notice the carnage across the street. "…to."

Her puzzled stare shifted across the scene, from me, staring at her with a gun in my hand and blood painting my side; to the snow, melted and littered with shattered glass and flaming debris; to Meticulous, staring at her with his dislocated arm and eyes wild with angry recognition.

"Ah." She politely cleared her throat behind the back of her hand. "Is this a bad time?"

I looked back to Meticulous to finish him off. But his instincts were quicker than mine and he didn't hesitate to seize on the opportunity presented to him.

Agne let out a cry as he leapt toward her, nimbly sliding behind her back and hurling his limp arm around her neck. I could see the agony painted on his face as he forced the injured arm to hold her tight. But he endured it, long enough to pull her against him as a shield, long enough to hold his knife to her throat.

"Should have known," he snarled through clenched teeth. "Should have known it was a setup. Should have trusted my instincts. Should have turned you away."

"Well, I'm flattered that you didn't." Agne's voice was calm, collected, even as the blade pressed against her jugular. She held up her hands in surrender. "Now, if we can all just stay civil about this—"

"Any appendage of yours that touches her," I snarled, pointing the Cacophony at him, "I'm adding to my collection, you greasy paunch."

"Or perhaps we could do the opposite of that," Agne said, pointedly glaring at me.

"Think twice before you threaten me with that cannon, girl." Meticulous scowled at me from behind Agne's shoulder. "I'm guessing it doesn't really do 'precision,' does it? You pull that trigger, I guarantee that your friend is going to get it worse."

He pressed his blade closer to her throat. Agne's eyes lit up. Her body froze. All the charm and confidence melted out of her like so much snow in spring. She may have been tall, she may have been powerful, but under a blade, we're all the same meat waiting to be carved.

I'd been under a blade before. I'd worn that same fear she wore.

"It does precision," I replied, calm as I could manage despite the wound in my side and anger in my throat. "And it does worse. You've got a choice here, Meticulous." I took the Cacophony up in both blood-slick hands and narrowed my eyes down his sights. "You can let her go and get precision. Or you can draw this out and get worse."

"Sal…," Agne whispered, but dared not say more. Even that word, soft as it was, made her throat brush closer to the blade. And while I didn't feel the blade, I felt that pained wince across her face as keen as anything.

"No, Vagrant," Meticulous replied, voice cold as the night. "*You've* got a choice. Chase me, maybe lose me, maybe kill me. Or stay and help your friend."

His eyes went narrow. Mine went wide. Agne screamed. He angled his blade over her jugular.

"Before she bleeds out."

And thrust.

TEN

TERASSUS

There was the sound of metal hissing. A woman's cry of alarm. A snarl of anger. Everything—color, noise, light—drained out of my eyes as that moment stretched out for an eternity. And when they returned in one painfully cold breath filling my lungs, I expected to see Agne's life painted all over the street.

What I didn't expect to see was a cold-blooded killer looking, with puzzled alarm, at the blade in his hands bent into a perfect crescent.

Impossible, I thought, for I couldn't think of anything else to describe it. *That was a perfect cut. I saw it.*

And yet, the knife had done nothing more than paint a bright red scratch across Agne's throat before it had bent into a useless piece of metal. And for want of an explanation, both Meticulous and I stared dumbfounded at each other.

Neither of us noticed Agne's hand until she wrapped it around the man's good arm and made a *tsk*-ing sound.

"Rude."

Then, she squeezed.

There was a loud snapping sound. Meticulous collapsed to his knees, screaming and pawing with one useless arm at the other useless arm, bent just like his blade lying on the ground.

"Oh, *lovely.*" Agne's voice was contemptuous as she touched the scratch on her neck—the scratch that *should* have been a killing blow—and drew back gloves tinged with red. "Now I'm bleeding. Do you *know* what a pain it will be to cover this up?"

"You...you..." Meticulous's lips fumbled to find words even as his eyes struggled to take her in, looming over him, somehow dainty and ferocious at the same time. "You're a...you're..."

"A mage," I whispered. "You're a fucking Siegemage, aren't you?"

That smile returned to her face like it had never left. And all six and a half feet of her bowed low in a delicate curtsy.

"Agne the Hammer. Siegemage, Vagrant at large, and poetry lover," she said, winking at me. "At your service."

"Lied...," Meticulous sobbed, staring at his shattered limbs. "You *lied* to me...you..."

"Oh, do keep things in perspective, darling. You're a *spy*." Agne sneered at him. "And let's not forget who's the aggrieved party here. You tried to cut my throat open."

"You *broke* my *arm*, you *bitch*!"

"Aw, honey." She took his face delicately in both hands. "Did I break your heart, too?"

And twisted.

Ereth Meticulous—spymaster, saboteur, hero of the Revolution—collapsed lifeless in the snow, as bent and broken as his weapon, his face wearing an expression of surprise, completely twisted around on his shoulders.

"Ah, poots." Agne cringed as she stared at his lifeless body. "I shouldn't have done that, should I? Jero is going to be quite cross with me. But he *did* try to kill me." She glanced at me. "You'll vouch for me, won't you, darling?"

It took my brain a minute to catch up to what my eyes had seen. "You're a Vagrant?"

"Yes, dear, I just said that." Agne rolled her eyes. "Mortal wounds are no excuse for inattentiveness, now, are they?"

"Why didn't you tell me?"

She shrugged. "Why would it matter?"

Before I could find outrage adequate enough to express why knowing she was capable of snapping a man's arm in two with her little fingers certainly *did* matter, another voice came lilting out of the alley, a slight figure following it.

"Agne? Is that you?" Urda poked his head out of the alley, glancing around. "Sorry about the delay. We were held back getting things all set up and—Oh my holy shit is that *blood*?"

The thin man immediately turned his head away, holding one hand up in warning as he clasped the other over his mouth, his body heaving with effort.

"Oh…oh my patron Scions, couldn't you have *warned* me before I…I…" He let out a heaving noise. "I'm going to throw up. *I will!*"

"So go ahead!" A hand shoved him rudely out into the street as Yria came stalking out behind him, wearing a scowl and dragging a limp leg behind her. "Puke's better than what usually comes out of your mouth, anyway." The anger on her face was replaced by awe as she spared an appreciative whistle for the destruction. "Damn, bitch, what'd you do?"

"What does it look like I did?" I gestured at Meticulous's corpse. "I *got* the guy we were trying to get, no thanks to you."

"Yeah, we'd have been here sooner"—she paused to gesture contemptuously at her brother, heaving in a corner—"but *this* narrow-lipped pussfoot had to get his tools just right."

"My *work* is an incredibly delicate art, you philistine," Urda protested, "and I wouldn't expect you to understand my—Oh no, I think I can taste it. I think I can *taste* the *smell*."

I ignored Urda's fresh round of heaving as he scampered away, glaring at Yria. "And how the hell did you get here so fast?"

She met my glare with one of her own, slapping her limp leg. "Is my leg numb from a Barter? Did I just appear from nowhere, as if by magic? How do you *think* I got us here, dumbshit? I'm a fucking *Doormage*! I made a portal!"

"Outstanding," I sneered. "Why didn't Jero bring you along, then? A portal would have been useful while chasing this paunchy fuck down."

"I didn't think we'd need it."

Jero emerged from the alley, Tuteng following close behind him. They both spared an appraising glance for the corpse of Meticulous, though only Jero bothered to wince. He shot an irritated look to Agne, who was busy daubing her tiny wound with a silk kerchief.

"So, out of curiosity," he said, "and considering this man knows everything we could possibly ever want to know about the subject, did the idea of taking him alive not cross your mind or did you just think it'd be more fun to attack the Iron Fleet completely blind?"

"He *tried* to *kill* me," Agne hissed in reply.

"And he *failed*," Jero shot back. "You are a *Siegemage*. Your skin is impenetrable."

"My mother taught me never to suffer insecure women, insincere men, or attempted murder." She snapped her fan out, fluttered it imperiously. "If you wanted him alive so bad, you should have found him first."

"Maybe we could discuss this somewhere a little less... *blood-filled*?" Urda suggested.

"He's right," Yria muttered. "We saw that fancy magicky birdshit from clear across the city, and so will the guards."

"Right. Just give me a second..." Jero knelt down beside Meticulous's corpse and reached into his coat, pulling free a sheaf of papers that he seemed to know to look for. He flipped to a page, nodded. "All right. We need to get *this* body to *this* location." He showed the paper to Yria. "Can you get us there?"

"Sure," she grunted, stalking back into the alley, grabbing her brother. "Not like I already gave up my fucking leg to the Lady Merchant to get you here. Why the fuck would I need *both* legs?" She tugged on Urda's collar. "Come on, you little fart."

"Agne," Jero began, "I hate to ask, but..."

"Oh, *fine*." She put her fan away and, with one hand, hoisted Meticulous's considerable corpse over her shoulder. "But only because you were nice about it."

She followed the others down the alley, Tuteng glancing around before silently disappearing after her. Jero spared a final look for the destruction before settling his eyes upon me.

"You said you could control that thing." He gestured toward the Cacophony.

"And I did," I replied.

"A city block is totally destroyed."

"Exactly. *One* city block. If I couldn't control him, the whole place would be in flames."

He opened his mouth as if to protest further, but a distant

sound caught his ear. Clanging metal, shouts of alarm, patrol birds squawking—they varied a little, city to city, but I knew the sound of guards when I heard them. And from the look of alarm on his face, so did Jero.

"Just as well, or they'd have been here quicker." He started down the alley. "Come on."

"Right behind you," I said, taking a step forward and promptly keeling over.

I felt cold. I felt numb. But, most importantly, I felt puzzled. It was the strangest thing—my legs had just gone out from under me, as though they had completely disappeared. I reached down to see if they were still there and drew back fingers sticky with my own life.

Oh right, I thought as blackness engulfed me. *I almost forgot I was bleeding to death.*

ELEVEN

METICULOUS'S SAFE HOUSE

Given the vast amount of people I've killed for a variety of reasons, I try not to be too judgmental.

The Scar being what it is, I recognize everyone has their own way of coping with its prowling beasts, extreme weather, and near-constant state of warfare. Be it religion, drugs, military discipline, sex—it takes all kinds of different people to make up this land.

Granted, I've killed most of those kinds.

But, like I said, I try not to be too judgmental.

However . . .

"What the fuck do you mean there's no fucking whiskey?"

I don't always succeed.

Jero looked up from his work just in time to avoid the angry haymaker I threw in what I thought was the direction of his head—it was a little hard to tell, given the amount of pain I was in. He merely frowned at my sloppy attempt to break his jaw and shook his head.

"Need I remind you that there are currently *several* guard patrols out searching for whoever set fire to a sizable chunk of downtown Terassus?" he chided. "Given that I'd rather *not* have to kill or be killed by one or more of them, could you possibly keep your voice down?"

"I don't know, asshole," I snarled through gritted teeth. "Could you *possibly* be more shit at what you're doing down there?"

Through eyes half blind with pain, I watched his fingers carefully apply a viscous, bubbling liquid to my midriff. I don't know why he was bothering being so delicate; the fucking stuff reeked of rot and dying things, it bubbled like stew as it sat upon my skin, and with every breath I took, it seeped deeper into my wound, sending a fresh coil of cramping agony that made my muscles so taut I could barely breathe.

"Vechine is an effective alchemic," Jero replied, not taking his eyes off my wound. "Not much I can do for the pain, but it's preferable to bleeding out."

He had me there.

The Revolution—routinely faced with enemies who could burn them, freeze them, and tear them apart with a thought—had struggled to find an effective and relatively painless medical treatment they could use in the field to answer the myriad ways the Imperium had to kill them.

And after they'd given up on that "painless" part, they'd come up with Vechine.

Half acid, half bandage, the alchemic sludge had been cooked up by some all-mad Freemaker and sold in bulk to the Great General's armies. It worked by entering wounds and inducing spasms to stanch the flow of blood, effectively cauterizing them until more proper treatment could be found.

Suffice to say, the sensation of a burning ooze sliding inside a raw wound to forcibly clamp it shut felt exactly as good as you would think, assuming you were appropriately intoxicated enough to even entertain the idea.

I, ruefully, was not.

"Fucking get me something, then." I spoke through clenched teeth, draping one arm over my eyes as I felt the ooze continue to seep into me. "Gin. Ale. Fuck me, Jero, I'll even drink *wine*, just grab me something to make this feel less like I'm going to shit my guts out."

"Charming," Jero hummed in reply. "Much as I'd love to help, Ereth Meticulous was a Revolutionary. By the order of the twenty-sixth of one hundred and one Immutable Truths handed down, he was forbidden to partake of liquor or intoxicants, save when absolutely necessary to keep up his disguise."

"*What?*"

"Take it up with the Great General. He thought alcohol was a tool by which the Imperium stifled the masses."

"*Birdshit*," I all but screamed. "I saw Meticulous chugging wine like a teenager back in the tavern. Fucking stifle me, Jero! Stifle the hell out of me!"

"He was a *spy*. He drank only as much as necessary to keep up his disguise. He doesn't keep any here. The place is as dry as a celibate skeleton."

That sounded stupid to me, but if I opened my mouth, I had a strong suspicion that something other than an argument would come out. With nothing left to me, I lay back down upon the table and tried to rely on my own willpower.

If I had known it would come to *that*, I would have asked Jero to just let me bleed out in the snow.

I had drifted somewhere cold and dark after falling onto the street. I didn't know how long I had lingered there before I was torn back to the waking world as surely as a scream tore itself out of my throat.

I'd had a moment to take in my surroundings—low-slung ceilings of a house nestled in the dark part of Terassus, alchemic globes burning quietly on bookshelves brimming with notes, painfully functional furniture sparsely decorating the room, including the table Jero had laid me out on and the chair he currently sat in beside me.

I'm sure there was more to the humble two-story apartment that Ereth Meticulous used as his hideout, but in another second, the Vechine had started smoking, the smell of rotten eggs filled my nose, and I became far less concerned with the décor and far more concerned with not shitting myself in pain.

I suppose, all told, I was still lucky—lucky that Meticulous had this stuff, lucky that Jero knew how to use it. Only because of him was I here and not bloodless and pale on the street. And even now, my breathing became steadier, the pain starting to subside to a dull ache.

"Bleeding's starting to stop," Jero muttered. "Good."

I groaned. "When does it end?"

"Right after the bad part."

I allowed myself a relieved breath. "Good. I can feel it starting to ease up a little."

"Yeah," he replied, "it always does that right before the bad part."

"*WHAT?*"

I wasn't expecting an answer, but if he had one, I didn't hear it. Every sensation—touch, sight, smell, sound—was overwhelmed by pain. Agony shot through my body, sending my limbs spasming and thrashing without me even realizing it. My body felt ablaze from within, acting like it was trying to smother a fire that was burning inside me. I could barely tell what was happening.

Except that he was there.

Through the pain, I could make out his silhouette against the alchemic glow—his eyes, locked on mine; his hands, holding me down by the shoulders; his voice, speaking through the sound of my pain. And though I only caught a few words, I heard him, cold and gentle as the snow falling outside.

"You can do this," he whispered. "You know you can."

I didn't. But he did. And, in another moment, one of us was right.

The thrashing slowed, then stopped. My breathing went shallow, then steady. The pain ebbed away, leaving me only with a ragged breath, a sheen of sweat painting my skin, and the old, familiar ache of my scars.

My vision was the last thing to come back to me, reasserting itself to reveal Jero, standing over me, sweat dripping down his brow and a large red mark across his face where one of my thrashings had caught him.

"Done?" he asked.

"Done," I replied, nodding wearily.

"Good?"

"Good."

He nodded. He eased trembling fingers off my shoulders. I could see the red marks left behind from where he had held on so long.

He hadn't let go.

"Two Lonely Old Men has a healer we can trust back at the Caned Toad," Jero said. "The spasms get easier the more you take. First time using Vechine hurts like hell, but it's better than dying."

"Whiskey would have helped," I muttered, rising up to my ass.

"If it would have kept you from hitting me, I'd have fermented some out of my own blood," he said, rubbing his cheek.

I grinned at that. I would have apologized, but from where I stood, he'd gotten off easier.

Without the whole "imminent death" thing consuming me, I could see that Meticulous lived sparsely and simply. A bed sat in the corner beside a staircase, every step laden with books, maps, and letters he had been studying. Food was left half eaten, dishes lying dirty. Notes and reports lay scattered about in an organizational system that invited madness to even try to comprehend.

"Our boy was busy," I noted.

"He was keeping notes of every movement of every day," Jero replied. "There should be valuable stuff in here."

"You haven't checked?"

"I had intended to." He shot me a glance. "But then you had to go and almost die."

I shrugged. "Well, be less shit at being spotted next time."

He shot a grin over his shoulder. "You're welcome." He waved a hand. "Anyway, I put the twins on it. This is more their area of expertise, anyway. Well, *one* of them, anyway."

I squinted. "Which?"

"Fuck me with a six-pronged fork at a twelve-course dinner."

My answer came tromping down the stairs, scratching her ass and spitting on the floor.

"What was going on down here, anyway?" Yria asked, glowering at me. "Sounded like one of you was giving birth to a rothac or the other one was shitting it out."

"It's been taken care of." Jero gestured at her with his chin. "What did you find?"

"You sure?" She squinted at him. "I haven't heard noise like that without paying for it. Was something fun happening?"

"It was a medical procedure," Jero sighed. "What did you find?"

"Because if you two are slapping hams during business hours, I'm going to have to start asking for more—"

"Fuck's sake, woman, did you find what we needed or not?"

"Oh, we certainly did." A voice and a step, both infinitely sprightlier than his sister's, heralded Urda as he came traipsing down the stairs, a bundle of papers under one arm. "And more."

"The correspondence?" Jero asked. "You found it?"

"He had it hidden under the *third* step from the top of his stairs," Urda said, tapping his temple. "Clever fellow, wasn't he? The first step would be obvious and the second step would just be insane, but who would even *think* to check the third step? No one." A smirk splayed across his face. "No one but a *genius.*"

Granted, I didn't know them that well, but I was swiftly having trouble deciding which of the twins needed a slap in the mouth more badly.

Yria was in the lead, but not by much.

"And the schematics?" Jero asked.

"Yeah, yeah, I got 'em." Yria waved a sheaf of papers haphazardly. "Don't see me getting stiff at the sight of a bunch of fancy letters, do you?"

"This is *far* more than just 'fancy letters,'" her brother protested. "The Revolution's codes are the most sophisticated in any realm."

"But you found what we need?" Jero asked. "The Iron Fleet's routes?"

"Oh, most assuredly," Urda replied, beaming. "It took me longer to read the bird-scratch that passes for Revolutionary penmanship than it did to decipher his codes." He chuckled, shooting me a sly glance. "Honestly, what kind of plebian uses both a glyphic *and* a numeric code to hide their work, am I right?"

He stared at me for an uncomfortably long time before I blinked and answered.

"Uh...yes?"

"We're all quite impressed, Urda," Jero said, leaning against a wall. "Or we will be, if you can replicate it."

"Can *I* replicate it?" Urda let out an incredulous laugh, then looked to Yria for support and, finding nothing but a blank stare, looked back at us. "You're speaking to *Urda*. Urda of the Wild Quill! Urda of the Impeccable Pen! Urda of the Hidden Parchment!"

I stared at him for a second before glancing at Yria. His sister shrugged, grunted.

"I don't fucking know," she grunted. "He just comes up with this stuff."

Urda skipped toward the table I currently sat upon, pulled out a chair. "All I need is a place to work and ten minutes of—" He paused, looked at my wound, then at the table. "Did you..." He shuddered, swallowed something back. "Did you... *excrete* on this?"

My glare must have been answer enough, because he pointedly looked away from me, pulled a handkerchief out of his belt, and thoroughly wiped down the surface of the table and the seat of the chair before sitting down.

"Might want to move, girl," Yria said to me. "He needs space when he gets like this."

I obliged—if only to spare myself talking to him more—and pulled my aching body off the table. Urda barely even looked up as he spread the sheaf of Meticulous's notes out across the table, flipping out his ledger to reveal a series of symbols and numbers that hurt my eyes just to look at. His eyes darting impossibly quickly between them, he began to work, his quill moving with mechanical precision as he began to write different sigils across a tiny sheet of parchment.

"Interesting," he muttered to himself as he ran a finger down one of Meticulous's notes. "There's no mention of Imperial movements in his notes."

"That's interesting?" I asked.

"It is for the Revolution," Jero said, peering at the notes. "He wasn't in Terassus on vacation. What *was* he tracking, if not Imperials?"

"Vagrants." Urda's brows quirked in surprise. "Not Imperial mages, just... Vagrants. And not just in Terassus, but all over the Valley. Look, he's been watching their movements: Cassa the Sorrow, Yugol the Omen, Rudu the Cudgel..."

I knew Rudu, actually. Nice guy for a murderer. But that wasn't the name that interested me.

"Darrish the Flint?" I asked, my voice cracking.

Urda shuffled through the papers. "I don't... see it here. But maybe it's deeper in the code? Give me a minute and I can—"

"Urda," Jero pressed.

"Yes, right, right."

Urda put the notes back down and started scribbling again, tucking away the sheet with the names on it.

I wanted to protest, of course. Darrish's name on my list was the whole reason I'd come to the Valley, after all. But Jero was right—we were here for another reason. And if all went to plan, I'd have her location, anyway. And more.

Urda continued to scribe, his pen moving in short, furious bursts of movement. It was fascinating in the same way watching birds fuck is fascinating—if there's nothing better to do, you might as well, but it's still weird.

But it wasn't until he pulled out another parchment from Meticulous's notes that my attention was seized. And so was Urda's.

His pen stopped moving. His hand began to tremble. His face screwed up so hard I thought it would fold in on itself as he stared at the sigils, teeth clenched.

"What's wrong?" Yria asked, leaning over. "Someone write a word you don't know?"

"No, it's just..." He squinted at the sigils, shook his head. "I don't...recognize these."

"What? Why not?"

His lips fumbled as he tried to stammer out an answer I knew he didn't have. Because I knew it.

I knew whose sigils those were. I knew the touch of the hand that held the pen that made them. I knew the last words she had ever spoken to me, because she still said them every time I woke up to find her ghost staring me in the face.

No, I told myself, shaking my head. *You're seeing things again. That's not her work. That's not her.*

That's what I said in my head. But when my lips moved to say it, too, something else came out.

Her name.

"What?" Jero asked, suddenly glancing at me.

"Huh?" I blinked.

"I said it's coded behind magic." Urda held up the parchment, turning it all directions as he tried to figure it out. "This isn't

Revolutionary work. It's a Spellwright's." He looked at Jero, worry crossing his face. "A Freemaker's."

My heart caught in my throat. I kept it there, forcing dread and fear off my face, all too aware of Jero's eyes upon me. Like he could see into me.

Like he knew.

"Birdshit," Yria grunted. "Those gear-fuckers don't work with magic, Freemaker or no."

"Oh, really, smart guy?"

Urda reached into his satchel and produced a small pouch. He emptied a pale dust upon the parchment, and in response, the sigils began to glow with a faint purple light.

"Shut your mouth." Yria gaped, eyes agog. "What kind of Revolutionary touches magic? Did he steal this?"

"No. Or...yes? I'm not sure." Urda shook his head. "Maybe it was sent to a noble and he intercepted it? It's good work. I've never seen it before. With enough time, I could—"

"Is it related to the Fleet's movements?" Jero interjected.

"Huh?" Urda glanced up. "Oh. No. I'm certain of that. Everything I *really* need is in Meticulous's notes. It's just an interesting little nugget of knowledge for purposes of—"

"Then do it on your own time," Jero said. "Because we're running out of ours."

"Of course, of course." Urda returned his pen to the parchment, making a few quick strokes. "And...*done.*"

He leaned back, gesturing to his work. I glanced from Meticulous's notes to the message he had scribbled and, fuck me, I couldn't help but whistle. If I hadn't seen it happen before my eyes, I would have sworn that the same hand had written both—a forgery so perfect it would make the Ashmouths weep to gaze upon its beauty.

"A perfect fucking match!" Yria guffawed, slapping her brother hard on the back. "What'd I tell you? Put a pen in this turd-skipper's hand and he makes magic!"

"It's nothing, really." Urda offered a grin as he rubbed the spot where his sister had struck him. "Well, nothing for *me*, anyway, not when you've had the kind of training I've—"

"And it says what we need it to say?" Jero plucked the forged message away and scanned it. "You were specific?"

"Of course I was." Urda looked vaguely offended. "You didn't seek out Urda of the Beastly Ledger for generalizations."

"Good." Jero rolled the paper up tightly and hurried toward the door of Meticulous's apartment. "Grab whatever else you need and get ready to leave."

He pushed the door open. Sitting upon the stoop of the apartment, Tuteng watched the streets, unmoving, the stumps of his horns poking out of his hood.

"Any patrols?" Jero asked.

Tuteng held up five fingers.

"How close?"

Tuteng tilted his head toward the north and stared thoughtfully for a moment before looking back down.

"Close," he answered.

"Two more patrols than there were an hour ago." Jero's sigh was as deep as his wrinkles as he glanced over his shoulder at us. "Terassus's guards are overpaid, underworked fops, but sixty of them combing the same city block will find us eventually. Grab whatever you need..." His gaze lingered on me for a second. "Or want."

"Time?" Tuteng asked.

Jero handed him the rolled-up forgery. "Time."

Tuteng nodded slowly, got to his feet even more slowly. He took the forgery with one hand, the other sliding into his cloak. My body tensed instinctively—I'd rarely had a night that featured a man reaching for something inside his cloak that ended well, except for one time. I was expecting to see a weapon in his hand, or an alchemic, or some other indication that this night was about to get much more complicated.

What I saw was a bird.

A Shekkai, specifically. Messenger breed—sleek, swift, and held gently in Tuteng's hand. Despite having been hidden beneath his cloak with who knows what else for who knows how long, the bird didn't do anything more than cast a curious glance around before the Clansman brought it up to his lips.

And began whispering.

The Shekkai sat in his grasp, suddenly attentive as Tuteng muttered to it in a language whose words didn't sound like anything I had ever heard. They didn't even sound like words, if I'm honest—more like some kind of soft whistle.

Whatever it was, the bird seemed to understand. And when Tuteng moved to fasten the forged message around its leg, it didn't fuss. It took up a seat on his shoulder as he stalked off into the night.

"Where's he going?" I asked.

"To take care of the message," Jero replied. He swept back into the house, pointing at Yria as he walked past. "Get ready to leave. We can't risk being seen on the streets."

She grunted an acknowledgment, tugging on Urda—busy arranging his supplies—before they hustled out and disappeared down an alley. Jero peered up the staircase and bellowed as loudly as he dared.

"Agne!" he shouted. "Time to go."

The floorboards shook with her stride as the Siegemage came down the stairs, an immense barrel leaking some foul-smelling fluid held effortlessly under one arm. She walked across the room, leaving a trail of the reeking stuff in her wake, before tossing it back into the living room.

"Everything go all right up there?" Jero asked.

"Does it look like it did?" Agne gestured to the dark stains across her dress. "*You* said we were going out for wine."

"I said we were going out to find and possibly kill a spy."

"*And* for wine," she protested as she stormed out the door. "You said nothing about burning down a house. My favorite dress smells like a candlemaker's wife's asshole now."

"We're burning his house?" I asked.

"And his body," Jero replied, reaching into his pocket. "If anyone else—Imperial, Revolutionary, or otherwise—finds this place, we run the risk of them figuring out what we're doing." He pulled a tindertwig from his pocket, struck it across the palm of his hand, and watched it spark to life. "And we can't have that, can we?"

He dropped it to the floor. The fire immediately caught the fluid, racing across the floorboards, up the stairs, and into the house. Blue and red danced, spreading in writhing tendrils to eat wood and paper and cloth.

I felt a hand on mine. Jero pulled me away from the house as the flames began to rise, smoke pouring out of it.

"The guards won't find this a little suspicious?" I asked.

"Ordinarily, they might," he replied. "But someone went and had the courtesy to set the rest of the fucking block ablaze."

I felt the Cacophony seethe with pleasure—he did so love it when people talked about him.

"Not like we'll be around to answer any questions, either." He started tugging me down an alley. "Come on. Yria should have a portal ready for us by now and—"

I dug my heels in, breaking from his grasp. He looked at me, caught between puzzled and irritated, but my eyes were on something else.

The house was a two-story pyre now, tongues of flame licking holes in the roof, painting the melting snow on the street in an eerie red glow. And against it, the silhouette of Agne stood, hands clasped, head bowed.

"What the fuck are you doing?" Jero snarled, storming up to her. "The guards will be here any second."

"I'm giving him a moment of silence," Agne replied.

"*Who?*"

"Ereth."

"Meticulous? What for?"

"Because he had excellent taste in wine." Agne didn't look up, her eyes closed. "And he loved to tell stories. And he had a wife once, and a charming smile."

"He was a *soldier*." Jero's face screwed up in confusion. "A fucking fanatical tool used by other fanatics, just like the rest of them. They won't mourn him any more than they would mourn a rusty shovel."

"Precisely."

Across Jero's face, I could see confusion give way to anger give way to cold practicality. The wrinkles settled on his features in dark, deep shadows as he turned away and stalked into the alley, casting an expectant glare toward me. I met it for a moment before looking back to Agne, so tall and powerful, head bowed humbly and silent before the inferno.

I walked up. I stood beside her. Silent.

Behind me, Jero spared one final glare before disappearing into the alley.

Far away, I could hear cries of alarm and the squawk of patrol birds as the inferno crested the roofs and caught the attention of the guards.

And even farther than that, there were more people that I would kill, like we had killed Meticulous—some that I knew, some that I didn't.

But for now, she and I stood there, at the pyre of the man we had both killed together. And together we stayed there, in silence, for as long as we dared.

TWELVE

ELSEWHERE

Y ou're hurt!"
I remember those words.

I don't always remember her voice—sometimes it's a ghost of a memory; sometimes it's sharp as a knife in my head. But those words, on that day, said that way...

Before she'd said those words, no one else had ever acted like I could die.

"I am?"

Including me.

"Huh. So I am." I glanced down at my arm and the gash that had been torn through it. "How'd that happen? Not in battle, surely. None of those nuls came close to touching me." I snapped my fingers as it came to me. "Right. I was supposed to ask the cadre commander to surrender, thought the presence of Red Cloud would intimidate him, and he tried to kill me instead."

Darrishana stared at me, slack-jawed, wide-eyed, dumbfounded. I cleared my throat, shuffled my feet, and stared out over my shoulder at the pillars of smoke being belched into the sky.

"He, uh...he didn't succeed."

On the morning of that day, it had been a fortress. An impressive one, according to both the Revolutionaries who'd built it and the Imperials who'd been trying for the better part of a month to capture it. Built on a hill with a dozen Revolutionary cannons pointing down its slopes, even the best Imperial cavaliers with the strongest warded shields couldn't make any headway against them.

That meant fuck-all against Red Cloud, though.

That's what they called me back then. Back when I still had my magic. Back when I was still a Prodigy, so beloved by the Lady Merchant that she never asked a Barter for my power. I asked for the sky and she gave it to me. I asked for light and she gave it to me. I asked for the flame . . .

And Red Cloud had brought it.

To that fortress. To a hundred fortresses. To a hundred, a thousand soldiers whose ashes painted the sky after I was done with them.

This was all the Imperium had ever asked of me, of Red Cloud. And it was all I had ever given them. In exchange, they gave me wealth, medals, titles, songs that didn't rhyme, and stories that didn't have any romance in them. I never cared. But they did. They were impressed.

Almost all of them.

"How many?" Darrishana asked.

"How many what?" I replied.

"How many did you kill today?"

"Don't ask me that," I groaned as I walked past her to the officer's tent. A wave of my hand sent the officer—some weary woman who'd given her best days to this war—scurrying as I helped myself to her wine. "I can't keep track of them all from so high up."

I plucked up the bottle, frowned. Althoun's Favor—a nice, deep red they gave to the higher-ups. Tasty, but she hated red—tasted too angry, she said. So I scrounged up some bottle of cheap white shit and poured us both a glass.

"They told me we're heading out tomorrow," I said. "All of us. You, me, Jindu, Vraki. To some nul fort. What was it called? Vigil? I don't know. But there are a lot of towns between here and there, so I thought we might as well celebrate before—"

When I turned around, she wasn't looking at me.

Her eyes had been on that pyre on a distant hill, on those twisting serpents of smoke that coiled up into the sky, on the people who had once been warriors and were now just cold ashes in a stale breeze.

Because of me.

"How many?" she asked again.

"I told you, I—"

"How many scholars?"

"Huh?"

"How many medics? How many farmers? How many carpenters? Wagon drivers? *Butter churners?*" She whirled on me, eyes wet with horror and mouth twisted into a shape short and pained. "How many people were there who weren't supposed to be there? How many did you kill, Salazanca?"

I narrowed my eyes, emptied the wine onto the ground. "It was a fortress. Fortresses have soldiers. Soldiers try to kill us."

"I...yes," she sighed. "Yes, soldiers try to kill us—"

"Kill *you.*"

"Kill *us,*" she snapped back. "But soldiers don't make bread. Soldiers don't make shoes. Soldiers don't write books." She gestured to that flaming wreckage. "That fortress held people who *don't* try to kill us. But they're ashes all the same."

"They're Revolutionaries," I growled in response. "They're *nuls.* They're the *enemy.*"

"And you're a Prodigy!" She wasn't a mighty voice, but when she threw herself into a scream, I could feel it. "Beloved of the Lady Merchant! You could have done something else with your magic."

"Like what?"

"ANYTHING!" she screamed. "You could have frozen them in place, you could have subdued them with a paralysis spell, you could have...I don't know, levitated them in the air until they surrendered."

"That's not something I can do."

"How do you know?" No more screaming. No more anger. The face she gave me was soft, tender, and in so much pain. "You have more power than almost any other mage in the Imperium, so much that you can do anything, shape anything, be anywhere."

She held out her hand to the smoldering wreckage on the hill.

From up there, when I had flown over it, the fortress had looked like any other fortress: a collection of shapes and dots that vaguely resembled a settlement. They all looked that way from up there—too small and distant to be real.

But now, even separated by the miles between us and the hill, it was too close. I could see the fires, the hundred red jaws laughing out columns of smoke into the sky. I could smell it, that living, breathing odor that magical fire always had. And if I closed my eyes, and fell silent, I wondered…

Would I hear them screaming?

"You burned them," Darrishana whispered. "Just like you burned the last ones. Just like you'll burn the next ones. All that power… and you can't even—"

"Say my name."

I remembered those words, too.

They come to me every time she's in my head again, the punctuation at the end of every sentence of every thought about her. Her memory faded with time, sometimes I can't even remember her face.

But I remember the first time we hated each other.

"Say it," I repeated.

She pursed her lips. I knew the name she wanted to say, the names we'd given each other over breakfasts where she did little happy dances when bacon was served with rations or when I'd dueled six mages in a row when someone insulted her hair.

But those weren't my name.

Not my real name.

"Red Cloud," she whispered.

Like a god's name. Fearful, revenant, and seething with contempt.

"I am Red Cloud," I spoke, terse and cold. "This is the Scar. And we're the Imperium. They didn't send me out here to coddle nuls or to indulge childish fantasies. They sent me out here to end a war."

"They didn't—"

"They did," I snapped. "This is what a war ending looks like. This isn't some two-coin opera where villains realize the error of their ways and we all join hands and sing about beauty or some shit."

I pointed to that pyre on the hill. To the people made into ash. To the sky painted red by the fires.

"*That* is what this is," I said. "This fort, the other forts, as many forts as there need to be for this to end so *you* can sit back, far from it all, and shake your fucking head like that's going to do anything."

I bit my lip and waited for her to start cursing at me. Or to scream at me. Or to grab something nearby—that bottle, maybe—and hurl it at my head. I waited for it to become a fight. We'd fought before. I could win a fight. I could move on from a fight.

But she didn't curse. Or scream. She didn't move.

She just...stared at me.

Like she didn't recognize me. Like she never had.

"This war," she whispered. "What is it doing to you? To *us*? Why can't we figure out something better?" Her breath grew short, her eyes distant. "We're going to keep burning them, and they'll come back with fire of their own. They'll keep burning and we'll keep burning until there's nothing left but...but..."

"Easy," I said, holding up a hand. "That's your Barter talking. You've used too much magic, given too much to the Lady. You're seeing threats that aren't there. Things aren't as bad as—"

"No." She looked at me, her eyes painfully close and full of tears. "They're worse."

I didn't know how to do this. I didn't know how to help someone fight an enemy I couldn't see, that cut wounds that didn't appear on her body.

That wasn't a fight. That wasn't anything I knew. It made me nervous. I walked over to her, reached out to her. The Lady's song rang out in a faint note.

"Darrishana..."

My hand hit something before I could find hers. The air shimmered in front of her, the light bending and becoming solid, like a pane of glass. I growled, curling my hand into a fist and smashing it against the barrier that had blossomed out of nowhere. I saw her staring at me, her eyes glowing faintly purple.

Fucking Wardmages.

"Darrishana!" I shouted.

"Don't," she whispered back to me.

"Don't be fucking stupid."

"I am not," she replied, cold as I had been. Did it cut so deep as it felt now, I wondered, when I had sounded like that? "You can't have that name. I gave it to Salazanca. Not to Red Cloud."

"I *am* Red Cloud."

"You are." She turned, started walking away, until she was just one more ash on the wind. "And I wish we were both different people."

Nothing ever happens like it does in opera. Stories don't end when the curtain falls and the audience leaves. Steel is answered with steel, blood with blood, a fire set keeps burning until it has nothing left to burn. And no matter what opera says, you can't really leave what you've done behind you.

But you can try your hardest.

Meticulous's house was far behind me, a distant pillar of smoke that faded into the night sky like the last glutted crows flapping lazily away from a stripped carcass. So, too, were the guards who had come to investigate—none of them motivated or stupid enough to come looking for me after I'd left. The numbness setting in from the cold and the Vechine wasn't comfort, but it was closer than I'd had in a while. Left alone with the dark and the falling snow as I made my way through the streets, I had a moment to breathe, to think.

"NO!"

So, naturally, some shithead decided to ruin it.

I followed the sound of a shriek of what I assumed to be a small child and instead found a full-grown man. On his knees in the middle of a small square, Urda was elbow-deep in his satchel, his eyes glistening with terror as he eviscerated the bag, scattering quills and papers out into the snow.

"No, no, no, no, NO, NO, NO!" he whimpered into the bag, as though some sympathetic creature inside would be moved to pity and give him what he was looking for. When that didn't happen, he clenched his fists and pounded futilely at his own skull. "It isn't... it's not... it isn't—"

"For fuck's sake, I said I'm *sorry!*" His sister stood nearby, alternately screaming at him and Jero. "It all looked like the same chicken-scratch shit to me!"

"It was the schematics of an *airship*." Jero thrust a finger in her face. "How the *fuck* do you not know what those look like?"

"They were *coded*, Sir Shitstain." Yria slapped his finger out of her face. "Don't go wiping my ass with sandpaper because you forgot to mention that little part."

"What about him?" Jero turned a sneer toward Urda, who was moaning into his own hands. "He was the codebreaker. That's why we brought him on."

"He was busy," Yria grunted.

"Busy?" Jero scoffed, stalking toward Urda. "So busy that he ruined the entire—"

His words, and his stride, were cut short as Yria imposed herself between her brother and Jero. She'd never had the most pleasant of demeanors to begin with—the only time I ever saw her laugh was when someone was farting, bleeding, or both—but the snarl on her face was so twisted with anger she could have carved it out of her face with her own knife.

"Don't. *Ever.* Touch him," she uttered. "You told him to break their code and he did. You told him to forge that dead fuck's writing and he did. You wanted him to make sure he got the right scrap of paper, you should have told him."

Jero's face went blank, his body stiff beneath his coat. I'm not sure Yria noticed it—hell, I barely did. When you meet a killer in the Scar, you expect some screaming maniac with a big weapon and a bigger ego, and most of the time, that's what you get. But those aren't true killers; those are thugs who view violence as a means to get what they want: money, food, fear.

A true killer moves slowly, deliberately. A man who's cut more throats than he's kissed doesn't waste time on threats or boasts. He goes soft and still as night, moves so slowly you don't even notice the knife he's reaching for until it's in your belly. His kills are special; they've earned the right to be—he doesn't waste them.

So I wondered, as I watched Jero's hand flit unconsciously toward the back of his belt where he kept his blade, what it was that Yria could have done to make him want to draw it.

"You had your job," he whispered. "My job was to find Meticulous and kill him. And I did."

"No."

His hand fell. His body loosened. The anger he kept hidden behind his face buried itself deeper as I approached.

"I did," I said. "Which means I'm owed an explanation for what's

going on." I glanced from their confrontation to Urda, quietly sobbing. "Because it looks like someone fucked up."

"Someone did." Jero pointedly looked away from Yria, rubbed his
eyes, and sighed. "We weren't after Meticulous just for his correspondence. He had information on the Iron Fleet. Specifically, the
mechanical layout of the airships."

I furrowed my brow. "How do you know he did?"

There. A flash of worry across his face. The briefest dart of eyes
as he searched for an answer before staring at me too intently. Meet
enough liars, you start seeing their little flinches and twitches. Even
the good ones have them.

"He's the sole point of authority for the Revolution out here," he
said. "Who else would have them?"

And Jero was very good.

"I thought I grabbed 'em," Yria muttered as she gestured to the
papers scattered on the ground. "But they're no good. Meticulous
coded some fake ones, left 'em out for me to find, paranoid bastard."

"A paranoid spy. Imagine that." Jero ignored the curse she flung
at his back. "Regardless, those schematics are essential for our plan.
Urda can't work without them."

"What do you mean?"

"*Can't change it, can't change it, can't change it...*" Urda's whim-
pering came accompanied by his knees pulled up to his chest, tears
streaming from his eyes. "If I can't change it, I can't fix it, and if I
can't fix it, I can't stop it, and if I can't stop it, I can't—"

"Hey."

Urda's frantic muttering fell silent. His eyes fell to the ground.
And his sister fell to her knees beside him.

"Look at me," she urged, taking him by the shoulders. "Look."

She wasn't a gentle woman. Nor even a kind one. She was firm
and coarse as old leather. That's what she gave her brother when he
looked up at her—something firm, something earnest, something
that wouldn't let him look away.

"We fucked up," she said. "But we've fucked up before and we've
fixed it before. We'll fuck up again and we'll fix it again. And we'll
fix this, too, all right?"

Urda licked his lips, wiped the tears from his eyes, nodded feebly, and began to draw in deep breaths. It was a touching scene—or as close to one as I was likely to see in this city—and while I hated to ruin the mood, I couldn't help but lean over to Jero and whisper.

"They're not going to fix it, are they?"

"Fuck no," he replied. "Not unless they can stop an airship by cussing and crying."

I squinted. "The schematics showed you how to stop an airship?"

"Not exactly." Jero sighed, scratched his throat. "Sneaking past an airship's guns is easy enough to do when you're *not* carrying around a gigantic Relic of unimaginable power. But once we've got that thing, we'll be easy prey for any one of those ships."

"Unless something keeps them occupied," I hummed.

"Precisely."

"I take it from the considerable pain in my spectacular ass this plan is giving me that just destroying them isn't an option."

"There aren't enough mages in the Scar, let alone the world, to bring down the whole Fleet. And we won't have the time or the tools to fuck with their engines." Jero gestured to Urda, who was slowly getting to his feet with Yria's help. "Our hopes rest on *this* little shit."

I stared at Urda as he stumbled on a stray piece of ice and fell flat on his face. I sniffed.

"So, we're fucked, then?"

"Essentially," Jero sighed. "A Spellwright can convince a sword it can burst into flames or a cloak that it's as strong as steel..."

The realization struck me square across the face. "Or an airship that it can't pursue."

Jero nodded. "With just a few sigils, Urda could stall their engines or silence their guns. Long enough for us to escape with the Relic, anyway. But he can't convince an object it's something else if he doesn't know what it *is* first."

Despite what my *numerous* injuries would have you believe, I don't consider myself to be particularly stupid. But it's true that I prefer simple things: strong whiskey, straightforward lovers, and problems you can solve with a sword or, if it's particularly complex, an explosion.

And shit like this was why.

Spellwrighting was an art in the same way math was: technically true but mostly birdshit. The act of wrighting relied on an intimate understanding of the object to be inscribed upon and the more complex the object, the more potential there was to go wrong—hence why a wright couldn't, say, turn a kitten into a fire-breathing monstrosity.

Not after the last time, anyway.

And while an airship wasn't as complex as the biology of a living thing, it *was* something big enough and complicated enough that any attempt to alter it would require a thorough understanding of its internal processes. On his own, Urda simply couldn't cut it.

But she could.

I didn't like the way I smiled at the thought of her. My smile was supposed to be confident, effortless, a Vagrant's smile. The grin that pulled its way onto my face without me realizing, though, was as dumb as a smitten kid's. She had a way of doing that to me. Of making me think things without realizing it. Just like I thought of her then.

Her eyes, brown and serious and so very big behind her glasses. Her hair, always so neatly tidied except for the few strands of black she could never force into obedience. Her face, always so stern and serious until I'd say the right thing, make the right joke, notice the right thing about her before she gave me a smile just as big and stupid as the one I wore.

I wonder what Liette would say if she were here now.

"Obviously," I could hear her voice even now, *"an airship is far too large and unwieldy to allow room for error that might be invited by stylistic decision. And given that the Revolution both possesses the only ones in existence as well as being a pack of short-sighted, propaganda-choked miscreants, we can assume that their limited capacity for creativity would likewise prohibit them from creating anything overly complex. Hence, we need merely deduce the most obvious means of constructing an airship, assume they followed that, then extrapolate what we need from that."*

Then she'd look at me, and I'd have this big, stupid grin I was wearing just from thinking about her face, and adjust her glasses and ask me why I was smiling. And she'd smile back. And I'd feel the scars aching on my body and the weight of the names on my list...

And I'd wonder how long it would be before she looked at me and saw only a monster again.

"I've got to handle these two." Jero lay a gentle hand on my shoulder. "Tuteng's ahead in that tower." He pointed toward a dark house a block away, a tower rising into the night sky. "Grab him and tell him we're ready."

I shot him a flat look. "I just nearly bled out. Why do I have to do it?"

"Would you rather stay here and deal with the twins?"

My lips pursed. My eyes narrowed.

"Has anyone ever told you, Jero," I said, "that you ask to get punched in the mouth a lot?"

"All the time." He shot me a wink as he turned around. "I promise you, by the time this is all over, I'll ask you to do worse."

THIRTEEN

TERASSUS

Now, don't let my frustration fool you, I've been a part of heist plots before.

Some of them even ended without everyone dead.

For example, in Sevric's Last Boast, myself and a few gentlepeople of peculiar talents and persuadable moralities were convinced to ambush a train. Now, never mind how it turned out or who started stabbing who—that part's not important and you can't prove it was me. What *is* important is that I'm well aware that a plot takes a lot of people with a lot of talents: some of them more hands-on, some of them more hands-off.

So, don't get me wrong, I *knew* that Tuteng was probably doing something very important at that moment.

I just wasn't sure if it was important enough to prevent me from hitting Jero for making me haul my busted ass up these stairs to find him.

Or maybe I was just in a bad mood.

Schematics. All of this had come down to drawings on a shitty piece of paper. All our plans to make a better world, all my ambitions to find the names on my list, all of it gone because Urda couldn't tell which shitty paper was the *right* shitty paper, Agne couldn't *not* kill the only guy who could have helped us, and Jero couldn't be bothered to tell me the plan so I could have stopped this.

It had all been for nothing. Everything. Every corpse, every scar, every drop of blood. All that I'd done and all that I'd killed and everyone I'd lost, all of it had led to this dead end. And all I was left with were shadows crowding around me and the ghosts waiting behind me.

Maybe that's what made me mad—no, not mad, hopeless; the cold cramp in my chest that came when people were more disappointing than I was—when I ascended the stairs of the tower and found Tuteng at its highest floor.

Or maybe it was because while I was getting shit done, he was busy stroking the feathers of his pet bird.

"It's not that far," he whispered to the Shekkai on his hands. "I promise. I would never ask you to..."

He glanced up, suddenly aware of me. In the shadows of the attic, the bony stumps where his horns should be looked like another set of eyes, wide and surprised. A contrast to his true eyes, which regarded me with annoyed indifference.

"We're going," I said to him. "The guards are closing in."

Tuteng's ears twitched. He hummed thoughtfully. "We've got some time."

"No, we do not have fucking time," I sighed. "This place is crawling with—"

"With humans," he said. "And they're crawling around everywhere. If Jero wants his plan to go off, he can wait. Now, if you don't mind..."

He continued to glare at me, waiting for me to be silent. Normally, I wouldn't have indulged that, but his bird was also staring at me and...well, if you'd seen the *way* it looked, you'd have given them space, too.

He muttered a few more words to the bird before it let out a soft chirp. He smiled, nodded at it, then rose to the window. With a quick flick, he sent the bird flying. It took off into the night sky, but Tuteng continued to wait, watching it.

Like he wanted to make sure it got out safely.

"Where's it heading?" I asked.

"Weiless," he replied. "Where Jero wants her to go. Where I asked her to go."

"Asked?" The realization hit me, made my eyes go wide. "You've got a Beast-Tongue."

"Humans call it that." He chanced a glance at me. "You know many Rukkokri?"

"Enough to know that the only ones who work with humans don't go back to their clans." I gestured with my chin toward his brow. "How'd you lose your horns?"

He smiled—or frowned, it was hard to tell with him, really. But the expression on his face was bitter, all the same.

"Money. Same as anyone."

"You sold them?"

"I might as well have," he sighed, looking back out the window. "Humans love killing each other. But they love one-sided fights the best. Makes them think their wars are good when they don't take a scratch. So when one group of them wanted to ambush the other, I showed them the way through the wilds to do it. For metal."

I winced. "Imperium?"

"And Revolution. Even Haven a few times. Made no difference to me." He ran a finger fondly across the stump of his horn. "Or to my mother when she lopped these off and cast me out. Neither of us could tell you whether it was Imperials or Revolutionaries who destroyed our home, choked our land, killed my nephew. All she saw were humans. And me helping them."

"Sounds rough."

"Being cast out of the only home you've known, shunned by your people, and forced to work with the same things that lost you your horns in the first place?" He sniffed. "Yeah. A little."

I paused, uncertain as to whether I wanted the answer. "What is Two Lonely Old Men paying you to work on this?"

"A lot."

I shrugged. "A man could do a lot with a lot."

"He could. My mother will do more with it, though, when I send it to her."

"What? Why the fuck would you ever do that?"

"Because she's my mother. They're my people. And you aren't." He continued staring out the window at the empty space where the Shekkai had been. He sighed wearily, turned around, and stalked toward the stairs. "I don't have anyone else here. And I won't when the crows take me."

He hesitated at the top of the stairs, turned toward me with those dark eyes. Eyes that had seen a suffering I'd never known, a unique pain that sang a different song than my own scars.

"What are you going to have when the crows take you?"

I wasn't sure how to answer that. When I signed on to this, I had so many: a better world liberated from war, the names of the people who gave me these scars, an end to the ghosts and the shadows and the nightmares...

But now...

Now, my mouth just hung open, trying to find a response.

"Just kidding." Tuteng smiled, clapped me on the back, headed down the stairs. "I actually don't care."

And there he left me. Without an answer. Without a reason to keep going at this. Without anything but two words that weighed on my mind.

The crows.

And the idea that came from them.

⊷ ⊷⊱≣≣⊰ ⊷

"The beggar."

Do this sort of thing long enough, bad ideas just become reflex. The words tumbled out of my mouth, an image flashed into my head—a man destitute in rags, huddled outside the Caned Toad in an alley, a large bird perched atop his head.

A crow.

"What?" Jero asked.

"The beggar," I repeated. "The one hanging around near the Caned Toad. With the crow. Remember?" I looked up as we made our way through the alleys. "He was in an alley just like this one."

"Yeah, he's there all the time. So what?" He chuckled. "What, did you think he'd make a better fit for us than Urda?" He squinted at the twins, hurrying ahead as they struggled to hold on to their papers. "Actually..."

"Listen." I took Jero by the shoulders, forced his eyes upon mine. "These schematics, they're secret, right?"

"Top secret."

"Which means people would pay a lot of money for them, right?"

"Right, but…"

I saw the realization in his eyes as they snapped wide open. He remembered the beggar, the fat crow. He knew what they meant, as surely as I did. And he knew what I was about to suggest.

"No." His voice went soft and urgent, his eyes draped in shadow as he leaned close. Seeing me about to protest, he raised a hand. "Yes, you're right. That beggar is exactly who you think he is. And no, we can't seek him out."

"We don't have any choice," I replied. "Without those schematics, we have no chance of escaping with the Relic. That's what you said."

"I did, but—"

"There's no one else but *them* who would have those schematics, right?"

"There's no guarantee of that—"

"And if we don't try, then all of this is for shit, isn't it?" I snapped. "That whole monologue about a better world was just second-rate opera, wasn't it? Without that Relic, we go right back to the way things were, right back to the killing, to the fighting, to the…the…"

To the looks she gave me. The thoughts wormed their way into my skull, impossible to keep out. *Right before I left to go back to killing.*

"To the revenge?" Jero asked.

I let out a cold breath. "That, too." I canted my head at him. "So, what, is Two Lonely Old Men afraid of them or something?"

Jero's face went empty. "Our patron prefers his name not to be spoken aloud in public," he said. "He was aware of the presence of malodorous malefactors in this city before he even arrived. His position—and I agree—is that this operation is complicated enough without bringing in a pack of murderous, greedy thieves that—"

"That aren't us?"

"That aren't loyal to anyone but other murderous, greedy thieves." He shook his head. "There's got to be another way."

"There was."

I felt a twitch at the base of my neck. The same twitch I get whenever someone's going to stab me there. I took a long step toward him, let my voice slide as harsh and low as a kick between the legs.

"You could have told me the plan."

Whatever we may tell ourselves to feel like we're more than a walking pile of envy and regrets, you'll learn almost everything you need to know about someone in the first five minutes of talking with them—namely, whether they want to kill you, how badly, and how soon.

Jero, I knew, would be different than that. A man who wore his wrinkles like scars and smiled as easily as he did was bound to have a lot of secrets. But when I spoke to him like that, when I saw that easy smile twitch at the edges, when he offered me nothing but an empty stare, I realized how he'd managed to keep so many.

He didn't trust me.

I suppose that shouldn't be surprising—you don't typically get put in charge of secret heists with the aim of toppling empires if you trust anyone. What was surprising, though, was the twinge of pain I felt upon realizing it. I hated myself for feeling it—I'd been doing this far too long to think he would have trusted me just like that.

And far, *far* too long to feel hurt by the fact that he didn't.

But... I don't know, maybe it just felt good to be around people who didn't look at me like I was a monster. For a little while, anyway.

"You're right."

I blinked, astonished. I hadn't expected *that*, either.

"About all of it." Jero sighed. "I should have told you the plan. And we don't have any other options." He glanced to Urda, frowned. "For any of this to mean anything, Urda needs those schematics. Or as close as we can get."

He looked at me again. No easy smile. No heavy wrinkles. And certainly no trust.

But it was closer, at least. And it made that pain go away.

For a little while, anyway.

"You really think we can find what we need?" he asked. "The Crow Market doesn't tolerate window-shopping."

Like I said, do this sort of thing long enough and bad ideas just become a reflex. I would have thought Jero was the type to know that. Still, as I pulled my scarf closer around me and set off, I don't think I could fault him for his caution.

After all, it was never a good sign when you went asking assassins for help.

Much less the Ashmouths.

FOURTEEN

THE CANED TOAD

Okay, so I know Jero said that the best way to avoid attention is to look like someone the rest of society doesn't want to pay attention to, as Meticulous did. And, okay, yes, I admit, that idea sounds very good, very practical, and, as Jero pointed out, very effective.

But since we had just fucked up Meticulous, it can't have been *that* effective, now, can it?

See, the Revolution may value its spies and saboteurs, but it still values its cannons and explosions more. And while Meticulous may have been an excellent spy—up until he was killed, and I hate to sound like I'm bragging, but I had a big part in it—he was still a spy in service to a nation that didn't quite grasp the use of the subtler arts beyond how it allowed them to make even bigger explosions.

For *our* purposes, we needed people who didn't simply dabble in the subtler arts as a means to an end. To find that which couldn't be found for purposes of pulling off the impossible, we needed more than what we could scavenge out of the carcass of an average spy. Meticulous had merely been a hobbyist in subterfuge. Hobbyists have larks. We needed a professional.

And professionals had standards.

Which was why, in the pale hours before dawn crept across the roofs of Terassus, a profoundly disheveled and greasy man awoke from the cry of an overfed crow to see a quartet of strangers in various states of distress and blood loss. A woman with white hair and a red scarf was at the head of the group, standing over him in a dank alley.

The beggar turned bleary eyes across us, apparently not impressed by our motley, let alone intimidated, and scratched himself.

"Oh, wow," he grunted. "I kind of hate to do this, since you guys look like shit, but"—he held up his bowl—"alms?"

"I'm afraid we're here on another matter." Jero stepped forward, clearing his throat. "We're here to make you a little offer of—"

He cut himself short when I held up my hand. Which was good, since that meant I wouldn't have to slap him. I knew he could get us where we needed to go after a doubtlessly charming little routine, but I'd been stabbed *multiple* times that night and I was in a bit of a hurry.

I fished into my satchel, pulled out a piece of metal, dropped it into the beggar's bowl with a heavy *clink.*

"You honor me, madam," he grunted, bowing his head. "My gratitude is—"

Clink. Clink. CLUNK.

Three more pieces of metal, each one thicker and shinier than the last, fell into his bowl. He pursed his lips, staring at the metal for a long moment, before looking back up at me through eyes considerably sharper than a beggar ought to have.

"I'm looking for friends," I said softly.

He glanced me over. "You a friend of mine?"

I reached into Jero's pocket, pulling a small pouch free before he could protest. I dropped it into his bowl, knocking it out of his hands and scattering its contents to the ground.

"We all are," I replied.

The beggar hastily scooped up the metal, sliding it into his rags— which I could now see concealed a very large, very sharp blade—but kept the shiniest one between his fingers. He glanced it over before looking up to the fat crow, perched on a rooftop's eaves overhead.

With one deft flick, he tossed the trinket into the air. And with equal deftness, the crow snatched it up in its beak. It ruffled its feathers, let out a pleasant chirp, and took off. The beggar, satisfied, crawled to his feet and started walking away. Urda glanced between us before starting to follow.

"Not him." I grabbed him by his shoulder, turned him around. "We follow the bird."

"Oh, thank *heaven*," Urda gasped. "I'm sure he's a very nice man, but that fellow looked as though he hadn't bathed in—Wait, we follow the *bird*? Why not the man?"

I furrowed my brow at him as I turned to stalk down the alley. "What sense would that make?"

"But what if it...*defecates* on us?"

"Ah, don't worry about it." Yria grabbed her brother by the lapel of his coat and dragged him down the alley after me, Jero hurrying to catch up. "Not even a bird would give a shit about you."

They descended into muted squabbling, which I didn't listen to. My eyes were on the crow, following the glint of its prize as its lazy half-flight, half-hop path led us down twisting alleys and through the bombed-out memories of the war that had ravaged this city.

To anyone else, it would have looked like just another bird giddily making off with its prize. Which was precisely the point. No one could have guessed that the path it took was deliberately planned by the hands that had fed it so much. Just like no one could have guessed that taking one step away from the path would end with our bodies bleeding out on the ground from a thousand quarrels.

I spared a glance into the shadowy windows of the ruined buildings that loomed over us. I couldn't see them. But I could feel them— the glassy stares hidden behind leather masks, the tips of crossbow bolts following our every move, the fingers trained on their triggers, ready to fire should we give any indication we weren't trustworthy.

Like I said, professionals had standards. And no one's standards were more exacting than professional killers'.

One misstep. One flinch. One wrong look in the wrong direction at the wrong moment, and we'd be dead. Which you would think would keep people from saying things that were painfully, blatantly, and stupidly obvious.

"I still think this is a bad idea."

And yet.

"If the Ashmouths get even a *whiff* of our plan, they'll start looking for a piece of it." Jero was no fool—he didn't look up as he spoke and he whispered just low enough that only I could hear him. But he was an asshole, which was why he was talking at all. "We can't afford that kind of complication."

"You should have thought of that before you burned a house down," I muttered in reply.

"You've burned down hundreds of houses, I've heard."

"And you don't hear me complaining about it, do you?" I pulled my scarf a little higher over my lips. "Yes, this is a bad idea. We've got nothing but bad ideas left. If Urda needs this shit, the Ashmouths are the only ones who will have it."

He cringed in that way people do when they know terrible people have made excellent points. Made me wish I could afford to smile at it. But smiles raise suspicions. And suspicions make trigger fingers itch.

"I'd feel better about it if we had brought Tuteng and Agne," Jero whispered.

"Yeah, yeah, everyone finds the presence of giant women with magical muscles very reassuring," I muttered. "Everyone *except* the Ashmouths. My bad idea, we do it my bad way." I shot him a side-long glare. "If you don't like it, don't fucking lie to me in the future."

Don't get me wrong—it's not that I'm sentimental. Or at least, not about this. Plenty of people have lied to me before—some are dead because of it, some aren't. It's a way of life, and of staying alive, in the Scar.

Jero's omission—which is what you call lying when you're too rich, smart, or good-looking to be a liar—didn't hurt me, it hurt the job. The job that was going to end in a better world and a lot of people I was going to bury in it. If his fuck-up had ended all of that, ended the list, ended that better world, ended any chance I had of pretending this could all be normal one day…

Well. Maybe I was a little hurt.

That would explain why it felt so satisfying to see him shut his face, anyway.

A squawk drew my attention overhead. The chubby corvid hopped happily across the eaves of a shabby building before set-tling into a nest over a splintering door. It let out a pleased caw as it wriggled its girth into a pile of branches, where it busied itself with fastidiously decorating its nest with its filthy lucre.

The building wore the crow's nest atop its eaves like a shabby hat completing a shabbier outfit. Splintering, crumbling, and sitting in the middle of a run-down neighborhood still wearing the scars of the war, it was noteworthy solely for the fact that its windows sported ugly, patchwork curtains instead of being boarded up and its stoop had been swept clean of snow while the other ruins had been left to collapse beneath white dust.

It was a sad, decrepit house in the middle of a sad, decrepit neighborhood, unremarkable but for the effort it would take to cringe and avert your gaze as you passed.

Which, as you might have guessed, made it a lovely little spot to set up an illegal market.

Or to kill us and harvest our organs for alchemic components. But if you get hung up on who's out to steal your kidneys, you'll never get anything done.

So, not for the first time, I pushed a door open, stepped into a dark room, and hoped for the best.

The pungent smell of herbs and weeds assailed my senses. And if my eyes hadn't adjusted, I might have sworn I was surrounded by all manner of illicit drugs. Once I saw the various jars lining a humble countertop, though, I realized I was just in a shitty teahouse. The tables stood empty but for one or two elders, staring glassily into nothing as cups of steaming, aromatic tea sat in front of them, the blare of a broken voccaphone playing in the background.

"Four cups?" a wrinkled voice rasped. A tiny woman wrapped in a plain coat and robe appeared before us, a kettle in one hand, a tray in the other. "The house special?"

My gaze drifted from her to the counter at the back of the room, to a small door tucked away in the corner. I sniffed.

"Got anything rarer?" I asked. "Something from Weiless, maybe?"

The voccaphone skipped a note. Slowly, the bleary eyes of every elder drew down upon me. So slowly, you'd barely notice them moving. And you *certainly* wouldn't notice them quietly loading hand crossbows under their tables.

The old woman held my gaze, just as I held my hands at my sides, clear of my weapons. After a moment, she sucked in a breath through her teeth and gestured with her chin toward the small door in the corner.

"In the back," she grunted. "Get it yourself."

"*Well*," Urda gasped from behind. "I must say, this service is *far* below the standard I would expect. Call me a dandy, but I don't think it's too much to ask for a little pride to be taken in one's—"

He was, gratefully, cut off by a swift elbow to the ribs before he could be cut off by a quarrel to the throat. I inclined my head in gratitude toward the old woman before heading off toward the door.

"Ah, ah, ah." The old woman's rasp caught me. "Four's too many. Not enough room back there." She squinted, her bleary eyes eventually settling on Yria. "She stays. The rest of you go."

My jaw clenched, my fingers twitched, instinctively eager for a weapon to hold. This was a precaution, of course—by dividing us up and keeping a hostage, they were assuring that we wouldn't cause trouble. Which, given that I was bloodied from head to toe and carrying a giant gun, fair enough. If we wanted in, we had no choice but to accept their terms, which I hoped everyone understood.

"*No!*"

But fuck me for being optimistic, right?

"No, no, no, no," Urda gasped, shaking his head. "W-we can't leave Yria. We're a team. You can't do this. You can't make me. You . . . you can't . . . I can't . . . *I can't!*"

He clutched his head so tight I thought he was trying to keep his brains from leaking out his skull. A sharp whine escaped his lips. My heart raced. I glanced between the two elders, watched their crossbows rise above the tables. I didn't know what the fuck Urda was doing and neither did they. Which was, apparently, all the reason they needed to kill us.

The Cacophony burned, beckoning my hand to his hilt. I wrapped my fingers around the wood. I let out a slow, steady breath and—

"Hey."

Every hand paused. Every hand but Yria's. She took her brother by the shoulders, forced him to look into her eyes.

"It's going to be all right," she said. "I'm going to be here. You're going to be there. You need me, just"—she leaned in close—"whistle, all right?"

Urda's lip trembled like he wanted to protest. But he eventually settled on closing his eyes, nodding weakly, and heading to the door with Jero. The hand crossbows disappeared back beneath the tables and I moved to follow them.

"Hey."

Yria's hand caught my arm. I turned and saw no snarling, cursing, rude Vagrant's face. Yria the Cell, Thief of the Rich and Ghost of Goodhome, looked at me with an expression that struggled to convey the worry in her eyes.

"Urda," she whispered, "he doesn't do good in tight places. I can't lose…" She licked her lips. "Just watch him, okay? Look out for him." She swallowed something hard. "He needs me, okay?"

"Okay."

I moved to walk away, she tightened her grip. "*Promise* me."

I held her gaze for a moment, plucked her fingers off my arms. "I promise."

She nodded, let out a long, nervous breath. "Right. Good. No stories that say the Cacophony breaks her promises." She found a chair, settled into it. "I'll be around."

I returned the nod before hurrying off to join Jero and Urda, my stride uneasier than I would have liked. It was always uncomfortable, seeing that kind of emotion coming from that kind of person. It turned them from monsters to people in a world where monsters survived and people didn't. What I needed right now was a monster, a remorseless Vagrant, not a worried sister. A Vagrant I could let down and not be bothered. A sister, staying up all night and staring at the empty spot where her brother should be…

Enough. I shook those thoughts out of my head. *Don't fucking look like this in front of the Ashmouths. Don't worry about her. Besides…* A cold cringe crept across my face. *If Urda's not getting out of this alive, you sure as shit aren't either.*

⸺ ⋇ ⸺

It's not always true, but—in my experience, at least—if you find yourself in a lightless basement, far away from anyone who might hear you, staring down a door behind which near-certain doom lies, you might be making some poor choices in your life.

"This is it?"

Also, you probably need to stop hanging around with assholes.

"What were you expecting?" I asked.

"I'm not sure. Something more mysterious?" Urda squinted over the door—a thick, ironbound barrier that had no business being in the basement of a teahouse. "I've heard stories about the Ashmouths and their...markets." He cringed so hard I could see the outline of his skull. "Filthy, terrible rumors of bodies being harvested for ingredients and elixirs that grant you six seconds of total knowledge before they make your humors burst out of your orifices and—You know what, why don't we just figure something else out?"

"Yeah, thieves always sound better in stories," I sighed. "Then you meet a few of them and you find out they're just assholes with money working for bigger assholes with money."

"So, the stories aren't true?" Urda offered a hopeful smile. "About the harvesting and...orifices?"

"No, those are completely true." Jero pushed him aside as he stepped up to the door. "The Ashmouths would tear out our livers if they thought they could make a copper knuckle off of them." He glanced over to me and Urda. "And if they didn't have stolen Revolutionary technology, we wouldn't be here. We go in, find what we need, get out. Agreed?"

A stiff nod from me. A fervent nod from Urda. Jero cleared his throat, turned back to the door, and raised his fist. Two swift knocks, a pause, then three slow ones, a longer pause, and six more quick ones. Then, with a satisfied smile, he stepped back and waited.

For a very long, awkward moment.

"The fuck was that?" I asked.

"Secret knock," he replied. "Just wait."

I opened my mouth to point out the stupidity of having a secret knock when we were already in a secret room in a secret teahouse that we were led to by a secret fucking crow, but at that moment, a wooden panel in the door slid open. A pair of weary eyes, rimmed with red, peered out and a voice that sounded like a six-day drunk with a mouthful of gravel rasped out.

"The fuck was that?"

Jero stepped forward, clearing his throat. "Friends. In search of something specific."

"Friends?" The red eyes squinted. "Huh. That's odd. All I see here is a bunch of stupid twats. But hey, if you see the dumbshit that was just knocking on the door, could you kindly tell him, her, or them that we don't do that shit anymore? Great. Thanks. Fuck along now."

"Wait, I—"

Jero's protest was cut short as the panel slid shut. His jaw clenched angrily for a moment before he closed his eyes, let out a breath, and rubbed his temples. Fury gave way to contemplation, the wheels of his mind creaking audibly as he began to formulate another plan to get in.

And I'm sure he would have come up with something great. But it had been a long night and I was very tired.

So I went with my plan.

I pushed him aside, walked up to the door, slammed my fist against it three times. The panel slid open, the same pair of red-rimmed eyes staring out.

"Okay, that knock was fine," the voice rasped from behind the door, "but I believe I told you to . . . to . . ."

The voice fell silent as the eyes fell upon me. I reached up, pulled my scarf back, and, with blood spattering my face and the long scar running over my eye, stared back. I'm not going to lie, the way those eyes widened as he realized who had come knocking?

"Ah, fuck . . . it's you."

Not better than sex. But close.

"You know me?" I asked.

Silence. Then the eyes bobbed up and down in a nod.

"You know I need in?"

A longer silence. A slower nod.

"You know how I'm going to get in?"

A lick of dry lips. "How?"

I shrugged. "I thought I'd let you decide. You can let us in." I slid my scarf back, rested a hand atop the Cacophony's black hilt, and drummed my fingers thoughtfully. "Or I can knock again."

A third silence—deeper, longer, and taut enough to strangle someone with—fell over the room. The red-rimmed eyes stared at me, twitching in appraisal, trying to figure out how many ways this could end and, of those, how many ended with someone painting the walls.

The panel snapped shut again. I sighed.

"I tried."

The Cacophony had barely left his sheath before there was the sound of something heavy and metallic clicking open. Then a pause. And then, the acrid stink of chemicals, dust, and money as the heavy door creaked open and a weary man stepped out.

Short, lean, and draped in loose, baggy clothing stained with food, he wore a shaggy mop of hair tied back in a topknot, his jaw coated in stubble and a long pipe dangling from his lips. One hand rested on a wooden sword thrust through his sash, his sleeve falling back to reveal a tattoo of a thick tree running the length of his forearm.

He was dirty. He was tired. He *reeked* of cheap silkgrass. And if you didn't know how many people Rudu the Cudgel had killed, you'd swear he was just another beggar.

Fuck, I knew and I still wasn't convinced he wasn't. But it didn't matter how filthy he looked or how much of a pain it had been to get down here—I couldn't help but smile.

"Well," he said as he stepped aside and gestured to the door, "welcome to the Crow Market, I guess."

Call me materialistic if you will, but shopping always put me in a good mood.

FIFTEEN

THE CROW MARKET

The first lie we're ever told is that we're better than beasts.

Imperium or Revolutionary, it doesn't matter—every society has a wealth of poems, propaganda, opera, and war songs extolling the grand causes of humanity. Our causes are nobler than the base instincts of the creatures that prowl these lands, we tell ourselves. We don't fight for food, territory, and sex. We fight for ideal, principle, and romance—which is like sex but with more talking.

Call me a cynic, but I long ago disabused myself of that notion. Countless battles, plenty of struggles, and a few choice scars had given me the clarity to appreciate that, when you get down to it, there's not a whole lot of room between humans and beasts. Sure, we're better at killing and we figured out how to make food better and relationships worse, but if you look close enough, you'll see we're governed by the same natures as they are.

Instead of predators, we have armies and warlords and Vagrants. Instead of prey, we have peasants and merchants and any number of unlucky fucks who run afoul of the former armies, warlords, and Vagrants. And instead of scavengers...

"WHO WILL BUY THIS MONSTER COCK?"

We have Crow Markets.

"Trouble in bed? Dissatisfied mistress? No respect from your offspring?" the woman in a stained apron waving a cleaver in one hand and an *unnervingly* large and greasy phallus in the other bellowed.

Her voice echoed through the dank aqueduct corridors, over the sound of rattling pipes and a hundred other voices. "This beast's organ, when properly cured, has the power to make your grandpa fuck for two nights straight! Put vigor in your step, spice up your bedroom, or sell it to someone else. I don't fucking care, just buy it, this thing smells terrible!"

If you were surprised at her sales pitch, you would probably have also been surprised at the small horde of well-dressed men who waved satchels clinking with money at her as they clamored for the monstrous member. And you *definitely* would have been surprised at the carcass of a monstrous feline Cacuarl, bristling with quills, being hacked from eyeballs to regular balls by three other industrious ladies behind her, who carefully placed each organ in a jar.

You'd have been alone, though.

No one has time for modesty in a Crow Market.

You won't find them in civilized places, the gentle and well-mannered cities with guards and primitive notions of the rule of law. But on the fringes of the world, where the air is thick with suffering and wars are met with the same weary indifference as bad weather, Crow Markets are as common as corpses.

They pop up after great battles, in the wake of devastating plagues and other places of misery—quiet people in quiet costumes show up on battlefields and in ravaged towns and efficiently pick them clean. Nothing is left behind, from the greatest fallen weapons and technology to the rings prized right off the fingers of the dead. The Ashmouths take everything and find a dark place to sell it.

Word spreads like rot to everyone but the law. And like flies to a carcass, the buyers come. Some are benign: collectors of exotic wares and hard-to-find antiques, Freemakers looking for wartime technology they haven't been able to steal. Some are less benign: warlords looking for weapons to give their boys an edge in the coming raids, Vagrants eager to find new toys to wreak havoc with. The Ashmouths don't mind. The Ashmouths don't ask questions.

So long as you have loose purse strings and tight lips, you're welcome in the Crow Market, no matter whether you're a collector, a criminal, or, say, an extremely good-looking and charming Vagrant embroiled in a plot to destroy two empires.

"Remind me what you're looking for again?"

Rudu the Cudgel did not seem particularly bothered by the grisly scene behind us. Nor did he seem particularly bothered by the pair of alchemists in a nearby alcove huddled over a cauldron from which a pale smoke billowed and carried the distant sound of screaming; or the goggles-wearing maniac in another alcove sitting atop a pile of bronze explosives and holding up a sign that read BOMBS. CHEAP. GUARANTEED KILL; or any of the other dozens of morbid, malicious, or malevolent tradesmen lining the aqueduct alcoves, each of them peddling something more horrific than the last, each of them with no less than a dozen buyers clamoring for their deadly wares.

Possibly because, as a Vagrant, he'd seen more than his share of horror already.

Or possibly because he was high as hell.

"Schematics." Jero shouted to be heard over the sound of something exploding behind us as Rudu led us through the labyrinthine aqueducts. "We're looking for schematics. Or Revolutionary technology. Same as we were the last six times you asked us."

To be fair, it was pretty easy to get distracted in a Crow Market. Who knew how long ago the Ashmouths had hijacked Terassus's underground aqueducts that twisted beneath the city, but they'd certainly made good use of the space since then. Not a single inch of the sewers that wasn't underwater or occupied by piping was without a seller hawking the obscene and macabre.

"I got you," Rudu said. Though the fact that he did not look up as he said it, as he was too busy focusing on packing his pipe full of more silkgrass, suggested that he did not, in fact, got us. "Sorry, it's so hard to keep track of stuff here. Especially when I'm three bowls deep into the grass."

"Maybe you could stop smoking so much?" I offered.

"Maybe you could stop being a pain in my ass." He struck a tinder-twig off the wall and lit his pipe, taking a deep drag and exhaling a cloud of pink smoke. "Guess we've got a real paradox here, huh?"

"That's not what 'paradox' means," Jero said.

"No kidding? Well, maybe if I smoke a little more, I'll figure it out. Or I'll stop listening to you. Let's find out."

Needless to say, I liked Rudu.

We'd had our differences in the past, of course, but show me a pair of friends who *hadn't* set each other on fire at least once. Since then, we'd come to terms.

And by "terms," I mean he was more or less legally obligated to do what I said.

As you might have guessed by now, what with all the explosions and killing, we Vagrants aren't a law-abiding bunch. The only real justice we recognize is the Redfavor: a single trinket, stained crimson, given from one Vagrant to another by their own free will. It entitles the bearer to the only thing a Vagrant has to give: a single favor.

A task, a payment, it doesn't matter. A Vagrant can call in their Redfavor for anything, from buying the next round to killing the Empress of Cathama. When the favor is called, it cannot be refused. When it's completed, it cannot be dishonored.

It happens, from time to time, that someone fails these rules. Sometimes someone refuses the favor. Sometimes someone doesn't honor the task. Whatever their reason for doing so, it doesn't matter, the result is the same.

A Vagrant who turns their back on the favor is a Vagrant who's fair game. No one will intervene on their behalf, no one shall offer them any comfort besides a knife in the dark.

We don't give it lightly. We don't spend it lightly. And as tempting as it was to call in Rudu's so he could find us what we needed, I wasn't about to waste it on this. Especially since it was his job to show us around anyway.

"Should, uh..." Urda glanced over his shoulder at the growing inferno raging in the alcove behind us. "Should you be concerned about that? Aren't you, uh, the security here?"

"I'm more like a consultant," Rudu replied through a cloud of smoke. "In that I am *consulted* on how they would like me to kill any Imperial mages that venture down here. Past that, I have strict orders not to interfere with business." He made a vague gesture. "Besides, those guys will take care of it."

It took me a moment to realize he wasn't just pointing to empty space. Lurking in the shadows between the stalls, the Ashmouths stood vigilant. Their bodies were hidden beneath their black uniforms, their faces obscured by the crow-shaped masks they wore. The only thing on display was the small arsenal of bows, blades, and flasks they carried, ready to be deployed on anyone they deemed necessary.

Somehow, this didn't soothe Urda.

If he'd been nervous before, he was falling to pieces with every step now. His eyes kept darting between the sellers, the buyers, and the Ashmouths, uncertain of which to be more terrified of. And every time he did, his hand went down to his pocket, fingering something inside that I only barely got glimpses of.

Something metal... silver. I squinted.

Was that... a whistle?

"Anyway, it shouldn't be too hard to find Revolutionary tech down here," Rudu said, pointedly ignoring the screams rising from behind. "The war left enough of it lying around, anyway. Tanks, cannons, those weird stabby-shooty-things..."

"Gunpikes?"

"Sure, whatever. All of it eventually ends up in the Ashmouths' hands, which means it eventually ends up here. Normally, they don't care who buys it from them."

"Normally?"

"Yeah, normally. And normally, I don't ask questions." Rudu came to a sudden halt, all of us stopping short just behind him. Slowly, he turned and cast a red-rimmed stare over his shoulder. "But then, normally I don't see Sal the Cacophony come sniffing after Revolutionary tech. So, I can't help but wonder if the Ashmouths would want to know if things weren't normal."

I didn't blink, didn't flinch, didn't move—I knew the eyes fixed on me from the shadows, the ears that lingered nearby, listening. I could feel Jero tense up beside me, his hand drifting toward a hidden blade. Without realizing it, my hand slid out to catch his.

Without realizing it, it stayed there.

It felt nice, almost. Holding something that wasn't a sword or a gun.

"I bet if they paid me enough to give a shit, I might ask." Rudu grinned, smoke leaking out between his teeth. "But you don't see me walking around in a rich man's clothes, do you?" He glanced up through the haze. "Oh, hey, here we are."

A nearby alcove, lit by pale alchemic lanterns, loomed before us. And out of the shadows cast by them, the Ashmouths emerged. The glass eyes of their masks swept over us, their crossbows held tightly.

"The Three don't want anyone near here they don't approve of," one of them grunted. "Move along."

"She's with me," Rudu replied. "Don't worry about it."

Their glassy stares lingered on him for a moment before drifting to Urda, like they could smell the fear coming off him.

"He looks familiar," the other one said. "Are those a wright's tools?" They stepped forward. Urda cringed behind me. "Let's have a talk, you and I, and then we can—"

He was stopped by my hands: one held up in front of the Ashmouth, the other resting on the Cacophony's hilt.

"He's with me," I replied. "No one touches him."

"And no one threatens the Ashmouths," they snarled in response.

"I'm not threatening anyone," I replied coolly. "I'm just saying, if you want to have a talk, you can talk to us." I patted the Cacophony's hilt. "Him and I."

I could feel their gazes on me: Rudu's irritated glare, Urda's terrified stare, the Ashmouths' glassy-eyed resentment. All of them knew this was stupid, what I was doing. If I offended the Ashmouths here, the only thing we'd leave with was the eternal enmity of an organization that could kill us all in our sleep. That was bad.

But not as bad as having it be said that Sal the Cacophony broke her word.

A professional rogue is still a rogue and a rogue is still a coward. The Ashmouths' loosening posture told me everything: whatever the Three paid them, it wasn't enough to be worth what I could do to them. They stepped aside, gestured with their chins. Rudu headed inside the alcove, Urda scampering after desperately.

Jero and I hurried to catch up, following the sound of metal creaking and a solitary hammer banging, and by the time we rejoined Urda and Rudu, we found ourselves standing in . . . how to describe it?

You ever been to one of those fancy brothels? The kind where all the workers are pretty and smell nice and they lead you into rooms full of silk pillows shaped like hearts and there's tapestries of nude people and statues of giant cocks and tits everywhere?

That, but machines.

Contrary to the haphazard messes of other merchants' wares, everything in the alcove was fastidiously organized, tagged, catalogued, and arranged in what could only be described as unnerving order. Gunpikes that lay neatly arranged from largest to smallest, tiny spheroid Relics that had been inappropriately and lovingly polished, a hulking Paladin armor that stood in the corner, surrounded by endless propaganda posters pinned to the walls depicting stern-faced Revolutionary soldiers gunning down comically exaggerated Imperial foes and beneficent faces of the Great General clutching Revolutionary children to his bosom. On top of all of this, upon neatly arranged shelves, were any number of machines, gadgets, and parts prized from the muck of the Revolution's battlefields.

It was a trove of Revolutionary technology. Exactly the place we'd been looking for. And don't get me wrong, I was glad we'd found it, but I had that creeping feeling on the back of my neck that I got when I was sure, but couldn't prove, that someone had just been masturbating before I walked into the room.

"You in here, Derimi?" Rudu bellowed into the room. "I swear to fuck, if you're naked again—"

"Uh, *excuse* me."

A pair of eyes—one gigantic, one frightfully tiny—peered out from behind the giant suit of armor. A thin and rodentine face, topped with a peculiar cap to which various loupes were attached and bottomed with an attempt at a beard, leaned out. It took me a moment to realize I was looking at a man and not some machine made of grease, hair, and glass.

"I believe I paid a handsome and exorbitant fee for this location as well as the extra protection?" he asked in the way that people who got punched in the face a lot did. "Ergo, if I *were* in the nude—which I must point out I am *not*—I would be well within my rights to be so."

I heard what he said, but I still tensed when he walked out from behind the armor. His thin face was matched by a tall, lanky body wrapped in a leather apron from which all manner of tools and instruments hung.

"And I am *exceedingly* certain that I left instructions that I am

not to be referred to by that name?" the man scoffed as he wiped his
hands on his apron. "I am, professionally, known as Forty-Pound
Barrel. Kindly do not forget it. Thank you."

"You're a Freemaker?" I asked, decidedly unimpressed.

"*You're* Forty-Pound Barrel?" Urda gasped, decidedly not. He
hurried forward, hands trembling like he wanted to touch the man
and mouth quivering like he knew why that was a bad idea. "*The*
Forty-Pound Barrel? I never thought I'd...I mean, I didn't think
you'd... *Wow!*"

"Fuck, you know him?" Rudu asked, tapping ash out of his pipe.
"I had a bet with some lady two alcoves over that he didn't have any
friends. You cost me six knuckles, kid. And after all I've done for
you, too."

"Know him? *Know* him?" Urda shot him a shocked expression. "I
mean, I know *of* Forty-Pound Barrel, the most renowned machinist
and Revolutionary technology expert outside Weiless!"

"Inside Weiless, too," Jero muttered, folding his arms. "Entire
regiments have been dispatched to get back what this bastard stole."

Forty-Pound Barrel removed his cap and haughtily cleaned its lenses.
"That Which Is Forbidden Is Mandatory," he replied. "If you will consult the Laws of the Freemakers, which are the only laws that matter,
for your information, you will find, forthwith, that the knowledge of
the Glorious Revolution of the Fist and Flame"—he paused to sweep a
glare across the room—"which is the *correct* way of referring to it, please
and thank you, was not meant to be hoarded and locked away, but to be
shared with the masses and/or anyone who can procure it, which I did."
He replaced his cap, adjusted its lenses, sniffed. "So there."

"Neat." Rudu took a puff of his pipe, blew smoke in Forty-Pound
Barrel's direction. "Anyway, these fucks are looking for some Revolution shit."

"Then you have, indeed, come to the right place." Forty-Pound
Barrel made a noble attempt at flailing the smoke away. "As you
no doubt do *not* know, as you are not capable of the same intui-
tive information-gathering as a Freemaker of my caliber *is*, there is
an abundance of hardware present in recent times. Revolutionary
desertion is on the rise since Proud and they're leaving their weapons
in droves."

"Proud?" I asked, feeling a surge of something hopeful that I thought I had done an admirable job quashing. "You mean Cav—"

"The Iron Fleet." Jero stepped forward, cutting me off. "The Ten Arrows. What do you know of them?"

"Uh, *only* all that there is to know," the greasy man said, pointedly coughing in Rudu's direction. "Though, since you are currently in what is colloquially known as a Crow Market, I assume you've come to purchase, not to discuss, which is a pity, as you are only cheating yourself out of a valuable learning experience."

Jero sighed. "So, are you selling or not?"

"Yes."

"Great, we're looking for—"

"*Provided*," Forty-Pound Barrel interrupted, "you can prove you are a connoisseur capable of *appreciating* the knowledge I have accumulated, as I am not some mere peddler of machinist smut, but a respected devotee of the mechanical form."

"For fuck's sake," Jero groaned. "Can I just pay you more to skip this part?"

"Do you happen to have a blueprint of the original iteration of the walking tank known by its military name of the Undeniable Face of the Anguished?" Forty-Pound Barrel inquired.

"No, I—"

"Then no, you cannot. I put an immense amount of effort into this collection and I cannot part with it knowing that it will be put to ill purposes."

"I assure you, Forty-Pound Barrel, sir, we'd never disrespect your expertise *or* your art," Urda said. "But we have a need to—"

"Urda, don't fucking play his game," Jero snarled. "We don't have the time to—"

"First of all, would you kindly refrain from cursing, good sir?" Forty-Pound Barrel offered a brief, perplexing bow toward me. "I would not like to offend the lady's sensibilities, if possible."

I squinted. "Huh?"

"Furthermore, if you do not have the time to *debate*, then you do not have the time to *appreciate*, as the old wisdom goes," Forty-Pound Barrel said, sneering. "And if you cannot appreciate what I am doing here, then I cannot bear to—"

"Please, he didn't mean to—"

"Oh, I did fucking mean to—"

"While I admire your candor, I cannot in good conscience—"

"You haven't *seen* candor yet, you greasy—"

And so on.

I don't want to sound rude, but once you get more than two men in the same room, you're basically either waiting for swords or cocks to come out. I had no desire to see either one of those happen and this seemed like one of those rare and annoying problems that couldn't be solved by shooting everyone.

I was angry, I was aching, and I was too fucking tired to do anything about either of those.

"Fuck me," I whispered, "what is it going to take to end this?"

My nostrils quivered at the pungent scent of burning leaves. A lazy tail of pink smoke drifted tantalizingly beneath my nose. I looked down to see a hand extended, a long-stemmed pipe full of illicit drugs proffered to me.

Needless to say, I *liked* Rudu.

SIXTEEN

THE CROW MARKET

A Vagrant is nothing without her vices, some say.

There's some truth to that. Those of us who went Vagrant, after all, did so because the concept of servitude no longer sat well with us. Even the more uncharitable descriptions of us as violent maniacs using our powers solely to pursue whatever twisted desires flit in and out of our magic-addled heads aren't *totally* off base—and some of my best friends are violent maniacs.

Personally, I prefer to view it a little more optimistically. True, we don't have a lot to spend our ill-gotten gains on except drugs, liquor, and pleasurable company. But vices serve an important role to Vagrants. For some, they're the only reprieve from the Barters the Lady Merchant extracts in exchange for our powers. For others, they're a chance to forget all the people who, deservedly or not, want them dead.

For me? Any moment I am indulging in a vice is a moment I am *not* making something explode or stabbing someone, so really, if anything, society should be *thanking* me for sitting in an alley and smoking silkgrass.

"Shit, woman, I offered you a *puff*, not a fucking dragon's breath."

If only Rudu felt the same.

I ignored his protests as I continued to suck on the pipe. The smoke flowed from my mouth to my lungs, and with every puff, I could feel aches fading, anger ebbing, and a strong desire for a sandwich.

I held the breath for as long as I was able before exhaling a cloud of pink. A lazy smile scrawled across my face as I watched the smoke dance and twirl overhead, tiny sparkles shimmering within.

"The Ashmouths don't care about you getting high on the job?" I asked as I handed the pipe back to Rudu. "I thought they had standards about that sort of thing."

"They do," he replied, puffing on the pipe. "But I have a sword and a lot of magic, so they're welcome to take it up with me if they want."

You might think that all Vagrants who rebelled against the Imperium did so in service of grander ambitions. Most rejected the new Emperor, who lacked any magical ability whatsoever. And no small number did so out of a desire for wealth, power, the classics. So, I wouldn't blame you for thinking there's no such thing as a "good" Vagrant.

And there isn't—we're all basically assholes. But Rudu was as close as they got.

In the army, he'd been best known for inexplicably coming down with life-threatening diseases when a battle was about to take place. Unbothered by the accusations of cowardice from his compatriots and superiors, he leapt at the chance to go Vagrant. Not out of a desire to acquire riches, but merely out of a bone-deep desire to not have to work.

I'd known many lazy men and I'd known many ambitious men, but never had I met a man whose laziness was so ambitious that he committed treason. In a twisted way, I had to respect that.

But not much else.

"Yeah, I've always wondered about that." I reached down and plucked up his wooden sword—a polished piece of tree you would be ashamed to see even in a trainee's hands, much less a hardened Vagrant's. "Why do you carry this thing around? You could do a lot more damage with an actual piece of metal."

"Metal costs too much," he replied. "Also, that thing broke three of your ribs once, if I remember rightly."

"It was two ribs and I broke six of your teeth."

"Three ribs are worth more than six teeth, so I win."

"You're high."

"*You're* high."

Shit, he had me there.

"You can't take back metal, you know." Rudu sighed as he stretched out, sprawling across the floor of the dank alcove we'd found to indulge in. "Once you draw it, it's not going back into the sheath until someone's dead, even if you put it back. You pull it out, people remember that you did and start thinking they should pull their own. You spill blood with it, someone starts looking for yours. You kill a man with it, you better be prepared to kill his whole family, because eventually one of them is going to come looking for you.

"Wood, though?" He smiled as he plucked up his sword. "Wood's solid. Sometimes it bends, sometimes it breaks, sometimes it burns, but it always comes back. You carry wood, the wood will do what you need it to. You carry metal, you live in service to that metal until the day you die."

I chuckled as I watched the shimmering clouds of silkgrass drift over us. "A Vagrant who's tired of killing. Imagine that."

"Shit, aren't you? I've heard the stories, Sal. How many people do you think are looking for you right now?" He glanced down to my hip, where the Cacophony seethed indignantly beneath his wary glare. "Doesn't that thing get heavy?"

Yeah. It did get heavy. Some days, the weight of it was so much that I didn't know how I was going to draw it again. But I always did. Because no matter how heavy the metal was, the piece of paper in my vest was heavier. Every name scrawled on that list weighed a world upon my shoulders. Every time I scratched one off, it got a little lighter.

Or... it should have, anyway.

"You probably took up the wrong job, then," I said. "I don't imagine the Ashmouths have a lot of use for a Vagrant who can't kill."

"I didn't say I *can't*. I just don't want to," Rudu replied, coughing out another cloud. "I didn't want this work, either. I had a real nice thing out on the edge of the Valley up until recently. Me and my partner were shaking down merchants coming in off the road. We never asked for much and they never put up a fight. Easy money, easy life. It was sweet."

"A partner, huh? Who was he?"

"Not important."

"Do I know him?"

Rudu paused, considered, and sighed. "Yeah. You know Yugol."

Another important role vices serve is keeping you from leaping up, reaching for your gun, and leaving in search of a fucker who richly deserved a messy, metal death.

Yeah. I knew Yugol.

I knew him when he went Vagrant and became Yugol the Omen. I knew him when he was known as Yugolamol, one of the Imperium's most talented Nightmages to ever join Vraki's conspiracy to overthrow the Imperium. I knew him from that night, that dark place below the earth where he and Vraki and Jindu and every other fucker on that list took the sky from me.

I remembered him as a simperer, a toady who could bring himself to worship at the feet of his betters, but couldn't muster the courage to face me down there. I remembered his stare, frightened and wild, as he stood in the background and watched me fall, watched me bleed...

Just like Darrish had. When she did nothing. And I lost the sky forever.

"*Eres va atali*," I whispered.

"Huh?"

"Nothing." I was too nice to tell Rudu I was going to kill his partner, but not too nice to ask. "What happened to him?"

"You did," Rudu replied, spite clinging to his voice. "Word reached him that you'd made it to the Valley and he took off. I could shake down caravans well enough without him, but he was the one who found them all. Without him, I had to find work with the Ashmouths."

"For how long?"

"Not much longer," he replied. "They aren't paying me enough to stick around for more than a few days more. After that, I'll head east to Clef's Lament again, but the point remains." He shot me as hateful a glare as a man that high could. "You made me get a *job*, Sal. I'll never forgive you for that."

"No?" I reached into my pocket, pulled out a feather, the tip dipped in red. "What if I gave you this?"

Rudu stared at the Redfavor he had given me so long ago with much more longing than he could muster for hate before he extended a hand. "Then all is forgiven. Hand it over."

"Fuck you, it's mine." I pocketed the Redfavor again. "You think I'd waste this thing on something as trivial as forgiveness?"

"I shared my grass with you."

"You *offered*. And you broke two of my ribs."

"And you broke six of my teeth."

"You're high."

"*You're* high."

Shit, he had me there.

I took the pipe as he passed it to me, took a hefty drag. The cloud of shimmering pink trickled out my lips, and with it went the fury, the pain, and the ability to sit upright. I felt everything seep out of me—bones, blood, muscle—and render me into liquid, sliding off the wall and onto a floor I suddenly no longer cared was filthy.

Was this what it was like? I wondered. To be normal? To wake up and not wonder who you were going to have to fight, who was out hunting you? Was this what it was like to sit next to someone and not even think they might have a blade and a grudge? I was probably romanticizing it a little, but in my defense, I was stoned off my ass.

"You know what I need?" I mused as I watched the sparkles dance in the cloud of grass.

"Yes, but if I say, you'll hit me," Rudu replied.

"A fuck," I said, pointedly ignoring the urge to hit him. "Nothing feels better after a pipe than a fuck."

"You aren't wrong," Rudu hummed. "It had to be...what, two years ago? I was heading through the Low Road, six pipes deep and absolutely incinerated."

"In the Low Road? That place is crawling with beasts."

"And beasts are very stressful and I handle stress with silkgrass. Can I tell my story?"

"Sorry, go on."

"I meet this guy. Older fellow, former Imperial, war record—you know the type."

"Gray hair?"

"Silver. Like the chain on a nice necklace."

"Nice."

"Normally, I can't stand them, but this one…" He chuckled, scratched an errant itch on his jaw. "Yeah, this guy knew how to take it slow. So slow I ended up staying in the Low Road for six months." He watched the smoke overhead twinkle, weary contentment seeping into his voice. "I liked that guy."

"What happened to him?"

I wasn't ready for the silence that came out of Rudu. That long funerary silence, the sound you get when people try to tiptoe past the empty space that someone else used to occupy… For some reason, I thought people like Rudu didn't have those kinds of silences.

"Same thing that always happens," he said at last. "The wars happened. The magic happened. The Barter happened." He sighed, a few lingering traces of grass smoke escaping his lips. "It was too much for him. He left. I didn't stop him."

I closed my eyes, scratched my scar. "Should have fought for him."

"Fight for him, huh? Like in an opera?"

"Operas are romantic. Everyone likes romance."

"Not everyone," he said. "And no one likes it enough to have to deal with a Vagrant. With the grudges, the fighting, the third person."

"Some people are okay with a third person. Once, in Lowstaff—"

"Not that kind of person. The other one. The singing one."

Ah, right.

Her.

"You were a Prodigy," he said. "You never had to pay the Barter. She never took anything from you. But us ordinary mages…" He frowned. "Could you do it, Sal? Ask someone to stay by you as the Lady Merchant chips off bits of you? Hell, it doesn't even have to be about the Barter. Could you ask someone to stay with you when there's always something out there to kill you? Always someone left to fight? To kill?"

"I could," I said. "I did."

"Oh, right." Rudu scratched his chin. "Jindu, right? Jindunama-lar? I remember him from the army. He was—"

"Not. Him."

Despite being baked more thoroughly than a loaf of potato bread, Rudu wasn't an idiot. He knew the voice I spoke with and he didn't press. Rather, he simply sighed and leaned back.

"What about the other one? How's that one girl? The really serious one with the glasses?" He glanced at me. "How'd that work out?"

And that silence came back. That empty, quiet spot that she used to occupy. Suddenly, it felt right beside me. Maybe it always was. Maybe that's all a ghost was, a big emptiness that was once a person that just follows you around.

I wanted to tell Rudu he was wrong, that I'd fought for her and won. And maybe sometimes I had. But how many of those fights had been with her? How many of those fights had she simply survived instead of won? How many times did I fight and let her wonder if this was the fight I wasn't going to win? I wanted to tell Rudu he was wrong.

Failing that, I wanted to hit him.

But I was too high for that. Too high to talk. Too high to keep my eyes open. The smoke dissipated, the tiny stars inside twinkling out, as my eyes drifted shut and a numb blanket fell over me.

Nothing was better than a fuck after a pipe.

But a long, unfeeling sleep was okay, too.

Do you ever wonder if dreams are like blood? That, if you get hit hard enough, cut deep enough, they all just...bleed out of you?

I sometimes do. I sometimes wonder if you can lose them all. I sometimes wonder what's left. Is it nightmares? Is it emptiness? Or is it just...you?

"Here. I procured something."

Just moments of your life. Fragments. Scraps.

"The hell is this?"

Sewn together by the scars so you can't remember them without the pain.

"It is a gift. For you," a calm, assertive voice said in my head. "The customary response to which is gratitude, as opposed to profanity, if you were not aware."

She was smiling.

Which is how I knew this was a dream.

Or something close to it.

"No, no." I was sitting in a bed that we once called ours before it was just hers. A bottle of whiskey and a bottle of wine stood nearby, both half empty. She was sitting beside me, her eyes big behind her glasses. And a box was on my lap. "It's not that I'm *un*grateful, just...I didn't think you the type."

Liette's brow furrowed over the rims of her glasses. "The type to do what? To show spontaneous expressions of affection in a materialistic manner?"

"Yeah," I replied. "Mostly because you say stuff like that."

"Then give it back," she said, reaching for the box.

I snatched it away, growling. "Fuck you, it's mine."

She smiled in that insufferable way she did whenever I did exactly what she was expecting me to do. "Then open it."

I did. It was a humble box—brown paper, simple twine holding it together, she always did think poorly of frippery—not big enough to be a weapon, not sloshy enough to be alcohol. I took it apart carefully before staring down at what lay within.

"A knife."

A very nice knife, don't get me wrong: a tiny, perfectly tempered blade, with a fine wooden hilt, an expertly sewn sheath.

"A *knife*," Liette scoffed. "I suppose if you consider a blade expertly honed by the finest smith, a hilt perfectly carved by the finest woodworker, and all of it treated against inclement weather, inadvertent damage, and overall wear-and-tear to be *merely* a knife, certainly. In my accurate assessment, the specifications I ordered render this a work of art." She adjusted her glasses, squinted over the blade. "Though, the tip is not quite as tapered as I would have liked. I bet I can fix that."

I picked it up, flipped it from hand to hand. Good weight, good balance, sharp as hell, but...

"What's it for?" I asked.

She blinked. "What do you mean what's it for? It's a knife. It's for...knifing. You know, cutting rope, cutting leather, that sort of thing."

"Knifing is the act of cutting a human," I said. "And this—thank you for it, by the way—couldn't tickle a man."

I remembered this day.

Only a few weeks after we met. After the first time I left and she assumed it was just an accident that we could move past, before the second time I left and she knew it wasn't. We'd fought that day—she said things that had hurt me, I had thrown something out a window. Then I held her in my arms and she put her head on my chest and in the space between us, we'd found a reason to keep going.

For a little while, anyway.

I remembered this dream, too.

It was different each time, so much that I had a hard time remembering what had actually happened. Sometimes I said all the right things and she laughed and smiled. Sometimes I said all the wrong things and we went right back to fighting. Once, I just grabbed her and kissed her and took a long time trying to figure out what she smelled like.

Jasmine. She loved flower smells.

But each time, it ended the same way. No matter what I said, what I did, how hard I tried or didn't. It was the same.

So was this.

Her smile fell. She turned away. I reached out for her. She was too far away.

"Sorry," I said. "I like it. I really do."

"No, you don't."

"I *said* I did, didn't I?" I snapped.

"You did," she said. "You also said it couldn't kill a man. And no, it can't. It's not supposed to. I didn't..." She clenched her jaw. "I don't want to give you weapons."

I blinked. "Why? I *like* weapons."

"You don't like weapons. You *love* weapons. You never stop thinking about weapons."

My lips pursed, something cold creeping up my neck. "I do. I did. I did last night, didn't I? When I said what I said, when we did what we did?"

She hugged herself, closing her eyes. "And I had to ask you to take that...that *thing* out of the room before we could." She looked over to the door, past which the Cacophony lay in the first sheath I'd gotten for him, the one he'd later burn to ashes. "I can still feel it looking at me."

I sighed, leaned back. "I told you, he can't—"

"It," she replied. "It's a gun, not a person."

"*He*," I snapped back. "The Cacophony is the Cacophony. He's the reason I came back alive. The Scar isn't a fucking picnic. I'm out there *fighting*."

"Do *not* presume to lecture me on dangers I am well aware of." She whirled on me, a glare hardened behind her glasses that steadily melted. She sighed, rubbed her temples. "I... I know it's hard out there. I *know* that. But... when's it going to be enough?"

"Enough what?"

"Enough weapons, enough fighting, enough killing." She leaned forward, stared at the scar that wound its way down my chest, from collarbone to belly. "When is it going to be... when am I going to..."

She couldn't find the words. Which was another reason I knew it was a dream. But it cut me deep, all the same. I fell back into bed, draped my arm over my eyes, let out a sigh.

"I'm sorry," I whispered.

I reached out, groped blindly around the bed. I don't know if she reached back. But I found her hand in mine all the same.

"I'm sorry for not knowing," I said. "I wish I knew as much as you. I wish I knew how to see things like you, but I don't. I don't know how to... make things work like you do. I don't know how to stop liking weapons or how to stop looking for fights or how to stop... any of it. I don't *know* because I don't *think*. I just find a sword and I find a name and it happens and... I don't know how to make it stop. I haven't figured that out. I'm sorry."

I squeezed her hand.

"But it's not all I think about," I said. "You are. Every time I fight, I think of you. Every time I bleed, I think of you. Every time I fall down and taste dirt in my mouth, all I can think about is getting up and limping away so I can get back to you. I don't know how to make it stop. But I'm figuring it out. I hope I am. One day I will."

Those were all the words I wish I had said that day.

All the words I carried around, deep and painful as any of my scars.

All the words I lost, like I lost that knife, somewhere out in that dark earth.

It was a dream because it wasn't happening. But it wasn't like dreams should be. It wasn't soft, it wasn't gentle. It still hurt.

It hurt when I said the words. It hurt when she squeezed my hand. It hurt when I felt the blood weeping between my fingers.

"Will you?" she asked.

I looked down. Her hands were knives.

"Will you figure it out?"

I looked up. Liette wasn't holding my hand anymore. She stood, miles away, on a dark plain. The sun vanished. Cold wind howled. A shadow appeared beside her.

"Or are you just going to keep fighting?"

Darrish. Pale-eyed and frowning, manifested out of the shadow. Another followed her.

"Are you going to keep looking for a weapon like what you had?"

Jindu.

And Vraki.

And everyone. All of them. People I didn't know, people I did, all of them I'd killed.

"What did it feel like," they asked me on breathless voices, "when you burned them?"

Flames exploded. I shielded my eyes. When I opened them again, the dark earth was gone, miles below me. So were the houses. And the people. And the flames.

I flew high and proud over them, a red cloud on a black sky. But the flames kept rising. And with them, so did the hands. Blackened, flesh sloughing off, skeletal fingers reaching out, screams rising on the smoke.

"What did it feel like," they whispered, "to fly?"

And I closed my eyes. And I held my arms out. And I let the flames reach up and swallow me, too.

It was easier to do that, to let the fire take me, than it was to admit...

It had felt glorious.

From a mouthful of cinders. On a breath kissed by ashes. Through a smile brimming with thorns. A voice whispered.

"Eres va atali."

And I was gone.

⊷⊷⊷ ▰◆▰ ⊶⊶⊶

"Is she dead?"

Voices. Distant. Soft. Fading.

"No. Look at the pipe. She's just stoned."

They dripped down to me, leaking through a crack in some hidden part of the dark place where I lay, soft gloom wrapping itself protectively around me.

"Of course, we're all going to be dead if we don't wake her up. Give me a hand."

Someone took me by the shoulders. I knew this, but I didn't feel it. I felt nothing.

"Er...are you sure? Are you supposed to wake people who do... that?"

Wait, no. It came to me. I felt something.

"For fuck's sake, can you be useful for *once*?"

"It's not my fault we're all going to die! I want that on the record!"

Annoyed.

I felt very annoyed.

My hand shot out, slapping a grip off of me. My eyelids fluttered open, light seeping back into my vision on relentless, desperate claws. Through the grogginess and haze, I managed to make out a face, its wrinkles contorted in a very alarmed frown.

"Hi, hey, hello," Jero said. He licked his lips, looked over his shoulder, then back to me. "So, uh, things did not go according to plan."

I blinked. I squinted. I cleared my throat. "Huh?"

"Okay, so," he sighed, "the Freemaker—"

"Who will never speak to us again," Urda's shrill voice chimed in, worried and frenetic.

"Shut up," Jero said. "He *did* have the schematics we were looking for. Not a complete set, obviously, but enough that we've got something to work with."

"Which doesn't matter," Urda said, "because the Ashmouths are going to kill us. Sweet heaven, we offended the *Ashmouths*. I knew this was a bad idea. I knew it, I knew it, I knew it."

"Shut *up*," Jero snapped. "Unfortunately, he wouldn't part with it at any price we offered, so we..."

"We stole it!" Urda sobbed softly. "We *stole* it! We violated every Freemaker law, we violated the sanctity of the Ashmouths' pact. They're going to say from Cathama to Weiless that Urda of the Wild Quill is nothing more than a...than a *THUG*!"

"*Shut up!*" Jero bit back his shout, pursed his lips, held up a finger. Beyond the alcove mouth, the fading light of an alchemic lantern swung in our direction before turning away. He sighed, turned back to me. "Understand, we had no choice. For our plan to work, we *needed* those schematics."

"And for us to avoid being killed by the Ashmouths," Urda said, "we *need* to get out of here."

"And for us to get out of here," Jero finished, "we need you. Got it?"

I blinked again. I smacked my lips. I coughed. "*HUH?*"

Jero's hand slapped over my mouth. Urda let out a frightened squeak, pulled out his pen, and started nervously scrawling a set of sigils upon the wall.

"What was that?" a voice whispered from nearby.

"I don't know," another voice replied. "Maybe we should stay here talking about it until they can get away. Come on."

One light was joined by another. And another. And then some crow masks, some glassy-eyed stares, a lot of shady-looking fuckers— I don't know, it was hard to tell. Except for the glint of arrowheads pointed our way.

Those were pretty easy to make out.

"There they are!" one of the Ashmouths shouted. "*KILL THEM!*"

A bowstring snapped. An arrow whizzed past my ear. Jero shouted, pulling free his blade. Urda furiously scribbled upon the wall. More boots came tramping up the hall, more lanterns swinging toward us, more arrows, more crow masks, more Ashmouths.

That was all really bad, don't get me wrong.

But I was still just...*incredibly* high.

Still, that's no excuse not to help out.

I pulled the Cacophony free, aimed it at the crowd of Ashmouths. Behind their masks, it was impossible to see their reactions. But the screaming and leaping out of the way, I understood well enough. I squinted one eye, pulled the trigger.

Click.

Ah, yes. Ammunition. Guns need that.

"Rush them! They've got Ashmouth property!" one of them shouted as the others, their folly realized, came to their feet.

"Oh no, oh no, OH NO!"

Urda's shriek was accompanied by a flash of light and a rumble of stone. His sigils burst to life, the wall following—the stones shot out in a wall, a barrier of rock, smooth and polished, erupting from one wall to the other as the Ashmouths crashed against it.

"You fucks!" they screamed behind the wall. "You think you can steal the Three's property?"

"A wall?" Jero asked.

"A spellwritten wall, yes," Urda replied, his voice babbling. "I convinced the wall that it was a different wall, no large task, no large task for anyone else, that is. I could have made it larger but they were coming and I can't think and I can't breathe and I—"

"Someone get an alchemic or an explosive or something. Bring this shit down."

Again, all very bad. Crossing the Three heads of the Ashmouths was no small offense, even without money involved. If we were lucky, they'd kill us outright once they got that wall down.

"This is terrible, this is terrible, this is terrible," Urda said, breathless. "Where's Yria? I need Yria. I need..."

He started fishing around in his pocket, pulled free that silver thing I saw him messing with earlier. A whistle? Yeah, a plain, ordinary whistle, except that it was scribbled with sigils I couldn't even begin to comprehend even while sober.

"Not yet." Jero held him by the wrist. "We don't need it yet, all right?"

"I need Yria," Urda gasped, barely fighting back tears. "I need my sister."

"That thing is powerful. We need to save it." Jero took him by the face, forced his stare upon him. "They haven't gotten in yet. It's just us here. We can think of something else, okay?"

Urda looked like he was on the verge of believing that. Or at least, he was until we all seemed to collectively remember that we'd come down here with three of us.

And there were four in this alcove.

"Ah, fuck." Rudu clambered to his feet, rubbed out a sore spot in his neck. "Did I pass out?" He paused, red-rimmed eyes taking in

the whole situation. With a tired sigh, he drew his wooden sword
out. "Shit. Do I have to kill you guys now?"

"No, no, no, no, NO, NO, NO!"

Urda shoved Jero away, put the whistle to his lips, and blew, hard
as he could. The sound rattled through our tiny alcove, the sigils
upon it lighting up. And upon the wall behind him, a faint pinprick
of light blossomed.

And then yawned to life.

A portal burst into being, a swirling hole of light and nothingness. But that was impossible... wasn't it? There were no Doormages
here—Rudu and I sure as shit weren't any—so how could—

"Yria!" Urda shrieked, leaping through the portal and disappearing.

"Fuck." Jero sighed as he took me by the shoulder. "I was hoping
we could avoid that."

I blinked again. "Wait, what are you—"

I'm pretty sure I've mentioned that I don't like portals, haven't I?
They're vile, nasty things that make you feel like your insides get
torn out and rearranged on the other side. Not everyone survives
them and sometimes the stress of that alone feels like it's enough to
kill you.

Anyway, turns out none of that is helped by being high on
silkgrass.

Jero gave me a stiff shove. I fell through the portal, into a world of
blinding light, hurtling through nothingness and space I didn't have
a name for, my screams lost on the void before, just as swiftly as it all
had began, it came to an ugly, jarring end.

I plummeted out of the portal and landed harshly on something
soft, a surge of pain lancing through my injuries. Urda grunted as I
collapsed upon him. And then he screamed as Jero came hurtling
out the portal to land on top of me.

"Well, look who showed up," a voice chuckled. "Thought maybe I
was gonna have to set out tea to get Lord and Lady Fancyfarts back."

Yria. How did she get here?

She wandered over to the portal, lazily, and waved a hand. The
light snapped shut almost instantly. I blinked, stared out from the
pile of men who had a knack for irritating me.

Agne and Tuteng, apparently ensconced in a game of cards, glanced up from the table. Snow fell against the window. Madame Fist came in with a tray full of tea and made a comment about people dirtying her floors. Yria just grinned as she reached out and pulled Urda free from beneath me.

"Neat trick, isn't it?" she chuckled. "Makes me wish we could do it more often. So…" She licked her lips. "You get your little papers or did I just blow my load for nothing?"

SEVENTEEN

LITTLEBARROW

D oes it?"

Sal looked up as the words tumbled out of his mouth. She tossed a piece of rubble atop the twisted wood and metal, held out her hands toward him.

"Does what?" she asked.

"Get tiring." Meret grunted as he struggled to pull a particularly large chunk of debris out of the earth with slightly more dignity than his noises would imply. "The fighting, the killing, the . . . I don't know, being a Vagrant."

She shot him a smirk too coy for a face as beaten and bloodied as hers had been.

"You were just talking about how lovely a Vagrant's life sounded. All that romantic talk about being able to change things. I thought I was listening to an opera." She chuckled as she came up beside him. "What changed? Was it the stabbing? Most people are less interested in this lifestyle once they realize how much stabbing is involved."

"No, it's not the stabbing." Meret cleared his throat as she pressed her shoulder against his and took hold of the debris. "I mean, *yes*, obviously, I would prefer there to be not so much stabbing in my future, but the sentiment remains the same. I can appreciate the—"

"Here." She interrupted him as she slid into a squat, tightening her grip on the chunk of metal. "Plant your feet. Bend down. Lift with your legs." He nodded, mimed her stance. "Ready?"

He nodded again. They started to pull. The sound of their grunt-
ing joined the hiss of snow shifting and the slobber of wet earth.
Slowly, they hauled the object—a wing, maybe? Or a figurehead? It
was hard to tell—out of the earth, sodden from melting snow.

The body came with it.

"*SCIONS!*" Meret shrieked, and dropped the object, eliciting
a curse from Sal, but he didn't care about any of that. He rushed
toward the person clinging to the wing, reaching for the satchel at
his hip. "Hang on, I can..."

His voice trailed off. His hand slid from his satchel. His eyes fell,
like the snow fell. Two more pieces of white, fallen upon a corpse,
helping no one.

You can do what? he asked himself.

He knew it was a man—or what looked like a man, anyway. But
nothing else. The fire had taken his skin, sinew, hair, face. What few
remains had been left behind had been shattered by the fall. He lay
there, clutching the wet earth where that piece of debris had been, as
though it would give him solace.

Solace, Meret realized, that he couldn't give.

Couldn't help him, he told himself. *Couldn't even comfort him in
the last moments. You could have helped him if he had a cold, though.
Or a sprained knee. That's what you do, isn't it? The small stuff?*

He turned and looked out over the field. What rubble could be
moved had been gathered into small piles that dotted the snow-
covered field. Like cairns.

How many other bodies were out there? he wondered. Buried
under rubble? Burned up in flames until only skeletons remained?
Crushed under metal or wood or the sheer weight of seeping, damp
earth?

How many of them might still be alive? he wondered. Trapped
there, screaming for help, begging for aid from gods they didn't
know they believed in? Bleeding out, broken, burning...

What could he do for any of them? How could he save them?
What if he did? How could he save the next ones? And the *next*
ones? How many empty-eyed, dead-inside people would he leave
behind on his way to other empty-eyed, dead-inside people?

What are you even doing here?

He wondered.

The field didn't answer him. No matter how long he stared.

"Were you still planning on helping?" Sal shouted at him.

He babbled a few apologies she couldn't hear as he hurried to catch up to her. He took hold of the wing, melting snow and burned flesh sloughing off it as they dragged it toward the pile, and together they tossed it upon another cairn.

Sal wiped her brow with the back of her hand. "So, what changed?"

"Huh?" he asked.

"You made it sound like a Vagrant's life was positively magical," she replied. "Now it sounds like you're not so sure."

"I'm not. I mean, I *am*, but...I mean, is anyone sure about such a...I mean..." He held his hands out, not finding the words there, either. "I don't know. I'm aware a Vagrant's life isn't magical. I'm aware that they tend to deal with, uh, rather a lot of blood."

Sal looked over the field of rubble-cairns and sniffed. "Yeah, I'd say that's accurate."

"But I confess, even with that, there's a certain...romanticism?"

She shot him a queer look. "Have I made this sound romantic? You know most Vagrants aren't as attractive as me, right?"

"*Romantic* isn't the right word." He thought of the dead person and cringed. "At all. But...the Scar's a difficult place, Vagrant or not. Everyone's suffering, everyone's bleeding, everyone's dying..." He stared at the rubble pile, at all the great things that debris had once been, built by great people. "Everyone's always dying."

"They were dying before Vagrants were a thing. If it wasn't the war, it'd be the outlaws. If it wasn't the outlaws, it'd be the beasts. If it wasn't the beasts, it'd be...I don't know, some kind of hellplague that made you shit your lungs out."

"That's not a thing," Meret countered sharply. "But if it was, you could probably do something about it. Just like you can drive off the monsters, kill the outlaws, stop wars—"

"No one can stop a war."

"But you could do *more*," he insisted. "Anyone else is just...just *prey*. All we can do is run away and lick our wounds. But a Vagrant can fight back, can't they? I mean, do you worry about bandits mugging you on the road?"

"Doesn't everyone?"

"Not everyone."

He glanced down to the big brass gun upon her hip. And it glanced back at him; he could feel it under its sheath. It was looking at him. It was smiling.

"All right, you've got a point." She brusquely shifted her scarf over the gun, hiding it from his view. "Once they see *him*, most trouble-makers don't tend to sniff around."

"But it's not just the gun, is it? It's the legends, the stories, all the *fear* that's heaped upon your name. Have you ever just spoken your name and sent someone running?"

She grinned. "Once."

"Have you ever had someone come looking for more after that?"

Her grin fell. "Once."

"When a beast attacks, what do you do?"

"Normally, I try to avoid it." She walked away from him, pulled something from the ground. "But if I can't, I'll blow it to hell."

"What about a warlord? When they attack a village you're staying in, what do you do?"

"Blow them to hell."

"What if a Revolutionary squadron tries to conscript you? Or an Imperial Judge billets himself in your house? Or—"

"There's only so many ways I can say it, Meret," she sighed. She trudged back to the pile, dragging a barrel behind her. She upended it, the rank smell of oil filling the air. "If everything about this life sounds so great, why don't *you* try it?"

"Well, uh," he said, clearing his throat, "a Vagrant is a mage, right? I don't have any magic, ergo—"

"There are a lot of famous outlaws that aren't Vagrants," Sal replied as she started dragging the oil barrel to the next pile. "Red Rinjar, Lucky Airo, the Grunch—she's an asshole, for the record. You think any of those warlords fear bandits or monsters?"

"Well, no, but they're probably all brutes from birth, right?"

"Red Rinjar was, yeah. But she was also a merchant's daughter. Lucky Airo is a grandfather of six. The Grunch was a chef. All of them started small."

"But they weren't apothecaries."

"If you know how to save a man's life, you know how to take it."
One by one, Sal visited the rubble-cairns and upended oil over them
before shaking out the last drops and adding the barrel to the last
pile. "The rest of it—the cronies, the weapons, the power—you get
along the way. The only thing that makes us what we are is whether
we're willing to kill someone."

She turned and looked at him. Not with the flippant grin she'd
sometimes offered him or the distant melancholy he sometimes saw
when she wasn't looking. She looked at him the way she had when
she'd first asked him to save that woman, Liette.

She looked at him like everything hinged on his answer.

"Are you?" she asked.

Are you?

He echoed the question inside himself. He'd seen his share of
death before. *More* than his share, if he was honest—and he still
stood strong where the sight of death would shake others.

Not that it hadn't shaken him. No one could look at that many
corpses, that much suffering, and not be. But lingering under all
that shaking, quivering fear, there was something solid, something
sharp and hot that he could never seem to grab hold of.

Anger.

Anger at the armies that had dug the mass graves he'd seen the
bodies in. Anger at the outlaws that had burned the villages he'd
left behind. Anger at the monsters, the fiends, the merchants of suffering who glutted themselves at feasts of misery and laughed while
they choked on blood.

Sometimes, he could grab that anger. Sometimes, he could hold it
in his hands and hone it until it was a sharpened point, fit for thrusting right through someone's—

"Yes." The words suddenly tumbled out of his mouth. "Yes, I am."

He didn't know what he had expected her reaction to be. Probably
disbelieving laughter or one of those smug-ass grins she shot him
when she was about to say something insufferably clever. But she
didn't give him either of those. She merely held his stare for another
moment, then nodded.

He had meant it. And she knew he had.

"There's a gang that runs outside the Valley. The Sad Lads." She chuckled. "Dumb name, but they're decent sorts, as outlaws go, and they could use someone who knows how to heal. They target rich fucks, military caravans, that sort of thing. You seem like the type that cares about shit like codes of honor."

"Well...I mean, I don't want to kill just *anyone* but—"

"They owe me a favor. I can set you up with them, if you want."

He blinked. "What? Really?"

Again, that stare of hers. That earnest, violent look. "You're doing something for me. For Liette. Something important. Sal the Cacophony doesn't shirk debts. If I can make this right by that, I will."

His mouth hung agape. Here it was. An answer. A way to hold on to that anger, a way to fight back, a way to *change* things. He stammered, looking for a reply, finding only a jumble of messy words.

"I mean, I'd be...I'd be...of course, my first duty is to my patients. I'd have to settle things with Liette—which I'd be happy to do even if I wasn't going to be a...or if I wanted to be a...wow, an outlaw? What kinds of codes of honor? Do I have to swear a loyalty oath or do an initiation? Will I have to put something in my—"

"Holy shit, calm down, I'm not talking about right this second." She reached into her pocket, pulled out a sheaf of tindertwigs. "But if you want that...or if you want anything, really...I'll get it for you."

Despite the morbidity of the situation, he found himself grinning. "That's not what I'd have expected from Sal the Cacophony."

"There are *nice* stories about me, you bag of ass," she replied, sneering.

She struck the twig, setting it aflame and tossing it atop the rubble pile. The rubble caught instantly, the oil and severium dust alighting in a purple-tinged flame that belched smoke into the sky.

"A word for the intrepid, though," she said. "Get used to this."

"To what?" He adjusted his glasses. "You never told me what you're doing."

"Burning," she replied. "For the dead."

"The...dead?"

A sad, tender smile—not something he'd have expected from her, either—crossed her face and was gone in an instant. One more cold and beautiful thing, burned and disappeared in the flames.

"Someone should remember them," she said. "When the killing's done, memories are all you get to keep."

⊷ ⚌✦⚌ ⊶

The trek back to Littlebarrow felt longer than it had taken to assemble the rubble piles. That task, he'd only been burdened with wood and metal. For the journey back, he'd been laden with heavier things.

This morning, he'd been ready to call Littlebarrow his home. But that had been before the sky opened up, before the fire rained down, before he knew that even here, war could reach him. Reach anywhere. What safety was there in a world where even the sky could erupt in flames?

Could he do it?

Could he leave it all behind? Not just Littlebarrow, but all of it: the herbs and the bandages and the patients, the finding a village and leaving it knowing that it would soon be destroyed, the helplessness and the empty words and the people...

The people.

What would they do without him? he wondered. Who would take care of the old wounds and the bad knees? Who would brew up tinctures for bronchitis and colds? Who would...

Who would protect them, he asked himself, *when the war comes to them?*

That thought settled heavy on his shoulders, along with the others. Tinctures and salves were all well and good for tiny problems. But what good would they do against falling bombs and fiery spells? How would a tea for fever help a man torn apart by magic or shot through the heart with a gunpike?

It wouldn't. *He* wouldn't. He'd just pick up his bag, move to the next village, start over. And the whole thing would just keep going.

But what if it didn't have to?

What if he met these Sad Lads? What if he learned to use a sword? A gun? What if he stood up to fight? Who would look to him as a hero? Who would come running to him for protection from the bandits and the outlaws? Who would go on living a long, boring life and die quietly in their beds at the end of a long, tiring journey, because of him?

He could do it. He could change everything.

He *would* change everything.

That's decided, then, he told himself. *Leave it behind. All of it. Once you do this for Sal, your life as Meret is over. You'll need a new name, like... Meret the Malice. No, wait, that's a Vagrant's name—they seem touchy about their names. Malicious Meret, then. Or something else. You can be anyone. You can do anything. You'll finally be able to—*

"Been busy?"

Sindra's voice cut through him cleaner than the cold—or a knife, for that matter. He started at her rasp, saw her sitting upon a chair on his porch, a cigarillo burning in her mouth.

"Uh, yes, as a matter of fact," he replied. "I was just out there helping Sal with some disposal."

"Sal." She repeated the name with the same dire ominousness with which one repeats the name of a plague. "You were helping her."

"I was." Without realizing it, he drew himself up. "She requested it. Liette needed quiet to convalesce. It seemed a good idea."

"You don't think that time would be better spent helping this town?" She gestured out over the village, over its darkened windows and doors left hanging open. "The people are leaving, Meret. Because of her. Because of what she's done and what she'll do."

He winced, as though struck. "Yes, that's... that's awful. Truly. But she fell here. She didn't choose to."

"And you didn't have to choose to help her, but you did." A sneer, old and deep as any of her wrinkles, painted her face. "Now these people are heading out, leaving everything behind, going onto roads crawling with outlaws and monsters, because they've got the good sense to realize a town with a Vagrant in it doesn't stay a town for long."

He sighed, rubbed his temples. "Sal wouldn't do that."

"She already blew the roof off one house."

"An *unoccupied* house."

"Did you hear the words she said? The threats she made?"

"She was... she was just trying to get them to be aware and to—"

"Listen to you," Sindra said, rising to her full height. "Sniveling. Simpering. Making excuses for her. If she's really as great as you say she is, why couldn't she think of something better? Why couldn't she *do* better?"

His lips fumbled for an answer that his mind couldn't find. The words she'd said, the look in her eyes, mingled together with the legends of murderous outlaws and the images of Littlebarrow torn asunder.

Sindra reached out, laid a heavy hand on his shoulder. "Meret, the people here need your help more than—"

"THEY ALWAYS NEED HELP!"

His voice. Cutting through the winter silence like a scythe. Echoing off every plume of smoke and snow that came drifting into town. His voice... but it didn't sound like it.

"And they will *always* need help." Still, the words kept coming, as he slapped Sindra's hand away, as his face twisted into an angry snarl he didn't know he could make. "If not from her, then from the Imperium, or from the Revolution, or from bandits, beasts, weather, magic, cannons, *anything*. The Scar is *brimming*, Sindra, with things that can kill them, things that can destroy their lives just as easily as any Vagrant, and all I can do is..."

He cringed at his own voice. It hurt to put into words. That's how he knew it was true.

"All I can do is pick up what's left and bandage them back together." His voice fell, a quiet hush. "And I'm tired of doing that, Sindra. I'm tired of setting up targets for big people with big weapons to knock over. Aren't you?"

The old soldier held his gaze for a second before the weight of her smoke-colored sigh slid her back to her chair.

"Yes, I'm tired of it," she said. "I was tired of it before I left the Revolution and I'm tired of it now." She rubbed her eyes with the heel of her hand before turning her weary glare upon him. "But I know I do a damned sight better than I used to. And I'll continue to. Because that's all I've got left."

"That's all we'll ever have, Sindra," Meret replied, trying to sound definitive in his coldness, yet even now, his voice sounded weak in his ears. "All we'll have is what's left. Nothing to call our own, nothing for *them* to call their own"—he gestured to the town—"except for whatever the people with the weapons decide to leave them." He shook his head. "There's got to be more. There's got to be *better*."

"And she's it, is she?" Sindra's face tightened into a scowl. "This Vagrant is going to give you what you need?"

"Not everything, no," Meret replied. "But better than we've got. Even if it takes a little bit for us to figure out how to use it."

The anger slid out of him with every breath, the tautness of his face relaxing to a very weary, very easy smile. It felt good to say that, he realized, like pulling a splinter out of a finger. The wound left behind might hurt, but it hurt a little less than it did before.

"Already, she's doing it."

He turned and pointed out to the field. The memorial cairns decorated the sad tragedy strewn across that snowy land, tiny points of red and purple light painting away the misery and banishing the wreckage of the airship to the shadows.

It wasn't going to solve everything, he admitted to himself. Hell, it might not even change that much—she was still a dangerous Vagrant. Littlebarrow didn't deserve to see its people set off into the wilds. The ruin of that airship would blight this land for months to come, if not years.

"But it's something," he said, both to her and to himself. "What kind of Vagrant would burn the dead and the wreckage if they were truly a monster?"

Not a Vagrant, he told himself. Not one of those fiends from the stories who kills and loots without a thought. She was more than that, he knew. Not a Scion, not a saint, maybe not even a particularly good person.

But different.

And enough for now.

"Is that what she told you she was doing?"

Sindra's voice came without scorn or anger. It came with the same weary benevolence his mentor had once chided him with, the sort of voice you take when consoling a gullible child who'd just been swindled out of their pocket money.

"Huh?" he asked.

She pulled herself out of her chair, pointed out over the field with her cigarillo. "Stop looking at the fires, Meret. Look at the smoke."

He followed the ember of her cigarillo, from the ground where Sal continued to burn, to the fires that flickered purple with latent severium charges, to the smoke that rose into the sky.

It became one colossal column, stark black against the winter sky like an infected wound, the tinge of severium making it glimmer in the air, bright and shining even as the gray skies roiled around it.

Huge. Bright.

Unmissable.

"We made signal fires like these back in the Revolution," Sindra said. "She's not memorializing the dead, Meret. She's calling out to someone. And every soldier, Imperium or Revolution, is going to see it."

Her eyes narrowed sharply.

"And they'll come running."

EIGHTEEN

THE CANED TOAD

No matter what the chroniclers, the sages, and the poets tell you, all deaths are equal.

To the dead, anyway.

No matter what you die for—a cause, true love, yourself—people eventually forget that. Great causes fall apart, true loves find other true loves, and you eventually become the same bones and dust as everyone else.

Pain, though...

Pain is different. Not all pain is equal. I've taken hits from warlords charging at me on birdback that dragged me for twenty feet and walked them off with a stiff drink. I've been given four words in a dark room that made me go days without sleep, they cut me so deep.

Pain is a weapon. And it all comes down to whoever's the one holding it when it sticks into you.

To that end, the ministrations of Madame Fist weren't the *most* painful thing I'd ever felt.

"*OW!*"

But they were close.

"Don't be such a baby." I could tell by the tone of her voice that the good madam was perfectly capable of sounding soothing, but was deliberately choosing not to be, as she pulled my arm so far back that it felt like it was going to pop out of its socket. "You're the one that asked for this."

"I *asked* for a *massage*," I snarled back, wincing as she put her namesake between my shoulder blades and began to knuckle them. "And I'm getting *tortured*."

"For free, I might add," she observed, moving her knuckles savagely down my spine. "In the capital, members of the Imperial court paid immensely for this pleasure."

"Were they high?" I clenched my teeth.

"Most of them, yes. That also cost extra." She lowered my arm and raised the other, the one over my wound, neatly stitched up and secured with an alchemic bandage, and began to massage my side. "I'll tell you the same thing I told them: you'll be begging for it later, you little shit."

She wasn't wrong. Vechine can keep you from bleeding out, but after it gets flushed out of the body, you might wish you had just died instead. The muscles it cramped up stay cramped until you loosen them up with a good week's worth of gentle massaging.

Since we didn't have that kind of time, Madame Fist had decided to go with two hours' worth of a much less gentle kind.

I'd have protested. Just as much as I'd protested when she pushed me into the bathhouse and stripped my clothes off. But she hadn't listened to me then, either. Instead, she'd forced me to be still as she flushed my wound, stitched it neatly, and applied the bandage before beginning to work life back into my muscles.

It hurt like hell. That I was used to. What I wasn't used to was being spoken to like that and not punching the person who did it. But call me a traditionalist, I still thought it bad manners to dispute a Master.

In Cathama, as you might expect of a city where magic has solved most of its problems, the arts are venerated and few are venerated more than the Masters. Magical arts, of course, rank the highest, but anyone who pursues a specific skill enough to be undisputed in their mastery of it is worthy of admiration and respect. That goes for a Master of the Intimate Arts as well, such as Madame Fist.

And while I wasn't *used* to being treated like trash, I hated to admit it, my injuries *did* feel incredibly better after her touch.

During her touch was another story.

"Fuck, woman." I groaned, tilting my head back as she worked at my hip and leg. "Why the hell can a Freemaker as rich as Two Lonely Old Men not afford a Mendmage or a proper healer?"

"He can," she replied.

"Then why—"

"Because you don't get as rich as Two Lonely Old Men by spending money frivolously." She fiercely worked the stiffness out of my legs. "Banished as I am to this backwater, I picked up a few talents here and there when the clientele proved unworthy of my more refined arts. There was no need to spring for something as ostentatious as a Mendmage when I can do the job just as swiftly. And besides…"

She leaned over me, her usually unpleasantly bitter expression twisted into a smile that I found much more unnerving.

"You *love* this."

She drove her knuckle into my side, eliciting a scream. But it lasted only as long as the pain did, my voice trailing off as my muscles shifted from agonizingly cramped to uncomfortably warm. She withdrew, set her hands on her hips, and looked me over as I lay on the table.

"Well, you'll be sore in the morning, but it's better than the alternative." She took me by the arm, helping me to my feet and guiding me to the bath—a marble pool of steaming water big enough for six women. "You'll be moving after a day."

"I'll feel better by then?" I asked as she helped lower me into the water.

"I didn't say that. I said you'd be moving after a day. That's when the next phase of the plan hits."

The plan.

The wounds were agonizing, even after the Vechine and Madame Fist had both done their work. But that wasn't what stung.

There'd been no time to berate Jero for not telling me about the schematics, or his theft of them, when we'd returned, much less time to punch him. He'd scurried off as soon as we'd gotten back to inform Two Lonely Old Men, leaving me with the good madame's ministrations. To inform. To plot. To scheme.

Don't get me wrong, if I had problems with dangerous, crazy plans, I wouldn't join them with such enthusiastic regularity. And I understood the need for secrecy when it comes to plans *this* dangerous and crazy. But I didn't like being left out of the planning part. Not that I didn't trust Jero and Two Lonely Old Men to know what they were doing, but...

When you're left out of the planning, you'll never know when they start planning what to do with you.

I grunted as I eased myself into the water. "How is it that the moody courtesan-turned-innkeep knows more about the plan than the woman who's supposed to actually *do* the plan?"

"I guess people just find me friendlier, you dumb bitch. Now sit here and soak for a bit. It'll help with the healing."

I leaned back against the edge of the tub, closed my eyes, and proceeded to try and do just that. It was made significantly harder, though, when Madame Fist upended a bucket of steaming hot water over my head.

I sputtered, pulling wet hair out of my eyes to stare up at her. "Does that help with the healing, too?"

"No. But it helps with the smell." She tossed the bucket aside and walked out of the room. "Do try to scrub more thoroughly, dear. I can't have you filling my inn with the reek of dead Revolutionaries and sewers."

I resisted the urge to get out of the tub and chase her down. I wasn't about to let it be said that Sal the Cacophony lets insults go unanswered. But if it happened to be said that Sal the Cacophony was fine with letting insults slide if it meant she could stay in a nice bath?

I could think of worse reputations.

I eased back in the tub and let the water seep into me. With every steam-soaked breath I took, I felt the pains melting off of me. My wound, the scrapes and scratches, the stiffness from the rides that had brought me to this dark stone hole of a city—one by one, every last pain felt like it dissolved in the water.

Except one.

My fingers went there before I even realized it, sliding across my body to my chest and finding a scar. My scar. The one that wound from my collarbone to my belly and painted my chest like a brand.

Years ago, it was given to me. A lifetime ago, a name ago, a lover ago—all cut short by a blade. In somewhere cold and dark, something had been torn out of me. Something I needed, something I loved, something that gave me the sky, had pulled itself out of my chest and fled into the dark.

I was someone else then. A loyal soldier of the Imperium. The greatest mage they had ever seen. Slayer of foes, ruiner of lives, destroyer of cities—and all I had left of that life was the scar.

It still hurt.

Just like it had the first night I had shown it to her. Back when she held my hand and gave me a name she had given no one else, and I knew that I wanted her to see me. All of me. We had gone to a dingy room in a dingy inn, drunk on wine and laughing at bad jokes that only we got. She tried to pull me on top of her. I resisted. I looked at her, as she looked at me, and I removed my clothes. And I showed her the scar.

She stared at it, this ugly thing that was a grave to the life I had once led, and I wanted her to scream, or to laugh, or to just be disgusted and leave. We could have both saved ourselves so much pain that way. But she hadn't done that. She had sat up. She had wrapped her hands around my hips. She had pulled me close, my chest against her lips, the scar close to her face.

And she had kissed it.

And I hadn't asked her to stop, no matter how bad it hurt.

And I whispered her name then, as I did last night, as I did now. "Liette."

For a while there, I thought that would do it. Just her lips. Just her name. I thought everything she could give me—all the gentle words and gentle hands—would make it stop hurting. I thought, if I just blocked it out, I could be happy with her and she with me and it wouldn't matter how bad this scar of mine ached when I woke up to cold mornings with her beside me.

For a while there, I really thought I could do it.

But like I said, not all pains are equal. The pain that I felt when I left her bed for the first time didn't hurt quite as badly as looking at that list of people who had given me this scar and thinking I'd never make them hurt just as bad. Through the years, as I came and went and tried a little less hard each time to make it stop hurting, eventually I realized that the only pain I was going to give was to her.

I could live with a lot of things. I'd gotten pretty good at it, actually. I'd walked away from townships I'd set ablaze without looking back. I'd put my sword through people who begged me not to and not lost a night's sleep over it.

But hurting her...

I shut my eyes, and with it, shut myself off to what I had seen in Meticulous's hideout.

Maybe that *had* been her work, her sigils, I had seen back there. And if I had them, maybe I could use them to track down where she had gone since I'd seen her last. Maybe I could find her and swear that this time was going to be different and say that it didn't hurt anymore.

But there would still be the list. And I'd still have this scar.

So I'd stay here. I'd help Two Lonely Old Men. And he'd help me. And if, in doing that, it spared her that pain...

Well, as far as trades went, I'd made worse.

I heard the door creak open behind me and bare feet padded across wet tile. I furrowed my brow and growled into the steam.

"If you're here to torture me again, I hope you're ready for a fight," I said.

The footsteps paused. She cleared her throat.

"I mean, if you want."

I turned at an unfamiliar voice. Agne the Hammer stood in the doorway, wearing a delicate purple silk robe that tried nobly to conceal her impressive musculature.

"But I *think* I can take you," she said, shooting me a smirk.

"Sorry," I said, turning away. "I thought you were...someone else."

"Someone fun, I hope." Rather delicately for someone that impressive, Agne padded to the other side of the tub and gestured to the water. "May I?"

"Oh. Sure." I reached toward the pile of my clothes nearby. "Let me get dressed and I'll leave you to it."

"Don't be ridiculous, darling. We just killed a man and burned down his house together," she laughed, untying the sash of her robe and letting it fall from her shoulders. "It'd be a little silly if we were so tragically modest around each other, no?"

I couldn't quite find it in me to blink at the sight of her, the silk robe pooling around her feet. I had to imagine that was a common reaction to anyone who happened to see all six and a half feet of Agne the Hammer unclothed. I'm sure that anyone might notice the perfect sculpt to her body, the rippling muscle shiny and pale like she'd been carved and polished from marble.

But my eyes were drawn to how clean she looked. Her skin was unmarred by scar or blemish, every inch of her perfectly polished and standing perfectly upright. That was an unusual look for a Vagrant—most of us carried scars and bent backs and long scowls, mementos of the roads we wandered etched into our skin. Yet she looked like she could have just as easily been at home in an Imperial court, some pristine maiden of effortless dignity and dainty laugh. Whatever anyone else might notice about her, I could only see that flawless poise.

Well, that and her thighs.

Damn thews looked strong enough to crush my head if it got between them.

"I always bathe around this time." She turned around, stretching, and across the muscles of her back, I could see her Vagrant's ink: a tattoo of a sledgehammer scrawled from the nape of her neck to the small of her back. "It gets rather dry in the mountains. Smart to keep your skin close to water before sleeping. I'd have been by earlier, but our esteemed employer insisted on a word."

"Yeah?" I let my gaze linger on her as long as I dared before she turned around and slipped into the tub. "Was he happy?"

"He will be eventually." She let out a contented purring sound as she sank up to the neck. "Mind you, he was just a *touch* cross at your wanton destruction."

"I was *trying* to kill a guy. There was nothing wanton about it." I rubbed my eyes. "What about what happened at the Crow Market?"

"The Ashmouths, smart as they are, aren't about to jeopardize relations with the Freemakers by raising too much of a fuss. Two Lonely Old Men managed to soothe them with considerable expense." She rolled her shoulders. "Jero, ever the silver tongue, managed to put the word out that the rest of the chaos was a couple of nobles having fun with magic. Once the guards caught wind of that rumor, they lost all interest in pursuing criminals they couldn't charge."

I stared at my reflection in the water. "The buildings we burned down...they weren't inhabited?"

"Oh, no, they were. Just by people who can't use magic." Agne flashed a bleak smile. "And if you think a guard will take up a common nul's complaint against a mage with money..." She glanced at my white hair, gestured. "Well, you're Imperial. You know how that goes."

Yeah.

I did know how that goes. The whole damn Scar did. It was the whole reason the Revolution started.

That wasn't what made my voice go soft and my eyes drift down to the water. That wasn't what made me look at my reflection and see a face full of regrets staring back at me.

"Was anyone killed?" I asked.

Agne hesitated before answering. "Somewhat."

"Somewhat?"

"No one was *outright* slain, but between the injuries, the loss of their homes, and winter coming..." She shrugged those broad shoulders helplessly. "I'd be shocked if Terassus didn't lose a few citizens."

"Fuck." I leaned back, covering my face with my hands. "Fuck, fuck, *fuck*."

"That's hardly going to help things," Agne chided.

"Oh yeah?" I glared at her between my fingers. "Are you about to tell me it wasn't my fault? It was just a freak accident?"

The warmth and smiles fled from her face and she regarded me coldly. "No."

"Good, because—"

"I'm about to tell you that if you weren't ready for people to die, you shouldn't have become a Vagrant." She raised her arm out of the water, stared contemplatively at the hand that had snapped a man's neck just hours ago. "That's what we do, after all. We destroy. We kill. When we served the Imperium, we did it for the Empress."

Her words hit me like a hammer across the head, cold and hard. I felt my scars ache. "And now that we're Vagrants," I muttered, "we do it for ourselves."

"Sometimes," she said.

She was right, of course. I knew that before I even opened my mouth. It wasn't a squeamish feeling, that sickness in the gut that comes when you've killed your first and follows you until your fourth. Rather, thinking about those people made my head heavy, my neck feel like lead.

I believed in this. I believed in making a better world. Enough that I was willing to accept the price it would take. But how much...

How many people did we get to kill to make a better world before it wasn't worth it anymore?

"Is there any other way to do what we do?" The question tumbled out of my mouth.

"We'll always destroy. I don't need to tell you that." She eyed the scar across my chest. It hurt beneath her gaze. "Sometimes we'll destroy something that needs to be destroyed. Sometimes we'll kill someone this world would be better off without. And sometimes we can do something good."

My voice was soft as steam. "When?"

"I don't know. But if you're not willing to try, you shouldn't be a Vagrant. Hell, you shouldn't even be a mage." She treaded across the water toward me, took me gently by the shoulder, and squeezed with a tenderness I didn't think those hands were capable of. "But you are a mage. So you have to try."

Her voice sounded foreign in my ears, like she was speaking another language. Words like the ones that came out of her mouth should be on an opera stage or in a book of love poetry. Words like those didn't belong in a place like the Scar.

This wasn't a place for trying. This was a place where people either did or died. The beasts prowling the night didn't care how hard you tried to escape them if they caught you. The armies didn't care how hard you tried for peace before they destroyed your home. This wasn't a place for people like Agne.

Words like hers, hands like hers—both so soft and gentle that I almost believed them—hit me harder than any blow could.

And maybe that's why I asked her what I did.

"You could have killed Meticulous any time you wanted," I observed. "But you didn't. Not until he tried to kill you. Why?"

She smiled softly, dropped her hand from my shoulder and slid back across the tub. "Do you know what Barter a Siegemage pays for our power?"

I nodded. The Lady Merchant asked a price from every mage for her power, but the price was never the same. Siegemages, for all their strength and invulnerability, paid in feelings. Fear, joy, love—they'd give up everything, eventually, if they kept using their power, becoming empty husks that lived for nothing and killed for anything.

Agne tilted her head to the right and pulled her hair back. There, between her ear and her jawline, I could see the faintest trace of a scar, the only blemish on her skin.

"I was eighteen," she said. "I barely even knew what my magic *was*, let alone what I'd have to pay for it." She lowered her hair, leaned back against the tub. "There was a boy. He had a knife. I didn't think before I acted. It was the last time I ever felt pain. I could take a hit in the face, be set on fire, take an arrow to the chest and I felt nothing. The Lady Merchant took that from me. I don't know what she'll take next if I keep using my powers…"

She closed her eyes, let out a slow, sad sigh.

"But I don't want to give it to her."

I suppose that made sense.

Or it would have made sense, to someone else. But with every word she spoke, my scar ached a little more.

"Well!" Agne rose from the tub, the water that came up to my waist barely reaching the middle of her thighs. "That's rather enough sentimentality for one night, I suppose, no?" She plucked a towel from the floor and began to dry herself. "Not that I haven't loved our little chat, but I'd hate to be responsible for people thinking Sal the Cacophony loved girl talk." She shot me a wink over her shoulder. "I know how much you love stories about yourself."

I glared at her. She was completely right, of course, but I wasn't about to have it said that Sal the Cacophony was vain.

"Besides," she said, tossing the towel aside and pulling her robe back on, "we've got business to attend to soon."

My glare turned to a puzzled look. "What kind of business?"

"They haven't told you?"

"I've been getting the crap kicked out of me by a surly masseuse since we got back. No one's told me shit."

"Urda's forgery of Meticulous's message will arrive, courtesy of Tuteng's bird, at Revolutionary headquarters within a few days," she said. "The command of the Iron Fleet will be advised that the route they intend to take is heavily guarded by Imperial forces and they should take another route."

"One where we can ambush them," I finished. "Assuming they don't figure out Urda's message is a fake."

"If there was even a possibility of that happening, darling, Two Lonely Old Men wouldn't have hired him." Agne cinched her robe. "The Fleet will go where we need them to, but there's still the matter of procuring a means of getting aboard. It's not as though airships are known for their accessibility, hmm?"

"And Two Lonely Old Men has a plan for that?"

"Well, he *is* a genius."

"Of course." I started to pull myself out of the tub. "I suppose I'd better get out, too, then."

"Actually..." Agne held up a hand, wincing. "It was requested that you spend a little additional time in the bath. With perfumed oils, if we can find some."

I wasn't quite sure *what* she was implying, but I was sure that I wanted to punch her for it.

"With all due offense, darling, you have a certain distinctive... aroma about you," she said. "Something akin to a...a 'raccoon having sex with the corpse of his dead sister in a puddle of puke,' I believe Yria described it as?"

"Was *she* the one who requested it?"

"Yes. Well, one of them. One of many, really." She cleared her throat. "All of us, if I'm being honest. It was rather democratic, actually." She waved a hand. "At any rate, the next phase of the plan requires us to be at our most charming, elegant, and fragrant."

I quirked a brow. "What kind of fucking plan is it?"

"Well, the only creatures capable of the kind of flight we need are Oyakai birds. And those are only found here in Terassus. Specifically, in the possession of—"

"The nobles," I finished for her. "Yeah, I remember seeing them. How does Two Lonely Old Men intend to get them?"

"Well, as it happens, the nobles are throwing a banquet tomorrow evening—a favorite pastime of theirs, I'm told." A sparkle I didn't like one bit glimmered in her eyes. "And it just so happens that Jero acquired an invitation for two young ladies of high refinement." She giggled behind her hand. "Or two Vagrants who can pass for them. And you know what that means."

My eyes widened and my heart sank. "Don't fucking say it."

She clapped her hands together, hopping from foot to foot, all dignity lost as she let out an *extremely* unpoised titter.

"Disguises!" she all but shrieked.

"Disguises." I groaned. "I fucking *hate* fucking disguises."

"Well, I advise you get over that." She walked around the tub, smiling. "And clean up your language while you're at it. You and I are the only ones in our little conspiracy that can pass for Imperials, after all." She leaned down and ruffled my hair. "So do try to look at least a little happy about it, hmm?"

She paused, raised her fingers to her nose, sniffed them, and grimaced.

"Also wash your hair," she said as she stepped out of the room. "We're going to bring down empires, darling. Let's try not to smell like a barn when we do it, shall we?"

NINETEEN

THE CANED TOAD

H is name is Keltithan. Keltithan yun Attoro."

Jero didn't look at me as he spoke, his eyes focused on the pot of cream in his hand, a companion to the dozens of other delicate-looking pots of brightly colored alchemic powders, plasters, and perfumes I had only ever caught glimpses of in the windows of shops too nice for the likes of me.

"He is—was, pardon—a Judge, a decorated war hero of the Imperium. His daughter, talented mage she may be, however, is *not*. Specifically, because he called in a favor to relieve her of service to the military."

"And they agreed to this?" I furrowed my brow in confusion. "I've never heard of the Imperium letting a mage out of the army."

"Don't talk. It makes your face move too much." He daubed a cloth circle into the cream and pressed it against my cheek, over my scar. "Anyway, yes. Considering that Keltithan had an extensive list of favors to accompany the extensive list of people he had murdered for the Imperium, they allowed him to retire to Terassus with his family to live out their days with their fortune in peace. Conditionally."

"What kind of conditions?" I asked, drawing a wince from Jero.

"Was I not clear when I said *don't talk*?" he muttered, hastily grabbing a brush and smoothing something across my cheek. "Honestly, it's like you have no respect for any craft that doesn't end in explosions." His composure resumed, he continued his work. "There were a few conditions—people he had to kill, donations he had to make, more people he had to kill, and so forth—but there's only one we're concerned with.

"In his time serving the Imperium, our friend the Judge was something of a consummate bird rider. From the backs of great fliers, he led over a hundred successful missions against the Revolution. Ever dutiful to the Imperium, he agreed that he would continue breeding Oyakai for his Empress. They're hatched, reared, trained, and groomed here, tamed for hunting and war with such doting affection from Keltithan that not a feather is out of place when they're finally sent to the frontlines to be gunned down by Revolutionary cannons."

I would have said "charming," but he seemed especially into what he was doing.

"I suppose that's why the good Judge enjoys throwing banquets in honor of each new generation that he rears," Jero continued, voice meticulous as he used a tiny brush to apply fine lines. "It's his last chance to show them any affection before they go and die in a war they don't understand for people whose names they don't know."

"Sounds expensive," I replied. "More expensive than just giving a mage over to the Imperium. Why not just give her over?"

This time, Jero didn't scold me for talking. He merely paused and stared past me, to some distant horizon.

"I guess," he said, "he doesn't want her to die."

I didn't know what to say to that. It was uncomfortable to hear. Even less comfortable to think about. Fortunately, Jero didn't give me a chance to do either before he resumed his work.

"Regardless, tonight is fortunate for both us *and* his birds, since they'll be getting a fancy banquet in their honor and then flying away with six dashing strangers instead of heading off to, you know, die horribly to cannon fire. Assuming, of course, you and Agne don't fuck it all up.

"You and she are the only ones who can pass for Imperials—well, you, she, and the twins, but I'm not nearly drunk, high, or stupid enough to send those two into a civil dinner," he continued. "You'll get in, find a place clear enough for her to open a portal, and Yria will do the rest."

"The rest being all the killing," I added.

"If we do it right, there won't be any killing," he said. "The Imperials will be distracted by their fancy banquet and we can slip away before anyone knows."

He pulled back and looked me over. A smile—the sort I had only seen him make when he saw Meticulous's cold corpse—spread over his face as he set the pots and brushes aside.

"Okay, *now* you can talk," he said. "Any questions?"

"Just three."

"The first one being?"

I glanced at his *very* extensive collection of cosmetics on the table. "How'd you get so good at makeup?"

He looked at me like I had just asked him something entirely less fair and entirely more dumb. But I couldn't help it—we'd spent the better part of three hours in his room, me in alternating poses of standing, bowing, and sitting in a high-backed chair, him busily applying powders, rouges, plasters, and creams to my face and body.

"Honey," he replied, voice dripping with condescension. "I'm good at *everything* I do."

I scratched the back of my head. "I just haven't met many men with such a"—I glanced back at his table—"collection."

"Well, I haven't met many women who look, smell, and laugh like they've just come out of a drunken fistfight that ended in an orgy, so I guess we're even." He shot me a glare. "Speaking of, be sure to curb that tongue around the Imperials. An uncouth mouth betrays a disguise quicker than anything else."

"I was still raised in Cathama," I replied, standing up and rubbing out the cramps that I had collected from sitting in the chair. "I can be a proper lady when I want to, you cock."

"Right." He sighed. "An intimate familiarity with cosmetics is useful to any man who doesn't want to look like shit. And since my line of work for Two Lonely Old Men requires me to look like *many* different kinds of shits, I'm better than most."

"Still," I said, "this is a *lot* of effort. Why not hire a Nightmage? A Vagrant could make me look like anything, flawlessly."

"And a Scrymage—of which there will certainly be *many* at an Imperial dinner—could see right through it. But they won't be able to see through my work. Magic is fallible. Fashion is eternal."

I guess that stood to reason. While there weren't *nearly* enough for my tastes, there were more than enough stories about Sal the Cacophony that a scarred woman with cloud and wing tattoos on her forearms would be easy to spot amid a banquet full of people who wanted to kill her on sight.

"Well, my second question was going to be how you managed to do my hair so nice," I said, "but I guess that answers that, too."

"Oh. No. *That's* because I used to run with a lot of courtesans."

I blinked. "Wait, but…"

"Don't think too hard about it. What's the third?"

I watched him as he packed his makeup. And though he appeared to have his eyes on his tools, I knew he had the corner of one on me. He'd always had that, hidden in the wrinkles of his eyes—wherever he appeared to be looking, he always had eyes on everyone in every room we'd been in. Agne hadn't noticed it, the twins hadn't, I'd be surprised even if Two Lonely Old Men had.

But I had.

Because I had been a soldier, too, once.

"When," I asked softly, "did you leave the Revolution?"

He didn't stop what he was doing. Not for long, anyway. He merely slowed as he kept packing. He'd known I'd ask this eventually.

"When did you figure out I'd been in it?" he asked.

"I started figuring it out when we first met," I replied. "You had a soldier's habits—walked too stiff, kept looking for enemies that weren't there. Then you knew how to track down Meticulous, you knew where he hid his documents, you knew how to use the Vechine." I folded my arms, stared at him. "Desertion from the Revolution is punishable by death. But you're still alive."

"I am." This time, he did stop. He paused, putting his hands on the table. His body shook, so hard that he seemed to shrink to someone more broken. "My brother isn't."

Ah. I winced. *That'd do it.*

He shook his head, tried to find his composure, failed. "He was older than me. When he went into the Revolution, I went with him. We fought. We killed. He died. Our sergeant wouldn't let me go retrieve his body. We gave the Revolution years of service, years of fighting, my brother's life." Bitterness crept into his voice. "The Revolution didn't even give him a grave."

I stared at the back of his head as he shook, quiet. I wanted to tell myself it was out of respect—Jero and I were fighters, silence was our way. We spoke with weapons and actions, not with words. I told myself that...

But I wasn't a good enough liar to believe that.

But it was easier to believe than the truth. Because I'd seen so much death, lost so many people, walked so many miles with so many scars weighing me down that something like dying somewhere with no one to mourn me, no one to bury me, was just something that I had always expected to happen. The truth was that all I could feel for Jero's words, cold and bitter and trembling as they were, was...nothing.

And that truth cut me deeper than any blade.

"What was his name?" I asked.

"Jandi," Jero replied.

"No," I said, "the name they gave him. The name they gave you."

Jero stiffened up. Over his shoulder, he looked at me cautiously.

"Erstwhile," he said. "Jandi and Jero Erstwhile."

That explained more than I thought.

A Revolutionary name was such a tangle of logic, meaning, and adjectives, but I had figured out the basics of it. Whenever a family entered the Revolution, they were given a name by the Great General, based on how loyal or valuable they were to his Revolution. Some names—Proud, Stern, Relentless, Graceful—were honorable.

Some names were not.

"Does Two Lonely Old Men know?" I asked.

"It's the whole reason he hired me," Jero said. "But the others don't." He shot me a look. "And they don't need to."

I nodded. "Where did your brother die?"

"Who's Liette?"

I recoiled, as if struck. And, as if struck, my first instinct was to punch that name out of his mouth. Instead, I settled for glaring at him.

"What?"

"You spoke her name in your sleep," he said. "I don't give away

secrets without getting them back. I'll tell you where Jandi died...
so long as you tell me who that person is."

How many other people knew Jero Erstwhile? Maybe a few.
Or maybe just me now. I knew it hadn't been easy for him to tell
me that. Secrets are like knives buried into your own heart—they
hurt to carry, but they hurt more to move. I knew from the way he
stood—still shaking, still small—that his had been buried deep.

Still.

Not as deep as mine.

"Right," he said, after a very long moment of me pointedly not
answering. "That's enough banter. We've got to finish your disguise."

I glanced down at my forearms, my tattoos hidden beneath layers
of makeup, and frowned. His work was impressive, don't get me
wrong—but so was the collection of cramps I had accumulated sitting still for this long. I understood the delicacy of this operation,
but I was also beginning to suspect I could have just shot my way to
these fucking birds by now.

Jero didn't seem to notice, though, as he flung open the doors of
his wardrobe and started sorting through the collection of clothes
with the enthusiasm of a dog in heat.

"My skill with cosmetics, impressive as you and I might know it
to be, isn't *quite* enough to carry this through." He poked through
an assembly of outfits, disguises, and hats—he had a *lot* of hats. "But
while you might *look* like a woman who can't belch the first six verses
to 'My Adoring Mother,' we both know that's not true."

"Impressed you enough at the time," I cast a mutter at his back.

"And while I have every faith in your ability to be presentable,"
he continued, ignoring me, "it's a pious corpse that operates on faith
alone." He paused, smiled as he found something in the wardrobe
and pulled it free. "My job..."

He turned to face me, holding up a garment in both hands, his
smile bright behind it.

"Is to give you *every* advantage."

A long piece of shimmering silk, the color of amethyst, hung from
his hands. Cut in the Imperial style—loose from the hips down,
tight from the waist up, cinched together with a thick sash in the
middle—it made me feel like I should be charged just to look at it.

"Well?" he asked, shooting me a glance that was half expectant and half incontinent.

"It's a dress," I observed.

The look he gave me suggested that punching him in the face and force-feeding him his own dog would have been kinder than what I had said.

"It's a dress painstakingly made to the very *pinnacle* of Cathama fashion," he continued. "This will allow you to blend seamlessly into the elite of the Imperium. Wearing this, you could shoot a man in the middle of that banquet and everyone would simply assume that was the latest trend." He held up a hand, considering. "For the record, though, *don't* shoot a man in the middle of that banquet."

"Yeah, it's nice and all, but"—I gestured to my leggings, somehow still dirty from the road despite repeated washings—"I'm really more of a"—my eyes lingered on that very long, very nice skirt—"*pants* kind of girl."

"You're going to a fancy banquet for fancy people," Jero replied. "Fancy people don't wear pants." He stepped toward me. "Look, you'll see what I mean once you try it on."

I took a step backward as though he'd pulled a weapon on me. "How do we know it even *fits* me?"

"Please. Madame Fist tailored this especially for you."

"How does she have my measurements?"

"I gave them to her."

My eyes went wide. "How...how do *you* have my measurements?"

⚔

I stared into the mirror.

"Well? What do you think?"

I didn't know who I was looking at.

To hear the stories, Sal the Cacophony was a woman whose very appearance made the wind hold its breath and birds flee from the sky. They spoke of a woman hard as the blade she carried who came out of the dark and carried fire in her hands, wearing her Vagrant tattoos like they were armor and her scars like trophies, striding across the land and leaving ashes and screams in her wake.

"Understand, without Fist actually having you on hand, there's some guesswork. But we didn't have time for that."

The woman in the mirror was not that.

She was someone small and slight in a purple dress that clung too tightly to her chest and too loose around her legs. She wore silk instead of leather. Her hair was done up in elegant braids rather than whipping around her face. And instead of scars and tattoos, she had . . . nothing. No wounds. No blood. No dirt.

I stared at her. And she stared back.

"It'll limit your movement, to be sure," Jero said. "But the skirt opens up along the thigh, good enough to do what you need to do if things go wrong. Which they won't, obviously, but no plot to overthrow empires ever goes flawlessly."

And neither of us recognized the other.

"You're hesitant," he said, sighing. "I understand. It's a difficult adjustment, but I assure you that—"

"I look normal."

It was my lips moving, but it didn't seem like my voice. It was the woman in the mirror who spoke. That woman who wasn't injured, wasn't inked, wasn't . . . broken.

She could go anywhere, this woman. She could go to a market to shop instead of hunting people down. She could go into a tavern without knowing someone might be waiting to kill her. She could go home, to a house without swords or guns in it, to someone who wasn't a ghost, and they'd drink together to enjoy their time together instead of to forget it.

She hadn't killed anyone, this woman who was under all my scars, all my ink, all my stories.

I didn't know her. But I envied her.

Jero stood beside me. No reassurances, no condolences, no words at all. He stared at the woman in the mirror alongside me and I knew he saw what I did.

"Yes," he said softly. "You do."

I knew he envied her, too.

I slid my hands down the dress. It felt weird, this silk without bloodstains or dirt on it.

"Can I keep this?" I asked. "After we're done?"

He nodded. I smiled softly.

"I guess I just want to . . . look normal. Even if I can't be—"

"You can."

For the first time, I looked at him in the mirror. He stood behind me—I hadn't realized when he had gotten so close. I hadn't realized how tall he was or how deep his wrinkles went or when his hands had found my shoulders.

"When we're done," he said, "there's going to be a place without the Imperium, without the Revolution, without soldiers or killers or hunters. Two Lonely Old Men is going to build it with that Relic. And we're going to help him. Once it's all done, we can be heroes."

He gave my shoulders a squeeze. His hands were delicate. Warm.

"Or we can just be nobody special at all."

He sighed. His face sank in the mirror. His hands slid from my shoulders. He didn't say it—he didn't have to. I already knew.

That was a nice dream. But it was just a dream. For now, we were still killers, him and I. For now, we were going to steal and lie and cheat. For now, we were going to make that place out of bloodshed and thievery and the death of empires.

We weren't normal.

For now.

"I guess it's fine." I walked—or did my best while in these shoes— across the room. The silk hugged me tighter than I was used to and I don't think I'd ever really get used to the feeling of so much makeup on my skin, but I could bear it. "Only one problem."

I turned around, trying to see my own ass.

"Where am I supposed to hide the Cacophony in this thing?"

Jero gave me that wincing smile that told me I was going to hit him in the testicles before this night was over.

"Yeah," he said, "about that..."

TWENTY

YUN ATTORO ESTATE

Wine is a drink for assholes.

Now, don't get me wrong, I know *many* fine wine drinkers. I count them among some of my oldest and dearest friends. That doesn't mean they aren't assholes, though.

Not that whiskey isn't a drink for assholes, too, but whiskey is for honest assholes. Whiskey is a drink that doesn't lie—within one sip of it, you know where it came from, how much it's worth, and whether or not you're going to survive the night with it. Wine is for an entirely different kind of asshole.

With whiskey, you fight and, if the company is nice, you make up. With wine, you mostly spend a lot of time talking.

"It's not that I hate the nuls."

Like this asshole.

"If anything, I have great respect for what they're able to achieve within their limitations." Keltithan yun Attoro paused to drain the last sip of wine and hummed. "Nuls build our bridges. Nuls pave our roads. Nuls *make* the Imperium what it is."

He waved a hand. A servant, toting a silver tray brimming with glasses, responded to his summons and walked over promptly. Empty eyes to match an empty smile were offered, along with the tray, as Keltithan took another glass and waved the servant away. The servant made a deep bow, accompanied by a crinkling sound, before wandering off to join the other dozen identical servants toting trays to bring treats and desserts to the other well-dressed guests.

I had to say, the quality of Keltithan's servants was impressive. They responded promptly, didn't drop anything, had very little tearing. Really, if it weren't for their empty eyes, the crinkling noises they made when they moved, and the fact that they were all identical, you couldn't tell at all that they were paper golems.

"But do they *fight* for it?" Keltithan mused, stroking his beard. "Do they know what it is to use the art? To pay the Lady Merchant her Barter so that the savages may be settled and civilization may continue? Of course not. How would you even describe it to them? How can you describe music to the deaf, or beauty to the blind?"

His gray hair and deep-set wrinkles spoke of his age, but his rigid posture and the *numerous* commendations he wore on his purple-and-black robes told me that Keltithan had never truly left the Imperial army. The blade he wore at his hip, though it hadn't seen combat in ages, was still polished and sharpened to a high sheen. Here was a military man, through and through.

"Nor would you trust them to lead," Keltithan continued. "Hence why this whole 'Revolution' business is utter tripe."

Which meant he actually believed the shit coming out of his mouth.

I suppose I could have been more understanding. The Imperium had given him quite a bit, after all, including the massive manor we currently stood in.

Bigger than any other house looming upon the cliffs, the Attoro Estate spanned almost three miles of sprawling gardens of plants kept alive by warming spells, corrals for riding birds, barracks for house guards, and wine cellars big enough to keep his many, *many* guests good and drunk.

In shades of purple and bronze, they milled about the immense banquet halls, their hair done up in Imperial styles, the more elite of them wearing Imperial masks, laughing and joking and singing along to ghostwritten instruments playing old opera tunes. Marionette specters of pink and purple warriors reenacted famous battles in ghoulishly vivid detail, illusionary though it may be, to the delighted applause of onlookers.

And looming over everything were the birds.

Oyakai. Ten of them. Each one twice as tall as a man. Legs long and thin like spears, ending in sharp talons. Beaks broad and shoe-shaped. Eyes bright and intelligent and surveying the party from their perches on high. Their plumage was soft, in black and white and red and blue, and occasionally on full display when one of them would extend their great wings and let out a keening cry, silencing the festivities as every eye looked up in awe at them.

Including mine.

My breath left me each time I looked at them. To ride just one of them for an hour, to feel the wind in my face again, I would have killed a hundred men.

"Now, if they wanted peace and to return to their old lives, we'd let them, surely."

Which meant I could stomach this shithead for another few hours, I guess.

He continued droning on, seeming oblivious to the fact that my eyes were wandering the hall. Somewhere, hidden in this sea of ass-holes, must be a room that would suit our purposes. All we needed was a forgotten quarters, a neglected storeroom, even a shit-filled stable—anywhere no one would notice a portal being erected.

Between the marionette illusionists, the spectral band, and the occasional besotted boast that turned into an impromptu duel between visiting mages with too much wine and too little self-esteem, no one would sense the magic. But a giant swirling purple door from nothingness tends to attract attention we specifically did not need. However, we weren't going to get the Oyakai we *did* need unless we found a place for Yria to portal in.

Though, as my eyes drifted up toward the ceiling, I couldn't help but wonder how even a Doormage, even one so criminally famous as Yria the Cell, would help us steal monstrous birds ten feet tall and brimming with claws.

Especially when said monstrous birds were situated in the middle of a banquet positively teeming with mages who can and would bring all their powers to bear in stopping us, including—but not limited to—summoning fire from nothingness, conjuring ghosts from one's darkest fears, and maybe spitting bees... and the bees are made of lightning or some shit like that, I don't know.

I didn't know what these sparkly fucks could do.

But I know they can kill me a lot fucking quicker than they could if I was armed, I thought, taking an *especially* spiteful sip of wine. *Fucking thank fucking you, fucking Jero.*

I could see the logic, of course. Missions relying on subtlety typically didn't benefit from the presence of a weapon called the Cacophony, after all. But without that weight at my hip, that heat from his brass, that knowledge that I could kill anyone…

I felt cold. Colder than I should.

I had an old fart droning in my ear and no whiskey to drown him out and no gun to bash his face in. So, I wasn't in the best of moods.

Still, that didn't mean I wasn't going to be a professional.

"Hey," I said, interrupting whatever he was blithering about—taxes or some shit, I think. "Is there a room around here that no one's using?"

Keltithan furrowed his manicured brows at me. "Beg pardon, my lady?"

"Like a…toilet?" I scratched the side of my head, drained the last of my wine. "Or a storeroom or something? I don't know."

I would have cringed at the entirely inappropriate blush that colored his cheeks, if I hadn't already been internally screaming when the much-worse-than-entirely-inappropriate smirk crossed his face.

"My lady," he said, "I…admit, it's been some time since the lady of the manor passed, but I don't know if…" He was positively beaming as he cleared his throat and straightened up. "May I ask what for?"

I rolled my eyes. "Because I'm just *gagging* for your wrinkled cock, *obviously.*"

After that, he turned an entirely different shade of red. "What did you just—"

"Darling! There you are!"

A charming voice interjected, followed by a charming six and a half feet of muscle wrapped up in silk. Agne, her hair elegantly styled and her dress flattering, imposed her prestigious self between the Judge and I. She took me by the arm—just hard enough to let me know she could break it, if she wanted to.

"I've been searching all over for you." She pivoted gracefully to Keltithan and cooed in a saccharine voice. "I do hope my companion hasn't dreadfully offended you, good Judge."

"As a matter of fact," Keltithan growled, narrowing his eyes, "she *just* said something that would merit a duel, were we in the capital."

"Oh, I *know*, isn't she just *terrible*?" Agne waved a limp hand at him, her smirk devious. "She's from the *lower* side of Cathama, you know. Their senses of humor down there are just *horribly* risqué, aren't they?" She took Keltithan's hand in her own, squeezed it. "You received the Esteem of the Capital medal, did you not, sir? You must know all about the raunchiness of the lower side?"

Keltithan blinked, shook his head like he didn't know what was happening. I barely knew myself.

"Uh, yes, of course," he said. "T-terribly raunchy down there, they are. But still—"

"Oh yes, I completely agree. Raunchiness aside, manners *must* be upheld. But surely you'd not begrudge a joke in bad taste." She took a pointed step closer to him, pouted. "She's my only friend here, sir. Please permit me to educate her as opposed to throwing her out and leaving me all alone?"

Keltithan glanced from me to Agne before smiling softly. He raised her gloved hand to his lips and placed a kiss upon it.

"My beautiful doe, I would offend myself if I did not honor your request."

Damn. I guess she *did* deserve to be the charm.

She made a low bow before damn near hauling me off my feet in her haste to get me away from him. She drew me in close and growled in my ear.

"What the *fuck* are you doing?"

"Being classy." We passed a fancy lady who was too slow to notice me snatching the wineglass out of her hand. "As hell."

"We're supposed to be searching for a means of bringing the others in," she whispered. "That is *not* helped by you being conspicuous."

"*Me?* What about you?"

"What *about* me?" she huffed.

I gestured across the room. She glanced toward the crowd of about a dozen men who had clustered together to gaze at her adoringly. She smiled, offered them a delicate wave of her fingers, and promptly sent them into an argument over whom that gesture had been meant for.

"That's different," she replied.

"*How* is it different?"

"Because *I'm* manipulating the attentions of *multitudes* of people who would otherwise notice *you* searching for a place to open the portal, like you *should* be doing." She sniffed, straightened her gloves. "Also, I look amazing. I can't help it."

I wanted to be mad at that, but she really did look stunning.

"What the fuck does it matter?" I hissed, gesturing to the Oyakai overhead. "Those things are in full view of everyone. How the fuck are we going to get them out of here?"

She waved my concerns down. "Don't worry about it. Jero will handle it."

"How?"

"There's a plan."

"What plan?"

"I...don't actually know." Agne sighed, looked out over the crowd. "Two Lonely Old Men is a Freemaker. A machinist. He's the one who assembles the moving parts to make it work. The parts themselves don't know their own function, yet if the machine moves, they've done their work."

"That would be an excellent metaphor if we were actually moving parts instead of two women who are going to be horrifically murdered if shit goes to hell," I growled. "Which we stand a *much* greater chance of being, considering we don't fucking know the plan."

Agne's face furrowed as she tried to think of a response. Failing to find one, she simply set a hand on my shoulder and sighed.

"I will get you out of here," she said. "No matter what shit goes to what hell. I promise you that."

She looked over my head toward the rear of the banquet hall. From the marching pillars, curtains hung, though between them I could see the shadowy outlines of furniture. The crowd there had thinned out from a raucous gathering to a few couples seeking the shadows. And *most* of them were either so deep into their cups or each other's lips that they wouldn't notice a cannon going off, let alone me.

"That will be our point," Agne whispered. "I haven't seen anyone go past there, not even the servants, and I've been watching it all night."

"That only makes it more likely that someone will notice someone who *is* going there."

"I'll take care of that," she replied.

"How?"

"I'd tell you." She winked at me. "But it'd only make you mad."

With that, Agne turned on her heel and started an elegant walk to the center of the banquet. She glanced around, pointedly dropped her glass to the floor with a shatter, and promptly fell down, neatly.

"*Oh dear.*" She barely raised her voice.

And she might as well have blared a war horn.

From the crowds of the banquet, a *truly* astonishing number of men—and more than a few women—came surging forward. Young upstart mages, old veterans, elegant dignitaries—all walks of life joined together, fighting and cursing at each other in their bid to be the first one to help Agne up.

As the throng descended around her, earning curious glances, she had just enough time to shoot me a smirk and a wink. I glared back. What the fuck had that been? All the powers of a Siegemage at her disposal and she just fucking *fell down* and got the attention of every slavering maw present? What kind of birdshit was that to—

Wow, she was right. That *did* make me angry.

And it did mean that nobody was looking toward me as I slipped away past the various bodies in various romantic positions and disappeared behind the curtains.

And into a room full of ghosts.

My hand shot for my hip as I saw them. They loomed out of the darkness, dozens of figures creeping out of the shadows, lurking closer to me. My heart lodged in my throat, made my breath run short as my fingers searched for my gun.

I realized that I didn't have him around the same time I realized the figures weren't moving.

Shapes. Furniture. Mirrors, maybe. Dozens of them, hidden beneath sheets. It had been a trick of the shadows, I think, that had made me think they were moving. Or my own nerves gnawing at me. They weren't moving. They weren't real.

They aren't real, I told myself, slowing my breathing. *They aren't real. The ghosts aren't—*

"I miss you."

A voice whispered in my ear. I turned. In the gloom, I saw someone standing there. Not something hidden beneath a sheet—this was a person, a woman, standing in the darkness. Staring at me.

I stared at her, waiting for her to move, to talk. But she didn't. Another ghost maybe. Or maybe I had been seen. Either way, I couldn't ignore it. I started creeping forward and, as I did, I could make out features: feminine curves, gentle lips moving, a pair of eyes.

Full of sorrow.

My heart froze for a moment before I realized those eyes were made of stone. Along with the curves. And the moving lips. A statue, talking, whispering in a distant, airy voice.

"I will always be with you."

I furrowed my brow. This wasn't *quite* how I imagined finally going fucking nuts—I had thought there'd be a lot more shooting and screaming.

"One ton of metal."

I whirled. Another figure, another woman, was standing behind me. This one, though, was no statue. She was flesh, blood, and a pair of twinkling purple eyes flashing in the dark.

Though I visibly bristled at the surprise, she paid me no mind. She walked, hands neatly folded behind her back, to stand beside me. Her posture was rigid, her gait flawlessly deliberate, and, even when standing still, she was noticeably tense beneath a long formal coat, as though even now, with only me and the statue here, she expected one of us to fight her.

While I couldn't speak for the creepy fucking piece of stone, the sword hanging off this newcomer's hip meant I sure as hell wasn't about to try anything.

"Two hundred for the statue itself to get her likeness, eight hundred for an opera actor to replicate her voice," the woman whispered, studying the statue. "But the most expensive part was the Spellwright who enchanted her. One thousand went to that."

She raised a slender hand wrapped in a white glove and drew a pair of fingers across the statue's twitching lips. Her eyes narrowed, amethysts so cut and clear I thought the statue might bleed under her scorn.

"Two full regiments of soldiers, each one equipped with the latest spellwritten arms, more than enough to hold a fortress in the most contested territory." She dropped her hands promptly. "That is what the good Judge spent on regrets."

"Regrets?"

She turned that sharp blade of a gaze upon me, and in the scant light offered by the room, I could see her in short, smooth fragments.

Hair, Imperial white, cut severely short and shorn at the sides. Fine boots and leggings offset a lean, muscular figure that her coat—military in make, I noticed—tried to obscure. Short, slender, a dagger of a woman, polished to a high sheen and sharpened to a killing edge.

"The late Lady yun Attoro," she said. "Slain in a Revolutionary counterattack when they overran the garrison at the edge of the Valley. He had this created to 'honor' her."

I looked toward the statue. "Romantic."

"Pointless." She studied the stone, as if she could find a weakness there. "He could honor her by staying in the service, by helping the Imperium, by *fighting*. Keltithan, like all these other overstuffed birds swilling outside, measure their worth only through things they can see, in trophies and ballads, like common Vagrants."

"And how ought a warrior measure their worth?"

"There is only one measure of a warrior." Her eyes fell. Her hand set upon the hilt of her blade. "It is in how many lives their sword saved."

I let out a low hum. With predatory swiftness, she fixed that gaze upon me.

"You disagree?"

"No." I cleared my throat. "Not in theory, anyway."

"Go on," she said, with a tone of voice that suggested doing so was a bad idea.

Still, that'd never stopped me before.

"What you say is all well and noble, truly," I continued. "I can't find a single fault in it, logically or emotionally. And yet..."

I felt her eyes, that sharp stare, digging into me with every word. But my own gaze was on the statue, on those stone eyes fixed on some forlorn horizon. Whatever truth she saw in the darkness, I dearly wanted to know.

"I guess," I sighed, "I understand not being able to let go." I turned toward the short woman and offered a sad, small smile. "Everyone does eventually."

At this, she furrowed her brow. Her stare went from cutting to confused as she squinted at me searchingly. Her mouth hung open for a brief moment before she spoke.

"Are you, uh..." She scratched the back of her neck. "Flirting with me?"

I returned her squint. "Are you fucking drunk?"

Suddenly her eyes snapped open. The sharp dagger of a woman was instantly replaced by fumbling lips, a shaking head, and hands waving in a flimsy declaration of peace.

"Oh!" she said. "Oh no. My apologies, madam. I only thought...it's just..." She sighed, lowered her eyes, and stared at me sheepishly. "This is the first time I've been in a city in a long time. I sort of...don't...talk to people..." She cleared her throat. "Much."

I quirked a brow. "I take it you've been busy on the front, then?"

A grin grew across her face. "What gave it away? The coat? The sword?"

"That," I replied, "and that whole rant about warriors and weapons."

"Oh. Right. In any event, you are correct, madam." She reached out to take my hand, folding into a stiff bow to press her forehead against my fingers. "Velline ki Yanatoril, Honored Sword of the Empress, at your service, my lady."

I couldn't help but grin. This is the sort of decorum you only saw in opera—hell, this gesture hadn't been used in Cathama for a hundred years. I'll be honest, it made me feel a little less like an infiltrator and more like...

I don't know. Special?

"You honor me, madam," I replied as she released my hand. I glanced out toward the party roiling past the curtains. "Though I think the army would prefer you to be out there honoring more important people."

She let out a low grunt of discontent. "If it were up to me, I'd be back on the front instead of wasting time swilling overpriced wine with overpriced people."

My eyes drifted down to the sword hanging from her hip and promptly threatened to roll out of my skull. I recognized the make of that blade, the tinge of dark purple that suffused the metal. That was an Imperial weapon, one bestowed with honors from the Empress herself.

And she never gave it to anyone who hadn't spilled an ocean of blood for her.

"*But*, as the honorable generals are keen to remind me," Velline continued, "money is what makes the army march and these squawking nobles love to get as close as they can to war without actually getting their hands dirty."

She gestured to the collection of sheet-draped furniture. "Hence why I'm here with Keltithan's less impressive trophies. It was the perfect place to hide." She shot me a smile. "Though I'm happy to share the company with a fellow warrior."

I had to stop myself from spitting my wine out in shock—it might have been a drink for assholes, but it was still a drink. I cleared my throat, put my best shit-eating grin on, and batted my eyelashes in a way I hoped wasn't *too* creepy.

"Why, madam," I said, "I'm simply a traveler from the capital, trying my best to—"

"I'm not going to reveal you, if you're worried about that," Velline said. "I'd sooner throw you to the birds than those fops out there."

I maintained my smile for a moment before the strain became too much. I sighed into my glass of wine as I took another sip. "How'd you know?"

She gestured to her cheek, right where my scar would be. "Your wound crinkles at the edges when you smile. I don't think anyone else would notice."

Anyone else, I noted as I glanced at her sword, *who hadn't given someone a wound like this.*

"Does it hurt?"

I blinked. "What?"

"Does it still hurt?" Her eyes were keen again as she stared at me, though no longer quite so sharp.

Smart thing to do would be to lie, tell her no. Then I could just keep lying, tell her whatever would get her out of here so I could finish what I had come here to do. But I didn't do that. I met her stare. And I spoke.

"Every day."

She nodded, pressed a hand to her side. "Mine too. Ten years old, but sometimes I wake up and feel like I just got it again."

Ten years, I thought. And yet she barely looked older than... twenty-six? Twenty-five? Younger? *How long has she been fighting?*

"Where?" I asked.

"Greenriver. My first battle," she replied. "At the edge of this very Valley, in fact." Her eyes unfocused, staring at something distant. "The wounds of the battles we fought over this land are still too fresh, the Revolution still too bold. They could sweep over the border at any time and overrun them."

"Overrun...who?"

She looked at me. "All of them. Every one of them. Every Imperial citizen that has come to this place seeking freedom from the war and strife and hate that plagues every other corner of this forsaken land. The Blessing is full of those souls."

My mind raced back to our meeting in the basement, to the map we looked at. The Blessing, Tuteng had called it—the land over which we had diverted the Iron Fleet to fly. It was full of Imperial citizens now? When had that happened? Why would the Imperium move so many citizens into a place so recently a war zone?

All reasonable questions, but it wasn't the one I asked myself.

Why didn't Two Lonely Old Men tell me?

"That's why Terassus has a surfeit of nobles of late," Velline sighed. "The Empress believes the Blessing to be ripe for settlement. The wealthy fops outside are keen to expand and reap the bounty. They'll buy it, settle it, charge far too much money for far too little space for it."

She smiled softly.

"But defending it falls to us."

"Us?"

She smiled. "I'm not a one-woman army, sad as I am to say it. I have certain help in the form of—"

"HEY! OVER HERE! I FINALLY FOUND HER!"

The sound of someone shouting filled my ears and fear filled my chest. I whirled, my body tensing, my hand reaching for a weapon I didn't have. The curtains parted. I caught sight of steel as a figure, blade in hand, entered. My hand curled into a fist, ready for the fight that had found me.

"Easy."

But before I could, Velline's hand found mine. And without knowing it, my breathing slowed.

"Easy," she whispered. "We're still safe. They're here for me."

"They" made themselves known shortly. Or at least "she" did.

She was tall, lean, and muscular—I know this because the dress she wore exposed so much skin I wondered if she might look more modest nude. Her hair, long and golden, hung in a free mane down her back as she walked in, wearing a grin as sharp as the blade she carried.

"Captain!" the woman said in a bellowing voice. "They're looking for you out there! Every fop in Terassus wants you to—"

"Shenazar," Velline spoke with curt authority, dropping my hand. "Are we in battle?"

The woman, Shenazar, blinked. "Uh...no?"

"Are you planning to kill someone?"

"Not at the moment."

"Then why is your blade out?" Velline asked, narrowing her eyes.

"Ah, come on, Captain." Shenazar raised her blade—Imperial, I noted. This woman had rank. "What's the point of having a sword if you can't wave it around? Also, every time I bust this thing out, someone puts another glass of wine in my hand."

Velline glared at her. "How many have you had?"

"Six"—she squinted, trying to recall—"teen?"

"You'll touch not another drop."

"*What?*" The woman's face contorted from confusion to rage to a piteous pout while mine was still stuck on annoyed. "But, *Captain—*"

"I warned you," another voice, accompanied by another figure, slid through the curtains. "The appreciation of these swine isn't worth the discipline."

A man. Delicate-looking in body beneath a delicate-looking coat and breeches, his black hair perfectly coiffed and his handsome face perfect in all the ways that makes a man look boring. Though it seemed the feeling was mutual, as he stared at me with an unimpressed pair of brown eyes over a wineglass. I couldn't blame him—compared to him, I looked downright shabby. He was flawless.

That is, if you didn't notice the unnatural bony plate jutting from his forehead.

"Regardless, Captain," he spoke, sounding bored, "your absence has been noted. The common rabble—"

"Dalthoros," Velline warned.

Dalthoros rolled his eyes. "Fine, the *un*common rabble is clamoring for your return." He gestured to Shenazar. "If you'd be so kind as to relieve your faithful troops of entertaining them?"

"Very well," Velline sighed. She gestured to me. "But may I have the honor of introducing—"

"Please, Captain." Dalthoros turned and left. "If I have to meet any more preening nobodies, I might start to lose my pleasant demeanor."

"Yeah." Shenazar moved to follow, pointedly sheathing her sword. "Hey, it doesn't count if Dal gives me *his* wine, does it?"

"You'll need that sword if you intend to take it from me."

Velline watched the two go with keen displeasure written across her face. She closed her eyes, took a deep breath, and snorted.

"Fucking mages," she whispered before turning to me. "Pardon. The other Hellions require my services. But even if they don't, I'd still like to know your name."

"Sal," I blurted out.

"Sal." She turned the name over on her tongue, finding its taste peculiar. But she smiled all the same and nodded toward me. "I am pleased you found me tonight. Please don't take long to do it again."

With another quick bow and a turn on her heel, she disappeared, leaving me alone in the dark with one burgeoning question.

Why the fuck did you give her your real name?

I shook my head. This was what wine did to you, made you sloppy, careless. Drinking whiskey only makes you punch people and write bad poetry. That's why assholes drank wine—they didn't care.

Velline had noticed my scar and now she had my name. It might take an hour or a day, but there's no way a woman like that wouldn't eventually figure out who I was. Which meant this operation was about to get a whole lot more complicated.

Kind of made me wonder why I had to leave my gun behind if I was going to fuck this up anyway, but I didn't have time to dwell on that. I didn't have time to do anything except drain my wine, toss the glass aside, and put a hand down my dress.

Hidden in the tiny pocket sewn into the waist, I fished out a piece of red chalk. I glanced around, ensuring there were no other charming, violent strangers lurking around in here, before heading to the back of the room and finding a spot wedged between two especially gaudy statues.

I grabbed the edge of a sheet and wiped down the wooden wall. I took the chalk carefully in hand and began to draw a rectangle big enough for a man to fit through. Upon the chalk, Urda's tiny sigils began to glow, their magic humming to life.

Portals were a tricky business—you didn't shit all over the laws of time and space without certain precautions, after all. To ensure a safe arrival, the portal had to be perfectly drawn upon a clean surface by spellwritten chalk. Just one slipup could be the difference between the portal working or collapsing, trapping everyone using it inside.

Which meant I probably shouldn't have drank *quite* so much wine before doing this, but as they say, drinkers can't be choosers.

Or...someone said that, probably.

Once the square was drawn, I rapped on it twice. The square sat silently in the dark. I furrowed my brow, rapped again, and again silence answered me. For ten minutes this continued, me knocking, the square being just a square. I had just started to wonder if I hadn't done it right—what with me having drunk two bottles of wine— when something happened.

I heard her song.

The Lady Merchant's tune, distant and whimsical, was barely a note amid the chorus of magic being expelled in the banquet hall. And when the portal sprang to life, it did so weakly, a dull purple glow lighting up as a swirling vortex of fading light blossomed into existence.

And from it, Yria sprang.

Breathing hard and covered in blood.

"Yria?" I asked as she fell out of the portal and collapsed, wheezing, upon the ground. I reached down to help her up. "What the fuck happened?"

A hand drenched in red grabbed my arm. She looked up at me with one wild eye, the other blinded by the blood leaking out of a gash in her forehead. Breathless, she wheezed.

"We got a problem."

TWENTY-ONE

LITTLE HAVEN

D ecadence!"
   A howl went into the night. A hundred torches were raised.
"Vanity!"

Swords followed, thick-bladed metal thrust into the sky like it
could cut the stars out.

"MAGIC!"

And then they started screaming.

Hundreds—it was impossible to tell how many, exactly—of them
threw their heads back, the long tails of their red blindfolds fluttering like flames as they let out a long, angry scream. They waved their
weapons, brandished their torches, carved bloody sigils into their
flesh, and burned themselves to demonstrate their immunity to pain.
Within seconds, the stones of the square were drenched in blood and
the sky was ablaze with fire and fanaticism.

And not for the first time, the good people of Haven conspired to
fuck everything up.

The throngs of men, each one adorned in bloodied marks and
wearing a cloth to hide his eyes, turned their blind gazes to the center of the square. Towering over them was a crude effigy of a human
made from rotted timber and bones, topped with the horned skull
of some incredible beast so freshly killed it still had gristle on it. It
stood twenty feet in the night sky, silent and immobile.

You almost wouldn't notice the gnarled woman standing at its feet.

"The time has come for the sin to be burned from this city!"

If she wasn't shrieking all the fucking time, anyway.

The Sightless Sister swept a glare across the crowd of the devoted. Within the empty eye sockets, the meat long gouged from them, two orbs of witch-fire burned, whatever dark power her god had given her coursing through her veins. She raised a rotted staff and, with a rotted mouth, rasped in a rotted voice.

"Your long ardor within these walls," she screamed, *"choking on the reek of excess, yearning to breathe the clean scent of ash, has come to an end! Rejoice, brothers, for tonight we…"*

She said more, but I kind of tuned it out. Once you've fought as many Haveners as I have, their rhetoric tends to run together. A lot of shouting about burning, killing, sinning, and so forth—whatever dark magic their Seeing God gave his disciples, he apparently didn't see fit to give them a wider repertoire of calls to violence.

Besides, I wasn't here for her.

Between plumes of smoke weaving through the sky, I could see a figure slumped over against the stake he was tied to. He was wearing different clothes than he had been when I saw him last and his face was painted a morbid shade of purple from the bruises and blood baking upon his skin, but I recognized him.

It was Jero.

Beaten. Bloodied. Breathless.

He hung there, suspended by the ropes, with his head bowed and his body unmoving. I only knew he was still alive because I knew Haveners didn't offer dead flesh to their god.

Which means, I thought as I scanned the crowd of shrieking crimson devils, *he won't be alive much longer.*

Outside of Haven, the Seeing Gods' disciples preferred to stick to small packs to avoid detection by powers hostile to lunatics trying to burn people alive. They only ever gathered in numbers this big for two reasons: to pray or to kill a lot of people.

Of course, they always tended to kill a lot of people after praying.

So just one reason, I guess.

Point being, whatever they were here to do, they weren't going to do it without giving an offering to their god. Which begged a question...

"How the *fuck* did this happen?"

I turned to face Yria, who squatted behind me, pressing a cloth to the gash in her temple. She blinked back at me, her wound giving her an extra glower as she narrowed her eyes.

"How the fuck do you *think* it happened, Lady Licktaint?" she snarled. "We got the shit kicked out of us!"

I held up my hand for her to stay quiet—not that I believed anyone might hear us over the roar of the crowd, but Yria had a voice like a broken harp fired out of a cannon.

Little Haven, as the collection of ramshackle and bombed-out husks of buildings had come to be known, was a relic of the war left to rot. Abandoned by its residents when the Revolution shelled this town, rebuilding the little square had proven less pressing than building a noble a third garden and it had remained dilapidated, splintering, and unfit for the residents of Terassus.

Deranged cultists, however, liked it just fine.

The already-crumbling houses had been further cannibalized by the Haveners. Eaves, doors, porches had been stripped. Any wood that could be pried apart was broken into kindling for the fires they loved so much and that dotted the square. The only buildings left intact were guarded and brimming with hoarded weaponry.

It was only through luck that Yria had managed to find a building still whole enough to offer cover so she could make a portal. And it was from that building we watched, staring through a cracked window.

"It's like this," she sighed. "While you and Agne were busy making kissy faces at the nobles, Jero and me were going to handle the other part. We were going to come down here, have a glimpse at these ash-sucking sons of bitches, and get out. Only, we weren't expecting—"

"*DRINK IN HIS BLESSING!*"

"Yeah." Yria gestured in the vague direction of the Sightless Sister. "Jero had his disguise on and it was working like it usually does when—"

"Like it usually does?" I asked. "How many times has Jero been here? What has he been *doing* here?"

"That ain't the part of the plan that's my job, now, is it?" Yria growled. "I don't fucking know what happened, but they saw through him this time. That socket-eyed strumpet looked at us like we had just drawn cocks on our faces."

"Sightless Sisters sense magic." I glanced out the window. "But they're blind beyond that. They can't see through regular disguises."

"Well, they fucking did *this* time, didn't they?" Yria muttered. "Would have been nice if we knew they learned some new tricks."

"Yes, it would have." I glared at her. "It would have also been nice to know *literally any other fucking thing that's happening right now.* Where did the Haveners all come from? What were you trying to do out here?"

"Spy on 'em, like I said."

"But *why*? What was the other part of the plan?"

Yria gave me the sort of look one usually reserves for the moment they wake up from a six-whiskey night and realize they went to bed next to livestock.

"I...don't know." She scratched her head. "Two Lonely Old Men only told Jero what to do with these freaks. My job was just to open the portals."

And my job was just to find a spot for the portal to be opened. Two Lonely Old Men hadn't told either of us and the only person within a mile who knew the entirety of his plan was about to be killed.

Why? I couldn't help but think. *If the fucking plan involves the Imperium* and *fucking Haven, why the hell wouldn't he tell us? Why didn't he trust us? What else isn't he...*

That would have been a productive and frustrating avenue of thought, I was certain, had I not suddenly been waylaid by a very distinctive reek. Over the odor of ashes and cinders, the aroma rose like a cloud of flies over a corpse.

It tasted coppery in my mouth, sent my senses aflame, my brain boiling as it seeped into my nostrils. I knew to cover my nose then, because I had smelled this particular stink once before.

And on that night, entire cities had burned.

I peered out the window and saw them: plumes of crimson mist rising here and there from low-slung braziers around which the

Haveners huddled, wafting the roiling clouds into their faces and breathing in, clouds of red disappearing down their throats.

"Fuck me," I whispered, "they've got Firelung."

"The fuck is that? Some kind of drug?" Yria snorted. "How come I ain't heard of it?"

Possibly because it was an incredibly rare, incredibly costly, and incredibly, *incredibly* toxic alchemic that only Haven knew the secrets of and ever only brought out when they were about to go to war. Firelung made a human feel neither pain, pity, nor fear, turning the average weakling into the most deadly warrior the world had ever known.

For the few hours it took for the drug to make their head explode, anyway.

A single whiff of it could change the tide of battle. And they were inhaling *bushels* of the shit. They wouldn't be taking it unless they were planning for an actual fight, rather than just slaughter.

"What's that big logs-for-cock thing they're looming on, then?"

The effigy's horned skull poked above the roofs of the houses, so huge that it required several mooring ropes to keep it from toppling over. Within its wooden rib cage, I could see a fire burning like a beating heart. And by its illumination, I could see the bodies.

Men. Women. The people of Terassus had been impaled on wooden stakes jutting from its body, morbid decorations weeping red onto the thing's crude body.

I didn't know how the Haveners had managed to build this thing without anyone knowing. I didn't know what the fuck it was for. I didn't know how they'd gotten so many drugs, so many weapons, so many *people* here.

But I knew why.

This wasn't one of their standard war parties, rampaging and butchering hapless civilians in the name of "purification." They wouldn't show up in this number, this well armed, unless they intended to fight an enemy that would fight back.

"The Imperium." The realization hit me like a brick to the face. "They're going to attack the fucking party."

"No shit?" Yria glanced over the windowsill. "Well, good thing we ain't there, ain't it?"

"Was this part of the plan?" I seized her by the shoulders, anger flooding my face. "To have the fucking *Haveners* fight? What the fuck was he thinking? What were *you* thinking?"

Yria blinked. "All good questions, I ain't denying, and I'm happy to suss 'em out with you." She jerked a thumb toward the window. "But if you're gonna do that, it might be worth plugging your ears, because—"

"BRING THE SACRIFICE!"

"Yeah, that."

Jero's body collapsed into the grasp of a pair of fanatics as they harshly dragged his limp form toward the colossal effigy of wood and bone. The Sightless Sister's face split apart in a broad smile as the fanatics lashed him to the thing's right leg.

"Witness now the herald of our victory." She swept her gnarled arms out toward the effigy. "We grant you a body, O Seeing God! We grant you legs to walk! We grant you arms to smite! We grant you eyes to see!"

She held a hand out. A fanatic placed a cruelly serrated dagger into her grasp. Her smile broadened as she swept her sightless gaze toward Jero, watching her through an eye sealed shut.

"We grant you blood to power you."

Fuck.

Granted, the intricacies of Haven's culture—let alone the role they played in Two Lonely Old Men's scheme—were lost on me, but I understood this shitshow clear enough.

It would have been smart to run away now—there were too many fighters, too many weapons, too much rage-inducing drug in the air. It would have been smart to figure out what the hell Two Lonely Old Men was originally trying to do. It would have been smart to do *anything* except what I ended up doing.

But fuck, you probably already knew that, didn't you?

I held out my hand toward Yria. "Give me your knife."

Yria shot me a peculiar look, but obliged all the same. I tested it for heft—too light to do real damage, but I'd killed with less. She watched as I took the blade to the skirt of my dress and cut it away, eyes widening as she caught a glimpse of bare leg.

"Er, yeah," she said, scratching the back of her neck. "I know the stories about you say you're, uh . . . but this doesn't seem like the—"

"I'm getting Jero and getting out of here." I tied the shredded garment around my face. "Whether you're coming with us or not depends on if you're smart enough to not finish that sentence."

She rolled her eyes. "Oh fucking boy. Sal the fucking Cacophony's got a plan. Where do I figure into it?"

"Stay here." I crept to the door, eased it open. "Keep an eye on the portal and get ready to close it the second we get through and—" My eyes narrowed as I spied a thick bracelet sitting on Yria's wrist. "Is that..."

She grinned as she flicked her wrist. Meticulous's retractable shield fanned out, dented but still solid.

"Slicker than a newborn, ain't it?" she asked. "Jero fixed it up for me and—HEY!"

I prized it off her wrist, affixed it to my own, and gave it a test for weight. Good heft. Good enough to crack someone's skull, at least. I didn't typically use Revolutionary gear.

But then, I thought as I flicked my wrist and retracted the shield, *I don't typically do this sort of shit for men, either.*

"That was mine!" Yria protested.

"I need it more," I replied, regarding her evenly. "And I shot the guy who had it last, if you really want to fight for it." She fell silent and I grunted. "Wait for us. You'll see us coming."

"Right." Yria snorted, crossing her arms. "Guess I'll just look for the half-naked crazy bitch." She waved a hand. "Well, go on, get out there. But don't think I'm going to be dawdling here if this shit goes any more screw-wise than it is."

I wasn't going to think about what that meant. I wasn't going to think about anything, if I could help it. If I started thinking, I'd start realizing what a stupid idea this was, how hopelessly outnumbered and outmuscled I was, how even if I got out of this, Two Lonely Old Men still hadn't told me everything and that meant—

Ah, but there I went again.

Thinking when I should be out there getting horribly murdered.

TWENTY-TWO

LITTLE HAVEN

I slid out the door, keeping low to the ground as I swept across the courtyard. The reek of the Firelung hammered itself against my makeshift mask, trying to seep past the cloth and into my nose. Even now, I could feel a twitching in my brain, ashes burning on my tongue.

But the Haveners didn't notice me as I crept around the outer edge of their gathering. Their attentions were locked upon the effigy looming over them.

"The hour is nigh!"

And the deranged woman at its feet.

"The fire paints the sky a bloody hue, brothers!" the Sister screeched. *"The Seeing God's eternal eye is upon us! Prepare! Prepare!"*

The Haveners roared in reply, their screams like feral beasts clawing their way out of their throats. To the effigy, they raised glimmering steel. And there was a whole fucking lot of it.

Be real fucking nice if I had a magic gun right about now.

Spear—too bulky. Sword—no, too short. I searched the raised weapons, looking for something more suitable than the feeble knife I carried. *Whip—who the fuck still uses those? Glaive...or is that a halberd? Shit, I always get them confused.* I shook my head. *Focus. Need something heavier than...*

My thoughts trailed off as my eyes settled upon the broad, jagged-edged head of an axe, bright and shining like a big, ugly moon.

A smile crept across my face.

Hello, beautiful.

I came up behind the Havener at the edge of the gathering, waving the axe around like a party favor. He was too lost in his fervor to notice me coming up behind him. His mouth gaped open wide, a formless howl tearing its way out of his throat.

For as long as it took me to jam the knife into it, anyway.

Throat. Lung. Kidney. It had been a while since I took care of someone this way, but I knew the old one-two-three rule of fighting Haveners. Vital organs, take them down quick, don't trust them to bleed out. So long as a fanatic is still breathing, he's fighting.

Even this one took a feeble swing at me as he crumpled to the ground. I glanced up; no one seemed to think one of their friends being murdered was more interesting than the Sister's lunatic ravings, but that wouldn't last.

I took the axe up, smiled at its heft. This little lady and I were going to do a lot of damage. All I had to do was find the quickest route through the human crowd, wait for an opening, then move swiftly, but carefully, sparing not even a single moment for—

"LET THE SACRIFICE BE MADE!"

Or I guess I could just do it right the fuck now.

I looked up. I saw the dagger raised in the Sister's hand. I saw Jero's chest heave, waiting for the blow.

I started running.

They roared, they howled, they shrieked at the promise of violence.

None of them even noticed the screaming until I was already halfway through the crowd.

I swung, hacked, hewed. Blood spattered the stones, my dress, my face. Everywhere I struck, a leg went out, an agonized scream rose, a Havener went down, clutching an axe wound in his side. The drugged-up ones barely seemed to notice until they looked down and saw themselves seeping out onto the street. The sober ones...

"HERETIC!"

Less so.

Haveners lashed out, with flesh and with steel, clawing their way over each other in a bid to be the one to kill me. I flicked my wrist, felt the shock of blows as the shield absorbed them and smashed against chins. Swords flashed, painting the edge of my vision with blood as they nicked at my flesh. Hands reached, tore at my dress, pulled at my hair.

I pushed through the pain. I pulled away from their grips. I kept moving. I kept swinging.

The Firelung was clawing its way into my mouth. My chest burned with every ragged breath. My head throbbed, torn between the drug making my brain boil and the sound of the Haveners' fanatical cries filling my ears as more and more of them came flooding toward me.

I couldn't see their faces beyond the lunatic grins and animal snarls beneath their blindfolds. I couldn't feel their blades, my arms gone numb from the shock of the axe cutting through so many people. I didn't look. I didn't think. I didn't stop.

My eyes, my thoughts, my blade were all on him.

I tore free from the throng in a burst of red and silver. The Sightless Sister's neck craned as she turned toward me, her mouth twisting into a gnarled frown just in time to catch the rim of my shield smashing against her chin.

I seized her withered form, pulled her against me as I pressed the axe's blade against her throat. I whirled, backing up against the effigy's legs as the tide of red-painted flesh came swarming toward me. I beheld a hundred gaping mouths, a hundred flashing weapons, a hundred blood-hungry bodies swarming up toward me, screaming, shouting, laughing, praying, bleeding...

And then... stopping.

The screams went silent. The weapons lowered. The tide of sinew and blood came close enough to drown me before stopping and slowly receding. The Haveners stood taut, every one of their blindfolded gazes locked upon me. Or rather, upon the crone I held against me, and the gnarled hand she held up, bidding them stop.

I didn't know what magic the Seeing God gave his followers. I didn't know how they knew, blind as they were, what was happening or how the Sister commanded a horde like that to stop. And I didn't know how the fuck Jero and I were going to get out of here alive.

"I sense a lack of foresight from you, child."

Neither did she, apparently.

"Why come to this hallowed place?" she rasped, mirth in her voice even as my axe drew blood across her throat. "Why profane the sacrosanct? The Seeing God would come for you, eventually, as he comes for all."

"And you're welcome to go meet him in whatever hell he happens to be," I replied, my eyes searching the crowd for anyone who might get inconveniently brave. "But you won't be taking us with you."

"Sal..." Jero's voice was thin with pain, his breath ragged as he spoke to me. "You...need to..."

"Shut up," I growled. I pressed the axe a little closer to the Sister's throat. "Tell them once we're free and clear of your little festival here, I'll be happy to return you. In how many pieces depends on how reasonable we're all willing to be."

Not to brag, but I've killed a lot of people. So many that I thought I'd seen every face a person can show before being sent to the black table. I'd seen the simpering pleas, the defiant cursing, the depraved cackling—and I've put a sword through each and every one of them without batting an eye.

I guess I should count myself lucky that I'd never felt the same chill run down my back as I did when the Sightless Sister just let out a long, slow sigh, as though she were talking to a dim-witted child and not a woman with an axe.

"I can tell them nothing, girl," she rasped. "For it is not my place to speak."

"Birdshit," I snarled, pressing my axe tighter against her throat. "Tell them your god wills it or something. They love that shit."

"Do you not see?" she chuckled. "It is beyond our will. Theirs. Mine. Yours."

"Lady, I'm the one with the fucking axe. I'll be making the rules."

"The omens led us here, child." She spoke breathlessly, awe dripping from her mouth. "One by one, they came to us. One by one, we came to this place. We were beckoned to this den of kindling filth, the sparks that will light the fire to set this entire world ablaze."

"What?" I screwed up my face—it was tough to understand what the fuck these lunatics said, but they usually weren't this coherent. "What fire are you—"

"Sal!"

I glanced over my shoulder. Jero stared at me with one good eye, an urgency on his face that he didn't have the strength to voice. What was that in his wrinkles? I wondered. A command? A plea?

No ... an apology.

"Kill me, if you like," the Sister rasped. "Save him, if you can. Run as far as you want into whatever shadows remain." Her smile spread like an ugly wound across her face. Her commanding hand trembled. "But when the great flame swallows every den of filth and heresy and there are no more shadows left to skulk in, remember this..."

She turned toward me. The bones and skin of her neck popped and creaked painfully as she looked at me. The lights in her eyes glowed, illuminating the sheer, terrifying joy in her smile.

"You will be the one to bring the fire," she said, "Cacophony."

I stared at her, into those lights in her sockets, for only a moment. Because in another, I saw her hand fall.

And behind her, I heard them scream.

The Haveners' howls tore into my skull, the thunder of their feet upon the street rattling my bones in my skin. They came surging forward, screaming and shaking their steel, pointedly not giving a shit about my hostage.

I spat out a curse, planted my boot in her back and kicked her forward. She struck the horde, causing them to recoil for as long as it took to keep her from falling before rushing toward me again.

My mind raced along with my eyes, searching the plumes of Firelung and tides of flesh for any escape. But all around me, they closed in, the tide rising. I looked to Jero, who regarded me with bloodied resignation. I looked to the sky and saw only the effigy: the timber of its legs, the skull that crowned its body...

And the ropes that held it upright.

I had no idea if it would work. I had no idea what would happen. I had nothing but an axe.

And that's what I used.

I hacked at the ropes. One by one, they snapped like whips across the sky, frayed by the tension of holding the colossus up. Over the sound of the fanatics' cries growing louder in my ears, I could just barely hear it: the snapping of rope, the whistle of wind.

And the creak of timber.

"*NO!*" The Sightless Sister's wail rang out as she reached with a gnarled hand, both gestures impotent. "*HIS BLESSED VESSEL!*"

The Haveners' blinded stares turned upward. And their blood-thirsty voices turned to screams of despair.

The effigy started to sway. Without the ropes to hold it upright, its colossal body started to lean backward. The remaining supports snapped and broke, leaving me barely enough time to cut Jero free from it before the mess of timber and bone started to plummet.

The Haveners came rushing toward us, over us, past us in a desperate bid to save the effigy from collapsing. No one raised so much as a word as I draped Jero's arm across my shoulders and started hauling him away toward Yria's hiding spot.

"I don't know how it happened," he rasped in my ear. "My disguise, they'd always fallen for it before...I can't...I don't..."

"Spend your breath moving, not talking, asshole," I snarled in reply as I pulled him toward the house. "They aren't going to keep ignoring us once they realize they can't...save...the..."

My words drifted off as I glanced over my shoulder and saw the effigy's massive body smashing into a house.

The same house they kept the Firelung in.

Okay, so maybe that *was* pretty stupid.

A burst of fire. Shattered timbers. A hundred voices screaming over the sound of wood groaning. And a great big fucking cloud the color of blood washing over everything.

The house erupted in a spray of cinders and splinters of wood. And like blood gushing from a wound, the Firelung caught aflame and spewed a great, roiling cloud over the square.

The Haveners vanished beneath it and, within the haze of the drug's smoke, I could see them beginning to change. Their lunatic grins almost split their faces in two. They clawed at their bodies, writhing with pleasure over the blood they drew. Their screaming twisted to laughing, shrieking, sobbing, cackling, vomiting, a grotesque and twisted symphony of bodily functions that tore its way out of the cloud like a newborn from a red womb.

A whiff of Firelung could make a man fearless.

I don't know what inhaling a whole fucking stock of it would do, but I bet it probably ended with me dead.

If I were a less humble woman, I might have taken a moment to marvel at my ability to take something like human sacrifice and somehow make it worse. And don't get me wrong, I'm not very humble.

"Fucking *MOVE*!"

I just didn't have the moment to spare.

I wrapped an arm around Jero's torso, holding him close as I stopped dragging him and started carrying him. The Haveners had lost all thought of pursuing us, but they didn't need to. The cloud of Firelung did that for them, chasing us like a predator chases wounded prey, leisurely reaching out with crimson vapor claws.

"It wasn't going to be like this," Jero groaned. "They weren't supposed to know...stupid...stupid..."

Maybe the Firelung was making him babble stupid shit. Or maybe the pain from his wounds. Or maybe he had always been this stupid and I hadn't noticed. Either way, if he didn't cut it out, I was going to leave him here.

The door to Yria's hiding spot loomed before us. I picked up speed, lowering my body as much as I could and smashing it open with my shoulder. I shifted Jero to one arm, turned and slammed it shut as the cloud of red smoke splayed against the window.

Yria looked up from scratching her ass to cast a confused look at us.

"The fuck happened out there?" she grunted.

"Get to the portal," I rasped, breathless, as I dragged Jero's limp form to it.

"What was all that fucking noise?" She stalked toward the window, squinted out it. "What's all this fucking red stuff?" She turned and scowled at me. "Where's my fucking knife?"

"*Portal*," I snarled.

"What? In *his* condition?" She eyed Jero warily. "I don't know. Portals are tricky things. If you ain't hale enough, they can—"

Glass shattered behind her. All eyes looked up toward the Havener, lodged in the window he had just broken with his head. He looked up, shards of glass embedded in his skin, and hissed.

"I want to lick your rib cage."

Yria blinked. Snorted. Spat.

"Yeah, all right," she grunted. "Let's go."

I stepped forward and jammed the axe's head into the fanatic's skull. Yria rushed to the back of the room, beckoning the portal to life. The Lady's song rose in my ears, the tranquility drowning out the sounds of people screaming, the sight of clouds roiling, the feel of the street shaking...

Wait.

I paused, listened. A faint sound, like a thunder crack, punched through the air. Again. And again. Louder each time until I felt the floorboards rattle under my feet.

"Hurry," I said to Yria, backing toward her. "*Hurry.*"

"You want it done quick or you want it done right?" she spat spitefully, shaking her head. "Fucking amateurs think shitting on the laws of time and space happens with a word."

She held her hands out. Upon the wall, a pinprick of purple light blossomed into a portal, stretching across the wood like a living thing. She studied it for a moment before looking back to me.

"Looks stable," she grunted, turning toward me. "I'll go through first to make sure. Then you ease Jero through and I'll be on the other side to gently—"

I couldn't hear the rest of what she said, seeing as the wind was knocked out of her when I shoved Jero into her and forced both of them through the portal. The purple light rippled like water as they vanished through it, leaving me alone.

Right up until the roof exploded, anyway.

Timbers splintered. Fire erupted. Shards of flaming wood rained down, forcing me to duck away as something huge punched its way through the ceiling. I glanced up, saw a colossal fist of timber and flame pull itself free, leaving behind a gaping hole.

And looming high overhead, a shadow painted black across the red mist, something immense stared down at me.

When you do this job as long as I have, you start to develop a certain instinct for recognizing when a situation has become incredibly, thoroughly, and irrevocably fucked. It feels like a heaviness at the base of your head, like an axe resting on your neck.

I looked up into that great shadow looming large over me. I felt that heaviness in my head.

I let it carry me as I fell backward, into the portal, and disappeared.

TWENTY-THREE

YUN ATTORO ESTATE

Understand, we're talking about changing the world here," Jero finally said at last, his breath heavy with pain. "This isn't some pedestrian heist of gold and silken underthings. The need for secrecy demands a certain independence in operations."

He paused to search my face for signs that my anger had abated.

Seeing that it hadn't, he cleared his throat.

"And though Two Lonely Old Men has no doubts about our intellects or loyalties, he suspected it would be wiser to have everyone know only *part* of the plan," he continued, "so that if any one of us were captured, tortured, or otherwise bribed, spilling our knowledge couldn't ruin the operation. That makes sense, doesn't it?"

He waited for me to nod.

Seeing that I didn't, he winced.

"Look, if we took the Imperium's finest birds without covering our tracks, they'd find us," he gasped. "We needed a distraction, a cat's-paw on which to pin the disappearance of the Oyakai and... and..."

He took in a deep, desperate breath.

"Any time you want to stop strangling me, just let me know."

"Sure," I replied, tightening my grip on his throat. "I'll tell you."

Ordinarily, I wouldn't react like this. Betrayal, subterfuge, lying—they were all part of even a peasant's life on the Scar, let alone life as a Vagrant. And while I'd inhaled some of the Firelung, it wasn't enough to make me want to do this—not after the shit I'd snorted over the years.

But it *did* make me wonder why *this* particular betrayal from *this* particular man rankled me in such a way. Lucky for me. Less so for him.

"Sal." Yria sounded meek—or as meek as she could manage—as she tugged ineffectually at my arm in a bid to free him. "C'mon. He didn't know this would happen."

"Well, then he's just one more fucking member of the Doesn't Know Shit Club, isn't he?" I whirled on her as Jero pawed weakly at my hand. "Do you not fucking get it?" I turned my snarl back on him. "Do *you*? You ask me to come onto this insane quest and don't bother telling me that it involves *Haven*? You didn't think a hundred-odd drug-fueled religious lunatics and that…that wood…*skull* thing they have was something that would warrant my attention?"

Jero rasped out a few words, trying to convince me. And had my fingers not tightened around his windpipe, he might have done it—he was very persuasive, which was one reason I was strangling the life out of him.

"You weren't even supposed to *know*!" Yria protested, trying to pull my hands off. Her arms were already too skinny for that *before* they'd gone half numb from using her magic, though. "Hell, you didn't even have to come! It could've gone off even if he did die! If you're so pissed at him, why'd you even bother saving him?"

That was a good question. A good question with a bad answer.

She was right—I both could have and should have left him there to die. This plan had already gone cockeyed before I knew Haven was involved. The smarter thing to do would have been to let him die and leave the city before anything else could have happened.

But when I'd looked at him, broken and bleeding, I hadn't seen a man who had lied to me, kept secrets from me, nearly gotten me killed. I had seen a man who had looked at me the way he had back at the start of the evening, with his smiling wrinkles and his bright eyes, and told me his secrets and asked me for mine and made me want to give them to him.

I'd been looked at that way before.

And I'd done crazy things to see that look again.

But that wasn't the answer I wanted to hear. And that wasn't the answer I was going to give Yria *or* Jero. Instead, I tightened my grip and spat something out.

"Because I won't have it said that Sal the Cacophony let someone *else* kill someone who screwed her over."

"Are you gonna have it said that Sal the Cacophony shat away a ton of money over some fucking pride?" Yria pressed. "Because that's what's gonna happen if you don't let him breathe now."

I actually *had* done that once.

All the same, with a final glower, I released my hand and let Jero collapse to the floor, gasping for breath.

Not that my faith in Two Lonely Old Men to reward us for our efforts meant much to me anymore, but the thought of letting Jero die, of one more person who had looked at me that way once and then never again...

I don't know. Maybe I'm capable of forgiveness. Or maybe I'm a huge fucking idiot. It's hard to tell the difference between the two sometimes.

But if the red fingerprints embedded around his throat were any indication, I'd at least made my point.

I glanced around the darkened room. In the banquet hall outside, the party continued to roar. The sounds of laughter and phantom instrumental quartets continued with all the tranquility of a bunch of people who didn't know how close they'd come to being brutally massacred by a bunch of religious lunatics. Neither my absence, my return, nor my subsequent strangling of Jero had been noted.

"The plan"—I glared at Jero—"whatever it was, has gone to shit. We can't stay here."

"Yeah, can't say as I disagree." Yria glanced me over, snorted. "You ain't looking like too much of a fancy Princess Sparklesnatch anymore, are you?"

I glanced down at myself. What skin was showing—and there was quite a bit more of it, now that I'd torn my dress apart—was peppered with cuts, bruises, and soot-stained sweat. Nobles loved eccentricity, but I didn't think I'd be able to convince them that this was just a new trend I was setting.

"You go and find the big lass." Yria stalked to the wall and started drawing a square in red chalk. "I'll put a portal together to get us out of here."

Jero's hand shot up and caught her by the wrist. His stare was hard, his wrinkles deep as scars, when he looked up at her.

"No," he said. "We stick to the plan." He gestured at her square. "Go. Bring back Tuteng."

"They fuck your head with a soldering iron or did your mama just love dumb babies?" Yria held up her hand. "I can barely feel my fingers. My Barter's cost too much. I got maybe *one* more portal in me and anything else means *permanent* nerve damage and that costs extra. You're painted redder than a horny radish." She gestured to me with her numb hand. "And *she's* half pumped on fucking wizard drugs. This thing is over."

"It isn't. It *can't* be. We *need* this to work." He staggered to his feet, breathing heavily. "Bring back Tuteng. We'll find our own way back."

"Your head's so far up your ass you got shit in your ears," she growled. "I *said*—"

"I heard what you said." Jero's voice turned deadly quiet, his eyes cold as winter. "Now hear what I tell you. If you go through that portal and leave, you had better hope they find an ocean wide enough to hide you from me, because once I get out of here, I will start looking for you. I will find you. And I will bring you back in one hundred different jars."

Yria's eyes went wide, her mouth silent. Hell, even *I* felt like I had just been hit in the head with a blade hearing that. He released her.

"Bring. Back. Tuteng."

She glanced from him to me, winced. "Good fuckin' luck."

She waved a hand. The Lady's song rose. The portal blossomed. She disappeared. And I was left alone with a man I sorely *wished* to kill but, for reasons that may or may not be birdshit, could not *actually* kill.

Which was a situation I was not entirely comfortable with.

"They'll be back shortly," Jero said, steadying himself. "We can take a moment to recuperate before—Wait, where are you going?"

And so I left.

"I'm getting Agne," I replied, "and we're getting the fuck out of here."

"Sal, I—"

"No," I spat as I pulled back the curtain leading to the banquet hall. "Fuck your plan. Fuck your employer. And fuck you."

His voice dropped into a soft, cold whisper. "Did you not hear what I just told—"

"I did." I turned, regarded him carefully. "And if you think you've got a threat that will stop me, feel free to make it now." I narrowed my eyes. "But you better be prepared to do it right now."

His mouth opened and hung there, wordless and heavy. His eyes followed, looking away from me and down at the floor.

"Yeah," I said as I pushed through the curtain. "That's what I thought."

"What is she wearing?"

I could hear their whispers as surely as I could feel their eyes upon me. Stained with blood and soot, my dress in tatters, and trailing the latent stench of Firelung, I couldn't really blame them. Nor could I really pay attention to them.

"Is it... was this supposed to be a theme party or is she actually..."
I ignored that.

"Summon the guards. Or the servants. Whoever takes out the trash."
I ignored that, too.

"Oh my sweet heaven, she's got thews like a Scion."
That girl I might look up later.

But the scorn and disapproval and whatever guards they might throw my way would have to be dealt with later. As I shoved my way through the revelry, the astonished and agog expressions cast my way didn't belong on the face I was looking for.

That one I found a moment later.

At the edge of the party, encircled by a truly impressive crowd of attentive men, Agne held a court of polite titters and swoons. As I headed toward her, the crowd became a wall of pushing, shoving, and hollering for her attention.

I sighed, cracked my knuckles, and waded in.

"Sal?" Agne shot me—or rather, the bedraggled creature that punched her way through the crowd of men to emerge before her—a confused look that quickly turned concerned as she took in my wounds. "What's going on?"

"We're leaving," I growled.

"But the..." She glanced upward toward the Oyakai birds, still regaling high over the crowd. "You know, the *thing*."

"It's off," I replied. "It's all off. Everything's off."

"What? Why? What happened?"

It would have taken far, *far* too long to explain that murderous fanatics hopped up on drugs had become involved in a plan that she and I had not been privy to, despite our lives being on the line for it.

So I shot her a look that tried to explain it.

I doubt I came close, but I gathered by the cringing realization on her face that she knew something had either gone terribly wrong or I was about to *make* something go terribly wrong.

"All right." She glanced around the multitude of men staring at us with increasing concern. "Let's be smart about this. I can find a polite reason to leave, so long as we're cautious and careful and—"

"Madam." A bold young suitor stepped forward, one hand on the pommel of his sword, the other on my shoulder. "If this foul-mouthed lout is harassing you, allow me the honor of—"

Since the end of that sentence wasn't going to be "swallowing my own teeth," my fist smashed into his mouth, which probably didn't help things.

Agne glared at me. "That is the precise opposite of what we needed to accomplish."

"I disagree." I turned and held up my bloodied knuckles to the crowd. "Unless anyone else has a better argument or a stronger jaw, we'll be going now."

You can't count on rich people to not be stupid, but you can at least count on them not to be stupid when it's their blood on the line. The assembled suitors took several collective steps back, permitting me a corridor to pass through as I took Agne's hand.

I could hear the music and laughter begin to quiet as word spread through the crowd about the dirty woman with the penchant for fop-punching. Over the muted conversation, I could hear the rattle of armor and weapons as guards entered. As more and more eyes turned upon me, I knew it wouldn't be long before they found me.

But that was fine. The curtains to the back room loomed before us. Agne was smiling politely and making excuses for her drunken friend as I hauled her through the banquet hall. We could find a back way out of the hall and return to the city. In another minute, we'd be far from this house and every last shitstain of a person inside it, just so long as—

"Sal?"

—nothing like that happened.

Velline stepped out of the crowd to interpose herself between me and my exit. She looked more curious than concerned, but her hand on her sword suggested that wouldn't last.

"What's going on?"

I was getting *real* tired of hearing that question.

"Holy shit."

The woman with the long hair—Shenazar, I think her name was—stepped forward, along with the morose man, Dalthoros, to appear behind Velline. She glanced over the myriad of cuts and bruises decorating my body with a grin growing steadily broader.

"Is that blood?" she asked, excited. "Was there a fight? Are we allowed to fight at these things now?"

"Obviously not," Dalthoros muttered, scratching idly at the bony plate jutting from his forehead. "Otherwise this wouldn't be quite so dull. As it stands..."

Velline held up a hand and the two obediently fell silent.

"Sal?" she asked, much less confused this time.

I started to reply, started to think of some lie, but the words didn't come soon enough. Not before I saw the realization dawning in her eyes.

That sharpened amethyst stare swept over me, taking in every drop of blood that marred me, before she locked gazes with me for a long, cold moment.

She slid her sword out of its scabbard by two inches. I clenched my fist. She lowered herself into a combat pose. I rolled my shoulder.

Be *real* fucking nice if I had a magic gun right about now.

Without a single word spoken between us, we both knew I wasn't going to stay here and she wasn't going to let me leave. I was tired, I was bloodied, I was unarmed, I stood no chance against her—but I was full of anger looking for a target and just mildly fucked up on drugs.

So, those odds seemed good enough to hurl myself at her.

"HALT."

As I turned around, I noted with some irritation that it would be a lot easier to get myself killed if people would quit fucking interrupting me.

I heard the Lady's song intermingled with the rattle of armor. Eyes blazing with purple light and brandishing a sword in his gauntleted hand, the Honorable Judge Keltithan emerged from the crowd, a battalion of guardsmen behind him.

"A great evil has been brought to my house," he bellowed, eyes narrowing to slits upon me. He leveled his sword at me, sigils upon its blade bursting with blue light as a hoary chill engulfed the metal. "And though I know not how you deceived your way here nor what nefarious deeds you intend to serve, I know that you won't be doing it."

"Sal." Velline spoke softly but sternly. "Whatever is happening, it doesn't have to end in bloodshed. Come quietly. Let's figure this out."

Given that "this" meant explaining that I had lied my way in here with the help of a vengeful Freemaker intent on stealing the Imperium's birds of war for purposes of launching an attack on a dangerous military power, I didn't see that happening.

Of course, given that I was flanked on one side by a woman with a sword and on another side by a man with a much more impressive sword, I didn't see escape happening, either.

Really, I admitted to myself as I surveyed the truly impressive number of people better armed than I was, I wasn't seeing much of any option that wasn't going to end with me getting gutted.

Except one.

And it came in the form of a shadow painted across the floor.

My gaze drifted upward to the skylight in the ceiling. I saw a silhouette looming, its shadow stark against the snow. I saw white cracks forming in the glass. I saw the flash of something metal in the darkness overhead.

Slowly, Keltithan's gaze followed mine. His neck craned up toward the skylight.

Just in time to see it shatter.

Glass rattled. Guests screamed. Something plummeted from above in a spray of glittering shards to land upon Keltithan in a rattle of armor and a spray of blood.

The guardsmen recoiled and Velline drew her sword, our quarrel forgotten as something crouched over Keltithan's prone form, mechanically pumping a blade in and out of his body until the body stopped twitching.

Slowly, the Havener rose to his feet. His machete was drenched in blood. His smile was broad and manic. Beneath the shredded remains of his blindfold, a pair of eyes stared out.

And from them, blood wept in bright red streams.

"Hello," he said in a lilting, lunatic voice. "We are coming."

"We?" Velline asked.

She didn't have to.

They came eleven seconds later.

TWENTY-FOUR

YUN ATTORO ESTATE

The walls were bleeding.
In rivulets. In trickles. In floods.
From windows. From doors. From the ceiling.
"MY BLOOD IS FIRE!"
And everyone was screaming.

The Haveners came pouring into the banquet hall, blades flashing and blood gushing from their eyes and mouths as they carved their way through in a drug-fueled orgy of red steel. The delicate guests and effete aristocrats ran screaming from them as the guards and armed patrons fought against the tide in an effort to meet their lunatic foe.

Tables were thrown up as barricades, were split in two by cultist axes. Glass fell and shattered to make wine-stained beds for corpses to rest upon. The illusory opera singers continued to bleat out lilting tunes as a backdrop to the shrieking, their phantom forms shimmering as maddened attackers rushed through them.

In the span of an instant, the banquet had become a slaughter.
"I CAN FEEL THEM ON ME!"
And I had become a target.

The cultist—a hulking brute bleeding from a dozen cuts and spitting blood out his mouth—came rushing toward me, swinging a machete half the size of me. Panic burned through his bloodstained face as he trampled corpses and the fleeing as he raised his weapon.

"THEIR LEGS BURN! GET THEM OFF! GET THEM OFF! GET THEM—"

He didn't finish that sentence.

Probably because his windpipe had just been crushed.

Agne's fingers tightened around the brute's neck, her eyes flashing purple and the Lady's song rising in our ears. She hefted him off his feet, her skin not so much as bleeding as he hacked wildly at her arm, and glanced at me.

"I take it this is what was going on?" she asked.

"Yup," I replied, drawing my sword and flicking my shield out.

"Huh." She glanced back at the cultist. "You were right."

With a snap of her wrist, she hurled the Havener face-first into the floor. His skull erupted with a wet popping sound, bits of white and gray sliding across the floor to mingle with the red.

"That *would* have taken too long to explain."

With a contemptuous flick of her toe, she kicked the dead cultist in the ribs and sent his carcass flying away. I had to admit I was impressed—she'd taken care of him without even blinking.

Now, if she could do that about six hundred more times, we might get out of here alive.

"WE ARE REBORN, BROTHERS!"

Maybe.

"IN FIRE AND SUFFERING, HE IS WITH US!"

My eyes were drawn to the top of a distant table, upon which stood another cultist, hacked near to pieces, blood flowing out of his mouth with every word. As wounded as he was, he looked a damn sight better than the poor sop whose severed head he was waving around like a trophy as he cackled.

"HE IS COMING! CAN YOU NOT FEEL IT? CAN YOU..."

I couldn't hear the rest of his words. In another second, my ears were filled with that wordless symphony without harmony. The Lady Merchant's song filled the room.

And a terrible power was awakened.

Behind the cultist, there was a shimmer in the air—as though the night drew in a deep breath and held it. And from nothingness, she appeared: short, slender as a blade, her amethyst eyes fixed on the cultist's neck, cold and sharp.

But not nearly as cold as her blade.

The cultist turned around just in time to see Velline's sword—or rather, the blur that had been Velline's sword—as it passed ghost-like through his neck. He had time to raise his weapon before his body shuddered to a halt. A thin line of red appeared across his neck. He swayed unsteadily for a moment before his head toppled from his shoulders and bounced across the floor.

Velline scarcely seemed to notice. She immediately turned her attentions to the swarming melee below.

"Get the civilians out!" she screamed. "Anyone with magic, protect anyone without! No Imperial dies today!"

She raised her sword, its Imperial purple stained with blood, and shouted, "*ONTORI TUN VATALA!*"

On red wings, we fly.

An Imperial war cry. The oldest. The first.

In response, a hundred songs rose.

The air exploded in a riot of cold and flame, of thunder and flight, of flashing steel and blooming portals and bodies flying. Their surprise given way to fury, the mages of the party launched into action against their attackers.

Frostmages and Embermages waded into the combat, flames and freezing cold pouring from their hands to mow down cultists. Doormages wove portals for Siegemages to leap through and come crashing down on cultist backs. Wardmages put up barriers to hold off the onslaught. Above it all, Shenazar—her already scanty garb rent to near scraps—flew, laughing with a Skymage's abandon as she dove in and out of the melee to carve assailants.

Such a frenzy of magical power would have made even the most hardened Revolutionary squadron break. Hell, even the cultists might have thought twice about this.

"LET ME TASTE YOUR SINS!"

You know, if they weren't all currently out of their minds on drugs.

From the corner of my eye, I caught sight of the Havener rushing toward me. I whirled, flicking my wrist out and deploying the shield. He collided with it, chest-first, barely seeming to even notice as he flailed at me with a sword, eyes weeping blood as he tried to get over the shield.

I growled, shoved him backward. He staggered away, then leapt toward me, receiving a face-full of axe as I brought it crashing down into his skull. He fell to the ground, the weapon firmly lodged in his twitching carcass.

Just as well, I thought as I plucked his weapon up. Swords always felt more classic to me, anyway.

Someone grabbed me by the shoulder. I whirled about with my newfound sword, smashing its blade against a rib cage.

Agne glanced down at the hole I had cut in her nice dress and frowned. "You know, this wasn't lent to me. I brought this dress from home."

"I'll pay you later," I muttered, turning back to face the melee. "Assuming we get out alive."

"We seem to be doing all right."

"*You* seem to be doing all right," I snapped. "Those of us whose skin *isn't* impervious to steel are in slightly dire straits." I scanned the brawl as magic and blood continued to erupt. "What the fuck is the plan now?"

Agne glanced toward the ceiling, gestured with her chin. "I assume it's *that*."

I followed her gaze to the perch of an Oyakai. Despite the chaos unfurling below, the great birds seemed oddly unfazed, launching not so much as a squawk. But once I noticed the cloaked figure standing at one of their feet, I started to understand.

I had no idea when he had even arrived, let alone how he made it through the brawl unscathed to scale the pillars up to the perches, but Tuteng stood beside one of the great birds, stroking its feathers gently and whispering something in words lost in the din of the battle.

Whatever he was saying, the Oyakai seemed to listen. The great avian lowered its head, eyes closed, and pressed its brow against his. The noise, the murder, the suffering—all went unnoticed by them as they exchanged a single, silent moment that lasted forever.

Then Tuteng patted the great beast's flank and whispered something. The Oyakai chirped, leapt off its perch, and landed at the far side of the banquet hall, lowering its head to disappear down a great hallway. Tuteng watched to make sure it had disappeared before glancing to the next bird's perch and leaping across to land on a chandelier and swing his way over.

"He's getting the birds," I muttered, all of it becoming clear to me. "The Haveners were a distraction. Two Lonely Old Men planned all of this."

"You have to admit, it's rather a clever idea." Agne cringed as a spatter of gore from a nearby battle washed over her dress. "Aside from the whole 'mass slaughter' part, anyway." She reached out, caught the offending assailants by their necks, smashed their faces together, and let them drop to the floor together. "Regardless, he won't get the birds out if the distraction doesn't last long enough."

"And?" I asked.

She shot me a deadly serious look. "All this"—she held her arms out toward the battle—"will be for nothing."

That hurt to hear. Most truths do. She was right—if we didn't come out of this with birds, then all this mayhem and murder were for nothing. While I still knew far too little about this plan, I knew that the *considerable* amount of people in this hall who wanted me dead wouldn't wait for me to debate the morality of it.

Never let it be said that Sal the Cacophony didn't make the best of a bad situation.

Or that she'd ever met a fight she couldn't make worse.

I took a breath. I took my sword. And then I turned and waded into hell.

The latent reek of Firelung coiling off the Haveners, the ringing of the Lady's song as magic flew through the air, the shock making my arm numb as I deflected blows from my shield—I saw the battle in fleeting senses and fragmented noise. I struck where I could, retreated where I had to, darted between blades and under spells as I made my way toward the Oyakai perches.

I had to keep eyes on me and off Tuteng as he continued to send the birds into the other hall. As more bodies fell and the battle thinned, eventually someone would notice the ten-foot-tall birds were missing.

Fortunately, there were still more than enough drug-addled fanatics and reckless, spell-spitting mages around that their eyes were kept off the ceiling and on the white-haired woman just *begging* to be killed.

Some girls have all the luck, am I right?

I caught a flash of movement. A cultist came rushing toward me—or rather, the upper half of him did. A throng of Haveners stood nearby, their blades flashing and axes cleaving at what appeared to be thin air.

Or it would, if you didn't know what to look for.

The air shimmered here and there, a breath held for a moment before she appeared. Cold and cruel as her blood-slick blade, Velline emerged out of nothingness, a bad dream given flesh. Her sword moved with ghostly ease, cutting through a cultist only to vanish, along with the rest of her, as the Havener swung at the empty air she had just stood in.

The Lady's song wailed as Velline moved, disappearing and reappearing, with ethereal grace and unblinking cruelty. One by one, wounds appeared on the cultists as if by magic, their faces contorted as if they could, through their drug-fueled haze, wonder what the hell had just happened.

They fell. One after the other. Petals cut from a red flower.

And she alone stood.

And stared at me.

"Impressive." I rolled my shoulder. "You're a Quickmage."

"And you"—Velline flicked red life from her blade, leveled it at me—"are Sal the Cacophony."

My body tensed, keenly aware of how many wounds decorated it. Granted, she hadn't *explicitly* said she intended to kill me, but I've never had anyone say my name that dramatically and not at least be thinking about it.

"Figured it out, huh?" I asked.

"I should have guessed sooner," she replied, cold. "I have studied the names and methods of every Vagrant documented within the Scar. And while each and every one of them has been an oath-breaking, murderous fiend, only one of them causes chaos like this wherever she walks."

I forced the longest, ugliest grin I could manage. And that pristine face of hers cracked with anger.

Good.

I had to keep her staring at my smile and not on my eyes. Fighting a

Quickmage, the old wisdom went, was like fighting a disease—the best you could hope for was walking away with at least two of your limbs.

The Lady gave them preternatural speed, unerring grace, and reflexes so sharp they could see an attack coming before their opponent even thought of it. Challenging any of them was a death sentence, let alone one who had just slain ten drug-fueled cultists in as many seconds.

But they could be survived. And they could be defeated.

I had the scar to prove it.

"I should be flattered," I replied, canting my head to the side. "Which story did you hear? Was it the one that says how pretty I am?"

"I do not heed the drunks who puke up your legend along with their wine," she replied, eyes narrowing. Good—if she was irritated enough to use that tone, she was irritated enough to miss. "I was trained by every master in sword, lore, and art under the Empress's patronage. I am the Sword of the Imperium, the guardian of her people, the bane of her foes, and the hope of her future."

"That's a long list of titles," I observed. "At least stories get you laid sometimes."

Her teeth clenched, her stance shifted, the air shimmered about her. My body was tensing up, sensing the violence behind her eyes, but I kept it off my face. If I gave her even a *hint* of what I was going to do, she'd immediately see how to get through it and I'd be another corpse on the ground.

"You had a similar list," she replied, "Red Cloud."

Her blade hadn't moved, but I felt like I was bleeding all the same.

That name. That life. It was the only scar on me you couldn't see, but the one that hurt the most. How did she know? No one who wasn't on my list knew that name, knew what I had done.

What I had lost.

"Why?" she asked. "You were the promise of the Imperium, a Prodigy. You could have saved thousands, made this land safe for generations to come." She stared at me, that gaze cutting deeper than any blade. "Yet here you stand, a Vagrant, one more petty thug among many. Indulge me one request."

The scorn in her eyes melted. And the look she gave me cut just as deep.

"Tell me why you turned your back on us."

Somehow, I thought I'd always have a good answer for that. One I honed until it was as real as any weapon. But a good answer isn't a true answer. And when the time came and I looked into that earnest, pleading stare she gave me, I gave her the latter one.

"Because when the time comes," I whispered, "and you're bleeding out on the floor, none of your titles make them hesitate when they step over your body."

Her eyes widened.

The rest happened so fast I couldn't keep up. The air around her shimmered. The Lady's song hit a painfully high note. She vanished. The wind behind stirred, as though through a faint breeze.

I whirled.

Sparks assailed me as I caught her blade against mine, driving her thrust away from my heart and into the air. Her eyes were wide with shock and anger. If she'd been even a little calmer, that blow would have come quicker than I could have blocked. But she'd wanted to be sure she killed me in one strike.

I have that effect on people.

"You," she whispered, unbelieving, "you blocked the Wolf's Fang Strike?"

Of course she fucking named her attacks.

I grabbed her by the wrist as I pushed her sword away. I drew my head back and snapped it forward. I felt the bone break, the blood spatter warm on my face as my forehead smashed against her nose. She reeled backward, blood pouring from her nose as she stared at me, astonished.

I wiped her blood off my face and flicked it away.

"Think I'll call that move 'Stephen.'"

Rage burned so hot on her face I thought the blood would boil right off it. She raised her sword, ready for another attack.

Good. If I could keep her angry, keep her making mistakes, I might make it out of here alive...

"*Captain!*"

Unless, of course, two other mages showed up.

Then I guess I was fucked.

Shenazar swooped down to land beside Velline, her sword thick with red. Dalthoros sauntered out of the melee, unscathed and unbothered, as he took a position at Velline's other side. The two of them took measure of their commander's blood on my face, raised their weapons, and slid into a familiar position of "ready to fucking kill."

I held my blade out, backing away as they advanced on me. They herded me away from the melee, toward the great bay window that overlooked Terassus's twinkling city lights. And with every step I took, I grew more tense.

Dumb luck had saved me from Velline, but all three of them could have killed me with a thought.

So what the fuck were they waiting for?

"The carnage is over, Sal," Velline said. "The Haveners will be dealt with shortly. Whatever insanity you were planning, it's over. Surrender."

So that was it. She wanted information—a plot foiled and another honor heaped upon her by the Imperium. That made sense, only...

"Please."

Why did she sound so damn pleading about it?

I couldn't say as Two Lonely Old Men wouldn't deserve me turning him and Jero over. But I couldn't say as Agne, Yria, and the others did. I definitely couldn't imagine that being turned over to the Imperium I had betrayed would end with anything but my carcass being preserved as a trophy.

So I did the only thing I *could* do.

I raised my sword. I set my feet. And hoped that I could at least muss her hair before she ran me through.

The three of them exchanged a look, a terse nod, as they came to the same conclusion. They started to advance upon me. I took a step forward.

Then the earth shook.

Faintly, at first, enough that I barely felt it through the soles of my shoes. But it hadn't gone unnoticed. Velline held up a hand for the others to halt, a suspicious look on her face as she wondered if she had just felt what I had.

The second time it happened, she was less suspicious.

The floor shuddered beneath my feet. Again and again, each time growing louder, until I could feel the impact in my rib cage. The chorus of the melee—the songs, the wails, the cries of horror and pain—fell silent beneath the thunderous, lumbering sound.

And the sound of something steady, distant and faint.

A heart beating.

And growing louder.

"LOOK!"

Someone screamed. Every eye, bleeding or not, turned upward and stared out of the window.

Amid the snow and darkness outdoors, a spark lit, a bright red glow in the gloom. With every beat of the heart, it grew brighter, illuminating a chest made of shattered timbers, a horned skull of a great beast, a great fist of wood and flame drawing back and—

FUCK.

I ran, along with everyone else, from the window as the wooden fist punched through the glass in a spray of snow and shards. The cold wind swept in, howling alongside the thunderous heartbeat and the shuddering stride as something huge lumbered into the banquet hall.

I stared up at the great skull scraping the ceiling.

The effigy stared down at me.

And it occurred to me that perhaps Velline had a point when she said I cause a lot of trouble.

TWENTY-FIVE

YUN ATTORO ESTATE

I've fought warlords and the armies behind them to the last outlaw. I've walked into the dens of beasts known only by the number of people they eat.

I've seen things more horrible and wondrous than you could imagine painted across this forsaken world, some I hesitate to say because I know you wouldn't believe me.

So trust me when I say I had never seen anything—*anything*—like this.

The sounds of battle had gone silent. Swords had lowered as gazes turned upward. Even the dying seemed to cease moaning. Under that thing's gaze, two pyres of light burning in empty sockets, any sound not the crackling of its fire or the beating of its heart seemed forbidden.

Profane.

It wasn't a monster, the effigy that loomed over us few that still stood. It didn't move with instinct or command, swinging its great skull of a head back and forth, smoke and cinders falling from its body. It didn't charge as a monster would, driven by hunger or rage; it merely stood there, staring down upon us from behind a veil of black smoke pouring from its heart. And though it saw us, it betrayed no rage, no hunger, no emotion beyond vague disinterest.

It wasn't a monster.

I knew how to kill monsters.

This thing... this was...

"MY LORD!"

A Havener came creeping forward, dropping a severed limb he had been carrying, heedless of the sword sunk three inches into his chest. His eyes, weeping blood, were glistening with an ecstasy matched only by the mania of his grin. He fell to his knees, staring up at the effigy.

"I prayed so long I...I didn't..." His lips trembled, struggling to find words that wouldn't come. "I am so happy I saw you... before... before..."

His head craned backward. His mouth stretched wide. A great torrent of blood erupted from his mouth, his nostrils, his eyes, draining him dry in six seconds. And by the seventh, the Firelung having completely burned out in his veins, he collapsed a dry, empty husk.

It said something about our situation that a man erupting blood from his eyeballs was only the second-weirdest thing going on.

"That thing," I whispered, staring up at the effigy, "that can't be..."

The most rational Havener is still a lunatic. A Havener so fucked up on drugs that his head was exploding was even less reliable. But if you could trust a Havener to do anything, it was recognize his god.

And yet, even as I stared up at the thing, even as his dying words lodged in my head like a spike, I couldn't be sure.

Is that, I wondered, *the Seeing God?*

As if in answer, the great skull turned toward me with the fire-eaten creak of wood. From behind veils of smoke, I felt its hollow stare upon me. Between the beating of its heart, I heard a voice.

You.

No. Not heard.

I remember you.

I felt it. As keenly as any wound.

The urge to run was distant inside me, buried so deep beneath a layer of fear that it was an impossibility. I couldn't run, couldn't move, couldn't think as I felt its voice inside my head, a fire crawling across a drought-stricken plain.

But you do not remember me. That fever-hot voice burned through thought and worry and left bare something inside me that I was afraid to acknowledge existed. *You do not feel me in your scars, as I feel you. You do not feel my pain, as I feel you. You do not hear me, as I have heard every moment of self-pity, every doubting boast, every prayer you think no one hears.*

Had to run. Had to move. Had to do something. But I couldn't will my legs to move, my eyes to blink. I couldn't feel anything but the searing pain of that voice in my head, the shudder of that beating heart in my skin.

I know the petty fears and sorrows that drive you. I know they have carried you here, seeking an end to the pain, the suffering, the scars you carry. And I know, no matter how hard you look...

Behind the black smoke, I saw something stir. The brow of the great skull cracked, a great gash splitting it down the middle. The bone split apart, revealing glistening red sinew that trembled with every beat of the heart. Slowly, like a red curtain, they parted. And something within the smoke awoke.

You will never find an escape from pain.

An eye.

A single blue eye, pure and bright as the first morning of winter, locked upon me.

The future is written in your flesh, Salazanca.

My name. My real name. It knew.

The ruin visited upon you, you will visit upon this virgin world. It will bring you no joy. But I cannot be satisfied with that. Nor can those who rely upon me.

My body was wracked by flame. My lungs were filled with smoke. My eyes were fixed, unblinking, upon that single blue orb. I didn't notice anything else. Not the smoke filling the room. Not the flames burning brighter.

Though, for what it is worth...

Not the great, wooden foot that loomed over me.

I am sorry.

And came crashing down.

Wood creaked. Flames laughed. The Lady sang. Two tons of wood came crashing down in a thunderous stomp, ash and cinders erupting in a cloud where the effigy's foot had struck.

And I was still alive.

Somehow.

It didn't become clear until that great eye disappeared behind the smoke again. Breath returned to my burning lungs and the fire went dim in my veins. Feeling returned to my body, enough for me to notice the arms wrapped around my waist.

"Why didn't you *move*?"

Velline. Her voice was sharp in my ears. Not as sharp as the sword pressed against my side, though. She must have pulled me clear, too fast for me to notice. By the time I thought to grab her hand, she seized my wrist and twisted it behind my back as she hauled me away from the effigy.

"Are the civilians out?" she shouted toward her companions as they rushed toward her. "Is everyone safe?"

"Not yet," Shenazar replied, glancing toward the end of the hall. A knot of civilians cowered behind a group of mages, fighting off those Haveners whose skulls hadn't yet exploded from the Firelung. "And they aren't going to, unless we do something *fast*."

She was right. All the tapestries and portraits and treasures of the banquet hall would become nothing more than expensive kindling, and the civilians with it, if the effigy's flames spread. If that thing so much as sneezed, this manor would become the biggest funeral pyre in the Scar.

I know skulls can't sneeze. Shut the fuck up. I couldn't think of anything better.

"We can't fight something like that," Velline said, eyes locked upon the effigy. "Shenazar, can you keep it contained?"

"*Contained?*" Shenazar gaped at the woman. "Captain, when I said I could shut down anyone, I was talking about drinking contests."

"Well, fucking *try*," Velline snarled. "Dalthoros, we need to get the civilians out of here while she buys us time."

"A pity." Dalthoros yawned as he looked toward the panicked guests. "This was just getting interesting." He looked toward me. "What of your friend?"

"She comes with us."

"The hell I do," I growled.

"Captain, we can't handle Haveners, civilians, a giant flaming pile of what-the-fuck, *and* a prisoner," Shenazar protested.

"She's a criminal against the Imperium and the entire reason *this*"—Velline gestured at the chaos—"is happening. She comes with us to answer for her crimes. Now *go*."

Shenazar winced, but nodded. She leapt into the air, her magic carrying her as she flew toward the effigy, sword out and ready to strike. Whatever she could do against it wouldn't be more than a fleeting distraction.

Which meant I didn't have much time to figure a way out of this.

"Listen to your friends, 'Captain,'" I spat as I struggled against Velline's grip. "If you think I'm coming quietly with you..."

I paused. Against the heat of my skin, the chill of her steel was like agony as she pressed it against my neck and hissed into my ear.

"You don't have a choice, *Red Cloud*." She spat the name, spite and pain dripping from her lips. "You abandoned the Imperium. You abandoned its people. *Thousands* could have been saved had you not turned Vagrant. You will answer for each and every one of them."

She leaned in, painfully close. She twisted my arm so that I could feel my shoulder straining in its socket. A trace of my blood wept out and splashed upon the metal of her sword. And deep within me, in some painful part that knew what it was like to be cut like this, something screamed.

"Whatever you were planning, it failed, and people died," she spoke, stark as winter. "You are not escaping this. No one else is going to die. No one is coming to help you. It's over, Sal."

I gritted my teeth, swallowed hard. "You're wrong," I rasped under her blade. "Stephen is coming."

"Stephen? Who the fuck is—"

My neck snapped backward. The back of my skull smashed against her face. I heard the bone of her nose snap—this time, for good—and felt a fresh spray of blood soak my hair. Velline screamed, her grip loosening enough for me to bring my fist crashing down between her legs.

She fell backward, sword clattering, the wind knocked out of her as I tore off running.

She was good, I had to admit. Maybe even better than Jindu. But trust me on this, all the training from all the masters in all the Imperium can't prepare you for getting punched in the snatch.

I sure as shit wasn't going to stick around to tell her that, though. I had to act fast, before either the giant effigy that wanted to kill me or the numerous deadly mages that wanted to kill me took notice of what I was doing.

I rushed toward the effigy. The great creature swung its burning limbs, trying to swat Shenazar out of the sky as she flew around it, striking at its neck and joints in a futile attempt to stop it. The winds of her magic twisted the smoke pouring from its body—I ran, coughing and searching through stinging eyes.

The earth shook as a colossal foot came crashing down. I stopped short just in time to avoid it, raising my arm to shield my eyes from its fire. I swept forward, found a jutting piece of timber lodged in its ankle, wrapped my hands around it, and pulled.

The heat from the effigy was incredible, agonizing. Sweat poured down my body as my lungs struggled to find enough air to let me pull. It hurt. Bad.

But I'd been burned worse.

With a roar, I hauled an arm's-length sliver of wood out of its ankle, burning like a torch. I ran clear of the effigy and its smoke. I drew a deep breath of clean air as I looked around the hall, all its priceless, precious, flammable treasures.

And then, I got to work.

I tore through the hall, leaping over corpses and rubble, darting between brawls as Haveners hurled themselves at mages and mages hurled spells back. In my wake, a garden of fire bloomed. Portraits of Imperial heroes smiled serenely as fire engulfed them, alcohol-soaked tables went up like so many candles, and the paper golem servants wandered the brawl, blissfully unaware of the engulfing flames they spread with every waking step.

I could hear the shouting, the screaming, the desperate wailing—I forced myself not to listen, not to think about what I was doing. I kept Agne's words in my head. If we were stopped here—if *I* was stopped here—everything, all these ghosts, all this blood, would be for nothing. So I shut my ears, I shut my eyes, I kept running.

In hindsight, if I had kept my eyes open, I probably wouldn't have run straight into Velline's boot.

She appeared with a whisper of wind and a note of the Lady's song, her boot driving the wind out of me as she drove it into my belly. I collapsed, my makeshift torch rolling away from me, as I tried to find my breath. I glanced upward, through vision clouded by pain and smoke, and saw a glimmer of steel.

My arm was up and my shield out just in time to catch her blade as she brought it down. Over the rim, through trails of blood painting her, Velline's face was twisted into a mask of anger.

"Why?" she cried. "What's the point of all this? Are you simply not happy unless people are dying and things are on fire?"

Maybe it was the smoke in my lungs or the drugs in my brain or the pain wracking my body, but I thought I saw tears sliding through the bloody mess on her face.

"What happened to you, Red Cloud?"

"Red Cloud is dead," I replied, setting my feet. "She died for a nation that didn't give a shit about her, burning people for a flag they would never burn, fighting a war that didn't matter. Red Cloud is gone."

I shoved, forcing her back. She raised her blade, eyes aglow with purple light, the Lady's song whirling around her.

"My name," I said, "is Sal the Cacophony." I smiled morbidly and gestured out over the banquet hall. "And I just did that."

Velline followed my hand. Her eyes went wide with horror.

The effigy waded through an ocean of flame, the fires having spread to every corner of the hall. The dead drowned beneath lapping red waves, smoke and cinders scattered like froth breaking on their crowns. And there, a tiny island, the civilians cowered.

"You're good, girl," I said. "Near as I can tell, you're the best the Imperium has ever made. I bet you could kill me pretty effortlessly. I bet you could save everyone in this hall." I snorted, spat blood on the hall. "But I bet you can't do both."

Horror, fury, hatred—emotion boiled beneath the blood on her face as she looked over me. Her sword quivered, as if begging her to end me. The Lady's song rose to a shrieking crescendo. Her feet were set, ready to attack.

But her eyes watered.

They shut.

And she whispered.

"I'll kill you for this."

She vanished.

And reappeared.

At the other end of the hall, far from me.

Fuck me, that had been close. For a second, I thought she was going to let them die to kill me. Hell, she still might not be able to save all of them. It was a dumb thing I'd done. A dumb, ugly, brutal thing that gave me a pain in my chest worse than burns or wounds.

But it had worked.

I wanted to vomit. I wanted to weep. I wanted to collapse, from exhaustion and horror, and just lie down until things stopped hurting so much.

And I might have.

But, you know.

The whole place was still on fire, so...

TWENTY-SIX

YUN ATTORO ESTATE

I ran through a hallway, blinded by smoke. My new wounds fought with my old scars for the right to kill me first. My lungs were full of smoke, my head was full of drugs, I was leaving an awful lot of blood on the floor behind me—but I was still running, I was still breathing, I was still alive.

I'd been through worse.

And if my skull stopped ringing anytime soon, I'm sure I could think of when.

At the very least, I'd shaken pursuit—five minutes of running through the halls and I couldn't hear any. Granted, it'd be hard to, over the screaming and all, but I had bigger problems on my mind.

The halls of the manor were big by design. Birds hated to be cramped and Oyakai were bigger than most—all I had to do was follow the halls large enough to allow a giant, surly bird to walk through. And, if this was anything like the home of your average Imperial rich asshole, there would be a rookery somewhere high enough to allow the birds to take flight. If Tuteng and Jero hoped to get them out, they'd head for those.

That made sense . . . didn't it?

It was hard to think. I'd been hurt too much, lost too much blood, inhaled too much of the Firelung—I wasn't sure what made sense anymore. I wasn't sure why I was here, now that I knew Two

Lonely Old Men had lied to me, now that I had been responsible for so many people dead, now that...

"Running again?"

No screaming. No songs. No fire. I heard her voice clearly.

Ahead, through the coiling smoke, I saw her. Small, slight, smiling. Too good to be here, in this wretched place, yet she looked at me with those gentle eyes, like she didn't even notice the blood painting me.

"Darrish?" I whispered.

No, I told myself. *Another ghost. The drugs. The wounds. Something. She's not real.*

She wasn't real.

So why wasn't I running?

"This is familiar, isn't it?" Darrish came walking toward me, unfazed by the cinders drifting through the air, unbothered by the red on my hands. "Fire at your back, bodies in your wake, hoping that if you run fast enough, you can escape the fire you set?"

"You're not real," I whispered as she approached.

"I'm not?"

She raised a hand, pressed it to my cheek like she used to back then. Back when I would come limping to the barracks after a mission had gone wrong, back when I would hang my head and stand for hours in front of her door before knocking, back when she would hold me and stroke my hair and tell me that it was all worth it...

It felt the same now as it did then. Warm. And so soft.

"Don't I feel real?" she whispered, her hand sliding down my cheek. "Wasn't I real when you came to me all those nights?"

"You were real when I looked to you, the night Vraki took my power," I snapped, snatching her wrist and pushing her away. "You were real when you did nothing to help me. You're not real now."

"Maybe. But maybe I was never real to you," she said. "Maybe I was always just a pleasant dream you could come back to when you ran from the bodies you left on the field as Red Cloud. Maybe I was something you could run away from when I needed you."

Her words cut me, but there was no malice in that smile. She wasn't capable of it. Even if she wasn't real.

And she wasn't...was she?

"Sal the Cacophony," she chuckled. "Vagrant. Killer of men and monsters. Wielder of the Mad Emperor's Legacy. But no story ever talks about how much running away you do, does it? So, what are you running from this time?"

"Nothing."

She looked over my shoulder. "Looks like an impressive fire. Not your best, but it's up there."

"I'm not running."

"No? Where are you going, then?"

I shouldn't talk to her. I should be moving. She wasn't real. She *wasn't.*

"Birds," I growled, starting to trudge forward. "We get the birds, we get the Relic, we end the war."

"Scions, but we're altruistic, aren't we?" she giggled, walking slowly backward to stay ahead of me, hands folded demurely behind her back. "Are you doing this all out of the goodness of your heart?" She canted her head to the side. "Or is it just to kill me?"

Don't talk to her.

"That's what this is all for, right? All these fires you set—they're just to get to the names on your list, to kill them."

Keep moving.

"Because nothing feels normal knowing we're out there, does it? Whiskey doesn't taste good, kisses aren't sweet, nothing seems right. Nothing except killing us. Every last name on that list."

She's not real.

"All the fires are worth it for that, right? Just like all the fires back then were worth it, so long as you got to keep coming back to me. You'll keep burning and burning and it's fine, so long as you can keep ahead of the smoke."

She's NOT real.

"And when you're done, Salazanca, and the last name is crossed out on your list, are you just going to keep moving ahead of the fire? Or are you finally going to stop, turn around..."

SHE'S. NOT. REAL.

"And see the ashes you left behind?"

Darrish stopped. She raised a hand and pointed over my shoulder.

I shouldn't have turned around.

But I did.

Flames lapped the hall behind me from doorways, red tongues from black maws belching smoke. There, standing frail and delicate and fleeting as ashes on the wind, I saw another woman.

She stared at me, with big eyes behind big glasses, and terror on her face. She raised a hand to me and whispered.

"Sal…"

I raised a hand to her.

And screamed.

"LIETTE!"

The flames swallowed her. She disappeared. Only ashes were left behind.

"The fire's getting warmer, Salazanca," Darrish chuckled behind me.

I shouted, flicked my shield out, ready to whirl and smash it across her face. But when I turned to her, she was gone. In her place stood a charred husk of a human, blackened but for the broad smile painted across her sunken face.

"Better run."

I blinked.

She was gone. Liette was gone. Neither had been real.

But the fire had been. And it wasn't gone.

I kept going. Stopping had given my body a chance to realize how tired it was. Every step was punctuated by a wince, a hack, an ache that would revisit me every morning until the day I died. Assuming I made it out.

But I kept going. Pursued by fire and smoke, I kept going until the great hall gave way to a great doorway that gave way to an immense room.

Cold wind buffeted me as I stepped in, plastering the blood and sweat to my skin. Nests, perches, toys, and the grisly remains of large animals that had been the birds' meals scattered the wooden floor. The rookery's northern wall was completely gone, replaced by a pair of gigantic doors that had been blown off its hinges, glowing sigils etched into its edges.

A Spellwright's sigils. But where was the Spellwright?

"Is it looking at me? Oh, Scions, I think it's looking at me."

Ah. There.

The Oyakai stood huddled upon the floor, unfazed by the

apparent destruction of their home or the death of their previous master. They crouched around Tuteng, the Rukkokri taking a moment to press his horned brow against each of their heads, whispering words I couldn't hear over the sound of someone screaming.

"I can't! I *can't!*" Urda stood in the grip of Jero, who was attempting to shove him toward one of the crouching birds. "It's . . . it's dangerous!"

"You just took a magical doorway from nowhere into the middle of a gigantic manor on fucking *fire*," Jero snapped as he struggled with the wright. "How the hell is a bird more dangerous than that?"

"It's unsanitary! What if it pecks me? What if it scratches me? I could get diseases! Like . . ." He swallowed hard. "*Featherwretch.*"

"That's not a real thing!"

"You don't know that! Nobody knows that! This is completely uncharted territory! I *refuse* to be the first patient to die of—"

"Fucking move it along already, Mayor Shitshoes." Yria shoved Urda toward the bird with the only arm that still worked. The portal magic had taken too much out of her—her right arm hung dead at her side, her left leg dragging behind her as she stalked after her brother. "My arm's fucking shot to hell, so you're gonna have to drive this thing."

"H-how? I've never even touched a bird!"

"Tuteng has handled it," Jero replied. "Just hold the reins and *get the fuck on!*"

"Th-there must be another way!" Urda protested. "There has to—"

Yria's hand shot out as she took her brother by the collar and forced him to look at her.

"What'd I tell you after Mom died?" she asked.

He stared at her, eyes quivering. He swallowed hard, nodded. She nodded back, released him. With only the faintest of whining sounds, they pushed him into the beast's saddle. With a grunt of effort, he helped Yria up behind him.

"Meet at the rendezvous. We'll be right behind you." He glanced to the Clansman nearby. "Tuteng!"

The Clansman's brows furrowed beneath his horns as he met the bird's stare. He gave the creature a brief pat on its beak and a whisper. The creature closed its eyes, rose on its long legs, and started sprinting toward the blown-off doors.

"*NonononoNONONONONONONONO*—"

Urda's protests were lost in the cry of the bird as the Oyakai spread its wings, leapt from the floor, and took flight into the night. Coiling smoke and falling snow parted before it, as though afraid of sullying such a creature. They did not resume until the Oyakai's dark feathers disappeared into the night.

"Okay." Jero wiped sweat from his brow. "We've got to get the rest of them—" He turned. And saw me. "Ah, shit."

His eyes didn't go wide with shock. His mouth didn't fumble for excuses. He stared at me, worry etched in his wrinkles, with wary disbelief. I'd seen that look before, in the hundred eyes of a hundred faces of a hundred people who thought me dead, right before I put a sword through them.

"Sal," he whispered my name as I approached. "You made it."

"Yeah." I wiped blood from my face with the back of my hand. "I'm good at that, turns out."

I didn't recognize the man staring at me, this mess of wounds and wrinkles like scars. I didn't see the man with the soft eyes that had met me on a cold night in the middle of nowhere. I couldn't find the man with the nice smile who had poured me wine and sat with me and pretended we were both normal. I had no idea where the man was who had traded with me, in quiet words that only people like us spoke, the secrets we kept close as our cuts.

This man—this man with every muscle drawn taut, bristling with pain and fear—I didn't recognize.

But that look... that wild-eyed, ready-to-kill look...

I knew that look.

"Listen," he whispered, letting out a breath. "I need to tell you—"

"You need to shut up," I replied. "And you need to get out of here." I gestured back toward the rising smoke. "Everyone does."

He opened his mouth like he wanted to say something. I narrowed my eyes like he really shouldn't. Whatever he had to say, I wanted to hear when I was in better shape to strangle him.

Instead, he nodded weakly and gestured toward one of the Oyakai. He held out his hand to help me up into the saddle. I stared at him until he withdrew it. And then withdrew ten more paces.

I reached up to grab the bird's saddle. Pain flared inside me—pain

from the drugs, the burns, the wounds. I gritted my teeth, bit them
back.

"Leaving so soon?"

But wouldn't you know it, that's when I found another pain in
my ass.

His voice came as languid as his stride, a slender man strolling
into the rookery as though he were leaving a nice restaurant and not
a manor filled to the brim with flame. His clothes were shredded,
torn by the dozen wounds and singed by the dozen burns across his
body. Yet for all that, his gaze was steady and unbothered beneath
the bony plate jutting from his forehead.

Dalthoros.

For a minute there, I thought I was really going to get out of here
without some last-minute birdshit like this.

"Personally, I can forgive the mess you made." He brushed ashes
from his bare shoulder. "Really, I lament the loss of the artwork
more than the loss of the nobles you slew. However."

He narrowed his eyes. Purple light flashed behind them. The
Lady Merchant's song rose, clear as a bell over the sound of flame.

He was a mage.

Of course he was a mage.

Why the fuck *wouldn't* he be?

"The captain is of the belief that all citizens of the Imperium, no
matter how foppish, are worthy of her protection. It is the mandate
of her rank as Sword of the Empress and the mandate of our mission
here."

His skin rippled like water. Across his body, his wounds began to
close themselves shut. The reddened flesh of his burns returned to a
healthy pink. In the span it took me to realize how deep the shit I
was in went, he stood up, hale, hearty, and ready to fight again.

A Mendmage.

A fucking Mendmage.

He was fresh, I was wiped. He was strong, I was weak. And even
if I *did* manage to somehow muster the energy to give him a bloody
nose, he could regenerate in the blink of an eye.

My skin burned, my blood burned, my skull burned. Yet somehow, I felt something very cold settle in the pit of my belly.

"An insult to the Imperium, I can handle."

Dalthoros started walking toward me. I set my feet.

"An insult to the Empress, I do not mind."

He raised his sword. I flicked my shield out.

"But an insult to the captain?" He shook his head. "That I cannot abide. Whatever Vagrant god you believe in, I suggest you make peace with, for I shall leave nothing to—"

He didn't finish that sentence.

Well, he *did*, but I'm not sure the gurgling noise he made when five delicate fingers wrapped around his throat counted as words.

The hand on his neck was joined by another that seized his ankle. His eyes bulged out in confusion, his mouth struggling to find the breath to scream as he was hoisted into the air. Terror bloomed across his face as he was leveled like a javelin at the wall.

And promptly hurled.

His body struck the stone. There was a thick, wet snapping sound. He crumpled bodily to the floor, where he lay.

Agne, covered in soot and stains, glanced from the man she had just hurled back toward me.

"Sorry," she said. "Were you and he about to do a thing?"

I blinked at the crumpled mess that had been Dalthoros before shaking my head.

"No, I'm fine."

"Good, good." Agne stalked forward and I could see there wasn't a scratch on her. She approached a larger Oyakai with deep azure feathers. "I'm taking this bird, if no one minds."

After that, she could have taken my virginity and I wouldn't have minded.

We mounted in short order, Tuteng at our head. He waved a hand. The Oyakai responded to whatever strange power he had, taking off at a run. One by one, the birds leapt into the air. One by one, they spread their wings.

And we took flight.

The smoke and heat fell away. The night air, cold and sweet and painfully clean, hit my face, filled my lungs. Snow fell and melted upon my skin and the pain melted with it. I breathed so deep I thought I might faint and fall off the bird's saddle.

But I didn't. I flew out into the night, behind the rest of the birds we had stolen, ahead of the fire I had set. With every breath I took, I whispered into the wind.

"I made it."

After everything, every lie, every wound, every shitty thing I did, we had done it. The birds were ours. The plan was secure. I was alive.

Somehow.

I looked over my shoulder. The fires had consumed the manor entirely, lighting up the night sky like a funeral pyre. And at its center, unbothered by flame or the carcasses blackening around its feet, the effigy stood.

Its empty gaze was canted upward. Its single eye, cold and blue, was fixed upon me. Its red heart beat.

Perfectly in tune with mine.

TWENTY-SEVEN

LITTLEBARROW

Suffering had a way of making the world seem too small.

It was the first thing Meret had learned when he came to the Borrus Valley, in the aftermath of that great war that shook the region. When faced with all of it—the broken limbs that wouldn't heal right, the night terrors that kept people from sleeping, the times when people just broke down crying for no reason—it all seemed so...suffocating.

It shamed him, sometimes, to think of it like that. But he had no other word for it. It tightened around his neck, the suffering, like a noose. Village to village, home to home, it was always there. Always present, in some form or another. Always closing in a little tighter, every time he took a breath.

Maybe that's why he kept moving on.

It hadn't occurred to him, until he had met the scarred woman with the big gun, just how big the Scar was and what kind of horrors he had been lucky to avoid. He'd heard stories of the fanatics of Haven and their monsters, but they'd always seemed just that: stories, far away from his work and the people who needed it. Hell, even the Imperium that owned the Valley sometimes felt like a myth—he'd only ever seen mages from afar.

But this story she told him...it was too much.

It had too much fire and screaming and death. There were too many monsters and not enough heroes to stop them. It was all the wars he'd struggled to avoid and all the blood he'd hoped to move on from. Now it, all of it, and the woman who sparked it all off had crash-landed in his township.

Maybe that's why he stood up and gasped out, "I need some air."

Sal looked up from across the table. "You feeling all right?"

No, he thought.

"Yeah," he said, his head bobbing in slack agreement. "Yeah, I'm...I just..." He fumbled with his hands before patting his legs. "Blood clots build up if you don't move around, you know? They can kill you."

"Really?" Sal leaned back, scratched herself. "What a sad way to go."

Better than being burned alive.

"Right. Sad," he said. "So I'm just going to...you know..."

She stared at him, her blue eyes empty and her lips pursed. For a moment, he wondered if she was about to call his bluff, if she knew what he was about to do. But if she did, she didn't show it as she inclined her head.

"All right," she said. "I'll be here."

He nodded again, dumbly. He stumbled toward the door. He walked until he was sure he was out of sight of the windows.

And he started running.

He tore his way down to the bottom of the hill, stumbling over rocks and bushes, letting cold air fill his lungs, not stopping until he'd run enough that exhaustion overtook fear. He bent over, hands on his knees, eyes wide and unblinking.

Monsters, he told himself. *She fights monsters. She burns cities. She kills people. She's a Vagrant, a fucking magical murderer in a war* brimming *with magical murderers. How long until they follow her here? How long until it's another war?*

He swept his gaze over Littlebarrow, over its humble houses that he'd come to know so well. He caught himself staring, trying to picture them engulfed in flames, trying to see the trenches that would be dug into fields to hold all the bodies. How long would it be before Old Man Rittish's house was kindling by some spell or cannon? How long would it be before Danisca and her three children were crushed beneath the foot of some monster?

How long, he wondered, would it be before they realized it had happened because of him?

Sindra was right, he told himself. *You brought her here. You let her stay here. You did this. You did this. You did this. You did this. You—*

"Meret?"

A raspy voice, one usually accompanied by complaints of bad joints and bad weather, reached his ears. Rodic, all thin angles and gray hairs, stood nearby, beside a run-down old bird yoked to an even more run-down old cart, brimming with possessions.

"Are you well, young man?" Rodic was years gone from Imperial territory, but his accent hadn't faded with age or distance. "You look as though you're going to vomit."

He hadn't actually thought he would vomit until Rodic mentioned it. So he kept his answer a short, gurgling, "I'm all right." He glanced to the cart, looked over its possessions. "You're...leaving?"

His face curled into a severe frown. "Not by choice. I've held this home for forty years and six children. I'd rather not abandon it." He gestured vaguely down the road. "But I'd rather less see *that* done to it."

Lady Kalavin's home. Opulent and austere, even in ruin. Sal's gun had shorn the top of it clear off, the shattered timbers of its second floor standing like a crown of splinters and broken furniture. That house had withstood six bandit raids, the local lore went. Over a hundred men with a hundred weapons.

And Sal had destroyed it with just one shot.

"More are leaving," Rodic said. "Except Sindra. I thought I'd wait it out with her, but she..." He sighed, a cloud of cold breath trailing out from weary lips. "She said there was no mercy in that Vagrant."

She's right, he told himself. *She was always right.*

"Rodic," Meret said, "I didn't mean to—"

"It's not your fault." Rodic held up a hand to stop his apology. "And you've done too much good for Littlebarrow for me to begrudge you trying to do a little more. But, Meret..." He looked back up the hill, cringing, as if he expected Sal to burst out at any minute and start shooting again. "She's not worth it."

He swallowed. "Not worth what?"

"The town, the struggle, whatever you're putting yourself through to try and help her." His eyes narrowed. "You ever seen a Vagrant's work, Meret?"

"I've seen some traces of the war around here and—"

"Then you've seen the work of civilized people pushed too far. But a Vagrant..." His lip stiffened, his breath coming more shakily. "I was traveling from Bentpine, up the road, after delivering some lumber there, six years back. I'd gotten half a day out when I remembered I hadn't gotten the credit notice signed. I went back and..."

His voice drifted off into the cold, became one more piece of snow falling on the ground.

"And what?" Meret pressed.

"And...nothing," he whispered. "The town was gone. Torn down to its foundations. The people were scattered about, impaled on the ruins of their homes, or smashed against the streets. Over six hundred people. Gone in less than a day. I learned later that it was the work of a Skymage—Vantha the Zephyr or something like that. She hadn't taken a damn thing from them. She hadn't offered any demands. She had no reason at all. She just showed up and..."

He shuddered, took in a deep breath. "War makes animals out of people, Meret, but they eventually change back into people. Vagrants, though...Vagrants aren't even animals. Animals have a reason for killing." He glanced back at Meret's house. "Listen... there's room in the cart. And the old lady"—he gestured to his bird—"is still staunch. She'll get us to the next town by sunup. Come with me, Meret. You don't want to be around when what happened to Bentpine happens here."

"Rodic, I don't—"

"What is it you're worried about? Pride? Courage? The bravest corpse is still a corpse, young man, and that Vagrant's appreciation for you will last as long as it takes to step over your body." Rodic sighed, placed a hand on Meret's shoulder, gave it an encouraging squeeze. "Listen. We don't need to have this conversation. These can be the last words we speak. I'm going into my house to get a few more things and then I'm leaving. If you're on the cart when I go, I won't say a word, one way or another. But it'll be there for you. And there'll be a new village for you. All right?"

Meret stumbled for an answer but could only manage a weak

nod. Rodic, with a grunt, returned the gesture before stalking back to his house and slamming the door shut behind him, leaving Meret in the worst possible place an intelligent person can find themselves.

Alone with his thoughts.

The inside of his skull rattled with them: concern battling fear, fear being strangled by terror, terror being stabbed and dragged into a dark alley by guilt. The thoughts clambered over each other to be heard, each one of them speaking too fast and too frenziedly to get any more than a brief, shrieking snippet of sound.

You don't belong here.

They need you.

Who can you help if you're dead?

Who will help if you're gone?

And so on.

It had always been like this. He kept himself busy with wandering, with healing, with worrying about wandering and healing precisely so he wouldn't have to deal with the thoughts. Thinking led to more thinking, which led to more thoughts, which filled up his head so heavy that they eventually pulled him to the ground where he would lie, paralyzed, until he was just too tired to hold them anymore.

But just as his knees began to shake, a singular voice whispered. Louder. Clearer. More forceful than the others.

Run.

Fear. Cold. Primal.

Run away. Run far. Run fast. Don't die here.

Sensible.

Please.

He eyed the cart, that tantalizingly empty spot between Rodic's pots and pans and his woodcutting axe. It was just big enough for him, like it had been made for him. He wouldn't have to do anything, wouldn't have to explain himself, wouldn't even have to think about walking. All he had to do was climb in.

And so he did.

Or he started to, anyway. With every step he took, his breathing became more labored, his legs grew more brittle, until he thought he might collapse before he got there.

"Are you leaving?"

But it wouldn't do to pass out in terror in front of a lady, now, would it?

Her bruises stark against the cold gray sky, Liette stood not six feet from him, her hands folded behind her back as she stared up at the snow falling overhead. Yet the snow seemed to...veer away, swirling around her instead of landing upon her shoulders. And the winds that stirred the falling flakes did not touch a single hair upon her head. She stood apart from the world, distant and colder than any winter.

"It's understandable, if you are."

He blinked, suddenly aware that she was talking to him.

"You, uh, you shouldn't be walking around...," he said. "Not with that injury."

"I'm not walking."

"I mean, not at the moment, but you really shouldn't—"

"Are you leaving?"

She was looking at him. He hadn't seen her move at all, but now her stare was on him. Through him. Like a dark-eyed knife. He fumbled for a lie, an excuse, but each time one came to him, her eyes narrowed just a little, like she could see it forming on his lips and already knew it was a lie.

"Yeah."

And so, the truth just fell out of his mouth.

"Yeah, I'm leaving." He swallowed cold spittle, licked chapped lips. "I don't want to be here anymore. I don't want to be here when the fighting starts. Or when it ends."

She continued staring at the falling snow, unbothered by the strange way it wafted away from her, as though it were simply getting out of her way so she could see something far beyond the gray cloud cover overhead.

"It's coming, isn't it?" he asked. "Fighting? Killing?"

"Most likely," she replied.

"Because of her."

She closed her eyes. "Most likely."

"She's going to bring ruin to this town." Words, hot and fervent, spilled out on cold breath and fell upon the ground like so much snow and slush. "And I brought her here. I could have pushed her away. I could have refused. But I brought her back and now we're all going to—"

"No."

A single word. Terse, though not spoken with any particular malice—yet he felt it rather than heard it. A single word with many legs, crawling through his veins.

"No?"

"No."

"No she's not going to bring ruin to this town or no it's not my fault?"

"It doesn't matter."

He blinked, glanced around the town. "Okay, that sounds really wise and all, but considering we're talking about the town being destroyed, do you suppose you could give me some more clarification?"

He wasn't sure why he suddenly started when she moved. Nor was he sure why he breathed a sigh of relief when she took her glasses off and began to clean them.

"Putting aside the other myriad laws, the observable world is measured in decision and impact," Liette said. "The former sets events in motion, the latter measures the event's influence, which in turn governs the next decision, and so on. Everything in nature is a cycle, after all."

"Okay, so does that—"

"Why did you bring us back here?"

"What?"

"You didn't have to. You and I are strangers to each other, likely to never see each other again after this. And she's..." Liette glanced up, gestured vaguely at the ruin of Lady Kalavin's house. "Well, you've seen. You'd be praised by any standard, ethical or intellectual, for disregarding both of us. But you didn't."

Meret rubbed the back of his neck and began to believe he liked this woman better when she was unconscious.

"I didn't...," he said. "Because you needed help."

"We could have found other help."

"But—"

"Or we could have died. Either outcome wouldn't have required you."

"I know, but—"

"Your presence could have been considered irrelevant, all things considered."

"For fuck's sake, you needed help and I was *here*!" he suddenly snapped. "If I hadn't done anything, then nothing would have gotten done."

An insufferably smug smirk creased her face. He wasn't *quite* sure how she could be more aggravating than Sal. Perhaps that's why they were together. Birds of a shitty feather flocked together in a big, shitty flock, as the old wisdom he had just now made up went.

"And thus, the impact." She replaced her glasses and stared out over Littlebarrow. The smirk disappeared, leaving behind something deeply sad. "Another town destroyed. More bodies in the earth. More blood. More death." She closed her eyes. "You're afraid of it."

"Aren't you?"

"Yes," she said. "But not for the same reasons you are."

"Then what?" he whispered, desperate. "What are you afraid of?"

"I'm afraid…" She turned and looked back to his house, through the windows. "Of what will happen to her."

"You mean what she'll do? She's a killer, a ruiner, a—"

"Fuck's sake, you simpleton, do you think I am not aware of that?" she snapped back. "She's a killer, yes. *That* is the impact. Of the scars she carries, of the gift she's lost, of the… *thing* that rides around on her hip. And whatever she does next will leave another impact, which will leave another one and another one, until she's burned this entire world down."

A gale picked up. A cold wind blew across the town, biting through his coat, sending his bag flapping at his side. He hugged himself to ward against it, turned his face away as a flurry of snow spattered him.

Yet she moved not an inch, not a single hair responding to the wind.

"The only way that cycle ends," she whispered, "is if a new decision is introduced." She adjusted her glasses. "Hence, it doesn't matter whether or not it was your fault. The impact has been made. We are alive because of you. And whatever happens because of her will have happened because of you."

She looked back up to the sky, back to whatever it was beyond the clouds that only she could see. And, respectfully, the wind quieted. The snow fell. She said nothing more.

And there, right beside her, he was alone again with his thoughts.

"Can you tell me..."

For just one frigid, eternal moment.

"Whether it matters," Meret whispered, "if I stay or go?"

She finally looked at him. Her eyes were deeper than he could have imagined. And in some part of those dark brown orbs, he thought he could see some small fragment of what had made Sal stand over her, weapon drawn and ready to kill.

Liette smiled and whispered, "Yes."

Meret blinked and coughed. "Uh...sorry, but do you mean yes I should stay or yes you can tell me if it matters?"

"Oh my fucking heavens." She rolled her eyes. "*Obviously*, I meant yes, as in—"

Her words died on the wind, became a scream that tore through the snows. She slumped to her knees, clutching her head. The wind shrieked—in sympathy, in time—with her, the snows quivered in the sky and suddenly swept themselves away from her in all directions.

Meret's hair whipped around his face with the force of the blast. The wind struck him like a fist, threatening to tear his clothes from his body and his feet from the earth. He shut his eyes tight, he raised a hand against the wind.

And he didn't run.

"*Liette!*" he shouted as he knelt beside her. "What's going on? What hurts?" He took her gently by the face, coaxed her gaze toward him. "Look at me."

The wind stilled. The snow hung where it fell. And his words died.

He stared into her eyes. A pair of orbs, black and deep as midnight, stared back at him.

"Don't tell her."

Her words in his veins, crawling and skittering. Her hand on his wrist, cold and ethereal. Her tears on her cheeks, freezing where they fell.

"Please," she whispered. "Don't let her think this is her fault."

"What...what's happening?" Meret, breathless, replied. "Liette, I can't—"

"Promise me."

Again, he felt her voice slipping through his veins. But instead of the cold and skittering thing it had been, it became something... alive. Something warm and hungry coiling around his rib cage, clinging to him with a desperate need. It sat unwell within him— too hot, too alive, too full of want and of sadness and of desire. Perhaps that's why he said what he did.

"I promise."

Or one reason, anyway.

She shut her eyes. She took a deep breath. And when she looked at him again, her eyes were wide and deep once more.

"Thank you," she whispered.

"Meret? Are you ready?"

A voice rasped from behind caught his attention. Rodic stood by his cart, tying down the last of his belongings. The old man gave the knot a tug before clambering onto his cart and taking up the reins as his bird let out an irritated squawk. He shot Meret an expectant look.

The space for him was still there.

Again, the thoughts came clambering over each other, rattling around inside his skull. They screamed at him, pounded on the sides of his skull, fought to reach his mouth. Only this time, they were all saying the same thing.

Run, they told him. *Run far, run away, run. Survive. Live. Breathe. Run.*

"No."

Rodic quirked a brow. "Pardon?"

"No, I'm not going," Meret gasped, the words coming breathlessly. "I can do more if I stay here."

"You can't do anything if you're dead."

"I know."

"And you will die, Meret. Sindra said soldiers were coming.

Imperium, Revolution, it doesn't matter—when one comes, the other follows, and neither of them give a shit about people like us."

"I know."

"Even if that Vagrant doesn't shoot you in the back—and she will, you know she will—she can't do anything against them. Are you sure about this?"

He wasn't, honestly. The stoic silence he offered Rodic was mostly to keep the terrified babble brewing behind his lips from spilling out. The thoughts still raged in his head, screamed at him for being a fool, begged him to run.

But he couldn't. Not this time. He couldn't find a new home to abandon, new bodies to leave behind, new people to watch die.

This cycle had to be broken. A new intent had to be made.

And he had found his.

Rodic didn't understand or approve—hell, if the look in his eyes was anything to go by, Rodic was just seconds away from dragging Meret bodily onto the cart himself. But that look drained from him with a sorrowful sigh.

"Look," he whispered. "If you come to your senses, my old wagon is in my shed. Wheels frozen, but you could get it moving with some muscle. Old Surly, my other bird, is out back in the corral, too—not my fastest, but she'll pull a load if you treat her right. Call her gratitude, apothecary, for what you've done for this town."

"Thanks, Rodic. I know you don't have much—"

"And I'll have a damn lot less because of that woman." His eyes lingered on Meret for a moment. "Thank you, Meret," he said. "For all you've done for us."

He snapped the reins.

The bird squawked.

The cart rattled off and Littlebarrow was that much emptier.

"I hope I did the right thing." Meret watched the cart disappear out the town's gates and vanish into the snows. "Do you think I did?"

He turned back to Liette. But she was gone, leaving behind not so much as a footprint.

The snows continued to fall. The wind sighed in the distance. He was left alone once more.

Alone but for the thoughts in his head, the fear in his heart, and the woman he had decided to stay behind for.

He hoped, as he trudged back up the hill to his house, that she would give him the same courtesy.

Or at least the courtesy of shooting him in the face.

TWENTY-EIGHT

THE CANED TOAD

In stories and other lies, you've probably heard of the Vagrant's Code.

Some performer or rumormonger or drunk has probably told you about the rules. *Vagrants don't attack anyone who won't give them a challenge, Vagrants won't steal your last coin, If you utter the right lyric from the right opera just before they strike, Vagrants won't kill you.*

I'm not saying *all* of it is birdshit. For all I know, there might be some Vagrants who do those things. But overall, the "Code" is no more solid than the beer on a drunk's breath. It's considered rude among most Vagrants to attack without introducing yourself—and that's mostly just so you can both figure out what your chances of killing each other are. Aside from that, there's no guideline, no code, nothing that makes a Vagrant any different than any other outlaw except their magic.

The myth of the Code serves a purpose, though.

If a Vagrant attacks your village, burns your house, and steals your money, you give up. You stop working, stop laughing, stop living because a Vagrant can come after you whenever.

But if there's a code, there's order. There was a rule somewhere that you didn't follow and, if you remember it next time, you'll survive.

The idea that a collection of superpowered maniacs are all following some law is soothing to people. Even the maniacs.

And maybe, if I had thought enough, drank enough, lied enough, I could have convinced myself, too, that everything that had happened last night was all part of some code and not a bunch of people burning and dying for no reason.

Fuck me.

I tried.

I woke up two hours after I went to sleep, six hours after we had dropped the Oyakai off outside the city and snuck back in, five hours after I had lain in bed, aching and sore and dirty with my own blood, and failed to convince myself that last night had been anything but a lot of blood, a lot of fire, a lot of...

Well, like I said. I tried.

I hauled myself out of bed. Snow was still falling outside, observed by a bird that had perched on my windowsill to seek shelter. Cold gnawed at my wounds, sank teeth into my bones. Every part of me that wasn't bloodied was aching, every part of me that wasn't aching was freezing. It hurt, but I didn't mind.

What came next would hurt a lot worse.

I felt his eyes on me. Two pinpricks on the back of my skull, burning red-hot against the cold. I'd tried to ignore him all night—his burning gaze, his hateful whispers. Even now, I wanted to just walk out, keep walking, never look at him again.

But we made a deal, him and I.

So I turned around.

And the Cacophony was still there. Staring.

Exactly where I'd left him—upon an old cloak on the room's desk. The cloak had been burned to ashes. The desk now bore a black spot. Coils of steam peeled off his brass. My eyes met his brass stare. I walked toward him slowly, feeling the cold give way to heat with every step until my hand felt like it was in a furnace when I reached out to him.

My fingers trembled. I closed my eyes.

I grabbed the hilt.

And screamed.

I couldn't call it pain, the feeling that shot through me. You know what pain feels like. Up until that moment, I thought I did, too. He'd burned before, sometimes enough to leave a harsh mark. But this...

It was like he was reaching through the hilt and into me. I could feel his brass burning, prizing the sinew of my arm apart layer by layer, through the marrow of my bones, into my chest, where fiery fingers wrapped around my heart and squeezed tenderly.

I was on the floor. I didn't know when that had happened. I was breathing, but I didn't know how. I couldn't feel anything through the fire burning through me. Nothing but the hilt in my grasp and his voice in my ears.

"*Fool.*" His voice was cinders on the breeze, the promise of disaster lurking over the next hill. "*Betrayer.*"

"Not...betrayer..." I forced my words out through my teeth. If I opened my mouth, I'd have bitten my tongue off. "Not...my choice..."

"*Your choice. Your failure.*" He burned bright, angry, hateful. "*You let them convince you to leave me behind. You bowed before their wills. How many are dead now? How many screams do you hear at night?*"

He didn't fucking care about the dead. He cared about all the mages he could have fed on.

Still...was he right? Could I have stopped it if he were there? When Jero had said that he'd have caused more trouble, I believed him. And look what believing Jero had gotten me.

If only I could think. If only this hurt less. If only...

"*More die without us,*" the Cacophony hissed. "*Without me, the wrong people die. Without me, the wrong people live. Without me...*" His brass rippled, shuddered, let out a hot breath. "*You are nothi—*"

"NO!"

My voice sounded so weak in my head, yet he made me pay for it, all the same. The pain surged through me, tore my body apart and turned my blood to steam under a lashing hot tongue. It hurt.

But it wasn't the worst pain I'd ever felt.

And he wasn't who I was going to take that shit from.

"Not nothing. Not your servant." Spittle fell down the sides of my mouth, sizzled as they dripped onto his brass. I pulled myself to my knees, took him in both hands. "My name...is Sal the Cacophony. You and I made a deal."

The pain abated. The steam ebbed. The heat cooled.

Just a little.

"You want out, then you can go out," I replied. "Without me, you go nowhere. Without me, you kill no one. Without *me*, you rot in whatever dark hole I throw you in."

His brass rippled again, agitated. But the heat continued to dissipate under my hand. I held him up.

"*With* me," I whispered, "you give me my revenge. And I give you—"

"*Ruin.*"

That word was the last pain to dissipate. My body slowly felt like it pulled itself together. My blood cooled. My body returned to its familiar chorus of pains. But that word, that grinning, delighted word...

I felt that one long after he stopped.

Slowly, I got back to my feet. I found his sheath, slid him in, and got to work putting the rest of my leathers on, buckling him around my waist. He settled against my hip with a familiar weight, my last and final ache.

Good. I needed to remember that pain. I needed to remember why I had come here. And why I had to leave here.

Not Jero. Not Agne. Not for the ghosts that followed me or the dreams that plagued me. Not for lofty ideals and old men's fantasies and all that tender, lying bullshit about making the world a better place.

Behind me, I had only ashes. Before me, I had nothing but the list. Nothing but the people in the dark who needed to die for what they did. Nothing but scars and names that had to answer for them.

Nothing but revenge.

And him.

I walked to the door, pushed it open, and together we went out to get it.

TWENTY-NINE

THE CANED TOAD

Terassus, I had been told, was a different place after that night. The Haveners had cut a swathe of destruction through the city on their way to the banquet last night, a scar of blackened footprints marking the effigy's path toward the manor. The snow tried nobly to bury the horror, but all it could really do was give the dead shallower graves than normal.

What Haveners remained had been hunted down and executed by the guards, whose regiment size had tripled since the remaining nobles ordered their guards to patrol the city. The dead citizens had been tallied and their families informed. A search party had arrived at the burned-out manor the next day, ready to confront the effigy. All they found was a morbid collection of ashen corpses and sticks with a skull for a crown, presiding motionless over the ruin, and crumbling into a pile of rotting wood when a stiff breeze had blown through.

Whatever evil magic had coursed through Terassus that night had left a wound all its own. The people, once content to let their biggest worry be griping about nobles, hid in their homes, too terrified to emerge and mourn their fellow citizens.

Some people, like me, wondered how many of them would never leave their houses again.

"Morning, neighbor!"

And some people did not.

Urda stood in the inn's kitchen, a kettle quietly hissing steam on the counter behind him. In his hands, he held a pair of cups full of steaming brown liquid. On his face, he wore a broad smile.

Like it was just a normal day.

"How'd you sleep?" He walked toward me, still beaming. "You're not going to believe this, but I slept *amazing*. I thought for sure I was going to die on the back of that giant bird. It was going to drop me or kick me or devour me and vomit a thick slurry that had been me into the mouths of its babies—did you know birds do that? Disgusting—but sometime after my voice gave out from screaming, it just became… *thrilling*. Coffee?"

He pushed a cup into my hands. I stared down at it. Coffee. Normal, average coffee. He had just given me this like everything was okay, like we hadn't done what we'd done, like people weren't dead because of us.

"Incredible, right? Me! Urda! With the wind in my face and my hair flowing and my clothes whipping about me and I didn't feel scared at all! Well, I did a *little* when those feathers came loose and I think one went in my mouth, but the rest of it was incredible! I can't believe we actually did that! I can't believe we're going to do it *again*! Wasn't it just amazing? Oh, are you not drinking the coffee because it's too hot?"

I don't know what it was.

Maybe it was his smile—too big and too proud. Or maybe it was the way he just kept babbling, talking like nothing was the matter. Or maybe it was just because I hurt and I wanted someone to hurt worse than I did.

I don't know what made something inside me snap.

I still didn't know when I smashed the cup across his face.

He fell to the floor with a shriek, clutching his face. I'd only cut him with the porcelain, leaving a faint red line across his cheek. But he looked at me like I had just stabbed his mother.

"S-Sal," he whispered. "What are you—"

"Did you know?"

"What?"

I snatched him up by his collar, hauled him to his feet, pulled him so close I could smell the coffee drying on his skin.

"Did you know?" I repeated. "Did you know about Haven? About the attack?"

"I...I don't...I'm not..." He shook his head wildly. "I...I was just supposed to draw...to draw the map...I don't know if—"

"The map." I slammed him against the wall. "All those dead people, all this gone to shit, and you just drew the fucking *map*?"

"Sal, please!" Tears formed in his eyes. He shook so hard I could feel him trembling through his clothes. His voice became a quavering torrent of fear. "I don't...I can't...I-I-I'm not...I don't know what you want!"

Truth be told, neither did I. This wasn't going to bring anyone back. It wasn't going to make what we did less bad. It sure as shit wasn't going to make up for all the ghosts, all the dead, all the lies, all the ways I thought this was going to end up that it didn't.

Those were problems for healers, for diplomats, for builders— people who fixed things.

Me? I was only ever good at hurting people.

So that's what I did.

I tightened my hands around his collar so tight that his shirt ripped. He stared at me, the light draining from his eyes, his body gone limp. Like he was already dead. He wouldn't even give me the satisfaction of fighting back, of giving me a pain I could hold on to.

"LEAVE HIM ALONE!"

But someone did.

Something landed on my back. Arms too skinny to strangle me wrapped around my neck. Feet too weak to hurt me kicked at my legs. Someone who was not at all good at it was doing their absolute damnedest to kill me.

I grabbed one arm, hurled the person on my back onto the floor. Yria landed with a thud, the wind knocked out of her. Yet she just leapt right back to her feet, wheezing and pulling her flimsy knife out as she imposed herself between me and Urda.

Weak stance—I could knock her off her feet with a push. Bad grip—I could tear the knife out of her hand. All I saw were the ways I could hurt her. But all she saw was someone she needed to stop.

"You touch him again," she whispered, thrusting the knife at me, "I will kill you."

No cursing. No bravado. I could see by the look in her eyes that she knew she couldn't even scratch me with that thing. Just like I could see by the tears in her eyes that she knew that didn't matter.

She was his sister.

No matter what had happened last night, they had each other.

Maybe that's why I woke up today and didn't feel like killing.

But that didn't help me. I didn't know what would. I sure as shit was willing to keep throwing punches until I was too numb or too dead to care.

I balled up my fists. I took a step forward.

"My friends."

A hand was laid on my shoulder, gentle as a falling feather. And just four delicate, perfectly manicured fingers pushed down gently on me.

And sent me to my knees.

"Brawling in any establishment is boorish, at best." Agne took one slow, delicate step forward and looked down at me, kept so handily in place with just one hand. "In the domicile of one's host, it borders on unforgivable."

Anger surged through me as I scowled up at her. I wanted to fight, to hurt someone, to *be* hurt, anything to keep me from thinking—and with four fingers, she'd ended that.

I swept my scowl from her to Yria, half expecting to see the girl coming at me with her knife. But her weapon lay on the floor where she had dropped it, and right beside it, she knelt, her brother in her arms.

Urda was...gone. I don't know how else to describe it. He was still breathing, still blinking, but his eyes were somewhere else, his mouth whispering something I couldn't understand. His body hung limp as a dead fish in her arms. For all I knew, I really *had* killed him.

"Hey." Yria's voice was soft, whispering, as she pressed her hand to her brother's cheek. "You in there?"

Urda didn't respond. He didn't even look at her. She just kept one hand on his cheek, another on his hand.

"Just breathe," she whispered, squeezing his hand. "Deep as you can. It'll pass. It always passes." She offered him a grin so gentle it looked obscene on her face. "Hey, I know I asked you before, but remember that one summer when she took us to the coast? Right before I left to join the army?"

Urda's mouth hung open. He swallowed hard. His breath came labored and heavy, like he was breathing through a wound.

"You remember, we were...what? Six? Seven?"

"Eight," he mouthed numbly. "M-magic...magic manifests at age eight."

"Right. Eight. Anyway, that one thing washed up on shore, some kind of quivering thing, and I dared you to eat it and you did and they delayed my recruitment for two months so I could stay with you until you got better. You read so many books in bed. Which one was the one I liked? Something blue? About animals?"

"Blue...blue..." Urda forced his eyes closed. He drew in a deep, wet breath. "*The Blue Veins of the Scar.* It was a book about river beasts in the Scar." He squeezed her hand. "It was a book," he repeated. "It was a book..."

When Urda's eyes opened again, they looked like he had aged a hundred years. His breathing was heavy, but steady. He smiled gently at her.

"Thanks," he said. "That was...it was bad that time."

"Yeah." She helped him to his feet. "It's bad every time." She put a hand on his back, guided him toward the door. "Come on. We don't have to stay here."

Yria the Cell, the stories went, was a ruthless criminal. She opened up portals into rich peoples' houses to steal their children in the night. She dropped entire caravans through doors in the ground and watched them fall from holes in the ceiling and picked through the shattered remains. She once bisected a man by closing a portal on him when he tried to take more than his share of a haul.

To think I had done whatever I had just done to her twin brother, of all people, I expected a similarly gruesome fate. Or a kick in the cunt. Or at least a chorus of dirty words hurled my way.

But as she helped Urda out of the room, she didn't even look back at me.

"Apologies."

Agne took me in one hand and pulled me back to my feet, dusting me off with her other hand.

"I had hoped to spare your dignity there," she said. "But I thought it better to try to defuse any potential violence."

"There wasn't going to be any violence," I muttered.

She met my stare for a moment and then smiled. "Of course. My mistake." She gestured to the nearby table, the kettle of coffee still steaming. "May I request you join me for coffee?"

I met her gaze this time and didn't bother disguising my sneer. "I've got shit to do."

I started for the door. Her hand shot out, pressing against the door frame and blocking my way.

"Madam." She squeezed the frame slightly, leaving a perfect handprint splintered in its wood. "I insist."

Like I said, there's no such thing as a Vagrant's Code. But, in general, your odds of survival in this business get better if you try to do right by each other and pay back what you owe. Agne had saved my life last night. If I could even the scales by having a cup of coffee with her, I suppose that wasn't so bad.

Also, you know, she could crush my head with two fingers if she wanted. So that was also a big motivator.

She smiled as I slid into a chair, her taking the one opposite me. I reached for the pot of coffee, only to receive a chiding slap on the hand. With a warning glance, she took the pot and proceeded to pour it into a kettle. I rolled my eyes, made a show of folding my arms as she got back up, procured two porcelain cups, saucers, and napkins, and arranged them on the table.

The Imperial style, I noticed. In Cathama, bored nobles eventually had enough time on their hands that they decided coffee and tea alike should be served a certain way or it just wasn't good. The capital was full of dainty people with dainty hands who dedicated their lives to mastering the various ways of serving tea. Agne, too, was no less delicate as she served—so delicate that I almost forgot I had seen those hands break men's necks.

You didn't see the Imperial style that often in the Scar.

Possibly because it took for-fucking-ever to pour.

I could tell what she was doing, dragging this out, letting this awkward silence hang like a corpse from the gallows. I wasn't going to give her the satisfaction.

"If you're about to say," I muttered, "that I should apologize to Urda..."

"You should." Agne did not look up as she poured—it was considered impolite to take your eyes off the cup in Cathama. "But you won't."

A surge of inexplicable ire furrowed my brows. "What makes you think I won't?"

"Well, are you?"

"Well...no, but—"

"But now you might?" She afforded an effete smile. "Just to spite me?"

"Not *just* to spite you. But yeah, that'd be a big part of it."

She tittered. "You know my favorite story about you, Sal the Cacophony?" She paused in the middle of pouring. "Do you prefer Salazanca?"

"Whichever hurries this up."

"I heard it in a wine bar in Greenriver," she said. "The tale of a woman with a gun in the shape of a grinning dragon who had visited the freehold just a week prior and had visited a tavern across the road. Yet, when I glanced out the window, I saw only an empty plot of land. Does this sound familiar?"

It did. "They got the wreckage cleared out in just a week, huh? I didn't leave much of that place standing."

"They said you went in there looking for a name and a glass of good whiskey. They refused to give you either. So you broke someone's arm. Then they gave you a bottle of cheap whiskey, so you upended a table. Then they gave you their earnings for the day, so you burned the place to the ground."

That was...mostly true.

I had been asking after a name on my list. Someone pulled a knife on me in reply, so I broke his arm. Then they tried to break a bottle over my head, so I broke a table over theirs. Then hand cannons had come out, someone offered to buy me off, and everything got a little hazy after that.

"No one died, I'm told," she continued. "When they came back, they found the bottle of whiskey and the earnings, left in the middle of the ruin." She finished pouring one cup, presented it to me, handle-first. "You burned a tavern just because they didn't give you what you asked for."

"Scar's a hard place," I replied, taking the cup but pointedly not drinking—it was impolite to drink before the pourer. "You don't get what you need if you don't fight for it."

"And yet, you take pleasure in it, no? Spite feeds you. Spite is what made you attack Urda."

I sighed. "You're saying I've got to make this right with him."

"I am not," she said. "It's irrelevant. You need spite. Urda doesn't. He has his sister."

"Huh?"

"Did you ever hear how they came to be partners, as it were?" Agne poured herself a cup, presented it to herself. "They were actually born in the Scar, if you can believe it. Not the Imperium, like us. They lived with their mother in a little seaside town on the eastern edge, closest to the Imperial harbors. I suppose that's why their village was chosen."

"For what?"

"To be made an example of by the Revolution," she replied. "An airship came out of the sky, they said, flattened the town with cannon fire and fled before Imperial Skymages could retaliate. Their house was destroyed, their mother along with it. Urda somehow managed to pull his sister out of the wreckage, but..."

My mind flashed back to that morning, to Urda shivering in Yria's arms, silent, frozen with those eyes completely empty, focused on some far-off horror that no one else could see.

So that's where he'd gone. I had sent to him a dark place today. Maybe even darker than mine.

"She was conscripted into the Imperial army, as all Doormages were," Agne continued. "He, lacking magical ability, apprenticed into a wright shop shortly after. Eight years old, they were all each other had, and then they didn't have each other. Tragic, no?"

It was. But I wasn't going to admit it. Not like I could take back smashing a cup against his face, regardless.

"Of course, twelve years later, she went Vagrant, picked him up in his town, and then the two of them went on to commit *multiple* frauds, extortions, and robberies across the Scar," Agne said, "but that's beside the point."

"What *is* the point?" I muttered.

"The point is that they will be fine." Agne, her coffee finally poured, raised it in both hands in the traditional toast. "Will you?"

I glared at her but returned the toast. "Are you saying what happened last night didn't bother you?"

"I am not."

"You're all right with Jero lying to us?"

"I didn't say that, either."

"Then maybe you can clear up"—I didn't hear the anger, the high-pitched shriek lurking on the edge of my voice—"how the fuck Two Lonely Old Men and his fucking plan are going to make the world a better place when he went and killed all those people last night?"

Agne took a sip of her coffee, stared at me over the rim. "I never heard a story that said Sal the Cacophony was concerned with casualties."

"You never heard a story that said I liked dogs, either." I stared into the coffee cup, wondering how I could break it, how I could smash it, to make her listen, to make this all feel better. "No one tells stories about that kind of shit. If they did..."

But the more I looked, the more I just felt... tired. Like even lifting it was too much effort. Breathing was too much effort. So the next time I sighed, all the words that I couldn't hold back anymore just slipped out and settled into my coffee.

"If they did," I whispered, "maybe they could tell me what everyone is dying for."

I expected the long silence that hung between us after that.

I expected her to tell me to toughen up, that our problems were bigger than this, that I was being whiny, selfish, weak. I expected her to lean over and simply slap me hard enough so that I'd go back to feeling okay. I expected Agne the Hammer to act like a hammer.

But she didn't.

She simply took a long, slow sip of her coffee and asked:

"How did you sleep?"

"What?"

"Did you sleep well?"

"No."

"Nor I." She set her cup down, stared into it. "There was a spider crawling across my bed this morning when I awoke."

"What does that—"

"Did you know I used to be afraid of spiders? Even when I grew up, they terrified me. They moved so quickly and could be anywhere, with gleaming fangs and eyes. But this time, I woke up and saw it and I didn't feel scared."

She took in a shuddering breath.

"I didn't feel anything."

It wasn't because of ceremony that she didn't meet my gaze, that she turned away and swallowed something hard and sour. She didn't want me to see the tears forming in her eyes. Over a spider.

"I looked down at it and saw just a thing," she said, "eight tiny legs that I could just crush, whenever I wanted. I used to be afraid of them . . . before last night."

I knew then why she wept.

Siegemages, some say, are the most favored of the Lady Merchant. They're given strength, endurance, the power to tear mountains apart and shake the earth.

In exchange, she takes their feelings. Their fears, their laughter, their sorrows, and their joys.

At the peak of their power, a Siegemage is like a glacier: unstoppable, impenetrable, and terribly, terribly cold.

This morning, Agne had woken up a little colder than she had gone to sleep.

"I suppose that's why I like the pouring ceremony so much, and pretty dresses and nice scents," she said, wiping tears away. "Because one day, I'll use a little too much power, and I won't like it anymore. I'll look at the cups and the kettles and just see more things I can break. One day, I'll use too much power . . ." She looked at me and smiled sadly. "And I'll see people the same way, too."

I knew what loss was like. I had the scars to prove it. But for everything that Darrish and Vraki and Jindu had torn out of me, they couldn't take the jokes I laughed at, the smells of sweat that made me want to kiss someone, the opera verses that made me mad and I couldn't explain why. One day, long after I couldn't lift a sword or fire my gun, I'd still have those.

And Agne wouldn't.

"I suppose that's why I joined when Jero asked me," she said, smiling as she sipped her coffee. "I wept for the dead, because one day I wouldn't be able to. I believe in this plan, to do something good for the world, because one day..." She smiled at her empty cup. "One day, I won't know what good is."

Then she laughed. A nervous, high-pitched giggle punctuated by sniffing and a little sobbing as she unceremoniously poured herself another cup of coffee.

"Sorry," she said. "Sorry, I know that doesn't help you. I just...I don't know..."

"Yeah." I poured myself a cup. "Me either."

"Still, you should speak with Jero," she said. "I'm sure he had his reasons for what he did."

"Everybody who does bad shit has their reasons," I muttered. "Doesn't make it smell any nicer."

"True," she replied, smiling. "If you find them unconvincing, you'll feel that much better when you break his face, fully justified." She took a sip. "Though I suppose just cutting to the chase with a man can be quite satisfying."

"Sometimes." I offered her a lingering smile. My hand slid across the table, brushed against her fingertips. "But I don't mind taking my time with a woman, either."

Agne the Hammer, who had just last night smashed her way through a horde of slavering, drug-addled murderers and emerged with nothing more than a scratch, stared at my fingers on hers with wide, astonished eyes.

"*Oh*. Oh wow." She laughed nervously, delicately lifting my hand off of hers and setting it down on the table. "Er, sorry, I'm really flattered..." She paused, looked me over, pursed her lips. "I mean, I'm really, *really* flattered, truly. But..." She cleared her throat, smiled sheepishly. "I like men."

I blinked. "Oh, I didn't..." Then I squinted. "Wait, really?"

She furrowed her brow. "You sound shocked."

"I mean, always, but you're so...so..."

She winked. "Not quite what you'd expect, hmm? And here I thought I was the pinnacle of effeteness."

She stood up to her full height, her smile warm and her muscles rippling beneath her shirt.

"My name is Agnestrada ki Dondoril," she said, closing her eyes. "I like flowers and wearing dresses, I *love* the color pink, and I can break someone's neck with two fingers." She laid a hand over her heart. "All of these things are true. For now."

She placed a hand on my shoulder, offered me a delicate squeeze that could have killed me with just a little more pressure from her pinky, and then walked out the door, leaving me alone with my thoughts, my pains, and the smell of cinders in my nose.

And I decided I didn't like it.

THIRTY

THE CANED TOAD

I didn't give him the courtesy of a knock, choosing instead to push the door open and simply walk in.

So I suppose it's understandable that Two Lonely Old Men didn't give me the courtesy of looking up at me.

His hunched-over, squinting attentions were fixed on the tiny city sprawled out on the table before him. Lastlight, in all its minuscule re-created glory, stood timid beneath his shadow. A jeweler's loupe over his eye, the Freemaker busied himself using a tiny brush to apply detail to the tallest tower looming over the rest of the city.

"Can I be of assistance?" he muttered into his city, barely audible.

"No," I replied curtly. "I just came to tell you I'm out."

I was prepared for accusations, threats, various slurs against my honor—just like I was prepared to break his jaw if he made them. What I wasn't prepared for was the low, noncommittal hum he made.

I came for a fight. If he wasn't going to start it, then I would.

"I didn't know if I believed your plan about making the world a better place," I continued. "But after last night, I know both your plan and your vision were shit."

"Oh?"

"How did you plan for this operation to work if you weren't going to tell us what you were doing? That you were involving *Haven*?" I shook my head. "How the fuck is this plan of yours going to work when everyone keeps dying because of it?"

"A fine question," he replied, still not looking up.

He wasn't listening. Maybe he thought someone with a list like mine didn't care about who got killed. Maybe there was a time when he would have been correct in assuming so.

But I wasn't a tool to be used. If anyone was going to die, it'd be because I knew they needed to.

"You got an answer?" I asked.

"I'm afraid not," he said. "I did not anticipate Jero to be captured, nor for Haven's construct to be present."

"So, what? It was an accident?"

"No. There are no such things as accidents. Not to victims, anyway. The Haveners were always intended to be cat's-paws, a useful distraction we could cultivate and unleash when necessary or to concern the city enough to allow us escape, were we discovered prematurely. My idea. Jero's execution. He saw it through quite admirably, until he didn't."

"You..." My blood ran cold. "You let the Haveners into Terassus, didn't you?"

"I persuaded certain people opposed to their presence to tolerate them. And with Jero's talents, I kept them pacified, aiming to ensure they would cause harm to no one but the people we intended them to."

"If that was your aim, you fucking missed."

"I am aware."

"So what are you going to do about it?"

He paused a moment before resuming his painting.

"How," he asked, "does one make amends for the dead?"

My blood surged. My jaw clenched so tight I thought my teeth might break. My finger twitched at the hilt of the Cacophony.

"I've heard the same sentiment from every warlord, every Vagrant, every fool who ever raised a knife," I growled. "Every corpse you leave behind is nothing more than a pile of meat. You'll shake your head and lament the loss and forget them in another second. And every person you forget that comes crawling out of the shit you made..."

The scar over my eye ached as I narrowed my eyes upon him.

"Is another me."

He finally looked up at that, took in me and all of my scars, and his lip twitched just a little.

"I don't know how many more of them I made last night, how many will come out of that with scars or how many will come looking for revenge," I said, the fire dissipating inside me and leaving behind something cold and sharp. "But I made them because of you. And when they come, I'll have to deal with them. Because of you. So I'm out."

"I see."

"If you want to come after me, that's fine," I replied as I turned away, hand on the Cacophony's hilt. "But whatever you send after me, I'm going to send back to you in pieces, so—"

"Would you pardon me for a moment?"

I seized the hilt as I shot a scowl over my shoulder. I didn't think interrupting me with that was going to be the reason I bashed his face in, but shit, it wasn't like I was going to be choosy.

When I turned to face him, he had turned away from me. He set his brush and paint aside, then slowly walked to the head of the table. He pulled a small pouch from his belt and removed from it a whistle. A silver whistle, gingerly inscribed with sigils.

Just like the one Urda had in the Crow Market.

He held it to his lips, hesitant, like he feared to blow it. He summoned up some courage, closed his eyes, blew a single, irritating note. And then...

They came.

People.

Women. Men. Children. Grandmothers and fathers, aunts and uncles. Carts pulled by sturdy working birds, unruly kids chasing dogs through the streets. Laughing. Singing. Arguing. Weeping.

Alive, in miniature, in Lastlight.

Tiny phantasms blossomed in bursts of light on the streets and in the houses of the tiny city as hundreds of illusionary citizens went about their day. Their voices were a gentle roar, telling the same stories and laughing at the same jokes they always had, completely unaware of their ghostly nature or the two people towering over them.

But Lastlight was alive again. Full of people.

"Fascinating, isn't it?" Two Lonely Old Men spoke softly, as if he feared the phantom people might look up and notice us. "All this, coaxed from a single note. I built the greatest city this world ever knew, yet I still can't figure out how they did it."

"Who?" I asked.

"The twins," he replied. "Yria and Urda." He ran a finger over the sigils adorning the whistle. "Did you happen to notice it, back in the Crow Market? When a Doormage opens a portal, they etch it out, make certain that it will go precisely where it needs to go. This is why they can't open portals to places they haven't been. And yet..."

And yet. Yria hadn't been there when Urda had whistled.

But the portal had come all the same.

"I suspect it's because they're twins. Whatever connection they have transcends mere biology and infuses itself into their work. It goes the other way, too, did you notice? Typically, a Spellwright like Urda has to be present for his sigils to work. Yet these were activated with just a whistle. Their powers work remotely. I could spend a lifetime figuring out how their abilities work."

He looked up and smiled.

"Yet all I asked of them was this small favor."

A reverent silence fell over us. Two Lonely Old Men stood there silently, watching over his resurrected people. A smile, serene and full of sorrow, spread across his face. He closed his eyes, let the sounds of their joy wash over him.

Then he reached back into his pocket, pulled out a tindertwig...

And set the city ablaze.

"Hey!"

I surprised myself with the urge to smother the flames as they raced across the city, consuming the tiny buildings and rivers and engulfing the people. But they were just illusions, unaware of anything but the script they'd been ensorcelled to follow. They just kept laughing as the fire washed over them.

I stared, incredulous, at the Freemaker. "The fuck did you do that for?"

"To remind myself," he said softly, "why I'm doing this."

"But Lastlight—"

"Is gone," he finished, "as is this pale imitation. No matter how many times I rebuild it, or how big it gets, it will never be safe so long as fate is decided by guns and spells. I did not realize how fragile my work was"—he stared into the rising flames—"until I watched it burn."

Life in the Scar was hard. I could tell you that better than anyone. I was no stranger to fighting, to killing, to crawling out of the darkest places and leaving behind more blood than I'd gone in with.

But up until that moment, I don't think I knew what hard was.

"You are correct."

When I glanced up, Two Lonely Old Men stood beside me, his weary gaze locked onto mine.

"It was foolish of me not to tell you the extent of our plan, foolish of me to treat you like a tool instead of a partner, foolish of me to think what we were doing outweighed what we'd do for it."

Granted, I never expected a guy who would make and burn a tiny city to be all that elegant with apologies, but it didn't matter. Apologies, excuses, philosophical musings—I'd heard them all come tumbling out of every mouth of every thug and soldier and warlord who wanted to avoid ending up in the same pit they happily put everyone else in.

The words a man trades when he stares down his sins are what he's made of. Apologies were just tin and wood.

"If you still wish to go, I will not stop you," he said. "I will not seek retribution, I will not speak your name again. All I ask is one favor."

I tilted my chin up, listening.

"Let me show you something."

I narrowed my eyes for a brief moment before sighing. I nodded. He flashed a bent wire of a smile as he pushed the door open for me and led me out.

Behind us, the people of Lastlight continued to laugh and sing as the fires swallowed them whole.

—— ≡✦≡ ——

I remembered his face.

When we'd served together in the army, he was just one more mage. A talented Nightmage, capable of weaving hallucinations with a thought, but there had been lots of talented mages and sowing fear wasn't so special an art as to be memorable.

When we'd both joined Vraki the Gate in his plot to overthrow the Empress and return the Imperium to the mages who had built it, he was just one more crony. He was just a chin nodding at whatever Vraki said, just lips muttering whatever disgruntled chorus he was expected to.

And on that night—the night they put a sword through me and pulled my magic out of me and left me bleeding out on the cold ground—he was just another pair of eyes in the dark, staring at me as I bled out, saying nothing, doing nothing.

Like Jindu.

Like Darrish.

Like all of them.

His face, I remembered. But his name?

His name was another scar on my body.

It was twenty-sixth on my list.

"Yugol the Omen."

I knew it was him. But in the dim light of the inn's cellar, it didn't look like him. The thin body chained to the wall barely looked human.

He was naked, his body emaciated, his papery skin littered with splits and wounds. His head—shaggy mop of black hair, pointed features bruised—hung to his chest, his mouth bound with cloth. Chains suspended his wrists above his head. His fingers were a mess of broken purple digits, to keep him from casting, no doubt. But it didn't seem necessary—the man shackled to the wall was barely breathing behind his gag.

Only the tattoos of laughing skulls that ran down his arms marked him as a threat.

"We located him a few nights ago, not far from here." Two Lonely Old Men spoke from behind me, observing the ruin of the man without interest. "His powers were formidable, I was told. Though I suspect even a Vagrant is less threatening after being poisoned. Still, you can see, there was some struggle." He gestured to the wounds across the man's body. "Once it was over, he wasted no time in ensuring this man could no longer use his powers."

"Who?" I asked.

I felt his weary eyes turn upon me. "Jero."

I could see it now. The short, deep wounds, each one a surgical strike to sever a cord of muscle. It was the knife-work of someone who knew what he was doing, someone who wanted his target unable to fight back, someone who wanted it to work.

His knife-work.

He did this. He found the man on my list. He made him suffer.

"We intended to reveal this to you in...well, I suppose there are no pleasant circumstances, in our line of work. Regardless." The Freemaker inclined his head toward me. "In gratitude for your work, as well as proof that Two Lonely Old Men makes no empty promises."

I blinked, glancing toward him. "Huh?"

"He is yours. His flesh and whatever trivial secrets lie beneath it. Do with them as you will."

I looked back toward him, to Yugol the Omen, and I just stared.

It's a strange thing, holding someone's life in your hands. You always think you'll know exactly what you're going to do, what you're going to say. In your head, they aren't people, they're monsters, collections of old wounds and bad dreams. When you look at them, like I looked at that broken husk on the wall, you realize everything you thought you'd say somehow doesn't work anymore.

It's a strange thing. Different every time.

Never gets better, though.

"Is something wrong?" Two Lonely Old Men asked.

"No," I replied, and that was true. Nothing was wrong—this is what he promised me, this is what I agreed to. And yet... "It's just... where has he been this whole time?"

"I beg your pardon?"

"What's he been doing?" I asked. "He had..."

Rudu.

The best people always have names like splinters. Names that stick into your body and brain and hurt when you think about them. And how you might hurt them back. Yugol didn't have a name like that. But I wasn't thinking about him.

"He had a partner," I said, more breathless than I wanted to be. "Once." I coughed, tasted something foul on my tongue. "Has he... had anything else? What's he done? Does he..."

Does he deserve it?

My throat was tight. Too tight to give that thought a voice. The taste in my mouth grew more bitter the more I thought about it.

"Does it matter?"

I couldn't answer that question. Not in any way I wanted to. Two Lonely Old Men's feet padded on the floor as he walked toward me.

"Perhaps he had a partner. Perhaps he had a family," he said. "Perhaps he doesn't. Maybe he's murdered more people than any Vagrant in the land. Or maybe he's simply been drinking himself to death in an alley before Jero located him. He's still Yugol the Omen, traitor to the Imperium, member of the Crown Conspiracy." He stopped beside me, looked at me. "He's still on your list."

"Yeah, but..."

The Cacophony seethed in his sheath. I could feel his heat creeping into my body, a red-hot finger coiling about my heart and giving it the faintest warning tug.

"Interesting dilemma, isn't it?" he mused, sparing the barest of chuckles. "What he did made you who you are. What we did made the people who crawled out of Keltithan's manor last night. Perhaps one day, we'll find ourselves on a wall in a cellar someday. We may deserve it. We may not. Our pasts belong to someone else."

He took my hand gently and placed something inside my palm, curling my fingers around it.

"His future belongs to you."

The Freemaker spared me a weak smile before he turned, shuffled out, and shut the door behind him. It wasn't until the echo of its closing faded that I uncurled my fingers and looked at what he gave me.

A key. The key. To Yugol's shackles.

I looked back up at him.

And he was looking at me.

At some point, he'd stirred awake and now regarded me through desperate eyes.

I wondered if he had heard us, knew the doubt that had lingered in my voice. I hoped I would see in his eyes that he hadn't. I wanted to see hatred there, to see fuming anger that he wouldn't get away with this, to see the glimmering eyes that I still saw in my dreams whenever I thought of that night, of people like him, like Darrish.

All I saw in those eyes was someone who didn't want to die.

Had I looked like that to him, on that night when Vraki tore my magic out of me, when they took the sky from me? Had he wondered what I'd done to deserve it? Did it matter? It still happened. He still did nothing to stop it.

It shouldn't have been this hard. I shouldn't have waited so long. I shouldn't wonder who he was, shouldn't care, shouldn't think of anything but the fact that he was on my list and because he was on my list, he had to die.

But...

I thought as I reached out to pull down his gag.

Maybe...

Pain seared through my arm, causing my fingers to coil into a gnarled claw.

"NO."

The Cacophony's voice, heat in my ears, in my heart, ringing through my body. His heat tore through me again, angry and red on a tongue of fire.

"Remember him," he snarled. *"Remember what he did to you."*

"But..." I gasped. "What if—"

"It does not matter." The heat abated, just a bit, to become something almost warm. Almost tender. *"He does not matter. Nor does anything he's done. His fate was sealed that night. He knows it, has known it ever since."*

I gritted my teeth as my hand lowered, drifted near my belt.

Near my sword.

And the pain abated even more.

"Whoever he helped, whoever he did not help," the Cacophony whispered, *"was for him and whatever guilts he carries. Never once has he thought of you, what he took from you, what they did to you."*

Yugol's eyes widened. He shook his head furiously. Behind his gag, he let out a noise—a cry? A plea? A curse? Could he hear the Cacophony's voice?

Or was he just making that noise because I had drawn my sword?

"Let him live, his name lives forever." His voice was something else inside me now, something that burned bright, not hot. Something that made me raise my blade. *"He will be a stain on justice, an affront*

to you, to everything. Kill him, it is your name they will whisper. Your name will shake men like him and keep monsters in their shadows."

I tried to remind myself that the Cacophony was not human, couldn't know what it meant to spill blood. The Cacophony was a weapon—he killed, he destroyed, he ate the remains. He was driven by that hunger, he needed it satiated. I tried to remind myself of that.

I was too busy trying to remember when I had placed my sword at Yugol's throat.

"How can this world be safe while creatures like him live? How can you be safe? How can she?"

I shut my eyes, swallowed hard. Yugol made a muffled sobbing sound beneath his gag.

"Everything you've given up, all to shear rot like him from this carcass of a world, it means nothing if you spare him."

I gritted my teeth, my fingers tightening around the hilt. Yugol rattled his chains, the blood from his wounds pattering on the floor.

"No justice without revenge. No future without judgment. Kill him. Become whole."

I felt a drop of blood slide down the edge of my blade and hit my hand. Yugol screamed until the only thing left was a wet wheezing sound.

And in my ear, a voice full of fire hissed.

"Take the sky back."

I stepped out of the room. The door creaked behind me until it fell shut with a silent click. I stared out toward the long hall that ran from the cellar to fourteen wooden steps that led back into the inn.

The tip of my sword let out a grating noise as it dragged across the floor, drowning out the sound of ragged breath and boots clicking as I walked toward the steps and took them up. One after the other.

I entered into the darkness of the kitchen. A pot of coffee sat on the table, stale and cold. A spider spun a web in the corner of the ceiling. I drew in a breath of cold air.

And tasted cinders.

THIRTY-ONE

THE CANED TOAD

"Seems we do this a lot, don't we?" Agne asked.

"How do you mean?" I replied as we made our way down the hall.

"I'm not sure." She hummed thoughtfully over the sound of liquid splashing. "I was as reluctant to go Vagrant as any loyal mage, I suppose, but I admit the stories I heard were rather tempting."

"Go on," I said as we walked backward down the stairs.

"Promise me you won't take offense if I say yours weren't my favorite," she said as we wound through the cold kitchen.

"I promise," I lied.

"Not that they didn't have their appeal—particularly the sexy ones, I don't mind saying—but they were all so...dire." We made our way through the common room, being sure to cover as much floor as we could. "I rather adored the stories about Vagrants striking out on their own, drinking in the freedom of the Scar and its vast spaces, forging our own destiny for ourselves, rather than the Imperium."

"Didn't live up to your expectations, huh?" I chuckled. "It never does."

"Well, I've had my share of highs and lows, I suppose." She sighed as we walked backward out the door, spilling the last of our oil out onto the porch of the inn. "I guess I just thought there'd be less..."

"Burning?"

"Treachery."

"Ah." I shook the last few greasy drops out of the can before I tossed it back into the inn. "Well, you get used to it after a while."

I turned around. Urda stood there with the rest of them, under the falling snow. He stepped toward me, a winter coat in his hands and a smile on his face as he proffered it toward me.

"The snow just started to fall," he said as I took the coat from him. "I thought you could use something a little warmer and a little less"—his eyes drifted across my expanse of scarred skin and he cringed—"*exposed*."

I pulled the coat around me and I had to admit, it felt pretty fucking nice. Oiled leather, trimmed with fur or something soft at the neck and cuffs—it didn't let me show off my ink, but I suppose I could forgive that. It'd been a long fucking time since I felt this warm.

"Where'd you get this, anyway?" I adjusted my scarf around my face as I fastened the coat around my waist.

"I had a few spare moments last night and I thought since Vagrants are always showing so much"—he visibly stifled a shudder—"*skin* that you probably needed something for where we're going. So, I got my needle and got to work."

I blinked. "Seriously?"

"I *never* joke about exothermic heat loss."

"In one night. Amazing." I held out a sleeve, admired it. "I suppose I shouldn't be surprised, after that trick you pulled down in the Crow Market."

"Not bad, was it?" He visibly puffed up, beaming. "Admittedly, it's not something we can do constantly—it takes a *massive* amount of Dust and sigils to make a whistle like that, for the record, but since signing on with our patron, we've had no shortage of either. Still, it was only enough to make him a whistle."

"The one for his little toy," I muttered.

"Right...wait, toy? No, it was for—"

"So, what?" I interrupted. "Why not a sword or something more useful? A weapon that can open portals is handier than a whistle."

"Well, yes, but it's the inverse material principle," he replied, like I should know what that means. "Something as pedestrian as making a sword explode into flame would be simple, but the more complex the task—say, reaching a sympathy with my sister's magic so that we can use it more often—the smaller the material it can affect. Hence why you don't see very many houses that are spellwritten."

"Huh. That makes sense. But why a whistle?"

He blinked. "I *like* whistles."

"Yeah. I guess you do." My grin held out another second before a pang of something cold hit my heart. I sighed, stepped up to him. "Listen, about what I said... and did... and thought. I'm sorry. You didn't need that."

Urda held up a hand to stop me. "Have no fear, my friend, and don't worry yourself. We all have moments where we get a little"— his face twitched slightly—"*tense*. I understand everything and I forgive you completely."

"I fucking don't," his sister spat as she stalked past, carrying a crate. "*She* didn't have to deal with your moaning ass as you whined about getting the right thread for your little fashion project all fucking night."

"Catgut is *necessary* to keep the seams secure." Urda hurried to help her as they loaded the crate into the back of a wagon. "There is no excuse for shoddy craftsmanship, after all."

"I'm walking around with an asshole I can't feel anymore because he made me use a portal to find fucking thread for your shitty coat because you're too fucking stupid to wear a shirt." Yria glared at me, snorting. "I only got one of those, you know. As far as I'm concerned, Lady Fancyfanny, you're still on my shitlist."

She trundled off to see to something on the cart. I frowned after her.

"Don't worry about her," Urda whispered to me. "She's fine with you, too. She just always gets crabby when the sensation starts returning to her." He cleared his throat. "As you know, Doormages sacrifice the sensation in their bodies to use their magic. Too much use and it becomes permanent."

"If you knew I knew that, why are you telling—"

"*But* my sister, for all her rough edges, is unique. She can walk off the numbness quicker than most. She says it's because she's so careful with her magic." He leaned toward me, whispered conspiratorially. "Personally, I think it's because she's too much of an asshole for even the Lady Merchant to stop."

"HEY!" Yria shouted. "Are you talking about my asshole over there?"

Urda smiled at me before hurrying off to soothe his sister. I watched him go, watched *them* go, with more envy than I was prepared to admit to. Yesterday, I'd smashed them into pieces. Today, they'd pulled themselves back together so tight you couldn't even see the cracks.

But maybe they'd been doing that their whole lives.

I envied that. My cracks went too deep to pull shut.

We'd assembled in the square at the crack of dawn, as per the plan. Tuteng had long departed to tend to the Oyakai. Agne was busy separating the twins as Yria, apparently enraged by something her brother had said, done, or breathed, went after a cringing Urda. Two Lonely Old Men sat with Madame Fist, talking quietly as she attached the yoke of the wagon to a pair of surly working birds. My bird, Congeniality, and a pair of other mounts lingered nearby.

Tending to them, Jero did his best not to be noticed.

But to me, he was as stark as a shadow in springtime.

We hadn't spoken since we had returned. That was a trend I hoped to continue, even during our travels today. Don't get me wrong—I wouldn't have it said that Sal the Cacophony wasn't a professional. I could work with someone I didn't like, even if they had almost gotten me killed and wound up killing more people than we needed to because they didn't think me worth sharing crucial information with.

But I wasn't going to have it said that Sal the Cacophony wouldn't break said someone's teeth in if they kept talking shit.

I hoped I conveyed all that with my scowl when he quickly glanced my direction and then glanced away, but if he hadn't understood, I could punch him later.

"Our time here is at an end." Two Lonely Old Men, wearing a coat far too thin for the cold and looking far too unbothered by it, sauntered up to the inn's door. "To think that the most important step in the history of the Scar was made in these humble walls. We bid farewell to the Caned Toad, with gratitude."

"I didn't let you stay here for gratitude," Madame Fist said, sneering as she came up beside him. "And I'm not letting you pull this shit for gratitude."

"Of course." Two Lonely Old Men reached into his coat, produced a thick sheaf of scrolls, and handed it to her. "All necessary arrangements have been made, all transport has been paid for, all accommodations have been planned. I do hope you enjoy your return to the capital, madame."

I'd known Madame Fist as both a Master of the Intimate Arts and a crotchety asshole who suffered fools only for the highest payment. So to see her staring at those scrolls as though they were a dead child returned from the grave, the tears that trailed down to the corners of lips opened in shock...

I wondered which one of her was the real one.

"Something wrong, madame?" the Freemaker asked.

"No, it's just"—she looked back up to the inn—"it's been years since my exile. I've run this inn for so long, I don't know if I..."

"We can leave no trace of our passing. Too much has been said in these walls." Two Lonely Old Men's voice turned severe, his features darkening. "This was agreed upon. It is too late to renegotiate. Far too late."

She cringed a little. "Yes. You're right. Of course." She sniffed. "It's just a shitty inn, after all. I'll be happy to see it gone."

The light returned to his features as he smiled. He reached into his coat again and produced a tindertwig. "Then would you care to do the honors?"

She nodded, took it, struck it against the heel of her shoe, and tossed it onto the porch.

The inn caught ablaze slowly, fire leisurely making its way across our oil trail. We'd made certain to leave it arranged so that it wouldn't draw attention until we were long departed.

Two Lonely Old Men turned to face us, fire rising behind him.

"You all have your directions," he said. "You all have your routes. Avoid detection. Stop for no one. Answer no questions. Leave no trace. We shall reconvene at the designated spot in four days."

"Yeah, yeah." Yria, in the wagon seat next to Urda, took the reins in hand. "All this fucking theater makes me wish I ever gave a shit about opera."

"It's a long ride," Urda offered helpfully. "I can teach you some!"

Yria forced a huge, fake smile onto her face. "Great! Teach me a fucking knot I can strangle myself with, too." She sneered at him, snapped the reins. "Come on, you ugly fucks, get going before I'm too drunk to steer."

The birds chirruped and took off, pulling the wagon behind them as they rattled off into the streets of Terassus. Agne, astride a massive thick-hewed motherfucker of a Rockeater bird, pulled her mount to a halt and extended a hand to Two Lonely Old Men.

"Shall we, my lord?"

"You honor me, my lady," he chuckled as he accepted her help. She effortlessly pulled him up and into the saddle behind her. He glanced down at me. "For the sake of everything, Cacophony, I hope you can handle the journey."

"Be easier if I went on my own," I said.

"And riskier if you were ambushed," he replied. "We cannot fail now. Not when we're so close."

I grunted, which seemed to be enough for him. He nodded. Agne gave her mount a spur. And upon a pair of legs as big as I was, it took off, leaving me with a fire, a nice coat, and...

"Ready?"

Jero came toward me, Congeniality's reins in one hand, his bird's in the other. Without saying anything, without even looking at him, I took them and mounted my bird. It felt good to be back in a saddle, even if it meant riding with an asshole.

"Did you miss me, princess?" I cooed, rubbing Congeniality's long, ugly neck. "Did you miss your best friend?"

Congeniality let out a low, ugly noise and shit on the ground. So... maybe?

"Was she any trouble?" I asked Madame Fist.

Madame Fist didn't answer. She was standing in front of the inn, her inn, watching the fires spread.

"Madame," Jero said softly.

"Huh?" She looked back.

"Are you going to be all right?"

"Oh. Yes. I just..." She turned back to the fire. "It's... nothing. Don't worry about me. Thank you."

He held her in his gaze for a moment before looking back at me.

He nodded. We spurred our birds forward, setting off as the fire rose behind us.

We left Terassus that morning. Houses were destroyed because of us. People were dead because of us. Lives were ruined because of us.

By that afternoon, we'd be ghosts.

And all the people who'd lost everything that night would never know our names.

THIRTY-TWO

THE VALLEY

I try not to make a habit of knowing too much, but there are three subjects on which I consider myself an expert: opera, hurting people, and what makes a fine glass of whiskey.

On rare occasions, such as that night, all three of them worked together in wondrous harmony.

It started with us overhearing two merchants who had stopped their wagons on the road to negotiate trade, which had apparently gone bad enough to devolve into insulting each other's tastes in opera. Two Lonely Old Men had instructed us not to attract attention to ourselves while traveling and we *were* going to pass right by without a word, but I felt compelled to intervene.

I mean, one of them said that Valcullen's *Serenade of Trenches* was superior to Arisidone's *Selania*. What was I supposed to do? *Not* say something?

Anyway, around the time I settled the argument, I noticed the crate of whiskey bottles in the back of one of their wagons. Given that the liquor we had at Madame Fist's inn went up with the rest of it, I thought I might try persuading him to sell me a bottle. And after I threatened to do to his fingers what Valcullen did to musical theater, he obliged.

Only several hours later did we find a place I might actually be able to enjoy it.

I pressed the bottle to my lips and, despite the urge to drain it, limited myself to a gentle sip. Tallmill & Tallmill, while not as robust as Avonin, wasn't a swigging whiskey. In every drop, there should be a symphony of earthy notes accompanied by a chorus that tastes almost of honey, with just enough burn at the end to get in your nose.

I took a sip. Then a longer sip. Then a long drink.

I smacked my lips. Sniffed. Sighed.

No good.

I could still taste the ashes.

I corked the bottle, turned around, and started heading down the trail. This deep into the Valley, woodlands fought with mountains for the title of Biggest Pain in the Ass to Traverse. The stones and trees that peppered the slopes of this land like arrows had been ancient when humans first started showing up to the Scar. Far removed from cities and their troubles, they stood silent and unjudging as I picked my way through them.

Not that it helped.

The cold air of the mountains assailed me, pushing through my coat, but all I could smell was smoke. The taste of whiskey still hung in my mouth, but I could still taste the ashes. I had put two days and eighty miles between me and Terassus…

And it still didn't feel far enough.

Maybe that was just how it was going to be now. Maybe it would never be far enough. Maybe I would always taste ash and smell smoke, no matter what I drank. Maybe that's what scars were—not just injuries, but memories, places…

"Hey."

People.

The sun had set completely by the time I arrived back at our campsite, a humble clearing of dried earth sheltered from the snow by encroaching boughs. The meager tent we had brought stood pitched nearby. The birds were tied up not far from it, Congeniality fighting—and winning, naturally—a battle for the last scrap of slop from Jero's bird. And Jero…

He stood there. Thrust in the middle of camp like a knife.

"You were gone awhile," he said. "Thought I'd have to go look for you."

Whatever beasts and outlaws dwelled out here, chances were strong that the girl with the magic gun and bad disposition was infinitely better equipped to handle them than the asshole with a knife and a nice smile.

I would have told him that. But that would mean talking to him.

Thankfully, he took my silent stalking past him and taking a seat by the fire as evidence enough. After he added another handful of brush to it, he likewise settled down opposite me. I was still convinced to see this operation through, but I could do that just as well without talking to him. Hell, maybe better.

"Cold out tonight."

Not that he seemed to agree.

"Those merchants said these kinds of storms last for weeks." Jero watched the snow falling around us as he munched on some rations. "Bad omen for them, much better for us. Thicker clouds mean more cover when we board the airship."

It also meant that we'd spend the next two nights freezing our asses off. The higher up we got, the less thick the coat Urda had given me seemed. The wind blew harsher here, the cold bit deeper. It was hardest on my scars, cold always was—I could feel them aching under my clothes, fresh as the day I got them.

"It might end up being the difference between pulling this off and falling to our deaths, honestly," Jero continued to muse, scratching at his cheek. "The Iron Fleet has the longest guns of the Revolution. On a clear day, they could pick us out of the sky. Of course, even if we land, we don't know how many forces they've got onboard. Airships are limited in capacity, but that could still mean a dozen suits of mobile armor, a Relic Guard, and who knows how many rank-and-file Revolutionaries."

His face turned dark a moment, shadows dancing across his features as he stared into the fire.

"Each and every one of them a fucking zealot," he whispered bitterly. "Every thought they ever had given up to their Great fucking General, every one of them ready to do whatever he tells them to or die trying."

A person's silence is more telling than his words. They can spin any fanciful lie they want—Jero better than most—with their mouth, but when faced with silence, they start saying what's really on their mind.

And something weighed heavy on Jero's.

His wrinkles were too deep, his eyes too cold, his body too tight beneath his coat. His feelings on the Revolution went deeper than just words, deeper than even dead brothers. If I didn't hate him, I'd have asked.

"So, you, uh, got any thoughts on that?"

But I did, so I didn't.

He stared at me expectantly for a moment as I took a long swig from my bottle. "Like"—he cleared his throat—"we're about to go into a life-or-death situation here. It'd be handy if I knew what you were thinking about—"

"We can do this one of two ways."

He fell silent. I turned toward him, and I didn't blink.

"Either you can keep talking and be satisfied with my silence," I said, "or you can keep talking through a mouthful of broken teeth and I'll start talking, too."

His lips pursed. He looked away. I expected that much and turned back to the fire.

"Fine."

That, though, I didn't expect.

"Huh?" I asked.

"I said fine." He stood up, held his hands behind his back, and presented his chin. "Take your best shot. Take as many as you need to." At my squint, he sighed. "I knew your past, I knew what people had used you for, and I did the same thing they did. But for this— any of this—to work, we've got to talk to each other." He took a step closer, gestured to his face. "So, if breaking my teeth will make that happen, go ahead."

I studied him for a long time, trying to figure out what trick he was trying to pull with this. When I couldn't find any, I pulled myself to my feet and walked over to him. When he didn't try to run or flinch away, I gripped the whiskey bottle in my hand as tight as I could, raised it up, and...

I should have hit him.

As it was, I settled for slamming it ungently into his stomach as I passed him the bottle.

"Here," I sighed. "I'll hate you less if we're both drunk."

I won't insult you by trying to convince you he didn't deserve it or by feeding you some shit about the greater good. I won't blame you if you hate me for not hurting him as bad as he hurt everyone else. But...

I don't know. I suppose I wasn't ready to put another name on my list.

It was too damn cold for hate, anyway. So cold that I pulled my scarf free and took it in both hands, and with a flick of my wrist, it became a cloak. I swaddled myself inside it like a spiteful little cuckoo inside an angry little nest and stared into the fire.

"That's a handy enchantment your scarf has," Jero said, finishing a long swig. "Did you get that in—"

"No." I sneered at him. "None of that."

"None of what?"

"Banter. No banter, no rapport, and if you even try persiflage, I'll stab you."

"Okay, so...." He fell back onto his log, taking another swig. "Are we back to not talking?"

I sighed, pulled my cloak tighter around me. "I don't know...you know any drinking games?"

He scratched his jaw. "In the Revolution, we used to play this game called Perch." He chuckled. "Drinking was against the Great General's truths, of course, but every now and then we'd get ahold of wine or whiskey from a confiscated shipment. Then we'd climb up a tree, right? And we'd pass around the bottle, everyone taking drinks, and the last person to fall out of the tree was the winner."

He turned toward me with the biggest smile on his face. In exchange, I offered him the biggest why-the-fuck-didn't-I-break-your-face-when-I-had-the-chance look I could muster. I don't know if he got that or not, but he quickly cleared his throat and changed the subject.

"We also sometimes played Tribunal."

I grunted at him to continue. This train of thought, at least, sounded less like one of us would end up bleeding.

"It's where one person is the witness and everyone else is the tribunal," he said. "The witness claims something they've never done and if anyone on the tribunal has done it, they drink."

"Oh, come on," I scoffed. "That's just Lady's Liar. We played that in Cathama all the time. I was *fourteen* when I first played it."

He shot me a glance. "So does that mean you don't want to play?"

"I didn't fucking say that, did I?"

I leaned back against the log that had been serving as my seat and let out a thoughtful hum. Jero could spin pretty words sure as spiders spun webs, but that didn't make either of them trustworthy. Still, nothing to the truth of a man quicker than a bottle—this could be a good opportunity to see just how much of him was a liar.

Also, we were in the middle of nowhere and it was really fucking boring, so...

"Okay, I've got one," I said, scratching at one of my scars. "I've never"—I eyed him curiously—"left a friend behind to die while I escaped."

I shouldn't have been so surprised by how quickly he took a drink. But I was. It must have shown on my face, because he sniffed, cleared his throat, and wiped his mouth.

"In the Revolution," he said. "I think it was...the battle of Ordro's Crossing?"

"Never heard of it," I replied.

"No one has. It was a crappy little township with a crappy little cadre—barely enough of us to keep order in the streets, let alone fight off the Imperials that were marching to claim it. But cadre command ordered us to stay behind and hold them off while they escaped. They said it was 'our duty to the future to ensure that the Revolution's greatest thinkers survived.'"

"Yeah, that sounds like them."

"Yeah." That bitter quiet crept across his face again. "They all believed it, of course. Every single fucking lie the propaganda ever churned out, everyone in my cadre believed it. They just stood there like pretty birds on the front line, singing Revolutionary songs...right up until the Imperials buried them under a wave of rock and ash."

He took another swig, tossed the bottle toward me. I caught it, pulled it under my cloak—it felt warm. He'd been gripping it hard.

"Me, I didn't see the logic in it."

"You just left them there?" I asked.

"After I tried, and failed, to make them see the stupidity of dying for people who would never lift a finger for us, yeah." He shot me a wry look. "I'm pretty sure I've heard stories about you leaving people behind, too. People you worked with."

"That was different."

"How?"

"They were assholes. Not friends." I gestured to him with my chin. "Your turn."

He squinted into the fire, tossed another log on. "Okay, I've got one. I've never made love to someone who once tried to kill me."

I quirked an eyebrow at that, opened my mouth to ask, but thought better of it and took a long drink.

"What?" He blinked at me, wide-eyed. "Seriously?"

"Well, I don't know if you'd call what we did making love, but..." I paused in the middle of wiping my lips. "Wait, did you mean sleeping with them before or after they tried to kill you?"

"Uh, after, I guess."

I grunted and took another drink. His stare remained on me, and I'd tell you I didn't feel a morbid pride at the shock splayed across his face. But I'd be lying.

"What?" A grin crept across my face as I tossed the bottle back to him. "Not what you were hoping for?"

"I just..." He caught the bottle, shook his head. "How? The Scar's got enough murderers without inviting them into your bed. With that kind of anxiety, how did you...you know...*perform*?"

"Same as I perform everything." I leaned back, let the fire soak into me. "Brilliantly." I shrugged. "I don't know. It was another Vagrant, we'd been fighting over the same bounty, one thing led to another."

"You need to explain that one," Jero said. "Because in my experience, the only thing failing to kill someone leads to is trying again with a bigger knife."

My tongue fumbled around with the taste of ash and whiskey, searching for the words to describe it. Without realizing it, my hand slid out of my cloak and traced a finger across the scar that ran down my eye. It ached at the touch.

"I don't know, it's like…" I clicked my tongue. "When you meet someone over a glass of wine or a really funny joke, that's all you ever really share. Once that wine's gone or you hear the same joke again, you realize maybe that's all you ever had. But when you fight someone, you share that pain, that heat, that anger. You can't carry it with you and it's stupid to try, but you have that." I glanced up. "Does that make sense?"

He stared at me, then glanced down at the bottle. "I mean, it would if I were a lot more drunk, I bet."

"Fuck you." The curse came on laughter I hadn't intended to give him. "Maybe, sometimes…it's just nice to be with someone who hurts the same way you do."

Jero had nothing to say to that. Just as well—I couldn't hear anything. The longer I stared into the fire, the more the shadows it cast began to look like someone I knew. The longer I listened to its quiet chuckle, the more it began to sound like words. Like a voice I once knew.

You make me feel like a fucking idiot, you know?" she said. "Knowing all of this, I'd still stay. I'd still be with you. If you just told me that someday this would stop."

That's how it sounded inside my head.

"Sal."

As cold and clear as the day she'd said them.

"Please."

Keen as any scar.

"Fuck me." I shook my head, glanced back at Jero. "Why'd you make this fire so hot?"

He shot me a casual look before glancing back to the fire. "Your scars hurt when it's cold, right?" He must have seen the ire crossing my face. "You've been scratching them since you got here. You didn't have to tell me." He smiled softly into the fire. "Mine do, too."

I didn't know what to say to that. And that bothered me.

"It's your turn," he said.

I leaned back again, pointedly *not* scratching my scar, a long moment passing as I tried to think up something to say. Normally, I'd have been quicker, but whiskey addled my thoughts, made it hard to focus on anything but the warmth creeping out of the fire and into my cheeks, hard to think about anything but how long it'd been since I'd felt like this.

Still, my reputation was on the line. I wasn't about to have it said that Sal the Cacophony let some Revolutionary shit beat her in a drinking game.

Why, they'd *laugh* at me.

"Got it." I shot him a wry smirk. "I've never eaten Saludi curry."

He stared back at me, the bottle hanging limp in his hands as he blinked. I squinted.

"Why aren't you drinking?" I growled.

"Because you only drink if you *have* done it?" He shrugged. "I've never had Saludi curry, either."

"Birdshit you haven't."

He chuckled, glanced into the fire. "You take this game very seriously, don't you?"

"I take *curry* very seriously because it's *delicious*, you dumb fuck. The Revolution occupied Saluda for ten years. You said you were stationed there, right?"

He nodded. "Spent two years of my service there. What of it?"

"They give you a bowl the size of an infant for two pieces of copper is what of it. How the fuck did you manage to spend that long in Saluda and *not* have any of it?"

"I don't know, I just…didn't." He shrugged. "They put garlic in everything over there."

"So ask for less garlic."

"Oh, wow, what a great idea. If only I, the guy who figured out how to put together a fucking *airship heist*, had thought of it." He snorted. "I don't eat garlic. At all."

I'd originally gone on this trip with the firm belief that I might end up murdering him out of anger. I'd since discarded that belief, but now I was strongly considering a mercy killing. Still, I thought I might as well ask first.

"Why the fuck not?" I chuckled. "Does it make you shit yourself? Because they make an alchemic that'll clear that right—"

"Jandi loved garlic."

My laughter died in my throat. The warmth bled out of me. No matter how hot the fire burned, I couldn't help but feel cold.

"When we were little, when our father left us alone..." Jero wasn't looking at me. He muttered so low he might as well have forgotten I was even there. Maybe he had. "We had to steal to eat. We'd always work together. He'd distract the farmers, I'd lift their food."

A faint smile dawned across his face like the coldest, darkest morning in the dead of winter.

"One day," he said, "we saw a farmer toting a gigantic sack and figured he must have something amazing inside it. So we didn't even bother distracting him, we just ran up, cut it off his back, and ran off with it. He must have chased us for miles, but we lost him. When we opened up the sack, there was nothing but garlic bulbs in it."

He wasn't staring into the fire anymore. He wasn't even here anymore. Behind those eyes, there was nothing but a dark place, far away and lightless, that he'd disappeared into.

I knew that look.

I knew that place.

"But winter was coming and we had nothing else to eat, so for four months, we..." He shook his head. "I hated the stuff since the first bite, but Jandi came to love the taste. He'd buy garlic wherever we went, trade his rations for it, thank the Great General every time he'd get some. Everyone in our cadre complained about the smell. They'd cover their noses when they spoke to him." He laughed, bitter and hollow. "And he *reeked* of the shit, but he'd always say it was the smell of Revolutionary fervor coming off him. He always had some stupid answer like that. He'd smile like that, and every time after that I smelled garlic, I'd..."

His voice trailed off. His eyes darkened. Wherever he went, whatever dark place inside his head he crawled into, it wasn't a place for laughter, for words. It wasn't a place I could follow.

Places like that, everyone has to go through on their own.

So I said nothing. I sat beside him. And I stared into the fire. And I let him have that dark.

"Sorry." He blinked, cleared his throat, like he was awakening from some kind of dream. "Sorry. I didn't mean to get all..." He made some vague gesture around his eyes. "Yeah. Sorry."

"It's okay," I said.

And I meant it.

I'd wondered who Jero was since the moment I met him—a dashing rogue right out of an opera, a callow thug who simpered and whined for wine, a murderous stain who lied and killed as easy as he breathed. Maybe he was all of those things. But under all of it, there was just this.

Just a broken person sitting next to another broken person.

I glanced up toward the sky. The trees rustled with a howl of wind. The snow went from pleasant, falling sheets to twisting shades of darkness. Congeniality and Jero's bird had curled up next to each other, sleeping off the carrion they'd just devoured, unperturbed by the snow.

"For the best, I suppose." I eased myself up, wincing as the cold seeped back into my scars. "We need to be at the meeting spot by tomorrow evening, right? I won't have it said that Sal the Cacophony didn't show up because she was busy puking out a hangover."

Not after last time, anyway.

I'd pulled the tent flap back before I realized he wasn't behind me. I glanced over at the fire, saw him still there. Feeling my stare, he looked up. The emptiness in his eyes vanished, replaced by a sort of awkward nervousness that I found, despite myself, rather charming.

Or I would have, had it not been so fucking cold.

"You coming?" I asked.

"Oh, uh..." He cleared his throat. "It's just that...the tent is small and I thought that you might still be...I mean, since the incident back at the manor, I thought you might prefer if I slept out... you know, instead of—"

"I'll make you a deal," I interrupted. "I'll share this tent with you if you stop fucking talking." I glanced at his hands. "And if you bring the whiskey."

He smiled at me. And he nodded. And he walked to me and whispered, "Thank you."

"It's okay," I said.

And I meant it.

THIRTY-THREE

THE VALLEY

Most nights, I do okay.

I find a small space in the Scar that isn't teeming with outlaws, beasts, or inclement weather—sometimes it's a bed, sometimes it's not. I make sure I'm not going to wake up to something stabbing, shooting, or gnawing on me—I've only ever been wrong four times. I fall into a sleep, occasionally assisted by drugs, alcohol, or exhaustion—if I'm lucky, I don't dream.

Most nights, I do okay.

But some nights I don't.

My body ached, my skin prickled with cold beneath the blanket, my scars begged for me to close my eyes and let them rest for a little bit. Still I couldn't sleep. The whiskey hadn't done anything to dull my thoughts and the warmth it had given me had worn off about an hour ago.

I lay there, under a scratchy blanket, as the wind murmured and mused outside and the cold seeped in.

He lay behind me.

I knew Jero was still awake. I knew what people sleeping breathed like and I knew he was only faking. Up until that night, I thought I'd known who he was.

A criminal. A killer. Some asshole with a blade and a need, like any of the countless bandits, warlords, and Vagrants I'd put in the ground before. He was ostensibly on my side, but that didn't mean he wasn't scum.

Or at least, that's what he was up until that night.

It wasn't like you're thinking. This wasn't some cheap opera—he wasn't a brooding hero who dared not be vulnerable for fear of what might hurt and I sure as shit wasn't some swooning maiden who collapsed weeping in a pile of skirts when a man opened up to me. Opera, especially the cheap opera, is exciting, fun, and satisfying.

This was not.

We were still scum, him and I. Still criminals. Still killers. Neither of us were good people. Hell, neither of us were even decent people.

And neither of us could let go.

We both wore scars that went deeper than our skin. We both carried a dark place behind our eyes.

We both were broken.

"How did he die?"

I half whispered it, half hoped he hadn't heard me. A long silence drew out as he lay there. And when he spoke, it was on a soft, weak voice.

"He charged the enemy." Jero waited a long moment to continue. When he spoke again, his voice shuddered. "Imperials. Outnumbered us five to one. He just took up his weapon, screamed, ran toward them, and...died."

I stared at the tent wall. "To protect you?"

"I sometimes wonder that."

"And?"

"And I don't think he did."

I didn't ask. I didn't sleep. I listened in the dark as he rolled toward me and whispered, "Did you ever love the Imperium?"

"Huh?" I asked.

"Was it your home?"

"I was born there."

"But was it your home?"

I considered.

"No."

"Would you die for it?" he asked.

I had.

"No."

"What would you die for?" he asked.

I knew.

"I don't know," I said.

The silence that fell over us wasn't like before. It wasn't the silence of nothing to say, but the silence of trying to not say something. Something I knew. Something he knew.

Like I said, this wasn't cheap opera. This wasn't even good opera. This wasn't going to have a happy ending. We wouldn't know what to do with one if we had it—we weren't heroes, he and I. We were just two people.

Broken.

I knew—in my scars, I knew—the road this led down. The same way I know which dark places not to go into and when someone's going to try to put a knife in me. It's a moment that draws out, when everything is a little darker and quieter, and when it ends you'll either walk away or do something stupid.

And just as I knew it wasn't going to end well, I knew what I was going to do.

The wind seeped in through the tent. I twitched under my blanket. I heard him shift, roll over toward me.

"Do your injuries hurt?" he asked.

"No," I said.

"You're lying," he replied.

"I am."

"The Vechine doesn't always flush out like it should. If there are traces left behind, they can cause infection."

His hand went to the edge of my blanket. I felt him hesitate, his fingers hovering over the thin fabric.

"May I?" he asked.

I closed my eyes. I nodded.

He peeled back the blanket. The chill that had been gnawing at me sank its teeth all the way in as he reached for the edge of my coat. He hooked a pair of fingers beneath it, paused. I felt his eyes on the back of my head, waiting for me.

I nodded again.

"Yes," I whispered.

He pulled the coat up. My skin tensed under the sudden cold. I felt the muscles of my belly bunch up, my breath catch behind my lips. I clutched the edge of the blanket to keep from shivering.

His hand found my side. His palm ran across the injury. His fingers ghosted across my skin, gooseflesh rising as they trailed across my body, over the wound, down to my hip.

He was warm. So warm.

His hand lingered there for a moment.

"You're okay," he said. "You're fine."

He began to pull his hand away.

And mine reached out to stop him.

I held his hand, there on my skin, not willing to let go of that warmth, that touch, that... feeling.

Of not being broken. For a little while, anyway.

I rolled over on the sheets, the coarse fabric scratching at the skin of my back as I looked up at him. The shadows rested comfortably on his face, painted him like a dream that lingers for a few minutes after you wake before disappearing. In the dark, I couldn't see the wrinkles from the faked laughter or the cunning smiles.

I only saw the contour of his cheek and felt the way he bit back a flinch as I touched him. I only saw the outline of his lips and felt his breath as my thumb glided across his lips. I only saw his eyes.

And the way he looked at me.

"Sal," he whispered. "About what happened... I'm sorry."

I smiled at him. I didn't know if he could see it.

"If that's not enough, don't feel like—"

I took him by the cheek, pulled him down to meet me. I pressed my brow against his and felt his warmth on mine.

"No talking," I told him, "for once."

I pulled him onto me, his lips against mine, and held him there in my hands, feeling his warmth. His hands found my body, palms sliding beneath my coat, fingers brushing against each one of my ribs, thumbs tracing the edges of my scar down across my belly until he took me by the hips and pressed me down.

His fingers hooked into my trousers, pulled my belt free. The cold swept across my legs, the skin prickling as I felt the leathers come free. I curled my legs around him, pulled his warmth into me as I reached for his belt, tore the buckle loose, started tugging his trousers down.

"Ah!"

I saw the wince across his face. I stopped, looked at him. He smiled, shook his head.

"Sorry," he said. "My leg. Old injury."

I nodded. "Should I..."

"Yeah." He looked away, the smile fading. "Just...let's go slow, okay?"

"Okay."

I slid him free of the garment. My hands found his back, the curve of his spine and the contour of his muscles, as I pulled him down toward me. His lips found my neck, tasting each inch of me until his teeth found the spot just between my earlobe and my jaw that made my breath catch.

I felt him pressing against me, the warmth of his legs against mine as I wrapped them around him, the warmth of his hands on the naked skin of my back as he pulled me up onto his lap, onto him.

And we started, slowly.

I could feel him only in moments, in fleeting sensations of his coat scratching against the skin of my belly, of the tangle of his hair as I seized it in my fingers and twisted, of the growl in his throat as I pulled his lips back against my neck. My eyes were only for the shadows of us, my nose was only for the scent of him pressed against me, my ears only for the breath that came slow and hot and the sound of us biting back our pain for this.

Everything else in me was for that warmth.

It flooded me. Each time I rocked against his hips. Each time his mouth found that spot. Each time we found a spot on each other—a scar, a scratch, an old wound from an old life in an old dream—and felt all the things that made us who we were beneath our fingertips.

Sometimes they hurt, those old wounds.

But I didn't stop. We didn't. Couldn't. He needed this, like I needed this, like I wanted this. It wouldn't make us less broken, it wouldn't take back what we'd done, and it wouldn't make anything stop hurting.

But sometimes...

Sometimes, it was real nice just being with someone who hurt like you did.

I hadn't felt that way since...

Since Liette.

The thought came unbidden. My eyes didn't want to open. But they did.

And I saw her. Her shadow was outside the tent, painted on the walls by the moonlight. Beside her was Darrish the Flint and Cassa the Sorrow and Yugol the Omen and all the ghosts that followed me. They crowded around the tent in a dark halo, staring at me, expecting an answer.

I didn't give them one.

I closed my eyes. I pulled Jero closer to me. I let the warmth wash over me again as he rocked beneath me, as I breathed in the scent of him, as he traced my scars under his fingertips.

As the shadows disappeared.

Slowly.

Until all that was left was the dark.

And us.

THIRTY-FOUR

LITTLEBARROW

Meret didn't recall much of his life before he became an apothecary.

Not for trauma or regret or anything nearly so impressive, rather there simply hadn't been much to tell. He had been born to a mother and father who had struggled to provide for him and his siblings. He'd worked hard and eventually became accepted as a student to a master and, years later, here he was.

But he remembered his uncle.

Or, specifically, his uncle's stories. Not that the man had been a bard—though he had been a drunk, so he wasn't too far off—but he'd traveled, seen villages beyond his own, met people who looked nothing like him, had conversations he never thought he would.

Those were all fine, but what he *really* liked were the stories about the Vagrants.

Back then, he'd been too young to hear the caution in the many tales about those dangerous, magical lunatics. Of course, he'd also been too old to be very impressed with all the explosions, garish costumes, and rampant violence that had spellbound the other children. Really, he wasn't sure until this moment, in that cold house in Littlebarrow, that he realized what he'd really loved about those stories.

Vagrants mattered.

For as savage as the Scar was, it was fraught with cowards like him. Farmers cowered from the Revolution, volunteered their harvests to avoid being conscripted. Merchants cowered from the Imperium, heaped flattery and riches upon the mages to escape their wrath. Even the barons of freeholds, the powerful and the wealthy, were only so because they suckled just hard enough at the asses of the even more powerful that they were permitted to hold on to their stations.

But not the Vagrants. The Vagrants cared nothing for boundaries, for heavy-handed philosophies or overbearing ethics. No one could tell them where to go, who to speak with, what they could or couldn't do. Revolutionaries and Imperials, Haveners and Ashmouths alike, all stepped a little more carefully when a Vagrant's name was even *mentioned*.

That was power. That was meaning. That was mattering.

Or so he'd thought.

He'd once cursed his parents for not being born magical so he could become a Vagrant himself—Mer the Plague, he'd always thought that would be a good name. Later, of course, once he realized how much gore would be involved, he promptly apologized to his mother and father, but he'd never really stopped believing that the life of a Vagrant was a life of self-realization.

Until now.

"What was it like?"

Sal glanced up as he blurted the question out. Rather than sneering at it, her eyes widened in surprise. She glanced him over, scrutinizing him with a tinge of disbelief before clearing her throat.

"Oh, um. Okay, wow. I thought you'd have known by now, but that's okay." She leaned forward, a serious look on her face. "All right, so before you do anything, make sure that you both want it, right? Talk about it, take your time, make sure you're not just ready but ready for *this* person and they're ready for you, too. After that, though, sometimes it's nice to start with kissing their neck or—"

"*NO!*" He hadn't meant to shout that. Or to leap out of his chair. He cleared his throat, settled back down. "Er, that's not... I mean, I *have* been... uh, back in Bitterbough, I met this..." He performed a thoughtful flail. "No, that wasn't my question. I mean... what was it like? To be with someone as a Vagrant?"

Her brow furrowed. "Listen, I don't know what you've heard, but it's not like we shoot fire out of our junk." She paused, considered. "*Most* of us don't, anyway."

"I mean... there are no stories about it."

"I mean, I'm flattered you'd think there would be, but we aren't *that* good." She paused, considered again. "*Most* of us aren't, anyway."

"I guess I just never thought that Vagrants did that," Meret said, looking down at himself. "Make love, feel those things..." He looked back up at her. "*Do* Vagrants fall in love?"

Another blurted-out stupid question, he chided himself. One that she would no doubt relentlessly mock him for. And by the long, leering grin that sprawled across her face like a snake in heat, he guessed she was getting ready to do just that.

But then a moment passed. And her smile shrank. Then disappeared. A troubled look came across her face, as though the answer that came to her lips wasn't the one she wanted to give. Or one she even knew.

"I don't know," she said. "I don't think so."

"But what you just told me with Jero, that—"

"That wasn't love," she interrupted with a glare he didn't notice.

"Then it was just sex?"

"I didn't say that, either. I don't have *just* sex. I—"

"Then what was it? Animal lust? An urge? Was it—"

"For a guy with such a cute face, you sure do fucking ask to be punched in the mouth a lot," she warned. "No, it's nothing like that." She scratched at a scar on her cheek. "But it wasn't *not* like that. It was... I don't know."

He opened his mouth to offer his help. But then he remembered what she had said about his mouth and decided, instead, to sit quietly for a moment. She leaned back, searched the table for whiskey that wasn't there, drummed her fingers as though it would make it appear, and when it didn't, settled for making a fist and slamming it on the table instead.

"It's just... being tired," she said. "Tired of running, tired of hurting, tired of..." She gestured vaguely to herself. "This. All of it." She stared up at the lamp hanging from the ceiling, sighed. "Sex is... nice, now and again. Not for everyone, but for me. It makes me feel like…like…" She squinted. "Like someone can look at all this blood and scars and think there's nothing wrong with me.

"But it's not enough," she continued. "Not really. You can't just cling to the nights where everything is going well. You start needing days where you wake up hurting and someone else is going to make the coffee for you. You start needing jokes that are just the right kind of bad and needing someone who isn't going to care if you don't say the right thing all the time. You need…you need…"

She held out her hands. And all the empty space between them was the answer she didn't want to give, but the only one she had.

"More," she said. "And you can't get that from a Vagrant."

He blinked. "Because of your code?"

"No, you dumbshit, because of our names."

There was anger behind her voice, hatred, even. But it was neither the all-burning fire nor the smug venom he'd come to expect. Rather, it was a weary anger, a flame that had been burning too long but couldn't be extinguished, so it settled for devouring the ashes.

She leaned back in the chair, her sigh so deep it came out of her scars, her wounds. Perhaps she'd been holding herself too proudly before, or perhaps the light had been too dim, but only now could he see the full extent of the injuries she carried. He could see the old scars, see the new wounds that would become more, as they wound a jagged map across her skin.

All that pain. All that blood. And still, her eyes were full of that fire. Still, she burned.

Long after nothing was left.

"It's like…" She held out her hands, trying to explain and still coming up empty. "You become a Vagrant, you break your oath, you get your ink, and you take your fancy name, and you think that's the end of it. But it doesn't end there. It doesn't end after the first caravan you rob, after the first village you burn, after the first man you kill.

"It keeps getting bigger, the name. You don't even realize it at first. It becomes something profane, something uttered in whispers and used to scare children. When someone speaks it, it carries weight. And that weight gets into everything you carry. The steel on your hip keeps getting heavier. The cuts you carve get deeper. The body counts get bigger and the flames grow higher. Until…"

She held her hands out.

"It's too heavy for you to carry anything else. Anyone else. All you have left is the name."

He stared at those hands. At the scars that wended across her palms like pink rivers. At the calluses and the burn scars that came from carrying that terrible weapon at her hip. At the emptiness.

For all that her hands wore, all the blood and suffering, they were still empty.

"You can still have it, can't you?" he asked, not looking up. "Love? Like, you and Liette..."

"We have something," she said. "We have something that's less than I should be able to give her. I can give her good days, good nights, some of them so good we can pretend they'll always be like that. But she deserves more than that. She deserves someone who's always coming back home, someone who doesn't make her cry so much."

She laid her hands on the table. She stared at them, as if she expected them to do something.

"And that's not something I can give her," she whispered. "That's not something I can even hold."

"Is that it, then? Hold a sword or hold someone's hand?"

"Pretty much."

Meret frowned, stared at his own hands. They still seemed too soft to him—a few calluses here and there, a stain from mixing the wrong tincture that one time. He used to hate them, too small to hold a sword, to do something *meaningful*.

But if they had to be this soft to hold someone close... if they had to be like this to still be himself...

"What about what she wants?" he asked.

"Huh?" She looked up, perplexed.

"What if she's willing to carry it with you? Or them? Or whoever?"

She shook her head. "You can't ask someone to do that."

"Why not?"

She furrowed her brow. "Why can't you ask someone to stand by a door, night after night, wondering if the last time you walked out is the last time they'll ever see you? Why can't you ask someone to hold you at night because you keep seeing dead men's faces in your dreams?" She sniffed, stared at him. "Would you?"

Would he?

In his dreams, it was so simple: pick up a sword, fight the bad guys. It wasn't that he *hadn't* considered that things would end badly—he wasn't an idiot, after all. But he hadn't exactly considered that the sword could reach farther than just him. Not like she had.

But then...those burdens existed, regardless of what he did, didn't they? He could mend wounds, stitch them shut, keep them clean. But he couldn't bring back the dead. He couldn't make the wars stop.

Pick up the blade, people die.

Leave it alone, people die.

Even she—Sal the fucking Cacophony—didn't know how to solve that problem.

What hope did he have?

"I think—" he started to say.

The glass interrupted him.

A faint rattle. Nothing too alarming. He looked up and saw the cups on his shelf trembling. Far away, a distant echo, was the sound of something great striking the earth. It lasted only a second.

Both of them fell silent.

And watched that shelf.

Until it rattled again.

"Meret."

He looked back at her. She was staring at him. Leaning over the table. Her hand was extended to him. Upon her palm, she held something.

A single feather. Stained red.

"Tell me what you remember about what we talked about," she said, "the part with the Crow Market."

"The Crow Market." He blinked, struggling to recall. "Uh, Ashmouths, a Freemaker, another mage...Rudu? Rudu the Club?"

"The Cudgel," she repeated. "Rudu the Cudgel. This is his Red-favor. You remember what that is?"

"I do, but—"

"Do you know where Clef's Lament is? It's east toward—"

"The edge of the Valley. Like a day's ride from here, I know it." Meret's eyes widened behind his glasses. "Sal, are you asking—"

"No," she said. "I'm not asking. I'm telling." She licked her lips. "I'm telling you that Liette doesn't deserve what's about to happen. I'm telling you that if you take this feather to Rudu, he'll take care of her. I'm telling you that..." She closed her eyes, drew in a shuddering breath. "I'm telling you that I don't have a lot. I don't even know if I'm walking out of this town. I can't offer you much...but..."

She swallowed hard, opened her eyes.

They didn't burn. They glistened.

"Liette," she said, "has to get out of here. I'm telling you that. I'm telling you that I need you to do it."

He stared at the feather. Something that small and simple. Just a feather with some paint on it. And she was extending it to him like it was a blade, like it was worse than a blade. She wept for it. A Vagrant would do anything for it. A town would...would...

"Sal," he whispered. "Is Littlebarrow in danger?"

She hesitated, then nodded.

"Because of you?" he asked.

Another nod.

He'd known it. But now he believed it. Everything Sindra had said was true. Everything he'd done here meant that Littlebarrow would burn.

He'd leave behind this town, the cinders and ash that it would be reduced to. And if he took that feather, that'd be all he'd have left of this place.

All for her. For Liette. For both of them.

Meret frowned. And he sighed deeply. And he looked into her eyes.

"Just so we're clear," he said as he reached out and plucked it from her hand, "if you *do* walk out of here, you come find her. Find me. Because you'll owe me a lot more than a fucking feather."

— ❈ —

"What are you doing?"

Somehow, Sindra's voice was so ripe with contempt that it rang out loud and clear over even the groaning of the wagon's axles and rime-coated wheels. Meret made a mental note to congratulate her when he wasn't covered in sweat.

"What does it look like I'm doing?" he wheezed as he pulled hard on the wagon's yoke, the wheels offering a faint, defiant squeak in response.

"You *appear* to be trying to move Rodic's old wagon out of his barn," she said. "But it *looks* like you're being fucking stupid."

"Good, good," Meret grunted, face screwed up in effort. "So long as one of us is on top of things."

Sindra watched him struggle, arms folded. "It's *got* to be one of us. Or have you not fucking noticed we're the only ones left?"

Meret paused, glanced up at her from beneath a sweat-soaked brow. "Did they get out okay?"

"I..." The anger from her face thawed, just a little. "Yes. All the elderly and children were given seats on carts. Everyone else is walking. But they've got enough food, water, and warmth to get them to where they're going. I made sure of that."

He nodded. "Thank you, Sindra. For everything." Then he returned to pushing.

"Everything I've done for you should warrant me more gratitude than a few empty words, boy."

"Anything left in my house is yours."

Her face fell. "Then you're really doing it, aren't you? You're leaving Littlebarrow."

"Soldiers are coming. You said it yourself."

"And you didn't believe me. What changed? Did *she* tell you what was coming?"

Meret grunted as he pushed. "She did."

"This wagon is for her, then, hence why you're not out on your own right now."

His jaw clenched. The wheels groaned. "It is."

"Moron," she growled. "Fucking moron. Do you know what that woman is? Do you know what she's done? To this town?"

This time, Meret didn't bother answering. She didn't seem to notice.

"Littlebarrow was their home, Meret. It was *our* home. And she just fell out of the sky and ruined it. For what? That *other* woman?"

"She's important."

"No one is *that* important."

"Probably not, no."

Sindra's brow furrowed. "Then why are you doing this? Why are—"

"Because I don't fucking know what else to do," he snapped. Salt dripped into his eyes, stung them, but he didn't blink. He forced his eyes on Sindra's, his hands on the yoke. "I'm an apothecary. I mix herbs and set bones and people still die. You're a fighter, you've got a sword. But people still die."

"People are always going to die, Meret. You can't stop that."

"No. I can't," he said. "Helping her won't stop that, either." He let out a hot breath. "I don't know what will stop it. I don't know if anything *will* stop it. But I know I can't watch it happen." He grunted, digging in his heels, shutting his eyes and pushing again. "So I'm doing this. I won't have it said that I didn't do everything I could."

He shoved as hard as he could. The wheels wouldn't so much as budge. Probably his imagination, but had they gotten *more* stubborn than they were a moment ago?

He opened his eyes. It wasn't his imagination. It *was* Sindra on the other side of the yoke, pushing back against him.

"No," she declared.

"No?" he asked, not moving.

"No, I'm not going to let you throw your life away," she said, shoving back against the yoke. "No, I'm not going to let you ruin yourself for that woman. *No*, I'm not going to watch another good man die for shitty ideas for the respect of people who don't deserve it."

"You can't stop me!" he shouted as he shoved. The wheels squeaked.

"I fucking put men six times your size on the ground, boy. I can stop you." She shoved back. The wheels groaned.

"A man six times my size doesn't *exist*! Get out of the way, Sindra!" He pushed. The wheels growled.

"Damn it, *no*! You want to leave, let's leave. But we'll do it so we have a fighting chance. Fucking see reason here." She pushed back. The wheels shrieked.

"No!" Meret shouted, shoving.

"You idiot, you can't seriously—"

"I am serious." He shut his eyes, he pushed as hard as he could. "I am serious and I am here and I can do something so *I'm going to fucking do it!*"

He heard the whistle of her prosthetic as she kicked the side of the cart angrily. "Not with this hunk of fucking—"

The wheels roared.

Mud and frost fell off their spokes and axles as the wagon came rolling forward suddenly. A body hit the earthen floor. A shout filled the barn as the wagon came rolling out.

Meret didn't open his eyes until he felt the cold air on his face. And when he did, Sindra wasn't there.

"Fucking piece of fucking useless..."

He turned at the sound of her cursing, saw her still in the barn, sprawled out on the floor. She struggled to find her feet, moving awkwardly. It took him a moment to realize what had happened.

The pistons, he thought as he looked at the limp mass of metal hanging from her knee. *The pistons in her prosthetic. They came undone. I told her not to wait so long to see someone to tend to those. I need to—*

He paused, stared at her.

Need to what? Help her? So she can get up and stop me? Stop all of this? He swallowed something bitter as she met his stare. *No. You can't go back to doing nothing. You can't just leave.*

He closed his eyes. He started pushing the wagon.

She'll be fine. She knows how to fix it.

The snow started to fall heavier. A cold wind swept through his hair.

She knows how to get up, anyway. The cold will bother her joints, but she's tough. She can take it.

The cold seeped into his body. The wind moaned softly.

She's a soldier. She'll be fine.

He kept pushing the wagon. Until he didn't.

"Fucking damn it," he sighed.

Sindra leaned against the door frame of the barn, struggling to reach down to her prosthetic, bashing it with her fist as though it could simply be beaten into working again. A litany of curses poured out of her mouth, each one more angry, more desperate than the last.

"Come on, come on, you stupid piece of shit." Her voice grew hoarse, squeaking with tears held at her eyes. "Fucking magic. Why won't you work? Why can't you just—"

She fell silent only as Meret approached. She looked away as he stared at her prosthetic.

"Can I help?" he asked.

She met his gaze, lips curled tightly, refusing to let the words come out of her mouth. After a time, she nodded so stiffly and swiftly that he would have missed it if he blinked. He returned it, just as tersely—she preferred it that way.

He knelt down, took a tool out of his bag, and got to work pushing the pistons of her prosthetic back into alignment.

"This changes nothing," she said. "You're an idiot."

"You're trying to save me, so what's that make you?" he asked.

"Also an idiot."

"I guess we'd have to be," he said softly. "Both of us could have found bigger towns than a hole like Littlebarrow."

She looked out over the town, its little houses disappearing under the snow. "It's a lot of shit swept together, true." She looked for a long time. "But it had its charm."

"It did," Meret said. "Good people, too."

"Idiots for building it all the way out here."

"Makes sense that two more idiots would come to stay here, doesn't it?" Meret looked up as he slid a piston back into place. "Makes sense that two idiots should leave together, doesn't it?"

She kept him in her gaze, her mouth twisted into a frown. Still, that was a step up from a scowl at least.

"You haven't changed your mind about those two," she said.

He shook his head.

"You're still going to try to help them."

He nodded.

"Even though they don't deserve it."

"I'm..." He sighed, clicked the last piston into place. "I'm not going to leave anyone behind, Sindra. Not them. Not you."

She stared down at her prosthetic, rolled her ankle. The sigils glowed with faint life. The metal squeaked comfortingly.

It wasn't fixed, of course. Without a machinist to work on it, it'd just pop out of place again. And the cold wasn't good for her joints, especially where the prosthetic connected. All he'd done, really, was push a few rods into place so she could walk again for a short time.

But it was something.

And she was still walking.

For now.

"I won't ask you if you're really sure," Sindra said, her voice soft. "Because I know you are." She looked up at him. "I just want to know two things. First, are you going to regret this?"

He frowned. "I don't know."

"No one does until it's too late." She sighed, nodded. "Second, do you expect me to be nice about it?"

He blinked, baffled. "Uh...no?"

"Good, because I'm not going to." She pushed past him, took a spot at the yoke, and glanced over at him. "Go and get Rodic's fucking bird. Moving this is going to take forever if we have to rely on your skinny ass."

THIRTY-FIVE

THE VALLEY

When I was a kid, I always dreamed of being a hero.

That evolved as I got older—sometimes I was a conquering warrior winning glory at the tip of a sword, sometimes I was a beloved ruler who led her people wisely, and once I really thought I'd be a great opera singer and would sing so hard that it'd lead to world peace.

The fantasy changed, but one thing was always constant. The day I became a hero, I would come riding in on a bird with the most regal amethyst plumage, heralded by the grateful cheers of thousands and the falling petals of blossom trees as I walked beneath the rays of a beautiful noonday sun. I would wave, smile, and change the world with nothing more than that.

However, as with love, sex, money, and war, the real things always end up being worse than the fantasy.

On the day I changed the world forever, it was gray, it was cold, and I was covered in bird vomit.

"Oh, *real* mature, madam. You're the fucking queen of civility," I groused, trying and failing to wipe the bolus of fur and bones off the front of my coat. "Do you want to be alone forever? Because I can tell you right now that it's hard to get a man when your answer to an argument is puking all over them."

Congeniality seemed as unmoved by that as she had been by my last six attempts to send her on her way. And, much like last time, she dug her spurs into the mountainside, let out an angry chirping noise, opened her beak wide, and—

"Oh, fuck *me*." I darted away as she expelled another wet, reeking bolus from her gullet—I knew it had been a mistake to feed her so much on the way up here. "This is a new fucking coat, you bitch. Do you *want* to die?"

The Badlander let out a challenging squawk, flapping her vestigial wings angrily as she clawed at the earth. I knew she couldn't *actually* understand human speech, but damn if there wasn't more lurking behind those yellow eyes than I knew.

Frankly, though? She was just being kind of an asshole.

This wouldn't be the first time we'd parted ways. Occasionally, I'd go to a place she couldn't follow and send her off on her own. Occasionally, she'd catch a scent she had to find the source of and leave me where I was. No hard feelings were held on either end because of it—after all, we were both professionals—and we'd always find each other again.

But this time... this time, she didn't want to go.

What the fuck was I supposed to do? Take a five-hundred-pound angry, stinking, ill-tempered asshole of a bird up into the sky?

"She's afraid."

His voice was as soft as the wind wending its way through the mountains. I looked up and saw Tuteng crouched on a craggy rock, his hood pulled back and his horn stumps stark against the gray sky. This far up, rocks were the only things in abundance—great stony fingers that reached up through the veil of fog that blanketed the mountainside.

The one he hopped off had to be at least ten feet high. Yet he didn't so much as flinch when he hit the ground on broad, flat feet and walked past me toward Congeniality.

I tried to stop him—the last person to approach her without being properly introduced had gone blind from the bile she had spat into his eyes—but it didn't matter. She let him approach with nothing more than a curious stare. When he gently reached out to rub behind her long neck, she closed her eyes and let out a pleased chirrup.

"A fine beast," Tuteng hummed, admiring her. "Resilient, strong, but lonely—that's why she chooses to walk with you, I bet."

"If she could choose somewhere else to walk, that'd be great." I tried wiping more of her vomit off me. "I can't take her up into the sky, now, can I?"

Tuteng leaned forward, closed his eyes. Somehow, Congeniality did the same. They pressed their brows together, his horns rubbing against her skull. His lips moved, speaking words I couldn't hear. Congeniality glanced up, spared a long look at me, before turning around and beginning to stalk down the mountain.

She paused, looked over her shoulder at me for one last look before disappearing into the fog.

Like I said, I know she can't understand actual language. She's a bird. A fucking fine bird who can eviscerate a fully grown hunting cat with just one foot, but still just a bird. There's nothing in her eyes beyond hunger and her usual surly temperament.

I don't know why, when she looked at me like that, she looked sad.

"Damn," I whispered as Congeniality's footsteps faded. "What was *that*?"

"I asked her to find you again, later," Tuteng said, pulling up his cloak and turning to head back up the mountain. "She agreed."

"Huh." I glanced over at the mist she disappeared into as I followed Tuteng. "What kind of magic is a Beast-Tongue's, anyway?"

"The magic of not being an asshole, I guess." Tuteng shrugged as he picked his way through the boulders. "Birds and beasts know things we don't. They talk in a language we can't understand. But they're still willing to tell you. You just have to figure out how to listen."

"What did she tell you?"

Tuteng paused for a moment. "She is worried. She thinks this time, you won't make it back."

I probably should have listened closer than I had. After all, "if a bird tries to tell you shit's about to go bad, pay attention" was an old rule of adventuring.

Or it should be, anyway.

But then, I'd always come back. This wouldn't be the first time she watched me go away. This wouldn't be the last time she watched me come back.

Right?

Right.

"Did you tell her I would?" I asked.

"I don't lie to them."

Despite myself, I grinned. "You're kind of funny, Tuteng. I wish we had gotten to spend more time together."

"Thanks," he said as we ascended to the peak. "I wish your people hadn't brought a war here that devastated my land and destroyed my civilization."

I mean, he wasn't *wrong*, but still.

We'd made camp the only place we could. The mountains that surrounded the Valley loomed so high that their crowns were lost in the clouds overhead. Stone tyrants, they loomed oppressively over the narrow pass that wound its way through their colossal presence—the sole defiance to their kingdom of rock and scrub. Our tiny plateau that overlooked the pass felt like a blind spot under their eyeless stares, and looking up into the low-hanging clouds felt like inviting their attention.

I kept my eyes and my voice low. To do otherwise felt like a bad idea.

"We've been over this," a tired voice sighed. "They're not going to bite. Just grab your balls, grab the saddle, and hold on."

Not everyone felt the same.

"Okay, for *one*"—Urda wagged a finger at Jero, who stood nearby wearing a weary expression—"that's incredibly hurtful. *Just* because I'm realistically, understandably, and wisely concerned doesn't mean I'm lacking"—he choked—"*balls*. And for *three...*"

He gestured to the huge Oyakai bird looming over him.

"How do we know that he hasn't been rolling around in feces? I am *not* getting on a bird whose sanitization is within reasonable doubt."

"He grew up in a house nicer than any of us will ever legitimately be in and ate dinners richer than any of us will ever taste." Jero patted the great bird's flank, eliciting a coo from the creature. "Trust me when I say Murderbeak here has better hygiene than anyone present."

"Murder...*beak?*" Urda squinted. "What kind of a pathetic cry for attention is *that* name?"

"Take it up with your sister. She named it."

Jero caught my glance from across the way as Urda made a show of inspecting the grime between the bird's toes. With his free hand, he mimed drawing a noose around his neck and drawing it taut, tongue lolling and eyes rolling back into his head.

I grinned at that and immediately hated myself for it. Not that it was the *worst* joke I'd ever heard, but it was still a bad joke. And I'd been around enough to know that when someone starts making bad jokes that you still smile at...

Well, that's something I didn't need right now.

Fuck me if I didn't want it, though.

The Oyakai seemed less interested in their squabble. As did the other birds. On their great legs, they milled about the plateau, occasionally staring uninterestedly into the sky. Like they had for the past day.

Like Urda and Jero had argued for the past day. Like Agne had sat in the wagon's seat, reading her fourth romance novel, for the past day. Like Two Lonely Old Men had stood in the middle of the plateau, staring up into the clouds, unmoving and unspeaking—like he was doing now—for the past day.

It wasn't the *most* boring heist I'd ever participated in. But it was number two, at least. And it didn't look like it'd be alleviating itself anytime soon.

What if Tuteng's bird hadn't carried our forged note to the Revolution? What if they'd read it and hadn't believed it? What if Urda's forgery was using old code and he'd in fact directed the airships somewhere else entirely?

What if, I thought, *the Iron Fleet just isn't coming?*

I'd asked Two Lonely Old Men that (among other things made more colorful by my frustration) and received only enigmatic smiles and one quiet repetition in response.

"They will come."

The first time he'd told me, I believed it. The sixth time, I didn't.

If I got that answer a nineteenth time, I knew that *my* answer would be violence. So I pointedly ignored him—and he me—as I went to the edge of the camp.

Where I found Yria waiting. Waiting and not cursing, farting, or scratching herself somewhere indecent.

Which is probably how I should have known something was wrong.

"What's going on?" I asked as I approached her.

"Nothing," she grunted, her eyes fixed on the ground. "*Probably* nothing, anyway."

Probably was a word whose mention I could abide only when I *wasn't* waiting to infiltrate a fleet of ships with guns that could blow us to pieces. I squatted down beside her as she gestured to the stone before us.

The earth was darkened in erratic patterns, barely noticeable against its deep gray hue. In bursts and slivers and designs that hurt my eyes to look at, I could just barely see what she saw: a thick black substance, halfway between ash and congealed blood.

Which, in case you were wondering, is a substance you only want to see in, like, *two* situations. This was neither of them.

"Someone was here before us," Yria muttered. She ran fingers across the substance, brought them to her nose, and cringed. "And they left this shit behind."

"Magic?" I asked, though I'd never seen anything like this before.

"Maybe," she replied. "Or alchemics. Or spellwrighting. Or maybe someone was up here slapping balls to ass and it all went horribly wrong. I don't fucking know, but I don't fucking like it." She wiped her fingers clean on her breeches, then glowered out over the mountains. "The trail of it leads up that hill there, and onward."

"Worth checking out?" I drummed the hilt of my blade. "I don't like the idea of someone else being up here with us."

"Oh, you don't, do you, Princess Picklepuss?" Yria sneered. "What, you fucking think I was sitting here waiting for a cock of mystery to come knocking at our asses? Of course I thought about checking it out, but that'd take magic to do it quick and magic takes Barter." She held up her stiff fingers. "And my asshole's only *barely* started tingling again after our last magical shenanigans, so I guess you, me, and the fucking spooky goop are stuck here."

That was probably the tension talking. Just like how, if I slapped her across her greasy mouth right now, it would be the tension slapping. But then Jero would get involved, then Agne would get involved after I slapped *him*, and the whole thing would be a lot of mess we didn't need right now.

This was a problem that couldn't be solved by violence. Which meant it was a problem I didn't want to deal with right now. So I merely pulled my scarf over my face, pulled myself to my feet, and turned away.

"No, wait." Yria caught my wrist with her hand, sighed as she pulled herself up. "Listen, I'm just..." She looked skyward, cringed. "It's *real* now, you know? Before, it was all tavern talk, saying big things over drinks. Now we're going to do this." Her eyes drifted toward her brother, who was screaming and running from Murderbeak as the bird followed him curiously. "All of us."

I followed her stare as Urda collapsed, cowering as the bird nudged him. "He's ready for this." I grimaced at the sound that followed. "Despite all appearances."

"Yeah, I know," she sighed. "Of course I fucking know. I just... I don't *know*, you know? What if this time it goes wrong? What if this time, I can't fix it for him?" She swallowed something hard and bitter. "I heard about what you did for him. Down in the Crow Market. He, uh, he doesn't do too good in those situations. Hasn't since we lost our mom."

I nodded. "To the Revolution."

"To big people." Her eyes remained locked on her brother. "The uniforms change, but they're all the fucking same. Big people with big things that make big noises. People like that, they don't give a shit about people like him." She glanced at me from the corner of her eye. "People like you don't usually, either. But you did. So, you know, I guess you're not the colossal asshole I thought you were."

I blinked. "Thanks?"

"Just... if I'm not there and you are... look out for him, okay? He's..." Her frown twisted the tattoo on her chin into messy lines as she wiped something away from her eyes. "I'm all he's got."

It's not that I expected Yria the Cell to be an emotionless collection of vulgarity and bodily functions—despite all the stories and despite knowing her. But she never struck me as someone to show them, tight as she held herself for her brother's sake.

Under any other circumstances, this would have been operatic. We'd cry and hug and celebrate our newfound growth with a song about friendship or some shit.

But here, atop this peak under these skies, it felt...final. Like she'd been saving these words for her deathbed. And now she'd given them to me.

They made something cold crawl into my craw. I didn't give her that in return. I squeezed her shoulder, nodded.

"I will."

"Great." And she wiped away her nascent emotional growth, along with her tears, as she slapped my hand away. "Now get the fuck off me. I got shit to do."

She was already screaming obscenities at her brother for his cowardice as she headed back to the group. I made to follow her when the wind shifted. And something caught my eye.

Upon a branch of thorny scrub that blossomed from the rock, something crimson flapped in the breeze. I pulled it free—a scrap of cloth, red and stained. Someone *had* been here before us. Someone who wore red cloth that smelled of ash, drugs, and...

Haven?

The thought made my palm itch for a weapon. They might have been long gone, if the faded odor was any indication, but long gone was still too fucking close.

"Hey," I said as I rushed back to the group. "I don't know if anyone else thinks this is weird, but I just...I..."

My voice trailed off, along with my attention, as something pricked at the back of my neck. A feeling I knew well.

You probably know it, too. It's the held breath of the bystander after the wrong person says the wrong thing to someone with the wrong intentions. It's the stillness of the beast before it leaps with claws out. It's the sensation of a man's eyes boring between your shoulder blades as his knife comes out to follow it.

The knowledge that somehow, without you even noticing, something has gone very wrong—I felt it. And when I turned around, I saw it.

"Urda?" I asked.

He was crouched at the edge of the plateau, hunched over with eyes wide and arms wrapped around himself. His breath was heavy, his fingers clawing at his sleeves like he was struggling to burrow a way even deeper into himself. His sister was kneeling beside him, watching him carefully.

She tensed as I approached, but didn't object as I knelt down before Urda and searched his face. Terror—not just unease, but the numb, unblinking horror that never really leaves you once you've got it—painted itself across his skin.

Just like it had before.

"I hear them," he whispered. "I hear them, I hear them, I hear them."

"Hear what?" I asked.

He looked up at me. His eyes were trembling and full of tears. He swallowed hard and spoke on a wet, rasping gasp.

"Locusts."

My scarf whipped in front of my face suddenly. A cold gale bit through my coat. The clouds swirled overhead as the wind shifted. Jero hopped up, rushing toward the edge, Agne discarding her book to follow. Tuteng tensed, stroking the beak of one of the Oyakai. Yria slowly helped her brother to his feet, whispering soothing words to him.

Their eyes were on the skies overhead.

And so were his.

"Ah," Two Lonely Old Men said softly. "Didn't I tell you?"

He turned, offered me a small, bitter smile.

"They're here."

The sound came first. The distant hum of blades, the whisper of wind, the whirring of engines.

And the airships followed.

A massive hand appeared, cleaving through the gray clouds overhead. A long, powerful arm followed, parting the skies for the prow of a ship. And affixed to it—titanic, unrelenting, stern—the Great General of the Glorious Revolution of the Fist and Flame flew through the clouds.

Just a figurehead—a man of harsh angles and harsher eyes wrought of metal with his arm extended in an aggressive direction forward. But even so, the image of the Great General was the second-most imposing thing I'd see that day.

The first was the ship he was attached to.

It came punching through the cloud cover a moment later: a great leviathan of wood and metal carved in a great-bellied whale of a ship that coursed along the clouds like they were waves. Massive wings stretched out on either side, keeping it on course. The multiple propellers attached to its flanks, fueled by whatever Relic engines kept them aloft, whirred, dozens of metal blades humming in iron harmony to keep the great airship flying, filling the sky with a thick buzzing sound.

Like locusts.

"My dear friends," Two Lonely Old Men whispered. "It's time."

I held no special love for the Revolution—as an Imperial, I'd seen no machine they could make that magic couldn't do better. But this…this flying thing…I'm not ashamed to say I was speechless. You would be, too.

Those fuckers.

They found a way to fly.

Wood creaking, metal humming, engines singing, the flagship of the Iron Fleet sailed through the skies with impassive, effortless bravado. With the flagship silhouetted in the clouds behind it, I beheld more airships flying Revolutionary flags. Each one was smaller and sleeker than their leviathan flagship, but all of them sailed with the same slow indifference, uncaring of what lay beneath them.

Or whom.

I didn't know how long I'd been gawking. So long, I think, that I forgot what those ships were, what we had come to do to them. Certainly, I'd forgotten how fucking stupid this plan was. But when Jero's hand came down on my shoulder and squeezed, I remembered why we had to do what we came to do.

Why we had to be the ones to do it.

"Go now," Two Lonely Old Men said. "I will meet you at our rallying point later."

I turned and saw them. Agne, Tuteng, the twins seated upon the Oyakai. And beside them, two more birds.

With empty saddles.

Jero smiled softly as he handed me my belt. Inside the leather of his sheath, I could feel the warmth of the Cacophony as the gun looked at me with brass eyes and smiled the cruelest, ugliest smile he could muster, just for me. And on that hot, hissing steam cloud of a voice, he asked:

"Shall we?"

THIRTY-SIX

THE IRON FLEET

The worst dreams I have are the ones where I'm flying again.

They're the ones where I'm not Sal the Cacophony, I'm not Red Cloud, I'm not anyone.

I'm just...flying.

Sometimes there are birds, sometimes storms. Sometimes the world is far below me, sometimes there isn't anything below me at all. Sometimes it's just clouds and wind and a sky so wide and blue that I can't believe I've never looked up and seen it there before. And it doesn't matter if I've seen it before or not, I'm flying again.

I used to fly.

Then I wake up and I'm not. I'm still stuck on the ground and the sky isn't so blue. And sometimes I cry and sometimes I don't. Sometimes I just tug my scarf over my eyes, start walking, and don't look up at the sky for a long time.

All the fighting and fucking and drinking and smoking in the world can't make me feel better than that feeling.

But on that day, when we changed everything...

"HOLY FUCK!"

That day came close.

Urda was screaming, holding on to his sister. Agne was laughing. Jero was shouting commands. And I wasn't listening to a damn one of them.

The Oyakai beneath me glided soundlessly through the sky, his wings cutting wounds in the cloudscape as we sailed across an endless gray. He moved so silently and effortlessly, barely flapping his immense wings. If I closed my eyes, I could almost pretend he wasn't there. All I could hear was wind screaming in my ears and all I could feel was hair whipping around my face and my body was so light that I completely forgot the burden of my scars.

There would be blood before the day was done—I knew it in my bones. I could never fly so far or fast that I'd forget that. And in the days to follow, there would be hardships and struggles and sad songs that I might or might not be alive to hear.

But those would be another time for another people and another world.

This moment, this sky.

This was for me.

A stray breeze caught my scarf, plastered it across my face. I breathed in a scent and my body grew heavier with the aroma of flowers. Though I desperately wanted not to, I couldn't help but think of the hands that had woven this scarf and given me that smell.

I wondered what she'd say if she could see me, smiling at something other than a kill or a bad joke. Would she have been happy for me? Or would she have known that this flight would end and, when it did, I'd still be the same broken person as ever?

The Oyakai glanced over his shoulder to regard me with a yellow-eyed stare, as if he could sense my thoughts and, in response, was saying: *"Holy shit, could you maybe be less of a sad piece of shit while I'm flying?"*

He was a good bird.

I named him Stephen.

And Stephen was right. I couldn't be weighed down with sorrows at that moment.

After all, I had a Revolution to destroy.

A sharp whistle caught my ear. All eyes turned toward Jero as he gave us the signal: a hand clamped over his mouth and a fist held upright. No talking from here on out or we'd all die.

Suited me just fine.

In another second, I couldn't even hear my own breath.

Not over the sound of locusts.

They moved like bad dreams. The airships glided through the clouds, painted black as ink stains on the clouds. Too large, too vast, too impossible to notice mere creatures like us, they pressed on through the sky, oblivious and imperious.

Beneath me, Stephen started to shift. Tuteng's bird angled upward ahead of us and the others followed, sweeping up into the cloud cover. We darted between the smaller airships, staying well out of range—the endless gray would afford us cover, but there was no sense in chancing it.

Not with what we were after.

We found the flagship, colossal instead of merely huge, drifting at the center of the fleet. It took us an eternity to fly along its hull, row after row of cannons staring out, a monster with a hundred empty black eyes.

They hadn't seen us—I mean, obviously they hadn't, or we'd all be in various states of plummeting out of the sky, on fire and shitting ourselves—but that wasn't what chilled me. If the other ships had even half this kind of firepower, just one of them could light up the sky.

Made me wonder what someone on the ground would see. The fire from the cannons? The ship itself? Or would they just hear the sound of locusts, look up, and see their world exploding around them?

Enough of that. I shook my head. *You want it said that Sal the Cacophony was waxing poetic when she should have been making things explode? Eyes up, idiot.* I paused as the clouds shifted around us. *Or... down, I guess.*

We ascended farther, until the cold made the air taste like fire, and below us, the flagship's deck stretched out. It was a good thing I hadn't eaten anything that day.

Because I *definitely* didn't want it said that Sal the Cacophony had shit herself.

Cannons. Armor. Gunpikes. Blades. And soldiers.

So many fucking soldiers.

Cannons and long-guns lined the railing, each of them glimmering with new steel and primed for launch. Firing teams scurried across the deck, toting severium charges and ever-burning alchemic torches. Paladins, mobile suits of armor, each one clutching a halberd the size of a very tall man in their enormous gauntlets, patrolled back and forth, staining the sky with the severium smoke of their howling engines.

One direct hit from *any* of those would kill me, luckscarf or no, in a blink.

I counted no less than forty of them.

So yeah, you could say things weren't looking great.

I stayed calm enough to avoid screaming at least. Jero and I had drilled the plan so much I was almost bleeding from it: let the Cacophony light up the deck, cast them into enough confusion for Agne to drop down and mop them up. Jero and the twins would move in from another angle to sabotage the engines.

All it would take was a little luck, a lot of firepower, and...

Oh fuck me, are those Dragonkillers?

I had to squint to find them among the *other* things that were poised to murder me, but I could pick them out. Men and women, each wearing an elaborate harness to carry the motorized personal ballista they clutched. A perfect fit for the quivers they wore on their backs, each one brimming with harpoon-sized bolts.

The Revolution's answer to the Imperium's air superiority, Dragon-killers sounded more impressive than they were. But you can't exactly name something "Dragon-irritants" and expect anyone to take you seriously.

That didn't mean I wanted to be on the receiving end of one, of course.

And it didn't mean anything changed. A man carrying a personal ballista capable of putting a lance through a giant bird was still just a man, after all. And the Cacophony burned all men alike.

I glanced across the sky toward Jero. He gave me a look, a nod, a whispered word.

And I got ready to kill an awful lot of people.

I raised the Cacophony, aimed his grinning brass toward the deck, and waited. A Hellfire shell would scatter anyone who couldn't be set ablaze and clear the way for Agne to do her work. I watched the patrols, waited for them to clump together, and...

There.

I closed one eye. I held my breath. I pulled the trigger.

Nothing happened.

No fire. No scattering. Not even a fucking *click*. I squeezed the trigger again and felt the brass stiff under my finger.

He wouldn't shoot. The one fucking thing he was supposed to do, and he wouldn't do it.

Jero shot me a nervous look. I shot the Cacophony a much more irritated look. In response, his brass grinned, seethed.

Spoke.

"Let's not be too hasty," he whispered to me. *"Do you not sense it?"*

I was sensing a plan getting imperially fucked up, but I guess that wasn't what he was talking about.

"What?" I muttered back. "An enemy?"

"Perhaps. Perhaps not. There is something aboard this heathen vessel… something I have not felt since…" I could almost feel his brass coiling into a smile. *"Since our introduction."*

My mind fell back somewhere, quicker than I could blink. Back to that dark place, back to that cold stone I lay upon, back to Vraki tearing my light out of me, back to Darrish just staring at me, to… to…

To that thing.

That horrible *thing*, screaming and shrieking and twisting into shapes that mortal things shouldn't take or know. It hadn't been of this world, shouldn't ever have come to it, but I had seen it come out of a portal of light, felt it come out of me…

I'd felt its screams.

"That night…that thing?" I held him close, whispered to his brass. "You feel that?"

The Cacophony stared back at me through that grinning dragon's mouth, offering me no answer except the lingering reek of powder and fire. I gritted my teeth, searched for some part of him I could strangle.

Guns of any sort ought not to be so enigmatic.

Talking guns, especially so.

"What's down there?" I whispered. "What do you mean?" Anger fueled me, made me forget where I was, what we were here for. *"What do you mean?"*

"ATTENTION!"

A metallic cry cut through the sky from below. My body froze, my breath catching in my throat. Had they heard me? No, they couldn't have. The engines were roaring and I hadn't screamed that loud.

Had I?

I glanced down. The frenzied rush on the deck had come to a sudden halt. The soldiers had shouldered their gunpikes in respect. The Paladin armors stood at attention. The Dragonkillers were lowered. Every last arm was raised in salute to one tiny, withered figure ambling across the deck.

A man. Old. Wrinkled. Bald but for a few wisps of gray hair and sporting a back so bent he could have found work as a crowbar. He looked like a strong breeze would have carried him over the edge if he had walked two inches to the left. Hell, even the medals pinned to his coat looked too heavy for him.

Yet somehow, this husk of a man commanded the attention of the entire fleet.

I squinted—I'd just begun to make out those familiar features, sunken and severe, when his name came rushing back into my head like an arrow through the eye.

Loyal, his name rang out. *Culven Loyal. Son of a bitch, that's one of the Great General's men.*

This man had heard every secret, seen every plot, spoken every name of every town ever to be burned to ash by Revolutionary guns. And every soldier on deck knew it, standing rigidly at attention as he shuffled across the deck.

Loyal, though, didn't seem to care. Hell, he didn't even seem to *notice.* The hundreds of people ready to kill and die at his command didn't warrant even a passing glance. His eyes were fixed on the stern of the airship, the looming cabin that marked the helm.

Yet he was unhurried as he slowly made his way across the day...

As he slowly came to a halt...

As he slowly turned, looked skyward, and fixed a baleful, sunken stare through the clouds...

Directly at me.

Oh. Fuck.

A surge of dread coursed through me, like I'd just swallowed something brackish and foul. It swept through my veins, making my muscles go rictus rigid and freezing my blood in my veins. Everything inside me suddenly hurt with a sleepless ache, a memory of a thousand years of pain.

And through all the distance of cold gray that separated us, I knew Loyal saw me. Because I could see his stare, his eyes black as pitch and seething with a scorn that I'd never seen even from the hundreds I'd sent to the black table. I felt those eyes, fixed on me with a contemptuous scowl. I felt those lips, whispering a word so dark it made the wind smell foul. I felt his voice…

You.

Echoing inside me.

Die.

I heard a commotion coming from my side. Suddenly, the dread left me, rushing out of me as swiftly as it had flowed. I felt weary, drained, yet I managed to look and see Jero gesturing frantically at me to move.

I looked down and saw movement. Beside Loyal, a soldier stirred. He raised his Dragonkiller bow high and a motor whirred, drawing back the huge string as he loaded a harpoon-sized arrow into it.

Now, I said that "Dragonkiller" was just a name and I meant it. Those things can't kill dragons.

But, as it turns out, they'll split a bird clean in half.

THIRTY-SEVEN

THE IRON FLEET

The wind howled. Clouds shuffled apart in frightened whispers. Metal screamed.

I saw my death flying up to meet me.

I jerked hard on my Oyakai's reins, pulling him sharply to the side. He let out a terrified squawk as the Dragonkiller's harpoon went shrieking past, tearing a clump of feathers free from his wing as it disappeared into the sky behind us.

He'd seen me. Loyal had seen me. But how? We were so high, hidden behind so much fog. Did he use some kind of machine? Some kind of *magic*?

Had he been what the Cacophony sensed?

I had a lot of questions that needed answering. But at that moment, none were more pressing than the question of how the fuck I was going to avoid being shot down by the absolute fuck-load of harpoons that suddenly filled the sky.

Motors whirred. Strings snapped. Metal shrieked. The Dragonkillers' shots tore through the clouds, leaving gaping holes in the gray as they did. Our birds tumbled and squawked, colliding with each other as we struggled to get clear of the fire.

Jero shouted something. I didn't hear it, but it didn't matter—we knew what to do if we got spotted. I sheathed the Cacophony and jerked hard on the reins, my Oyakai chirping as I drew him back, letting the flagship get away. I glanced to the others, saw them doing the same.

Jero and I exchanged a look, sour and defeated. This wasn't part of the plan. Of course, getting seen by some weird old fuck with pitch-black eyes who spoke inside my skull hadn't been part of the plan, either.

But we could come back from this. Jero had spent years plotting this. He wouldn't let us be defeated by just one setback. He'd think of something.

Or he would have if a harpoon hadn't just punched a man-sized hole through his bird.

The gray sky was suddenly painted red. A terrified screech filled the sky. Jero let out a noise as he tumbled from the saddle. His bird fell out of the sky in three parts.

The front half.

The second half.

And him.

"JERO!"

Agne screamed as he disappeared through the clouds. Yria and Urda exchanged frenzied screeches at the other to do something. Tuteng watched. And me?

I guess I'm just a romantic.

I jerked Stephen's reins hard, sent him into a dive. The Oyakai responded, folding his wings at his sides as we plummeted through the clouds. I felt the wind pulling at me, threatening to tear me out of the saddle. Tears formed in my eyes, froze on my cheeks. Around me, above me, ahead of me, I couldn't see anything but endless gray as I kept diving until—

There.

I spotted him. A black shadow against the sky. His limbs were spread to keep him from falling so fast—smart. Or it would be if he hadn't been falling faster than my bird could dive, anyway.

He spotted me the same time I spotted him. He shot out a hand for me and I reached out for him, an impossible distance of screaming wind between us. I grit my teeth, kicked Stephen's flanks. The bird screeched, struggled to go faster. My heart pounded, muscles no longer frozen by dread but now throbbing with desperation. My body was wracked by a singular need, sharpened and honed into a singular thought that lodged itself in my head like a knife.

Please, I thought, praying to no god I knew. *Please, don't let me lose another one.*

He drew closer as we fell faster. I could make out the fear on his face, the light in his eyes, the fingers that trembled as they reached for me. I leaned out of the saddle, so far I could feel my feet leave the stirrups. The wind pulled my legs out, sent them flying behind me. The bird's reins snapped taut, the only things that were keeping me from disappearing into the sky.

Jero's hand reached out. His mouth opened as he screamed a name at me. I reached for him, shouted something back, both our words lost on the wind as we fell.

As I reached.

As I closed my eyes.

And felt his hand wrap around mine.

I snarled, clenching him by the wrist and swinging him around. He found the saddle with one hand, my belt with the other, hauling me down onto the bird's back. He reached around me as I fit my feet in the stirrups. Together, we pulled hard on the reins, pulling Stephen out of a dive.

And up into the sky.

"You all right?" I shouted to be heard over the wind.

"Yeah," he grunted.

"You shit yourself?"

"Would you judge me if I did?"

"No," I replied, "but I'd kick you back off."

"Noted."

"Hang on." I pulled Stephen upward. Already, the silhouette of the flagship could be seen through the clouds. "I'll get us back."

"No! We go back there, they'll open fire again, except this time it'll be with cannons." He pointed toward a distant shape, one of the smaller ships. "Take us to that one."

"But the others—"

"Tuteng knows the plan. Just *go!*"

I spat, let out a wordless curse. I didn't see what else the hell I could do.

Don't get me wrong, I was starting to get used to plans going to shit. But this was different. This wasn't like what had happened back in Terassus. Jero couldn't have known about Culven Loyal, about those black eyes, about that dread feeling that had coursed through me. Hell, I'd be shocked if Two Lonely Old Men had known, either.

But there was someone who did...

I glanced down at my hip. In his sheath, the Cacophony sat, pleasantly warm. Whatever had happened up there, he had sensed it, he knew, and he'd *liked* what he'd seen.

More than anything else in that shitshow of a day, that scared me.

<hr>

We spotted the others not long after, their shadows stark against the sky. I swung Stephen up to join them, settling in the lead as Jero leaned out to point at a distant shape.

"There," he said. "That one."

It was the smallest of the ships, lingering behind the rest of the fleet. And even from here, I could see that it didn't have nearly as many guns or soldiers as the flagship had. That hardly gave me much joy—a fraction of a shit-load of guns was still a fuck-load of guns.

But the only other places to go were into the aforementioned shit-load or...I don't know, the ground, I guess.

I swung Stephen toward our target, gliding low beneath the airships. My eyes were fixed on their shadows overhead, looking for the flash of fire, listening for the sound of thunder that would herald the cannons firing.

I saw nothing but the clouds and the shadows. I heard nothing but the roar of the engines. As we sailed toward the ship, not a single shot was fired to challenge us. That struck me as odd.

Fuck if I was going to complain, though.

The stern of the ship was adorned with a railing-lined platform for rear cannons, but the guns stood silent and unmanned. Jero pointed toward it and I swung Stephen over. Once we got close enough, Jero leapt from the saddle and onto the platform. He pushed open a door leading into a darkened cabin, glanced around, then turned and gestured for me to follow.

"What?" I asked, furrowing my brows. "What about all our birds?"

"Don't worry about them. Come *on*."

I thought to protest, but it didn't seem the right moment—what with the entire Fleet knowing we were here and all. I pulled my scarf closer around me, gritted my teeth, and leapt.

The others came up behind us in short order. Yria leapt first, tumbling onto the platform. She turned and glowered at her brother, who clung tightly to the saddle.

"I . . . I can't . . . I . . . don't want . . . ," Urda was stammering, his eyes fixed on the yawning void beneath him. "I can't . . . I'm sorry, but—"

"Look at me."

He pried his eyes up to fix on his sister's.

"You can," she said. "I know you can."

He closed his eyes. Swallowed hard. Nodded. And leapt.

"Not with your eyes closed, moron!"

She lunged out to catch him, arms wrapping around his wrists as he flailed. Agne came up a moment later, daintily leaping off her bird to land beside Yria. With one hand, she took the girl by her belt and hauled her—and her brother—up and tossed them into the nearby cabin before following herself.

Tuteng swung past, offering a stiff nod to Jero before wheeling off. With a squawk, the other birds followed, disappearing into the clouds.

"How is he going to find us again?" I asked.

"He's not," Jero grunted. "He's not coming back."

"What? What sense does that—"

"We can't retreat. Because we can't fail. Now *move*."

He took me by the hand, pulled me into the cabin, and slammed the door shut behind us.

"But how—"

"Quiet," he whispered.

"What kinda fuckin' plan is—" Yria began to growl.

"QUIET."

We paused. In the darkness, I could see him staring at the ground, eyes unfocused. He was listening, I realized.

"No guns," he whispered after a few moments. "No sirens, either. No alarms."

"That's . . . that's good, isn't it?" Urda asked wheezily. "It feels like no guns is a good thing." He glanced to his sister. "Doesn't it?"

"How'd those wrench-fuckers even spot us?" she growled, sweeping a glower between us. "Clouds were so thick I couldn't even see my own tits, but they picked us out like peasants at a ball. You ask me, this whole thing—"

"Loyal."

She fell silent as I spoke. And as I spoke, I felt that aching feeling, that liquid dread coursing through my body once again. Like even speaking his name was enough to summon it.

"It was Culven Loyal," I said. "He was there. He spotted us."

A gallows silence hung between us, brows furrowed and lips pursed as everyone struggled to figure out the same thing. But it was Jero who actually gave it a voice.

"How?"

"I don't know. He..."

He what? He turned his eyes pitch-black? He spoke with a voice inside my head? He made something hurt inside me, some part of me I didn't even know could feel pain?

I shook my head. "I don't know."

"Revolutionaries don't seem the type to discriminate between what they shoot at," Agne offered, far too cheery for how fucked we were. "Perhaps they merely thought us birds passing in the sky."

"They wouldn't have used that kind of firepower for just birds. They knew we were there." Jero slowly looked around the darkened hold of the ship. "So, why aren't we being torn apart by soldiers right now?"

"Maybe they thought they got us after you went down faster than your dad did on me." Yria grunted, scratching herself indelicately as she walked around the hold, giving a nearby crate an idle kick. "Or maybe we're in the fuckin' wrong ship. What the hell is this crap?"

Yria was as right as she was vile. Darkness shrouded the hold, only the dim light of a poorly maintained alchemic globe offering a glimpse of what lay within. You'd expect a Revolutionary ship to be brimming with weapons, ammo, and at *least* a few bloodstains.

What I saw... was not that.

Tools ranging from picks and shovels to delicate brushes and loupes to mechanical monstrosities I didn't have a name for lined the walls, stuffed into crates and haphazardly strewn. Charts, graphs, and other diagrams indicating everything from geological surveys to ancient history were pinned to the walls. And books—mountains of them, brimming from every shelf and covering every horizontal surface, each one as thick as my arm with titles so long they damn near could be their own country.

If this collection were anyone else's, I'd call it impressive. For the Revolution, whose list of approved reading materials consisted entirely of propaganda, I called it impossible.

"Freemakers," I muttered. "These are a Freemaker's tools."

"Are you quite certain?" Agne picked up some manner of drill and sneered at it with distaste. "I was under the impression those barbarians preferred not to consort with Freemakers."

"They're forbidden to, by Revolutionary law." Jero took the drill from her and glanced it over. "But Sal's right. Those fanatics don't make anything that doesn't make someone else explode." He scrutinized the drill, glanced over the other tools. "What's with all the digging tools?"

"Excavation tools, not digging," I corrected.

"What's the difference?"

I'd asked the same question once.

One's a careful study of archaeology and the origins of species and the ancient world. The other's what you do when you need to bury your poop.

And that's what she'd told me.

"Meticulous's notes." Urda's voice came out breathless. "Remember? I said there were some sigils on it I didn't understand. A *Freemaker's* sigils." He scratched his chin. "This is all starting to add up."

"Yeah?" Yria grunted. "To what?"

"To...to..." His face screwed up. "To something. Shut up." He rubbed his temples. "If I'd been given more *time*, I'd know whose sigils those were already, and we'd be a *little* better informed. But *noooo*, no one ever has time for Urda of the Feral Print and now we're all paying the price." He sniffed. "I'll take an apology whenever you're ready."

"What you'll take is a fist to the fucking scrote if you don't—"

"*Shut up.*"

Jero's hiss decapitated that particular squabble, sending us into a silence punctuated only by creaking wood and the distant hum of the ship's engines. His wrinkles deepened, brow furrowed in thought as he tried to make sense of things that didn't make any.

I'd been ready for things to go wrong—they always do.

I'd been ready for someone to get captured or killed. I'd been ready for the fights to get messy or for us to get spotted. Hell, I'd even been ready for us to miss the Iron Fleet completely and spend the rest of the day getting drunk and cursing our failure.

I hadn't been ready for...this. Any of it.

There were more soldiers than anyone could have expected, more firepower than even a ship in the Iron Fleet would need, and Culven Loyal...whoever he was, *whatever* he was, he was more than an officer. He might have been more than human.

Humans didn't have eyes that went pitch-black.

"There might be no alarms," Jero said softly, gathering his thoughts, "but that doesn't mean they aren't looking for us. Whatever we do next, we do so with the assumption that they know we're here and on high alert. Agreed?"

We exchanged terse nods. All save Urda, who timidly raised his hand.

"So, uh...what *do* we do next?"

"Our objective is still the same: get the Relic, hinder their ability to pursue us, get out. Which means our plan is still the same...just on a different ship. Our first step is to get between the ships and sabotage the engines." He looked to the twins. "Can you still handle it?"

"Of course!" Urda produced a thick sheaf of papers from his satchel and held them up triumphantly. "Nullification sigils, from Two Lonely Old Men himself—with a little help from your old pal Urda. Once I apply these to the ships' engines, they won't know what hit them. *Literally.* See, the sigils actually confuse whatever they're applied to, so instead of using them to convince the airship it's something that it's not, it's convincing it that it doesn't know what it is and what it can do and you're not even listening to me anymore so I don't know why I bother to..."

"What about you?" Jero turned toward Yria. "Can you get us between the ships?"

"It'll be tricky," Yria muttered, scratching the tattoo on her chin. "Jumping—teleporting, that is—between two points is basic.

Jumping through the air between two moving points is possible. Doing it with two other people and still having enough of a Barter to get out of here with a Relic is—"

"Yes or no."

"Of course I can fucking do it," she growled. "I was just giving you a chance to appreciate how bad you've shit this bed." She stalked to a nearby area of open space and pulled her chalk out. "It's gonna take some time, though. I'll need Urda's sigils to help anchor the points we're jumping between."

"Not like we were expecting him to do anything else, anyway," I muttered.

"*Hey*," Urda whined.

"I'm sorry," I snapped, "did you want to pick up a sword and start fighting?"

"Well . . . no. But *still*."

He turned and sulked after his sister, the two of them going to work creating their portal while Jero turned back to us.

"We don't know what's going on, how Loyal spotted us, or how far the flagship is," he said. "But someone on this ship does. The rest of us are going to make finding that out a priority."

He leveled a pair of fingers at me and Agne, then craned his fingers up toward the ceiling.

"About two floors above us, at the stern of the ship, is the helm. The captain, navigator, and command will be in there. You two are going to make for it as quietly as you can." He paused, reconsidered. "*Extremely* quietly. We'll need a way of getting back to the flagship, and this ship is going to be how we do it. Kill the others if you have to, but keep the captain alive and steering the ship until I can make my way back to you."

"What makes you think they'll cooperate with us?" Agne asked, cringing. "Revolutionaries are not exactly famous for obeying people who *aren't* their Great General."

"Fanatics break just like any other man," Jero said, voice black. "You just have to break them a little more. He only needs one arm to steer, anyway."

"Dear me. This really sounds like it'd be easier if you came with us."

Jero shook his head. "We need information and we're not going to find it if we're all stumbling around together. Ship archives and captain's quarters will have what we need. I'll find those while—"

"Wait." She paused. "How exactly do you know all this?"

There. His mouth opened and I saw his wrinkles deepen exactly the way they did before he was about to lie. And since we were in a hurry, I thought I'd save him the trouble.

"Because you've been on this ship before," I said, "haven't you?"

The look he shot me was almost wounded. It's the only reason I wasn't mad at him. Lying was one thing, but this wasn't lying. This was a secret he simply hadn't told me yet.

Secrets, I understood. They're sharp, shiny little things, full of cruel tips and jagged edges. And once you give them to someone, they have everything they need to kill you.

"Yeah," he said. "Once."

I nodded. "So, how many soldiers should we expect?"

"A lot," he said.

"What about Paladins and Dragonkillers, like on the flagship? An operation like this must have Relic Guards, too."

"They were supposed to, sure. They're currently recovering from stomach ailments in the township they were supposed to leave from. You're welcome." He shook his head. "This ship's too small for heavy power. You can expect normal resistance."

My mouth fumbled around some words—another question, another curse, I didn't know. But I couldn't find them. Not until he spared me a small nod, a smaller smile, and turned away and disappeared through a door and into the shadows.

Only then did I realize what I'd wanted to tell him. And why I couldn't.

Because when we had been falling through the sky...

It hadn't been his name I'd shouted.

A heavy hand fell upon my shoulder. I looked up into Agne's smiling eyes as she offered me a gentle grin and brushed a hair out of my face.

"Shall we get to it, then?" she asked.

"Sure," I replied as my hand went to my hip. "Only..."

I unsheathed the Cacophony, his brass burning bright enough in the dark that I could see my own grin reflected in his.

"How quietly do you think is *extremely* quietly?"

THIRTY-EIGHT

THE IRON FLEET

"Ten...no, wait. Twelve? More?"

Agne furrowed her brow as she whispered, listening intently. She stuck her tongue out in concentration.

"About twelve," she said. "I'm sure of it. And I hear...metal banging. Cups clanking. Chewing." She glanced up at me. "I think it's a kitchen?"

"In the Revolution, they call it a mess hall," I replied.

"A mess...hall?" Agne looked aghast. "They truly are savages, aren't they."

"Uh-huh." I searched in my satchel, wrapped my fingers around a shell, hesitated. "When you say 'about twelve,' you mean more than twelve or less?"

She pressed her ear to the door again. She squinted, struggling to make out whatever noises lay beyond.

"Less," she said.

I nodded, fished a different shell out of my satchel. I slid it into the Cacophony's chamber with a satisfying *click*, slammed his cylinder shut, and drew back the hammer. I took a step away from the door, took his black hilt in both hands, and raised him high into position.

I glanced back down the hall we'd come from. Nothing but the distant hum of the ship's engines greeted us. No ambush coming.

I looked back to Agne as she stood to the side of the door, hand on its knob, and gave her a nod.

"Quietly?" she asked.

"As something called the Cacophony can be," I answered.

She looked like she didn't like that answer. But she was perfectly free to come up with a better plan if she didn't. Instead, she simply shrugged, twisted the knob, pushed the door open...

And got the hell out of the way.

A dozen faces—or so I thought, I didn't have time to count—of men and women looked up from tables with eyes full of confusion and mouths full of food. It wasn't until they saw the gun in my hands that they realized what was happening and started shouting, scrambling for the gunpikes they'd left leaning against the table.

Of course, by then, I'd already pulled the trigger.

The shell shot out of the Cacophony's grinning maw, speeding into the mess hall and exploding in a bright blue flash. All the shouting and scrambling was drowned out in a crystalline snap and an ensuing hiss, a blinding cloud of white erupting and swallowing the room.

I pulled my scarf up over my face as the cloud, frigid and twinkling with frost, came roiling out of the mess hall. A few flakes settled upon my shoulders, the cold gnawing through my coat and creeping into my bones. It was a frost deeper than any I'd felt in the Valley or in the sky.

I had to admit, I was impressed. He'd really gone all out for this one.

The cold dissipated, settling from a blinding cloud into a freezing mist, as I walked into the mess hall. The soldiers stood—some with mouths open in warning cries, some with their hands wrapped around gunpikes, one poor fucker trying to hide behind his plate like a shield.

They stood. And they did not move.

Being frozen will do that to you.

Ice crunched under my feet as I walked in, checking each soldier as I walked past them. Every inch of skin was drained of color, a sheet of rime covering them like a second flesh. They were frozen in their last seconds, their faces betraying no pain, nor even fear, the Hoarfrost shell having taken them before they could figure out what was going on.

It had been fast and painless at least. The sole mercy I could give them.

One...two...three... I counted their faces as I walked past them. *Ten...eleven...twelve. Wait a minute...*

Ice crunched to my left.

I whirled, saw the gunpike's barrel leveled at me. And the pair of very-much-*not*-frozen hands attached to it as the Revolutionary touched the trigger on the shaft.

"Ten thousand years," she snarled.

"LOOK OUT!"

Ice snapped. The trigger clicked. A bright flash of gunfire and severium smoke exploded in my face.

Fast. Painless. The same mercy I'd have wanted.

Or would have, anyway, had there not been a very large woman between me and the gunpike, at that moment.

I looked up from the ground Agne had so tersely shoved me to. The Revolutionary blinked, staring agog at the woman who had just taken a severium charge straight to the chest and was still standing. Agne stared at the gunpike for a moment, then glanced down to the blackened hole in her shirt exposing the impervious flesh beneath, before looking back at the soldier.

"Rude," she said.

Her hands shot out, one seizing the gunpike from the soldier's hands, the other seizing her throat. The Revolutionary flailed for a moment, her scream choked beneath Agne's grip, before the Siegemage brought down the gunpike over her skull with a sickening crack.

The soldier hit the ground knees-first before toppling over, the weapon embedded in her skull landing against the floor with an iron thud.

"Less than twelve, you said," I grumbled as I got to my feet, brushing red-flecked frost off my coat. "My ass."

"Oh, you poor dear. If only there had been some stunningly gorgeous woman immune to bullets who could have saved you." Agne frowned down at the hole in her shirt. "They shot my favorite tit."

I blinked. "You have a favorite?"

She blinked. "You don't?"

I made a firm decision never to answer that as I turned and stalked toward the door on the other side of the hall.

That could have gone better—I could aim and pull the trigger, but the Cacophony shaped the magic. Freezing all of them was a precise feat, one he could have pulled off had he been given accurate numbers. But, as no one had died and only *one* tit had gotten shot, I was willing to call that a success.

Hell, ordinarily I'd be willing to call the fact that those thirteen soldiers were the only ones we'd seen aboard this ship a *rousing* success. But, if you were there, you'd notice I wasn't currently dropping my pants and doing a happy little jig.

Not that I was exactly displeased about the uneventfulness of our foray through the ship's halls. But I'd grown used to fighting Revolutionaries a certain way: they came heavy, they came screaming, and they came in endless numbers. To see one of their great airships *not* crawling with guards was disquieting.

But not nearly as disquieting as what I *had* seen on this ship.

Maps. Tools. Diagrams. And *books*.

Every cabin had been converted into a tiny workshop, a tiny library, or a tiny combination of both. Sketches had been pinned to every wall—some of things I knew, some of things that hurt my face to look at. Maps of regions and surveys had been left scattered everywhere. Books open to various subjects, none of which I understood, dominated every horizontal surface.

Anywhere else, that'd be the sign of someone in desperate need of someone more interesting to talk to.

Aboard a Revolutionary airship . . . it was worrying.

Not that the Revolution is packed full of blithering morons, per se, but their operas are sparse, their classes are just propaganda pamphlets, and their trashiest novels read like instruction manuals. They're not stupid, but they don't value knowledge. Not enough to displace hundreds of soldiers to make room for it. I didn't know anyone who liked books enough for that.

. . . except her.

Fuck's sake, I scolded myself, shaking my head. *You just sentenced twelve people to a frigid, icy death. Fucking* act *like it, woman.*

Right. Solving mysteries was Jero's problem. We had a ship to hijack.

We'd figured out that the mess hall was the quickest way to reach the helm and the most efficient way of killing a bunch of soldiers who could ambush us later. As we picked our way through the tables, dinners frozen to their plates, it felt like our plan had paid off. However bad things had gotten up there, they were turning around now.

"Did you sense that?"

So, if you were betting this would be the moment when shit got bad: congratulations.

I tensed up, sliding a shell out and slamming it into the Cacophony as a voice reached my ears. I aimed him at the door at the other end of the mess, waiting for whatever body to which that voice belonged to come barreling through.

The body didn't come.

"Felt like . . . magic?"

But the voices did.

"Sal."

Agne was kneeling beside a thin copper tube set against the wall of mess, its length ending in a trumpeted shape. She held a finger to her lips as I approached, tapping her finger.

"I didn't feel anything."

Another voice, this one feminine, emerged from the tube. Some kind of communication device from above, I assumed, intended to allow people above deck to scream at soldiers in the mess.

Convenient. Especially for us.

"Why would there be magic here, anyway?" the woman's voice, soft and gentle in its chiding, asked. *"This is a Revolutionary ship."*

"Fuck if I know," the other voice rumbled, gravelly, male. *"I figured it might be another Vagrant. There's no way these nuls hired only us two."*

Agne looked to me, brow furrowed, and mouthed, "Vagrant?"

My mind flashed back to Meticulous's house, to Urda sorting through the spymaster's notes. He'd been tracking Vagrants, Urda had said, and I'd assumed that was merely good sense—it paid to keep track of where magically powered criminals were going, after all. But this must have been the true purpose.

The Revolution had hired Vagrants. Whatever they had on their ship, it was worth breaking the first and most important rule of their Great General's teachings.

That wasn't just concerning. That was terrifying.

So you might have wondered why I wasn't presently losing my shit over that.

"*Entirely possible.*"

And it was because of that voice. That woman's voice, so soft and unhurried, that settled around me like a warm cloak. I'd heard it before, felt it before. I'd let it carry me off to sleep, a warm blanket on a cold night, before.

But now...

Now it felt like a blade sliding into my back.

"*Regardless, I remind you we were hired to guard, not to loiter,*" she continued. "*Remain vigilant.*"

"*Against what?*" the other voice grumbled. "*We're on a fucking airship. The only thing that could get us up here is more mages. And if they show up, these nuls are screwed, anyway.*"

If they did know about our tussle with the flagship, they wouldn't be talking like this. That was comforting, at least.

"*Anything,*" she said. "*And everything. Whatever you might think about this... cooperation, the nuls carry the Relic. And the Relic carries the world, if the Freemaker is to be believed.*"

Freemakers. Relics. Vagrants.

I should have been thinking about them. I should have been worrying about them. But the longer I listened to that voice, the deeper that knife went. My body went cold. My scars ached. My head drifted back to that dark place.

That dark night when I'd made my list.

"*Yeah, sure,*" the male voice scoffed. "*If I believed a nul could change the world, I'd have stayed with the Nul Emperor.*"

"*The Freemaker says—*"

"*I don't give a shit what the Freemaker says. And if you weren't dreaming of her bed every night, you wouldn't—*"

There was a loud banging sound, the din of something smashed against a wall. The tube shook violently as something was smashed against it. The voice that followed was cold and harsh.

"*Do not ever speak of her that way.*"

"*Fuck... you...*" The male's voice came out choked.

There was another smashing sound. A scream. Something fell to the ground and did not rise.

"Say whatever you want about the nuls. Think whatever you want about this mission. Take your money and crawl back to whatever tavern you want to drown in when it's done. But so long as you are here, you will not utter a word against her. Am I clear?"

The blade twisted inside me. My body seized up. All feeling left me except for the burning anger of the gun in my hand.

"AM I CLEAR?"

Nights, I'd lain awake wondering what I'd do when I heard her name again. I'd gone through all the things I wanted to say, all the tears I wanted to shed, all the curses I wanted to hurl at her. I'd gone over a hundred different speeches in a hundred different scenarios in which I'd tell her exactly what she did to me and exactly why she had to die.

But on the day I finally heard her name again?

"Yeah...you're clear, Darrish."

I didn't say a word.

"Sal!"

Agne called after me, but I couldn't hear her. I couldn't feel the cold of the ice spraying my face as I kicked the door down and stalked down the hall. I couldn't think of anything as I found a set of stairs and pushed my way up.

Except her name.

Darrish the Flint.

Who'd spoken to me with such soft words and touched me with such soft hands.

Darrish the Flint.

Who'd shared nights that turned into days with me, days that turned into weeks.

Darrish the Flint.

Who'd stared.

And said nothing.

And did nothing.

On the night they took my magic from me.

Agne was calling after me as I charged up the stairs, hurrying to catch up, but I didn't have any blood in my ears to hear her. Every part of me had gone cold except for my scars, my feet, and my fingers that slammed shells into the Cacophony's chamber.

The stairs ended in a steel door. Beyond it, I knew she was there. When I opened it, I'd look into those eyes that had looked into mine on the night she'd betrayed me. And when I killed her, when I finally crossed her name off my list...

I wasn't going to say a word.

I took the Cacophony in both hands, took a cold breath, and kicked the door in.

A pair of eyes glanced up at my entrance.

They weren't Darrish's.

"Who the fuck are you?"

They belonged to a man with a thick skull and a foul mouth. He stood taller than me by a head. His body was long and thick with muscle and left generously exposed by the breeches and boots he wore, the bruises from where he'd been thrown around plainly visible on his pale skin. His hair was a dark brown mess loosely tied back by a red bandana, a match for the red spear he wore strapped across his back.

And both, in turn, were a match for the Vagrant's ink tattooed across his chest: a set of animalistic jaws, twisted open in a horrific smile.

"Shit," he muttered, rubbing one of his bruises, "did the nuls hire you, too? Have we not met? Or..."

His eyes drifted away from mine to the gun I held in my hands. As the Cacophony looked back at him through that brass grin, a dread realization dawned upon his face.

"Holy shit," he whispered, "you're—"

"Tenka?"

A voice came from behind me as a large hand gingerly pushed me aside. Agne peered forward, a smile blossoming across her face as she looked at the young man.

"Tenkalogones?" she asked.

That fear across his face shifted suddenly to a blushing joy. "Agnestrada," he whispered, breathless, through a smile. "Agne the fucking Hammer."

"I love that you still put a profanity in my name," Agne said, smiling as she placed her hands on her hips. "You always did have a way of making me feel powerful."

"Uh..." The cold anger and purpose slowly drained out of me, replaced by a much less purposeful befuddlement. "Am I...missing something?"

"Gracious, where are my manners." Agne gestured to the young Vagrant. "Sal the Cacophony, I have the devout pleasure of introducing to you Tenkalogones yun Gorathi, professionally known as Tenka the Nightmare." She shot me a wink. "We used to date."

"More like she used to blow my mind nightly." I'd seen holy men who hadn't looked at their gods with the same devotion with which Tenka looked at Agne. "Shit, remember back in Greenriver? With the chains? I thought I wouldn't walk for a fucking *week* after you took me in your—"

And that befuddlement, in turn, was replaced by a long, loud, internal shrieking.

"I'd love to reminisce." Agne mercifully held up a hand to end the conversation. "But I'm here on business."

"No shit, huh?" Tenka canted his head to the side. "You're with the Cacophony now? Nice, nice. What brings you all the way here?"

"I'm here to hijack this ship! What are you doing here?"

"I'm here to protect this ship from hijackers!" he laughed, bitterly. "Wild, huh?"

"Rather," Agne replied, her voice growing colder.

Tenka's head bobbed in an awkward nod as a tense silence fell over us. He cleared his throat, pulled the spear from his back.

"Welp," he said, "guess I'll be killing you, then."

THIRTY-NINE

THE IRON FLEET

Okay, so, it's not like we all sat down and decided what the naming conventions for Vagrants ought to be. People who can make other people explode into tiny pieces with a thought can, by and large, call themselves whatever they want.

But it's still considered both polite and aesthetically pleasing for a Vagrant to take a name relevant to the art they practice. A Siegemage is the Hammer, a Quickmage is the Razor, and so forth. It's not an ironclad rule, of course, but we generally adhere to it, otherwise you get situations like—

"WHY DO YOU CALL YOURSELF 'THE NIGHTMARE'? YOU'RE A SKYMAGE, YOU FUCK!"

Yeah. That.

I shared Agne's concern, but I didn't bother shouting it like she had. After all, it's not like Tenka was going to hear me, anyway.

Not over the sound of the hurricane he was hurling at us.

The sound of the Lady Merchant's song rang and it beckoned the wailing wind. Great unseen serpents of air came flooding in through open hatches, shrieking as they coalesced at the tip of a spear to become a great, howling gale that tore down the hall. At the center of it all, positively insignificant in the face of the screaming wind, Tenka the Nightmare, no matter how inappropriate his name, sent the sky itself against us.

A Skymage's powers are as fickle as the winds that love them. A few, knowing the wind's barest affection, can only content themselves with flying a few feet off the ground. A few more are loved enough to call the wind to them and send flying anything not nailed down.

And people like Tenka...

Well, he must be really funny or something, because the wind fucking loved him.

Planks creaked, were torn up from the floors. Pipes trembled, were ripped free of the walls. Scrap metal, furniture, crates, stray weapons—anything that wasn't nailed down, and some things that were, became part of the wind's wild song, just errant notes carried on a disharmonious chorus to smash against us.

Or one of us, anyway.

Agne stood against the hurricane, arms crossed over her face, as the debris struck her, one item after another. A stray pipe tumbled out of the wind and broke itself across her arms. A flying crate smashed against her, the clothes inside scattered in the gale as the box broke into timbers. A stray gunpike came twisting out of the gale and splintered across her body in an explosion of severium and metal.

The Lady's song coursing through her, fueling her Siegemage's power, she shrugged off each blow, unbothered by them. Or, at least, I hoped she was unbothered by them, since my plan, at that moment, consisted solely of wrapping my arms around her leg while the rest of me flailed in a wind desperate to add me to its maelstrom of trash.

Given that she was all that stood between me and being battered against the metal walls like a broken toy, I guess I can forgive you if you think I was ungrateful for saying what I did.

"DO SOMETHING!"

But fuck you, I was out of ideas.

"I get any closer and I go flying!" she shouted back.

"Use more of your magic! Get...heavier or something, I don't fucking know! Give up another Barter!"

She shot me a cold glare that told me two things: that would not be happening and if I asked again, she'd be using me as a shield. More magic would have allowed her to tear this fucker's wind *and* his stupid name apart, but whatever emotion the Lady Merchant would demand, Agne would not give.

We were stuck here until Tenka killed us or made enough noise for more people to come and *they'd* kill us.

Which, I guess, left things to me.

Or rather, to us.

I let out a whispered prayer lost on the wind as I took one hand off Agne's leg and reached into my satchel. I felt my legs flailing behind me like reeds as I fished around, running my fingers along the shells within.

Discordance? No—I tear this hull apart and we all go flying off, but he can *fly. Hellfire? Probably not a great idea to use in a ship made mostly of wood. Hoarfrost? No. Sunflare? No.*

Steel Python?

NO.

We might have been about to die, but that was no reason to consider it.

Fuck, fuck, FUCK. What's left?

My fingers wrapped around a shell. The only one left that wasn't an utterly terrible idea. And with a resigned sigh, I shut my eyes, fished it out, and fumbled with the Cacophony to load it.

From behind Agne's leg, I aimed. Tenka looked like an impossible target at the other end of the hall, his spear guiding the gale against us. An impossible target made all the more impossible by the wind whipping my arm around and the barrier of debris between us.

But what else could I do? I had no choice but to shut one eye, pull the hammer back...

And pull the trigger.

Anyway, turns out that was the wrong choice.

The shell sped out from the Cacophony's maw—whatever evil magic gun juice kept him going, it was stronger than wind. At least by a little. In a spray of cobalt electricity, it exploded. Across the walls of the ship, lightning danced in jagged arcs, brushing electric fingers against the walls, the pipes, the floor.

I shut my eyes.

I held my breath.

And...nothing happened.

Agne shot me one of those "the fuck was that" looks. Even Tenka, far away as he was, gave me a clear look of befuddlement. But though he might not be a proper magic, the Cacophony was an art, same as any. And every art has its philistines that just don't get it.

Not until they do.

The pipes in the walls began to tremble. The metallic struts of the hull shook and quaked. Even the screws and nails holding them in place began to jiggle.

Against most of my foes, Shockgrasp isn't much of a shell. Outside the rare occasion I meet someone with a lot of armor and an urge to kill me, it's not a lot of use against the various beasts and bandits of the Scar. But in the proper time and the proper place, a spell that magnetizes every piece of metal within forty feet is pretty handy.

As it turns out, in the bowels of a ship positively laden with metal is neither the proper time nor the proper place.

"HOLY SHIT!"

You know. In case you were wondering.

I heard Tenka's scream over the wind. But not over the sound of several hundred pounds of metal being torn out of the walls.

Pipes. Plates. Struts. Screws. In brass and copper and iron, the Shockgrasp shell pulled them free and sent them into the maelstrom of wind. The whine of metal twisting in the wind was added to the hurricane chorus as metal clashed with metal, sparks bursting in bright angry kisses as they collided, separated, and flung themselves into the wind with jagged, glistening edges.

I cowered behind Agne's leg, wincing each time a shard of metal struck her. Pipes and struts came twisting out of the wind to bounce off her. She let out a grunt, a cry, a snarl—but she did not give an inch.

The same could not be said for our foe.

Skymages, as you might imagine, are not exactly renowned for their self-control and a guy with as stupid a name as Tenka the Nightmare wasn't going to be breaking any molds that day.

The metal torn out of the sides proved too weighty for his wind to control. They began to fly in every direction, including toward him. A shard went shrieking by, grazing his temple and sending a spurt of blood into the vortex. His scream was accompanied by the Lady's song as he summoned another gale, sending out a new wind in a desperate bid to keep the metal debris from killing him.

Admittedly, the finer points of anemology are lost on me. I have no idea what makes the wind do what it does. But on that day, I learned that introducing two hurricane-force gales in opposition to each other to a whole mess of metal garbage...

"No, no, no, no, NO!"

Turns out it's a bad idea.

Tenka was screaming as he went from certain victory to certain death. He waved his spear around wildly, hurling the winds this way and that in a futile struggle to keep the metallic debris from smashing into him. With each gesture, the maelstrom became more chaotic, the hall shuddering as wild winds sent pipes and plates smashing against the walls and the floor and each other.

About the time I narrowly avoided an iron spike the size of my forearm plunging into my eye socket, I suspected I probably should have thought of a better idea.

But this could still work. Agne, despite her clothes being torn, was unscathed. Tenka was unfocused, panicked, using too much power. Skymages gave up their breath to the Lady Merchant to keep their magic working and he was going through his like a wineskin with a hole in it.

Either he'd run out of magic or an errant piece of trash would tear a hole in him. One way or another, he'd have to stop and then we could take care of him.

There was an ominously deep creaking sound.

The hull shuddered.

Metal screamed.

Or everything could go fucking wrong, I thought. *That's fine, too.*

An explosion of screws and sparks. A great sheet of metal the size of a man tore itself free from the ship's hull. Jagged edges went twisting into the winds, hurled against the ceiling, the walls, the floor. Splinters shot up as it carved a massive hole in the deck before it tumbled back into the wind and went flying...

Straight toward us.

"AGNE!"

I shouted into the wind. The Lady's song rose in my ears. Agne let out a low growl, setting her feet, clenching her fist...

And swinging.

Her punch split it in twain, turning one gigantic fucking metal sheet into two gigantic fucking blades. One of them tumbled, struck the floor, and bounced up to cut along my arm. I screamed and I bled and both were lost into the wind as a great gout of red swirled. Pain lanced up my arm, loosening my grip.

And I flew.

I went twisting into the wind, my blood trailing behind me, just one more piece of trash in the maelstrom. I shouted, flailed, struggled to find purchase as I bounced off the walls, the floors, my bones shuddering with each strike.

Flying toward the ceiling, I saw a blur of movement beneath me. The floor trembled as Agne charged toward her foe, undeterred by wind or trash. I reached out, caught her by the shoulder, trailing behind her like a fleshy string on a fleshy kite as she rushed toward Tenka.

But I'd lost too much blood, my body ached too much. Even holding on to her clothes was too much effort. I lost my grip. I collapsed to the floor. I rolled across it.

And I fell.

The splinters of the hole raked against me as I tumbled through the hole in the floor and crashed into something. Glass shattered. Wood splintered. Something wet and reeking washed over me.

I told my body to get back up. My body screamed back that it couldn't. I tried to argue with it, but I couldn't hear myself think. My ears were full of the wind's wail and the Lady's song, growing fainter. My vision swirled, darkness sweeping in from the edges. The only sensation not overwhelmed by agony was scent.

Which, unmercifully, was how I recognized the wet stuff covering me.

Somehow, this felt oddly fitting.

Sal the Cacophony, who'd set out to end the greatest of all wars, somehow managed to die by her own incompetence.

Covered in shit.

Are you there?

A voice. Or a dream. Or whoever waited for me at the black table.

I can feel you.

Echoing in the darkness. Not a sound. A feeling.

Such a fragile thing. So easily broken.

In my bones. In my blood. In my skin.

What makes you want to get back up? Why do you bother?

Reaching. Clawing. Probing.

Tell me.

Infesting.

Tell me.

Screaming.

TELL ME.

Everything came back to me in a massacre of light and sound and color. I shot up with a ragged gasp, pulling cold air into cold lungs. My vision came flooding back, darkness swept aside as a nauseating wave of color swept over me. My heart started beating again, pumping blood back into my veins, and the pain came with it, that slow, dull ache that told me I was hurt.

But still alive.

Yet, as I sat there, I could still feel it. That voice. That feeling. That noisy twitching that had crawled through every part of me. Its skittering legs, its whispering claws, the harsh and desperate *need* in it...I could feel it, surely as I could feel my own blood.

How long had it been inside me? How long had I been *out*?

I looked up above. The jagged rent in the ceiling stood a silent, open wound. The sound of wind was gone, the Lady's song fled, not a single noise but the distant hum of the airship's engines. And Agne...

"Agne," I whispered. I shouted into the ceiling. "AGNE!"

Had she won? Had Tenka? Had either of them survived? I didn't know what had happened or what had reached inside me or how I'd ended up here. I had to find her, if she was still alive, but I didn't know how. It all felt like a long and terrible nightmare.

Well, except for the fact that I was covered in shit.

That part felt—and smelled—all too real.

I cringed as I pulled myself to my feet, realizing that, not for the first time, I was covered in way more fluids than any woman should rightly be expected to. Pools and puddles of liquids of scintillating colors were smeared about the floor, shattered vials, beakers, other sciencey birdshit beside it, along with the fragments of the table I'd just crushed.

And books. Everywhere were more fucking books.

It looked like I'd crashed onto a bunch of alchemists having an orgy.

Or a laboratory.

I didn't like this.

I mean, *obviously* I didn't fucking like this. Agne was gone, the others were gone, I was bleeding, broken, bruised, and far from the helm and hijacking the ship like I was supposed to be.

More than that, I didn't like what I'd seen here. The Revolution, if nothing else, was reliable. You could usually count on their propaganda-addled brains to act predictably: they liked guns, they hated dissidents, and they loved using their guns on dissidents. Nowhere in any of my long experiences with them did they like studying.

Yet here I was. On an airship full of Freemaker's tools, alchemist's laboratories, and books.

I didn't like it. Worse, I didn't know what was going on. Like most people who feel angry and stupid, I decided the best course of action would be to find someone and hurt them.

I wiped off the shit and blood as best I could. I bit back the pain that surged up my leg as I started toward the door. Circumstances might have changed, but the goal hadn't: find the helm, take control of the ship, wait for Jero and Agne. If either of them was still alive, they'd be making their way there as well.

"You have an astonishing amount of faith in them."

There would never be a pain so sharp that I couldn't hear the Cacophony's voice through it.

"What if they've been captured? Or killed?"

"What if they have?" I growled back. I make it a point to try not to answer when he starts talking—sets a bad precedent—but I was too angry and hurt to think.

"Then it would seem this mission is folly. Hence, we should seek a new conquest."

"Yeah, no, I'll just ask the Revolution to land the ship so we can go off to the nearest tavern. Are you out of your fucking mind?"

"Many thought so. They're dead now, of course." He giggled, steam rising from the sheath. *"But there's no reason we have to be. I have a plan."*

"No."

"You haven't even heard it."

"Are you a talking gun?"

"Yes?"

"Then I'd be out of *my* fucking mind to listen to you." I winced as I grabbed the door and made ready to shove it open. "No plan you came up with would get us all out of here."

"And?"

"And I'm not going to have it said Sal the Cacophony abandoned her people."

"Tch. That's hardly bothered you before… but it's different now, isn't it? You've grown fond of them. Ugh. How disgustingly cliché."

I ignored him, pressed my ear to the door. No sound greeted me. None but his voice, anyway.

"You jeopardize more than just good taste by indulging them. We made a bargain, you and I. Your affection for collecting broken miscreants continues to hinder our efforts."

I ignored that, too. I grunted, shoved the door open.

A pair of dark eyes met me.

She was exactly as I remembered her. The same short, slender thing in dirty, functional clothes. The same writing quills stuck in her black hair, the same scrolls and inkwells affixed to her belt. The same slender face with the same wide eyes behind the same big glasses wearing the same expression of anger and shock and hurt she always did whenever I came back to her.

Her memory was as much a part of me as my scars.

Yet looking at her then felt like someone had carved a fresh new wound in me.

"Sal," Liette whispered.

And from his sheath, the Cacophony giggled.

"Told you."

FORTY

THE IRON FLEET

Another ghost.

A hallucination.

A bad dream, a hangover, a nervous breakdown, *something*—she couldn't be here. She couldn't be real.

I stared at Liette for a time that drew out longer and crueler than any blade, waiting for it to happen. Waiting for her to say something ominous, to attack me, to laugh cryptically and disappear back into the fucked-up void of my skull like all the other times she'd come to me.

But the more I stared at her, the more I saw that it was the same face, those same big eyes reflecting that same angry pain that I'd put into them every time I left, every time I said I was done killing, every time I lied. The longer time drew out, the more I wished she *had* attacked me. She could kill me, so long as I didn't have to look at those eyes again.

But she didn't attack me. She didn't disappear. Every moment just made her more real. I felt the floorboards shiver slightly under her soft footsteps as she approached me. I smelled the coffee and tea on her breath as she came close enough to look into my eyes. I remembered the pain—that old, familiar ache that came back any time she touched me—as her hand, painfully real and impossible to escape, came to rest upon my cheek and thumbed thoughtfully at the scar across my eye.

She looked into my eyes. Just like she had all those times when she'd said she forgave me and it killed me. And her lips, the ones that always tasted of dust and sweat when I came back to her, parted softly. And she spoke in that voice that I always heard in my dreams.

"What the fuck did you do to my workshop?"

Fuck me, that really was her.

Liette dropped her hand to my shoulder, pushing me aside with some considerable effort as she approached the wreckage that had been her laboratory. She adjusted her glasses on the bridge of her nose, made an irritated humming noise as she surveyed the damage, then looked back to me.

Standing there.

Covered in shit.

Fuck, I thought to myself. *Say something.*

"This, uh..." I gestured to the filth staining my clothes. "This isn't mine."

Beautiful.

"Obviously," she replied as she wearily collected a vial and scalpel from her belt. "While I am well acquainted with your exploits, both embellished and tragically accurate, I do not recall, either in our time together or apart, an ability to defecate yourself to such an impressive degree while fully clothed."

I blinked. "Huh?"

"However, you *are* covered in something decidedly valuable and it might be the only sample we get, so kindly hold still a moment, would you?" She sighed as she began to scrape the filth into the vial. "It would be presumptive to refer to the substance as offal, though, despite the smell and...consistency. While we've determined it *does* exude from our candidate, it's impossible to determine the nature of it beyond its toxicity if ingested." She paused, stared at me with horror. "You didn't get any of it in your mouth, did you?"

My mouth hung open. "*What?*"

"Given that you're not currently exploding, dissolving, or otherwise excreting electricity, we can assume not...unless this is a new reaction we aren't aware of?" She squinted at me behind her glasses before turning back to the wreck of her workshop and looking up at the hole in the ceiling that I'd tumbled through. "Tch.

My alchemical apparatuses were destroyed, naturally, and my notes along with them, otherwise I would have a more definitive idea of what was about to—"

Her voice fell deathly silent. Her eyes went wide with horror as they settled upon a book covered in ash.

"No. You didn't," she whispered. She lunged down, picking it up and frenetically poring over the book carefully to make sure that neither page, cover, nor binding had been damaged before allowing herself a sigh of relief. "Thank fuck you didn't hurt the book." She glared over her shoulder at me. "If you could ever walk into a room using a *door* like a normal person, I wouldn't have to experience mild cardiac palpitations any time you got near one of my books. Honestly, Sal, is it so much to ask that you—"

One of my hands went over her mouth, gently silencing her. The other went to her shoulder, squeezing her softly. With all the composure I could muster, I bent down and looked into her eyes and whispered, oh so gently.

"Liette," I said, "am I fucking high?"

She blinked as I lowered my hand from her mouth. "No?"

"Then what the fuck is going on?"

Ire returned to her face as she prized my fingers away. "I should have thought the sequence to be obvious. I heard sounds of a scuffle, found it drifting closer to my research, and came to investigate. Because, apparently, I'm the only one concerned about getting anything *done* around here."

"No, I mean…" I searched for the words, found them hard to locate. I'd come here prepared to kill a lot of people, hijack an airship, and steal an arcane object of impossible power—*not* to see her. "What are you *doing* here?"

"I could ask you the same thing." She adjusted her glasses again as she looked me over. "Did you come here by yourself?"

"No, I…" My head drifted back to the hole in the hull, the rush of wind…Agne. I shook my head, forced myself to focus; there was only time for *one* calamity right now. "I had some people with me."

"That makes sense, assuming you are, of course, here to steal the airship."

I furrowed my brow. "How did you know?"

She smiled sadly at me. "Because," she said, voice painfully soft, "you only ever show up to destroy something."

No malice. No hatred. The only pain in her voice was her own. It wasn't an accusation. It was a fact.

To say it hurt her more than it hurt me to hear it. I couldn't help but feel sorry for her.

Because hearing her say that made me want to tear my own heart out.

But that was in the past, along with all the other ghosts that had followed me out. I swallowed that feeling down, buried it under the ache and the smell of shit and the gun burning on my hip, and I spoke.

"Yeah," I said. "That's what I'm here for. Are you going to stop me?"

She stared at me. "Could I if I wanted to?"

I stared back at her. "Yes. You could."

She could. Anything she wanted bad enough, she could do. She could think of something, create something, devise something. There was a time when she could have asked me to jump off this ship and I would have done it.

In her stare, I could tell she was wondering if I still would.

Maybe I was, too.

Instead of that, instead of saying anything else, she took her glasses off. She rubbed her eyes and she sighed.

"You shouldn't be here, Sal."

"Neither should you," I replied.

She shot an iron-hard glare at me. "*Here* is exactly where I should be. Where I *need* to be. The future is aboard this fleet. It only arrives if I'm here to guide it."

I furrowed my brow. "You mean the Relic?"

About the time her eyes almost popped out of her head, I realized I had said the wrong thing. She swept up to me, her voice in a low place caught between reverence and fear.

"How do you know about the Relic?" Before I could answer, the realization hit her like a brick to the skull. "Sal," she whispered, "are you here to steal it?"

Not for the first time, I wondered what was the most honest way to confess to a crime.

"Well, I'm going to try my best not to destroy it."

That wasn't it, if you're wondering.

"*No!*" Her shriek came with a fist, an angry flailing motion as she swatted furiously at me. "No, no, *no!* You can't take it, Sal! Not this time! This time, it's too important! It's too...too..."

"Too *what?*" I seized her by the wrists, if only to keep her from going for my eyes. "What is it? What are *you* doing here with it? Liette." I held her eyes in mine. "Talk to me."

Not for the first time, she gave me the look that told me we both knew I didn't deserve that chance. When I saw those eyes softening and realized she was going to give it to me again, I knew I'd said a hundred wrong things.

She sighed deeply. Her fingers traced a long cut across my arm where Tenka's metal had cut me.

"You can never come to me uninjured, can you?" She turned and began to sift through the wreckage of her workshop. "My informant was in worse shape when he returned to me after I relocated from Lowstaff when it was..."

Destroyed.

By me.

But she was too nice to say it. Too nice to hold me accountable. Too fucking nice.

"Anyway," she continued as she searched through broken vials. "I pay a few Revolutionaries to keep me apprised of the goings-on in their Great General's capital. Some months ago, one of them, half dead from wounds, dragged himself to my temporary residence to deliver important information. Deep in the mountains, the Revolution discovered something. Something big."

She shot a meaningful glance over her shoulder.

"The Relic."

Obviously, I thought, but kept it to myself. She was trying so hard to sound dramatic, bless her.

"I take it, since you know about it, you know the specifics." She held up an unbroken vial, sniffed at its content, then blanched and tossed it away.

"Roughly," I replied. "Big, important, never-before-seen, could-potentially-kill-us-all, et cetera, et cetera."

"What a wonderfully obtuse way of suggesting you don't understand at all." She sniffed. "The Relic itself isn't important."

"I'm pretty sure things that will kill us all are a *little* important."

"*Potentially* kill us all," she corrected. "Or potentially change the world. The Revolution understood about as much as you do when they excavated it. While they're normally the only ones who know how to use Relics, this was beyond them. While a brain fattened on propaganda and weaned off logic makes for an admirable soldier, it produces a less-than-ideal scholar for plumbing the mysteries. Hence—"

"Hence they found you." A surge of anger coursed through me, that readiness that came with knowing I'd break every finger of every hand that had touched her. "They tracked you back, captured you, forced them to work for you."

She paused. "Are you perhaps confusing me with someone whose cranium and rectum are interchangeable? I've remained hidden from the Revolution, the Imperium, the Ashmouths, and every faction with someone dumber than me at their helm—that is, all of them. The Revolution couldn't track me out of an outhouse, much less out of the Valley. No, Sal." She smiled softly. "I came to them."

"What?" I blinked. "Why?"

"The 'how' is more interesting than either of those," she replied. "The Revolution realized their own inadequacies faster than I would have given them credit for. By the time I'd approached them with an offer, they'd already sought the help of multiple other parties, various Freemakers and a handful of Vagrants."

That explained things. Sort of. At least now I knew why they had so many Freemakers' tools. But what could be so important about the Relic that they'd seek the help of their hated foes? Sure, it was big. But bigness wasn't directly correlated to power.

Or... was it?

"They'd been hurling themselves at the Relic—sometimes quite literally—with little to show for it but incinerated soldiers and one unfortunate Freemaker who began his career *not* being turned inside out and ended it..." She cleared her throat. "At any rate, I wasn't having much better luck until I heard a certain sound emanating from it. A song, discordant and unfortunate. I recalled a description of it before." She paused. "You once told me what it sounded like."

The Lady Merchant's song.

I'd tried explaining it once. Back when she was curious about me. Back when I really believed I could be better.

"But it wasn't like what you described." She found another vial, sniffed it, nodded to herself. "It was too . . . jarred. Screeching. Angry. I couldn't make sense of it." She approached me, uncorked the vial. "But a mage could."

"They could understand the song?" I asked as she took my wounded arm. "How's that possible? How's it possible that there's even more than one sooooooooo*HOLYSHIT!*"

My voice trailed off into a formless scream as the alchemic she poured onto my wound began to sizzle and steam. I jerked my arm away, clutching it and staring at her accusingly. She rolled her eyes and tossed the empty vial away.

"It's a moderate compound of benign acids and a latent strain of a flesh-eating disease, each grown by me. Don't be such a baby." She produced a cloth and seized my arm again, wrapping it around my wound. "You had open wounds when you crashed, I assume, and everything in this laboratory came out of that Relic. I'd rather you not blame me for whatever diseases it might have."

"Wait, came *out* of the Relic? Things don't *come* out of Relics unless they make things explode."

"And it does, as I already explained."

"What is *it*?"

"*Who* is it," she corrected. "It doesn't have a name that we understand. We only just recently figured out that it can be released." She looked up at me as she tied the bandage tight and smiled. "The Relic isn't a relic. It's a *cell*."

As if the pain came with that knowledge, I felt that cold ache again. It came creeping on cold black fingers into my bones, up my rib cage, into my chest. It was like just hearing it, becoming aware of it, was enough to summon that dread into me. And when I spoke, it choked me.

"A cell," I asked, "for what?"

⸻

A tumor.

A rock?

Some kind of…flesh…poop…thing?

I wasn't sure what I was looking at, honestly. Which meant I sure as shit wasn't sure what made the brown-and-red lump I was staring at worth all the fuss of recruiting Freemakers, Vagrants, and the entire Iron Fleet to protect it.

But given that they *had* deployed several small armies for purposes of keeping it secret, it did seem *slightly* unwise to keep it in a jar.

I held it up, squinting through the glass at the thing. It was, to all appearances, a lump. No bigger than my fist. An unpleasant shade of brown with hues of crimson running through it. I would have called it a stone, but I'd never seen a stone with colors like that before.

Also, stones didn't float.

It was floating.

That seems important to mention.

Hovering in the air inside the jar was impressive, but it nonetheless remained motionless. While I was duly impressed, I was also duly bored as shit.

"So, what?" I glanced over my shoulder. "You brought me here to look at a flying turd?"

That was probably the wrong thing to say, if the expression on Liette's face was any indication.

Her quarters—already cramped—were made even tinier by the small hoard of books in various stages of been-read she kept around. Yet the ire on her face made her loom as she folded her arms and scowled at me.

"It is *not* flying and it is *not* a turd," she replied sternly. "It suspends itself in air via no summoned magic that we can deduce and responds to no stimulus, nor attempts to damage it, in any way that we know."

"So…it's a very dry, floating turd?" I stared back at the jar, tapping at the glass. "Does it do anything else?"

"We didn't think so," she replied. "But then…Relentless got better."

"Who?"

"Relentless. Lieutenant Relentless. Brother of Agent Relentless—you recall him, I hope?"

I did recall Agent Relentless. I had three scars on my side from Agent Relentless. Or rather, the abomination that had been wearing

Agent Relentless's skin like a suit at the time I had been left trapped in an abandoned mine after it tried to rip my flesh off.

It was a whole...thing.

"He was suffering from an ailment—Hollow Fever. The disease takes an incredibly long time to recover from." She glanced at me. "As you no doubt know."

Point of interest: if you throw up in someone's lap, even for perfectly good reasons beyond your control, they will never, ever let you forget it.

"As he began to spend more time guarding the Relic, we noticed his symptoms began to clear up rapidly." She clicked her tongue. "So, naturally, I decided to cut him open with a scalpel."

"Naturally...Wait, what?"

"To my astonishment, the wound healed near instantaneously. Further experiments yielded further effects. Plants grew and withered at an accelerated rate around it. Food changed flavors. Water caught fire once." She grinned. "Do you see what it does?"

I squinted at the jar. "It's...a *magic* turd?"

"It does impossible things we can't even begin to comprehend." She reached out to snatch the jar back from me. "While its exact nature eludes us, I am fucking sure that it *doesn't* appreciate you teasing it."

"I'm not teasing it!" I let the jar go as she took it back. "I don't even know what *it* is, much less why you'd come all the way here to find it. You despise the Revolution."

"I despise lots of things that I'm able to look past for greater purposes."

"You never told me."

She regarded me evenly for a moment. "I grew tired of explaining it to you."

Honestly, at this point, it would probably be less painful if she just beat me to death with one of those books.

"How can you even say it's a turd?" She held up the jar. "It looks nothing like one."

"It's brown. Red. A lump. If you've never seen a turd like that, I envy you."

She scrunched up her face. "What? It's not..." She paused, her eyes going wide. "Wait...you see a lump?"

"I see a lump because it *is* a lump."

"Incredible." She stared at it, more breathlessly than anything that weird deserved. "We knew it had the power to influence cognition, but we thought it was limited to shape alone. To think it could alter its material state, too..."

This was certainly *way* more reverence than was owed any turd.

"Liette," I said. "What the fuck is it?"

She set the jar down with an almost terrified caution. Her eyes lingered on it for a long moment before she spoke.

"Our progress on the Relic was stagnant, despite my best efforts. Months of work and the finest minds we could locate couldn't deduce what it was or what it could do. Then, roughly two weeks ago, we returned to it and discovered this."

She gestured to the jar.

"Hovering in the middle of the air before the Relic. I couldn't believe it myself. But there it was... a perfectly smooth, polished orb of pitch-black obsidian."

I squinted. "But that's—"

"Some looked at it and saw a rough, jagged crystal. Others saw a gray stone. Some saw a limestone cube. All of us were staring at the exact same object, and all of us saw completely different things."

"So it's a—"

"If you say 'magic turd,' I will strangle you until my hands go numb and then use my feet." Liette scarcely missed a beat as she returned her attentions to the lump. "This thing can be whatever it wants to be. Or rather, whatever the *viewer* wants it to be." A smile creased her face. "Do you know what this means, Sal?"

She turned toward me. She gave me a look without hatred, without anger, without fear or confusion or pain or sorrow or any of the terrible things I'd painted on her face.

In those big eyes behind those big glasses, there was a shine. I'd seen it in her eyes only three times before. The first time I gave her my real name. The first time I'd put my gun down and she thought I meant it. And now.

It was a rare thing. So rare that every time I saw that shine, I swore I'd never see it again. But when it came back, when I saw it again...

I started to forget what dark places looked like.

"We can change everything," she whispered. "No more war. No more killers. No more—"

She caught herself. That light in her eyes went soft. She didn't have to finish the sentence. I knew what she was going to say.

No more people like me.

It hurt too much to say it. It hurt to think it.

Fuck, it hurt just to look at her.

It would have been easier if she was another ghost. If she was just a bad dream I could have woken up from I could have handled it. I could have bitten it back, swallowed it down, washed the taste out with the nastiest liquor I could find.

But she wasn't. And I couldn't.

Not after seeing her again. Not after knowing she bit back her hatred for the Revolution just to make a world without me in it. I couldn't blame her. And I couldn't make it stop hurting.

So maybe that's why I said what I said.

"What makes you think," I whispered, spite creeping into my voice, "that the Revolution will let you use it?"

She blinked. And the light went out again.

"Sal," she said.

"You said it yourself," I replied. "Brains eating propaganda."

"*Fattened* on propaganda were my exact words."

"The words don't change a fucking thing," I snapped. "What are you going to do once you open it? Once whatever that thing is gets out? How are you going to keep a bunch of brainwashed killers hell-bent on annihilating anyone not them from using whatever's in there to kill everyone? Appeal to their humanity?"

She pursed trembling lips. "I have a plan."

"Birdshit. If you had a plan, that thing would be out of here already and you'd have it in one of your studies."

"I'm rapidly running out of those," she replied, coldness in her voice. "After you destroyed the last one."

"You won't have any fucking left if you let the Revolution get their hands on that thing," I said. "They'll sweep over the Scar, over its people, over *everything*. What could the Great General do with even *that* tiny piece in the jar?"

"They already have the Relic, Sal," she replied, her voice becoming a growl. "I can do more to effect change from here than I can by letting them just open it on their own. What else was I supposed to do?"

"I don't know. Let someone else take it?"

Her eyes narrowed sharply. "Like you?"

"It'd keep it out of the hands of maniacs, at least."

"And deliver it to the hands of other maniacs. Or maniac, singular."

"Fuck, it's not like I was going to take it for *myself*, woman. What the shit would I even do with a box full of magic turds?"

"It's an undiscovered, reality-altering form of energy yet unknown to mortal minds, you *ass*!" Her voice was alive now, all the courtesy flooding out of her mouth on a torrent of anger. "Who the fuck did you intend to deliver it to? The Imperium? A Vagrant? Or some rich asshole with enough money to make you do something stupid?"

"A Freemaker," I replied.

"A Freemaker." She paused. "Which Freemaker?"

Ideally, this being a secret operation, I shouldn't have said anything.

But I was pissed.

"Two Lonely Old Men."

"*Him?*" Her eyes snapped wide. "And what did he offer you? Money?"

I said nothing.

"Whiskey? Weapons?"

I clenched my jaw.

"Or . . . don't tell me . . . your list."

I didn't reply. I didn't move. I didn't even blink.

Somehow, she still knew.

"Of course." Cold. Sharp. Cruel. Curt. She spoke like a dagger speaks to a spine. "Of fucking course, it's for your list. For them. For all the people you have to kill. Because even now, even at the *cusp* of changing the world, it's still about killing people for you."

"YOU'RE FUCKING RIGHT IT'S STILL ABOUT KILLING PEOPLE!"

Screaming was a bad idea. Storming toward her was a bad idea. But I was full of those lately.

"It's still about killing people because it's *always* been about killing people. Even when it's about changing the world. *Especially* when it's about changing the world. Because what the fuck do you think people do when they get the power to change the world?"

She backed away from me, swallowing hard. "I . . . I don't . . ."

"You don't what?" I reached up to my coat, undid the top button, seized the collar of my shirt. "You don't know?"

I yanked it down.

"Because I do."

My scar hurt. It hurt from the chill air hitting it as I bared it. It hurt from the fights and the fighting. It hurt from the fact that, for the first time since we'd met, she looked at my scar.

And looked away.

"I've known. I've had *years* to know. Ever since some asshole who thought he could change the world gave me this scar, ever since they took my magic."

I raised my shirt collar. I stalked toward the door. There was more to say, more to understand, I'm sure—she had her reasons maybe, and maybe they weren't so different from mine. Maybe, with a little talk and a little patience, we could have understood each other. And I'm sure if I'd been slightly less pissed, I might have been the person who could have done that.

But I was pissed. And I seethed. And I hurt.

So I wasn't that person.

"Stay here if you want," I muttered, "tinker with whatever magic birdshit you want, pretend it won't end like it's always ended, if you want." I seized the door handle. "But you're too fucking smart, Liette, to think that you're going to get anything but more killing from giving that thing to the Revolution. All you'll do is make it bigger."

"Sal, wait," she replied. "It's not that simple. We didn't—"

"And another thing." I shoved the door open, glared over my shoulder. "What's this fucking 'we' thing you keep talking about? Have you and the Revolution decided to make it official? Should I bring a fucking bottle of wine for the two of you next time?"

"Don't be so fucking absurd," she snapped. "I'm talking about my partner."

Something dropped into my throat.

"What partner?"

From the other side of the door, a voice whispered.

"Salazanca?"

Live long enough, make the wrong decisions and the right mistakes, you'll meet someone in your life who makes you forget who you are. I don't mean in the back-alley opera about tragic lovers kind of way. I mean in the real way. The way where all the wounds and the grudges and the terrible things that make you who you are slide off you like skin off a serpent's back and leave something glistening and raw behind.

I had a person like that.

And she was standing in front of me.

Short, pale, and slender as a willow tree, she stood there. Her eyes were wearier than I remembered, her hair paler and in an unkempt braid, and though she'd always been slender, she now looked... starving. Her coat and leggings hung off her like they couldn't wait to get away from her. She stood awkwardly and uncomfortably, out of place in a world so cold and dark. I almost didn't recognize her.

But I recognized that smile.

I remembered it. I remembered the days I woke up next to it, the jokes that got it as a reward, the night I looked for it and it wasn't there.

I recognized it. And once I did, all those things came sliding off me, and what was underneath...

I didn't like it. It hurt too much. But it was me. No matter how hard I tried to forget it.

"Salazanca," she said again softly, her smile growing as she stepped toward me. "I'm so happy to see you."

She held out a hand to me.

Darrish the Flint held out her hand.

I stared at it for a long moment. Then I took it. Then I put my other hand on my sword.

And that's when I stabbed her.

FORTY-ONE

THE IRON FLEET

So many names later, I still never know what it'll feel like when I kill one of them.

I always think it'll be dramatic, like in an opera. I always wonder who will beg, who will threaten, who will lament before I plunge my sword into them. I always wonder if this one will make me feel better, feel normal again.

They never do.

Every time I do it, every time their blood splashes onto the floor and they slide off my steel, all I feel is a short rush and a long emptiness. But that brief moment, where it feels like this name, this kill, will be the one that's enough, even for just a second, is worth it.

It feels good.

It would have this time, too.

But then she had to go and be a Wardmage.

The tip of my blade hovered an inch away from Darrish's belly, striking only shimmering air where it should be cutting through her flesh. I looked up, saw her staring back at me, a faint purple light in her eyes and the Lady's song in my ears.

"You're angry," she said, more softly than anyone else I had tried to eviscerate. "I understand and I—"

Unless the end of her sentence was *"am about to get chopped in the fucking face,"* she didn't.

My sword came up and down in a savage chop. She hurled her

hand up, the Lady's song rising. The air shimmered as my blade struck another barrier. I snarled, came in from the side, found another song and another invisible wall to go with it.

"*Sal!*" Liette shouted.

Or I thought she did, anyway.

I couldn't hear her. Or anything. I couldn't even see. Sight and sound had sloughed off me, along with the wounds, the grudges, the hurt, the mercy, the tears and blood I shed over her and all the things she ever said to me when we still understood each other, until nothing was left but the sword in my hand, pumping mechanically as I tried to find a place to cut.

And her.

"Sal, stop!"

Darrish the Flint. Who rested her head against my chest and listened to my heartbeat.

"Stop it! Stop it, please!"

Darrish the Flint. Who was the first person I ever gave a damn about the way they looked at me.

"PLEASE! PLEASE STOP!"

Darrish the Flint.

Who turned her back on me the night they took the sky from me.

And did nothing.

I loved her. And for anything to make sense again, I had to kill her.

So I kept cutting. I kept chopping. I kept hacking and stabbing and smashing myself and my steel against her walls. They kept shimmering, but each time, they weakened. Each time, she staggered back.

Wardmagic isn't a high art. The ability to conjure impenetrable walls at a moment's notice is impressive. But the Lady asks a steep price: your ability to heal. I don't mean like how many hits you can take; she asks for more than that. She takes your ability to forgive, to forget, to move on—every blade and bullet that bounces off your walls is a memory you won't escape, a mistake you won't ever live down. It does things to a person's mind, makes them start seeing only ways things can go wrong. The trauma is too much for some Wardmages— the more they did it, the harder it became to keep it up.

Darrish had been doing this for a long time.

So I kept slashing. Liette was screaming, pleading. Darrish was backing up each time I swung, collapsing to her knees. I couldn't think beyond putting the sword in my hand into her, couldn't see beyond its flashing steel, couldn't hear beyond the sound of it ringing.

"You hate her. Why?"

And that.

"Tell me. Tell me what she did. Who she is."

A voice. A feeling. That cold dread language that crept through me. I could barely feel it, barely hear it. I didn't even think about it.

"Tell me. Show me. Let me know. I have to know."

But if I'd known what it was, I would have.

"SAL!"

I was too tired to keep swinging, exhaustion finally filtering through the cold. Or maybe whatever that voice was that I heard made me hear more of them. Or maybe some other magical birdshit, I didn't know.

I only knew that I paused for a minute. And that was all it took for everything to come back to me.

Darrish was on the floor, gasping for air, her eyes shut tight. Liette was on my arm, putting every ounce of her strength into holding my sword back. And I was there. Me and the sword.

Like always.

"Let go, Liette," I demanded.

"I can't, Sal," she replied, gasping. "Please. I can't let you kill her."

"You don't know her."

"She's helping us, Sal. She's helping *everything*. She's—"

"YOU DON'T KNOW HER."

I whirled on her. The sword fell from my hands, clattered to the ground as I took her by the shoulders, pulled her so close to me that I could see my spittle on her glasses. There was no other way. I couldn't think of another way to make her see.

"You don't know who she is!" I screamed. "You don't know who she was! *You don't know what she did!*"

"*What?*" Liette shrieked back. "*What* did she do, Sal?"

"She...she..."

Hurt to say. Hurt to talk. Hurt to think about it. Every thought but picking up the sword again hurt.

"Did nothing."

Darrish leaned hard on the wall, her breath coming out in great gasps as she struggled back to her feet. Her face was contorted in agonies from long ago, her body trembling as she looked back at me through eyes devoid of light, of joy, of anything but a deep and abiding weariness.

"I did nothing," she said. She turned and looked at me through those eyes—the same ones I saw shining in the dark that night. "When I should have done anything."

I held my sword, narrowed my eyes.

Meet enough of them, you find a villain of every flavor: the warlord with dreams as long as his sword, the rich baron who specializes in making ends justify means, and, occasionally, the penitent monster.

My least favorite.

I've heard this pitying rhetoric a hundred times on a hundred different lips and it just gets more tiresome each time. Sometimes they whine about their circumstances, sometimes they blame their mothers or their wives or the loves they thought they were owed. Sometimes they just beg. But no matter what fancy words they choose, they always end the same way, just like this would.

The sole comfort Darrish the Flint would take to the black table was the knowledge of what she'd done to deserve it.

Good for her.

I took up my sword in both hands, raised it over my head as she bowed hers, and prepared to run it through her until every last drop of blood painted the floor and she fell lifeless, empty of everything but regrets.

"WAIT!"

Of course, *someone* had to go and ruin it.

My blade stopped its descent two inches from Liette's chest. She stood there, imposed between Darrish and my steel, arms thrown open wide and eyes alive. Behind her glasses, I could see the terror in her stare as she looked at me.

Like an animal.

Like she thought I would have killed her.

"I need her." Liette found her composure, along with her breath, as she forced iron into her eyes. "I need her, Sal. She can hear the song."

I narrowed my eyes. I clenched my jaw. I didn't lower my sword. But I didn't stab her either.

So... progress.

"The Revolution can't hear it and neither can I," Liette continued. "But mages can. *She* can. Once she started listening, we were able to get *that* thing"—she gestured to the jar—"out of it. I need her, Sal. *We* need her."

"You can find another Vagrant," I growled. "I passed one on my way here."

"Tenka won't work."

"Well, what the fuck do you keep him around for? Is he great at eating—"

"No."

Darrish's voice. Weary and shaking as she pulled herself to her feet and gave me a slow drawn blade of a look.

"He can't hear the song. Not like I can." Darrish gestured vaguely to her ear. "He hears something, but it's... not right."

This didn't sound like something I was more interested in than stabbing her to death. But Liette wasn't moving, either.

"Just like we see something different, we hear something different, too," Darrish said. "He heard something angry and foul, like a curse. And I..." She laid a hand on her chest, drew in a cold breath. "I heard something cold, like it was reaching into me and..."

She hesitated, lips trembling as if the words hurt just to hold in her mouth. She shook her head.

"It's not magic, Salazanca," she said softly. "It's not explosions or flying or making nightmares. It's... something more. It doesn't just destroy—it *changes*. Sounds. Sights. Itself. There's not a magic or machine in the Scar, the Revolution, or the Imperium that can do that."

She smiled softly. Not at me. Never at me.

Never again.

"Whatever you heard about the Relic, whatever you know or don't know," she whispered, "it's not enough. Nothing we know is enough. With this, with what's inside, we can change things."

She looked at me. No. She looked past me. Through me. To something that wasn't broken so badly, something she hadn't sung to at night, something else.

"We can change this world."

Like I said, do what I do long enough, you can meet every kind of villain. But you only ever need to meet one to know they all want great things. I don't mean gold or weapons, though they all certainly want those, too.

Every villain—every warlord and baron and murderer and poacher and Vagrant—wants to change the world. They want to live on longer than the terror they've sown, to leave a mark on the world deeper than their swords can cut. They try a lot of different things—magic, alchemy, charity, conquest.

But in the end . . .

"Who gives a shit?"

Nobody is ever anything more than the bodies they leave behind.

"Sal."

Liette said my name. An hour ago, I would have killed to hear her say it. But now my sword was lowered, my eyes were on Darrish, and my chest felt cold.

"What the fuck do you think you're going to change?" I asked.

"With the Relic," Darrish replied, "we can—"

"Fuck the Relic. Fuck whatever's inside it. What do you think *you*, Darrish the Flint, are going to change?"

She furrowed her brow. "I don't—"

"What, are you going to end wars? Are you going to feed the hungry?" My lips trembled. My eyes grew wet. "Are you going to take this back?"

I reached up.

I pulled down my collar.

I let her look at my last memory of her.

She cringed away, as if it hurt to look at that scar twisting down from my collarbone. Good. I wanted it to hurt her. I wanted it to do more than hurt her. I wanted to sharpen it—this scar, that night, that moment she looked away from me—into a point and jam it in her chest and let her look at it every day she woke up.

"Look at me, Darrishana," I growled. "LOOK AT ME."

She looked back at me. Quivering. Trembling. Weak.

"You may have fooled her into thinking you care about the world—"

"I haven't fooled anyone," she tried to protest.

"I'M FUCKING TALKING!" I roared. "You can fool her, you can fool the Revolution, you can fool yourself and the whole fucking world if you want. All your ideas and your speeches and your hopes don't count for shit. You can save every child, stop every war, give every home a puppy and it won't change a fucking thing."

My face was hot. I didn't remember when that happened. Nor was I sure when the tears started falling down my cheeks.

"You took the sky from me," I whispered. "You took *everything* from me. Nothing can change that."

She swallowed hard, opened her mouth to respond, found nothing but a sour taste and empty breath. The Barter she'd given for her magic, I knew, made her feel every wound like it was fresh, even one as old as this. But I didn't care.

It didn't hurt as bad as mine.

And it wasn't going to hurt as bad as this.

"Except this."

I snarled, raised my blade. Darrish took a step back, eyes wide with terror. I moved to swing, found myself unable to, with the sudden addition of a very small, irritated woman clinging to my bicep.

"Run," Liette said, giving an urgent look at Darrish over my shoulder. "GET OUT OF HERE!"

Darrish made a move as if to intervene, as if to protest, and maybe she realized that either of those options would end with my steel in her chest because she chose, instead, to rush out the door and slam it shut.

Like that was going to stop me.

Before I could reach the handle, Liette darted out in front of me. Before I could stop her, she'd pulled a writing quill free from her hair and an inkwell free from her belt. Her hands moving quicker than my feet could, she hastily scrawled a series of sigils upon the door frame and gave them a flick.

They hummed to glowing life, taking on a pale purple hue that hurt my eyes to look at. But even as I glanced away, I knew those sigils. Back from that time we didn't want to be disturbed at that one inn in Murmursoft. And that one other time when I was tripping hard—and I mean *hard*—on doom pepper.

A locking sigil. No one was getting in or out of that door without breaking it down.

Which I would have.

Just as soon as she got out of the fucking way.

"Sal."

Soft words. Small, delicate hands spread out, demanding I stop. Short, slender body pressed against the door. That's all that stood between me and that name on my list, all that stood between me and getting one step closer to feeling this ache in my chest go away. I'd cut down murderers, generals, monsters, and worse to get to my quarry before. I wouldn't even have to use my sword to get through her. Blood, red-hot and angry, was draining out of my head and into my hands, demanding I reach out and remove her, hurl her aside, *break* her.

Which I would have.

Only…

Murderers, generals, monsters—none of them looked at me the way she looked at me now. That plaintive, urgent stare that made me feel like I could breathe deeper, stand straighter, do anything…

When she used to look at me like that.

"There's more at stake here than—"

"Than what?" My words. Hard. Cold and sharp. I'd never used them on her before. "Than me?"

She looked like I had just punched her in the face. Fuck, maybe it would have been nicer if I had. Her lips fumbled for the words, hands searched for something she could do, could pull out to convince me.

"Than all of us," she whispered. "Than everything. Can't you see that?"

"See what?" I asked. "This magical world you're going to create? These great things you're going to do? Let me ask you, Liette." I stepped toward her, my footsteps echoing in her chamber. "Can you see me in that world?"

She looked up at me. Her eyes glistened. And I wanted to leap out the window.

"No," she said. "I understand you're upset, but—"

"I'm not upset," I replied. "I'm Sal the fucking Cacophony. And nobody… *nobody* gets in the way of Sal the Cacophony."

A sigh, deep and annoyed. *"Tiresome."*

"Fucking right it is," I snarled as I tried to push Liette aside. "Get out of the fucking way."

"NO!" Liette clung to my arm, tiny and tenacious, digging her heels into the floor. "I won't let you ruin this, Sal! Not like everything else!"

"Ruin *what*? Ruin your perfect world? Ruin your perfect plans?"

"Ruin *everything*! With your gun! With your list! With your fucking *revenge*!"

A long, irritated grumble. *"Petty."*

"The hell it is," I spat, trying to dislodge her. "Let go of me, Liette."

"I can't."

"Fuck me you can't. Let *go*."

"Or else what, Sal?" she demanded. "Or else fucking what?"

"Or else I'm going to burn this ship, every ship, and every last piece of your precious fucking Relic and cram every last *ounce* of its ashes into every ass I can find from here to Cathama!"

A weary, bemused chuckle. *"Interesting."*

"And if you don't fucking shut up whatever noise-tube is making that sound, I'm going to start *and* finish with Darrish's ass and stop for tea halfway through."

That was a good threat.

Hell, maybe my best one.

Made me wish anything had been said to warrant it. Or anything said at all, really. As it was, though, Liette just stared at me, puzzled.

Liette paused, echoing her look. "What noise-tube?"

"Those fucking tubes on this ship that you talk through." I growled as my voice slid into snide mimicry. 'Tiresome,' 'petty,' 'interesting.' If everyone doesn't fucking stop talking and let me get stabbing, I'll...I'll..."

My voice trailed off. Liette quirked a brow, torn between curious and thinking I might have finally lost what was left of my mind.

"I don't have one of those," she said. "I blocked it up when they gave me this room."

I blinked. "Really?"

She adjusted her glasses. "Really."

Not to brag or anything, but I know liars when I see them—their emotions are rehearsed, their words are impeccable, and they always have this look at the corners of their eyes like they're about to get their teeth punched down their throats. I didn't see that in Liette's eyes. She wasn't capable of it.

Whatever I'd heard, she hadn't.

But that didn't make sense. If I hadn't said it, and she hadn't said it, the only thing left in the room was...

My eyes were inexorably drawn to the jar. From behind its glass, I could feel a certain presence, like...like...

You know when you've just met someone and you instantly regret it?

"Ah. I interrupted."

It was talking. The floating turd was talking to me.

Which made sense, I guess.

Since it was also now looking at me with one huge, bloodshot eye.

FORTY-TWO

THE IRON FLEET

When it comes to survival in the Scar, I like to consider myself something of an expert.

There are those who might disagree with that statement, but as they are all currently dead, you might as well just believe me. The reason I have spent so long avoiding my turn to be called to the black table is because of a simple adherence to three rules.

One: If something calls to you, don't call back.

Two: Don't stand in the way of anything bigger than yourself.

Three: If you can't tell how to kill it by looking at it, run away.

Now, I recognize that "don't talk to a flying, magical piece of shit" isn't *explicitly* on there, but as far as I was concerned, it covered all three, as well as being just good advice. At the very least, a grotesque lump of flesh that was currently staring at me through an unblinking eye was something I was not prepared to see that day, in addition to being something I was completely unprepared to handle, which made it a damn fine reason to turn around and walk right out that door.

I would have, if not for two reasons.

The first being the magical Spellwright lock that Liette had scribbled upon it, and the second...

"Oh, sweet scientific process, I'm a fucking genius."

Yeah.

That.

All Liette's ire and fear toward me dissipated in the blink of an eye, along with any attention she had for me at all. She abandoned the door and rushed over to the jar, pressing her face against the glass like a kid admiring a particularly greasy, profoundly unwholesome and decidedly glistening puppy in a window.

I could have kicked the door down—hell, I could have blown it off and she wouldn't have noticed. But...

Well, I mean, it's not like I was going to leave her *alone* with that thing.

"Incredible," she gasped. "It possesses not only the ability to alter its appearance depending on who's viewing it, but it can also change its appearance *at will*, suggesting supreme adaptability unseen in any predator. It has an eye! Or at least... I see an eye. Do you see an eye? I see an eye."

"Yeah, I see an eye," I muttered, approaching with significantly more caution, as all flying turds should be approached with. "And I heard a voice." I swallowed hard, looked at her. "Did... you?"

"She did not."

Its voice—if you could call it a voice—was not gentle to hear. Possibly because I didn't "hear" it. Not like I should have. I couldn't...

You know those moments when your chest tightens up and your breath goes short and you don't know why? The moment the rest of your body figures out something and your brain is always the last to catch up? The moment when every inch of you knows something is about to go horribly wrong but you haven't realized just how bad?

Like that, except it's coming out of a piece of shit.

"My presence is attuned solely to you." Every word a heartbeat, every breath a rush of blood. *"For though extending my presence to another is trivial work, it is you alone who has seized my attention, where all the splendors in all the worlds beyond these could not. I bestow my esteem upon you and you alone."*

I stared at the object—creature? Being? Entity? I cleared my throat. I rubbed the back of my head.

"Uh, okay," I said. "But *could* she hear you? That would make this a lot easier."

A pause. A long, irritated sigh.

"Fine."

Liette's eyes went wide. "I heard it." She turned to me, breathless. "I *heard* it! Do you know what this means?"

I didn't. But she only ever asks that question when she doesn't know, either.

Her enthusiasm might very well have been infectious, but I'd have no way of knowing. Whether she could feel that thing's voice like I could, I didn't know, but my ears, my blood, my *body* were full of its amusement.

And I didn't like the sensation.

"*Such emotion from the tiniest of gestures.*" Its eye slowly swiveled inside its socket, surveying us, surveying *me*. "*Is it truly so easy? What else lurks inside your fragile cocoons? What horrors? What delights? What beauties do you still remember?*"

I knew this feeling, this seeping unease, that its voice instilled in me. But I couldn't place it. It felt like staring into a dark spot, like looking too closely at it would mean disappearing into it.

In the face of the unknowable, the overwhelming, my general reaction tended to be to spew curses and threats. I knew that wasn't going to cut it this time.

But fuck, I couldn't think of anything better.

"If you don't want to see what lurks over the edge of this ship," I growled, "you'd better tell us what the fuck you are, exactly."

"*Sal,*" Liette chastised. "We're clearly dealing with sentience, hence it would be a *who* the fuck it is." She squinted at it. "Or... *are* you a 'who'? Do you possess an age? A gender? A—"

"*It does not matter,*" the thing replied. "*Perhaps it did once. But I can no longer remember.*" Its eye glanced around at grotesque leisure. "*Nor do I recall this land. Nor your breed.*"

"You are... ancient, then?" Liette whispered. "An ancestor?"

The eye narrowed in indignation... or amusement? Anger? I don't know, it turns out the expressions of flesh-sacs are pretty hard to read.

"*I stood here once. I traveled this land. I left it behind.*" It paused, thoughtful, as it stared at us. "*You would have called me a person. Or close enough to it that you would not be able to tell the difference.*"

"Did you have a name?"

"It does not matter."

"Well, I suppose not." Liette scratched her chin. "But for purposes of record-keeping, it would help if we could call you *something*."

I opened my mouth to offer a suggestion. She held up a hand.

"Not 'the turd.'"

"It's right, though, it *doesn't* matter. It's fucking with us," I muttered. "Nobody with anything of value to say speaks in cryptic birdshit like this."

"If it will soothe you, I was once known as Eldest."

"Eldest." Liette tasted the name—normal enough, but the way it said it was unnerving. "How long ago were you here, Eldest?"

"Vast ages, untold spans of time."

"See?" I asked. "What did I—"

"Six hundred thousand years, ten months, two weeks, four days, ten hours, forty-eight minutes, and fifty-eight seconds ago," Eldest spoke suddenly. *"If you truly wish to know."*

"Six hundred...," Liette whispered, her eyes growing so wide she could barely open her mouth. "That would mean... Hang on."

She turned, immediately rushed over to a pile of books, rifling through it and ignoring me. Would that I could say the same of this... thing. It continued to stare at me through the glass. While I didn't know exactly *how* this thing could talk, I wasn't going to let it say that Sal the Cacophony averted her gaze from a flying turd.

"You knew all that, huh?" I asked. "Just like that?"

"That, more, everything. I know every sinew, every bone, every nerve of a human's body. I know the deep things that sleep between the stars. I can follow a drop of blood from a body, into the earth, across the years, into the fibers of the leaves of the tree that it fed. What I know is limitless. And tedious."

I furrowed my brow, looked over my shoulder. "Yeah, see? This thing is full of—"

She wasn't looking. She was picking up books, flipping through them, tossing them aside. She hadn't even heard me.

"She hurts you."

But it had.

When I looked back, Eldest's eye was wide open. A single slit pupil expanded to black orb, growing wider with every breath I took.

"To look upon her causes you pain. What do you see? What do you remember?"

Wider. Larger. Until the eye was nothing more than a gash of darkness, impenetrable and dark.

"Tell me. Tell me everything."

I didn't have a word for what I felt upon staring into that blackness. All the dread and the creeping cold that came with its voice suddenly seemed so insignificant in comparison to what I saw within its gaze. It was too... engulfing, too attentive, an abyss that stared at me no matter where I turned. I'd known nothing about this thing when I first laid eyes upon it, and now I felt like I knew even less than nothing.

So I can see how you might have thought smashing it would be a bad idea.

But fuck, I couldn't think of anything else. I couldn't think of *anything* except that wide stare and how badly I needed to get away from it.

Liette was still rummaging through her books. She didn't notice as I slid a hand down to the Cacophony, nor did she notice me wrapping my hand around his hilt. Whatever this thing was, I wagered a magic gun would stand a better chance of breaking it than any sword.

But when I reached out to him, when I tried to draw him, he would not come.

That hadn't happened before.

I pulled on his hilt, but the gun remained firmly in his sheath, refusing to be drawn. I squinted at him, waiting for some snide remark, some hissing chastisement, some sign that I'd insulted him. *That* wouldn't have been surprising. But he remained quiet, cold, and useless as a lump of brass.

Mind you, when you deal with a magical firearm that eats people, you learn not to let a lot of stuff bother you. But this did.

This was the first time I'd seen the Cacophony afraid.

"Ah, here it is."

Liette came back, taking several breaths to blow a considerable layer of dust off a rather flimsy-looking tome that looked bound together in straps of rawhide and wood.

"The hell is that?" I asked. "A how-to guide for flying poop?"

She squinted at me. "What? No. How would...what would the parameters of that even be and..." She waved a hand, promptly derailing whatever train of thought that had been. "No, this is a history book."

"That's too thin for a history book."

"I will take both your observation, and the fact that you have only ever read books that use the word *throbbing* liberally, into consideration." She hummed as she flipped through its crumbling pages. "On the histories of nations, customs, and kings, we are inundated with records. On the histories of what came *before* them, less so. But..." She tapped a page. "Here. Look."

I squinted at the page. There, in faded and withered ink, was an illustration of buildings. Though, only barely. Those parts that weren't in utter ruin were of indecipherable geometry and incoherent purpose. I didn't know their function, but I knew them.

You saw these ruins crop up across the Scar now and again: ancient sites found anywhere from rolling plains to hidden beneath caverns. Sometimes, people built freeholds around them. More often, they ended up destroyed by scavengers or bandits, or in battles between the Revolution and Imperium. Occasionally, they just... disappeared, vanishing overnight to appear somewhere else in another year, as though they'd always stood there.

Don't get me wrong, that was weird. But in the Scar, I don't have a lot of attention to spare for things that are *merely* weird and not actively trying to kill me. I'd seen these around before but never gave them any thought. Judging by the flimsiness of this text, I doubted anyone else did, either.

Except Liette, apparently.

"This is the work of a Freemaker, Cold Comfort for a Dying Widow," she said. "She dedicated her life to detailing the history of those who occupied the Scar before us. The fact that she could accumulate so little is a testament to the difficulty of the task. But she was able to date this ruin accurately."

Liette beamed at me the way she did whenever she was about to solve a puzzle. Or whenever she saw a dog. She fucking loves those things.

"This ruin goes back over five hundred thousand years. Do you see?" She gestured to the turd. "The entity is an Ancient!"

I glanced at the turd. "Is that what you call yourself?"

"There is no people that refer to themselves by such a pretension, but if it elicits joy from you to do such, I would not deny you such trivial pleasure."

I wondered, absently, if that book mentioned these Ancients being assholes.

"However, your information is accurate. That structure was wrought by our hand."

"Incredible," Liette whispered, breathless. "Who built it? Which one of you? How did you do it?"

"It does not matter."

"What? How could it not? We haven't even begun to guess the function of them!"

"It does not matter for the same reason their function does not matter. We wished it to be there, so it was. We wished it to serve us, so it did. We plucked it, whole and complete, from where it was and placed it where it needed to be."

"How...how is that possible? Through magic?"

"If it pleases you to think of it as such. We had no word for what we did. We simply did. We simply were." Eldest's eye narrowed. *"And when that was no longer enough, we simply were not."*

Liette wanted to ask more, I could tell by the way she was vibrating in her shoes. But in my experience, anyone annoying enough to speak in cryptic gibberish tended to tell you everything, whether you asked or not.

"When this world was young..."

See?

"We were not unlike you. We strove to collect knowledge, to understand the land we walked upon, the air we breathed, the stars we looked upon. We were concerned with such petty things back then, and our knowledge was in pursuit of that pettiness. We discovered ways to defy age, to free ourselves from hunger and desire, to cast out our weaknesses, in our quest to know everything. And one day...we simply did."

"Everything?" Liette whispered, wrinkling her nose. "That's impossible."

"Everything is impossible. Until it is not. For us, nothing was. And when nothing was, we saw no need to remain here. And we ascended."

"Ascended..." I squinted. "To where?"

"We have no name for where we went. It was unimportant to us. In time, we saw that it was not so far away from this world as we thought it was. As time went on, we realized it was painfully close. Soon, we could hear whispers without mouths, see visions of lives not our own."

"Ours," Liette whispered. "You saw us. Is your world that close to us?"

"Closer. When the time is correct, and when we are invited, we may even cross over."

My eyes widened. My voice died. My breath died in my throat.

One after another, the realizations came flooding into me on a cold-blooded river: the dread sensation that came with its voice, the emptiness in its stare, the terrible familiarity that came from looking at it. I knew this thing. I'd *fought* this thing. This thing had nearly killed me. *Twice.*

My hand shot out, seized Liette by the shoulder. She let out a cry as I hauled her back, putting myself between the jar and her. She shot me a furious scowl, but I could live with that. More than I could live with her getting torn apart by what this thing could do, anyway.

"Sal!" she snapped. "What are you doing?"

"Protecting you," I said. "Get out of here before it moves."

"This is unnecessary," Eldest said.

"I quite agree," Liette added. "What do you think—"

"I don't think *shit*," I snarled, whirling on her. "I *know* what that thing is." I leveled a finger at Eldest. "It's the smallest one I've ever seen, but I know a fucking Scrath when I see it."

I felt Liette wither behind me. I heard her breath run dry. I knew whatever objections to my reaction she might have been thinking of, they were gone now.

When it came to Scraths, there was no such thing as an overreaction.

We didn't know much about them, those things that came from somewhere else, that warped reality with every unnatural breath, that wore humans like clothing and discarded them just as fast.

Everything we *did* know came only by sifting through the body parts they left behind.

We knew they could be called to our world by a select few—fewer, now that I'd killed Vraki. We knew they could exist only by occupying a human host. We knew they couldn't be stopped, killed, contained, reasoned with, appealed to, bribed, seduced, or anything that didn't end up with them tearing apart everything they came across.

Now, I guess, we knew that they could do...whatever the fuck Eldest was doing.

"Is that true?" Liette whispered. "Eldest, are you a..."

Its eye quivered for a moment. *"Yes."*

"There, see?" I reached for the jar. "Once again, we could have saved ourselves valuable time and energy if you'd just let me smash the shit out of it to begin with. Open a window, would you?"

"And no," Eldest suddenly interjected. *"To your eyes, I would not be dissimilar. Yet there remains a difference between myself and that which has come before."*

That was a good point, I had to admit. *But* I was already excited to destroy this thing, so...

"Wait." Liette, like the adorable little pain in the ass she was, seized my arm to stop me. "What do you mean by that?"

"Your heart beats, pushes blood through your veins, propels you to motion. The process is the same in any beast. Yet you are not the same as a bird or a cat, are you?" If there were a way for an eyeball to look smug, Eldest would. *"The principle is the same. We share lineage, the Scraths and I. We are not siblings."*

"But if Scraths can only come here when called," Liette whispered, "then how did you get to be here?"

"Don't talk to it, Liette," I warned.

"Simple. I was cast out."

"What? By whom?"

"It doesn't *matter*, Liette," I growled.

"Family, you would call them. Compelled by envy. Or resentment. I do not know. And ages spent inside that prison—the Relic, you called it—have diminished my curiosity toward their motivations. I think of only one thing now."

"Incredible," Liette whispered, pushing closer. "How did you send yourself out of the Relic? Are there more of you inside other Relics? What is it you want?"

"*I...want...*"

Eldest's eye widened. I shouted her name. I pulled her back. The thing uttered a single word.

"*OUT.*"

Pain. Not dread. Not unease. Pain shot through me at its voice, lancing through my bones, my sinew...

My scars.

I clutched my chest, gasping for breath. Agony flooded my senses, painting my vision dark, my body numb, filling my ears with the sound of a ringing, wailing, *screeching* disharmony that shook me down to my skull. I couldn't think, I couldn't breathe, I couldn't hear...

"*Sal.*"

Except one voice.

"*No, no, no. Not like this.*"

Whispering. Urgent. Terrified.

"*I was so close.*"

And it made everything hurt less.

Just a little.

Feeling returned first, the sensation of her hands on my cheeks, and everything else followed the tips of her fingers. My hearing brought me back to the din of the airship. I felt the splintered deck under me—when had I fallen down? My vision returned.

She was standing over me.

"Are you all right?" she whispered. "It...it spoke and you just—"

"Yeah," I muttered, clambering to my feet with no small effort. "I did. Which is why we need to destroy it."

"I...I don't..." She looked from me, back to Eldest—to the Scrath—and doubt painted her features. "It's...so..."

"*Liette.*" I forced her name through my teeth. "It's a *Scrath.* You know what they do. You've *seen* what they do."

"I have," she replied, pointedly not meeting my gaze. "And I've never seen one speak before. Not like this."

"For fuck's sake," I almost whined. "You're too smart not to realize that an unnatural killing machine that talks pretty is still an unnatural killing machine. Get *rid* of it, Liette."

She closed her eyes. She swallowed something bitter. "I can't. Second law. It helped me. I can't turn my back on it."

"The fuck you can't. Just step aside and let me do it, then."

"I can't do that, either." When she could bear to look at me again, her eyes were pained. "Sal, whatever this thing is—Scrath or not—it can do things we thought impossible. It heals illnesses, it creates matter, it alters *time*. Think of all that we can do with that."

"I *am* thinking of that," I said. "I'm thinking of what illnesses it can cause, what matter it can destroy, how fucking insane it is to try to alter *time*. You could do amazing things with it, I don't doubt." I reached out and tapped her head. "Now think of all the terrible things it could do with *you*."

She slapped my hand away. "I am *always* thinking. I have considered everything and any eventuality that may come up will be dealt with in a manner befitting my—"

"Oh, listen to your fucking self. No matter how fucking smart you are, that thing is a *Scrath*. You can't reason with it. You can't outsmart it. You can't *use* it."

"Don't fucking tell *me* what I can't do," she snapped back, composure trembling out of her through her fists. "I am Twenty-Two Dead Roses in a Chipped Porcelain Vase. I brought down cities with a formula and killed barons with a sentence. If there is anything in this thing that can be used for any good and *anyone* in the world capable of using it, it's *me*. So if you can kindly remember that you're speaking to a fucking genius, it would be vastly appreciated."

"It's a *MONSTER*!" I screamed.

"SO ARE *YOU*!" she screamed back.

I recoiled. I stared. My mouth hung open.

I've been stabbed before. I've been shot. I've been strangled, punched, gored, bitten, burned, hurled, and broken before.

I would have rather gone through each and every one of those for every day I drew breath on this dark earth than hear her say that.

Shock painted her face. Pain was there, too. But there was no apology. There was no need for one. We both knew what I'd done to deserve that name. We both knew there was no taking it back.

"Sal," she whispered, "I..."

"Don't." I shook my head. "No more words."

That was more for me than for her. If I said anything else, if I even opened my mouth, well...

I wasn't going to have it said that Sal the Cacophony broke down crying.

It had been a mistake to follow her here. A mistake to look into those eyes of hers again. A mistake to think that this was anything other than what it had always been: a bunch of bodies for me to kill so we could steal something and use it to kill more people. I knew that now. Maybe I always had.

I pulled my scarf up around my face. I headed back toward the door. I ignored her eyes upon me, the words dangling on her lips as she searched for something to say, the perfect word to make this better. My hand lingered on the handle, like I was waiting for her to find it.

But she was the smartest person in the Scar. She knew fucking well no such word existed.

So I made ready to leave again. Maybe I'd find the nearest squadron of Revolutionary soldiers and start shooting and hope for the best. Or maybe I'd just head to the edge of the deck and hurl myself off. Either way, I'd be leaving her here.

Her, I thought as I glanced behind me, *and that fucking piece of...*

I paused.

In the jar, Eldest was staring at me. Staring...and smiling.

Through the mouth it had suddenly grown.

How had it grown that? Could it always? What made it do that? My mind flooded with questions, but once I looked at its eye and saw it darkened by that hungry void of a pupil, I realized the answer.

And that's exactly the moment the door exploded.

An eruption of sound and smoke. The sting of a severium charge assaulted my nostrils. Wood splintered and metal hinges went flying as the impact of a bullet punched through the door and caught me square in the belly.

Liette screamed as I went flying backward. My breath rushed out of me. My body was alive with pain. But it was still alive—I saw the sigils on my scarf glow brightly before fizzling out, the luckwritten enchantment on it having kept me alive through the blow.

I skidded along the floor. Through a cloud of severium smoke, a figure came rushing toward me. I jerked my sword free, reached out to thrust at my assailant. Another blade shot out quicker, though, batted mine aside and brought a hilt cracking against my jaw.

I fell to the floor. A boot came down upon my wrist. A blade came down to level its tip at my throat. A voice, jagged and sharp as a rough-hewn dagger, punched into my ears.

"Sal the Cacophony," a woman snarled. "In the name of the Great General and the Glorious Revolution of the Fist and Flame, I hereby sentence you to death."

I looked up into a pair of dark eyes looking just as pissed off as the day I'd first seen them. The day they sentenced me to death the first time.

"Tretta Stern," I said, coughing up blood. "Had I known you'd be here, I'd have brought flowers."

FORTY-THREE

THE IRON FLEET

Okay, so.

The initial attack on the airships did not go as planned. That's bad.

The Relic we've been chasing is actually some kind of cell for an otherworldly being capable of changing reality. That's really bad.

That otherworldly being is actually a creature of unimaginable horror and unstoppable power and it wants out. That's *extremely* bad.

I would forgive you for thinking that I was being just a touch short-sighted for thinking that running into ex-lovers all day long was probably the worst thing to happen to me that day.

"I've been waiting for months for the chance to kill you, Cacophony."

But I hope you could see where I was coming from.

Granted, Tretta Stern—the woman I was captured by, about to be executed by, then escaped from by setting fire to her city—wasn't exactly an ex. But she *was* currently tying me up. So, you know, close enough.

"Every moment I'm awake, every dream when I sleep, I see your face."

See?

She spoke sharply between the hissing of hemp as she secured my hands behind me. "All these months after my failure, the only thing that's kept me going is that image and the thought of putting a bullet through it."

It was kind of a shame that she was getting ready to kill me, because except for that last bit, that all sounded kind of sweet.

"Well, fuck, if you'd left me an address, I would have written you," I replied, testing my bonds. It turns out she'd had enough time to practice knot-tying in all those months of dreaming about killing me. "I kind of lost it after...well, you know."

A pair of forceful hands seized me by the shoulders, spun me about, slammed me against the wall of the airship's corridor. My breath left me in a rush of air, a forearm trapping what remained beneath my throat as she pressed it against my neck. Though I'd been getting a *lot* of people giving me hateful looks lately, Tretta Stern's was something special.

When I'd met her on that fateful day she was to execute me, she'd been a well-honed edge of a woman: poised, coiffed, not a hair out of place. Now, in the bowels of the airship, I recognized nothing but the anger in her eyes. Her black hair was longer, unkempt. The angles of her dark face were not so much polished as hewn, worn ragged by too many scowls and too few smiles. And her uniform, once proud and bearing the medals of a Governor-Militant's office, was now...

Shit.

It was a shit uniform.

"After you escaped," she said. "After I failed to stop you from killing and burning your way across the Scar. After I was demoted to serving on the lowest, meanest wreck in the Iron Fleet and babysitting counterrevolutionary Freemakers. After I lost *everything* because of you."

With her arm pressing down on my throat, the last remnants of my breath failing, I had just enough air left in me to speak once, to make her see reason.

"Reeks...to...be...you..."

Why do you do these things, Sal?

"I should kill you." Cold flooded into my body as the pressure on my throat tightened, my last gasps of air feeling like icicles in my lungs. "For everyone you killed after you fled, for everyone I failed to protect, for everybody who weeps when they hear your name."

Usually there's a "but I won't" after speeches like these, but she sure was taking her time.

When she did finally relent and remove her arm from my throat, I didn't have enough left in me to keep upright. I collapsed to my knees, then to my side, gasping for air. I had taken about two breaths before her boot came down upon my chest.

"In all those months, Sal," she whispered, cold and harsh as the metal under me, "what kept me awake most was wondering if you ever even wondered about what you'd done. Did you think about the towns you burned down? The people you'd killed?"

Yeah.

I did.

On the mornings when my scars ached for no reason and I couldn't figure out a reason to get back up, I thought about them. Some days were worse than others—sometimes I could shake it off, sometimes the thoughts were so heavy that it took everything in me just to breathe. And each and every day, I wasn't really sure what made me get back up—maybe the list, maybe the gun, maybe...

Maybe someone else.

Fuck if I was going to tell her any of that, though.

"What did you figure out?" I asked.

She stared at me for a moment. "I figured out," she replied tersely, "that it's foolish to ask a fire why it burns. You simply extinguish it." Her boot came off my chest, her hand settling pointedly upon the hilt of a thick blade strapped to her belt. "Were it not for one thing, I would do exactly that."

I would have asked "Because I'm so pretty?" but I didn't feel like getting the shit kicked out of me three times in one day. Just know that I *could* have said something clever.

"Had you just wandered into a township or a freehold, I'd kill you on the spot and think nothing of it," she said. "But you're on the Iron Fleet. The pride of the Revolution. You had something planned. You had to know we were coming. You had to have found a way onto the ships. Until I find out how, I won't kill you."

"Aw, Tretta," I said, "has the relief of command made you more sentimental?"

She kicked me in the ribs as soon as I said that, so I guess not.

"I won't kill you." She seized my arm as I rolled, groaning, onto my belly. "By blade, by blood, by boot, I'll draw every answer out of you. Willing or unwilling, your last act on this dark earth will be to help people." She hauled me to my feet, leaned so close I could feel her spittle sizzle on my cheek. "Only once I am convinced I have stopped you, Sal the Cacophony, will I permit you the privilege of being called to the black table."

I bit down the agony that lanced through me with each heartbeat. I forced iron into my eyes and held my lips tight. That groan would be the last word I gave her.

In the innumerable experiences I'd had being attacked by both, you can be either a single-minded person or a clever person, but not both. And if the *numerous* beatings she'd just given me weren't enough of a hint, Tretta was the former.

She hadn't said anything about Jero and the others.

She hadn't said anything about Liette.

And, most importantly, she hadn't said anything about the other-worldly horror in a jar.

She doesn't know, I told myself. *She doesn't know or she'd still be talking.*

Which meant I wasn't going to tell her anything, either. Whether Eldest was telling the truth or if it really was just another Scrath, it had a power like nothing anyone had seen. That power was something that shouldn't be in the hands of a bunch of fanatics with a lot of guns.

If the only other person who knew about Eldest was Liette...

Better me than her, then.

"Sergeant!"

A small squadron of Revolutionary soldiers came tromping down the corridor, gunpikes in hand. They skidded to a halt, fired off hasty salutes toward Tretta before launching into breathless speech.

"We searched the ship, as per orders," the one in the lead, a young man with a face that several fists had loved intimately, said. "We found evidence of a skirmish, but no other intruders."

No other intruders? How could that be? Jero might have been that stealthy, but Agne and the twins sure as shit weren't.

"No intruders, soldier?" Tretta asked. "Or no *sign* of intruders?"

The soldiers exchanged nervous glances before a middle-aged woman stepped forward. "We *did* find square outlines drawn with chalk in the storage room, Sergeant. Nothing I'd have called unusual, but—"

"But if you were smarter, you'd know what a Doormage's magic looks like," Tretta hummed. "There were intruders. And if they aren't here now, they'll be back soon." She glanced to the man. "Raise communication with the rest of the Fleet. Tell them we've been breached and need reinforcements." She looked toward me, spite welling in her eyes. "And send for an interrogator. I have a prisoner who knows something."

The young man snapped a salute before scurrying off. The others stood at attention as Tretta swept a gaze back over them.

"The rest of you, get back to the storage room," she said. "I want eyes on that chalk at all times. The minute something steps through that portal, shoot it."

"To kill, Sergeant?" the woman asked.

"Kill, capture, decapitate it, and throw it overboard if you have to," Tretta spoke, her voice hard as iron. "We are not losing one more soldier to this menace." She offered a salute. "Ten thousand years."

"Ten thousand years!" the soldiers barked back before hurrying off to see to her orders.

This was not good.

I know that's not exactly news, coming from someone leaking as many vital fluids as I was, but I didn't think anyone would hold that against me. Considering the whole, you know, "everything going to shit" aspect of the situation.

I had exactly as high an opinion of a Revolutionary's perceptive ability as a brainwashed fanatic would warrant, but even *they* could have found Jero or the twins or at least Agne. There wasn't a lot of room to maneuver on a ship. If there was no sign of *any* of them, that meant they'd gone.

Which meant that I was on an airship teeming with people who very much wanted me dead, captured by said death-craving people, with a Scrath capable of changing reality just waiting to be let loose in the middle of it. Alone.

My heart pounded. My breath went short. Panic tightened around my neck closer than any rope could. I had to think of something, some way to escape, some way to get off this ship, some way to get

Liette out of here before the curtain rose on whatever fiery, screaming shit-opera this situation was about to become.

But I couldn't think. It was all…too much. Too much blood
lost, too many enemies against me, too many friends leaving me. I
couldn't see a way out, couldn't think of a plan, couldn't even come
up with something fucking witty to say.

As Tretta sank her fingers into my arm and started bodily hauling
me down the corridor, I supposed it didn't matter.

What with me about to be tortured and killed, anyway.

⁘

"Being captured isn't so bad," an old Vagrant—Verrim the Dirk, I
think it was once? Or Dirk the Vigil? Something stupid like that—
once told me. "They can bind your hands, they can gag you, they
can gouge out your eyes. But they can never cage your wits, they can
never tie down your instincts. So long as you have those, there's not a
prison out there worth the metal it's made of."

They were good, sturdy words. Words you could lean on in hard
times, words you could fashion into a shovel to dig your way out of
any pit. All the times I'd been stupid, drunk, or unlucky enough to
fall into someone else's hands, I remembered them.

Except this time.

This time, all I could remember was how that guy had been executed, like, two days after he told me them. Beheading. It was a
fucking mess. They shot his skull out of a cannon afterward.

As the cell door slammed shut, its iron echo smothered by the
claustrophobic confines of the brig, I was starting to think that
maybe sometimes, no matter what fancy aphorisms you had in your
back pocket, you were just fucked.

Or at least I was.

Tretta went about securing the cell in silence, twisting the lock
shut before moving to secure my weapons, pointedly holding the
Cacophony by just two fingers as she lowered him into a pack. I
caught a spiteful glare from his brass eyes before she shoved him,
along with my blade, into the satchel.

No weapons. No tools. Nothing I could do to keep her from carrying out my execution, to save Liette.

Calm down, I told myself. *You've escaped worse… Wait, have you?*

Not important. Think. I narrowed my eyes upon Tretta as she hoisted the pack. *She's got a short temper. Get her talking. Get her attention.*

"Hey," I said, "handsome?"

Oh, for fuck's sake.

"Don't," Tretta snapped without looking at me. "No lies, no insults, no clever wordplay. Face your death with some semblance of dignity." She spared a fleeting glance. "Or does Sal the Cacophony not know how?"

"Sal the Cacophony," I replied tersely, "does not face death. Death can't bear to look."

Fuck me, that's good. Why do you only come up with these things when you're about to die?

"Precisely the sort of pointless rhetoric I've come to expect from you," she replied. "It was too much to hope you'd spare the memory of your victims such pointless posturing. Only for their sake do I keep the Revolutionary fury in check, else you'd join them in—"

"Oh, fuck off with that."

No one's ever truly in control of themselves, no matter what they like to say. And the ones who appear the hardest have the biggest weakness. All you have to do is find it and give it a good jab.

Once Tretta turned on me, all that cold, professional composure came sloughing off like so much ash and mud.

"I know it's been months, Tretta, but did you really forget I'm not an imbecile?" I asked, pressing against the bars. "You really expect me to believe you're doing this all for victims? For people you never knew and never cared about until I came along and humiliated you?"

Her lips pursed, her eyes narrowed. "The Revolution protects all," she replied, mechanical. "The downtrodden, the oppressed, all who languish beneath the heel of decadence, of corruption, of—"

"Woman, your Revolution has killed more than I ever had even in the most ridiculous stories they tell about me." I leaned on the bars of the cell door, my arms dangling over the bars—lazily, cockily, just until she got into range. "You didn't give a shit about them, just like you don't give a shit about whoever you think I've killed. When you think of me, you don't see them. You see yourself."

She wasn't moving. She wasn't talking. She wasn't leaving, either. I licked my lips, leaned closer. All I had to do was get her close enough.

"You see yourself getting bashed in the face when I freed myself," I whispered, low enough to make her come closer to hear me. "You see yourself, chained up and used as a human shield, when I got out of your shitty little jail and escaped your shitty little town. You see yourself, Tretta Stern, so devoted and so dutiful, outwitted, outmaneuvered, out*matched* by the petty Vagrant you scorned."

Her face twisted with restrained anger. Good. She took a step toward me. Better.

"Go ahead and tell yourself it's for the victims," I said, my grin long and lazy and begging to be punched. "Or for the Revolution. Or for whatever lie you make up. It won't change what happened. I'll still have outwitted you. You'll still have lost me." I leaned so close as to offer her a free shot. "I'll still do it again and again."

Her body shook beneath her coat.

Yes.

Her hand drifted toward the sword at her hip.

Come on.

Her grip tightened on its hilt.

Hurry the fuck up already.

"You're right."

Wait, what?

Her grip relaxed. Her head sank beneath a heavy sigh. "You're right," she said. "I do crave vengeance. For the humiliation. For everything you did. For everything you *could* have done because my life was in your hands." She looked up at me—neither cold, nor warm, nor anything but hurt. "You shamed me. My rank. My cadre. I would give anything to see you dead for that."

"Yeah?" I chuckled, taunting. "You haven't got what it takes."

"I don't."

For fuck's sake, what's it going to take?

"But I don't have to." She stiffened, folded her hands behind her back, regarded me coolly. "In another hour, every interrogator we have will be here with every instrument they need to tear you apart. You will tell us what we want to know and then you will die."

She turned on her heel, picked up the pack, started walking out the door. I slammed the bars, snarling at her.

"Yeah? And it won't be you who did it!" I shouted, desperation creeping into my voice. "You'll be a bystander, a witness to your own failure, *again*! Everyone will know that Tretta Stern couldn't kill Sal the Cacophony even when she had her locked up in a cell for the *second* time!"

"No one will know." She paused, looked over her shoulder. "We will burn your body and throw your ashes out on the wind. With every year they twist in the wind, people will remember you less and less until you're a bad dream. With time, you will fade."

"But you won't have gotten the honor! The pleasure! You won't—Hey! HEY!"

I had been so close. I could have just grabbed her, used her, figured some way out of here. But the problem with having all these clever taunts is that they don't do much good against a door swinging shut.

I screamed a variety of very clever, and very graphic, curses at her as she disappeared out of the brig. I banged on the bars, I kicked the walls—she didn't come back and my anger didn't go away. So, with no other targets, I turned and, snarling, kicked the bucket sitting in the corner of the cell.

I promptly received a half-gallon reason why that had been a bad idea.

I was angry enough to kill, angry enough to cry, but neither would help. The fact that I would die on a day I'd been covered in shit twice was less alarming than the fact that Tretta was right.

I'd die here. I'd die affecting nothing, saving no one, for no reason. People would forget me. They already had. I don't mean the slack-jawed dopes who plow earth and each other like it's their job. I mean...

Liette hadn't forgiven me.

She wanted a world without me.

She was going to build it.

And that hurt. It hurt worse than shit. Than wounds. Than anything.

"Were you going to try to strangle her?"

Almost anything.

I suppose whatever cruel whimsy that pens the opera of fate *would* see fit to grace me with one last insult. And she was standing, weary and broken, in the doorway.

"Darrishana," I muttered.

"I go by Darrish now," she replied. "Darrish the Flint." She frowned. "But you knew that, didn't you? I'm on your list."

I sniffed. "Liette told you about it."

"I had heard about it. There are stories. But...yes. She told me. Many times."

I don't know why I asked. I don't know why I wanted to hurt more. But I did.

"You and she," I said. "Have you..."

A cold glance, the ghost of a frown. "And if we did?"

I couldn't respond to that. She was right. It wouldn't be any of my business.

"But...no." Curt. And a little sad. "We...tried, one night." She winced, unable to look at me. "We started talking and we shared your name and..."

"All right, all right." I sighed, skulked to the lone bench decorating my cell, and flopped down. "Shit's bad enough with you telling me my name kills the mood dead."

"I didn't say *dead*," Darrish replied. "Bleeding, certainly."

"You're not funny."

"I didn't come here to be funny."

"Yeah? Well, you didn't come here for me to break your teeth in, either, or you'd be standing closer. So, if you're not here for either of those, you'll have to wait until I can scrape this shit back into this bucket so I can hurl it on—"

"I came to tell you I'm sorry, Sal."

She stood, feet planted on the ground, hands clutched into fists at her sides. Her mouth was contorted and trembling like she was about to carve a bullet six days old out of her. I didn't know what pain ran through her, what memory the Lady Merchant wouldn't let her forget. But I knew she was looking straight at me, unflinching.

And there was only pain in her eyes.

"For?" I asked.

Her eyes sank a little, along with her frown. "I...don't know."

"You came all the way down here to say *that*?" I placed a hand to my chest in shock. "Well, gracious me, all is forgiven, then. Don't I feel fucking silly for holding a grudge over you leaving me to die on the floor?"

She winced. "I deserve that."

"You deserve worse."

"That too." She closed her eyes, pursed her lips. "All these years, all this time, I haven't been able to think about anything else. I've spent days of my life trying to think what I could have done, what I might have—"

"Fuck's sake, do you think that makes it *better*?"

I stormed off the bench, seized the bars, like if I just got angry enough I could bend them and get at her. But contrary to whatever stories you've heard, anger isn't enough. With steel, with flame, it's something terrible and great.

By itself, anger is just something you do when you've run out of tears.

"What did you think? Did you think this was some bad opera? That I just needed an elaborate enough apology? That you could sing a pretty song about how bad you feel and I'd forgive you?"

She said nothing. In her silence, the rattle of metal echoed as I slammed my fist against the bars.

"DID YOU?"

"No!" she shouted back. "I didn't think that! I didn't... I wasn't thinking about that... about..."

"About what?" I roared back at her. "About what you took from me? About *this*?" I gestured to the scar running down my body. "It was my magic, Darrishana. It was a part of me. And you just stood back and watched them do it. You didn't say a word. You couldn't even look me in the eye."

Just like she couldn't now. Just like how she hugged herself the way she did when she wanted to disappear. Just like how I used to think that was adorable, how I lived to see her happy. And how all it did now was make some part of me wish I had a sword.

"It was mine," I growled again. "And you took it from me. You took the sky from me. I was Red Cloud and you took that from me. Why, Darrish?" Silence. I smashed the bars again. "WHY?"

"BECAUSE I WAS TERRIFIED OF YOU!"

Now she looked at me. Now with tears. Now with legs shaking so bad she had to lean on the wall and with a face that looked like she would rather I have just punched her.

"Of you," she whispered, "of Red Cloud. I watched you fly into the sky, I watched you burn people, and when you came back down, I recognized you a little less. I didn't know when you would come down one day and Salazanca would be gone and there would just be Red Cloud. I guess I thought...when Vraki said he could take your power...I thought...I..."

Behind money, war, and sex, the world is built on lies. We need them—the little ones we tell to get out of duty, the big ones we tell to get people to do what we want, the cold and cruel little ones we tell ourselves to keep going. Lies are like liquor—even the bad ones still make you feel good.

Until they don't.

The truth is worse. The truth is harder, messier, uglier. No matter how good it may be, no one's ever happy to hear it.

This was easier when I thought she was a villain, easier when I thought she didn't care, easier when I thought I could cross her name off and be done with it.

This...

"How long did you spend thinking of that?"

This was worse.

"How long did you tell yourself that those words would make things better?" I snarled. "It was *my* power, Darrish. *MINE*. I don't care how bad it scared you, *it wasn't yours to take!*"

"I know. I always knew. I just..." She slumped to the floor. "I didn't know how to make it right, Sal." She stared out into nothingness for a long time. "I went Vagrant because I...I mean, I didn't know what else to do. Then when I found out about the Relic, when I knew what it could do, I thought maybe—"

"That I'd forgive you? Because you found a flying piece of shit in a box?"

"Honestly, I thought they'd just shoot me on the spot."

I paused. *That*, I hadn't expected.

"The Revolution, the *nuls*, looking for help from mages? From Vagrants? I thought it would be a trap. Honestly...I didn't care. When it turned out not to be, when I met Liette, when she told me about the world she could create..."

I slumped back down onto the bench, the fight draining out of me along with the blood. Liette's words came flooding back to me, built themselves into a cold stone monument on my shoulders that bent my neck so low I felt like my head would fall off.

"Her world without me," I whispered.

"You heard, then," Darrish replied quietly.

"She told you?"

"Often. Does the thought scare you?"

"I don't get scared."

"Yes, that's something someone who is scared says often."

"Well, fuck, how would *you* feel if someone like *that* told you that someone like *you* didn't belong in her world?"

She stared at her feet. "Relieved."

She really had a talent for making me want to punch her in the face. I wonder where she picked that up.

"Do you enjoy this life, Sal?" she asked. "Being a Vagrant? All the fighting, all the killing, all the…" She gestured vaguely at nothing. "*This?*"

"I'm good at it."

"That's not what I asked. That's not what Liette said, either." She pursed her lips, stared so hard at the floor she looked like she was waiting for it to open up and swallow her. "Liette wants to make a world where you don't have to kill. Where you don't have to hurt. Where you don't have to be Sal the Cacophony or Red Cloud or…" She sighed, looked at me. "You could be whoever else. Anyone else. With her. Without her. Wherever. She wanted that. For you."

Something sour lodged itself in my craw. "Then why didn't she say that?"

"Because she's pig-headed, stubborn, and so prideful a lion would envy her, obviously." Darrish sniffed. "One of the many reasons we didn't…well, you know." She blanched. "Also, she gets really excited about…stuff that comes out of other stuff. Like, *really* excited. It's weird."

"Fuck you," I grunted. "It's adorable when she does that."

She smiled at me. Like she used to. I remembered a time when it didn't hurt so bad to see her face again.

"I guess that's why I stayed here with her," she said. "I wanted to see that world. I wanted to make things better. I wanted..." She shook her head. "Fuck. I wanted to do something good for you."

"I wouldn't have forgiven you."

"I know."

"It wouldn't have changed anything."

"I know."

"You'd still be who you are. I'd still be who I am."

"For fuck's sake, I *know*," she snapped. "I have spent *years* knowing. I know and I don't care and I still want to do it."

"Why?"

A frown deep as a scar. A pair of eyes, too sorrowful to look up. Gone, as she turned on her heel.

"You and she were meant for each other," she muttered as she walked toward the door.

Like I said, truths never make anyone feel good. It's not like opera. There's no great moment of revelation when the heavens open up and bestow an immutable law upon a society grateful they don't have to think about it and come to their own decisions anymore.

If you're lucky, you just go on lying until you can get far enough away from them when they come collapsing down. But more often, you get this. No resolution. No satisfaction. Just a realization that some scars are too deep for the truth to heal and nothing really changes.

If you're smart, you'll just accept that and make peace with it. It's not something that'll make you happy. But it's something that'll let you rest.

"Darrish."

You should know by now that people like me don't get to do the smart thing, the happy thing, *or* the thing that lets them rest.

She stopped as I called out to her, an ear up, attentive.

"I'm not going to forgive you," I said.

"Sal, I fucking get it," she replied. "If you wanted to rub my face in that fact, you could have at least used fancier words this time."

"Let me finish," I snapped. "I'm not going to forgive you...but I need a favor."

She paused. "I can't let you out."

"You could, if I asked real nice, but that's not what I wanted."

She turned. The hurt was still there, but there was just enough curiosity in her eyes to make me lean out from between the bars.

Maybe Liette was right. I was a killer, a destroyer, an outlaw—and maybe she could make a world where people like me wouldn't exist. But it wasn't going to happen with that Scrath. I knew that.

In my scars, I knew it.

"Look." I sighed. "What happened with us, nothing's going to make right. But I believe you want to try. If you still do after this shitshow, then do me a favor."

She didn't say yes. But she didn't leave or spit in my face, either.

In this business, we call that a win.

"Stop her," I said. "Convince her to find another way, destroy her research, kill the fucking thing in the box if you have to, but don't let it get out."

"Sal, Liette's certain that—"

"I know she's certain. She's too fucking smart *not* to be certain. And fuck, maybe she *can* control that thing, but not forever and not before it starts controlling the Revolution. You need to stop her from letting that thing out." I licked my lips—when did they get so dry? "Please."

Even as I spoke, I could feel my scars aching, that sensation of something reaching into me, crawling around inside me. Like just speaking of the Scrath was enough to draw its attention. And the longer it lingered there, slithering through my veins, the more I recognized it.

The same feeling that I had when I looked upon the effigy in Terassus.

The same feeling that I had when I'd fought one in the dark.

The same feeling that I had on the night I lost everything…

I couldn't let that happen again. Not to her.

"*Darrish!*" I slammed the bars.

"I'll try!" she blurted. "I'll try, Sal. But…what are you going to do?"

"Don't worry about me." I rubbed my neck, looked around my cell. "I'll figure out something."

"How?"

"If I knew that, I wouldn't have said 'I'll figure out something,' would I?" I waved a hand. "Sometimes, it's all about waiting for the right opportunity."

Darrish's face screwed up in irate bewilderment. "You're hinging your entire plan on *that*? Like some shitty opera? Like the third act from *Speaker for the Ghosts*?"

"Fuck you, I loved *Ghosts*."

"It was trite and full of clichés. Opportunity does not just show up like that and—"

The door burst open. On a trail of blood, clutching her side, Tretta Stern—wounded, breathless, and wearing a face wild with desperation—limped in. I folded my arms and shot the smuggest smile I could manage at Darrish.

"Now," I said, "admit that *Ghosts* was good."

"Sergeant!" Darrish, ignoring my excellent line like an asshole, rushed to Tretta's side to support her. "What's going on?"

"Intruders...," Tretta gasped, collapsing to one knee. "Ambushed me..."

"It wouldn't have happened if you had bothered to look behind you, Commander."

Slowly, a knife dangling from his hand, blood trailing in his wake, he came out of the gloom of the corridor. And though I thought I'd seen all his faces before—the laughing one, the loving one, the wounded one—I only barely recognized this man who came into the brig. His eyes were clear and calm, his tone cool and even, and his face was expressionless behind the mask of blood that painted it.

His voice I knew, even drained of passion and humor as it was now.

As he walked into the brig, the pack with my weapons slung over his shoulder, I knew him.

"But a fanatic can't look anywhere but where they're told, can they?" Jero said, each word a knife wound. "You didn't, Commander. You didn't look back when you were ordered to retreat. You didn't look back when my brother hurled himself into the fray." He flicked Tretta's blood off his blade. "You didn't look back for his corpse."

"Erstwhile," Tretta spat, pulling herself up to her feet and reaching for her own weapon. "Deserter. Counterrevolutionary. *Traitor.*"

"And still alive," Jero replied. "While Jandi isn't. Do you even remember his name, Captain?"

"I remember the Staunch brothers," Tretta replied, anger in her voice. "I remember one being the bravest Revolutionary I ever had the privilege to command, one who gave his life for his cause, his comrades, his cadre. And I remember you, Erstwhile. You're not fit to share his name. The Great General knew that when he took it back."

"And you're not fit to speak it," Jero snarled. "It doesn't matter. Your whole farce of a Revolution is about to answer for his death. For every death."

"Jero?" I whispered from behind the bars.

"I'm sorry I'm late, Sal," he replied, smiling sadly. "I had some business to attend to outside the ship."

"Sal?" Darrish looked at me, eyes wild with terror. "You know this man?"

Needless to say, three people under the same roof who've either loved you, tried to kill you, or both, made for an incredibly awkward situation. So awkward, in fact, that I would have given anything for something to change the—

An explosion. A quaking deck beneath my feet. A distant avian screech followed by the blare of warning sirens.

"ALL HANDS, ALL HANDS! REPORT TO BATTLE STATIONS IMMEDIATELY! IMPERIAL ATTACK! IMPERIAL ATTACK!"

Yeah, that'd do.

FORTY-FOUR

THE IRON FLEET

It's true that the battles between the Revolution and the Impe-rium have ravaged the Scar, put millions out of their homes, and resulted in some of the most widespread destruction known to humanity, but there were a few upsides of their battles.

For one, they made an excellent cover for illicit activities—such as escaping from a cell.

There were other advantages, too, but I couldn't really take the time to list them since I was about to die and all.

"There they are! Open fire!"

The rattle of the decks beneath my boots was sharply punctu-ated by the crack of gunpikes. Sparks erupted in a halo around me as severium bullets shrieked past, biting into the pipes and hull of the corridor. I pulled my luckscarf over my head as a shot whistled past and took a chunk out of the hull—a stray shot, I'd survive, but given the generosity with which the Revolutionaries pursuing us were handing out bullets, I didn't like my chances.

"All hands to decks! All hands to decks! Glory to the Great General! Glory to the Revolution!"

The sirens continued to blare, mechanical voices echoing off each other as commands were barked and soldiers raced to follow them. In the noise and fury, I'd lost Darrish and Tretta both. And my search for either of them was abruptly cut short by the—

"DIE, IMPERIAL SCUM!"

Yeah.

A Revolutionary came barreling out from behind a corner, leaving me just barely enough time to pull my sword up as the head of his gunpike came crashing down. I caught the serrated blade against my weapon, but he had weight, momentum, and years of fanatical propaganda on his side. His blow brought me to my knees, the second knocked my sword away, the third would cut clean through me.

Or it would have if Jero hadn't cut him first.

He leapt out of the shadows behind me, catching the gunpike's haft in one hand and swinging around to get inside the Revolutionary's reach, where his weapon would be of no avail. In his other hand, a knife leapt out of a hidden sheath before Jero buried it in the soldier's neck.

Three quick, mechanical pumps of the blade—throat, kidney, lung—and the fanaticism, along with the rest of him, bled out of the soldier and onto the floor. He collapsed, his final moments of bewildered agony frozen on his face.

"All right?" Jero asked, breathless as he reached down to me.

"Not fucking all right," I replied as he hauled me up. "Where the hell have you been?"

"Busy."

"With *what*?"

Through the din of the sirens, I heard the click of triggers. Gunpike shots rang out as Jero seized my hand and led me down the twisting corridors of the airship. Turn after turn, he jerked me into the shadows before we came across an alcove ensconced in a twisting mass of rattling pipes. He pulled me in, pressed a finger to his lips, and waited.

The boots came not long after. A gang of Revolutionaries came rushing past, sparing us not even a glance as they thundered by. Jero waited until the sound of their boots had faded before turning toward me with a shit-eating grin.

"Not bad, eh?" he said. "No one else knows about this spot. I used to come here to smoke on patrols when—"

He didn't finish that sentence, as it turns out it's pretty hard to speak with a mouthful of fist.

"Where the fuck did you go?" I snarled as he reeled from my punch. "I was almost killed and you left me! *AGAIN!*"

"Is it at all possible for you to make a point without violence?" Jero muttered, rubbing his jaw.

"It is exactly as possible as you doing something without making people want to inflict violence upon you." I gave him a coarse shove. "You said there wouldn't be more lies! You said you were going to handle something on the ship!"

"And I did!" he snapped back. "I went into the armory and the engine room...and I handled it." He spat on the floor. "The sigils needed to be applied, remember? The twins and I were leaping from ship to ship to handle it. And...a few other things that needed taking care of."

I narrowed my eyes. "What did you do?"

He met my stare, unblinking. "I took care of them."

In those eyes—those laughing eyes I first met, those sorrowful eyes that told me his secrets, those deep eyes I stared into and let hold me in the night—I saw it. Older and deeper and clinging to him with hungry, hateful intensity, a wound carved so deep it hadn't even begun to heal, all these years and corpses later.

The same thing she'd seen in mine.

The lies, the things he hadn't told me, they were all a part of the same wound, ragged edges of skin over which the blood bubbled. His pain, the same as mine, kept him doing them. Just as mine kept me killing.

Was this all we gave to each other?

Was this all we *could* give?

"Fall back, you fools! FALL BACK!"

A call rang out. The corridor shook with the rumble of twenty boots. Then ten. Then six. By the time a Revolutionary turned the corner, the sound of a frenzied retreat had been whittled down to a ragged, limping pair of boots.

Bleeding, gasping, dragging her gunpike behind her, a single Revolutionary soldier hauled herself down the corridor. She'd made it to our hiding spot when something came hurtling through the air behind her—or rather, someone.

Someone wearing the same coat as her. And screaming.

The soldier's shriek faded into nothingness as he was hurled through the air like a toy from a frustrated child's hands, clipping his comrade in the shoulder and sending her collapsing to the ground. She managed to pull herself to her ass, taking her gunpike in hands and thrusting it, trembling, down the hall.

"S-stay back!" she shouted. "By the Great General, I shall not be—"

Unless the end of that sentence was going to be something other than *smashed worse than a teenager at a wine tasting party,* she was sorely mistaken.

I heard the Lady's song, a note clear and painful in my ears. I heard her cry as the gunpike was torn from the soldier's hands, tossed into nothing by some spectral force. Then I heard the bone-deep echo of a body smashed against a wall.

Her scream was cut off as her body flew straight upward and was pinned against the ceiling. A figure, tall and lean and draped in the ostentatious violet-and-bronze armor of an Imperial mage, walked into view, his hand extended in a gesture that bordered on flippant. Through an emotionless bronze mask, he glanced up at his victim, crushed against the ceiling by his magic.

"T-ten . . . ," she gasped, her mouth filling with blood, "ten thousand years."

He let out a tired, tinny sigh. "Typical."

He made another gesture. She was hurled down onto the floor, leaving an ugly smear of blood across the deck. He gestured to his right. His magic dashed her against the wall, bones snapping as they smashed against the pipes. He flicked a pair of fingers. What had once been a soldier was now nothing more than a piece of trash, tossed aside to lie in a rotting, fetid pile.

I fucking hated mages.

But I *really* fucking hated Graspmages.

"Was that propaganda I heard?" Another mage, a woman in similar armor and flicking electric sparks from her fingertips, came down to join him. "No begging for mercy?"

"A nul is nothing more than a parrot that learned how to hold a weapon," the Graspmage replied, voice dripping with contempt. "They regurgitate whatever word they're taught."

"Barbarians," the Sparkmage muttered behind her mask. "They're fighting like savages above. Whatever they've got on these mechanical horrors, their master desperately wants."

"Then we must be quick." The Graspmage turned a hollow-eyed stare down the corridor. "Whatever research they have on their Relic is on this ship. The Empress wants everything, down to the last scrap."

My blood froze. My breath with it.

How did they know about the Relic? About the research? How did they even know how to find the ships?

"Ah, the research," the Sparkmage said. "You really think someone has been doing it for them?"

"Have you ever known a nul capable of writing down anything more than propaganda?" The Graspmage beckoned his companion as he set off down the hall. "If I'm wrong, oh well."

"And if there is an associate?" the Sparkmage asked, following.

"Our orders were to kill all nuls," he said. "Let's not disappoint the Empress, shall we?"

Liette.

The other fears in my head fell silent against that word.

Liette.

The other thoughts followed. Everything in me—every pain and ache, every worry and doubt—disappeared, drowning beneath the name that kept appearing in my head.

Liette.

They would find her. They would hurt her. They would kill her.

"*Unless...*"

A word. Hissing. Burning. Seething.

The Cacophony whispered from his sheath, his grip burning as my hand brushed against his hilt. As soon as I wrapped my fingers around him, even her name left my head. And all I had left...

"*We stop them.*"

Was him.

He leapt into my hand. As soon as he did, I felt it. That burning brass, seeping into my veins and searing away all the cold and pain. It whispered to me on a tongue of fire, a voice of ember and ash that spoke sweet lies and simple truths. It told me not to worry about the collateral destruction, about the fear with which people would look at me, about anything else.

But the people who needed to die and where to find them.

Later, I'd be ashamed to admit it, but right then?

It felt good.

"Hey! *Hey!*" Jero's hand shot out to stop me as I slid out of the alcove. "The hell are you doing?"

I didn't answer him. Sal the Cacophony didn't need to tell someone why it was a bad idea to get in her way.

"The Imperials will keep them tangled up in combat for hours," he hissed urgently. "Their strongest forces will be away from the Relic. We aren't going to get a better chance than this."

I jerked my hand free from his grip. I could have told him that we didn't understand dick about the Relic. I could have told him that whatever was inside it was something I didn't want *anyone* getting their hands on, including Two Lonely Old Men. I could have...

But we were broken people, him and I. No matter how badly either of us wanted that not to be true. And though ours might have been similar, our hurts were still our own. His made him lie. And mine made me leave.

That didn't make us even.

But it was close enough.

I shot him a look. I pushed my way out of the alcove. A hand clasped down on my shoulder. Firm. Insistent.

"You walk away from this, you walk away from *everything*," Jero warned. "Your revenge, a better world, anything Two Lonely Old Men promised you and everything the villains of this world deserve." He drew in a sharp breath, gave my shoulder a tug. "Now if you *really* want to throw all of that away, you just—"

I don't think the end of that sentence was "*smash me in the face with the hilt of a gun.*"

But I did it, anyway.

Bone cracked. Blood spattered. He fell back, screaming, as he clutched a pulped mess that had once been a very pretty forehead. I liked to *think* he got the message. But I didn't have time to make sure.

That voice was still whispering to me.

"Pity," the Cacophony hissed. *"I liked him."*

I only barely heard him. My ears were full of the sound of my boots on the deck as I rushed toward Liette's room. My thoughts were on the shells in my satchel as I fished them out, one by one, and slid them into his chamber.

Discordance. Loud. Angry. Hateful.

"But I suppose we all outgrow our toys, don't we?" he chuckled. *"And work does come before play."*

Another shell. *Hoarfrost.* Frigid. Vengeful. Agony.

"Can you hear their songs? Through the sirens and screams? There must be hundreds of them. Their spells sing. They ring out so beautifully, child."

The final shell. *Hellfire.* I wasn't going to leave them anything to bury.

"Do you ever stop and wonder how many of them know who we are?"

I slammed his chamber shut.

"Do you ever wonder..."

I tightened my grip on his burning hilt.

"How many of them wake up in the dead of night..."

I rounded a corner.

"Screaming our name?"

And hell came with me.

I heard their song before I saw them. The Sparkmage stood beside Liette's door, her arms folded, toe tapping impatiently for a chance to release her power. The Graspmage stood in front of it, his hands flexing, the air shimmering as the door resisted his attempts to pull it off its hinges.

"This is taking *forever*," the Sparkmage sighed.

"Don't blame me," the Graspmage grunted. "This thing is spell-written. Whoever's in there is using some..."

Maybe it was the sound of the hammer clicking. Or maybe it was the cold fear that alights upon the back of a man's neck when someone wants to kill him that made him look up. Or maybe I just smelled bad.

But he looked up at me. And through the hollow sockets of his mask, I saw eyes widen.

"Holy shit," he whispered, "is that the fucking Caco—"

I pulled the trigger.

The hammer clicked.

And Discordance flew.

The Sparkmage's cry mingled with the Lady's song. Her hands flew out, lightning arcing from her fingertips to lash at the shell. A frightened reflex maybe, or maybe that trick worked on regular bullets.

Against an exploding one, it worked about as well as you'd expect.

With a wail, Discordance erupted into a wall of sound pushing outward. Timbers snapped. Pipes burst. The two mages were flung in opposite directions, him hurled against the nearby staircase, her flung screaming into the shadows of the corridor.

I spared a moment to make sure Liette's door hadn't been blown away in the burst. Which turns out is a mistake when you're fighting a Graspmage.

A screeching note. A rush of wind. A great hunk of wood and jagged metal came flying toward me, caroming off the walls as it barreled down the corridor. I narrowly darted to the side, splinters falling across me like snow as the mass of timber and iron flew past me.

The Graspmage hovered off the ground, his mask broken and revealing a furious grimace beneath. He extended his hands and I could feel the pull of his magic as he tried to pull me into the air. I rolled out of the reach of his magic—the art of the Graspmage wasn't the most accurate, hence why most of them tended to focus on inanimate objects. Such as the giant mass of wood and metal he was pulling toward me to smash into my back. I couldn't give him that chance.

I raised the Cacophony. Fired. Hoarfrost wailed out, speeding toward him. I grit my teeth, waited for the explosion of frost.

It never came.

The shell stopped in midair, quivering as frigid vapor struggled to break free of the telekinetic magic that had seized it.

"Who the fuck do you think you're dealing with?" the Graspmage snarled.

He swept another hand out. Wood and metal peeled themselves off the walls and floors, bending and snapping and re-forming into a cocoon of debris around the shell.

"You come to me with tricks? With *toys*? Who the *fuck* do you think you're dealing with?"

It fell to the ground and shuddered as the shell burst harmlessly inside it, cold mist seeping impotently out.

"In the name of the Empress, for the virtue of the Imperium," he said, raising his hands. The Lady's song rose, mournful and agonizing. "It will be my *distinct* pleasure to tear you apart, Cacophony."

"Oh, see? He has heard of us," my gun whispered. *"Isn't that nice?"*

He raised his hands. There was a deep, suffering baritone as the hull trembled. Wood groaned. Metal screamed. Nails popped out of their sockets and screws burst from their pipes. The corridor was rent asunder as fragments were torn free in a creaking agonized noise, bones torn from a dying behemoth's carcass.

Which, in another second, came hurtling right toward me in a maelstrom of shards.

And I sprinted into the heart of it.

There are only two rules to keep in mind when fighting a Graspmage.

First of all, don't stand still. If they can't keep a bead on you, they can't reach out and crush your ribs with telekinetic force. Hence why I went rushing toward him, even as massive chunks of wood and metal flew toward me.

Splinters painted my face. Sparks showered me. The fragments of the ship's hull flew past my head, beneath my feet as I leapt over them, bounced and shrieked off the walls as each chunk of debris failed to find its mark. My sword slid into my hand as I drew nearer, my eyes locked on the expanse of his throat left bare by his broken mask.

The second rule of fighting a Graspmage: get close. They might have the power to lift boulders with their minds, but it turns out that boulders are incredibly unwieldy and inefficient weapons. Get in tight with them and they're defenseless.

Just like this fucker was as I leapt over a streaking tangle of pipes, raised my sword high, aimed for his throat, and thrust. It was a heroic leap, an expert strike.

I bet it would have looked really good, too, if he hadn't brought up a sword to block it.

He saw the confusion on my face. It left him chuckling.

"You've been gone too long, Vagrant." He shoved me away with a sudden burst of strength, sliding seamlessly into a dueling posture. "Too long fighting drunkards and bandits. Have you forgotten what an Imperial's swordswork looks like?"

Whether or not I had, I was reminded of it all the same in a flash of crimson and a whisper of steel as he thrust, his blade biting through my sloppy parry and drawing a gash across my cheek.

The blow caught me off guard and he was quick to capitalize on the opportunity. He launched into a flurry of blows, thrusting low, slashing high, batting away every feeble counterattack I managed to retaliate with. My breath gave out quickly, my feet even quicker—I was weary, beaten, bloodied, while he was fresh, strong, and had a lot of fucking magic at his disposal.

His blade flew from his hand, held aloft by a phantom force as the Lady's song rose in my ears. He waved a pair of fingers this way and that, a conductor of an opera of steel, directing his blade to continue the assault even as he backed away.

Clever fuck—he was putting range between us. Every time I tried to dart past his blade, his magic put it back in my way. With each strike, his blade herded me farther back, away from the rubble, away from the walls...

Away, I realized with a cold shock, *from any cover.*

That's when I remembered.

There were two of them.

The Lady's song rang out behind me. I heard the telltale crackle of electricity, felt the fine hairs rise on my back. The Sparkmage. She'd recovered. Her partner wasn't driving me back. He was giving her a clear shot.

In addition to swordsmanship and how to be an insufferable anus, the Imperium trains mages to work together, their powers synergizing to take down the Empress's enemies more efficiently. And that training had allowed them to conquer the world, annihilate their enemies, and, more pertinently, find a way to tear an electric hole in my spine.

But there were a few things the Imperium couldn't prepare their soldiers for. A few incredibly unpredictable and amazingly stupid things.

One of which I was about to do.

I bowed low, rushing forward. The Graspmage cursed, waved his fingers—his blade followed, caught my shoulder, drew a gout of blood. When I didn't retreat, his cursing grew louder. When I rushed past him, his anger turned to confusion. And when I spun, caught his shoulder, and shoved him rudely away, his only response was a befuddled look.

He didn't catch on until he heard the lightning crack.

The Sparkmage's electric blast exploded out of the corridor, too powerful for her to call it back. The Graspmage screamed a warning at her, waving a hand and pulling up a piece of rubble to hold in front of him as a crude shield. Her lightning sparked off the fragments of wood and metal, casting the corridor in a blinding azure light.

Which meant neither of them saw me raise my gun, pull the hammer back, and whisper:

"Eres va atali."

I pulled the trigger. Hellfire erupted. The blue light was swallowed whole in a pair of red, laughing jaws as the gun's magic exploded in a chorus of fiery delight. Blazing tongues lashed out, devouring rubble, wood, metal.

Flesh.

The Graspmage screamed, flailing wildly as the flames consumed his uniform. He swung his arms erratically, his magic casting flaming debris haphazardly as he struggled futilely to put out the flames. But Hellfire was tenacious. And flesh was flammable. And the Cacophony was no magic he'd ever seen.

He collapsed into a smoldering pile of embers, revealing the Sparkmage standing behind. Electricity still sparking off her fingers, her eyes wide behind her mask, she stared down at her partner's burning carcass.

"No," she whispered, her voice shuddering behind her mask. "NO! You dare...you *dare* defy the Empress?" She turned her gaze up, vengeful and brimming with hatred. "I swear to all Scions that you shall pay for—"

She didn't finish that sentence.

Turns out it's hard to talk with a sword in your neck.

I pulled my blade free. Blood bubbled out of her throat. She pawed futilely at the hole I'd carved in her, reaching out to strangle me with bloodied, trembling hands, even as she slumped to her knees and then fell, unmoving.

I took in a breath of ash and dying embers. I looked around the blackened, shredded corridor. Cold wind blew in through the holes carved in the hull, through which the sounds of battle could be heard. My body ached at the prospect of more violence beyond, begging me to lie down and just . . . stop.

I won't lie, the idea was tempting. I might have given in, too.

"Holy shit."

But I had bigger problems.

I looked up. Liette stood in her doorway, the magical sigils dissipating as she broke the seal. She took in the carnage, the fire, the distant sounds of pain and fury, and looked at me.

I snorted. Spat blood on the floor.

"Hey," I said. "We, uh . . . we should probably go."

FORTY-FIVE

THE IRON FLEET

If your priorities are straight, you've seen a fair share of art. And if you've been anywhere in the Scar, you've seen a war painting.

In the Imperium, they're living portraits, woven by magic and paint to portray heroic Imperial legions subduing nul interlopers with flashes of magic and sound. In Revolution territory, they're miles-long murals wrought by a thousand artists depicting, in grueling agony, the struggle against Imperial oppressors. Even the freeholds have their own paintings depicting someone—usually someone rich—bravely beating back monsters or bandits.

No one loves war more than someone who doesn't have to fight it, after all. But they find the collateral—you know, all the blood— rather inconvenient. So they pay the artists to make their paintings, to make themselves feel grand, to dazzle the peasants, but most importantly, to trick themselves into believing their own lie that war is some grand adventure.

Once you see it for yourself, though, you'll never be able to look at those paintings again.

Maybe he was a father, or someone's lover, or just some poor dope who was promised a better life in the Revolution. But the young man lying at my feet as I stepped out into the cold wind on the deck wasn't even human anymore. His eyes were twisted into some amalgamation of rage and horror, forever frozen in the moment he realized everything he had been told was a lie.

A coarse match for the hole carved into his chest.

Smeared blood painted the deck from where he'd dragged himself to the gangway in a feeble attempt to escape belowdecks, a red road that twisted its way across the deck and led to more carnage. The corpses, mages and Revolutionaries alike, were strewn across the deck like discarded favors from a rich man's party. Each of them stared up at the gray sky passing overhead. Each of them wore the same face as this poor bastard.

Above it all, the sirens blared, beckoning soldiers to battle. Though, if you'd looked out upon the gray skies that day, stained with fire and smoke, you'd swear it was a dirge.

Only the people it was eulogizing didn't know it was for them.

Soldiers thundered across a deck thrice as large as any ship I'd ever seen, and bled upon the deck, and died upon the deck. Revolutionaries stood in tight packs, pointing massive crossbows at the sky and squeezing off shots as their comrades rushed around with bundles of bolts in their arms to replenish their comrades' ammunition. Flashes of magical lightning and flame erupted across the deck, mingling with the miniature explosions of severium charges as Revolutionaries with gunpikes struggled to fight off Imperial boarders who, in turn, struggled to massacre their comrades.

The eruption of flame and smoke, the wail of sirens, the macabre symphony of steel punching through flesh, all coagulated into a noisome miasma of sound. And yet, through all the din of suffering, the song of the Lady Merchant rang out in one clear, sustained note, rising higher with each body that fell broken to the deck.

It was no work of art that anyone had ever seen. No glorious painting, no amazing story. It was a bland, bitter joke told by some insatiable god, who simply kept repeating it over and over for his own amusement.

"How?"

I recognized that quavering tone in Liette's voice as she stared out over the carnage from the safety of the gangway. It was the sound of certainty shattered, of a learned person staring out over something deliberately senseless and struggling to make sense of it.

And failing.

"How did they find us?" she whispered, stepping out onto the deck. "Our plans were so precise, we were so careful." She clenched her teeth. "We were so *close*! They can't get in the way! They can't ruin this like—"

She tried to rush out. I caught her by the shoulder, pulled her back into the gangway. She made a noise like she was about to protest. I held up a finger for silence, pointed it to the sky.

And on shrieking wings, hell came.

A shadow appeared across the deck, a black ink stain that blossomed to the size of a carriage in the span of an instant. It swept over a squadron of shooters, who turned their crossbows and terrified eyes skyward, launching bolts and panicked screams into the sky.

You always see their talons first: four black daggers punching through the clouds to snatch a hapless bastard. Then you see the wings, huge ivory feathers stained with red flecks. By the time you hear the screech, it's too late.

Like it was for those fucks on the deck.

The Tamkai, huge and spear-beaked and bearing an Imperial rider, crashed into the pack of shooters and snatched them off the deck. The remainder either scattered or futilely tried to squeeze off panicked shots as the giant bird took flight again, disappearing into the clouds with their comrades. A moment later, their meager defense turned into screaming retreat as the bird dropped their comrades.

In ten different pieces.

"Tamkai," I muttered. I spied their dark silhouettes diving and gliding through the clouds, striking at the decks of the other airships. "Fighting Shrikes. They came prepared."

"But how?" Liette asked. "How did they know? No one knew!"

No one except me, I thought. *And the people who told me.*

I cringed as another soldier was carried off by Tamkai claws. "I mean, I can always ask them," I muttered. "Or we can get the fuck out of here." I scanned the railing. "These things have escape vessels, don't they?"

"I . . ." Liette found her composure in a sharp breath. "Yes. They do. Each airship has a skyskiff."

"Great, let's get one."

"We can't."

She pointed toward the railing and a pair of pulleys designed to hold a smaller vessel. A smaller vessel that was, fittingly, not presently there. Someone had already made off with the skyskiff and our chance of escape.

"Lovely," I sighed.

"There are more on the flagship," Liette said. "At least six."

"Unless those have already been taken, too."

"They haven't," Liette said. "The flagship's crew was hand-selected by the Great General for their loyalty and their absolute willingness to go down with a ship." She adjusted her glasses. "In any event, there aren't any other ways off this ship that don't involve us dying horribly in a fiery wreck."

I peered out the gangway. The flagship hovered ominously in the sky, impassive and unbothered by the attacks swirling around it, explosions from its cannon lighting up the sky as it fended off boarders. That was our way out.

And all that stood between us was miles of open sky filled to the brim with gigantic murderbirds.

So, you know, not *great*, but...

"Neat." I sniffed. "Well, if you've got any better ideas than 'sit here and wait to die,' I'm all ears."

"Let me think." Liette rubbed her temples, hummed. "We're still aloft and in formation, which means the captain is still alive. The Imperium haven't breached the helm." She pointed across the blood-soaked deck to the helm's cabin. "But we could."

"You know how to land this thing?"

She glared at me. "It's a colossal ship given the impossible power of flight by incomprehensible technology. Of *course* I can land it." She adjusted her glasses. "But we're over the mountains. I couldn't land without everything, you know, *exploding*. I could pull us closer to the flagship, though."

"Good enough," I grunted. I flipped the Cacophony open, slammed a shell into his chamber. "If we don't draw attention to ourselves, we should be able to make it. Stay low, stay close, and we just might..."

Warmth. Pressure. Familiar as an old scar. I glanced down and saw five tiny fingers wrapped around my hand. I looked back at her. She looked back at me in a way I had sorely missed.

Maybe I was a monster in her eyes. Maybe there would be another world, one day, without people like me. And maybe that would be a better world.

But I still walked this dark earth and I still watered it with the lives of hundreds. If I was going to be a monster...I could be the one that protected her from bigger monsters, at least.

We nodded at each other. We sprinted out onto the deck. Severium charges exploded in the air around us. Crossbow bolts whizzed past us, were answered by flashes of lightning and bodies hurled through the sky by magical force. We held on to each other, her grip in one hand, the gun in the other. The helm's cabin loomed large before us.

You can do this, I told myself. *You're going to make it.*

I won't have it said that Sal the Cacophony was a liar, even to herself. But if someone said that Sal the Cacophony was inattentive, I couldn't rightly argue.

Considering I didn't see the man with the giant crossbow until he fired.

The Dragonkiller bow launched with a whirr of a motor. A harpoon-sized bolt plunged into the deck in front of us. I jerked hard on Liette's hand, leaping behind a slain Tonkai for cover as another bolt punched into its carcass.

I peered over its corpse. A trio of Dragonkillers—two of them reloading their massive weapons as the third kept hers trained on me—stood atop the cabin. How the fuck hadn't I noticed them?

"It's fine," I muttered to myself. "Dragonkillers are made for shooting down birds, not people. They're too inaccurate to pin us down." I tensed, readying myself to run as I peered over the bird. "On my signal, make for—"

"No!"

Liette's shriek was accompanied by the whine of metal cutting through the sky. She jerked me down to the deck just in time to spare my face a harpoon-sized piercing. The bolt whizzed past, two inches from my head, to impale the deck beside me. I glanced, horrified, from it to her.

"They shouldn't be able to do that," I said.

"They couldn't." Liette offered a smile so sheepish I wanted to shear her lips off. "Until I, uh, recalibrated them."

"You *what*?"

"They were inefficient!" she protested. "And I had some free time! What was I supposed to do? *Not* fix them?"

"Yes, you dumb fuck, that's *exactly* what you should have done." I peered back around the dead bird, wincing. The Dragonkillers were reloading. Even if I stayed put, they'd shred my carcass cover eventually. "Fuck. Fuck, fuck, *fuck*."

"*No matter,*" the Cacophony hissed inside my head. "*The most glorious weapon in the hands of a primate is no better than a very fancy stick. Unleash me upon them.*"

"You'll damage the helm," I muttered, trying not to let Liette overhear me talking to my gun. "We need it."

"*I promise to leave enough of it to operate.*" He paused, contemplative. "*I promise to try to—*"

"No," I snarled.

"*Do you have any better ideas?*"

I didn't, no. But there had to be a better way of doing this than just pulling the trigger and hoping for the best.

Then again, that strategy seemed to work out for me most of the time.

Sort of.

"All right." I took him in both hands, stilled my breath. "One shot. Then we run. Got it?"

"Got it," Liette said.

"*Oh, let's,*" the Cacophony hissed.

I came up, hammer drawn back, expecting to be greeted by a hail of harpoons. But none came. In fact, not one of them was so much as looking in my direction. The shooters' weapons were empty, their mouths agape, and their eyes were fixed upon the great shadow falling over them.

They screamed frenzied instructions at each other, cursed the slowness of their weapons' motorized winches as they reloaded, shouted as they aimed the massive crossbows skyward and unleashed a trio of harpoons...

...and then ducked as all three of them bounced off something inside the clouds and fell back to the deck.

I said before that Dragonkillers were wildly misnamed, but until that moment, I didn't know just *how* wildly. Because, as it turns out, while a Dragonkiller can split a bird in half, against an actual dragon?

"HOLY SHIT!"

It does dick-all, apparently.

A glimmer of obsidian scales flecked with amethyst. The beat of feathered wings. A great roar and a lash of a long, spiked tail. That was all any of us saw before the three Dragonkillers, as well as the entire fucking helm, collapsed beneath six tons of angry, red-eyed reptile.

"A dragon..." I uttered the word with the same reverence with which one utters the name of a god. Made sense, since they're both giant fucking things from the sky that can kill you if the mood strikes them. "They brought a fucking dragon."

Depending on who taught you your Imperial history, the painfully rare Imperial Dragons were either a gift to the First Empress after she conquered the territory from which they came or a creature sent by the Lady Merchant to indicate her favor for the Imperium. Their exact numbers: an Imperial secret. Where they come from: also an Imperial secret. But their purpose was well known, from the highest Imperial noble to the lowest nul.

The Empress only sent a dragon when she didn't want someone dead.

She sent a dragon when she wanted them burned so thoroughly to ash and cooked fat and skin that she could make ink out of their corpses to pen a letter reading: *don't fuck with me.*

In a spray of gore and splinters, the mighty beast crashed down upon the helm's cabin and perched atop its ruin. A long, serpentine neck craned up, a crown of horns and ridges framing its eyes in sinister slits as it scowled across the deck. Toothy jaws craned open, a sac beneath inflating as it drew in a deep breath and—

Oh, fuck.

"RUN!"

I seized Liette by the hand and tore off at a sprint, all but dragging her behind me as we made for the gangway. The deck plunged into chaos. The Imperial boarders rushed to the railings, leaping off into the howling void and trusting their birds to catch them. The few remaining Revolutionaries degenerated into a screaming mess. I bashed, kicked, cursed my way through them as I shoved Liette into the gangway, leapt atop her, and drew her up in both arms as I pulled my scarf around us both and shut my eyes.

But I couldn't shut my ears to the screams.

The roar of fire erupting from the beast's gullet was powerful as it raked across the deck, but not so powerful that it could drown out the agony of those incinerated by its powerful breath. I could feel the heat licking against my back, the scarf's enchantment only barely keeping us safe. I don't know how long it lasted or when the sounds of their terror finally stopped, but when it did, I could hear only one voice.

"Glorious."

I looked over the deck, its vast sprawl awash in crackling flame and charred carcasses, as the dragon surveyed its gruesome work. Through the smoke, I could see figures clinging to the beast's scaly back via specialized harnesses. And atop its crown of horns, her white hair a stark contrast to the black blade she wielded naked in her hand, a pair of imperious purple eyes scowled down at me.

"CACOPHONY!" a familiar voice screamed, her fury carrying over even the dragon's.

You know, I had hoped to go at least a month before Velline came back to kill me.

But as shocking as it might sound, I had bigger problems than either the colossal, fire-breathing hellmonster that had plummeted out of the sky or the vicious, talented magical bitch with an admittedly very good reason to want to stab me to death.

Those fuckers had just destroyed the helm. Which we kind of needed to not crash.

So, you know. Things weren't going *great*.

A hand fell upon my shoulder.

Not Liette's.

I whirled around, Cacophony in hand. The eyes that stared down the barrel, wide with terror, were not hers, either. Nor was the surprisingly feminine scream that ensued as those eyes flinched away, hidden behind a pair of ink-stained fingers.

"Oh shit, oh shit, oh shit, don't shoot!" Urda shrieked, cringing away. "I swear, I thought you were right behind us!"

"Urda?" I lowered the weapon. Not because I had ruled out shooting him for abandoning me, but I'd at least wait until we were somewhere less cramped. "Where the fuck were you?"

"An *excellent* question." He peered between his fingers, mostly satisfied that I wasn't going to kill him. "One I would be happy to answer in exquisite detail if we weren't—"

The deck shifted violently beneath our feet as we started to plummet out of the sky.

"Yes, exactly," he said, gesturing down the stairs leading belowdecks. "Shall we?"

Not like we had any other options.

Our boots rattled the timbers as we rushed down the halls, the floors splintering and dipping beneath our feet. The wail of wind became a scream as the speed of the airship's descent picked up. Through the twisting corridors, we ran until we came to a crossroads.

That's when I realized Liette wasn't following me.

I turned. She was standing at an intersection of the corridor, staring down a hall. The hall that led back to her room.

"Liette!" I shouted. "Come on!"

"But..." Her voice was brimming with despair. "The sample. The jar. My *work*."

"You can't save it now! Come *on*!"

"But without it, I can't..." She stared at me, tears in her eyes. "I still need to fix..."

My hand shot out, took her by the wrist. I pulled her close.

"You can't fix me," I hissed. "But I can save you."

Whether I could or not was up for debate. So was whether it was polite to pick her up, throw her over my shoulder, and rush off in pursuit of Urda even as she screamed and begged me to turn back. Later, I'd apologize and maybe she'd forgive me and maybe she wouldn't.

She'd be alive to do it, at least.

"Fucking *finally*!" Yria's exasperated wheeze reached us as we rounded a corner and found the Doormage leaning against the wall, barely able to stand, though apparently still very capable of spitting. "You running a fucking sewing circle up there or some shit?"

"We don't really have time for—"

Urda didn't get to finish his point before the airship made it for him. The floor twisted violently beneath our feet, sending us sprawling to the floor as the ship went into a nosedive, the floor going vertical and sending us sliding, and screaming, toward the jagged mess of shredded pipes and timbers at the other end of the hall.

Urda screamed. Yria cursed. Liette wailed. I said nothing.

I pulled her close. I wrapped the scarf around us. I whispered something to her that I couldn't hear. Not over the sound of the Lady Merchant's song as a singular note rang out.

In the blink of an eye, a swirling portal of purple light gaped open between us and the pile of jagged rubble. We disappeared into it—hearing lost to her song, sight lost to the miasma of violet light engulfing us. Senses abandoned me. I could only be certain of touch.

Because, as we vanished into nothingness, she never let go of my hand.

FORTY-SIX

THE FLAGSHIP

I don't know if I told you, but I hate portal magic.

Walking through one always feels like shitting your guts out, flushing them down a toilet, and then hoping they fall together on the other side in roughly the correct order. Every time you come out of one with your anatomy intact is a cause for celebration.

Unless, of course, your anatomy has been shot, stabbed, beaten, thrown around, and otherwise abused.

Then you just come out feeling like a bird's dinner.

I emerged into the sweltering innards of a great beast. Severium-tinged steam hissed out in plumes, filling the darkness with an explosive odor. Metallic guts churned, pumping precious blood through a skeleton of wood and cloth. Every few seconds, the great creature would shudder, as if drawing a deep and ugly breath.

The claustrophobic darkness, the rattle and whirr of metal closing in, would make anyone feel a little terrified. I suspect the only reason I didn't was that I was in too much pain to feel anything else.

The adrenaline that had carried me this far ebbed out of me through innumerable cuts. The leather of my coat—what wasn't in tatters, anyway—was sticky and stifling with drying blood. My nose was full of the stink of my own wounds, my ears were ringing with the echo of the dragon's roar, my body found itself unable to move until my new wounds and my old scars finished arguing over which one of them hurt worse.

But I was still alive. Still alive and . . . and . . .

"Where am I?" I asked.

"An airship," a voice whispered back from the gloom.

"Another one?" I groaned.

"Aw, gee, I'm sorry, Baroness Bitchybritches," another voice growled back. "Between our imminent death by explosion and the entire plan going to shit, I forgot to consult with you where our life-saving portal went to. I hope you can for-fucking-give me."

Yria was alive. Oh, good.

"So, if you've got any other criticisms, you can kindly . . . kindly . . ."

Yria's breath ran short, her words started to slur. In the dark, I could hear Urda shuffle close to her.

"Yria," he whispered, "you used too much power, didn't you? You're numb again."

"Not in front of her," Yria hissed back in a tone that hadn't been meant for me.

Just as well, I was only half listening. Yria was fine. Urda was fine. That just left . . .

My hand shot out, slapping around in the dark, searching for her fingers and finding nothing but the wooden floor.

No.

I'd lost her. I'd lost her again. Yria had fucked up. I'd fucked up. Everything was—

"Hey."

Soft voice. Calloused fingers. Her hand found my shoulder, pulled me to my feet.

"You're alive," I whispered. I didn't mean to let that breath come out the way it did.

"So are you." Liette didn't mean for it to sound like a prayer.

"Hang on a second." Urda's voice was followed by the sound of leather rustling, something scratching against the wood. "Let me just . . . aha, here we go!"

A spark illuminated in the darkness. A soft green glow emanated from a small collection of sigils scrawled upon the walls. It grew brighter until it shone as bright as a torch, illuminating Urda's smile as he admired his own handiwork.

"Not bad, huh?" he asked. "It's an uncomplicated sigil, one that *should* be all right so long as I didn't wright it on any important parts of the ship." He paused, alarm spreading across his face. "Oh no, did I? I did, didn't I? Oh no, oh crap, oh no, we're all going to die, *WE'RE ALL GOING TO*—Oh wait, no, I just put it on the hull. Never mind, we're fine."

He might have said more, but I, like any rational human, stopped listening.

Instead, I turned my attentions to the bowels of the ship. Labyrinths of pipes intersected with the humming symphonies of cogs and gears, collided with the whirring blades and pumping pistons in a great tangle of guts that only the Revolutionary engineers who built them could have possibly understood. Even by the light of Urda's sigils, I couldn't see an end to them. The sprawl of the ship's mechanical guts seemed to go on forever, coiling into endless dark.

It was huge. Bigger than the hull of the airship we'd just been on—sorry, the airship we'd just destroyed—had been. Which could only mean...

"The flagship." I turned and looked at them. "We're in the flagship."

"Congratulations on winning the position of Mistress of the Fucking Obvious. I always believed in you." Yria's scowl was a mess of green light and ugly shadows as she limped forward—her leg must have gone numb from the power she'd spent. "Yeah, we're in the flagship. While you were off sucking face, we were setting up portals, no thanks to you."

I narrowed my eyes. "What do you mean 'no thanks to me'? *You* fuckers abandoned *me*."

"Aha, well, I can appreciate how it might *seem* like that," Urda replied, pointedly stepping in front of his sister. "However, if you'll recall, once we *obtained* our prize, there was the little matter of escaping the fleet of airships that would inevitably be after us. Hence, we took just a *little* more time in going from airship to airship, with the aid of my dear sister's power, to apply the—"

"Sigils."

Liette's voice was a whisper, but it came with such weight that Urda completely lost what he was talking about. Or maybe I had just stopped listening. Either way, we turned toward the sight of her shadow, slight as a wisp of smoke among the tangle of moving parts inside the ship.

She adjusted her glasses, standing up on her tiptoes to get a better look at something scrawled across a peculiar-looking whirring part. By the green glow, I could just barely see what she was looking at.

A Spellwright's sigils. Scrawled immaculately across the metal. And repeated, a thousand times, across the other parts.

"Expert work," she hummed, more to herself than anyone else. "Doubly so, considering the intricacy of the material." She glanced back toward us. "Yours, I assume?"

"Er, yes! Mine, as a matter of fact!" Urda bumbled his way forward to her side. "And thank you, you're so nice to notice!"

"Exquisite," Liette murmured, her eyes fixed on the sigils. "Near-flawless penmanship. Clean, efficient sigils. Barely an ounce of wasted power." She adjusted her glasses. "This pattern you're using... the Cillusian Line?"

"Ah, see, that's what I thought at first, too." Urda smiled sheepishly. "Er, that is, the penmanship is my work, but the pattern came at the specific client's request."

"Of course," Liette hummed. "Thick skulls are the second direst impediment to progress, thick purses the first. Pardon me a moment."

She produced a scrap of paper from her satchel, a quill from her hair, and hastily scrawled something across it. The writing glowed a second later and, two seconds later, burst into flame.

Urda gasped. Even Yria blinked, astonished. Not me, though. I knew she'd be insulted if I dared react to something as trivial as creating a perfect, self-contained flame out of nothing. Besides, she wasn't even looking at any of us.

"These aren't universal sigils," she said, studying the work by the light of her impromptu torch. "They're tailored. *Specifically* tailored for this ship, which I presume you'd never seen before. How on earth did you manage that?"

"Well, the *bulk* of the sigilwork was my own—the lines, the curvature, and so forth—*but*, I must confess, I had *some* help. The pattern came specifically requested, after thorough research of the airship's schematics—er, that is, *mostly* thorough, since we couldn't steal the whole thing—but our *employer* insisted and provided the remaining—"

"Fucking *cram* something in those greasy lips," Yria snarled, shoving her way toward her brother. "You wanna go telling every stranger we meet what we're doing here?"

"I was *just* explaining the intricacy of my craft to *someone* who can appreciate it," Urda replied, sneering.

"Individualized sigils. A prompt written specifically for one machine and one machine alone. Burdensome. Illogical. But impressive. Well done." Liette, ignoring their spat, shot a sparing glance toward Urda. "What's your name?"

"Oh! I'm, uh, Urda. Urda of the—"

"No, your *name*. What do the other Freemakers call you?"

He blushed, rubbing the back of his neck. "Oh, um, I'm no Freemaker. I work with my sister. My name really is just Urda. May I, er, have yours?"

"Twenty-Two Dead Roses in a Chipped Porcelain Vase," she replied, without sparing a beat or a look. "Charmed."

I don't know if you've ever seen the totality of a man drain out of him until nothing's left but a shocked expression and a faint urge to piss himself, but it's not a pretty sight. Usually, you see it when he's staring down the length of a sword about to go into him.

Unless you're Urda of the Wild Quill, I guess. Then you just do it at completely inappropriate times like this.

"Twenty...Twenty..." He struggled between finding words to express his astonishment and breath to keep upright and settled for something that didn't quite accomplish either. "Twenty-Two Dead Roses in a Chipped Porcelain Vase," he gasped. "You're Twenty-Two Dead Roses in a Chipped Porcelain Vase!" He turned, seized his sister by the arm, and shook her. "She's Twenty-Two Dead Roses in a Chipped Porcelain Vase!"

"I fucking heard her," Yria snapped, shoving him off. "Shit, if she knew you were gonna get this excited over fancy names, Mom would have given you a better one."

"I hope you'll forgive me but I am *such* an immense lover of your work." Urda didn't even seem to notice his sister's presence, much less her insult, as he turned back to gush toward Liette. "I mean, I bet you get that all the time, but I just... I mean, I got to see a *frag-ment* of your penmanship after the Immortal Vaults of Linchvin had been blown apart and I was just... *wow*. I mean, who would have thought of a sigil to convince the stone that it was actually grass and set fire to it? Who else but you, that is?"

You wouldn't have noticed it in the dim light, but the barest hint of a smile, valiantly hidden, creased her lips. That is, you wouldn't have noticed it unless you were one Vagrant who'd been with her before and was now currently rolling her eyes.

She fucking loved it when people did this.

"I assure you, that was a complicated task. But as you've so adroitly noted, every sigil is unique and once I was liberated from the tyranny of the pattern, it proved to be a less monumental effort," she replied. "Not that it *wasn't* monumental, of course. The Immortal Vaults are, in fact, not named thusly because they are *easy* to break into."

"No, of course not, obviously," Urda said, bobbing his head eagerly. "But... I mean, you made it *look* effortless. We—my sis-ter and I, that is—were halfway across the Scar and the news *still* reached us. We had to ride for six days straight to reach it so I could acquire a sigil left behind." He held out his hands. "Just having you, *the* Twenty-Two Dead Roses in a Chipped Porcelain Vase even *look* at my work is an honor beyond... beyond..."

"For fuck's sake, Urda," Yria sighed, "this is the worst possible time for you to erupt in your trousers."

"Would it *kill* you to guard your tongue *once*?"

"It'd be a fucking pleasure to die if it meant not having to listen to this!"

He whirled on her with a glare and a harsh word. She whirled on him with a sneer and *several* harsh words. The smallest fight in the world took place wherein she shook a numb limb at him and he limply flailed at her. A twin thing, I assumed. Or a sibling thing. Or a stupid-pair-of-dumbshits thing, I didn't know.

My eyes were on Liette.

Or rather, where she had been.

At her absence, I followed the sigils—as I knew she would do the same. The twisting patterns of shapes made my eyes hurt, each one glowing faintly as I passed to illuminate a language that only a handful of people could speak. They painted a path through the twisting pipes and machines that kept the airship flying, into the bowels of the ship. The darkness of the hold became illuminated by a soft, gentle glow, pulsating like a heartbeat.

That's where I found her.

And the Relic.

Sitting atop a pedestal, attached to apparatuses I couldn't begin to guess the function of, let alone name, like the heart of a beast I never wanted to meet. An object of stone and light and baffling geometry hung there, its radiant glow feeding into the apparatuses. A Relic Engine, a tiny version of the one we were after, pumped its power into the airship. This little lump of stone, barely the size of an over-fed housecat, carried this entire monstrosity.

Just think, I thought, how much a Relic as big as what we were after could power.

Liette peered around the pedestal. I could see Urda had been here, too, his lines so thick across the Relic's apparatus that I could barely see the metal beneath them. But Liette saw more. She always did.

The look she wore—eyes forward, barely blinking behind those huge glasses, brow smooth even though it should be furrowed, afraid to miss a single detail if her eyes so much as quivered—wasn't one I wanted to see on her face. I could recall only witnessing it three times, not including this: the first time I left her, the first time I came back, and the first time she realized those hadn't been accidents.

It killed me when I'd seen that look fixated on me. But now that I saw it as she scanned the lines of sigils, I was downright terrified.

That was the look she wore when she realized things were far, far worse than she thought.

"Problem?" I asked, pushing past the squabbling twins and coming up beside her.

"No, no problem," she replied curtly.

I pursed my lips. I waited.

"No problem beyond a mission impeccable in its discretion and paramount in its secrecy being so thoroughly and utterly compromised that a band of ragtag thieves *and* the Imperial army managed to find it."

There it was.

She bit her lip, contemplative as she looked down through the engine room, studying the sigils twisting across its myriad parts. "How the fuck did he manage to scribe so much?"

"He's got a talent for reproducing script," I replied. "But it's nothing to worry about."

The hull shook suddenly. A distant explosion, a chorus of screams, echoed from above. Liette shot me a glare.

"I didn't say *there* was nothing to worry about. I said *this* isn't anything to worry about," I shot back. "These sigils are just to stall the airships while we make our escape. A contingency."

"A contingency," she repeated. "You know that?"

"I do."

"Do these sigils look like contingency sigils to you?"

"I...don't...know?"

"Of course you fucking don't," she said, spiteful. "Because no matter the subject, no matter how much you *don't* know, you solve it by crashing in and firing your fucking gun off, and who gives a shit what happens or what gets ruined so long as you get what you're after, am I right?"

I let out a sigh so deep it hurt. "It's a pack of airships brimming with guns, bombs, and fanatic fucks eager to use both. Crashing in with my gun was *objectively* the correct action to take."

"Yes, it's working out *so* wonderfully, isn't it?" she sneered.

"Well, it fucking *was*," I snarled back. "And it fucking would have if you hadn't been here."

"Oh, so this is my fault now?"

"This? No. This is my fault. Delivering a Scrath—a fucking *Scrath*, Liette—to the Revolution? That is your fault. Whether I came here or not, that would have been a fucking stupid idea and you *know* it."

"I have a duty. A duty to seek knowledge, to understand the incomprehensible, and to—"

"BIRDSHIT!" I roared. "It's never been the duty. It's always been about doing what others can't, about *proving* only you can do it." I scowled at her, challenging. "Am I wrong, Liette? Did you really just come here for a better world?"

"I DON'T GIVE A SHIT ABOUT THE WORLD!" she shrieked back at me. "I came here for...for..."

"For what?"

Her lips quivered. Moisture welled up in her eyes.

"For what, Liette?" I pressed.

Her mouth fumbled for a word she didn't know, an explanation that didn't exist. A tear fell from her eye. She turned away.

Here we were again. Like we were the first time she told me to go. Like we were the last time I left.

Opera will have you believe that love lives and dies in dramatic moments, that two people find who they truly are in declarations of affection unending or in grand gestures and noble sacrifices. But that's a lie.

Love dies the same way everything dies.

Quietly. Softly. With no one bothering to try to save it.

I should have done something, I knew. I always knew. I just never knew *what*. Should I have reached out to her? Should I have apologized? It felt like every word I'd ever spoken to her had been hollowed out, left empty and meaningless. Maybe I could have thought of something better.

But fuck me, I hurt. I hurt so bad.

"For what it's worth," I muttered, turning away from her, "it wasn't about killing this time. We had a plan. Two Lonely Old Men and the others, we—"

I stopped. I stiffened. On my shoulder, I felt her. That light touch, those calloused fingers, the tiny warm spot that lingered whenever she touched me. She came back. She reached out. She...

"What did you say?"

She promptly spun me around, seized me by both shoulders, and stared at me with the dire intensity one usually reserves for wide-scale arson or small-scale warfare.

"What?" I asked, baffled. "About the killing? Is it so hard to believe that—"

"I didn't see it soon enough," she interrupted. "Two Lonely Old Men. You're working with Two Lonely Old Men? This was his plan?"

"Well, I *helped* but—"

She wasn't listening.

She whirled back on the sigils, adjusted her glasses, brought her tiny torch back up. "Now it makes sense," she muttered heatedly. "He specializes in Relic study. Of course I would have thought it was a Cillusian Line. He wanted it to look like a Cillusian Line. But with his penmanship, and these sigils..."

She squinted, her lips quietly moving as she carried on a dialogue with herself. But as she leaned closer, her eyes snapped open. She recoiled from the sigils, placing a hand over her mouth. Only then did my blood run cold.

The most terrifying sound in the world is someone with all the answers rendered speechless.

"They're not nullification sigils," she whispered, turning toward me. "They're meant to look like nullification sigils, but they're *not*. They're command sigils."

"Command...sigils?"

"These things won't stall anything. They're designed to compel the material to do something it's already capable of. Like...like commanding a door to open on its own or...or..." She shook her head. "Fuck me, only Two Lonely Old Men could do that. *Only* that fucker could—"

I drew in a sharp breath. "Are you sure?"

"It makes perfect sense," she said, shaking her head. "Urda said that the pattern was provided by your employer—Two Lonely Old Men. He disguised them so that they looked like nullification sigils. Urda wouldn't have noticed. *I* barely noticed."

I furrowed my brow, stared down the hall. "Command sigils," I muttered, "to do what?"

"I'm...I'm not sure. Two Lonely Old Men is the only one who knows how this works. His lines are too dense. I can't figure out what they're supposed to do, but..."

Her voice trailed off. Along with her gaze. My eyes followed hers as we both stared down into that long darkness of twisted metal. I reached down, picked up her torch, held it up as I took a step deeper into darkness.

They looked like ink stains at first: just little blobs of shadow squatting in the darkness. But every step brought more features. The sharp curve of metal. A weight at the bottom for a swift plummet. The Revolutionary slogans imprinted on their steel hides. And that smell...that reek I'd inhaled on every battlefield that any Revolutionary had ever walked.

Severium. Densely packed. Ready to blow.

Side by side, we stared down the hall.

A hundred bombs resting comfortably atop Urda's sigils stared back at us.

FORTY-SEVEN

THE FLAGSHIP

People fear what they don't understand.

It's an immutable fact in life that's been used for all manner of people to do all manner of horrible things to all manner of other people. To fear the unknown is to build a bridge in your mind and promptly burn it down. With one exception, it's always better to confront the unknown and understand it.

That exception, of course, being when a shit-ton of bombs are involved.

"We're leaving."

Liette started to say something in response to that, but between the sound of my voice echoing off the multitude of sigil-wrought metal, my boots tromping as I rushed back toward the rear of the ship, and the sound of my heart pounding in my ears, I didn't hear it.

Sigils of command.

They were fucking sigils of command. Painted a hundred times over on the hull, enough spellwrighting to make a city turn into sand with just an errant punctuation mark. A command to do what, precisely, I didn't know. And that thought chilled me, but not as bad as the thought that came next.

He played us. I struggled to keep it in my own head; I didn't have the strength to say it aloud. *That fucking Freemaker played us. All these fucking lies, all the things he never told me, it was all for this. He never wanted the Relic. He wanted these sigils, this airship, these bombs.*

For what? What's his plan? Why the fuck didn't I see it? Why the fuck did I listen to him? Why the fuck . . .

And so on.

They rattled around in my head like bullets, the thoughts colliding with each other in angry explosions. It made my head hurt as bad as the rest of me did, forced me to suck in breaths through my teeth as I tried to keep my eyes up, my neck straight, and my brain from erupting out my ears.

Whatever Two Lonely Old Men was planning, whatever his real goal was, I could deal with it once I got her clear of this airship-turned-deathtrap.

Her, I told myself. *Think about her. There will be time enough for regret once she's safe.*

Right.

Her.

If I could get nothing else out of this, I could get her out.

By the light of a green glow ahead of me, I could make out a tangle of snarling, sputtering, whining limbs that had once been the twins.

"How *dare* you embarrass me in front of my colleague!" Urda shouted, slapping angrily at his sister. "How *dare* you!"

Yria spat, slapping back. "You weren't gonna impress anyone because no one was gonna fucking listen to you go on about—*HEY*!"

If I were significantly more drunk and significantly less about-to-be-blown-apart, I would have found this amusing. As it was, I seized both of them by their collars and hauled them to their feet.

"We're leaving," I said. "Open a portal."

"Huh?" Yria squinted. "A portal to where? We already did the other airships."

A cold pang of fear twisted in my belly. The other airships—these sigils were on the other airships, too.

"Anywhere," I said. "To the nearest town, mountaintop, anywhere that isn't an airship about to explode."

"Far be it from me to point out the obvious," Urda meekly offered, "but it's clear from the sounds of battle overhead that the fighting hasn't breached the hull of this particular airship yet, so we are in no danger of—"

"Command sigils." I pulled Urda close, forced my stare into his. "You wrote command sigils. Not nullification sigils. Command sigils."

"W-what?" Urda stammered, immediately looking down at his satchel as I released him. "No, I didn't. I followed Two Lonely—"

"If you think you can impugn my brother's work with your fucking slanderous sass," Yria grunted as she pushed away from me, "you better be fucking ready to answer to Two Lonely Old Men and *both* of my—"

"It *was* Two Lonely Old Men," I shouted. "Don't you fuckers see? How did the Imperium know where to find us? How did *Jero* know what was going on when we didn't? The shit with Haven, the schematics, *all* of it came from Two Lonely Old Men. This wasn't about stealing a Relic, it was about putting those sigils in these airships!"

Yria opened her mouth to protest—or, more likely, to suggest something horrific about my parentage—but confusion dawned across her face. "I mean...there was some stink on him, but I thought he was just one of those eccentric geniuses. Also, all those Freemaker types are fucking shady, so I didn't think anything of it." She muttered toward Liette, "No offense."

"Of course."

"And he was paying, so..." Yria's face screwed up. "But why this whole plan if he just wanted some fancy scrawling on some bombs? There's gotta be an easier way than—"

"She's right."

Urda's voice came with morbid finality. He stood beside the sigils he'd scrawled upon the ship, a sheaf of papers in his hands. He glanced between them, checking them against one another, and each time, his face grew longer and paler.

"She's right." He started to breathe heavily, his hands trembling. "They're command sigils. I...I didn't know...I didn't even check. I just thought the ones he gave me were the ones...the ones..."

The papers fell to the floor. His knees followed. He clutched his head, as if he could tear out whatever terror was boiling inside his skull.

"No, no, no, *no, no, no,*" he gasped. "It was...it was me...I did it. I should have...I couldn't...I...I..."

"Easy." Yria was at his side in the blink of an eye, taking him by the shoulders. "Breathe deep." She squinted up at the sigils. "What are they commanding this thing to do, anyway?"

"I-I'm not sure," Urda said, struggling to get his breathing under control. "It's made for this airship, it's mechanical in nature, it..." He rubbed his temples. "Maybe I can figure it out if I can get a little more—"

"Unlikely," Liette chimed in, analyzing the nearby sigils. "Two Lonely Old Men is an incredibly accomplished Spellwright, and he layered the command sigils under the nullification sigils. I can't deduce what they're intended to do and I have extreme reservations about anyone else's ability to do so, either." She offered Urda a brief incline of her head. "No offense."

"Well, can't you fucking undo 'em?" Yria hummed. "Like...erase them or scribble on 'em or some shit?"

"What a fascinating way to illustrate you have no idea how this works." Liette shook her head. "The sigils are intricate, layered upon other sigils. I could undo them, but it would take days, and I guarantee you we don't have those."

Urda's frown deepened. "Then...what? Are we supposed to just...wait for them to activate?"

"Sure," I replied. "Let's do that about six or seven hundred miles somewhere else." I looked toward Yria. "Can you get us out of here?"

The twins shared a wary look before she rubbed her arm, deadened by her magic use. "Listen, I've got about one good jump left in me for four people, including me and my brother. Any more than that and...well, I'm not *too* sure what'd happen, but I'd bet it'd leave a stain."

The sigh that escaped me took the last pieces of me that didn't hurt with it.

Four people. All of this. All the killing, all the corpses, all the lies, and we were going to walk away with only four people.

Should have known.

My thoughts scratched at the back of my skull on long, rancid claws. The sound of them made my head feel like it was bleeding.

Should have known this would happen, I told myself. *Should have left after the manor burned down. Or after the first lie Jero told you.*

Fuck, you shouldn't even be here. What were you thinking, that a few extra names on your list was going to be worth all this?

A silence just long enough to be painful lingered in my head before the next thought came, an iron nail pounded directly into my skull.

Or were you really so stupid as to believe that any of this was going to make a better world?

Maybe I had.

Shit, maybe more than maybe. Maybe I had *wanted* it to be true. Maybe I had wanted to think I was doing more than just going down names on a list, more than just watering the ground with blood. Maybe I wanted to believe that I could have done something good here...

Something I could have shown Liette.

And showed her I...

Well, I thought with another sigh, *not much good that's going to do you now, is it? Shall we?*

Yeah.

Yeah, we should.

"All right, then," I said. "Fuck it. We have no choice. If you can take four, we've got four. Open a portal, let's get out of here, figure out our next move."

"What?" Urda gasped. "But...what about the others? What about Agne and Jero and—"

"Agne's a Siegemage," I replied. "If she's not already dead, she's found a way to survive. And Jero..." I clicked my tongue. "If he's not already dead, I'll have more work to do on the ground."

"That all sounds right-brained to me, I suppose. I ain't gonna stay around and die for them, either." Yria scratched the tattoos on her chin, glanced at me. "But, uh...you sure about this? Whoever you leave behind ain't coming back."

Darrish.

Her name.

Darrish.

Like a heartbeat. Over and over in my head.

What did she say? Was that sorrow in her eyes? Don't you want to talk to her? Don't you want to—

"I'm sure," I said. "We leave now or we die. So, everyone, just get close and we'll—"

"No."

In opera, there's a point called the *raicu yu onodoria*. Roughly translated, it means "veiled reason." It refers to the moment wherein a character, who has been hiding a deeper motive than they've claimed, reveals their true reason for being and the plot takes on a new and complicated twist.

In opera, it's one of my favorite parts.

In real life, turns out it's really fucking annoying.

"What the fuck do you mean, no?" I growled as I turned toward Liette.

She stood there, a slender slip of a woman in the darkness, hands curled into fists at her sides, eyes shining behind her glasses.

"I mean," she said sternly, "no, I'm not going to leave behind the most important research of my life."

"Liette, listen—"

"NO," she snapped. "You listen. This isn't some mechanical trinket or alchemic we're discussing. This is *change*. The creature on this ship defies reality. It *alters* things in ways we can barely *perceive*, let alone understand." She pointed out into the darkness, to some faraway thing only she could see. "The wars. The empires. The suffering. We could change it *all* with what's on this ship. With it, I could make crops grow bigger, I could end war, I could make it so that *no one...*"

Her voice trailed off. Her eyes fixed on mine in that way she does. Somewhere inside me, some dark place I struggled to hide from her but she always managed to see, she looked at something broken, something hurt, something that hadn't stopped bleeding since I'd stopped being Red Cloud.

And it hurt her in ways I'd kill to make them stop.

"I can fix things, Sal," she whispered. "Let me fix things."

Fuck me, when she gives me that look, I can't help but believe her. Almost always, anyway.

But I knew this war. I knew these stakes. I knew things she didn't. And I wasn't going to let any of them hurt her.

I sighed, stepped up to her.

"I know," I whispered. "I know, it's awful. And I know it won't be the same, but we can fix this. I can scavenge through the remains, I can find more of what you need, I can even live with you hating me for this."

I reached out. My fingers found her shoulders, glided up to her neck, felt the tangle of her hair fall over them.

"But I can't let you stay here."

She opened her mouth, thought better of it, sighed. She slowly bowed her head. She placed her hand on top of mine. And she whispered softly. "I know you can't," she said. "And because you can't..."

Her fingers tightened on my wrist. Before I even saw her move, her quill was out. She drew it hastily across my arm, painting a short series of sigils upon my skin. She shot me an apologetic look.

"I can't leave this behind."

I said something. It wasn't intended to be a scream, but as soon as she pressed her fingers to them and the sigils burst into glowing life, I didn't have a choice. An arc of electricity, crimson as blood, raced up my arm and across my body. In its wake, my muscles locked up, my body went rigid, my jaw clenched.

I toppled over, stunned still as a statue.

"I'm sorry." Liette turned to the twins and made a deep bow. "There's a cache of wealth under a dead tree just outside a township called Vert's Fear, two days south of Terassus. It's yours, for your trouble, just please"—she shot me a pained frown—"take her with you."

Then she was gone. Racing off into the darkness. To face every last soldier out there if it meant preserving knowledge.

It was hard to hate her for that.

Or it would be, anyway, if the little shit hadn't just paralyzed me.

"Did you see that?" Urda came stumbling forward, hands over his mouth in awe. "Did you *see* that? The deftness of her lines! The speed of her application! I didn't even *know* you could put a nullification sigil on human flesh and have the subject live through it. But that's Twenty-Two Dead Roses in a Chipped Porcelain Vase for you, isn't it? I should have gotten her autograph. Do you think there's still time? Do you think she remembers my name or—"

"Hold on a second there." Yria's face hovered into view. "*Is* she still alive? Blink twice if you're still alive."

My muscles refused to work more than that, but I managed. Yria frowned.

"Ah, fuck, she is. Thought things were about to get easier. Teach me to be optimistic." She glanced at her brother. "What should we do?"

"Well, Twenty-Two Dead Roses in a Chipped Porcelain Vase *asked* us to take her with us." Urda's face joined hers as they both looked down at me. "It'd be rude to refuse, but..." He looked over my body and cringed. "She's covered in a *lot* of... fluids." He squinted at my arm. "The sigils she wrote were hasty. I could probably undo them."

"Well, hold on there, she offered us a sizable bounty for *not* doing that." Yria reached up, started picking her nose. "Of course, if we did take her with us, Sal would probably beat us to death for doing so." She looked down at me. "Hey, blink twice if you'd beat us to death."

I did. Fervently.

"Ah, see, I knew it. Not worth it." Yria sighed. "Yeah, you better undo it. Let these two face-battlers sort their own shit out." She grimaced. "Er, listen... we'll wait for you as long as we can, but if shit starts going south, we kind of... uh..."

I closed my eyes. She didn't need to say it. Honestly, I felt a little touched that she'd even entertain staying behind for our sake.

But as Urda began to scrawl some counter-sigils, I knew it was just a courtesy. At the first sign of trouble, they'd be gone and I'd be left here. The minute my legs could work again, I had to find Liette.

And survive the two armies tearing each other apart.

And hope I didn't run into one of the numerous people on this ship who wanted me dead.

And somehow procure the unholy abomination that altered minds and reality at will and hope it didn't use my body as a host or worse.

Also—

Actually, you know what? I probably shouldn't have thought about it too hard.

It was all starting to sound a little impossible.

FORTY-EIGHT

THE FLAGSHIP

Vagrants have a way of getting noticed.

From our costumes to our names to the ink we wear on our skin, everything about a Vagrant is intended to tell everyone within a hundred miles that trouble is coming and it was wisest to just give us what we want. Sometimes that works and sometimes that doesn't, but outside of a very few select circumstances, a Vagrant always gets noticed.

"FIRE! FIRE! SEND THAT THING BACK TO HELL!"

Select circumstances such as, say, the midst of a battle between a dragon and an airship.

I emerged from a gangway onto the deck for only a second before I was forced to duck back into the shadows of its corridors.

A squadron of Revolutionaries toting crates of ammunition came charging past me, responding to orders barked by commanders who occasionally fired hand cannons into the sky to better motivate those who might be entertaining thoughts of desertion. They hurried to the railing, where long lines of glistening, gigantic cannons were situated. Like the machines they operated, the firing teams worked with mechanical precision as they took the ammunition, loaded it, primed their firing mechanisms, aimed, and—

"FIRE!"

At the commander's shout, a chorus of flame and smoke lit up the foggy sky. Severium shells went screaming out into the gray and, by their purple-tinged fire, I caught sight of the great winged reptile streaking through the sky. There was a disgruntled roar from the gray and a shudder of air as a great breath was drawn.

"DOWN! DOWN! SHIELDS UP!"

With rehearsed precision, the firing teams fell to one knee and flicked their wrists out. Retractable shields sprang out just in time to ward off the great gout of flame that came sweeping out from reptilian jaws to rake across the firing line. Those who kept their cool weathered the fiery breath. Those who didn't...burned.

Some fell off the railings, fiery cinders lost in the breeze, to be replaced as the commanders barked up more soldiers. Others went fleeing, desperately trying to put out the hungry fires engulfing them.

A young man, his crisp uniform blackening every second, came shrieking toward me, having given up trying to put out the flames and now simply flailing and screaming like a panicked animal. He tripped, left a black skid across the deck, looked up at me through a face red and blistering from the flame.

"Help...I...can't..."

That's as far as he got before the next squadron was called up and ran over his carcass.

If the sky was on fire, the deck was drenched.

The Imperial dragon continued to sweep overhead, darting in and out of the clouds, kept at bay by cannon fire. Mages leapt from their attack birds, rushing to slay the firing teams, being met with Revolutionary zealots as they came.

And died.

Bodies went flying across the deck and screaming over the railings as Graspmages hurled debris and bent weapons into packs of soldiers. Squadrons disappeared beneath waves of cold and fire as Embermages and Frostmages waded into the fray. At the center of it, an impressive pile of corpses stood beneath the feet of a towering Imperial Siegemage who, patiently and methodically, weathered blasts and skewers from gunpikes as he reached out, plucked up one of the myriad soldiers, and casually dismantled him like a toy.

"Does it not seem futile?" the Siegemage called out across the carnage, holding up a bloodied torso that had once been a person. "Cease your resistance, nuls. Your Great General cannot save you—"

That might have been true. But it turned out a gigantic suit of Relic-powered armor could.

The Paladin armor came shrieking across the deck, belching severium smoke as its engine carried all two tons of its immense armor into the Siegemage. With a resonant *clang!* it struck the mage with a shoulder the size of a beer keg and sent him collapsing to the ground. The Siegemage leapt to his feet just in time to see a gigantic halberd, its shaft the size of a small tree and its head a whirring mess of metal sawblades, come crashing down into him.

Gore erupted, painting the armor scarlet, and when the mage was no more than an ugly smear on the deck, it turned around. The massive helmet of the Paladin's armor flipped up and the slender pilot inside leaned out of her cockpit and screamed out into the fracas.

"TEN THOUSAND YEARS!"

The cry was taken up, from soldier to soldier, as they pressed back against the incursion of mages. Magic and metal erupted in clashes of blood and flame across the deck. Attack birds swooped in and out of the sky to snatch up soldiers and be gunned down by autobow fire. Cannons roared into the fog to be countered by the fiery breath of the dragon.

Across the sky, the scene was painted over and over, iterations on carnage from the same uncaring artist's hand. The remaining airships of the Iron Fleet erupted in cannon fire in a desperate bid to fend off Imperial attackers. The skies were aflame. The decks were soaked in blood. The sounds of battle were so thick that nothing could be heard.

"LIETTE!"

But I had to try.

"LIETTE!"

My mouth full of her name, my sword clenched in my hand, I waded out into hell. Whatever looks were cast my way were quickly forgotten and turned toward Imperial attackers, not so much as a word of challenge raised—I suppose, bloodied and stained as I already was, I blended in with the rest of the carnage.

"LI—"

My voice was cut short as the deck shifted under me, knocking me to my knees. The airship veered hard to port, as elegantly as a colossal mechanical monstrosity can, just in time for me to see a craggy mountain peak erupt out of the clouds and narrowly graze the railing.

We were flying low, I realized. Too low. The crowns of the mountains rose out like greedy fingers, eager to tear the airships apart. The Fleet must be trying to shake the birds, forcing them to close in to where the cannon could get them.

One more way for us to die.

One more voice in my head, screaming at me to find her.

I searched the deck for her, sifting through the charred carcasses burning beneath an Embermage's magic, around the attack birds twitching on the decks with harpoons lodged in their breasts, through the corpses and past the metal and sparks and through the choking veils of severium smoke. I searched for her, for that small, delicate wisp of a person that shouldn't be in a place this gorged with blood.

I found it.

But it wasn't her.

Bent and withered beneath his overcoat, the old man stood at the center of the carnage. Unfazed by the blood spattering his boots, unbothered by the corpses piling up around him, barely noticing the hellish flames painting the sky red, an old man bowing with the weight of his many medals watched the fight impassively.

Loyal.

Culven Loyal.

He didn't bother barking orders. His hands remained folded behind his back and far away from the sword he wore at his hip. He didn't look a thing like a Revolutionary officer should, much less one of the highest-ranking confidantes of the Great General. And yet...

Wherever he glanced, an enemy appeared seconds later. Whenever he blinked, the cannons followed. With a mere look, he sent squadrons of soldiers rushing to restock ammunition, to replace fallen firing crews, to intercept some new foe. And each time, they were exactly where they should be.

It was as though he were directing the battle entirely without words. Like his thoughts alone were the orders his soldiers responded to.

Kill him.

The idea came unbidden, like all bad ones do. Killing the only one keeping a lid on this mess would end with this entire ship going down...but not before every soldier aboard rushed to his aid, leaving me free to search for her.

A bad idea. Hell, it was a terrible idea.

I didn't have anything left but bad ideas.

And the brass at my hip.

I fished a shell out of my satchel with one hand, reached for the Cacophony with the other. My fingers wrapped around his hilt, felt his heat seeping through my glove. My eyes were fixed on the center of Loyal's back—a man that old, one shot would break his spine. I let out a cold breath, I seized the Cacophony's hilt, pulled, and...

Nothing.

I snarled, spat curses, pulled viciously on the hilt. But the gun wouldn't budge, refusing to come out of his sheath. Exactly as he had done back when we'd seen...

"*No,*" the Cacophony hissed. "*Not now.*"

"What do you mean 'not now'?" I spat back at him. "Is this not glamorous enough for you?"

"*He'll see me,*" the gun whispered. "*And once he does, they all will.*"

Normally, I don't begrudge him these cryptic little whispers—a gun's hobbies are limited, after all—but now was not the fucking time.

"What the fuck are you talking about?" I growled. "How do you—"

You.

A voice. A sensation. A thought. I didn't know how to describe it. It was a word, echoing inside my head, but it wasn't my voice. The longer it echoed, the more it felt...alive. It became a cold and hateful venom, a potent killer that coursed through my veins into my bones and froze my blood so cold I had to fight to stay upright.

I knew you would come.

I searched for the source of the voice. But even as I looked around, the sounds of carnage fell away, growing soft and distant even as fire rained and bodies fell. There was no more room in my head for them, or for terror, or survival, or anything but that voice.

For what? What do you covet?

My eyes settled, inexorably drawn to the center of the deck. To the lone, bent shape of Culven Loyal. Standing there. Staring back at me.

What do you seek?

Through eyes black as pitch.

Ah. There it is.

His voice, rasping and withered, reached deeper into my head. He sharpened his words to claws—I could feel them peel back the folds of my mind. A scream tore itself out of my mouth as I felt him probing, clawing, raking, my thoughts laid bare and shriveling beneath a hateful stare.

A human? No, a woman. He continued to murmur inside my skull, to peel, to pry. *What does she mean to you? What does she give you? Tell me. Tell me who she is. Tell me what she gives you. Show me. Give it to me.*

They came. I didn't want them to. But they came.

Give me everything.

Images. Scents. Memories. Dreams. His voice tore open a wound in my head through which they came bleeding. I couldn't tell one from the other, which parts I had lived, which parts I had hoped, which parts I wished had happened.

But they were of her.

Her smile, the first time she'd ever shown it to me. Her laugh, raucous and snorting, when I told her a crude joke she thought she'd hate. Her scent of oil and machines and alchemics I'd breathe in every night before she went to bed. Her eyes, big and bright and telling me what her voice never would.

Her hair. Her touch. Her ideas. Every part of her. As deep in me as my scars.

"Liette."

Her name. So heavy on my tongue it bore me to my knees. I fell. I couldn't hear the sound of my body striking the wood. I couldn't see the plumes of fire from the cannons. Darkness ringed my vision. A cold deeper than the wind could muster seeped into me, drank the light from my body until I was empty.

"I'm sorry," I gasped, but even my voice felt like it was bleeding out of me. "I'm sorry...I wanted so badly...for us..."

Ah, regret. His voice again, edged and bloodied. *How dreadfully common. I am disappointed. Is this all you have learned in your time here, my sibling?* Across the deck, a cruel smile curled across Loyal's face. *You always were the most ambitious of us. I had thought so much more.*

Slowly, his head started craning across the deck.

But tell me…

Slowly, it drifted toward a pile of rubble.

This woman you dream of…

Slowly, it settled there.

What do you think she will offer me?

My eyes followed his. And we both saw the same thing.

Liette huddled there, between a destroyed cannon and the smoldering body of a Siegemage. Her eyes darted around the chaos, drifting back to the helm of the ship clear across the deck, searching for a way through.

Trapped.

"No," I whispered.

I feel you quicken, my sibling, Loyal mused. *What does she have that you crave? Tell me.*

Across the deck, soldiers in the midst of carrying out orders suddenly stopped.

Tell me what she has. Tear her open to find it. Shred her to the last piece.

With stiff, trembling movements, they slowly turned around to fix their eyes toward Liette. She saw it, the stiffness in their bodies, the murder in their eyes, the glint of their weapons.

Bring it to me.

They charged.

She screamed.

And I…

I started killing.

I didn't feel my legs under me as they brought me to my feet. I didn't know what I hoped to accomplish as I rushed toward a hundred soldiers bearing down upon her.

But I didn't fucking care.

My sword was in my hand. My feet were moving beneath me. My lungs filled with cold air. I knew these. And nothing else.

Nothing but the fact that I had to get to her.

A body loomed before me. A soldier turned, saw me rushing toward him. He let out a scream, brought his gunpike up to stop me. My sword pushed past his guard, into his throat. His life painted my face as I tore the blade free. His body struck the deck after I had kept running.

More soldiers saw me. More steel flashed. Gunpikes, swords, shields came up to stop me. Some missed me. Some didn't. I was struck. I was cut. I bled. I knew this.

But I didn't care.

I couldn't stop killing. I didn't want to stop. Not as my sword punched through throats, chests, severed arms, cut tendons, skewered livers. They fell, one after the other, sometimes wearing their own blood, sometimes wearing mine, and each time I came back harder. More of them appeared, two for every body that I sent to the deck, but I didn't care. I wanted more. I wanted them to hear my steel, to see me.

I wanted them all to know that Sal the Cacophony had come and no one was getting out of this alive.

A shield caught my chin. I staggered. A blade lashed out, gouged my arm. I swung at a body, missed. I roared, but they still came. Hundreds? Thousands? I didn't know. I didn't care. They didn't, either.

But I couldn't let them stop me.

My hand went to the black hilt at my side. He didn't want to emerge. He resisted my pull. I wouldn't let him hide.

We made a deal, him and I.

Agony lanced up my arm as I tore the Cacophony out of his sheath. That was fine. I didn't need this arm. I didn't need my blood. I didn't need to be alive at the end of this. So long as she was.

I flipped open the chamber, slammed three shells in. I turned toward a mass of soldiers. I pulled the trigger.

Hellfire roared out. A great whirlwind of laughing fire tore across the deck, swallowing their screams inside its cackle as it swept through them. Ashen, red, blistered, cooked, charred, they fell.

I whirled, aimed for another knot of soldiers. I pulled the trigger.

Hoarfrost hissed, erupted across the deck. A pale field of frost blossomed in an instant, spears of jagged ice punching up to catch them through tendons and groins, to lance them through rib cages and spines. Impaled, screaming, twitching, they fell.

I turned. I saw them. I pulled the trigger.

Discordance sang, sent them flying. The luckiest were cast out like ashes on the wind, swept up to be dashed against the mountain faces or disappear shrieking into the gray void. The unluckiest were shattered, broken bodies crashing against cannons and rubble. Broken, bleeding, wailing, they fell.

They kept falling. Body after body. Life after life.

And I didn't care.

I didn't see their faces, hear their voices, know if they were men or women, had families or didn't, believed in their cause or not. I didn't know, I didn't care, I didn't think about them or my wounds or the ship or how we got here or anything.

Anything but her. And how she had to walk away from this. From the blood. From the fire.

From me.

Even if I had to burn this earth to cinders to do it.

Maybe I had slain them all. Or maybe I was already dead and didn't know it. I couldn't tell. Not until I kept pulling the trigger and heard only a clicking sound. Not until I swung my sword and bit only empty air. Not until there was no one left to fight.

Only then did I stop. Only then did I draw in a long breath that tasted sweet with my own blood. Only then did I see.

In heaps of smoldering ash. On spikes of ice. Broken on the deck. Some screaming as they clutched at great holes carved into their bodies. Some twitching, faces painted in shock, still trying to comprehend what had happened even as darkness fell around them. Some still and quiet, once lives, now footnotes on a long and ugly essay whose arguments still raged in the distance.

I'd done it. Whoever they were—whether they were believers or conscripts, whether they had families or not, whoever they had been before they met me—I'd ended them. And whatever else happened here, it would always be said that Sal the Cacophony had come and left corpses in her wake.

And I didn't care.

"Sal."

Not so long as she was okay.

I didn't want to turn around. I didn't want to see her, to have her see me, standing at the center of this carnage, every bit the monster she feared I was, every bit the mistake she'd made so long ago. I wanted to walk away, or leap off the railing, or just fall down and die—already, as the fight ebbed out of me and became one more stain on the deck, I could feel my legs giving out, my vision going blurry, my breath turning to ice in my lungs.

But the thought of doing that, of just lying down and letting everything go dark...

Without seeing her, at least one more time...

I turned around. She stood there, slight and delicate and too damn good and beautiful to be here among all these monsters. Her mouth was open. Her eyes didn't blink. She took me in—all of me, every drop of blood, every scar and metal—and I knew what she saw.

Same thing everyone else did. Same thing everyone would say on the day this was all over.

That when an army stood between Sal the Cacophony and someone who needed her, she burned it to the ground.

And spared not a single word for them.

"They were...," she whispered, "they were going to kill me?"

"Yeah," I said.

"But we worked together. They were supposed to..."

"Yeah." I spat something onto the ground. "You all right?"

"I...yes. I'm all right."

I nodded. "Good."

And then I fell.

My legs gave out. Or I'd lost too much blood. Or Loyal had done something to me. Or I just couldn't see much of a reason to stand upright. I was too tired to know, too wounded to care. So long as Liette was okay...then this was fine.

The deck rose up to meet me.

And then it stopped.

Arms around me. Hands on my body. The scent of oil and flowers in my nose. I was eased down to my knees, down to the deck by that touch, that smell. Distant sensations, like I was feeling them through a sheet, but they were there. Her touch. Her scent. Her eyes, wide and staring into mine, as she held my face up. And smiled at me.

"Die on me here," she whispered, "and I won't forgive you."

And so... I couldn't.

"Come with me," I said through ragged breath. "We shouldn't be here, Liette. Neither of us."

That smile faded. It hurt to watch.

"I can't," she whispered. "My research—"

"Don't." I shook my head weakly. "Don't die for it. It's not worth it. No matter what oath you took."

"Fuck me, Sal, this isn't about oaths. This is about you." She steadied me with her hands. "That thing in the Relic can change reality. With it, I can make a new world."

"A new world isn't worth it."

"It is, Sal. A hundred worlds are worth it." Tears blossomed in her eyes, too clean for this mess, too gentle for this place. "I would burn all of them down and build them back up, every time."

She pulled me close. She pressed her brow against mine. She was warm. And so was her voice.

"Until I found one that didn't hurt you anymore."

Life isn't an opera.

People die shitting themselves instead of giving poignant last words. Love doesn't last forever. No one ever fought for romance when they could just as easily fight for money.

But there are moments.

Moments where all the fighting seems worth it. Moments where you don't think twice about bleeding for someone else. Moments where one person's tears, one person's smile, are enough to convince you to get back on your feet, to keep breathing, to keep living.

Moments like this one.

Where I fell into her. Where she caught me. Where my lips found her lips and my hands found her hair and her arms found my waist. And we disappeared into each other for one long, held breath in that fiery sky.

For a long moment, it didn't hurt so bad.

The deck shuddered beneath us. The wail of grinding metal filled the air. We looked up and beheld the looming suit of armor not forty feet away. The Paladin wrapped giant metal fingers around its whirling halberd sunk deep within a foe and pulled it free. Its visor, black and empty, stared down upon us.

Its engines roared. Smoke poured out of it. It started rushing toward us.

I got shakily to my feet, stepped in front of her, held my sword up. But I could see the metal shaking in my hand, feel my grip trembling. She saw it, too, as she stepped beside me, wrapped her arms around me, and buried her face in my neck. In between our breaths, we realized that I would never stop that thing.

Without a word, we agreed...

If neither of us were going to walk away, then we'd both go together.

Her fingers dug into my skin. The Paladin raised its immense weapon, sparks spraying as its whirling blades ground against each other. I closed my eyes. I made my peace.

I whispered her name and waited for the end.

The deck shuddered, shaking into my bones as the armor drew near. I heard the wail of its engines as it closed in. I felt the kiss of sparks on my flesh as its colossal halberd swung down.

And I felt nothing else.

FORTY-NINE

THE FLAGSHIP

Sorry, I meant I *didn't* feel it cleave me in half.

I probably shouldn't have stopped there. Apologies.

I heard the grinding steel, the roaring engines. I felt the sparks raining down upon me. I heard the tinny voice of the pilot inside the armor snarling. But no pain, no blood, no—

"Madam."

I opened my eyes at the sound of a familiar voice. I looked up and saw a pair of perfectly manicured hands, missing a few nails, wrapped around the halberd's haft and trembling as they struggled to push back two engines and three tons of metal behind it.

Her jaw clenched, her entire body trembling, Agne the Hammer looked down at me imploringly.

"Would you mind terribly doing something about this?"

She was alive. We were alive.

Agne shuddered as the Paladin pushed her back a step. "And could you hurry the fuck up about it?"

Oh, right.

My hand scrambled into my satchel, fishing out a pair of shells. I flipped the Cacophony open, slammed them in, aimed, and—

Discordance shot out, the Cacophony seething as he shaped the magic. The wall of sound knocked us away from the Paladin, but only sent the metal monstrosity back a pair of steps. Its metal armor groaned as it lowered its halberd, readying for another charge.

I fired again. It went better this time. For me, anyway.

Discordance burst against its metal hide, the shrieking wall of sound blasting it backward. With a metal wail, the Paladin collapsed backward, its helmet flipping open as its pilot rolled out, unmoving.

"Really, I don't see the purpose in such mechanical abominations. They seem so impersonal." Agne rose to her feet, dusted off her clothes, as though that made a difference when they were already shredded. "Why can't they make more devices like the voccaphone? Those are lovely." She turned toward me and grinned. "Anyway, I trust you've been—"

I threw myself at her. Wrapped my arms around her. Drew her as close as I could draw a woman twice my size. She chuckled, laid a hand on my head, and stroked my hair.

"Why, Sal," she said, "am I going to have to nearly die every time I want a hug from you?"

"How?" I ignored her jibe, reached up and grabbed her face in both my hands—I had to be sure she was real, that I hadn't just died and gone to Large Woman Heaven. "How are you alive?"

She winked at me. "I'm quite good at what I do." She looked over my head toward Liette, extended a dainty hand. "But I'm being rude. How do you do, madam? I'm Agne the Hammer. Sal and I do murders together from time to time."

Liette, wide-eyed and sweating, stared at her hand before taking it and giving it the tiniest of shakes. "Uh...hi?"

"Charmed." She glanced up. "Pardon me a moment, would you?"

Before either of us could say dick, she turned and launched herself into a knot of soldiers rushing toward us. Their blades bounced off her, leaving little more than nicks, as she swatted at them in a dainty, head-crushing sort of way, sending them broken to the floor.

"She's with you?" Liette asked.

"She is," I replied.

We both stared at her for a brief moment before Liette whispered: "She's big."

"She is." I rolled my shoulder, tightened my grip on my sword. "Hang on, I should probably help."

I said that, but by the time I got there, she seemed to have it well in hand. As well as two Revolutionaries by the throat. She tossed them aside as I approached, pausing to glance out over the surrounding carnage. The Revolution had the upper hand as the last desperate mages were backed into a corner, but they weren't going out without at least a few explosions.

"Things have rather gone to shit, haven't they?" Agne hummed.

"Two Lonely Old Men betrayed us," I said. "He's rigged this whole airship and its bombs to do...something."

"Something?"

"Explode, probably."

"Ah. I rather suspected something was amiss. How could a man know so much about the airships and not know there were Vagrants aboard?"

"Right. Speaking of Vagrants, what happened to Tenka?"

I didn't need to ask. He answered for me.

Lean, powerful, and screaming, he came swooping out of the sky to crash upon the deck with a whirlwind that sent the Revolutionaries flying. With each swing of his spear, a great gale swept out to hurl more of them aside. And every time he did, he looked toward Agne, a great grin on his face seeking her approval. She indulged him with a gentle wave and a quiet smile.

"We had a discussion," she said. "There were some threats, some tears, a little bit of passion. We came to an understanding and he agreed to fly me back up here and help out."

I blinked. "Seriously? You managed to do all that?"

She offered me another, much more lascivious wink. "I'm *quite* good at what I do." Her smile didn't linger. "Regardless, if the operation is shot, we should get out of here."

I gestured toward the gangway I'd emerged from. "The twins are down there. Follow the sigils. Yria's got enough left in her to get four of us out of here."

Her lip stiffened. She swallowed a nervous breath and closed her eyes, nodding solemnly. "Then you go. I'll stay behind. With my magic, I can survive."

I shook my head. "No. You have to go."

"I'm a Siegemage, darling," she sighed. She stared out over the sky, cringing. "Blades can't harm me, guns barely tickle me, and I can't—"

"You can't stay," I interrupted, "not without giving up what makes you who you are."

Her frown deepened to something painfully tender. She knew I was right. Just as she knew that the price it would take, the feelings she would have to offer the Lady Merchant to survive, would render her into something else.

Something she lived in horror of becoming.

"But you can't survive," she whispered. "Sal, if you stay behind..."

"I'll think of something," I said. "I just..." I shook my head. "We've already given too much to Two Lonely Old Men. To this operation. To this fucking war. None of them are getting one drop more."

She opened her mouth. To protest? To convince me? I didn't know. And she didn't argue. She looked over my head toward Liette, smiled sadly.

"Is she..."

"She is," I said.

"And you're going to stay...for her?"

I nodded. "For her, anything."

"I've never heard a story that said Sal the Cacophony was this generous."

"And you're never going to. I'm not giving you a gift, I'm calling in a favor." I pointed out toward the carnage. "I've got to get to the helm. You've got to keep them busy."

"*Ocumani oth rethar!*" Tenka's laughter carried across the winds, along with his victims. "Agne! Hey, Agne! Did you see that one?"

"I rather think the boy and I can handle a little distraction." She rolled her shoulder. "What do you need? An hour?"

"Shorter," I said. "The minute you see us go through that door, you get the fuck down to the twins. They're not going to wait if something happens."

"Bully, then." Agne smirked out over the carnage. "A few cannons, a few Revolutionaries. If this is all we're facing, then I suspect we'll be—"

She had to say something.

Fuck me, why does everyone always have to say *something*?

A roar cut through the air, drew my attention skyward. In the clouds overhead, I could see the dragon pivot and come swooping down. Cannon fire burst fiery blossoms across the sky, but all of them shot wide as the great beast came plummeting down.

A gap in the firing line. I saw it as soon as Agne did, as soon as the whole fucking ship did. A trio of cannons at the railing lay in hunks of twisted metal, its crews either tossed overboard or shattered on the deck nearby. Had I done that? The Cacophony and I? Or had Tenka or another mage or...or...

Well, I suppose it didn't matter.

Since we were all about to die anyway.

The dragon roared as it swept low across the deck, its great wings beating back Revolutionary soldiers. They flicked out their retractable shields, huddling up in a mass to defend themselves from the beast's breath. A good plan.

If the Imperium had been planning that, it might have gone well.

The dragon lingered for only a moment, barely slowing down before swooping away into the clouds, screeching as cannon fire raked its hide and left smoldering wounds. But in that brief moment, its aims were accomplished. From its hide came leaping Imperial soldiers, clad in purple and wearing bronze masks. Only four of them, far too few to challenge the Revolutionaries.

But they only needed one.

She leapt from the beast's back, disappearing in the air as crossbow bolts shot at where she had just been. The Lady's song rang loud and clear through the carnage as she reappeared on the deck, her sword raised, her white hair slicked back, her face a purple mess from where Mendmagic had failed to heal her broken nose all the way.

"Leave no nul alive!" Velline shouted to her soldiers as she raised her hand. "Every soul down there requires our victory."

I'd have asked what she meant, if she weren't suddenly in the midst of killing a lot of people.

Gunpikes opened fire. The Lady's song rose. Her blade became a ghost, impossible to see but for the sparks where her steel parried away the severium charges. She vanished. She reappeared, a ghost of white and steel in the midst of them. Her blade started its grisly work, carving through the pack of soldiers with grotesque efficiency. Where their weapons bit, she disappeared. Where they weren't looking, she returned.

A keen eye—or a lucky shot—caught her. A gunpike punched through her shoulder, eliciting a scream. She whirled, punishing the attacker with a savage slice across the face that sent him screaming to the deck. She tore the weapon free, clutched her wound. The Lady's song was joined and I watched as the wound sealed itself shut.

I glanced across the deck. Dalthoros, the bony plate in his forehead wet with sweat, extended a hand, his eyes glowing as his magic mended the wound in his captain's flesh. Overhead, Shenazar came swooping down, cackling as she whipped great gales across the deck.

Two of her Hellions, I noticed as all three of them waded into the battle. *Then who are the other two?*

Instead of rushing forward like the others, these two hurried away from the fracas, rushing toward the walls of the ship's helm. Saboteurs? No, mages—their song was faint, but familiar. I'd heard it before.

But I didn't figure it out until they pulled out chalk.

"Doormages," I whispered. "Those are fucking Doormages!"

"What? Who?"

Agne hadn't seen them. I couldn't wait to point them out and I couldn't let them finish.

I started running. Blades flashed out, gunpikes cracked, but I kept them in my view only as long as I needed to get away from them. I found a soldier aiming an autobow into the fracas, swept up behind her. She turned around just in time to see the Cacophony's hilt smashing down upon her face. With a grunt, she dropped to the floor and the weapon dropped into my hands.

I aimed it at the helm, squeezed the trigger. The motor in the autobow whirred, threw off my aim—I fucking hate these things—sending a pair of bolts wide. They struck the wood of the helm, the Doormages not even looking up as they finished sketching their portals. The Lady's song reached a crescendo as faint pinpricks of light illuminated beneath their hands.

Growing wider.

I cursed, took a steadier aim. I held my breath, squeezed the trigger. A flurry of bolts streaked out, punched through the Doormage's back. The light died, along with him, as he collapsed to the deck.

One down.

I let out my breath, drew on the other one. The pinprick of light was growing, a flower of swirling purple light that grew bigger with every breath to fill out the chalk outline. I held mine, squinted, aimed down the sights of the autobow and squeezed the trigger.

Between "I love you" and "I'm leaving," the most terrifying sound in the world is the *click* of an empty weapon.

I pulled the trigger again, disbelieving, like that would make a fucking difference. The motor whirred, but the string plunked with the sound of empty air firing. The magazine—there hadn't been enough bolts left in the fucking magazine. I hated these things. I fucking *hated*—

A noise severed that thought, ringing in my ears like a stained glass bell shattering into a thousand pieces. Not a song, nor even a tune, but a hundred different choruses striking off each other with bone-rattling resonance.

It drove me to one knee. Liette rushed forward to steady me. Agne shouted, clutched her head. Even Velline and Dalthoros winced at the noise. But whatever discomfort the sound brought paled in comparison to the horror wrought by the sight.

They leapt. They charged. They flew.

Graspmages. Siegemages. Skymages. Mages I'd never seen before.

In plumes of flame and the shudder of wood and the howl of wind and always, *always* in the echo of her song, they emerged from the portal. They ran toward the battle, a sea of purple-lit eyes with the Lady's song as their crashing waves. They rallied behind Velline as she raised a blood-slick blade, pointed it at the Revolutionaries, and uttered, cold as her steel:

"*Ontori tun vatala!*"

FIFTY

LITTLEBARROW

Life as an apothecary had never been easy, despite what complaints Meret had about it.

Perhaps it wasn't as demanding a profession as a Revolutionary field medic or an Imperial Mendmage, but the healing arts all shared a need for precision. A broken bone required an exact knowledge of how to set it, a wound needed a precise hand to suture it, a fever required a painstaking knowledge of exactly how much silkgrass would be needed to dull the pain without exacerbating it. A single mistake, a single misspoken word, could be the difference between life and death.

Meret kept that knowledge in mind, wore it around his neck like a heavy chain, as he squinted over his situation and applied the carefully honed, expertly polished methodology that he had been trained for.

"So." He cleared his throat, looked to Sindra. "We're fucked?"

She grunted. "We are fucked, yes."

They returned their stares to the road stretching out before them. Or rather, what had once been a road before it was drowned beneath an Imperial ass-load of snow and ice.

Winter in the Valley was not unlike the relatives who know everyone hates them: it came too quickly for anyone to object, made itself comfortable before anyone could notice, and then proceeded to loaf around and make everyone else work around it for the next several months.

That was a good analogy, he thought. He'd have to remember it if he survived.

His eyes were drawn skyward. The clouds hung thicker, unloading soot-singed snow as the smoke columns from Sal's pyres twisted into the sky. In another few hours, he wouldn't be able to see twenty feet ahead.

But he could see the birds.

They came and went like bad thoughts: nimble shadows fleeting through the clouds, darting at the edges of his vision, there and gone again before he could even look. They would come and go at random—sometimes hours would stretch between each sighting, sometimes minutes. But every time they came, they came closer. He could see the details, the edges, and the points of their wings, their beaks...

Their riders.

They'd be here soon, he knew. More of them. With weapons. With magic.

With the road thusly buried, it would take a swift bird, a sturdy wagon, or a lot of luck to escape them. The wagon part, he knew, was already out—with some solid hammering and a lot of cursing, Sindra had gotten it to a point where it would only *sound* like it was going to fall apart. Luck, too, was a nonstarter, since this had all started from a fucking airship falling out of the damned sky.

Which left the bird...

Old Surly.

Once pride of Rodic's flock. A champion showbird, once.

Why couldn't I have gotten that one? he thought disdainfully as he observed the weary old creature yoked to the wagon. One eye a useless rheumy orb, one leg trembling with arthritis, a lot of feathers lost to age, and one beak stained with his own blood from where she had nearly taken off his ear. *Why'd I have to get* this *old shit?*

Old Surly looked up, glared at him through her one good eye. His eyes widened in astonishment. A bird that could read his thoughts *could*, ideally, be useful in some other situation. However, he suspected he would have precious little worth relaying to her once Littlebarrow started burning.

"Rodic said she could get me out of this town," Meret observed, frowning.

"A few hours ago, she probably could," Sindra sighed. "Of course, a few hours ago, Rodic probably thought you weren't a fucking fool." She cast a sidelong look at him. "I still say—"

"We're not leaving them," Meret said.

She sighed. "Right." She clapped him on the back briefly before starting to stalk back off to her house. "I'll pack enough that we can go it our own, if we need to. Then we'll just hope for the best and—"

The wind whispered. They stared overhead. Black against the clouds, a shape flew. Not a bird, but a human: slender, laughing, and carrying a sword as they disappeared into the void.

A Skymage.

They'd be here soon.

"We'll hope," Sindra muttered. "We'll hope."

He watched her disappear into the swirling snows until only her tracks remained. He started counting in his head as he watched the snow fall until her footprints, too, vanished beneath the white.

Six minutes, forty-eight seconds, he told himself. *That's how long it took for her footprints to disappear.* He looked out over the snow-choked road. *So, roughly, if you died out there, it would take less than an hour for your body to disappear, too.* He took off his spectacles, polished them. *Assuming there was anything left of you, mind.*

He'd come to the Valley a few springs ago and his first sight had been the tank. It had looked ancient, rusted-out and overgrown, buried by snows in the crater that had become its tomb. But it had only been about two years old when the Imperium had destroyed it, a local had told him.

It was a Valley tradition, seeing what relics of the war came out during the thaw. Freemakers, Ashmouths, and independent collectors alike would show up when spring arrived to start plucking off the best parts. A Valley child's earliest money usually came from hawking spare machine parts or Imperial weaponry to buyers passing through.

He wondered what they'd find on his body when he thawed out.

He wondered what they'd sell his medicine bag for.

He hoped it would be a good price, at least.

"More than we'll get for you, I suppose," he sighed to Surly without looking at her. "Not much of a good price for a mind-reading bird."

"I disagree."

Liette's voice, unexpected, caused him to emit a rather high-pitched shriek. She was too polite to mention it, though. Or maybe she hadn't even noticed. When he turned around, she stood beside Surly, gingerly stroking the bird's neck as Surly leaned into her.

How had she gotten here so quickly? But when he looked down at the snow, he no longer wanted to.

No tracks, he noticed. *She didn't leave a single footprint.*

"An avian that could detect thoughts would be exceedingly valuable," Liette observed as she studied the bird. "It would reduce difficulties in training and promote a more harmonious existence with a species that benefits us immensely, as well as furthering our knowledge of their processes."

"Oh, uh..." Meret fumbled over his own cough. "I didn't mean she could...I mean, I was just joking."

"As was I," Liette replied, "hence why I was using my joking face."

Meret opened his mouth, squinted, studied the very hard frown and severe stare that comprised her joking face and then thought better of saying anything.

He had that old healer's reflex to try to urge her back to bed—her bruises and cuts were still fresh and the cold couldn't have been good for them, after all. But to look at her...he didn't think he could muster the nerve.

She stood straight as an arrow, her face frozen in pristine severity, neither expression nor posture betraying pain. Yet even looking upon her wounds made him cringe. She didn't so much not feel pain as...not consider it worth noticing.

Snow didn't collect on her shoulders. Footprints didn't follow her. Everything—the cold, the wind, nature itself—was unworthy of her attentions.

And that thought terrified him.

"I never used to like birds very much," Liette interrupted his thoughts as she scratched beneath Surly's chin. "I found their hygiene atrocious, their attitudes deplorable, and they were far too...too..."

"Smelly?" Meret offered.

"I believe I covered that, albeit without pointing it out specifically, when I criticized their hygiene." Liette glanced at him. "No, I found them too...unpredictable. A machine does what you design it to. A sigil does what you wright it to do. Provided you have the knowledge to make it. But you can know everything about a bird and it'll still be moody, still have needs." She cringed. "And they do this thing where they scream *right* when you're trying to do something delicate that would *not* be helped by them screaming."

Hey, you do *do that,* he thought, glowering at Surly with an accusing stare. Then the bird scowled at him through that terrible eye and he quickly looked away and cleared his throat.

"But you like them now?" he asked Liette.

She grimaced. "Honestly, I'm not sure. While they *are* smelly, noisy, and angry, they're also gentle." She smiled, stroking Surly's last few feathers. "If you're gentle to them. They're comforting. They're strong. I suppose, after a while...you come to appreciate unpredictability."

Meret waited a moment before mustering the nerve to speak. "Are we still talking about birds?"

"Obviously, I was attempting to allude discreetly and poetically to a different subject." She winced. "But I don't actually want to talk about that subject at this moment, so I'm not quite sure what my aim was beyond acknowledging something is irritating me." She glanced at him with something that might have been bafflement. "Does... that make sense?"

He blinked. "Uh, yeah. It does. People do that all the time. Talk-about-but-not-talk-about things, that is." He coughed. "Which, uh, I'm sure you *knew* they did, but..."

She stared at him for a long moment. So long that it took him a good minute to see the frown tugging at the edges of her lips.

"I'm not...good with people," she said. "They're like birds. I can figure out their patterns, where they go and what makes them want things and it's almost like I understand them. But then I remember they're big, huge things that can destroy me if the mood hits them and..." She turned away. "I'm glad, I suppose is what I'm trying to say. That you're helping her."

"Uh, sure," he said. "But I'm helping both of you." He glanced at her wounds and cringed. "No offense, but you kind of look like you need it more than her."

"Oh." She looked at a large cut across her hand, suddenly aware of, but no more concerned with, the bloodied bandage. "Technically true."

"*Technically?* You're kind of...bleeding a lot."

"That's a correct assessment, but I can fix blood," she replied, "and wounds, and broken bones. But she...she can't fix things." She turned to him and offered him the barest of smiles. "But you can. That's important. I recognize your aptitude."

That was an extremely weird way to say thank you, but it was probably also as close as he was going to get.

"I'm glad I could, too," he said, daring to edge a little closer. Surly punished such impudence with a quick snap of her beak, sending him sulking away. "I wish I had any talent in fixing broken, shitty birds, though." He nervously cleared his throat. "Uh, again, no offense, if you were, like...developing a bond with this one."

He looked to her, hoping to see the last remnants of that smile. But her eyes were somewhere else, him being relegated suddenly to the same category as the snow, the blood, and all the other things that didn't matter.

She was staring at the bird. And she was not blinking.

"Fix," she whispered to herself. "No...not fix. *Understand.*"

That last word...she hadn't spoken it. He hadn't heard it. He'd *felt* that word, reverberating inside him, as though every strand of sinew inside him had been plucked like a violin string.

"Arthritic leg," she whispered, her unblinking eyes sliding slowly across Surly, appraising. "Bone and muscle loss. Cataract rendering eye unusable. Sixty-six nerves damaged, forty-two sets of muscles degraded..."

Her voice trailed off into murmuring, words and numbers he couldn't keep up with. But her eyes remained fixed: unblinking, unwavering, staring at a horizon only she could see, one that kept getting farther away until suddenly:

"Ah. I see now."

She leaned down beside Surly before he could stop her—the old bird was prone to kicking, after all. Surly didn't so much as flinch as Liette held her palm out against the avian's trembling leg. Before Meret could blink, she ran her hand across the bird's limb and...

It stopped shaking.

More than that, it was bigger. Leaner. Strong again. Surly, as if disbelieving it herself, warily tested the leg but settled upon it confidently. The bird's leg was whole again, thanks to Liette.

As though she'd simply reached inside it and...fixed it.

But that was...

"The other one needs to be equivalent." Liette hurried to the other side of the bird, touched her leg. It, too, became strong. "The eye next."

"Wait, Liette, what's going—"

Surly clucked a little, pulling away as she reached up toward the bird's face, but allowed Liette to trace a circle around the rheumy orb. The bird blinked and when its lid opened again, the eye was a perfect, pale yellow match for the other one.

"*Holy shit.*" There was probably a more appropriate exclamation for the sheer awe of what he was witnessing, but this was the best he could muster. "What did you..." He smiled broadly, clapping his hands together. "No Barter, no explosion...Liette, what kind of magic *is* this?"

"It isn't." Liette continued studying Surly as the bird preened over its newfound vigor. "It is *understanding.* I can see how it works, every muscle, every nerve, every..." She looked to Meret. "You said she's angry?"

"I mean, her name *is* Old Surly, but—"

"I can fix that, too."

Before he could protest, she waved a hand. The light in Surly's eyes dimmed, then diminished entirely, leaving her staring ahead, unblinking, unthinking, barely even breathing.

"Wait, this isn't..." Meret placed a hand on Surly's neck—she didn't even flinch. "What did you do to her?"

Liette wasn't listening. She was still staring, still searching. Her fingers were trembling. And Surly was still changing.

"White plumage would be more effective in the snow for evading detection," she whispered. "That's easy enough."

"Liette, wait."

She didn't. She waved a hand. Surly's feathers sprouted anew, a brilliant ivory.

"This whole breed is ill-suited to our purposes in general," she hummed. "I know something better."

"Liette, stop!"

She didn't. She waved a hand. Surly's flesh rippled, bones popped, going from an old draft bird to a tall, regal Imperial charger.

"Why be limited to that?" Excitement, desperate and dry, lingered in her voice. "Why not longer legs for running? Broader wings for flying? Why not *fire* breathing? All it would take would be a new organ and…"

"LIETTE!"

She didn't listen. She continued to wave her hands. Surly's flesh trembled, her form breaking and being remade, over and over, as she assumed new and terrible forms.

"STOP!" Meret ran toward Liette, seized her by the shoulders, turned her toward him. "I don't know what you're doing, but *please*, don't—"

She turned to face him. His hands fell away from her. He stepped back, mouth agape and breathless as she stared back at him.

Through eyes black as pitch.

He wanted to run, but his legs wouldn't move. He wanted to scream, but his lungs shriveled inside his chest. He wanted to blink, but that stare of hers wouldn't let him. He felt the hairs on his arms stand up, like they were trying to pull themselves out of his body. The skin of his limbs started to stretch, to ripple, to change.

He struggled to gasp out a word, a plea for her to stop, but his voice sounded not like his own: a warbling, quavering sound that came from outside his body. His head pounded, a heavy sledgehammer blow of a noise filling him instead of breath. He tasted copper as blood dripped from his nose onto his tongue. He held up a hand in a desperate bid to ward off whatever was happening to him, and saw his digits disappearing into his hand, sinking beneath the flesh to become a long and twitching tendril.

He shut his eyes. He opened his mouth. He heard a scream.

Not his own.

When he opened them again, his skin was whole, his hand was a hand again, his body felt like its own save for a horrifically unpleasant tingling. Even the blood weeping from his nose had vanished.

You're okay, he told himself, breath returning to his lungs. He glanced to Surly, saw her unpleasantly discombobulated, but once again an aging, angry avian. *You're both okay. But...how did—*

"I'm sorry."

Liette was on her knees, her arms wrapped around herself, shivering. The snow collected upon her shoulders, a funeral shroud for a body that hadn't realized she was dead yet. Tears fell from her face, sliding over her cuts to fall, red-tinged, upon the snow.

"I'm sorry," she whispered. "I didn't mean...I don't...I..."

Meret leapt away as she looked back up at him. He cursed himself for doing so. The eyes staring at him were big and brown behind her glasses. Human, again. And full of tears.

"I don't know what's happening to me." The traces of that expertly clinical voice that she'd greeted him with had vanished from her mouth. She spoke through tears, through shuddering breath, through wracking sobs. "I can...*feel* something inside me. It keeps talking, it keeps telling me secrets I don't want to know and answers I don't want to hear and...and..."

She looked at him with a desperate stare. She extended a trembling hand. That shaping hand that had turned Surly into something else, that had almost done the same to him.

He still wanted to run. Everything inside him from brain to bone was screaming at him to run. Whatever he had signed up for, whatever dangers Sal had brought with her, this wasn't something he was ready to deal with. Fuck, this wasn't even something he'd ever *seen* before.

Reshaping, reforging, *changing* things like that...that was no magic. That was no technology. And while he wasn't religious, he knew in his bones that such a power was something that should not be. In heaven *or* on earth.

He should have run. He should have run until he couldn't see her or Littlebarrow or even remember any of it.

One day, he hoped, he would know why he didn't.

"Easy." He took her gently by the hand, knelt down beside her. "Breathe. Slow and deep. Just like this."

He drew in a deep breath, exhaled, showed her. Just like an

apothecary should do, he told himself. Only this time it was a woman who could make and unmake with a thought instead of, say, a child panicked over a sprained ankle, but the principle was the same.

He hoped.

"But what I did," she gasped, "I almost—"

"Let's worry about that later," he replied, taking another deep breath. "Come on. Just like this."

He breathed, she breathed with him. In and out. Once, twice, three times. When it was done, the terror had diminished in her eyes. The tears hadn't.

"I...I can't tell you what happened," she whispered. "I don't remember."

He nodded. "Does Sal?"

She shot him a look torn between wounded and horrified. "Don't tell her."

His brow furrowed. "Why not? Whatever's going on, if she knows something, we should—"

"It's not about 'we'; it's about her." Her frown deepened. "Have you treated her?"

He shook his head. "I wanted to, but—"

"She wouldn't let you. She thinks she can't be hurt. But she can. She is. You've seen it, haven't you? The way she moves...her scars hurt her." She shuddered. "Every day she wakes up, walks out into a world that wants to kill her, and even if she doesn't see a single foe, she still comes back hurting and I...I..." She swallowed hard. "I can't be another thing that hurts her."

He frowned. "You think keeping this from her wouldn't?"

She shook her head. "It would hurt less than telling her. I can live with being disdained by her. I can't live with burdening her."

He hadn't known them long, either of them, only enough to know who they were. Sal the Cacophony: the most feared Vagrant in the Scar, bringer of ruin, she who left only ashes in her wake. Twenty-Two Dead Roses in a Chipped Porcelain Vase: famed among Freemakers, a genius even before she'd gained this terrible strength. Two people who had the power to make the earth shake and the heavens weep.

There was something comforting, Meret thought, in knowing that even the very strong could be stupid like this.

He sighed. He sat down beside her. He stared at the same salt-stained patch of snow she did.

"Sal told me," he said, "on the airship, you said you would burn down the world for her." He paused. "Did you really say that?"

She nodded. "I did."

"Did you really mean it?"

She looked at him. "I did."

He returned her look. He smiled sadly at her. "What are you going to do when you *do* burn it all down, when all you're left with is the ashes and her, and neither of you can talk to each other?"

She blinked, eyes wide with astonishment. Then they squinted, her mouth hanging open as she struggled to find a clever enough answer. Then her mouth pursed and folded into a deep, wearying sigh.

"It's going to hurt," she whispered. "It's going to hurt everyone."

"Probably." Meret stared up at a sky free of shadows, for now. "But everything hurts, eventually."

He felt something warm. Her hand—the one that had nearly killed him—was on his. She squeezed his fingers gently.

"Thank you, Meret. For everything."

He smiled. "Is that the Freemaker's code?"

"That's for you." She smiled back. "Technically, since your assistance was unrequested and did not further the cause of the summation of all human knowledge, you don't *quite* qualify for compensation under the second law." She rose to her feet, helped him to his. "But still...thank you."

He nodded. He watched her go as she turned and headed back to the house, back to Sal, back to all the pains that awaited them, him, all of them. Most of those pains he'd never be able to understand, let alone fix.

But this one...it felt nice to help with this one.

"Well done," a gravelly voice rasped behind him. Sindra was loading a few more supplies onto the cart.

"You saw that?" he asked, worry creeping into his voice—getting her to sign on to this *without* her knowing what Liette could do was bad enough.

"Just the end part," she grumbled, securing the load. "Since you're apparently in the practice of solving *everyone's* problems now, I figured you might as well be praised for it."

"Well...thanks?"

"Don't thank me yet." She pointed skyward. "There'll be a break in the snow soon. It'll be hard getting out now, but impossible if we wait. If we don't—"

Her words were cut short by a distinctly avian shriek. A shadow, low and dark in the clouds, slid overhead. The silhouette of a great riding bird's head rose, its beak opening to loose a cry.

A cry taken up. And echoed. Over and over, across the sky.

"We go in the next hour," she growled, "or we use that time to pick out where we're buried."

Meret was tired. Exhausted, if he was honest. It turned out the threat of imminent annihilation stressed him out quite a bit. So, while he certainly *felt* like curling up into a ball and dying, his trip back to his house was marked by desperate wheezing, frenzied trudging through snow, and no small amount of flailing.

By the time he had reached his door, he was ready to burst in, gasping for breath to deliver the news that their departure had to come soon.

The door opening suddenly and slamming into his face kind of ruined that, though.

He fell back to the ground, clutching the spot between his eyes where the edge of the door had struck him, his face contorted in pain. When he looked up, it was into a pair of big brown eyes behind a pair of glasses being adjusted by a pair of tiny hands.

"You really should be more observant of your surroundings," Liette chided. "Given that the door opens *outward*, the chances of anyone attempting to access it from the outside being involved in an accident are much more likely. It's simple mathematics, really."

"Thank you. Truly," he muttered.

Far too late, Meret was beginning to understand why someone might want to kill these two people.

She offered him a hand. He flinched, his skin quivering in memory of what that hand had done. But he saw it was wrapped in a grubby bandage, a match for the other ones that adorned her myriad cuts and bruises. Seeing his hesitance, she cringed a little.

"Ah, yes," she said, gesturing vaguely at her bandaged injuries. "Sal thought it prudent—that is, *we* thought it prudent—that my injuries be more thoroughly tended to for purposes of avoiding... further incidents." She cleared her throat. "Which I would prefer to avoid, for the time being."

That *might* have been an apology? He wasn't inclined to push it. Instead, he took her hand, let her help him up as she dusted snow from his coat. Her hand paused on his shoulder in the midst of sweeping some snow off.

"We talked," she said. "She and I. I'm... I'm glad that you had that idea."

He blinked. "Oh! Um... good. I'm glad I did, too... I mean, I'm glad you talked, but..." He sighed. "Listen, we can't stay here any longer. So anything else you need to take care of—"

"Anything else I need to take care of, I will take care of," she interrupted, curtly sweeping the snow from his shoulders. "Beginning with the cart. I expect I can fix it enough to alleviate some burden on the animal pulling it."

He shot her a dire stare. She winced.

"Through mundane and conventional means," she assured him. "As I said, there won't be... further incident."

He let out an exhausted chuckle. "Great. I mean, that's good. It'll be hard enough getting four people and an angry bird out of here without *incidents*." He took off his bifocals, cleaned snow from them. "The fewer feathers ruffled, the better, am I right?"

That one was pretty good, he thought. Not *good*-good, but just terrible enough to be funny. Yet, when he put his glasses back on, Liette wasn't smiling.

Her lips were curled into a frown.

Tears appeared at the corners of her eyes again.

"Oh, um, I'm sorry," he said. "I didn't mean to imply that your... uh, incidents, were... were..."

"She's inside," Liette said softly as she turned and started walking toward the cart. "You should..."

She paused, considered what to say next, and settled on simply letting out a soft, weary sigh and continuing. She did not look back.

Meret frowned, eased the door open to a sight he wasn't ready to see. The last of his wine—*including* the bottle of The Last Lastlight he had been saving—lay scattered across the table in various states of being drunk. The last of his bandages and salves lay tattered and drained—what wasn't already wrapped around corded, tattooed muscle, anyway.

And under those bandages, a pair of hands were slowly, patiently loading shells into a gun with a great, brass grin.

"Sal," Meret gasped. "We've got to go. There's a break in the snow and we just—"

"You heard a bird." Sal didn't look up as she methodically loaded another shell into the Cacophony's chamber. "Loud scream, right? Flying low?"

"Uh...yes?"

She grunted. "Scout bird. Annoying fucks."

"It'll be back to attack soon. We should—"

"If they were going to attack from birds, they would have done it already." She shook her head. "They don't have enough to hit us from the sky. A bird wouldn't do much good in these snows, anyway. They'll come on the ground."

He paused as she loaded the last shell into her gun. "How do you know?"

The Cacophony's chamber clicked shut with a sound that echoed through the tiny house.

"Because," she said softly, "that's how I'm going to kill them."

His eyes widened. "What? We don't have time for that. We need to get going *now*."

"You do, yes."

"No, *we* do, Sal, whatever's coming—"

"Was invited," she finished for him. "I've been sending out invitations since I got here, each one of them perfumed with smoke. They'll come, however late they deem fashionable. They'll come with friends. And they'll come expecting to see me."

The gun and she shared a look, too long to be normal and too intimate to be right, before she slid it back into its sheath.

"I won't have it said that Sal the Cacophony was a bad host."

The realization would have been easier to handle had it come out and struck him out of nowhere, a sledgehammer blow to his skull. But instead, he sank inside of it; it had been gathering at his ankles since she'd arrived and now the truth of the situation was over his head.

And he'd known it.

The threats she'd made, the pyres she'd built, the people she'd chased away—he'd understood what was going on back then. No matter how much he'd wanted to believe it was for some grander purpose, he'd known.

"You're going to fight them," he whispered. "You're going to turn Littlebarrow into a battleground."

She sniffed, got to her feet, winced. "That's the idea, anyway."

He should have been angry. Outraged, even. Screaming curses at her for turning this village into a war zone, at Sindra for not warning him more, at himself for letting this all happen. He should have been, but...

"You can't," he said. "You *can't* fight them."

"No," she replied. "I can't."

"You're too hurt to fight them," he said. "The Imperium, the Revolution—"

"Both," she said. "You're right. I am too hurt to fight them." She rolled her shoulder, twitched. "I'm guessing I've got it in me to hold them off for...a little bit. Longer, if they do what I think they will."

"But you'll die!"

"And everyone else won't." Her voice was curt and final, a headsman's axe falling fast. "Or, at least, they'll stand a better chance if everyone with guns or magic is looking at one little village and not the entire Valley."

"But that...there's *so* many reasons why that plan won't work."

"True, true," she hummed. "On the other hand, considering I managed to come up with it while plummeting out of the sky in an airship that was on fire, it's not too bad, is it?"

He should have just thrown up his hands and left. Left her, left Liette, left Littlebarrow. Hell, he should have done it ages ago. There was no real reason why he should be concerned for her. No *practical* reason, anyway.

And yet...

"Sal, that's...no." He shook his head. "Come with us. We stand a better chance of escaping if we all stick together."

She grinned. "Yeah? A merry band of outlaws?"

"Of people," he replied. "People trying to help each other stay alive. Like we should be doing."

Her eyebrows rose. "Damn. That was almost inspiring, Meret."

"Thank you," he replied. "I mean, you're being stupid and you need to come with us, but thank you. Still."

She walked toward him—fuck, had she always been taller than he was? She rested a hand upon the Cacophony's hilt, stared down her nose at him through blue eyes that didn't blink. She raised a hand and he fought the urge to flinch away from it as she rested it on his shoulder.

"That's why you need to survive," she said. "The Scar has too many people like me and not enough people like you. Like her. Like that cranky lady with the sword."

"Sindra. Her name is Sindra."

"Sindra." She sniffed. "Pretty name. She didn't deserve what I brought to this Valley, either. But I brought it, all the same. This village, this whole land will be crawling with soldiers. Once the bombs start dropping and the spells start flying, no one's getting out."

He opened his mouth to protest. She pressed a finger to his lips.

"Don't," she said. "Don't fucking say anything else. The more you talk, the more sense you make and that's not something I can afford right now." Her sigh was ancient and rife with pain. "Yes, you're right. We might stand a better chance with each other. But not with me. This metal I carry is raw meat, Meret. They'll follow its scent for miles. Maybe it saves us once or twice, but it'll kill us eventually."

She thumbed the butt of the Cacophony's hilt. The same way she thumbed her own scars.

"This is what I do, Meret," she said. "I destroy things. You've trusted me this far. Trust me one more time. Let me destroy something that needs destroying."

This, if the stories were any indication, was the moment he should do something. He should deliver a stirring rhetoric that would make her see reason. He should seize her and refuse to let go until she either broke him or relented. He should…kiss her, maybe? They did that in the stories, right?

Of course, two of those ideas would definitely end up with her breaking his face and the other one had face-breaking as a distinct possibility. So he did what he always did, what people like him in the stories always did…

He sat quietly. He stared at his shoes. As she pushed past him. And walked to the door to her death.

Come on, you idiot, he scolded himself. *Do something.* Do *something.* He gritted his teeth, his hands clenched into impotent fists. *You can't just let this happen. You can't…* He sighed to himself. *You can't fight her. You're not a hero. Not a Vagrant. This isn't a story.*

He drew in a long breath, released it.

You're Meret. And this is your friend.

"I trust you," he said softly.

She stopped.

Halfway out the door, hand on her gun, she stopped. She glanced over her shoulder at him like she hadn't actually expected that to work. To be honest, he hadn't, either. To be *perfectly* honest, he wasn't sure what he was doing right now.

And yet…

"I trust you," he said. "I think it's a bad idea, but I trust you. And I'll believe in you." He puffed himself up as tall as he could manage. "But you have to trust me, too."

"Uh, all right," she said. "But I'm already asking you to get Liette out of here, so—"

"That's a favor. That's not trust. I won't do any favors for you, Sal. But I'll help a friend get out of here alive as best as I can." He held her stare. "Before that can happen, you have to tell me. Tell me what happened on that ship. Tell me what happened to Liette."

Now *that* was definitely going to end with him getting his face broken.

Or that's what he thought, seeing her face, anyway. Her scars pulled at her cheeks as her frown deepened into a grimace and her eyes narrowed so sharp he expected to look down and find himself bleeding. Whatever insult or anger he might have hurled at her, she wouldn't have bothered retorting.

But for Liette...

Well, he reasoned to himself as he closed his eyes and waited for her to punch him, *it's not like you didn't know.*

A long moment passed without a broken nose. Perhaps she was just stretching beforehand. Or perhaps she was drawing her gun. Or perhaps—

"All right."

The door closed. He opened his eyes. She stood before him.

"I'll tell you," she said. "If you'll get her out of here, I'll tell you."

He nodded. "I promise."

"Don't promise. Not yet." She sighed, rubbed at her scars. "Not until you know."

FIFTY-ONE

THE FLAGSHIP

"All squadrons to the deck, all squadrons to the deck!"
Fire. Thunder. Bones breaking and metal crashing and songs rising and the screech of birds.

"The Imperial swine have breached the flagship! All ships, all ships, converge immediately!"

The reek of powder. The spatter of blood. The staccato song of guns bursting and wood breaking and the sound of pleas and cries to uncaring skies punching through.

"In the name of the Great General and the Glorious Revolution of the Fist and Flame, do not fail! The future of the Revolution rests in your hands!"

Fighting. Dying. Killing. Screaming. Bleeding. Weeping. Singing.
"TEN THOUSAND YEARS!"

And twisting through it all out of the blare of sirens, the sound of people commanding other people to their deaths, the foulest chorus in the world's ugliest song.

Survive enough fights, battle starts to have its own harmony, its own chorus. Get into enough fights, it all starts to sound the same. I told myself that this was like that: just another tired song, just another dance I knew all the moves to, and all I had to do was pull them off and I'd be out of this. I'd survive. I'd be okay.

I told my ears this.

My eyes didn't believe it.

The sky was painted with bodies. Revolutionary soldiers flew, coats flapping behind them like too-small wings as Siegemages and Graspmages hurled them aside like toys. Birds swooped from the sky to snatch targets from the deck and carry them to hell. Waves of fire, of frost, of twisted song and writhing doom swept across the deck as the mages marched forward.

"TEN THOUSAND YEARS!"

And were met.

The doors to gangways burst open. A river of blue and flesh and steel poured out, great Paladin engines spewing smoke as they waded among the tide of Revolutionary soldiers answering the Imperial challenge. Graspmages exploded beneath clouds of gunfire, gunpike shells chewing off limbs and great chunks of flesh. Siegemages were cut down by the rattle of repeating guns as Paladins waded forward with the great weapons, spinning barrels spewing severium charges. Bodies vanished under swarms of Revolutionaries, their mouths full of anger and hands full of steel, as they carved their foes apart.

Corpses. Blood. Noise. Anger. Hate.

I knew the notes, but not this song. Not something this bloody, something so utterly devoid of any meaning beyond people killing. It hurt my ears to hear, my eyes to see, my—

"Sal."

Her voice in my ear. Her hand on mine. Her eyes—fuck me, her eyes.

Life isn't like an opera. Not usually. Wars are fought for stupid reasons instead of noble ones, people are weeds instead of flowers, love doesn't conquer all.

But it doesn't have to. It doesn't have to conquer anything. It just has to make things feel okay for just long enough to make you realize you want to live. For her. For us. For the world she wanted to build.

The world I was going to give her. Or die trying.

I tightened my fingers around hers. I slid my blade into my free hand. I met her eyes, those big brown eyes behind her glasses.

"No matter what happens," I said, "don't let go of me."

She nodded. "I won't."

I glanced out over the deck. "You ready?"

"I am," she lied.

I drew in a cold breath. I tasted my blood freezing on my lips. I felt the gun's heat, seeping into my skin.

"By the way." I paused to spit out something on the deck. "If we die here, I love you."

She smiled. "If we don't, I love you, too."

I nodded, smiled a little.

Together, we ran into hell.

Head down, sword up, don't stop moving. The old dance steps came back to me once I started running, instinct beating down pain and fear alike. *Eyes ahead, keep breathing, don't think about the blood.*

Bodies fell around us, screaming and cursing and dragging foes down with them. Explosions lit up the sky, cannons erupting in gouts of flame. Clouds of severium smoke veiled the deck, broken only by the talons of attack birds swooping down from above. The Lady's song rang out, an agonizing melody reverberating off itself, shaking my skull in my head, my bones in my body.

I didn't care.

I didn't have eyes for the dying, the suffering, the pointlessness of it—my stare was locked on the cabin across the deck and the iron door looming in it.

I heard no song, no explosion, no scream—all I listened for was the sound of her footsteps behind mine as I pulled her to keep up.

I spared no feeling for my wounds, my scars—everything in me was in my fingers, clinging to her with everything I had.

I cut when I had to. I leapt when they got in my way. I took a hit that had been meant for her. And we kept running. We kept moving. Through the smoke and the blood and the fire, we made it. The stairs leading up to the cabin loomed before us. I counted each one as we rushed up them. In my ears rang the sound of our footsteps, the thunder of my heart, the Lady's song...

Rising to a single, crystalline note.

The air shimmered before me. A blade flashed. My hand shot out, shoved Liette backward even as I fell, steel narrowly missing my throat.

I pushed her behind me as I held my own sword up. And there, standing where there had been only empty air a second ago, was a woman as cold and sharp as the blade she held, staring down its length at me through amethyst eyes alive with hate.

"Every disaster," Velline ki Yanatoril, Sword of the Empress, said simply.

I blinked. She vanished. I heard the air part behind me. I seized Liette and twisted us out of the way as Velline's blade cut a path two inches away from my heart.

"Every ruin," she said.

I couldn't say anything before she disappeared again. I hurled Liette to the side, narrowly blocking the next bite of Velline's blade as she appeared on my right.

"Every war," the Quickmage said.

Her voice was seething, anger heated and quenched and hardened into a fine point. She vanished again. The air whistled above me. I tumbled back down the stairs as she dropped from above, her sword punching through the wood and cutting the steps in half.

"Every puddle of suffering that forms on this forsaken land, you're there," Velline said, her eyes narrowing. "How are you always there, Sal the Cacophony?"

If I had the time, I would have said something cleverer than: "Get the fuck out of my way, Velline."

"All the Imperium, all the Revolution, every rancid soul to ever hold a blade has stood in your way," Velline snapped. "Still, you wreak devastation. Still, you bleed the people of the Scar. Still, you have the utter *gall* to think, at the throat of the Imperium, I would step aside."

"I'd ask you what the fuck you're talking about," I replied as I raised my blade, "but I don't have time."

Not quite a lie. I *didn't* have time, it was true—whatever Two Lonely Old Men's sigils would do to this airship was something I didn't want to be around for. But even holding up my sword felt like agony, my entire body shaking. I'd gotten sloppy, careless, taken too many stupid hits. I couldn't kill Velline. I couldn't even fight her in the state I was in. All I could do was stall until I could think of something.

"Is there any way you could summarize this for me? Maybe a pamphlet I could look at later?"

Fortunately, I wasn't too bloodied to be a dick.

"What did the Revolution offer you, Sal?" she growled, advancing toward me. "Money? Whiskey? Or are you so base and low that the mere promise of this much bloodshed was enough to lure you to their services?"

"I don't work for the Revolution." I took a step back. She noticed.

"You expect me to believe you simply happened to be aboard a ship poised to slaughter Imperial citizens?"

"Look, this shit just happens to me," I said before squinting. "Wait, what do you—"

"Do not insult me. Do not insult the people you were meant to destroy," Velline said, leveling her blade at me. "This airship is heading straight for the Blessing. Any fool can see that."

"The Blessing?" Liette adjusted her glasses, got to her feet. "The Imperial villages? No, there must be some mistake."

"There are many mistakes aboard this ship. If you ally yourself with the Cacophony, you are one of them." Velline's eyes flashed with purple light. "And I will remedy every last one of you."

Her eyes drifted toward Liette. She vanished. I swallowed every ounce of pain and fear and exhaustion, choking on them as I lunged toward her. Liette shrieked, falling beneath a shower of sparks as our blades met over her. My arm snapped out, caught Velline by the throat. I couldn't let her disappear again, couldn't let her use her magic. She twisted in my grasp, pulling us closer so I couldn't bring my blade against her. She knew what she was doing. She knew my arm was already tiring.

She knew all she had to do was wait.

She pressed, I gave. She leaned into me, my arms shook. Her eyes, hardened and sharpened to cold iron, stabbed a hateful stare into my skull, telling me to give up, that I deserved this, that I couldn't beat her. My eyes...

My eyes were on the figure standing on the deck behind us holding a ridiculously large gun.

I leapt away, falling over Liette. Perplexity covered Velline's face—of all the ways she expected this fight to end, that wasn't one of them. Then again, I bet neither was the sound of a repeating gun whirring to angry, bullet-spewing life.

At the center of the deck, so bloodied and battered she might as well have been a corpse herself, Tretta Stern stood, muscles straining to hold a Paladin armor's gigantic repeating gun. She narrowed her eyes as the barrel whirred.

"Ten thousand years," she spoke.

So did the gun.

A scream of metal and severium filled the air as the massive weapon spewed its bullets. They raked across the deck, an implacable tide of metal and severium surging toward Velline. She disappeared, emerging a second away as the bullets shredded the staircase, but the gun kept tracking her. She continued to dart away, batting away shots where she could, fleeing where she couldn't, but the hail of bullets was endless and Tretta refused to stop firing.

That gun was made to be held by a Paladin—without the suit of armor to brace it, it would shake her to pieces eventually. I supposed I should be flattered that Tretta would go to such lengths to deny Velline the pleasure of killing me, which she felt she deserved.

Torn between two women who both wanted my head. What *was* a girl to do?

Ha.

No, seriously, though, this was really bad.

"Come on, come *on*." I hauled Liette to her feet, helped her up the stairs to the helm, and shoved her at the iron door. "Open it, open it!"

"Yes, yes," she muttered as she took out a quill and an inkwell.

I glanced over my shoulder, saw that Tretta had chased Velline off. "What the fuck are you doing? I said *open* it!"

"I don't have the fucking key!" she snapped. "I need to wright it open. Just hold on."

She daubed her quill into the ink and began to scribe across the door's hinges.

The roar of the repeating gun died to a shrill whine as its ammunition ran out. Tretta cursed and started reloading, slamming a canister of bullets into its chamber.

I glanced back to Liette. *"Could you possibly maybe hurry the fuck up, please?"*

"There's a fast way to do things and a right way to do things," she replied, not looking away from her sigil. "Why do so many women want to kill you, anyway?"

"There's no time to explain it," I growled.

"Do you . . . *know* them?"

"I SAID THERE'S NO TIME!"

The repeating gun's chamber snapped shut with an echoing *clack*. The barrel whirred to life again.

"And . . ." Liette's voice hung for a painstakingly long note as she finished the sigil. "Done."

A faint light emitted from them. A heavy *click* sound emitted from behind the door. A blossom of gunfire emitted as the weapon started firing. I shoved the door forward, hearing it groan as Liette scampered inside. A hail of splinters fell over me as bullets raked across the deck. I ducked in, slammed the door behind me.

I held myself up against it, my eyes shut, my body wracked from the shudder of iron against my body as hundreds of bullets slammed futilely against the door. I waited until the song of the gun ebbed to a faint, discontented murmur.

Still alive, I told myself. Bloodied, battered, bruised, and with my skeleton vibrating inside my skin, but still alive. Once I told myself this enough times to believe it, only then did I allow myself to collapse.

"Sal," Liette whispered. Her hand was on my shoulder.

"I'm fine," I gasped. "Just need a moment to not puke my guts out."

She guided my chin up from the floor. "Look."

I looked.

Twenty empty eyes looked back at me.

I scrambled to my ass, fumbled for a weapon—I'd been so concerned with who was trying to kill me on the other side of this door that I'd forgotten there would be people on *this* side of the door waiting to kill me.

"No, Sal." Liette took me by the wrists. *"Look."*

The cabin of the helm was arranged sparsely into two levels. Upon the lower, tables for charting courses and mechanical apparatus for navigation stood huddled together. On the upper, dominated by viewing ports that showed the swirling gray beyond, stood the captain's chair, the helm wheel . . .

And the Relic.

The Relic. Bigger than three draft birds together, made up of impossible geometry, hovering in the air between a series of hastily arranged, spellwritten apparatus keeping it in place. It hung lazily there, as though defying gravity were something it did with such routine as to be mundane, pulsating with a faint light that brightened and dimmed with every heartbeat.

My heartbeat.

I couldn't look at it—even trying to make sense of its shape made my head hurt. But I couldn't *not* look at it. It was grotesquely fascinating, radiating the same morbid curiosity that makes you pull up a funeral sheet to see the body underneath. The longer I looked, the less I wanted to look away. And the closer I stared, the more I realized...

It was staring back at me.

An eternity passed before I noticed that I was still breathing. No gunfire, not even a blade drawn—surrounded by enemies and no one had bothered trying to stop us or even said a word.

That's when I noticed the blood.

Draped across a charting table, lying on the floor, their blood spattered against the windows at the rear of the helm and their bodies splayed across control apparatus. Each one of them lay there, some with daggers plunged up beneath their chins, some with messy holes in their skulls from hand cannons long gone cold fallen from their hands.

"They killed themselves," Liette gasped. "They *killed* themselves."

Grim, I thought, but not surprising. I'd seen too many commanders who presided over losing battles choose to take the quick way out rather than see a more gruesome outcome. But...that didn't make sense. This was the flagship. These were Culven Loyal's soldiers, the *Great General's* soldiers. The battle hadn't even been going that poorly for them.

Why would they...

"Scions..." Liette invoked a power she couldn't see. Which was what she always did when she was too distraught to think. She leaned over a body on the charting table, set her back into a chair, revealing the dagger plunged into her throat that she still grasped. "These were my...I *knew* them. What...*why?*"

"Apologies."

The answer came as a faint thought, like a bad idea you're trying to ignore. In my head, in my blood, in my bones, I could feel it. And as Liette's gaze was drawn upward, along with mine, I knew she felt it, too.

We stared up at the Relic.

And Eldest stared back.

"Eldest?" Liette whispered. "You did this?"

"I am sorry. I had no choice." Its voice came distant, ghostly, like a fading dream. *"Time is more limited than you know."*

I cringed—that had to be the second worst thing I could have heard aboard an airship rigged to possibly explode.

"They are coming."

And that was the first.

"Who?" Liette asked as she ascended the stairs to the Relic. "Who's coming?"

"Forces beyond what you are capable of comprehending, let alone stopping."

"Yeah," I growled. "I've heard that before."

Liette shot me a glare. I held my hands up. She was right, I knew—we'd come this far for her, I couldn't very well waste what little time we had backsassing a magic piece of shit.

But, in my defense, it wouldn't have killed it to show a little gratitude.

"We have to go," Liette said, turning back to the Relic. "We're going to get you out of here, Eldest." Realization spread across her face, hastily smothered by despair, as the gravity of the task of extracting something of such a size settled upon her. "But I don't know how…"

"Permit me."

A crack appeared in the Relic. No, not a crack, no jagged natural hew—a line, perfectly even and spanning the Relic's wild geometry. I stepped in front of Liette, blade out, as one line became a spiderweb. The ancient sound of stone grinding against itself filled the air as the pieces slowly parted from each other. A mist, reeking of long-mourned things and places long abandoned, came pouring out. First as a hiss. Then as a howl.

I pulled her close, draped my scarf over us. The mist slithered across the floor, writhing and twisting like a living thing, as it fled for the cracks and crevices of the helm, escaping out. If it was poisonous, it didn't kill us. Yet. But that quickly became the least of our concerns.

When I lowered my scarf, the Relic had opened. Its vile angles had folded back on themselves to lay bare an interior that glistened like an open wound, mist weeping out of it to reveal...to reveal...

"Holy fuck," I whispered.

And that about did it.

I didn't know how to describe it. Him? They? I didn't even know what the fuck I was looking at.

Flesh, twisted and knotted and the color of a long-dead tree, clung tenaciously to the trembling interior of the Relic. It pulsated, shuddered, *breathed* with a life that seemed ancient and unnatural. It coiled over itself countless times and, within the folds of its flesh, I could see...things.

Wings, insectine and shivering. Faces, eyes closed and mouths open in some ancient slumber. A woman's arm, long and delicate. A child's leg, chubby and nascent. An eyeball swirling madly in its socket. Organs that belonged in no monster I ever knew, let alone a person.

A great tumorous mass of...*things*. As though whatever had occurred within this husk had just begun growing whatever it wanted. And as the great mass of skin and sinew and bone trailed upward, I could see what crowned it. Or rather, what it had grown from.

Eldest. Whatever the fuck Eldest was. The left half of its body disappeared into the grotesque mass, but from it came an androgynous form, skin radiant and polished as bronze in a sunset, carved to the closest thing I could think as perfect. And its face...

Ethereal? Ancient? Angelic? Terrifying? All of those words were true.

Yet...words seemed altogether too limited, too trifling and insignificant, to encompass what looked at us out of the Relic. Alive. And aware.

"Could you..." Liette approached Eldest with a reverence she'd never offered anything before. "Could you do that the entire time?"

"*No.*" Outside the barrier of the Relic, Eldest's voice reached deeper into me, its every word like the plucking of a vein inside me as though it were a harp string. *"Not until this moment."*

"Why?"

"Because this was the moment...I would need you."

"Yeah, uh..." I stepped forward, glancing over the horrific, tumorous mass as much as I could stand. "I'm not sure how"—I gestured vaguely toward the thing-that-should-not-be—"*this* is going to help us get you out of here. You didn't get any smaller, just... squishier."

"A body is a husk. Nothing more. I require it no more than you require clothes."

I didn't want to think too hard about that.

"All that is required is this."

I didn't want to watch, either. But I couldn't look away.

With the one arm that wasn't a part of the skin, Eldest reached toward its chest. Its skin rippled, liquid and meaningless, as its fingers reached inside itself. The great mass of its entirety shuddered, tensed, as if holding a collective breath. Slowly, it withdrew its hand and reached out to Liette, its fingers unfurling. She studied it for a moment before tentatively cupping her hands together as it dropped something into her grasp.

It was beautiful.

A light. Radiant with colors I couldn't have seen in my darkest dreams. They swirled over each other, clashing against each other, a chorus of brightness that fought, lived, died entire lives in the span of seconds.

"Is it..." Liette's voice fell. Words seemed too impure to describe it. "Is this your heart?"

"If you wish it to be," Eldest's voice resonated from the light. *"It is all that I have ever been. All that I ever will be. All that I have ever wanted...and all that I have ever failed to achieve."*

Her fingers shook as they curled around the light. Slowly, its radiance softened, weeping out between her fingers, until all that remained was a perfect sphere: prismatic, polished, and tiny.

"You will...," Eldest's voice ebbed out from it, *"forgive me...one day..."*

And it fell silent.

The great knotwork of flesh and sinew that had been Eldest's body stiffened, going from tense to rictus taut. The mass grew darker, its glistening vibrancy draining with every moment and being replaced by a cracking, calcifying sound.

That noise crept across the abandoned husk. In its wake, every limb, every face, every eye and stalk and wing and finger was left petrified in pristine stone. The ethereally beautiful face of Eldest fell limp on its neck and, in the moments before it was forever frozen, I wondered if it didn't wear a look of sadness.

Then I let my breath go. And Eldest became just another ancient thing, like all ancient things: gone without answers, having left us too many questions and not enough time to figure them out.

What had Eldest meant? Who was coming? What had it failed to achieve? What the fuck kind of horror was out there that a fucking *Scrath* was afraid of it?

Maybe I was being unrealistic expecting an ancient horror that had been, up until a few hours ago, a flying turd to make some fucking sense, but still—

"Huh. So it was real."

A voice. Thick with exhaustion and long-dulled pains. A perfect match for the man who met my eyes when I whirled about, gun in my hand, to see him standing on the lower level.

Jero Erstwhile, a thick knife in his hand and blood painting his face, stared past me, past Liette, to the calcified husk of Eldest.

"I had no idea," he said.

FIFTY-TWO

THE FLAGSHIP

Jero," I whispered. I lowered my gun, let him hang from my fingers behind me—out of sight, but close.

I could feel the question boiling on Liette's lips as she stepped back. Just as she could feel the answer as I deliberately stepped in front of her and tightened my grip on my blade.

"How did he get in here?" Liette whispered.

"Did you know the Revolution builds escape hatches for its command centers? Cadre offices, garrison posts...airship cabins." Jero smiled hollowly. "They always leave a way for themselves to escape. Even while they tell their soldiers to die for them."

"How are you alive?" I asked.

"Same way you are," he replied. He took a long, limping step forward. "I couldn't die until I got here." His eyes were still on the Relic. "Fuck me, we really could have done something magical with that, couldn't we?"

"It's the whole reason we're here."

"The whole reason we're here is to bring down empires," he replied. "The Relic would have been a nice way to do that, wouldn't it? An object of unimaginable power and unknown origin that only Two Lonely Old Men knew how to use? One that could build bridges and change the world?" He grinned hollowly. "You couldn't find a better story in an opera."

I felt the ache in my muscles before I realized I'd been holding myself tense since I saw him. Every move he made, every direction his eyes wandered, made me hold my blade a little tighter. It was the blood painting his face, or the empty look in his eyes, or the ugly bend of his grin, or all of that but...

I didn't recognize him.

"It was a lie, then," I whispered. "The whole plot, all that shit, it was all a lie to get here."

"A little, yeah," he replied. "Or at least, we thought it was. Two Lonely Old Men had a few leads, but we thought them just Revolutionary propaganda." He chuckled. "Fuck, if he could be here to see this, I wonder what he'd say." His smile faded to a thousand miles away. "Or would he even care? Real or not, the Relic was never the point."

"Then what was?"

He turned his smile toward me. That same smile I'd seen in those dark nights. That same smile he greeted me with.

And it made me die a little to see it.

"Exactly what we said it was," he said simply. "Bringing down empires. By showing the world just how much blood comes out of them."

He wasn't there, the man I'd met back all those nights ago. That laughing man, who hid his pain in the dark parts of his smiling wrinkles, was gone. In his place was this killer, this man whose many faces had slid away and revealed nothing underneath. Jero was gone, I told myself. He'd had the goodness beaten out of him or just let it go to get a better grip on his weapon. This wasn't Jero, I told myself.

And I almost believed it.

I wish I could have told you I didn't recognize this man. This man with the empty eyes that had seen too much, with the blade that fit too easily in his hand.

I wish I could have told you this wasn't really him. He was someone else: the man that I had shared pain with, the man who hurt like I did, the man who was too clever, too funny, too good to be this person.

But the truth is... this was him. This was who he'd always been. The laughter, the soft voice, the gentle hands; *those* had been the act. Underneath all those faces and laughing wrinkles, he'd always been this.

Just like I was.

"Revenge," I muttered. "For Lastlight. For his precious, ruined city."

"Yeah, it sounded weird to me, too," Jero replied. "He could have just built another one. He's the greatest Freemaker the world ever knew." He tipped his head toward Liette. "No offense."

She cringed away from him. I held her a little closer to me. She knew this face, those eyes, too well to be at ease. She'd seen me wear them often enough to know.

"But then he told me something that made a lot of sense to me."

He took a step forward. We took a step back.

"He told me that a city isn't just stone and water and wood. A city is imagination, a city is ideas, a city is a dream. You pour yourself into it, everything you have, and it comes out as its own thing."

He took another step up the stairs. My pulse quickened. My chest tightened. The Cacophony seethed.

"He told me that a city can be destroyed and a city can be rebuilt. But when it comes back, it's something else. And when it's gone... it's gone forever. All those dreams, all those memories, all those things that made it what it was... just gone."

He ascended to the second level. My eyes were locked on his. And his eyes were somewhere else, some long-ago place where he had once been happy, where he'd held so tightly to something that still slipped out of his fingers.

"Even if you get another one, what you had is still never coming back. Like a person. A child. A mother."

All that remained was this man. This blade. And nothing else.

"A brother."

At the corners of his mouth, at the edges of his eyes, something trembled. The last twitch of the corpse of a good man who'd died along with his brother.

"They take, Sal. This is all these fanatics do. They take your mind, they take your body, they take your..." His lip stiffened. Wetness rimmed his eyes. "They took him from me. He was all I had and they took him apart, piece by piece. They took his heart, his voice, they carted him off like cuts of meat. Once he was totally gone, when there was nothing left of him, they sent him out to eat a bullet so they could escape."

The wetness froze on his face, disappeared, leaving behind only a long, cold dark.

"He didn't get a burial. They didn't leave enough for that. So, this is going to be his grave. This airship. This Relic. The whole fucking Scar."

I narrowed my eyes. "Killing won't bring him back, Jero."

"Don't fucking chastise me with two-copper opera rhetoric, Sal. I don't care that it won't bring him back." He sneered. "Or is killing only okay when you've got tattoos and a fancy gun?"

"I've got those, sure." I reached up, pulled the collar of my shirt down, exposed the knotted flesh of my long and winding scar. "I've also got these. Killing didn't make them go away, either."

"I know that—"

"No, you fucking don't. I mean, killing doesn't make it stop. All the blood in all the Scar that I've spilled, and every morning I still wake up hurting like hell, my scars still ache when it gets cold, and when I look in the mirror, I'm still not Red Cloud. Not anymore." I shook my head. "We kill. We do some good by killing. But it never makes us happy."

"Well, shit, Sal," he said, grinning. "You're in the wrong fucking business if you're looking for happiness, aren't you? It's gone. Along with Lastlight, Jandi, and Red Cloud. They're all gone. I know we can't make it hurt less and I know we can't bring them back…"

He raised his blade, pointed over our heads toward the viewports.

"But we can take them with us."

I turned. As the clouds parted, I saw.

Far away, so far that I could almost pretend they weren't real, I could see them. The farms, the homes, the townships, and the villages sprawling across a vast plain. The Blessing. The patch of land that everyone had decided was worth killing so many people over years ago during the Borrus War.

People. Thousands of them. Daughters and fathers and grandfathers and drunks and farmers. Sprawled across the land, so tiny from so high above, like insects ready to be crushed underfoot.

And we were heading right for them.

"She was right." The words hung icy in my craw, so jagged that I feared to speak them lest they tear my mouth apart. "Velline was right. We're heading for Imperial land." My eyes narrowed as the realization hit me. "Because someone told them we were."

"Honestly, I was surprised they took the bait," Jero said. "But what's an Imperial but a Revolutionary pointed in the opposite direction? A fanatic is a fanatic, no matter what colors they wear."

I whirled back on Jero, my jaw clenched, my blood boiling.

"This was the plan, then," I spat. "The *real* plan. Divert the Iron Fleet to the Blessing, get the Imperium to attack, and then... then..."

Cold and cruel as dawn rising on the aftermath of a battle, it hit me. The sigils in the belly of the ship. Command sigils. Etched on the Relic engine. On the hull. On the bombs.

"The bombs," I whispered. "That's what the sigils do. They're going to drop the bombs."

Jero's smile was bleak, sad, and terrifying. "This world has become so used to a fanatic's boot on its neck that they don't even notice anymore, Sal. We're part of it, you know. Vagrants, outlaws, killers... someone needs to show them. Someone needs to do something."

He reached into his satchel. I tensed, trying to draw my gun. My hand was stayed as I felt Liette's hand wrap around my wrist. Slowly, so delicate and careful I barely felt her do it, she slid the Cacophony's chamber open.

I was ready for a weapon. I wasn't ready for the tiny tin whistle he produced, laden with inscriptions.

"Urda's whistle," I breathed, recognizing it from the Crow Market so long ago.

"Close. Urda's too delicate to know what we had to do up here, but the principle is the same. Two Lonely Old Men bound the sigils' command to the sound of the whistle, just as Urda bound his sister's magic to one. Not sure why our patron decided to keep it a whistle... homage, maybe?"

I kept my eyes on his, forced his stare on mine, held every other part of me completely still. I couldn't let him notice Liette, or her hand slipping into my satchel.

"Two Lonely Old Men said he couldn't understand it," I growled.

"He couldn't, at first. But he's the greatest Freemaker the Scar has known. He figured it out. I didn't think it was necessary, personally.

If there's anything you can trust the Revolution to do, it's kill people for no reason. All we had to do was set this up and then trust them to do the rest." He sighed. "But neither he nor I wanted anything left to chance."

"So that's it, then? All this shit about building a better world? About freeing people from the Imperium and Revolution? All of it was a lie?"

"None of it was a lie. A lie worthy of the name, anyway. This world will be born again, beautiful and free of the sicknesses that plague it today. It's just going to be messier than we thought it would be."

I felt Liette's fingers wrap around a shell in my satchel. Slowly, subtly, she began to extract it, her other hand holding the Cacophony behind my back.

"But it's going to be worth it, Sal," he continued. "I know it doesn't seem like it—it was hard for me to believe at first, too. Once we deal a blow to the Imperium, to the Revolution, to *all* the fanatics out there, when we cut them so deep they can't get back up, we can start again. Once we show the world how—"

"No."

He fell silent. His words fell, cut off and bleeding on the floor.

"You're about to kill thousands, Jero," I said. "There's no grand scheme to it, no high ideal, no magic way this all works out. You're about to kill thousands. For no other reason than you want someone, *anyone*, to hurt as bad as you do." I sharpened my eyes to a scowl. "If you're going to kill them, you fucking grant them the dignity of admitting why."

I wanted a clever retort. I wanted a grand speech. I *wanted* to be wrong about him. Fuck, I needed it. I needed him to have some great words prepared to make me doubt, to show me how wrong I was, to prove this wasn't all as simple as that.

But as I looked into those empty eyes, free of wetness or pain or anything that wasn't cold and dark, I knew I was right.

And so did he.

He looked out the viewports. The mountains started to thin out, giving way to hillside villages. We were here.

"You're right, Sal," he whispered. "You're absolutely fucking right. You deserve honesty, just as they do."

He raised the whistle to his lips. Liette slipped the shell into the Cacophony.

"So believe me when I say," he whispered.

The sigils across the whistle began to glow. The Cacophony's chamber snapped shut.

"I'm sorry."

"Yeah."

Then I drew.

"Me too."

And I pulled the trigger.

A burst of smoke. A searing heat. A wall of sound. Discordance sped toward him. He'd seen me draw, flicked his wrist, a retractable shield starting to deploy. He was quick. Too quick.

But that's the thing about the Cacophony. You can be the quickest, the cleverest, the most ruthless, it doesn't matter. He breaks them all the same.

Discordance erupted in a blast of sound. The viewports cracked, bodies and equipment scattering like toys in a tantrum. Jero's shield protected him enough to send him rolling instead of flying, but it caught him off guard.

He'd dropped the whistle.

I bolted for it, ignoring the agonized shriek of my body. Any pain, any exhaustion, any fear, I'd have time enough to feel later, if I were still alive. Because if I stopped now, I wouldn't be. None of us would.

Jero got to his feet quicker than I wanted. His own injuries barely seemed to faze him as he ran for the whistle as well. He leapt. I leapt. We landed. Him atop me.

Me atop the whistle.

"Jero, don't—"

He didn't let me finish before his fist found my side. No more words, no more stalling, the only sound was my scream as he punched at me. I curled over the whistle, but he didn't even bother trying to get at it. He kept punching and each blow hurt worse than the last one. He knew where I was injured, knew where my scars were, knew where to hit to make me hurt the worst.

"GET OFF OF HER!"

Two screams. One of anger. One of pain. Neither of them mine.

Liette leapt onto his back, a sharpened quill in her hand. She jammed it into his neck, trying to find a jugular. But we were thrashing too much and all she managed was a deep carve from his jaw to his shoulder. Ugly, but not fatal.

Pity.

If she'd been a little cooler, a little more patient, she could have done some spellwrighting—paralyzed him, made him explode, I don't know. But she hadn't. I was more important to her than reason.

Only then, bitterly and blood-soaked, did I realize it took me until now to see that.

Heh. Maybe life was like an opera.

Sometimes.

Jero snarled, whirling around with an elbow that found her ribs. He'd struck exactly where he needed to. I heard a sick crack, I heard her scream, I heard her body hit the floor.

I roared, trying to turn on him, to smash his face, claw his eyes, find some part of him I could hurt. My fingers found his wound, sunk in, tore. He screamed, returned it with a punch to my face. And another. And another. Until my voice ebbed out of me, my breath ran short, my vision went dark...

And my body fell, limp.

He caught me by the collar, held me aloft as he stared down at me through empty eyes. No pity. No remorse. Nothing but the hurt. And the reflection of steel as he drew his blade and leveled it at me, hanging there for a long, breathless eternity.

"Fuck," I grunted, struggling to find breath. "*Now* you want to talk?"

"No," he replied. "We know how this is going to end. I just want to tell you it didn't have to be this way. Whatever the reason, whatever the methods, there's going to be a new world. A better world. You could have been a part of it. We both could have." He flipped his grip, raised the blade high, ready to punch it down. "Just know, Sal, that it's going to be worth it."

"Yeah." My eyelids drooped. Things started to go black. But I'm glad I had enough left in me to see his face when I spoke next. "I'll tell that to Jandi when I reach him at the black table. I bet he'll understand."

Every wrinkle, scar, and wound contorted in anger. There for a second, gone in another, leaving only the emptiness behind. But for a brief, glorious moment, he knew exactly the monster he was about to become, and it would haunt him forever.

Coldest fucking comfort in the world.

At least it was something to hold on to.

As he tightened his grip.

As I closed my eyes.

And the blade came down.

FIFTY-THREE

THE FLAGSHIP

Whoever else she had been, Red Cloud was me.

Butcher. Criminal. Warrior. Loyal servant of the Imperium. I wouldn't dispute any of those titles—she'd earned them all and we both had to live with that.

But she was also Salazanca ki Ioril. She loved opera, loved wine, loved certain people who loved her back. She kept trying to pick up painting but never had the patience to be good at it. She liked stand-offish cats, loved affectionate dogs, and adored unpleasant birds. When her spells were cast, the Lady Merchant's song never rang out more clearly or more beautifully.

Maybe every mage thinks that about their own magic. I don't know. But my spells, the good ones and the bad ones and all the ones I can't take back, had a song like nothing I'd ever hear again. Even when I just waved my fingers, when I just *thought* about using my magic, I'd hear her—as clear as a single bell played in the middle of a field just before dawn, a note meant for me and me alone. I didn't feel powerful when I heard it, nor murderous or any of the other things they said Red Cloud should be.

I felt close to the sky.

I always wondered...when I finally died, when I went to the black table to take the place that had been set for me so long ago...

Would I hear her song again? Just once? Just for me?

I thought I had. When I closed my eyes and waited for Jero's blade to fall, I heard it. Distant. Soft. Quiet and shy like an opera singer's understudy on her first night. I knew that song. I'd fallen asleep to it on nights when I couldn't stop crying, woken up to it on mornings when I'd never wanted to wake back up, looked for it on that dark night when the Lady's song was taken from me forever. I knew that song. I loved that song.

But it wasn't mine.

I opened my eyes. Jero's blade, wet with blood, hung over me, an inch away from plunging into my eye. A droplet of crimson slid down its length, spattered upon my cheek.

And that's all that came.

He released me, slid off of me. I wasted no time in scrambling toward Liette, even as my body screamed from its wounds, throwing myself over her. I waited for the blow to come then, too.

It still didn't.

What was he playing at? What long game had he been plotting this entire time? I whirled to face him, expecting that ugly grin, that empty face. Anything but the dark wetness I saw in his eyes.

"Sal," he said softly, "I...don't make me. Go wherever you want. Take whoever you need. Leave me and all of us to die here, if you have to. Just don't..." He swallowed hard. "Don't make me kill you."

No matter how many scars you carry or how tough you are, there are words that can cut you. Sometimes they're sharpened specifically for you, sometimes they find just the right place to stab. And sometimes it doesn't matter what words they are, just the mouth they come out of.

How could he do this? How could he show me that face again? The face that he showed me over the fire. The face with kindness stewing beneath the sorrow. How could he show me *mercy*?

It wasn't any stupid warrior's pride that made me incensed. It was the gall, the brazenness, the utter *arrogance* with which he showed it. He didn't get to pretend that he was doing this for me.

"Make you?" I laughed blackly, tasting my own blood. "I didn't make you do shit. No one *makes* people like us do these things, Jero. We do them"—I narrowed my eyes—"because we *need* them."

He couldn't hold my stare. His eyes drifted toward the Relic, the empty husk, then back down to me.

"This world needs the Revolution gone," he muttered. "The Imperium, gone. The Ashmouths, Haven, the Freemakers, *everyone* gone. And if this Relic makes it to any of them..." He lowered his eyes, now cold again, back to me. "But it doesn't need you to die here, Sal. Drop the whistle. Walk away. Let me finish this."

I offered him no more words. No more meaningful glances. I wasted no more hope on the belief that he'd change, that his final mask would fall away and reveal the person I'd seen in the dark.

He didn't offer anything, either. The face he showed me now— whether it was his, another mask, or someone I'd never know—was empty but for the coldness in his eyes.

All we had left for each other was the steel in our hands. Our blood weeping down our skin. And the sound of boots faintly rapping across the iron floor.

Not his.

Nor mine.

I looked to the shadows of the cabin. Something emerged from there. My eyes went wide. I felt a droplet of blood weep down my temple, dangle from my cheek, and fall to the floor.

My heart fell with it.

FIFTY-FOUR

ELSEWHERE

In my dreams, their faces are always different.

Sometimes, they're like opera masks: noses so sharp, eyes so big, mouths twisted into grotesque smiles. Sometimes, they're shadows: features painted black and smooth so that I can't even tell they're humans. But to the last of them, in my dreams, they're monsters. All of them. Whether they cut me, burn me, bleed me, break me, or just stand by and watch, their faces are always monstrous.

Except hers.

In my dreams, I remember her face. Never a mask, never a shadow, never a monster. In my dreams, her eyes are stained by salt and her lips are dry and her breath is like sand. She never looks twisted, nor fiendish, nor even sorrowful.

In my dreams, Darrishana looks…tired.

Like she looked that night.

"Hey."

The Imperial Gardens were quiet that night. The great birds that had sailed through the sky all day had returned to their roosts. The evening's entertainment had been brief and somber and was long since over. Beneath the black eyes of the darkened windows that stared down upon the tangle of flowers and greenery below, only the chirp of insects could be heard.

"Darrishana," I whispered to her shadow as I saw her enter. "Over here."

More than anything, I wanted her to answer back. I wanted her to curse me. I wanted her to scream at me. I wanted her to hate me, as vocally and furiously as she could, if she had to. Anything to tell me I still existed to her, to tell me she still saw me as I was. As I had been, before the day she left.

To serve as a shield on the Unending Front, I'd heard. Or sometimes, to go and help lift the siege of Thalmassia. Or sometimes to shield the Siegemages in their assault at Mount Hornbeak. In those days, my mind was filled with rumors—some I'd heard from the other soldiers, some I made up myself.

Had she been sent to another unit because the generals needed her elsewhere? Or had she requested to be removed because of me? Was she not writing because the letter carriers had been ambushed, like I thought I heard? Or was she just out of words for me? Was she all right? Was she suffering? Was she worrying about me as much as I was worrying about her?

I didn't know. In all the battles and all the days and all the bodies that followed that long time since she had left, I never knew anything but that she was far away, she was fighting, and she wasn't speaking to me.

It had been months since Vigil. Months since she'd spoken to me. Months since she'd looked at me like I was a monster. Months since she'd spoken the name Red Cloud with all the fear and hate that my enemies had.

What we'd had…

Whatever we'd had…

It was gone. I knew that now. Maybe I even knew it then. I'd denied it, still waiting for her to come back to my chambers each night. I'd accepted it when I saw her turn her eyes away from me. I'd mourned it the nights we'd spent together, I'd found another pair of arms to slide into, I'd deluded myself into thinking I didn't care anymore.

Until that night.

When I called out to her.

And she came.

Darrishana's silhouette paused at the field of my vision, just beneath the southern archway to the gardens. We'd been filing in all night, trickling in one by one so as not to be noticed. I'd been instructed, that night, not to loiter—it might attract attention, even if the Empress had no reason to doubt our loyalties. But I'd stayed near the southern gate—the one closest to where she used to live, the one I was sure she'd come through—to see her.

She lingered there a moment, maybe debating whether to come out, I don't know. But she still came to me. And when she stepped out of the shadow...

It was still her. Still Darrishana. Still with the soft hands and gentle eyes. But it wasn't the woman I'd known. Even before we spent those nights together.

There are no war heroes. Not really. That's just another opera trick they came up with to avoid another reality, one that the Imperium found too useful to let go. There are no conquerors, no triumphant heralds of Imperial Law. Like every conflict, there are only varying degrees of survival.

The luckiest lose something important they can live without. They get sent back and learn to live with the price they paid. The less lucky give everything, but only at the end, their bodies broken by battle and their magic Bartered until there's nothing left but Dust and a few solemn words half-heartedly delivered by someone important in nice clothes. But the unluckiest...

They looked like her.

It was her body, but it bent a little lower. It was her face, but it hung empty and slack. It was her eyes, but they were empty.

Sometimes...sometimes it hollows people out. The war. The tension. Just the knowledge of knowing that someone out there, someone you don't even know, is going to try to kill you. It burns through you, eats you away piece by piece, taking the parts of you that were meant for other things and devoting them to the fight.

Sometimes, you feel it happening and you stop it. Sometimes, you feel it happening and you don't. And sometimes you don't even notice it until you're walking on legs that aren't yours and looking out of eyes that you can't remember how to use.

"Sal." Her voice. Still her voice. But no laughter in it anymore. "We should go. We're going to be late. Vrakilaith said—"

"Vraki can wait." I cut her off. I did that a lot back then. "I haven't seen you in ages. I was hoping I could..." No, that wasn't right. "I wanted to..." That, either. "Where have you been?"

That wasn't what I wanted to say, what I should have said. But it was what came out. It was what made her look up at me with hollowed-out eyes.

"The war," she replied softly. "I've been at the war."

"Yeah, it's..." I winced. "It's been rough."

She didn't say anything to that. Her eyes slid downward, staring into nothing. At nowhere.

The last vestiges of my talent for diplomacy faded with my sigh. "Look," I said, "I'm sorry. For what happened. For how it happened. I don't know. It's just..." Frustration leaked out between my clenched teeth on a hot breath. "I'm not good at this. I've never had to be before. I flew, I burned, and I came back and everything was fine. Maybe that's what you meant. Maybe I never had to learn how to be..."

I trailed off, hot with anger. This was always the part where she'd take my hand and help me. Then she'd say something encouraging, I'd say something witty, and everything would go back to the way it was. That's how we used to do it.

I guess some part of me thought that's how it was always going to be.

But it wasn't. I know that now. She wasn't Darrishana anymore. Hell, maybe I wasn't even Red Cloud anymore. Red Cloud solved problems effortlessly and, when she couldn't, she flew away and disappeared into the sky until all of them, and the little people who had them, were ants on the ground.

I could have done that. It probably would have spared me a lot of pain if I had.

But instead...

"I don't know how to tell you," I said, my voice painfully soft to my own ears. "I don't know how to explain it or what to say or what the right words are for this part. I never did. I don't know if I ever will. But I need you..." I swallowed something bitter. "I need you to help me. To tell me what to say or what to do or how many times to do it so that you..." I closed my eyes, unable to look at her anymore. "I need you to not hate me, Darrishana."

"I don't hate you, Sal."

There was something sad about her voice that night. Not sorrowful, not the heart-wrenching kind you see after loss. This was... empty, mechanical, an echo of something that had once been vibrant. The way she stared into nothing as she spoke...

I should have paid more attention.

"I don't know if I have any hate left in me anymore, after what I've seen," Darrishana said. "I can't tell who my enemies are or who my allies are anymore. I don't know who I'm supposed to be protecting and I don't know how killing people is supposed to do it. This war... this Imperium... the Empress..."

Her eyes widened. To the point where I could see the last vestiges of fear dangling off the edge of their hollowness. Her words came with a terrified breath.

"And it's *everywhere*," she said. "Every place I go, it's the same. They get changed. They turn into you. To me. No matter what I do, no matter how I try to help them, or what I change, I can't... I can't..."

There should have been tears that came after that. A wracking sob that I could at least try to fix by holding her close. But all that came out of her was the longest, tiredest sigh I'd ever heard.

It's not dramatic, the Barter that Wardmages give. Most people don't even think of it, really. There's no physical change like Skymages losing their breath, no personality change like Siegemages losing their memories.

But giving up the ability to feel safe... to walk without worrying someone's behind you, to look at people without realizing how fragile they are, to know no home without knowing the fear that it'll one day be lost...

What must it have been like, I would one day ask myself, to look at the world and see only the ways it can hurt?

If I had asked myself that on that night, maybe things would have been different.

"Sal," she whispered. "Would you forgive me?"

I recoiled, that question feeling like a slap in my face. "For what?"

"For..." She swallowed hard. "For anything."

I've sometimes wondered...

If I knew what she was truly asking, if I knew what was going to happen, would I have said what I said? Would I have still taken her hand in mine, would I still have held it the way I did and smiled at her like I did?

"Never give up on me," I said, "and I'll never give up on you."

I don't know.

I don't think I ever will.

I wanted her to smile at that. I wanted to have even a glimpse of how things used to be. I wanted to be able to pretend that somehow, things could go back to the way they were.

But she didn't. She said nothing. She did nothing.

She just...stared.

Until I released her hand. My smile fell. She walked off, numb, to a dark place, her shape growing hazier in the darkness, until I couldn't see her anymore.

I can't remember how long I stayed there, staring after her, only that I did so until I heard the Lady's song in my ears and felt the wind stir behind me as someone appeared from nothingness.

"Are you all right?" he asked.

"Yeah," I lied, wiping my face with the back of my hand. "She's fine. I'm fine."

"She's not," he said. "She gave everything to the Empress's war. To her nul son. Now there's nothing left."

Up until a few weeks ago, it had been our war. All of us.

"But we'll make a better world. For her."

His hand appeared on my shoulder. I leaned into it, breathed in the scent of his fingers, of his hilt's leather and oiled metal. He pulled me closer to him and I let him.

"For us," he whispered in my ear.

"For us," I repeated.

We stayed that way as long as we could. Until his hand slid to mine, the other on his blade, and he coaxed me deeper into the garden.

"We should go," he said. "Vraki and the others will be waiting."

I nodded. I squeezed his hand.

I followed Jindu.

Out of that night.

And into that dark place.

—⊷ ≡✦≡ ⊶—

She didn't look like she should.

She clutched a wound in her side. Her breath was ragged and her face was fallen. She stood proud on legs that wanted to kneel, stared out of eyes that wanted to close. She wasn't the monster from my list, the shadow from my dreams, the woman from my past.

She was Darrishana. Standing there. Alive. Tears streaming down her face.

"How was it supposed to end?" she asked.

Jero's face screwed up. My mouth fell open. Neither of us knew then that she was asking both of us, neither of us, whoever could answer it.

"In your darkest dreams," she continued, "when you've won, when everyone who needs to be punished is dead and all the problems that haunt you disappear, how does it end?"

Her eyes, wide and desperate, drifted toward me. I wasn't ready for those eyes. I wasn't ready to see her like this. I fumbled for an answer, fumbled for one of the many dreams I'd had where I could still fly, where I didn't hurt, where I knew only people who wanted me there.

And I found…

I couldn't picture them.

"You're the Vagrant," Jero observed coldly. "You've been help-ing these fanatics. I found evidence of your presence, but I never thought—"

"HOW DOES IT END?"

She screamed to be heard over him, winced as she did. Her legs buckled with the exertion, sent her leaning against the wall. I had to fight an urge I didn't know I had to rush forward and help her. But Liette, breathing ragged, leaned hard on me, as if fearing I would leave her.

"Do you think this ends with the Revolution? The Imperium?" Darrish asked. "Do you think this ends with a weary people crawl-ing out of the rubble and weeping gratitudes for you, the people who killed them?" She turned her glare to him, trembling and brimming with tears. "In your darkest dreams, does it even *end*?"

"We are here *because* it needs to end," he snapped. "Because *some-one* has to show the world, someone has to stop them."

"You're not going to stop it."

It wasn't with scorn that Darrish spoke. Her voice quavered, shook, naked with terror, every word heralded by ragged, desperate breath.

"You're not going to stop anything. I heard your plan. I know your ambitions. You dream of a world where things go back to normal." Her frown scarred itself across her face. "But they aren't going to."

"They will. They *will*," Jero insisted. "The survivors will—"

"Will hate you," Darrish finished for him. "The ones who don't die from despair will spend every moment of every hour dreaming of *you*. Your face, your voice, your dreams, and how *they* can take those things away from you. They will never stop dreaming of their own normal. They'll never be able to imagine a normal where *you* live."

Jero cringed. As though she'd struck him so hard his face flew clean off and revealed behind the same terror on her face, in her words. For a moment, he believed her.

For a moment.

"Is that it?" His face hardened again, became the mess of shadows and wrinkles and emptiness I knew. "Some banal observation on the cycle of hatred? Or are you about to tell me about the power of friendship and a kind and loving god?" He sneered at her. "Did you expect me to believe some shitty lecture by a *Vagrant*, of all people?"

She shook her head slowly, stiffly. "I'm not lecturing you. I'm showing you." She placed a bloodied hand to her chest. "My name is Darrishana ki Kaltua. I fought for the Imperium. I betrayed the Imperium. I betrayed…"

She stole a glance at me out of the corner of her eye.

"Someone I shouldn't have," she said. "I wanted her to go back to the person I knew. I wanted us to become the people we wanted to be. I wanted…I wanted things to be normal again." She swallowed hard and pointed that same bloody hand, that red finger, at me. "And what I did to her…she did to everyone."

My heart froze in my chest. My breath caught in my throat. I couldn't speak. Couldn't run. Couldn't move. That finger…those eyes…I never wanted to see them again. I wanted her to look at me like I was a monster, like I was a killer, not like this…

"I'm sorry, Salazanca."

Not like she meant it.

"I'm sorry for what I did to you, for what I tried to make you, for what you did to the Scar." The tears cut clean trails down her grimy face. Her body shook with every sob, so much that I wanted her to stop, for both our sakes. "I'm sorry I'm here, I'm sorry you even have to think of me again, but I can't let this happen.

"Do this," she gasped, looking back to Jero, "and you'll make more. More killers, more murderers, more people who hate and kill and betray as easily as we do. But walk away..." She breathed hard. "Walk away...and your sins...they'll be yours to live with. But they'll end here."

I had dreamed of moments like these.

Moments where Darrish was bloodied and broken, tears streaming down her face as she begged for mercy. In those moments, sometimes I killed her quickly, sometimes I killed her slowly. But always, I woke up with my blood pumping and my teeth clenched and a hunger to get out there and find her, find all of them, and make them pay.

But now...I couldn't feel my blood, or my teeth, or the steel in my hand or the gun on my hip. I had been ready for her words. I had been ready for the lies, the pleas, the curses I imagined she'd say. I wasn't ready to see her like this...

I wasn't ready to see her in pain.

Liette groaned softly at my side, clutching her ribs. I wrapped my hand around her, helping her stay up. Jero had hit her harder than I'd thought, hurt her deeper than I believed he could.

Maybe too deep.

"Walk away," Jero repeated, staring blankly at the floor. "Walk away. Save the world."

"Save the people," Darrish replied. "Save everyone who would be turned into a killer by this."

"Walk away," Jero whispered to himself, over and over. "Walk away...walk away...Let it all fall apart, let it all end here...walk away..."

He looked back up.

His eyes were cold and empty as winter.

"And let my brother die"—he tightened his grip on his blade—"for nothing."

"SAL!"

He moved faster than her scream, faster than my eyes. Jero was rushing toward me, his eyes on the whistle in my hand, his blade aimed for my throat. No fear, no remorse, nothing in his eyes but the glitter of the whistle and the need to have it, the need to hurt. I couldn't raise my steel in time, I couldn't defend myself holding Liette up, I couldn't hear—

Anything. But the Lady Merchant's song.

The air shimmered beside Jero. An invisible wall burst into existence, striking him harshly and shoving him, his body sent flying across the floor of the cabin. I looked from his prone form to Darrish, her bloodied hand extended and her eyes alight with magic.

"GO!" she shouted.

I pulled Liette as tight as I dared, made our way quick as we could manage to the door. But I already heard the scrape of cloth as Jero pulled himself to his feet, the rush of boots as he came charging toward us. We rushed for the door—I could still open it, still escape. All I had to do was get out of here before—

A hard jerk on my neck. Jero grabbed my scarf, pulled hard. I choked, flailing to shake him off. The Lady's song rose again, another wall bursting between us. Jero staggered back. I turned to see his scowl affixed upon the pale figure in front of him.

Darrish, her arms spread wide, the Lady's song pouring out of her. Jero rushed toward her, lashed out with his blade. The air shimmered as he struck her shield, shuddering like a living thing. With each blow, she winced.

"Darrishana!" I shouted at her.

"Get out of here, Sal," she replied, not looking back at me. "Hurry."

"You can't stop him," I said. "You're not a fighter."

"No. But you are." She glanced over her shoulder, toward Liette. "Protect her, Sal. She's what you need to get out of here."

"Darrish, I..." I searched for the words, the right ones. "I want to...I want to forgive, but..."

"This isn't for forgiveness." She smiled at me. The way she used to. The way she still did in my dreams. "This is for love."

The shield shuddered. Behind it, Jero let out a long, hateful scream. Darrish winced, looked at me pleadingly to go. I held that look for as long as I dared, and I wondered, briefly...would that be what I saw when I dreamed of her again?

Liette groaned beside me. I tightened my grip on her. I turned toward the door.

I tried to ignore the sound of the Lady's song growing fainter behind me.

I struggled with the latch. I don't know how we made it out. I didn't even know we were outside until the wind was blowing in my face, howling so hard I couldn't even hear the sound of the Lady's song, or the sound of Jero's screaming, or anything.

Anything... but a single, desperate voice screaming into the wind.

As steel flashed and cloth of crimson, deep as stained blood, appeared over the edges of the airship.

"GAZE UPON ME, O SEEING GOD!" one of the Haveners shouted as he crawled over the railing, machete held high.

And that cry was taken up. Echoed by another. Then ten.

Then a hundred.

FIFTY-FIVE

THE FLAGSHIP

N⁰. "Carve them apart, brothers! Let their lives atone for their sins!"

No.

"Do not relent, sons and daughters of the Imperium! Strike down every nul!"

NO.

"Destroy the zealot! Purge the corrupt! The Great General is with you!"

This couldn't be happening. We were going to escape. I was going to fix things. We were so close.

The air was soaked with the sound of suffering: screams and cries of terror fighting to be heard over the blare of the Revolutionary anthem playing dutifully over the sirens, the resonant song of the Lady Merchant, the cackling glee of Haven butchery.

The deck was laden with the afterthoughts of slaughter: the groaning bodies trampled underfoot, limbs twisted and broken and scattered like ashes, broken weapons and churning machines mingling with flesh to form a barrier of carnage I couldn't hope to cross even if I wasn't already torn up.

How? HOW?

I got my answer as a mountain peak whizzed by out of the gray. The range was thinning out. We were flying even lower. From the cliffs, Haveners were launching themselves with grappling ropes to crawl upon the deck and indulge in wanton slaughter. The Revolutionaries and Imperials had been suddenly forced into a desperate battle against the boarders.

Whatever order there had been to the melee was now cold and stiff on the ground. Swords turned to flailing steel. Gunpikes discharged in all directions. Screams flew through the air more than crossbow bolts did. It was chaos. It was carnage.

It was impossible.

How the fuck were we going to escape? How the fuck was I going to get out of this one? We were too injured, there were too many of them, this was too much to—

"BURN, PAGAN!"

A flash of flame and steel. A Havener came rushing toward me, torch and blade brandished. His battle cry was depraved laughter, unbroken by the many wounds painting his body. His stride was a frenzied dash, legs pumping furiously as he leapt, his grin broader than any blade I'd ever seen.

Right up until he saw the Cacophony leveled at him, anyway.

I pulled the trigger. The hammer clicked. Discordance caught him square in the face, an eruption of sound scattering teeth and pulped bone aside as his body went flying, limp as a fish, back into the throng to disappear beneath the brawl.

"Foolish."

The Cacophony's hiss could only barely be heard over the violence, but I felt his contemptuous sear all the same. He was right, it had been foolish—stupid to waste a shot on one man, stupid to have used the gun at all. Even the sloppy way I had found a shell and loaded it had aggravated my wounds.

But I didn't have a choice. I was too broken, too bloodied, too hurt. To fight, to run, to do anything but pull a trigger. I couldn't... I couldn't...

I looked out over the battle, gun drawn and loaded, for a moment that drew out like a knife. I couldn't pick out people anymore. All I saw was a tide, a drowning wave of steel and blood into which soldiers and fanatics and mages alike were churned, drowned, and dissipated. These weren't people anymore. This wasn't a battle. It was a sea of violence.

Soon enough, it would rise to my feet. It would sweep over my head. I would disappear beneath it, like all the others.

The Cacophony fell to my side. My heart fell into my belly.

It takes a lot to make a woman with a magic gun feel hopeless. But I knew a rigged game when I saw it. Even if the twins and Agne hadn't escaped through a portal yet, I'd never get through that carnage. Not with both of us alive. Whatever skiffs or ropes or cheap operatic last-minute hopes for escape might exist would be destroyed.

Can't escape. The thought flooded into my mind on a tide of horror. *Can't escape, can't fight, can't—*

The thought was interrupted by a surge of heat coursing through my palm, into my arm, into my chest. I looked down at the piece of brass burning hot in my hand. And he looked back at me, grinning.

Without any words, he told me how this was going to end. How it always was going to end.

I nodded solemnly. I quietly loaded the gun. I held Liette close to me. I stared out over the battle.

I waited for it to take us.

"Prow."

Liette's voice. Desperate as her hands as she reached up for me, clinging to my arm. She looked up at me through a face wracked with pain as she clutched Eldest's heart to her breast.

"Get to the prow," she grunted through clenched teeth. "We have to...to..."

She couldn't finish, either because of the pain or because she didn't know what the fuck was going on. It didn't matter which. If these were our last moments, if this was the last thing I ever did for her...

I would carve through every last killer on the Scar to give it to her.

I held her close, propped her against my body, draped my scarf around us, and held my gun out as I maneuvered us down the stairs back to the deck and around the helm's cabin.

Every step hurt; even a particularly harsh glare could have knocked me over. But I kept going. Stepping over bodies and around the broken husks of people who sat, drenched in blood, minds

broken by the horror. Edging around knots of brawls and under
shots that broke through the brawl. Around the eruptions of magic
and through the bloody path wrought by the Paladin armor as it
charged through the battle, Haveners clinging and hacking futilely
at its metal hide.

Step by step, breath by breath, I pulled us free of the carnage,
around the helm and toward the prow.

At the bow of the airship, against the roar of wind and clouds, a
morbid tranquility settled. The deck here wasn't drenched in bodies
and fallen weapons. The hum of the airship's motor drowned out the
sound of violence behind us. The figurehead of the Great General,
eyes forward and hand extended in warning to the world we flew
over, seemed almost serene, blissfully unaware of the horrors occur-
ring behind his back.

Or maybe what lay ahead was just more interesting to him.

Almost free of the mountains, the world opened up beneath the
veil of clouds. And the Blessing, its verdant fields and hills rolling for
eternity, sprawled out before us. Across its rolling land, villages dotted
like plant life, mushrooms growing in the shadows of enormous trees.

This was what Jero had hoped to destroy. What Two Lonely Old
Men had hoped to ruin. What I had helped to bring the war to.

The war...

I saw the other airships, far ahead of us. Missing one, their hulls
rent apart by birds and magic, the last of the Iron Fleet sailed on over
the Blessing, over its fields...

Over its villages.

You stopped Jero, I told myself, my breath caught in my chest. *You
took the whistle. You stopped their plan. Their sigils can't work now.
You stopped it. You saved everyone. You stopped it.*

Hope has a way of torturing time. The long, cold dread that fills
your chest when you desperately want something to be better than
it is makes your head swim. Seconds draw out to hours draw out to
days. And every breath you take or hold while you wait for something to happen is agony.

Just like it was as I stared out over the Fleet. As I watched them
for minutes—for hours, for days, I couldn't tell anymore—hanging

in the air like the lie you knew you'd regret or the truth you never wanted to tell. As I waited. And watched. And held my breath.

Until, so far away I could almost pretend it wasn't real, the first airship's belly swung open.

And a tiny black shape, small and insignificant and utterly inconsequential, fell to the earth.

And a house was gone.

A plume of fire erupted from the earth. From up here, it looked so small, like I could close my eyes and pretend it hadn't been so bad. Then another fell. And another. And a garden of flame burst across the Blessing.

I remembered what it was like to look down from on high onto a sea of fire.

And who it would be that drowned in it.

"No."

My voice. Breathless. Weak. Lost on the wind.

"No."

Cutting my mouth as I spoke it.

"They did it," I whispered. "Those fucking... those shitheads... those... those..."

What good would words do anymore? Words wouldn't be able to take those bombs back. They couldn't explain what sense it made for the Revolution to attack a village to punish an army. They couldn't fix anything...

And yet.

"That's not fair," I said to myself. "I stopped him. I stopped it all. They can't do this." I clenched my teeth. "THEY CAN'T DO THIS."

You would think so, would you not?

A voice. A thought? No...

It takes so little to convince them to hurt themselves.

A heartbeat.

Time passes, mountains crumble, rivers dry, and they still kill themselves for no reason.

In my head. In my body. In my blood.

Ah, well.

In the clouds ahead, a mountain peak loomed large in our path. Towering, twisted, with things that looked like limbs.

Perhaps that's why they fascinate us so much.

It wasn't until I saw the collection of massive animal skulls serving as its head that I realized it was no mountain.

And by then, it had me.

The airship groaned to a sudden halt, sending us skidding along the deck to slam against the railing. My body exploded in pain, just enough of me left to scramble away from the sides as a colossal hand made of briars, trees, and wicker reached up and seized the hull of the ship, each finger twice the size of me. It was followed by another, and another, three misshapen limbs holding on to the airship and keeping it from moving.

They pulled the railing down low. A morbid display of skulls and bone, lashed together by wire and rope, peered over the edge of the airship. I stared at it, clutching Liette, mouth agape.

The effigy stared back.

It was different than the one back in Terassus—bigger, angrier, more skulls and limbs—but I knew its stare. I knew the fires burning inside its body of bone and wood. I knew the sound of its heart beating in perfect time with mine.

"I can feel you," its wooden body rumbled, a voice so soothing having no place coming out of a creature so foul. *"I can feel your body crumbling. I can feel your thoughts swirling about inside you."* Its collection of skulls canted to the side, almost quizzical. *"Is that fear? Love? Both? Or are you so pedestrian as to be consumed with wondering how I found you? Would that I could provide an answer that would not break you."*

Splinters and twigs popped from its colossal body as it moved. Its great mass swiveled toward Liette, its fires stoked inside the empty sockets of its many skulls.

"Would that any of us had time."

Without thinking about it, without even breathing, I stepped in front of her. I held the Cacophony out, his grin leveled at the effigy's heads. The great mass of wood and flame and bone did not seem impressed.

Not that I could tell, what with it being a bunch of fucking skulls strapped together.

"Ah, a moment. I recognize this sensation consuming you." A wistful sigh escaped the effigy on plumes of smoke seething out its many holes. *"That yawning sense of futility. That dawning realization that all that you possess, all that you can do, all that you are is not enough. And never will be. It lurks in every prayer and every desperate hope."*

It leaned over the railing. Liette took my free hand, the two of us backing away from the shower of cinders and splinters as the effigy's shadow fell over us.

"My faithful, too, radiate it," it hissed. *"Would that you could feel them as I feel. The fervor of their devotion, the rush of their fear, the sheer ecstasy of feeling both of them break at the same time. As I offered them salvation, so, too, do I offer it to you."*

I saw it for the first time. A flash of pain and light across my eyes, like the flickering ache of an old wound. I saw within the effigy, past the wicker and bone, past the blood and flame, to the burning heart within. To the eyes that stared back out at me.

The Seeing God stared at me. And it extended one of its massive hands, beckoning.

"Render unto me what is mine and I will give it all to you," it said. *"Safety. Security. Whatever you need to convince yourselves such things are attainable. Everything your feeble person craves that you refuse to acknowledge yearning. It can be yours. Simply return my sibling to me."*

Its wooden fingers extended, popping and creaking, as it held out a colossal, splintering palm.

"Return Eldest."

Eldest?

Sibling?

Shit. Shit, shit, shit.

You wouldn't think there were many things that could make a ten-story-tall monster of bone and fire that could crush you with one finger more frightening. But a ten-story-tall monster of bone and fire that was also a fucking Scrath sure as shit would do it.

This thing—monster, effigy, Seeing God, whatever the fuck its twisted devotees called it—was no god, no savior. It was a parasite. A fetid tick riding a host, drinking the blood offered it. What had it offered Haven that they agreed to follow it? Did they even know?

I didn't. But I knew what it was offering me.

The beating of my heart flickered in time with the quivering of its fires. I could feel its voice inside me, reading my thoughts, my feelings like they were graffiti on a wall. I could feel the promises it offered, the sincerity of its sensation. How easy would it be, I wondered, to just reach out my hand and simply take it?

But to do that... I'd have to let go of her first.

I looked back to Liette. And she looked at me. No pain in her eyes, no fear, no scorn. It spoke to her as it spoke to me, offering promises, rewards, things even she couldn't put into words.

I wondered... did visions of me flood her mind as visions of her had flooded mine?

Our eyes met. She gave me the slightest smile, as soft and gentle as the first one she'd ever given me. She squeezed my hand tightly.

And I knew what our answer was.

I turned toward the effigy. I showed it my smile. I closed my eyes, reached out my hand...

And pulled the trigger.

Discordance smashed against its skulls, the eruption of sound tearing bone and wood from its body, sending a pair of colossal craniums flying into the wind. Its remaining hollow sockets stared at me and I wondered if that was disappointment I saw in its stare.

Maybe.

If it wasn't, though, that sure as hell was disappointment I saw in the giant fist that it clenched, that it raised high into the sky...

And brought down upon us.

I had always thought I wanted to die in song. In great fires or bloody wars that would be sung about in taverns once everyone had exactly two drinks more than they should have. Or maybe in solemn ballads sung by bards on street corners about the day I put down my sword, walked away, and disappeared into legend.

Now I knew there wouldn't be enough left of me for a song.

But if there was...

I hoped it would be something slow. Something soft and tender. Something young women sing to their lovers or mothers soothe their children to sleep with. Something about how Sal the Cacophony had stared down her end, with the smell of her love's hair in her nose, with the feel of her love's fingers around her own, gently rubbing a finger across a scar on her palm, and when it finally came...

It hadn't hurt at all.

I held my eyes shut. I breathed in the cold wind. A warmth neither searing nor angry coursed through me. And with her beside me, I waited.

I felt the deck shift beneath me. I felt a great rush of wind. And then...

I felt a scream.

A great wail coursed through my blood, a pain that went deeper than a human body could handle. I opened my eyes, saw the effigy's great fist hovering three feet over my head, halted and trembling.

Its wooden hand began to change. The deep crimson of its splintering lumber bled to a pale gray. The wood creaked and groaned as it began to change, the wood becoming brittle and calcified. Twigs and branches turned to pale stone, snapping off to splinter into dust.

Just like Eldest's body.

"In all your great eons and all your great wisdom, am I to understand that you still have no idea how these things work?"

A voice, sneering and snide like the nicks in an uncared-for knife, cut through my ears. I whirled and beheld a man, frail and bent beneath his Revolutionary coat, approaching, his hand outstretched.

And his eyes pitch black.

"Truly," Culven Loyal, commander of the Iron Fleet, muttered at the effigy. "Your standards have grown lax."

Loyal tightened his hand into a fist. The effigy's fist exploded into a rocky powder, cast out upon the wind. The effigy watched its hand, reduced to nothingness, dissipate and leave behind a splintering stump. It turned its collection of skulls toward Loyal, fires burning in their sockets.

"*Sibling*," it acknowledged.

"Sibling," Loyal replied, inclining his head.

"SIBLING?!" I screamed, glancing between them. "You're fucking family?"

"We share common origin." Loyal smiled bitterly. "We are not family."

Undeterred by the looming horror staring down upon him, Loyal walked forward, hands folded behind his back. He glanced up at the effigy and sneered with the same distaste with which one regards a pile of trash on the street.

"Am I to understand, then, that you have decided against all experience and wisdom to challenge me?" he asked of the effigy. "Or did you merely wish to reconnect?"

"I have no desire to experience the unpleasantness of your presence, nor any of our wayward kin," the effigy rumbled in reply. *"Yet is that arrogance I see tinging your countenance? When did you learn such a thing?"*

"It comes with power," Loyal replied, his face coiled into a seething smile. "As does hatred. Contempt. Terror. All that we sacrificed for her, all that we were denied, this land bleeds. From every creature on this desolate husk of dirt." His smile faded. "But surely you realized that. I've seen your pets."

"Pets?" I asked, agog. "You mean...the Haveners?"

"My devoted give me only so much," the effigy said. *"Neither they nor I have any interest in you or your deranged minions."*

"Is that so?" Loyal hummed. "I had assumed otherwise by the fact that yours are currently trying to slaughter mine."

"Shit," I whispered to Liette, taking a step back. "Shit. Haven, the Revolution...they're both answering to these...these..."

"I am here for Eldest," the effigy said. *"When our sibling is returned to me, you may take your toys and make them march around as much as you see fit."*

"I would have thought it obvious that I have no intention of doing that," Loyal snapped. "Yet you have always failed to live up to expectations. Perhaps the error is mine. Why would I give our sibling to you when I have only just now broken them free of their cell, Wisest?"

"Do not mistake your haughtiness for intellect, Strongest," the effigy seethed in response. *"You stand here only by virtue of having been the first to be cast out. Eldest's knowledge would be wasted on your decaying shell."*

"Cast out?" I blurted out. "Wisest? Strongest? Just what the fuck is—"

"Contrary to whatever belief you may hold…" Loyal turned his void-dark stare upon me, face seething with contempt. "Your befuddled interjections are neither charming, contributive, nor desirable. Have you nothing else to offer us?"

"As a matter of fact," I replied, raising my gun, "I do."

I pulled the trigger. Right into his shriveled face, Discordance flew.

Slowed.

Stopped.

Inches away from his nose, the shell came to a sudden halt, hanging in midair, unexploded and useless. Loyal's left eyebrow twitched. And it all fell apart. With precise dismantling, the shell split in half, emptied its contents, and fell to the ground in a collection of useless metal and Dust.

"Shit," I whispered.

"Rather," Loyal replied.

He raised a hand, leveled a finger toward me, curled it.

And fire shot through me.

It flooded through my body, into every fiber of muscle and every droplet of my blood. My legs gave out from under me, my arms ceased to work, my brain ceased to think. All that was left in me were my lungs and just enough air to scream.

And I did.

"Two hundred and six bones, seven hundred–odd layers of muscle," Loyal muttered, contempt dripping from his voice. "A tangle of fragile nerves, a collection of gases and fluids, all bound together by a singular lump of soft gray."

He curled his finger a little more. I no longer had a voice.

"This is all that it takes to create you. Nothing more than a collection of glistening parts and luck."

A little more. I didn't have breath anymore.

"And to unmake you?"

He curled his finger again.

"Even less."

My heart ceased to beat.

Breathless. Dying. Unraveling. I didn't know. I couldn't think. Not as the darkness swirled around me, not as I struggled to find the voice to call out for her, not as I tried to reach for her, for the gun, for anything with hands that no longer worked.

As I went rigid with pain, the effigy stiffened up. Its titanic body groaned, wracked with a pain its skulls couldn't convey. The fires inside its chest began to dim, plumes of smoke and cinders escaping its body to dissipate on the wind.

If there was any blood left in my brain, I might have found that odd. If I could think or feel anything except animal panic hurling itself against the walls of my useless body, trying to break free, that would have been nice, too. But I couldn't. Nothing worked. My body wouldn't obey. My lungs wouldn't fill. My heart wouldn't pump blood. I was going to—

"STOP!"

A moment. A word. A blink of an eye.

And it all stopped. The pain. The fire. I could breathe again, could feel again. I could see Liette, standing in front of me, her hands held out wide.

Eldest clutched in her hand.

"Truly?" Loyal arched one brow. "That's all it takes? Predictable. But acceptable." He extended his hand. "Return Eldest and take your collection of flesh and be gone. Consider this our only mercy—"

"Second law."

"I do not—"

"Second law," she reiterated through clenched teeth. "A Freemaker, upon accepting assistance, must compensate fairly for said assistance, by whatever means necessary." Her eyes narrowed, her fist tightened around Eldest. "Anyone who helps me—everyone who helps me—I will never abandon."

She leaned down, pulled me close against her. Her warmth seeped through me. Her smell filled my nose.

"Ever," she said, tears streaming down her cheeks. "No matter the cost."

Loyal's sneer twisted to a disappointed frown. "The purpose behind human affection for pointless dramatism continues to elude. Am I to assume you will not surrender Eldest?"

Liette's face burned with a searing anger she only ever used for me. Her mouth opened, for a stirring rebuke, a defiant speech, or maybe just a few good cusses. But whatever she had been holding on to couldn't find its way to her mouth. Her anger fell, her face with it. She closed her eyes, held Eldest closely to her chest, and whispered the two words I never wanted to hear her say.

"Forgive me."

Loyal's face turned to a twisted smile. "I am certain the sentiment would be appreciated, if Eldest were capable of it."

"I wasn't talking to Eldest. Or to you."

She turned to me. She gave me a smile. Soft. Tender. Apologetic.

"NO!"

That was my scream.

That was my hand, reaching out as she raised Eldest above her head.

That was me trying to stop her.

And me failing.

Loyal's eyes widened. He reached out with that terrible hand, stared through those terrible eyes, but it didn't matter.

In another instant, I couldn't see him. Or her. Or anything.

Sound died—the wind, the carnage, the airship. Color vanished—the gray of the skies, the red on my hands. The world disappeared, swallowed up by a great light, a spectrum of colors too beautiful to behold, too terrible to look away. The barest crack appeared on Eldest.

The light erupted.

A great pillar of twisting hues and radiance erupted, snaking serpentine through the sky and painting a halo above us. I stared at it through burning eyes I couldn't blink, my mouth agape in a soundless scream at its majesty. It was beautiful. It was incredible. It was indescribable.

Eldest. A Scrath. In its purest, rawest form.

It hung in the air there—for a second, for twenty years and two days, I didn't know. So radiant that it could abide no other light to besmirch its beauty. And though my ears were too primitive, too useless to understand all of it, I thought if I listened, I could hear a song condensed into a single, perfect note.

It sounded...sad.

Then, the great column of light twitched, shivered, and came sweeping down into a pillar. Out of the sky, out of the world.

And into Liette.

The light flooded into her, through her mouth, her eyes, her very pores. The radiance tore at her, threatened to break her apart with its splendor. Her mouth craned open, the song escaping into the sky. But all I could hear was her scream.

I forced my body to rise, I didn't care how much it hurt. I forced it to run. To leap.

As the light and song faded. As the world returned. As she fell, unconscious, into my arms.

"Stupid," I snarled as I pulled her close, my tears hot on my cheeks, my hands aching for some way I could fix this. "Stupid, stupid, fucking stupid. Why the fuck did you do that? Why the fuck did you think that would work?"

"A reasonable question."

Loyal stood. Hands folded behind his back. Utterly unfazed by any of what we had just seen.

"Eldest was always reluctant to occupy hosts," he observed. "Our dear sibling always was too delicate. They must have come to this conclusion together, Eldest and the woman." He shrugged, extended a hand. "Still, separating them should be no matter. If messy."

I couldn't force my body to stand up and fight him. I couldn't see a reason to get up without her. I couldn't think of anything to do except pull her close to me, press my face against hers, and wait for the darkness to take us both.

"Sibling."

I looked up. As did Loyal. We both beheld the effigy's gigantic fist hanging in the sky.

"A word."

A great impact. A burst of flame and wood. A metallic wail that cut through sky, skin, and steel.

The effigy's fist smashed through the deck, tearing a colossal hole in the hull. The airship's motors shrieked as it tore free from the effigy's grip. The figurehead of the Great General punched through the effigy's chest, an eruption of flame heralding the collapse of its body.

As the effigy fell to pieces, I wondered if I didn't see a column of light escaping it.

The deck shifted wildly beneath us as the airship, an iron beast maddened by pain, tore recklessly through the sky. We were hurled against the railing. I felt the shudder of explosions as the ship began to come apart, its delicate machines screaming out in voices of flame and melting metal, one after the other.

Timbers and pipes burst from the hull, went flying through the air. Propellers and wings came loose, disappeared into a thinning gray void. Bodies, both limp and flailing, fell like snowflakes brushed off the shoulder of a rich man's suit. The airship's voice was one of agony and screeching metal as the ground rose up from beneath to meet us.

I always thought I would die in song. But maybe that's just because I didn't want to think it would end like this: just two more bodies in a pile, meaningless and indistinct. It felt wrong to die otherwise, to let what she'd done, what she was to me, go without a song.

An opera. A ballad. Or maybe just a simple tune.

I couldn't think of anything else.

So I held her close. I shut my eyes. And I whispered the only song I could think of.

"*Aias va Indaria*," I whispered to her, the old Imperial tasting strange on my tongue. But the song came all the same, the lilting tune I remembered from a happier time before I was Sal the Cacophony or Red Cloud or any kind of killer.

When I was someone else...

...someone I wish she could have met.

"Sal."

Her voice? But... her lips hadn't moved. And yet I felt it.

Like a heartbeat.

Her arms rose, mechanically stiff. Around us, the hull began to quiver, to tremble, to change. Her eyes snapped wide open.

Inside them, I could see only stars.

Before I could ask, weep, scream, or curse, the deck changed beneath me. The wood became as water, something soft and liquid that beckoned me in. With her in my arms, we slid beneath it, became enveloped by it. The liquid surrounded us, the pipes and metal and timber and flame changing to become something warm, soft, like a blanket.

It closed around us. Was she doing this? Or something else or...

I suppose it didn't matter.

Live or die. In song or in flame. With all the stars in her eyes and all the smiles she would give me.

So long as she was with me, I was unafraid.

As I pulled her to me, and waited for the earth to take us both, I knew that when it came...

It wouldn't hurt at all.

FIFTY-SIX

LITTLEBARROW

Y ou're bleeding."

"I'm always bleeding."

"Because you're always doing stupid shit like *this* stupid shit."

"I know."

Her voice fell. The wind murmured anxiously.

"You could use some more armor."

"If I find some, I'll use it."

"You're not *going* to find any out here, you stupid…"

The wind howled. They lost the rest of her words upon it. Just as well, since it wasn't what either of them wanted to say to each other.

"Your hair is a mess. Let me fix it."

"Liette…"

"Just hold still for a moment."

"Liette, you can't stop me by fixing my hair."

Her teeth gritted. Her eyes trembled, forced to choose between anger and tears and settling on something in between. She reached out, took Sal's face in her hands, more harshly than she had probably intended.

"I know I can't stop you," she whispered. "I can't do anything to stop you. And you won't let me help you. So just let me fucking do *something* for you, all right?"

Sal frowned. She wouldn't, it was true. She *couldn't*. She couldn't let them come—the soldiers and the twisted things that commanded them—looking for Eldest and finding Liette. She couldn't let them cut her open or tear her apart or do whatever it was they were planning to do to get the thing dwelling inside her. She couldn't let Liette be here.

They knew this.

They had agreed on it. It wasn't a good plan, but it was the best plan. A sound plan. A plan that might work.

For they could do nothing else, they knew.

And so Sal the Cacophony, killer and destroyer, stood perfectly still and let Twenty-Two Dead Roses in a Chipped Porcelain Vase, among the most feared and renowned Freemakers in the land, fix her hair.

Sal looked up as Liette smoothed out a lock of hair, forced a weak grin onto her face. "How's it look?"

Liette frowned. "Terrible."

Sal's grin grew a little broader. "Thanks for trying."

They both looked long to the cart. It stood only twenty feet away—a ragged, weary thing, despite Liette's best efforts—yet it felt a world away, at once too far to ever approach and too close to ever ignore.

Sindra and Meret continued strapping things down—tightening wheels, checking what meager supplies they'd scavenged from the houses—and talking softly. But not a word came and went without them looking expectantly to the two women.

How long had they been standing here? Sal wondered. It had that familiar ache of longing, the ancient and instinctive pain that came from seeing someone for the last time without knowing it. And yet, it wasn't enough time. Not enough time to feel her hands in her hair, not enough time to breathe in her scent, not enough time to... to...

"I wish we hadn't done this," Liette whispered, her voice choked with sorrow. "I wish I hadn't worked for the Revolution. Or gone on that airship."

"No, you don't," Sal replied. "If you hadn't, you'd have been angry at yourself for never knowing what was on there. Then you'd have figured out something terribly clever, like shooting it down and piecing through the remnants to see what they'd been hiding. Then they'd be coming for you, anyway."

"You don't know that."

"I know you. And you know me. We'd both have ended up there, one way or another." She took Liette's hands in her own, pressed them to her lips. "It's fine."

"It's not fine."

"I know."

"It's the complete fucking opposite of fine."

"I know."

"If I had just a *little* more time to think, I could—"

"Storm's broken," Sindra called out from the driver's seat. Old Surly squawked in agreement, eager to get on. "We go now or we don't go anywhere."

And that was that.

No more stalling. No more wishing or lamenting. No more words—none save the ones she couldn't bring herself to say.

Sal held out her hand. Liette took it. Together, they walked beside each other through the snow. As they'd always wanted to do and never found the time, the words, the will to do so.

For the first time. And the last.

Sal helped her into the back of the cart. She got her settled into it, cushioned between a soft sack of rations and a few books she'd managed to find in Meret's house—medical texts, each one about six hundred pages, she'd be done with them before tomorrow's sunset.

But they'd help.

Sindra settled in at the front of the cart, taking Surly's reins in her hands. She glanced over at Sal, spared her a curt nod. There was still contempt in her eyes—there always would be, Sal knew—but it was settled beneath a layer of resolve. A soldier's eyes, Sal recognized. She could be trusted to hate Sal for the rest of her days and that was fine. She could be trusted to get Liette out of here safely, too, and that was better.

She turned back to Liette, stared silently at her.

It was so easy in opera, she mused. They always said everything succinctly, poetically, and poignantly just before the curtain fell.

But here? Now? There were too many words to be said, too many words she *hadn't* said. She'd never told Liette that she loved that one dress she'd worn. She'd never told Liette that she loved the way she made eggs. She'd never told Liette how her hands...

Her hands.

Calloused, but still soft. Stained with ink, frequently. Gentle in ways she'd never imagined anyone's hands could be. Delicate and careful around her scars, her hair, her neck when, for no reason at all, she'd reach out and trace the slope of her throat and smile at her the way she herself smiled at a good opera.

She held her hands in her own. And the words just came.

"Seru vo talati."

Liette's eyes brimmed with tears. Her face fell. Her lips trembled.

"Now?" she whispered. "You waited until now to say that to me?"

"I wasn't going to have another chance."

Her body shook. "You're an asshole, Sal."

"I know." She leaned forward, kissed Liette upon her brow. "Be safe."

Reins cracked. A bird chirruped, irate. Wheels groaned. The wagon began to plow forward through the snow and down the road, disappearing into the gray cold that swirled below. Sal watched it go, watched her go with it.

No words. No waves. Just a look that lasted until the wagon vanished into the snow.

And so did she.

Snow crunched as Meret started walking after them, a heavy pack upon his back. He was fairly strong, Sal noted. He could have actually swung a sword halfway decent if he hadn't been so nice.

Meret paused as he set foot on the road, turning to offer a look at Sal.

"This isn't a gift, Sal," he said, curt. "What I'm doing for you. This is a loan. Whatever you're planning to do here today, whatever you destroy, it won't mean anything if you don't come back." He stiffened up. "So come back."

"I'll try," she said.

"You will," he replied, forceful as a voice as gentle as his could manage. "Or are you going to have it said that Sal the Cacophony doesn't repay her debts?"

Sal quirked a brow. Or maybe he wasn't so nice.

"Huh," she said with a grin. "You're kind of a prick, aren't you, Meret?"

"Yes." He nodded stiffly. "Sorry."

Her grin lingered on him a little longer before he turned and hurried to catch up to the wagon. She'd miss him, of course. Miss all of them—even the cranky lady. She wondered, idly, what life would have been like if she'd found Littlebarrow before all this. Would she have been happy here, with Liette and a little house to call their own? Seeing neighbors every day and baking cookies for kids?

She expected to cringe at the idea. But now . . .

Now, it didn't seem so bad.

But, she chided herself, listen to her prattle away time with whimsical dreams. She'd almost forgotten she was about to go die in a glorious blaze.

The winds howled. Snow twisted in white columns. The cold seeped in. And she felt none of it. Not against the burning sensation coming from her hip.

She drew the Cacophony out of his sheath, met his brass eyes and broad grin.

"Shall we?" she asked the gun.

And the gun answered.

With searing heat, with silent laughter, and a broad, brass grin.

Hilt in hand, they walked together through the emptiness of Littlebarrow, their music an unrehearsed symphony of snow crunching underfoot and wind murmuring anxiously in her ears.

She stopped at a house, seized the small stool off its porch, and glanced apologetically upward at the building's face. This stool was meant for better things, but she needed it now.

The dark windows of the house looked down upon her and the gun, glass eyes brimming with memories of soft beds and days spent watching the snow fall. Imploring, they followed the woman and her gun as the two of them walked to the tract of empty snow that served as a town square.

Sal took in her surroundings. The mist and snow closed in around her, drowning the alleys and roads in a gray fog. No cover here, she noted. Nowhere to flee to if things got bad.

And things were going to get bad.

Still. It would have to do.

Sal squinted up at the gray-and-white emptiness swirling overhead.

She raised the Cacophony skyward—he always did want to rattle the heavens. She turned her head away, closed her eyes, and pulled the trigger.

The shell flew into the sky. And for a bright, glorious moment, the clouds fled. Sunflare exploded, a tiny and angry sun burning in furious defiance over the bitter cold. She pulled the trigger again. Another Sunflare shell shrieked skyward and exploded, another bright and glorious scar across the sky. A third pull of the trigger sent her last Sunflare to join them, a third and final blaze whose bright roar silenced the howl of the wind.

For a little while, at least.

For a little while, it was bright out. For a little while, it was warm. For a little while, things didn't seem so bad.

But the light lasted only briefly, its incandescent shout dimming, softening, quieting with every passing breath. The cold seeped back into Sal's lungs, the light faded, and the gray came creeping timidly back to settle into the space that the Cacophony had chased it out of.

It was cold again. And dark. And that was fine. For those few moments, things had been bright again. Those few moments were all she had needed. Once she had told herself that enough times that it almost sounded true, she pulled up her stool and sat down and began to wait.

Time passed. Hours, she hoped. Minutes, she feared. It was difficult to tell without the sun—the snow certainly wasn't going to help her. She continued to wait, all the same, in soft, sunless silence.

She hated silence. Always had. Silence typically meant things had gone bad and always meant things were about to get worse. More than that, silence meant she had no choice but to be alone with her thoughts. And those, usually, were the start of things going worse.

"You can't burn a bit hotter? It's fucking cold."

She didn't usually talk to the gun. It wasn't the best habit to get into. But fuck, what else was she going to do with her last minutes?

The Cacophony didn't answer. Neither with warmth, nor words. She expected that.

"I know this isn't what you wanted," she said. "We made a deal, you and I, and I'm not holding it up. My fault on that, I'll admit. I wasn't expecting this to come up."

A weak excuse. She knew it. So did he.

"You're not getting a body. You're not getting your ruin. I'm not getting my revenge. Neither of us are happy." She stared out into the swirling gloom. "No one will remember that about us, anyway."

She leaned back in her stool. She reached into her satchel and pulled free the last dregs of Meret's wine. She swirled it a little, watching the crimson lap up against the glass.

"They won't remember if we got what we wanted or if we deserved it or not. When they talk about Sal and the Cacophony, they won't waste time figuring out why we did it. They won't ruin the story by wondering if it was a good enough reason to do what we did. But what they *will* say..."

She breathed in some of the cold, biting wind. She stared up into the gray clouds. She ran her thumb across the scar that ran down her eye.

"They'll say that Sal and the Cacophony, armed with nothing but each other, called everyone who thought they could kill to their side. When they went to the black table together, they took every last poor bastard who ever had the bad idea to pick up steel with them."

She looked down at the gun and offered him a weary smile.

"That doesn't sound so bad, does it?"

He didn't reply. Not with words, anyway. He was too proud for that. He was still who he was, still the Cacophony, still the terrible weapon that they spoke of softly in stories. And so when his hilt offered just a little delighted heat, like the blush that comes right before a first kiss...

Well, she'd settle for that, at least.

She patted his hilt with as much affection as he'd allow. She turned back out to the swirling cold. She upended the bottle of wine, drained the last drops, smacked her lips.

Still tasted like skunk-ass.

She tossed it aside. She waited. Hours passed. Or minutes. Or seconds.

And then they arrived.

Her ears pricked up at a sound. Through the wailing wind, through the falling snow, through the vast and empty noise, she heard it, too pure and beautiful to be hampered by such a trivial thing as nature.

The Lady's song. Resonant. And echoing.

Sal looked up once more. She saw them. In shadows that came and went with the parting sheets of cold. Some stood proud and tall, hulking and unscathed by carnage. Some stood slender and short, wielding weapons in one hand and magic in the other. Some hovered in the air, the cloth of their uniforms blowing gently in the wind.

Some were wounded. Some were not. Some had hands stained with another's life. Some shook beneath their uniforms. She couldn't see their wounds, their pains, whether they carried their hatred in their hands along with their weapons. Through the bitter winds, all she could make out was the cold, empty expressions of their masks.

As the Imperial mages, regal and innumerable, surrounded her.

In the alleys. On the rooftops. Lining the streets. Siegemages, Graspmages, Skymages, and more. They came out of the gray to stand in the snow, called by her and her gun, and stood.

Waiting.

She could have guessed for what. But it didn't matter.

Velline arrived a moment later.

A shadow fell from the sky. Shenazar came floating down, the scanty remnant of her uniform stained and torn by her own blood, but still with enough strength in her to carry her captain. They landed, Shenazar scowling at Sal as Velline stepped forward, blade naked in her hand.

Eyes full of tears.

Sal stared at her. She glanced around the assembled mages. She snorted, spat, scratched her side.

"Took your fucking time, didn't you?" she asked.

Velline said nothing. Not with words, anyway. Her eyes trembled, quivered, struggled to speak what her mouth couldn't. But she wouldn't let her tears speak—not a woman like her. Not a captain of the Imperium.

The sword in her hand would do that. For a long, tense moment, Sal wondered if she might do just that—move and, in the blink of an eye, strike her down. Sal tensed, tightened her grip on the Cacophony. She couldn't let that happen.

Not yet.

"You were Red Cloud."

Velline's voice wasn't strong, barely bold enough to be heard over the wind. That name wasn't new—she wore it as close as one of her scars. But it cut her to hear it, all the same, spoken like that. With reverence. With fear. With betrayal.

"You were the best of us," Velline whispered. "The best of the Imperium. You led us in the Scar. You protected us. You built us up." Her mouth hung slack, searching for the explanation that would make these words hurt less. "And you killed us."

"It's what I do," Sal replied—spat the words, really. She needed Velline mad. She needed those eyes on her for as long as she could manage. "I'd do it again if—"

"Do you know how many?"

Sal's voice fell. Velline's eyes trembled.

"How many people live in this Valley?" Velline pressed. "How many of them have homes here? Families? Lives? Do you know..." She swallowed hard. "Do you know how many of them are going to die because of this war? Because of you?"

No retort. No clever taunt. Sal had nothing to tell her. Because Sal knew.

Velline slowly shook her head. "Why? What could make you do that? What could make you hate your own people so much?"

There were a hundred things she could have said. A thousand, really. She had more than a few right on the tip of her tongue—cruel, hateful words that would have cut Velline to the quick, enraged her so that she'd spend the next six years burning Sal's corpse and then burning the ashes.

But none of them could cut as cold or as deep as the truth.

"I know," Sal replied. "Not specifically, but I know. I couldn't count them all from so high up, but I remember..." She closed her eyes. "I remember when I was Red Cloud. I remember seeing them. Little black shapes in the fires. And then... nothing. They burned away."

"I'm not talking about foes of the Imperium. I'm talking about—"

"I know what you're talking about," Sal interrupted. "I know you think everyone Red Cloud killed deserved it. Maybe in your darkest dreams, you're willing to admit that only almost all of them deserved it. But you don't know what I did. Who I burned. I do." She looked up at Velline, her own eyes cold and still as the snow on the ground.

"You don't. You say I was the best of you and then weep for the lives I took? Whether Red Cloud or Sal the Cacophony, I've always been a killer. You're just pissed off because now you don't get to pretend you and I didn't kill for the same reasons."

She narrowed her eyes.

"Because the Empress told us to."

A sound stirred. The Lady's song rose. And so did Shenazar, sword in hand, fury on her face. The other mages began to move, their own songs rising.

"You *dare* insinuate the captain is as sullied as you," the Skymage snarled. "I'll cleave your lying tongue from your—"

"No."

A word. A raised hand. A single step forward.

The mages stood still. Velline took up her blade in both hands.

"I will do it."

"But, Captain," Shenazar said, urgent, "we're all—"

"She's been here for hours, Shenazar," Velline replied. "She could have any number of tricks planned. And I…" She bowed her head, bit back her tears. "I will not lose one more life to this monster."

She pointed her blade at Sal.

"Stand up, Cacophony," she said. "Face your judgment. *Ontori tun vatala.*"

Sal rose. Her body creaked. Her old wounds grumbled. Her new wounds screamed. Every part of her begged her to sit down or, failing that, to just wait for death. But she couldn't do that.

Not yet.

So, she raised the Cacophony to her brow in salute. His burning brass singed her scar. And she whispered:

"Eres va atali."

Sal blinked.

Velline disappeared.

The wind behind her stirred.

A flash of sparks. A verse in steel. A smear of disturbed snow where her feet had just been. Sal gritted her teeth as she caught Velline's blade against her own, her arm numb from the shock of the blow as the woman's attack drove her back one step, then two. She'd caught it four inches away from her throat, but that was too close. She was too slow. Too wounded.

And Velline was so fast. So strong. So full of anger.

She broke the deadlock. Sal snarled, swung her blade at her. Too sloppy, too slow, its steel sailed gracelessly through the air as Velline effortlessly stepped out of its reach. Sal brought up the Cacophony, but he was so heavy—fuck, when did he get so heavy—and her fingers shook with the effort of drawing his hammer back.

By the time the brass clicked, Velline was already gone.

Sal swept a scowl across the snow, searching for the flash of steel, the stir of wind, the swift note that would denote where her foe would appear. But she saw only the stillness of the cold, heard only the murmur of the wind, felt only the cold metal faces staring back at her, patiently waiting for her to die.

"Oathbreaker."

A word. A whisper. Sal whirled, caught the thrust as Velline reappeared and lashed out with her blade. Two inches from her throat, Sal caught it. She swung the Cacophony around. The air stirred. Velline was gone.

"Murderer."

The hiss of steel. The rush of wind. Sal twisted as Velline struck from her side, narrowly avoiding the sword that cut past her. One inch from her throat. She snarled, lashed out with her blade, bit empty air as Velline's magic sang and delivered her away.

"I've tried to find the words for you, what you've done to this land, to these people."

Her voice came from nowhere, whispers lost on the wind, as Sal searched the empty air for her. Blade held close, Cacophony outstretched, mind empty, she searched for her foe. But her arm ached, the metal too heavy to hold in muscles so tired, and in the moments between her hands shaking, the thought came.

I can't do this.

"Every word I come up with seems too small, too trivial," Velline's voice came. "And all the torments I could visit upon you seem too narrow for what you've done."

I won't even slow her down. A wound opened in her head. The thoughts bled out. *She'll kill me quick. She'll find Liette. She'll find them all. All of this will be for... for...*

"How do I give them justice?" Velline whispered—two inches away, sixty feet, a hundred miles. "How do I protect this world from you? How do I protect them all?"

"I'll tell you how." Sal spat the words, hot and angry, into the wind. "You stop pretending you give a shit about them, about the Imperium, about anything but the sword in your hand."

She focused everything in her, every shaking muscle and aching wound, into those words. She had to make Velline angry enough to make a mistake, to delay her just a little longer.

But Velline said nothing. And no song of magic answered for her.

"Is this what you settled on?" Sal roared into the gray. "Some beautifully tragic duel? Some vainglorious farce at pretending this was ever about you and me?" She held her hands out wide, gesturing to the other mages. "You think you're protecting *them*? How long are you going to let them believe that? How long are you going to pretend that..."

Her breath came. Heated. Hateful. Burning as bright as the hilt in her hand.

"That this is anything," she spat, "other than you wanting the pleasure of killing me yourself?"

The wind whispered. A shape appeared before her. She struck with her blade. Velline struck first, knocking the weapon from her hand. A brass voice hissed hot and urgent in her ear.

"*Now.*"

She raised the Cacophony, pulled the trigger. Hellfire screamed, a great and angry roar of flame that swallowed the figure of Velline. Her shadow vanished beneath sheets of flame. Clouds of steam burst into hissing life as the snow and the ice and the water were devoured by the flames and spat out like white, vaporous bones.

Sal kept the gun raised as the flames roared, as the steam shrieked, as both of them sang fractured verses of a tortured song before ebbing, dying, disappearing, and leaving only a bare patch of earth and a...

Sal's blood froze. Her eyes widened.

A corpse. There should have been a corpse. But there wasn't anything there.

Cold wind on her back. Hot blood hitting the air. She fell to her knees before she even knew she was bleeding. Her strength left her before she even knew she had been cut. Everything in her wept out across her back and the clean, numb cut that had been carved into it.

Boots appeared before her, curt and polished. A blade hung from a slender hand, slick with her own blood. She struggled to lift her hands, but found she couldn't. She struggled to breathe, but found it too hard.

"Yes," Velline said. The wet blade found Sal's chin, tilted it up to look into the cold purple stare of the woman who'd cut her so swift and so deep. "I wanted this. I wanted to end you. I wanted to be the one who ended Sal the Cacophony, the traitorous Red Cloud."

No more hate in her stare. No more anger or righteous fury. Those purple eyes shone with the bleak light of someone liberated from the pomp and grand ideas, from the fake codes of honor and all the grand speeches that made people think their steel cut cleaner than anyone else's. She stared at Sal with the cold clarity of a woman who wanted only to kill, only to try to soothe the injury in her heart.

And in those baleful eyes, Sal saw her own reflected. As cold. As empty.

"And when you're dead, I'll relish it, Sal," Velline whispered, brimming with spite. "I'll gladly ruin every lover I ever take for never finding their scent as sweet as this moment." She drew in a sharp breath. "And I will still protect them. Lives will be saved because of this. No matter what I want, how base my desire, it will still do good." She drew her sword back. "Take comfort in that, if nothing else."

Sal simply... grinned.

"Is that what you think?"

Velline's hand stayed. Her eyes narrowed.

"You don't think I planned for this?" Sal tried her best to chuckle. "You don't remember that I had friends?"

Velline's lips pursed. Her jaw set.

"Why would I lure you to this shitty little town and let you beat the shit out of me if I didn't have a plan?" Sal asked, grinning. "A plan like, say, a timely ambush from my associates—you remember them, don't you? The ones on the airship with me—due to attack precisely when you think victory is assured?"

Velline's eyes twitched as she fought the urge to look away. Sal forced her grin even wider.

"Wouldn't that just be," she gasped, "so perfectly dramatic?"

Her blade hung there a long moment. Her face remained crystalline in its composure. The wind stirred around them. And Sal simply kept grinning—wounded, bleeding, too tired to do so much as move.

She smiled. Like this was just one more part of the plan. Like she knew the punch line to an awful, awful joke and knew it was even worse.

And maybe that confidence was why, that horrible certainty. Or maybe it was because Velline really believed her own birdshit about protecting people. Or maybe it was just who she was.

But she turned.

And she looked.

All around her were only cold gray mists and cold metal faces. The snow betrayed not a single footprint that wasn't hers or her foe's. No surprise attacks. No glorious war cries. No master plan, only the cold and the desperate lie of a broken villain. Nothing else.

"A lie," Velline muttered, spiteful. "And a pathetic one." She turned back to Sal. "Really, what were you trying to accomplish with—"

As it turned out, it was pretty difficult to sound derisive with the hilt of a gun smashing into one's teeth.

Blood burst from Velline's mouth as she staggered back. She stared at Sal, astonished, as the woman crawled to her feet, grinning weakly. The mage's bleeding mouth contorted in rage.

"What was the point of that?" she asked, sneering through the blood painting her face. "A feint? For what purpose?"

Sal shrugged. "I don't know. It made you look kind of stupid, I guess."

"That won't save you."

"No," she said, smiling. "But tell me you aren't going to think of me the next time you kiss someone and taste blood."

She held her hands out, smiling. She didn't have anything left in her. No more tricks, no more fight, not so much as a quip. Not even the angry thoughts that had hounded her.

This was good, she thought. For that, she'd die. And die slowly. Velline would take her time, loose every ounce of hatred she had into Sal at the tip of her sword. And that would be another moment Liette had to escape.

Not a good death. Far from a clean one. But the best one she could give.

And that, she thought as she closed her eyes, would have to be enough.

She held her breath, waited for the blow. In her ears, the song of the Lady rose. Above her, the wind stirred. A single, crystalline note, painfully beautiful, rang out. She felt a warmth coursing through her. Slowly, the note was joined.

First by another. Then, another. And then by some manner of tinny, droning noise blaring out a most unpleasant tune. It crackled as recorded voices sang out a verse graceless. Inelegant. Fanatical.

Familiar.

"Fucking *finally*," she gasped.

And in response...

"TEN THOUSAND YEARS!"

A single scream. An eruption of sound. A rush of wind.

And then, just as she had convinced herself she intended, everything got much, much worse.

All eyes went up to see the red-hot cannon fire falling from the sky. All bodies went running as it struck the earth, gouging up a rain of hot, sodden earth. All attentions turned to the other side of the town.

As one shadow emerged from the cold. Then ten. Then a hundred.

"FOR THE GLORY OF THE GREAT GENERAL!" a Revolutionary screamed. *"FOR THE GLORY OF THE REVOLUTION! TEN THOUSAND YEARS!"*

"TEN THOUSAND YEARS!"

The cry came hoarse and ragged from hundreds of throats. It came accompanied by the salvo of gunpikes and the roar of cannon fire and the rush of Paladin armor. It came burdened with hatred, with anguish, with the tender pain that is only ever soothed by steel and fire.

Before she saw the ragged tear of their coats and the blood

painting their faces, she saw their eyes. Wide and white with horror, with agony, with all the new wounds they'd carry from this day, the Revolutionaries came rushing. There was no formation, no strategy, nothing beyond the enemy in front of them and the sheer need to make them suffer that burned bright and painful on every one of their faces.

Of course, Sal realized as they came rushing forward, the list of the Revolution's enemies was long and, while she might not have been on the top, she was probably in the top fifteen.

As fast as her weary legs could carry her, she ran. The air split behind her as a Paladin armor went roaring behind her to charge a Siegemage, magic and metal colliding in a spray of shrapnel. She ducked under the salvos of flame and thunder launched by Sparkmages and Embermages into the crowd of Revolutionaries to be answered by staccato blasts of gunpikes and the shriek of repeating guns. Skymages swooped from overhead, blades out and hungry. Dragonkiller harpoons flew to cut them down before their wielders fell beneath savage strokes of steel.

And Sal kept running. And gasping. And breathing. And staring at the narrow corridor of space not occupied by fire or steel or flesh that wended through the town. Her way out. The *only* way out. She ran for it. She ran as fast as she could, as much as her lungs could handle.

Until she couldn't.

A puddle of melted snow. A stray pebble. A blast that cut too close. It didn't matter. She fell, her body screaming out in pain as she tumbled across the snowy earth. She scrambled to her ass, turned around, beheld the melee closing in around her. She couldn't fight. She couldn't run. So she clung to the only thing she had left.

"Together?" she asked the Cacophony.

"As ever," the Cacophony answered.

She pulled the trigger.

Hoarfrost struck the earth. Great barbs of ice erupted, impaling Revolutionaries charging toward her.

She pulled the trigger.

Discordance shot out, erupted in the air, gouged a hole in the gray and sent Skymages screaming into the void.

She fished out her shells, reloaded, pulled the trigger again.

Hellfire blackened a Paladin, a plume of smoke bursting from its cockpit as its pilot crawled out, gasping for air.

Again.

Shockgrasp howled, jerking steel to steel, metal to flesh.

Again.

Hoarfrost painted skin, froze faces into agony.

Again. And again. Until there was nothing to her world but the smell of smoke and the flashes of flame from the Cacophony's muzzle and the bodies falling. Again, until she didn't even see who was dying, what she was hitting, where she was firing. Again. Again.

Until she pulled the trigger and heard only a *click*.

She reached into her satchel and found only leather.

And that's how it would end, she realized. Not with noise or drama. But empty leather and empty brass.

"Sal."

And a bloodstained blade.

Velline stood before her. Her face was empty and covered in blood. Her hands were stained with the lives of many. And her blade was raised.

"Velline," she said. "I thought—"

"No." Velline adjusted her stance. "No more." The song of her magic rose. Her eyes flashed violet. "And never again."

Sal wanted better last words than that. A better ending. A happier ending. Or at least, one where she'd saved some of that wine. They'd never sing songs about how Sal the Cacophony had died, flat on her ass, at the hands of a woman who very badly wanted to kill her.

But they didn't matter. None of them—the Imperium, the Revolution, the heavy names on her list—mattered. The only thing on this black earth worth saving had already fled.

She let that comfort her as she closed her eyes and waited.

The wind rushed. The earth trembled beneath her. A blade struck flesh.

"Madam."

A voice, familiar and comforting, bid her to open her eyes.

The flames and blood couldn't touch her. Even as her coat hung off her in tatters, even as the horrors of the battle painted her body, every part of her was pristine, untouched and delicate, not so much as a scratch on her.

Even as she held Velline's sword by the blade, Agne the Hammer looked perfect.

"You really must stop getting into things like this."

"*You*," Velline gasped, struggling to pull her sword free. "You traitorous, oathbreaking piece of—"

"Apologies, my good woman," Agne interrupted. "I'm sure that barb is very good and venomous, but unfortunately..."

She swung her arm in a limp swat. Her empty palm struck Velline's shoulder. And the Quickmage went flying, screaming as she was struck away by four perfectly manicured fingers.

"I'm in a bit of a hurry."

Sal gaped as Agne walked toward her, plucking her up with one hand and making a vain attempt to brush debris from her clothing.

"Agne," Sal whispered, breathless. "I didn't—"

"If the end of that sentence is 'put any thought into this before shooting everything and hoping for the best,' I quite agree. Unless, of course, those three sparkly shells you hurled into the sky were for my benefit."

"I didn't think you were alive," Sal said, "much less that you would come."

"I am, I did," Agne replied. "Once again, I'm in the midst of a poorly plotted, pathetically excused quarrel because of your—"

Sal collapsed forward, wrapping her arms around Agne. She hadn't meant to do that. Nor had she meant to let out a gasping, choking breath that sounded almost like a sob. And she certainly hadn't meant for Agne to place a comforting hand atop her head, pull her closer, and smile gently.

But she was glad she did.

"Really, now, Madam Cacophony," Agne cooed through the sounds of battle. "Whatever will they say if they see you like this?"

"The wagon," Sal said. "There's a wagon. My friends, my..." She smacked her lips. "We have to get to it."

"A wagon?" Agne glanced over her shoulder. "All this is because of a *wagon*?"

"I was trying to keep the Imperium and the Revolution busy until it could escape."

Agne twitched as a Sparkmage's bolt struck her shoulder. She turned around and glared before plucking up a fallen gunpike and hurling it, driving it through the offender's chest.

"Well done, in that case," she muttered.

Sal furrowed her brow. How had Agne merely flinched at that bolt? How had she survived? How had—

"Your magic," Sal whispered. "You used too much Barter. You can't use that for—"

"I assure you I can," Agne interrupted. "And I did. For you." She smiled, patted Sal's cheek. "Apologies. I'm sure you had some delightful guilty soliloquy ready, but I suppose I prefer living without a few feelings than I do without you."

Sal swallowed hard, a bitter bile mixed with tears and guilt, and smiled. "Thank you."

"You're fucking dreaming if you think a few pleasant words are going to make this up to me." Agne turned and scowled over the battlefield. "But before we can start discussing how much wine you're going to buy me, we need to get out of here."

"We can't," she said. "I drew them *both* here. I didn't plan for an escape."

"Lucky for us," Agne said, glancing skyward, "that not everyone is as shortsighted as you."

He came plummeting out of the gray. Wounded, bloodied, wheezing, but alive. Tenka the Nightmare almost collapsed as he landed in front of Agne, steadying himself as she reached out for him. His breath was ragged and worn, the painful Barter the Lady extracted from her Skymages having left him close to asphyxiation.

"Easy," Agne whispered, holding him up. "Breathe slowly."

"Trying…" Tenka struggled to speak. "The ships…they're close."

"And the twins?" Agne pressed.

"Almost."

"Wait, the twins?" Sal asked. "What are you—"

"And yourself, you dear little man?" Agne asked the Skymage, pointedly ignoring Sal.

"Can't fly," Tenka rasped. "Not anymore. Too much magic . . . too little . . . too little . . ."

He fell. Agne let him. With one powerful arm, she scooped him up, holding him like a child as he struggled to regain his breath.

"There, there," she whispered, stroking his hair gently. "I'll handle the rest."

The rest of what?

The thought had just begun to form on Sal's lips when it happened.

Snow erupted. The earth groaned. Around the battlefield that had once been Littlebarrow, great sheets of stone and earth rose up. Solid and unyielding, they ripped across the blood-soaked snow, herding the savagery into isolated pens of carnage.

"Fuck me, that wasn't worth it."

A voice. Footsteps behind her. Sal whirled and saw Yria and Urda staggering toward her. His hands were stained with ink, frayed writing quills stuck in his belt. Her arm hung limp at her side, paralyzed.

"We did like you said," Urda said to Agne, breathless. "Of course, with a little more time and proper planning, we could have accomplished more than a few flimsy barriers. Furthermore, if anyone asks, I want it clarified that this was *not* my best work and—"

"How long, Urda?" Agne asked.

"A few minutes maybe," he answered. "But they'll break through them before long." He paused and offered a smile and wave. "Hi, Sal! We're not dead! Isn't that great?"

"No thanks to fucking you," Yria snarled, glaring at Sal. "You got any idea how fucking hard it is to jump around a battle full of magic-asshole-lickers?" She shook her deadened limb. "*NOT FUCKING EASY, IF YOU WERE WONDERING.*"

"Your arm," Sal gasped. "You used your magic, too. For . . . for . . ."

"That's right, for you, Princess Poutypuss." Yria glanced down toward her arm, rubbed it a little. "Gonna be a little nerve damage, maybe a few fingers lost, but . . . fuck, we've lost the job, lost everything else, so I guess . . ."

"What she's trying to say," Urda chimed in helpfully. "We're all we've got left." He smiled at his sister. "Right?"

She grinned at him. "Aw, you're gonna make me cry if you don't slam that sentimental shit right up your dickhole."

"You all..." The words just tumbled from her mouth, dumb and insensate and heavy. "You all came back... for me?"

"The fact that you're surprised by this suggests you've got some issues to work out." Agne shuddered as an explosion shook the earth. "Which you'll have to do on your own time, I'm afraid."

Agne glanced to the twins, nodded. The twins offered her a smirk. All eyes turned to Sal, the killer, the murderer, the oath-breaker they'd come back for. Urda appeared at her left, Yria at her right—they draped her arms over their shoulders.

And everything ached a little less.

"Shall we?" Agne asked.

A cold, deep breath. A rush of wind. And they ran.

Earth shuddered, groaned, burst beneath their feet as spells and cannons tore frozen chunks of soil free. They kept running. The sky bled with flashes of lightning and volleys of autobow bolts and the hateful wails of Skymages. And they kept running. People fought and bled and died and killed around them, screamed for mercies and screamed back curses until it was all a maelstrom of noise, hundreds of people screaming as loud as they could until things made sense.

Sal didn't hear it. Didn't feel it. Didn't feel the numb pump of her legs or the cold air raking her lungs. She had left everything on the soil when she had been ready to die—every ounce of fight and anger, save for one small part of herself that she had hoped to carry to the black table with her. And now that part was all she could feel, all she could hear, all she clung to.

She had to see Liette again.

She had to pay Meret back.

She had to live.

Through the melee, as Urda's walls came down and the battle was joined. Through the carnage, as Agne charged through throngs of battle and sent foes flying. Through the smoke and cold and hate as Yria cursed, trying to keep Sal aloft. They kept running. They had to live.

She didn't realize until she drew in a breath without the tinge of smoke that they'd done it. Even when she looked over her shoulder and saw Littlebarrow, its houses crumbling and its streets paved with bodies, growing smaller, she didn't believe that they'd made it. She wouldn't believe it. Not until they were free. Not until—

"*Oathbreakers.*"

Of course.

Agne skidded to a halt in front of them. The twins and Sal collided with her back. Ahead of them, pristine in his uniform, a man stood, the bony plate jutting from his forehead painting his face into a severe scowl. Dalthoros, blade in hand and a quartet of mages at his back, stood between them and the vast plain of snow.

A rearguard. Of course. Why the fuck *wouldn't* have Velline left a rearguard?

"Such strange vermin that crawl across this land." His words came accompanied by the Lady's song. Across his flesh, his wounds began to close, along with the wounds of his soldiers. "You shun the light, cringe from the warmth of civilization, living every second of every day of your miserable lives searching for carrion to glut yourselves on. And now that you behold a feast of carnage, so thick with decay and blood as to make yourselves burst, you scurry away."

He stepped forward. He raised his blade. His mages called magic to hands and eyes as they, behind him, stood tall, whole, and ready to kill.

"Nature abhors a hypocrite, Vagrants," Dalthoros said. "Grant me the honor of soothing her."

Sal blinked.

Now *that* was opera.

She knew he was about to kill her, of course, and that was certainly bad, but she couldn't pretend that *wasn't* a properly dramatic insult, rife with metaphor and poetry. It was the sort of thing you'd see onstage in Cathama, the audience breathless, moments before the great duel.

It was *not* the sort of thing you'd imagine seeing a giant bird at, but Sal was thrilled all the same when one showed up.

With a shriek and a dark rush of feathers, she came charging out of the snow to take down Dalthoros in a tackle. His scream was lost beneath the tearing of flesh and thrashing of claws as a savage beak tore at him and giant talons rent him.

When Congeniality *did* deign to look up, her eyes were bright and her beak was painted. Flecks of red flew from her maw as she raised a head and squawked triumphantly over the bloodied body of Dalthoros.

The other mages looked astonished. Sal couldn't blame them. How often *do* you get to see something like that? Just like she couldn't blame them when Agne seized the opportunity to rush forward, snapping one of their necks with a well-placed chop and sending the others vanishing into the snow as they tore Dalthoros's body from Congeniality's claws.

The great bird snapped as them as they did and made a move to give chase, but a hand on her neck stayed her.

"Good bird," Sal said, stroking the flabby skin of her throat before forcing her body onto the saddle. "Good fucking bird."

"Fucking finally," Yria sighed, rolling out her shoulder. "Not enough that I lose my fucking arm coming back for you, you gotta pull my fucking shoulder out. Your fucking bird can carry your tight little ass from here on out."

Sal glanced over Yria's head to the battle in Littlebarrow. "We've got until one of them kills the other one to get out of here. Easier to do that apart. There's a wagon farther up the road with Liette. Rally there." She looked down at the Doormage. "Thanks for saying my ass was tight, also."

"There's wisdom in that," Agne said as she adjusted Tenka on her shoulder. "We'll find each other again." She winked at Sal. "You still owe me some wine."

"Suits me just fucking fine." Yria pulled out a piece of chalk, cleared a small patch of snow, and hastily drew a portal. "Don't fuckin' think I'm going to be satisfied with wine, though. You're going to be polishing my taint before I call us even."

"What she means is—" Urda tried to offer helpfully.

"I know what she meant," Sal interrupted. "And thank you. Both of you."

The twins exchanged a look. "See?" Urda said. "I told you she'd be glad to see us."

"Yeah, yeah." Yria snapped her fingers. A note rang out. A portal opened. She took her brother's hand and leapt. "See you later, asslords."

They vanished. Agne glanced toward Sal.

"This woman," Agne said, "Liette. Was she...worth all this?"

Sal looked back at her as a cut bled into the corner of her mouth. It seeped past her lips as they curled up into a smile. The taste was foul, coppery, alive.

"We're all we've got left."

Agne didn't look convinced as she turned and tore off into the snow with her burden. Who would, really? But that didn't matter. Nothing else did.

She had made it.

She was alive.

And all it took...

All it took...

In the distance, Littlebarrow shuddered. A house—something simple, suitable for a small family that she never knew—trembled and collapsed, vanishing into the melee. Another corpse to be buried there, another relic of another war, to be drowned beneath the snow and the earth and the blood until they were all gone.

And no one would even remember it.

All it took, the thought came bitter and bleak, *was everything.*

The crack of guns and magic disappeared. Carried faintly on the wind, a horn blew a desperate chorus—the Imperials? The Revolutionaries? She didn't know. Nor did she know to which side the dark shapes that went fleeing suddenly from Littlebarrow's ruin belonged.

But the sound that followed—the song of iron and oil that drew her eyes to the sky, the droning melancholy and rumbling echo of metal—she knew that.

She knew the sound of locust wings.

An airship descended from the clouds, wings black against the clouds and propellers scattering the snow as if doffing a cape of white and gray. For the first time, Sal saw it as it was meant to be seen, as every poor fucker who'd ever seen it. Huge. Impossible. A black shadow across the sky.

Raining fire.

Cannons burst. Fire fell from its railings. Littlebarrow vanished in clouds of smoke and plumes of flame. Graves were dug from shrapnel and soil. The gray was painted with a hundred red wounds, a hundred blazes of brilliant flame, falling like stars.

Sal spurred her mount. With a shriek and a spray of snow, they were off. Yet even as the smoldering devastation shrank behind her, the cloud of red and black rose ever higher.

There, over the town where once lived a small collection of people who would never know why this had happened to them, the cloud of smoke settled. From on high, it stared down at her through eyes of cinders.

Dispassionate and baleful, its stare followed her.

Long after she had fled from it.

Until she disappeared.

FIFTY-SEVEN

THE VALLEY

It was worth it.

They had begun as a salve, those words. Whether they were true or a lie, it didn't matter—she needed them. She repeated them until her lips were numb and then continued in her own head. She balmed herself with them, applying them to her wounds and her aching muscles, until they could keep her on her feet and walking.

They didn't soothe her as she trudged through the snow, Congeniality's reins in her hand. White cloaks and gray scarves whipped around her, snow and wind swirling and becoming an ocean around her, drowning sound and sight and sun. The cold plucked at her skin, pulled at her hair, bit at her scars, problem children pestering her with a question she would never be able to answer to their satisfaction.

Or to hers.

It was worth it.

They became a cloak, those words. Something she wrapped around herself, so tight she could barely breathe for how they crowded her thoughts. They didn't keep her warm. They never could. But she didn't need them to do that.

She needed them to smother the sounds.

Through the wind, she could hear them, but never see them. There were shouts, panicked and desperate, that came through—wagon leaders trying to keep track of their charges, families searching for each other through the blinding white, sometimes just desperate pleas to whoever might listen. But she saw no shadows of people on the other side of the snows and she would not seek them out.

There were roars—animal, feral, and painfully human. There were wails of the defeated, shrieking the last ounces of their beings into the wind before they were silenced forever. There were maddened cries of the victorious, so drunk on hate and carnage that they no longer could tell the difference between triumph and agony. There was laughter. Single. Solitary. Senseless. The unnerving joy of someone who just figured out the punch line of a joke they'd heard too often and realized it wasn't funny the first time.

There were explosions. Flashes of crimson snuffed out like candles. Pillars of fire that howled defiantly against the snow. Clouds of soot-flecked flakes that fell and settled upon the earth like bruises.

Or so she thought. Perhaps it was just the wind. Perhaps it was just her imagination. She couldn't bear to think of anything else.

It was worth it.

And now they became a crutch. Those words. Keeping her upright, keeping her moving, keeping her believing that all of it—Littlebarrow, Terassus, everyone and everything—had to mean something.

It was worth it.

She walked with them.

It was worth it.

She leaned on them.

It was worth it.

And they splintered a little more with every step.

Congeniality chirruped warily. Ahead of them, a shadow appeared through the snow, drawing closer.

Liette.

It wasn't her. Sal knew that, in the cold parts of her. The figure that came limping out of the white and gray was solitary, too tall, dragging something long behind them. Yet that word grew softly in feverish hope. It made excuses—maybe she'd been separated from Meret, maybe she was always that tall and Sal had never noticed. It burned, small and soft and hot.

For a few moments.

Tretta Stern emerged, haggard and bloodied, wounds painted

across her skin and uniform, a broken gunpike dragged behind her like a loved one she couldn't bear to leave behind. Her breath was ragged, every gasp torn through laboring lungs. How long had she been out here? Sal wondered. How had she survived?

She didn't ask. Tretta didn't answer.

She looked up at Sal through one eye, the other so concealed behind caked-on red-and-purple bruises that it had vanished entirely. She opened a mouth in a bare-toothed scream. She took up the gunpike in her hands. And she charged.

Sal didn't move. Didn't draw steel. Didn't blink. She watched Tretta's legs pump numbly beneath her for a few steps. She watched Tretta raise her weapon and scream. She watched Tretta take one, final, futile swing. Too slow. Too far. Too little.

The woman collapsed to her knees. Bereft of a weapon that worked, a body to carry it, of anything but the fury that had kept her going, she collapsed. She thrust the gunpike into the earth, leaned upon it, head bowed and body wracked with desperate breaths.

Fallen. Halted. Defeated.

Sal waited. Waited for the urge to draw steel and finish Tretta off. Waited for Tretta to find the strength to stand up and kill her. But when she searched her heart for either, she could find nothing. And when she searched her head...

It was...worth it.

On the splintering crutch of those words, she started walking again. Through the snow. Through the wind. Past Tretta.

"You won't kill me."

Not a question. Not a plea. Tretta's voice, tattered and threatening to fly off in the breeze, spoke a truth both of them knew. And Tretta's eye, burning bright and hateful, did the same.

"But I will kill you," she said to Sal. "I will...wait as long as I have to. I will do whatever I need to. I will gather every drop of blood you've spilled, every sorrow you've left in your wake, every life you've ruined. And then...I will rain down upon you, Sal the Cacophony, with everything I have. Until everything you are is ash and dust and then I will cast you out on the winds." She bowed her head again, belabored from even those words. "I swear this. To the Revolution. To the Great General. To you. I swear this, Sal."

Not a threat. Not a promise. Tretta coiled around the truth she had spoken, to the great pain that had borne a great hate. She clutched it to her breast, let it burn brightly into her. Perhaps it would comfort her in her final moments. Perhaps it would smolder and die out, like so many other things.

But it wasn't Sal's hatred to take. Nor her fire to extinguish. She left Tretta with that. In the snow. In the wind.

It was worth it.

On four words that grew softer in her head with every step.

— ◅◆▻ —

She heard the music two hours outside of Littlebarrow. The soft crackle of a voccaphone, the dulcet song of an opera she couldn't remember the name of, that came swirling through the wind. Faint and fleeting.

By the time she convinced herself she wasn't imagining it, she began walking toward it. Through the thickest part of the snows. Up a steep hill. Until the winds ebbed softly and the white fell not so thick.

By the time she knew it wasn't Liette, or Meret, or anyone she wanted to see, she was too close to it to turn back. She crested the top of the hill to find a small tent situated at the center of a patch of grass, the snow cleared by the warmth of an alchemical globe. A voccaphone played an opera recording she didn't recognize upon a teak table, accompanied by a bottle of wine and two glasses. Beside it, a man sat in a chair, an empty one beside him, and stared out from on high.

By the time she realized it was Two Lonely Old Men, she had already sat down beside him.

He did not look up at her as she took a seat. He said nothing as they stared out over the Borrus Valley sprawling below. He merely reached for the bottle of wine, poured a glass, and handed it to her.

Together, they watched the fire.

From so far away, they couldn't hear anything—the explosions of the bombs falling, the drone of the locusts, the screams of the battle. As silent and small as a miniature replica, they watched. Seven airships glided silently over the Valley, dark fish in a gray sea, dropping shadows upon the floor.

Red wounds burst where the bombs fell. And beneath them,

villages disappeared. Great plumes of smoke painted the sky, black headstones, colossal and hazy, for the graves of homes and families. Over a hundred of them reached up. And more grew every time the Iron Fleet, the Seven Arrows, glided away.

"In truth, I never forgave you."

Two Lonely Old Men spoke. His voice was weaker than it had been when she last saw him.

"Or them," he said. "In my head, I did. I used reason, rationale, reality to explain why they destroyed Lastlight. Why I should have let it go and rebuilt. But in my dreams…" He pursed his lips. "In my dreams, it was never Lastlight. It was my city. Mine. And they had taken it from me. And you had taken it from me."

Sal sipped the wine. It tasted sweet and fragrant. Below, another village disappeared in a wave of fire. Tiny black shapes vanished beneath the red.

"In my dreams, I hurt," he said. "All the reasoning didn't matter, nor did all the ways I told myself that it couldn't have been avoided. In my dreams, I couldn't see what purpose it served or what knowledge could be gleaned from it. I saw my city, I saw its spires and its lights, and I saw them go away, one by one. And all I had left was the hurt."

From the floor of the Valley, a salvo of lightning and frost magic flew skyward to bounce off an airship's hull. Cannons retaliated. Another village vanished.

"Doesn't that seem strange?" he asked. "To let dreams dictate reality? It seems strange now, but at the time… at the time, it felt like I was sleeping. Like I just kept sleeping until one day I couldn't tell if I was awake or not." He sipped the wine. "Maybe it was my dreams that came up with this. With punishing the Imperium and the Revolution for what they'd done to my city. With using you to do it. For that, Sal, I am sorry."

She did not forgive him. Another fire burst on the ground.

"Jero knew," she said softly.

"He did."

"And Tuteng?"

"Him too. He took the money I paid him and disappeared. Back to his home, I like to believe. But Agne, the twins… you…" Two

Lonely Old Men let out a bone-deep sigh, settled into his chair. "Jero could see the wisdom of my actions. To see the Imperium and the Revolution and all the other terrible powers of this world would never give up their influence willingly. We had to make them destroy each other. We had to make the world see how vile they were. Jero agreed with me. He believed you would, too."

She didn't. Another headstone of smoke rose into the sky.

"Did you come to punish me?" he asked. "I'm afraid...you're too late."

She glanced at the table beside him, where the voccaphone played. Beside the bottle of wine, a tiny vial lay empty. Blood dripped out of Two Lonely Old Men's nose. He discreetly dabbed it away.

"Grandmother's Kiss," he said. "Did you know I invented it? Long ago. The Ashmouths requested of me a painless poison that could be used for some nefarious purpose. I didn't ask questions. I didn't even care about the money they offered me, I just wanted to see if I could do it. And I did. It's a potent poison, shuts down the nerves first, then the organs." He tried to raise a hand, couldn't. "My nerves are growing insensate. Any horror you might want to visit upon me would be fruitless. I figured it fitting to be my end. As fitting as anything else."

She quirked a brow. He smiled.

"I didn't poison yours," he said. "You'll realize that soon enough, if you don't believe me. I didn't forgive you...but I didn't blame you."

His eyes drifted to her scars.

"You know what that's like, don't you? To live with a thing that you can neither ignore nor remedy. That was my hurt. I could do nothing for it. Nothing but make them pay. To show them that I could hurt them worse than they hurt me. In my dreams, I could not see any way of feeling whole again."

He reached for his glass of wine. Numb fingers tipped it over.

"I don't think you believe me," he whispered. "You don't think this was for a great cause, or that I knew what I was doing. That's fine. It isn't what you should tell people, anyway."

He looked back out over the Valley and frowned bitterly as the smoke rose. The singer on the voccaphone broke into an aria.

"What you should tell them about Two Lonely Old Men," he

said, "about the man who burned this world to the ground to expose the rot beneath it, is..." He took a deep breath. "Is that a broken, tired man stood against the two strongest forces in this world. And shattered them with a few clever words and some ink. Tell them that Lastlight was worth avenging. Tell them that the people of this world—"

"No."

Sal didn't look at him as she interrupted. The voccaphone crackled dimly. She took another sip of her wine.

"You didn't do any of that," she said. "Neither did we. We didn't do anything but kill a lot of fucking people. That's all. We're not great people. Not broken people." She took a long swig, spat it onto the snow. "We're killers, you and I. Whatever else we did, that's all we were. And whoever else we hurt, we didn't care. You didn't. Jero didn't. I didn't."

The sky over the Valley was black now. Black with smoke. Black with flying machines that rained death. Black with the screams she couldn't hear. Sal set her glass upon the armrest of her chair and stood up.

"The Scar's full of people like us," she said. "People won't remember us. They shouldn't. They don't deserve that. Neither do we."

The wind murmured. She looked up. The clouds began to swirl overhead and snow began to fall once more.

"Whatever happens because of what we did," she whispered, "whatever it's going to mean...that's theirs. That's for the people who could make a better world than we could. That's for them. You and I..."

She looked down at Two Lonely Old Men. He stared up at the sky, mouth open, snow falling upon his glassy, unblinking eyes.

"If there's any mercy in this dark earth, you and I will be forgotten."

Sal the Cacophony took one last look over the Valley, over the black smoke headstones and the bright red graves. She stared at it exactly as long as she had to. She pulled her scarf a little tighter around her face. She took her bird's reins in one hand. She let the other rest upon a burning black hilt at her waist.

She turned and went back down the hill. Away from the Valley.

THE STORY CONTINUES IN...

BOOK THREE OF THE GRAVE OF EMPIRES

extras

orbit

meet the author

Photo Credit: Libbi Rich

SAM SYKES—author, citizen, mammal—has written extensively over the years, penning *An Affinity for Steel*, the Bring Down Heaven trilogy, *Brave Chef Brianna*, and now the Grave of Empires trilogy. At the time of this writing, no one has been able to definitively prove or disprove that he has fought a bear.

Find out more about Sam Sykes and other Orbit authors by registering for the free monthly newsletter at www.orbitbooks.net.

if you enjoyed
TEN ARROWS OF IRON

look out for

LEGACY OF ASH
Book One of the Legacy Trilogy

by

Matthew Ward

Legacy of Ash is an unmissable fantasy debut—an epic tale of
intrigue and revolution, soldiers and assassins, ancient magic
and the eternal clash of empires.

A shadow has fallen over the Tressian Republic.

*Ruling families—once protectors of justice and democracy—now plot
against one another with sharp words and sharper knives. Blinded
by ambition, they remain heedless of the threat posed by the invading
armies of the Hadari Empire.*

Yet as Tressia falls, heroes rise.

*Viktor Akadra is the Republic's champion. A warrior without equal,
he hides a secret that would see him burned as a heretic.*

extras

Josiri Trelan is Viktor's sworn enemy. A political prisoner, he dreams of reigniting his mother's failed rebellion.

And yet Calenne Trelan, Josiri's sister, seeks only to break free of their tarnished legacy, to escape the expectations and prejudice that haunt the family name.

As war spreads across the Republic, these three must set aside their differences in order to save their home. Yet decades of bad blood are not easily set aside. And victory—if it comes at all—will demand a darker price than any of them could have imagined.

Fifteen Years Ago

Lumendas, 1st Day of Radiance

A Phoenix shall blaze from the darkness.
A beacon to the shackled;
a pyre to the keepers of their chains.

from the sermons of Konor Belenzo

Wind howled along the marcher road. Icy rain swirled behind.

Katya hung low over her horse's neck. Galloping strides jolted weary bones and set the fire in her side blazing anew. Sodden reins sawed at her palms. She blotted out the pain. Closed her ears to the harsh raven-song and ominous thunder. There was only the road, the dark silhouette of Eskavord's rampart, and the anger. Anger at the Council, for forcing her hand. At herself for thinking there'd ever been a chance.

Lightning split grey skies. Katya glanced behind. Josiri was a dark shape, his steed straining to keep pace with hers. That eased the burden. She'd lost so much when the phoenix banner had fallen. But she'd not lose her son.

Nor her daughter.

Eskavord's gate guard scattered without challenge. Had they recognised her, or simply fled the naked steel in her hand? Katya didn't care. The way was open.

In the shadow of jettied houses, sodden men and women loaded sparse possessions onto cart and dray. Children wailed in confusion. Dogs fought for scraps in the gutter. Of course word had reached Eskavord. Grim tidings ever outpaced the good.

You did this.

Katya stifled her conscience and spurred on through the tangled streets of Highgate.

Her horse forced a path through the crowds. The threat of her sword held the desperate at bay. Yesterday, she'd have felt safe within Eskavord's walls. Today she was a commodity to be traded for survival, if any had the wit to realise the prize within their grasp.

Thankfully, such wits were absent in Eskavord. That, or else no one recognised Katya as the dowager duchess Trelan. The Phoenix of prophecy.

No, not that. Katya was free of that delusion. It had cost too many lives, but she was free of it. She was not the Phoenix whose fires would cleanse the Southshires. She'd believed – Lumestra,

681

how she'd believed – but belief alone did not change the world. Only deeds did that, and hers had fallen short.

The cottage came into view. Firestone lanterns shone upon its gable. Elda had kept the faith. Even at the end of the world, friends remained true.

Katya slid from the saddle and landed heavily on cobbles. Chain-mail's broken links gouged her bloodied flesh.

"Mother?"

Josiri brought his steed to a halt in a spray of water. His hood was back, his blond hair plastered to his scalp.

She shook her head, hand warding away scrutiny. "It's nothing. Stay here. I'll not be long."

He nodded. Concern remained, but he knew better than to question. He'd grown into a dependable young man. Obedient. Loyal. Katya wished his father could have seen him thus. The two were so much alike. Josiri would make a fine duke, if he lived to see his seventeenth year.

She sheathed her sword and marched for the front door. Timbers shuddered under her gauntleted fist. "Elda? Elda! It's me."

A key turned. The door opened. Elda Savka stood on the threshold, her face sagging with relief. "My lady. When the rider came from Zanya, I feared the worst."

"The army is gone."

Elda paled. "Lumestra preserve us."

"The Council emptied the chapterhouses against us."

"I thought the masters of the orders had sworn to take no side."

"A knight's promise is not what it was, and the Council nothing if not persuasive." Katya closed her eyes, lost in the shuddering ground and brash clarions of recent memory. And the screams, most of all. "One charge, and we were lost."

"What of Josiri? Taymor?"

"Josiri is with me. My brother is taken. He may already be dead." Either way, he was beyond help. "Is Calenne here?"

"Yes, and ready to travel. I knew you'd come."

"I have no choice. The Council . . ."

She fell silent as a girl appeared at the head of the staircase, her sapphire eyes alive with suspicion. Barely six years old, and she had the wit to know something was amiss. "Elda, what's happening?"

"Your mother is here, Calenne," said Elda. "You must go with her."

"Are you coming?"

The first sorrow touched Elda's brow. "No."

Calenne descended the stairs, expression still heavy with distrust. Katya stooped to embrace her daughter. She hoped Calenne's thin body stiffened at the cold and wet, and not revulsion for a woman she barely knew. From the first, Katya had thought it necessary to send Calenne away, to live shielded from the Council's sight. So many years lost. All for nothing.

Katya released Calenne from her embrace and turned wearily to Elda. "Thank you. For everything."

The other woman forced a wintery smile. "Take care of her."

Katya caught a glint of something darker beneath the smile. It lingered in Elda's eyes. A hardness. Another friendship soured by folly? Perhaps. It no longer mattered. "Until my last breath. Calenne?"

The girl flung her arms around Elda. She said nothing, but the tears on her cheeks told a tale all their own.

Elda pushed her gently away. "You must go, dear heart."

A clarion sounded, its brash notes cleaving through the clamour of the storm. An icy hand closed around Katya's heart. She'd run out of time.

Elda met her gaze. Urgency replaced sorrow. "Go! While you still can!"

Katya stooped and gathered Calenne. The girl's chest shook with thin sobs, but she offered no resistance. With a last glance at Elda, Katya set out into the rain once more. The clarion sounded again as she reached Josiri. His eyes were more watchful than ever, his sword ready in his hands.

"They're here," he said.

Katya heaved Calenne up to sit in front of her brother. She looked like a doll beside him, every day of the decade that separated them on full display.

"Look after your sister. If we're separated, ride hard for the border."

His brow furrowed. "To the Hadari? Mother . . . "

"The Hadari will treat you better than the Council." He still had so much to learn, and she no more time in which to teach him. "When enemies are your only recourse, choose the one with the least to gain. Promise me."

She received a reluctant nod in reply.

Satisfied, Katya clambered into her saddle and spurred west along the broad cobbles of Highgate. They'd expect her to take refuge in Branghall Manor, or at least strip it of anything valuable ahead of the inevitable looting. But the western gateway might still be clear.

The first cry rang out as they rejoined the road. "She's here!"

A blue-garbed wayfarer cantered through the crowd, rain scattering from leather pauldrons. Behind, another set a buccina to his lips. A brash rising triad hammered out through the rain and found answer in the streets beyond. The pursuit's vanguard had reached Eskavord. Lightly armoured riders to harry and delay while heavy knights closed the distance. Katya drew her sword and wheeled her horse about. "Make for the west gate!"

Josiri hesitated, then lashed his horse to motion. "Yah!"

Katya caught one last glimpse of Calenne's pale, dispassionate face. Then they were gone, and the horseman upon her.

The wayfarer was half her age, little more than a boy and eager for the glory that might earn a knight's crest. Townsfolk scattered from his path. He goaded his horse to the gallop, sword held high in anticipation of the killing blow to come. He'd not yet learned that the first blow seldom mattered as much as the last.

Katya's parry sent a shiver down her arm. The wayfarer's blade scraped clear, the momentum of his charge already carrying him past. Then he was behind, hauling on the reins. The sword came about, the killing stroke aimed at Katya's neck.

Her thrust took the younger man in the chest. Desperate strength drove the blade between his ribs. The hawk of the Tressian

Council turned dark as the first blood stained the rider's woollen tabard. Then he slipped from his saddle, sword clanging against cobbles. With one last, defiant glare at the buccinator, Katya turned her steed about, and galloped through the narrow streets after her children.

She caught them at the bridge, where the waters of the Grelyt River fell away into the boiling millrace. They were not alone.

One wayfarer held the narrow bridge, blocking Josiri's path. A second closed from behind him, sword drawn. A third lay dead on the cobbles, horse already vanished into the rain.

Josiri turned his steed in a circle. He had one arm tight about his sister. The other hand held a bloody sword. The point trembled as it swept back and forth between his foes, daring them to approach.

Katya thrust back her heels. Her steed sprang forward.

Her sword bit into the nearest wayfarer's spine. Heels jerked as he fell back. His steed sprang away into the streets. The corpse, one booted foot tangled in its stirrups, dragged along behind.

Katya rode on past Josiri. Steel clashed, once, twice, and then the last wayfarer was gone. His body tipped over the low stone parapet and into the rushing waters below.

Josiri trotted close, his face studiously calm. Katya knew better. He'd not taken a life before today.

"You're hurt."

Pain stemmed Katya's denial. A glance revealed rainwater running red across her left hand. She also felt a wound high on her shoulder. The last wayfarer's parting gift, lost in the desperation of the moment.

The clarion came yet again. A dozen wayfarers spurred down the street. A plate-clad knight rode at their head, his destrier caparisoned in silver-flecked black. Not the heraldry of a knightly chapterhouse, but a family of the first rank. His sword – a heavy, fennlander's claymore – rested in its scabbard. A circular shield sat slung across his back.

The greys of the rain-sodden town lost their focus. Katya tightened her grip on the reins. She flexed the fingers of her left hand.

They felt distant, as if belonging to someone else. Her shoulder ached, fit company for the dull roar in her side – a memento of the sword-thrust she'd taken on the ridge at Zanya. Weariness crowded in, the faces of the dead close behind.

The world lurched. Katya grasped at the bridle with her good hand. Focus returned at the cost of her sword, which fell onto the narrow roadway.

So that was how the matter lay?

So be it.

"Go," she breathed. "See to your sister's safety. I'll hold them."

Josiri spurred closer, the false calm giving way to horror. "Mother, no!"

Calenne looked on with impassive eyes.

"I can't ride." Katya dropped awkwardly from her saddle and stooped to reclaim her sword. The feel of the grips beneath her fingers awoke new determination. "Leave me."

"No. We're getting out of here. All of us." He reached out. "You can ride with me."

The tremor beneath his tone revealed the truth. His horse was already weary. What stamina remained would not long serve two riders, let alone three.

Katya glanced down the street. There'd soon be nothing left to argue over. She understood Josiri's reluctance, for it mirrored her own. To face a parting now, with so much unsaid . . . ? But a lifetime would not be enough to express her pride, nor to warn against repeating her mistakes. He'd have to find his own way now.

"Do you love me so little that you'd make me beg?" She forced herself to meet his gaze. "Accept this last gift and remember me well. Go."

Josiri gave a sharp nod, his lips a pale sliver. His throat bobbed. Then he turned his horse.

Katya dared not watch as her children galloped away, fearful that Josiri would read the gesture as a change of heart.

"Lumestra's light shine for you, my son," she whispered.

A slap to her horse's haunch sent it whinnying into the oncoming wayfarers. They scattered, fighting for control over startled steeds.

Katya took up position at the bridge's narrow crest, her sword point-down at her feet in challenge. She'd no illusions about holding the wayfarers. It would cost them little effort to ride straight over her, had they the stomach for it. But the tightness of the approach offered a slim chance.

The knight raised a mailed fist. The pursuers halted a dozen yards from the bridge's mouth. Two more padded out from the surrounding alleys. Not horsemen, but the Council's simarka – bronze constructs forged in the likeness of lions and given life by a spark of magic. Prowling statues that hunted the Council's enemies. Katya swore under her breath. Her sword was useless against such creatures. A blacksmith's hammer would have served her better. She'd lost too many friends to those claws to believe otherwise.

"Lady Trelan." The knight's greeting boomed like thunder. "The Council demands your surrender."

"Viktor Akadra." Katya made no attempt to hide her bitterness. "Did your father not tell you? I do not recognise the Council's authority."

The knight dismounted, the hem of his jet-black surcoat trailing in the rain. He removed his helm. Swarthy, chiselled features stared out from beneath a thatch of black hair. A young face, though one already confident far beyond its years.

He'd every reason to be so. Even without the armour, without the entourage of weary wayfarers – without her wounds – Akadra would have been more than her match. He stood a full head taller than she – half a head taller than any man she'd known.

"There has been enough suffering today." His tone matched his expression perfectly. Calm. Confident. Unyielding. He gestured, and the simarka sat, one to either side. Motionless. Watchful. "Let's not add to the tally."

"Then turn around, Lord Akadra. Leave me be."

Lips parted in something not entirely a smile. "You will stand before the Council and submit to judgement."

Katya knew what that meant. The humiliation of a show trial, arraigned as warning to any who'd follow in her footsteps and dare seek freedom for the Southshires. Then they'd parade her through the streets, her last dignity stripped away long before the gallows took her final breath. She'd lost a husband to that form of justice. She'd not suffer it herself.

"I'll die first."

"Incorrect."

Again, that damnable confidence. But her duty was clear.

Katya let the anger rise, as she had on the road. Its fire drove back the weariness, the pain, the fear for her children. Those problems belonged to the future, not the moment at hand. She was a daughter of the Southshires, the dowager duchess Trelan. She would not yield. The wound in Katya's side blazed as she surged forward. The alchemy of rage transmuted agony to strength and lent killing weight to the two-handed blow.

Akadra's sword scraped free of its scabbard. Blades clashed with a banshee screech. Lips parted in a snarl of surprise, he gave ground through the hissing rain.

Katya kept pace, right hand clamped over the failing left to give it purpose and guide it true. She hammered at Akadra's guard, summoning forth the lessons of girlhood to the bleak present. The forms of the sword her father had drilled into her until they flowed with the grace of a thrush's song and the power of a mountain river. Those lessons had kept her alive on the ridge at Zanya. They would not fail her now.

The wayfarers made no move to interfere.

But Akadra was done retreating.

Boots planted on the cobbles like the roots of some venerable, weather-worn oak, he checked each strike with grace that betrayed tutelage no less exacting than Katya's own. The claymore blurred across grey skies and battered her longsword aside.

The fire in Katya's veins turned sluggish. Cold and failing flesh sapped her purpose. Too late, she recognised the game Akadra had played. She'd wearied herself on his defences, and all the while her body had betrayed her.

Summoning her last strength, Katya hurled herself forward. A cry born of pain and desperation ripped free of her lips.

Again the claymore blurred to parry. The longsword's tip scraped past the larger blade, ripping into Akadra's cheek. He twisted away with a roar of pain.

Hooves sounded on cobbles. The leading wayfarers spurred forward, swords drawn to avenge their master's humiliation. The simarka, given no leave to advance, simply watched unfolding events with feline curiosity.

Katya's hands tightened on her sword. She'd held longer than she'd believed possible. She hoped Josiri had used the time well.

"Leave her!"

Akadra checked the wayfarers' advance with a single bellow. The left side of his face masked in blood, he turned his attention on Katya once more. He clasped a closed fist to his chest. Darkness gathered about his fingers like living shadow.

Katya's world blurred, its colours swirling away into an unseen void.

Her knee cracked against the cobbles. A hand slipped from her sword, fingers splayed to arrest her fall. Wisps of blood curled through pooling rainwater. She knelt there, gasping for breath, one ineluctable truth screaming for attention.

The rumours about Akadra were true.

The shadow dispersed as Akadra strode closer. The wayfarers had seen none of it, Katya realised – or had at least missed the significance. Otherwise, Akadra would have been as doomed as she. The Council would tolerate much from its loyal sons, but not witchcraft.

Colour flooded back. Akadra's sword dipped to the cobbles. His bloodied face held no triumph. Somehow that was worse.

"It's over." For the first time, his expression softened. "This is not the way, Katya. It never was. Surrender. Your wounds will be tended. You'll be treated with honour."

"Honour?" The word was ash on Katya's tongue. "Your father knows nothing of honour."

"It is not my father who makes the offer." He knelt, one gauntleted hand extended. "Please. Give me your sword."

Katya stared down at the cobbles, at her life's blood swirling away into the gutter. Could she trust him? A lifetime of emissaries and missives from the north had bled her people dry to feed a pointless war. Viktor's family was part of that, and so he was part of it. If his promise *was* genuine, he'd no power to keep it. The Council would never let it stand. The shame of the gallows path beckoned.

"You want my sword?" she growled.

Katya rose from her knees, her last effort channelled into one final blow.

Akadra's hand, so lately extended in conciliation, wrenched the sluggish blade from her grasp. He let his own fall alongside. Tugged off balance, Katya fell to her hands and knees. Defenceless. Helpless.

No. Not helpless. Never that.

She forced herself upright. There was no pain. No weariness. Just calm. Was this how Kevor had felt at the end? Before the creak of the deadman's drop had set her husband swinging? Trembling fingers closed around a dagger's hilt.

"My son will finish what I started."

The dagger rasped free, Katya's right hand again closing over her left.

"No!" Akadra dived forward. His hands reached for hers, his sudden alarm lending weight to his promises.

Katya rammed the dagger home. Chain links parted. She felt no pain as the blade slipped between her ribs. There was only a sudden giddiness as the last of her burdens fell away into mist.

Josiri held Calenne close through the clamour. Screams. Buccina calls. Galloping hooves. Barked orders. Josiri longed for the thunder's return. Bravery came easier in moments when the angry sky drowned all else.

The church spire passed away to his left. Desperate townsfolk crowded its lychpath, seeking sanctuary behind stone walls. People filled the streets beyond. Some wore council blue, most the sea-grey of Eskavord's guard, and too many the garb of ordinary folk caught in between.

Ravens scattered before Josiri's straining horse. He glanced down at the girl in his charge. His sister she may have been, but Calenne was a stranger. She sat in silence, not a tear on her cheeks. He didn't know how she held herself together so. It was all he could do not to fall apart.

A pair of wayfarers emerged from an alleyway, their approach masked by the booming skies. Howling with courage he didn't feel, Josiri hacked at the nearest. The woman slumped across her horse's neck. Josiri rowelled his mare, leaving the outpaced survivor snarling at the rain.

More wayfarers waited at the next junction, their horses arrayed in a loose line beneath overhanging eaves. The town wall loomed through the rain. The west gate was so close. Two streets away, no more.

A glance behind revealed a wayfarer galloping in pursuit. A pair of simarka loped alongside. Verdigrised claws struck sparks from the cobbles.

To turn back was to be taken, a rat in a trap. The certainty of it left Josiri no room for doubt. Onward was the only course.

"Hold tight to me," he told Calenne, "and don't let go."

Thin arms redoubled their grip. Josiri drove back his heels.

Time slowed, marked out by the pounding of hooves and the beat of a fearful heart. Steel glinted. Horses whinnied as wayfarers hauled on their reins.

"For the Southshires!"

The battle cry fed Josiri's resolve. The widening of the nearest wayfarer's eyes gave him more. They were as afraid of him as he of them. Maybe more, for was his mother not the Phoenix of prophecy?

Time quickened. Josiri's sword blurred. A wayfarer spun away in a bloody spray. And then Josiri was through the line, his horse's greedy stride gobbling the last distance to the west gate. The mare barely slowed at the next corner. Her hooves skidded on the rain-slicked cobbles.

Calenne screamed – not with terror, but in wild joy – and then the danger was past, and the west gate was in sight.

The portcullis was down, its iron teeth sunk deep. A line of tabarded soldiery blocked the roadway and the branching alleyways to either side. Halberds lowered. Shields locked tight together, a flock of white hawk blazons on a wall of rich king's blue. Wayfarers filled the street behind.

Thunder roared, its fury echoing through the hole where Josiri's heart should have been. He'd failed. Perhaps he'd never had a chance.

"Everything will be all right." He hoped the words sounded more convincing to Calenne than they did to him. "Mother will come."

Calenne stared up at him with all the earnestness of youth. "Mother's already dead."

Spears pressed in. An officer's voice bellowed orders through the rain. Josiri gazed down into his sister's cold, unblinking eyes, and felt more alone than ever.

if you enjoyed
TEN ARROWS OF IRON

look out for

ASHES OF THE SUN
Book One of Burningblade & Silvereye

by

Django Wexler

Long ago, a magical war destroyed an empire, and a new one was built in its ashes. But still the old grudges simmer, and two siblings will fight on opposite sides to save their world in the start of Django Wexler's new epic fantasy trilogy.

Gyre hasn't seen his beloved sister since their parents sold her to the mysterious Twilight Order. Now, twelve years after her disappearance, Gyre's sole focus is revenge, and he's willing to risk anything and anyone to claim enough power to destroy the Order.

Chasing rumors of a fabled city protecting a powerful artifact, Gyre comes face-to-face with his lost sister. But she isn't who she once was. Trained to be a warrior, Maya wields magic for the Twilight Order's cause. Standing on opposite sides of a looming civil war, the two siblings will learn that not even the ties of blood can keep them from splitting the world in two.

Prologue

Gyre and Maya were playing ghouls and heroes. Gyre had to be the ghoul, of course. Maya would never tolerate being anything less than a hero.

Summer was in full flower, and the sun was alone in a pale blue sky, with only a few wisps of cloud at the horizon. They'd already had the dramatic sword fight, and Gyre had been defeated with appropriate hissing and choking. Now he lay on his back, dead, and Maya had planted one foot on his stomach, hands on her hips in a heroic pose.

"...an' now I'm *queen*," she shouted at the top of her lungs. "An' there'll be peace an' justice an' all, an' everyone's got to do what I say. Stupid Billem Crump an' his stupid brothers have to help Mom dig the new well, an' there's going to be apple pudding every day with dinner. An' my brother Gyre can have some," she added generously, "even if he never beat a ghoul all by himself."

"If we had apple pudding every day, you'd get sick of it," Gyre said.

"Would not."

"Would too. And anyway, queens are for barbarians. We have senators and consuls."

"You shut up. You're dead."

She pressed down on Gyre's stomach, and he let out an *oof.* At five, Maya was heavier than she looked, plump and broad-shouldered, with their mother's light brown skin and curly crimson hair. Everyone said Gyre, darker and black-haired, took after their father.

"I'll be consul, then," Maya said. "Everyone still has to do what I say forever an' ever."

"You only get to be consul for a year," Gyre said.

"That's practically forever," Maya argued. "An'—"

694

She stopped, and a moment later vanished from his field of vision. Gyre sat up, brushing dirt and dried vulpi dung off his back. All around him, yearling vulpi snuffled over the rocky ground, looking for tender green shoots. Yearlings were Gyre's favorite age for vulpi, soft-furred and playful, before they grew into bristly, irritable layers and then huge, sedentary terminals. They didn't take much watching as long as the gate to the pasture was closed, which was why he had time to fool around.

Even so, Gyre had a guilty moment while he made a quick count of the herd. He relaxed when he came up with the requisite thirty-three. He was eight and a half years old and had never lost one of his father's vulpi, not even the time when the fence had washed out in the rain and six of them had made a break for it.

"Gyre!" Maya shouted. "Gyre, it's a *centarch*! He's riding a war-bird!" She was standing at the fence with her feet on the second rail, leaning as far over as she could. "*Gyre*, you have to come see!"

"It can't be a centarch."

Gyre hurried to the fence, absentmindedly grabbing the back of Maya's dress with one hand in case she leaned too far over. Maya was reckless, and often sick to boot, spending months with fevers and racking coughs. Keeping his sister out of misadventures was as much a part of his daily chores as tending vulpi. But her excitement was infectious, and he found himself leaning forward to get a better view of the cloud of dust coming down the main road. It *was* moving awfully quickly.

"It was *too* a centarch!" Maya said breathlessly. "I *saw* him an' all. He had white armor an' a blaster an' a hackem!"

"Haken," Gyre corrected. The legendary bladeless sword, weapon of the centarchs of the Twilight Order. "What would a centarch be doing here?"

"Maybe he's come to arrest Billem Crump for being an ass an' all. Dad said he was going to go to law with him if he kept picking those apples."

Gyre pulled his sister back. "Centarchs don't arrest people for stealing *apples*."

"They arrest people who've got"—she lowered her voice to a stage whisper—"*dhak*." The word, with its connotations of filth, infestation, and immorality, was inappropriate in polite conversation. If Gyre's mother had heard Maya saying it, she'd have gotten a smack on the ear. "Maybe Billem Crump's got ghoul *dhak* in his shed and the centarch is going to drag him away!"

Gyre watched the dust cloud with something less than his sister's wide-eyed wonder. He still didn't believe it was a centarch, and if it *was*, he wasn't sure how to feel about having one of the Order's champions on their farm. He'd caught on to the hard expression his father and the other farmers wore when the subject came up. Everyone knew the Order kept the people safe from plaguespawn. But...

Nothing else, just the significant "but." And Gyre knew, as Maya did not, what was in the locked shed off the south field. Last summer, when a plague of weevils had threatened their potatoes, Gyre's father had taken him out there by night. They'd both equipped themselves with a double handful of bright green seeds, like hard young peas, from a half-full sack, and spent the evening planting them between the rows of potato plants. By the next afternoon, the field was *full* of dead weevils. Gyre had swept them up and buried them in the compost pile, proud and guilty with the shared secret.

Was that dhak? Gyre suspected it had been. *Dhak* was anything from the Elder times, before the war that had destroyed both ghouls and Chosen, unless the Order had approved it as safe, sanctioned arcana. But his father had assured him it was fine and that every farmer in the valley had something like it laid away. *A centarch wouldn't come after him, just for that. Would they?*

"We should get back to the house," he told Maya. Or, he discovered, he told the empty space where Maya had been, since his sister had already jumped down from the fence, wriggled out of his grip, and set off up the path as fast as her short legs would carry her.

Gyre looked at the dust cloud. It was rounding the point of the hill now, going past the turn for the Crump farm and definitely heading their way. He wanted to run after Maya, but there were the vulpi to think of—well behaved or not, he couldn't just leave them on their own. So he spent a few frantic minutes rounding the animals up, ignoring their affronted blats and whistles at being turned out of the pasture early. Only once they were safely back in their pen, jostling for position at the water trough, did he hurry toward the house.

The path led directly to the kitchen door, which was undoubtedly where Maya had gone. But a smaller side route led around the low, ramshackle farmhouse to the front, and Gyre went this way. He had a notion that if the visitor *was* anyone important, his father would banish him and his sister to their room before they got a good look. Coming in through the front door, Gyre hoped he would be able to get an idea of what was happening.

There was indeed a warbird standing in the gravel drive, looking incongruous next to their battered farm cart. Gyre had seen one of the creatures before, years ago, when they'd been in town on the day the magistrate's guard had come through. This one seemed bigger than he remembered, its long, curving neck layered with overlapping plates of pale white armor with the iridescent shimmer of unmetal. More armor covered the warbird's plump body. Two long, knobbly legs each had four splayed toes and a single enormous backward claw. The head, ridiculously tiny compared to the rest of the animal, was encased in segmented white plates, with its beak covered by a long, curving blade, shrouded in turn with a black velvet cloth.

It was easily twice Gyre's height. The magistrate's warbird hadn't been nearly as big, he decided, and in retrospect its plumage seemed a bit ragged. It certainly hadn't been armored in unmetal. Whoever the visitor was, he was considerably better equipped than even a county official. *Maybe it is a centarch.* Gyre gave the warbird a wide berth, creeping around the edge of the drive toward the front door, which stood partially open.

It led to the parlor, which the family used once a year at Midwinter. The rest of the time, the good furniture was covered by dust sheets, and life at the farm centered around the kitchen and the back door. Gyre and Maya's room was in that part of the house, an addition that leaked when it rained. Looking into the parlor, Gyre had the feeling of being a stranger in his own home, the shrouded shapes of the sofa and end table looming and ominous.

Gyre's father stood in the doorway that led to the kitchen. He was a big man, broad-shouldered, with dark hair tied at the nape of his neck and skin the color of the soil he spent his time tending. Gyre could tell at once there was something wrong, just from the way his father stood. He was slumped, defeated, his eyes on the floor.

In front of him, in the middle of the parlor, stood the visitor. He was tall and thin, with short hair that gleamed purple-black in the light. He wore an unmetal breastplate and shoulder armor and carried a matching helmet under one arm. On his right hip there was an implement a bit like a capital letter *T*, or a sword hilt and cross guard with no blade.

It was, without question, a haken. The highest of arcana, able to manipulate the power of creation in the raw. And that made this man a centarch of the Twilight Order, since only they could use the haken. Gyre had never seen one, of course, but he recognized it from a hundred stories. With haken in hand, a centarch was unstoppable, invincible.

Now that he was confronted with one of the legendary warriors in the flesh, Gyre realized he very much wanted the man to be gone. *Just go away and leave us alone,* he thought. *We're not ghouls, and we haven't got any* dhak *except for seeds that kill weevils. What harm can that do to anyone?*

"You're certain?" Gyre's father said quietly. Neither of the men had noticed Gyre yet, and he pressed himself against the sofa, desperate to hear their conversation.

"Quite certain," the centarch said. He had a highborn accent. "Believe me, in these matters, the Order does not make mistakes."

"But..."

Maya screamed, and Gyre's father started. Gyre's mother came in through the other door, holding Maya under her arm. The girl was kicking furiously, tears running down her cheeks, and shrieking like an angry cat.

"It's all right," Gyre's father said. "Maya, please. Everything's going to be all right."

"Yes," the centarch drawled. "Everything's going to be fine."

"No!" Maya said. "No, no, no! I don't want to go!"

"You have to go," Gyre's mother said. "You know how you get sick. They can help you."

Gyre frowned. Bouts of a strange, feverish illness had been a regular feature of Maya's life for as long as he could remember, especially in the winter. But she'd always recovered, and by summer she was herself again. *Though Mom did say this year was the worst she'd ever been.* Maya hated doctors, who could never find anything wrong and prescribed bitter medicines that didn't work.

Did Dad call the Order to help her? Gyre hadn't heard of the Order doing anything like that, though they had access to arcana medicine far better than any doctor's. *But why would they need to take her away?*

He bit his lip, watching as his mother transferred the squirming five-year-old to the centarch. The thin man donned his helmet, which made him look like a white beetle, and took Maya under his arm, lifting her easily.

"No, no, no!" she screamed. "I don't *want* to go! Mom, Dad, don't let him take me!"

She hates doctors, Gyre told himself. *She screamed her head off when she cut her hand and Dad took her to get it sewn up.*

But something was wrong. The way his father stood, hands clenched into fists. His mother's eyes, brimming with unshed tears, her hands clasped to her chest. *It's* wrong. *Why are they letting him take her?*

Gyre stepped into the doorway, trembling, as the centarch turned to leave. Maya saw him first and screamed again.

"Gyre! Help, help, *please!*"

"Let her go," Gyre said. He wished his voice didn't sound so small, so like a little boy's.

"Gyre!" Gyre's father took a half step forward. His mother turned away, her shoulders shaking with sobs.

"Ah," the centarch said. "You must be the brother. Gyre, is it?"

Gyre nodded. "Put my sister down."

"It is commendable, of course, to defend one's family," the centarch said. "But I am afraid you have made a mistake. My name is Va'aht, called Va'aht Thousandcuts, a centarch of the Twilight Order." His free hand brushed across his haken.

"I know what you are," Gyre said. "Put her *down*."

"If you know what I am, you know that the Order helps wherever it can. I am going to help your sister."

"She doesn't want to go," Gyre said.

"I don't!" Maya wailed. "I'm not sick, I'm *not*."

"Children don't get to make those decisions, I'm sad to say," Va'aht said. "Now, if you would stand aside?"

Hand trembling, Gyre reached for his belt. He drew his knife, the knife his father had trusted him with the day he found all the vulpi. It was a wickedly sharp single-edged blade almost four inches long. Gyre held it up in front of Va'aht, heart thumping wildly.

"*Gyre!*" Gyre's father shouted. "Drop that at once and come here!"

"I see," Va'aht said gravely. "Single combat, is it? Unfortunately, boy, I'm afraid I don't have time at the moment. Once you've grown a bit taller, perhaps." The centarch turned. "If there's—"

Gyre moved while he was looking the other way. Va'aht's torso was armored, and Gyre's steel blade wouldn't even scratch the unmetal. But his legs were protected only by leather riding trousers, and Gyre swung the knife down as hard as he could into the man's thigh. It sank to the hilt, blood welling around the wound.

Va'aht shouted in pain, and Maya screamed. Gyre's mother was screaming too. Gyre tried to maintain his grip on the blade, pull it out for another stab, but Va'aht twisted sideways and he lost his hold. The centarch's knee slammed into Gyre's stomach, sending him gasping to the floor.

"Gyre!" Gyre heard his father start forward, but Va'aht held up a warning hand. The centarch still had hold of Maya, who was staring down at her brother, too scared even to keep shrieking.

"That," Va'aht said through clenched teeth, "was unwise."

"He's just a boy," Gyre's father said. "Please, I'll answer for it, I'll—"

"That's Order blood, *boy*," Va'aht said, raising his voice. "The blood of the Chosen. Every drop is worth all the flesh and bone in your body. Consider that, and reflect on my mercy."

"Mercy, sir," Gyre's father said. "Please."

Gyre heaved himself up onto his elbows.

"Let her go," he croaked.

Va'aht put his hand on his haken. He didn't draw the weapon, just touched it, and crooked one finger.

Pain exploded in Gyre's head, a line of fire from cheek to eyebrow. He was falling backward, hitting the floor shoulder-first, feeling nothing but the searing agony in his face. He mashed his hand against it, and blood *squished*, torn skin shifting nauseatingly under his fingers. He only realized he was screaming when he had to stop to take a breath.

Va'aht loomed above him, an outline shimmering in a haze of tears.

"You'll live, with care, though I daresay there'll be a scar." The centarch gave a humorless chuckle. "Let it be a lesson to you."

He limped past, still carrying Maya. She screamed Gyre's name again, but his thoughts were already fading into a fiery blur of pain. By the time his father reached his side, darkness was closing in around him.

orbit

Follow us:

 /orbitbooksUS

 /orbitbooks

 /orbitbooks

Join our mailing list
to receive alerts on our
latest releases and deals.

orbitbooks.net

Enter our monthly
giveaway for the chance
to win some epic prizes.

orbitloot.com